'I NEED TO GET OUT. ... NEARLY TIME!'

'Time for what?' Eva's heart sank. Her mother's voice sounded so young.

In the moonlight, the old woman's eyes were glinting with an icy fire. Youth still lived there, and power. 'Something I doubt you'll be happy about. Something I deserve. They've come back, Evie. Like it or not, they've come back!'

Eva had pressed herself against the wall. Her lungs ached as if the air had been punched from her body. It couldn't be. No. That was all over, over and done with. She only had to wait for her mother to die now. There could be no return.

The old woman looked at her daughter with clever, glittering eyes. 'You can't stop it. I know what you think, but there's nothing you can do to stop it.'

Storm Constantine has written stories all her life. In 1985 she began work on the first of her Wraeththu novels, *The Enchantments of Flesh and Spirit*, which was published in 1987 and was followed by the concluding volumes, *The Bewitchments of Love and Hate* and *The Fulfilments of Fate and Desire*. Her fourth book, *The Monstrous Regiment*, appeared in 1990, and was described by her editor as 'quintessential Storm'. In 1991 *Hermetech* was published and was praised in *Interzone* magazine as 'a mythic journey replete with picturesques, grotesques and poisoned earth elegy'.

Storm has also worked with rock bands a great deal, either as an illustrator or contributing written work. In 1991 she took on the management of the band Empyrean, which greatly enhanced her profile in the music world. In February 1992 *Burying the Shadow* was published, a reinvention of the vampire myth which also incorporated mythology from *Paradise Lost* and the Nefilim legends. This was followed a year later by *Sign for the Sacred*, exploring the complexities and manias of religion. Storm has also written a multitude of short stories for various science-fiction magazines and anthologies. At present she is working on a fantasy trilogy based upon the legends of fallen angels but set in the contemporary world, of which *Stalking Tender Prey* is the first volume. The next two volumes are forthcoming in Signet Creed.

STORM CONSTANTINE

STALKING TENDER PREY

A SIGNET BOOK

SIGNET

Published by the Penguin Group
Penguin Books Ltd, 27 Wrights Lane, London w8 5tz, England
Penguin Books USA Inc., 375 Hudson Street, New York, New York 10014, USA
Penguin Books Australia Ltd, Ringwood, Victoria, Australia
Penguin Books Canada Ltd, 10 Alcorn Avenue, Toronto, Ontario, Canada m4v 3b2
Penguin Books (NZ) Ltd, 182–190 Wairau Road, Auckland 10, New Zealand

Penguin Books Ltd, Registered Offices: Harmondsworth, Middlesex, England

Published in Signet 1995
1 3 5 7 9 10 8 6 4 2

Filmset by Datix International Limited, Bungay, Suffolk
Printed in England by Clays Ltd, St Ives plc
Set in 10/12pt monophoto Baskerville

Contents

Acknowledgements

Thanks, as usual, to all who have accompanied me on this journey, and who held me on the path. To Luigi Bonomi at Penguin for essential cutting and polishing; Debbie Benstead for all the rich and invaluable material that helped create the visions and dreams of this book; Andy Collins for sharing his knowledge (and his personal library) and for writing 'The Grigori Cometh'; Tigger Nelson-Gennard for dreaming up the scandals!; my long-suffering partner, Mark, for suffering quite quietly; Vikki Lee France and Steve Jeffery for their enduring hard work on Inception and all the support they have extended which has made the smooth continuation of my work possible; Paula Wakefield and Lynn S. for professional and personal soothing in times of crisis; Anne Sudworth for her enthusiasm, organizational abilities and the superb cover artwork; Carl McCoy for his music and sterling example of keeping the faith; Steve Chilton and Debs Howlett for listening and nodding; Empyrean – Mark Haines, Shaun Nelson-Gennard, David Raddon and Richard Thacker – for sticking around; Jamie Spracklen for that vital introduction; and finally to all those who have been with us from the start, thanks for your presence and support.

For more information on Storm Constantine's work, write to:

Inception
c/o Vikki Lee France and Steve Jeffery
44 White Way
Kidlington
Oxon OX5 2XA

Foreword

For those of you who regularly read my work, this novel will be a return to familiar territory – that of the fallen angels, who have featured in my novel, *Burying the Shadow*, and various other shorter pieces, as well as providing some of the inspiration for my first work, the trilogy of the Wraeththu. However, I have long wanted to write a novel set in a contemporary world rather than a fantasy universe, and, in this, *Stalking Tender Prey* is new and uncharted territory. The novel began life as a short story, 'A Change of Season', in Midnight Rose's *Weerde* anthology, a collection of stories about a shape-changing race (created by Neil Gaiman, Roz Kaveney and Mary Gentle). I always knew I wanted to expand this story at some point, although it was unlikely I'd be able to write a *Weerde* novel as Midnight Rose was no longer running. The only way to achieve my aim was to remove all the attributes linking the story to the world of the Weerde and transform it into something else. There were similarities between 'A Change of Season' and my novel, *Burying the Shadow*, so the direction became clear. The novel would be based on the theme which has lured back my attention again and again: the Fallen Ones.

I have delved into the subject of angels, fallen and otherwise, for a long time, which back in the late Seventies led to my discovery of the legends of the Watchers and the Nefilim. These myths tell of a race of people, who were identified as 'messengers of God', who were very tall and who could fly between the earth and the heavens. The Watchers were members of this race.

Perhaps their name was a title, like police or army. Certainly it suggests they had a supervisory function, as they were also known as the Sleepless Ones, who were forever 'watching'. According to the old stories, some of the Watchers rebelled against authority, for which they were severely punished. Their crimes involved taking human wives, as well as imparting 'forbidden' knowledge to humanity. The Nefilim were the hybrid offspring of Watchers and humans, monstrous because of their size and strength and their apparently bloodthirsty habits. There is a bewildering array of different names and terms for various offshoots of the Watchers and the Nefilim, which is confusing to say the least, and caused more than a few headaches in the editorial stage of creating this book! However, the chapter entitled 'The Grigori Cometh' (pp. xv–xviii) introduces and explains the terminology I use throughout the novel.

Those interested in the occult will notice that in the scenes depicting magical rituals, although I have followed tradition with the elemental correspondences for north (earth) and east (air), I have not done so for south and west. The correspondences given here, water (instead of fire) for south and fire (instead of water) for west relate to earlier beliefs, and seemed more in keeping with the spirit of the novel.

Legends of fallen angels imparting knowledge to humanity crop up in many mythologies, in different forms, so much so that it is easy to imagine they must have once had a basis in truth. Modern non-fiction writers are now investigating this possibility. Some have been attracted by the 'angel' connection, while others have a broader view: there must have been an advanced race before the Ancient Egyptians, but who were they? Where is the evidence for their existence? Why can't we find it? Is it already visible for all to see, but simply unrecognized for what it is? In researching this book, I explored the work of writers who are attempting to answer some of these perhaps unanswerable questions. Primarily, I have drawn upon the hard work of Andrew Collins, whose forthcoming book *From the Ashes of Angels* is a comprehensive study which examines the true origins of the Watchers. Just as influential was the music of Carl McCoy, the driving force behind the band Fields of the Nefilim, and more recently, The Nefilim. Carl's affinity with this subject predates the work of many of those now drawn to it.

Also, the dreams and visions of psychic Debbie Benstead provided a fascinating insight into the more subjective aspects of lost civilizations, and offered a deeper understanding of the symbolism behind the story of the fallen angel, Shemyaza, and the human maiden, Ishtahar.

For those of you who share my fascination with this subject, and would like to investigate it further, I want to list some of the material I used for research and as inspiration. I have included Graham Hancock's *Fingerprints of the Gods*, even though the book is not yet published at the time of writing, because I attended a lecture he gave on the subject in 1994 at Andrew Collins's Psychic Questing Conference in London. I do not take a religious view of the Nefilim, such as that of Elizabeth Clare Prophet, nor believe they were spacemen, like Zecharia Sitchin, but I have included their work in the list below simply because I drew upon certain aspects of their books in the creation of *Stalking Tender Prey*.

This book is a supernatural novel, and as yet I have no real evidence that the material it is based upon is hard fact, yet there is still the enticing possibility that once the Nefilim walked among us, and that they perhaps still do, and that is where the fascination lies.

Storm Constantine, January 1995

Bibliography

Bauval, Robert and Gilbert, Adrian Geoffrey, *The Orion Mystery*, Mandarin, 1995.

Charles, Canon R.H., ed., *The Book of Enoch*, SPCK, 1991.

Byron, Lord, *Heaven and Earth: A Mystery* (drama)

Collins, Andrew, *From the Ashes of Angels*, forthcoming publication by Penguin.

Collins, Andrew, 'Rosslyn's Fallen Angel' in *The Templar Legacy and the Masonic Inheritance within Rosslyn Chapel*, The Friends of Rosslyn, 1994.

Davidson, Gustav, *A Dictionary of Angels*, Free Press, 1994.

Godwin, Malcolm, *Angels: An Endangered Species*, Boxtree, 1993.

Hancock, Graham, *Fingerprints of the Gods*, Heinemann, 1995.

Milton, John, *Paradise Lost*.

O'Brien, Christian and Joy, Barbara, *Genius of the Few*, Turnstone Press, 1983.

Prophet, Elizabeth C., *Forbidden Mysteries of Enoch*, Summit University Press, 1983.

Sitchin, Zecharia, *The Twelfth Planet*, Bear & Co., 1991.

The Grigori Cometh

Long, long ago, when the earth was a little younger, there came into this world a strange race – human in many respects, but also somehow different.

These people were tall, with legs, arms and fingers that were attenuated and slender. Their complexions were pale, their looks gaunt, but it was their long faces that really set them apart, with their elongated features, high foreheads, sharp cheek bones, small, well-shaped lips and bright, piercing eyes – the bluest ever seen.

To look directly into their faces was a forbidden act, for they exuded a hypnotic brilliance of supernatural origin, while around the locks on their heads was a divine glow that made them different to any other men or women in this world. Some said this lustrous radiance was caused by the strange oils they rubbed upon their skin, while others claimed it was a sign by which they could be recognized as gods walking among humanity.

No one knew where they came from, but all knew they were not like us. To some they were known as Anannage, the Shining Ones, to others they were known as angels, devas and djinns, while still others knew them as the Cabari, Gigantes and Titans.

Some even called them bene ha-Elohim – the sons of God – or Watchers, *those who watch*, because of their ever-watchful eyes, like those of serpents and lizards, and their houses, which they set high above the world on lofty crags, similar to the eyries created by eagles and vultures. And the Anannage must have been much taken with these great birds, for on their brief incursions into the homesteads of humanity, they came looking like vultures, with their long white hair and cloaks of dark feathers.

Initially, they kept themselves to themselves, these Anannage, never mingling with the men and women who made their homes in the forests and lowlands. Then a time came when they were forced to take on labour to enable them to fulfil their mammoth building and engineering projects in the high places. Here the men and women would help them to dig irrigation ditches and reservoirs, domesticate animals, make vessels of clay and metal and grow strange cereals, leaving the Anannage free to tend the sacred blue flame deep within the mountain where the Seven High Lords met to decide the affairs of humanity.

Eventually, against all the ancient laws that forbade it, many Anannage took wives for themselves from among the peoples of the lowlands, and to these women great secrets were revealed, concerning the movement of the stars, the wielding of magic and sorcery, the fashioning of weapons for war, the art of cunning, the pleasures of the flesh and the beautification of our womenfolk.

And to the women of the rebel Anannage were born children, monstrous because of their great height, and with the long features of their fathers. They were half-breeds, shunned by all, and were called Nefilim – *those who have fallen* – because of the inexcusable sins committed by their Anannage fathers and human mothers. Embittered, the Nefilim raged across the land, making war and plundering the settlements of humanity. It was said they ate human flesh and drank human blood. No one was safe from them.

The Anannage who had remained true to the ancient laws then sought out and punished those of their kind who had dared to break the oaths and traffic with the daughters of men. Those children born unto the wives of the rebels were seized and destroyed, or else provoked into warring with one another, until it was assumed no further Nefilim remained.

As for the leader of the rebel Anannage, one called Shemyaza, a most terrible fate awaited him. For revealing the sacred oaths of his forebears to his maiden lover, Ishtahar, and inciting his half-breed sons to violate the lands of the Anannage, he was cast over a rocky precipice to hang upside-down by one foot until every ounce of life had been expended from his body. Furthermore, his soul was banished to remain for all eternity within the starry gate of Orion, never to return to this world and never to experience the knowledge of the One existing beyond the heavenly portal.

His example would be a reminder, for all to come, of the sins committed by the rebel Anannage in the name of lust and desire.

Despite all their efforts, the Anannage's infanticide was to no avail. Too much intercourse had taken place between their kind and the daughters of men for the High Lords to vanquish the Nefilim completely. New generations saw the birth of Nefilim-featured babies among families of men and women who had themselves never had loves among the rebel Anannage. Sometimes the bodies of these babies were so large they had to be cut from the bellies of their mothers to allow entry into this world.

Women grew to fear these hideous births and many charms were used to try and prevent such devils being born. Those who did bear such children were accused of lying with demons or rebel Anannage, while their offspring were often shunned and disowned by their families. Even so, many were destined to grow into huge, fearsome warriors, wicked sorcerers and great prophets, with the power to wield either ultimate good or ultimate evil. Of these, some even created the first members of races who still bear their name: families of giants, demons and cruel warriors, such as the Anakim, the sons of Anak, who lived in the underground cities of Basham and built rude monuments of stone that still litter our lands. The Anakim also travelled the world and created settlements on the southern shores of Ireland and England. They were the truth behind all the legends of giants in the folklore of these regions. Other branches of the half-breed families included Zamzummim, the Achievers; Emim, the Terrors; Rephaim, the Weakeners and Gibborium, the Giants. Eventually, those half-breed families that thrived agreed to co-operate in their manipulation of human affairs, and took for themselves the name of Grigori, which originated from a Greek word for Watchers. They bred and grew stronger, hidden among humanity, yet wielding great power in human commerce.

All evidence of the great race of the Anannage has vanished from our world, and no one knows what became of them. But their half-breed descendants, the Grigori, live on among us today, their presence clear to those who have eyes to see. Their tall stature, their great strength, their long faces, their reclusive clans, their power to understand the ways of the ancients and their ability to wield forbidden magic are all signs one must watch out for.

Yet many go unseen now, their past features lost through the many generations since the demise of their culture. Some recognize their origins only through dreams and visions, while others simply want to forget their forbidden heritage. Some, as you might say, have become almost human . . .

Andrew Collins, 1995

Prologue: The Arrival

Friday, 16th October: a journey by train from Cresterfield in the North of England

The child watched him from across the carriage. His eyes were closed, leaking only a shining sliver, as if tears gathered there in darkness, but he could feel the girl's intense scrutiny, the half-formed butterfly questions flitting through her focused child's mind. He did not mind. Children, untainted by experience, might recognize him sometimes.

His long hands lay loosely clasped in his lap. He felt empty, neither guilty nor exultant. What had happened further north in the city was finished with now. There were no victories to savour, no mistakes to lament. He was not running away but running onwards.

A man came to check tickets, to clip and stamp them. The traveller was forced to open his eyes, search for the square of card. The guard, braced on stiff legs against the movement of the train, did not look at the traveller's face. He moved on. 'Tickets please. Passengers since Cresterfield.'

The traveller smiled at the wide-eyed girl who continued to stare, then he looked out at the world through glass.

Beyond the train, the countryside had changed. It looked both younger and older than the flattened areas of industry and human overpopulation he had recently left behind. Spiky hills, raw rock poking through. Blankets of forests, rough heath; a place of ancient legends. The summer was fading into that frowzy, tired interim period – the earth masquerading as overdressed and sadly declining female − before a brief spurt of harsh colour leads the unforgiving winter in by the nose.

He spent so much time in the city places; the only time he ever saw the seasons change was from the inside of trains or coaches or cars. The land rushed by beyond the dust-veiled window, and he rested his head against the glass.

There was a star in the afternoon sky.

The traveller raised his head, and a flash of light burned against his eyes. Perhaps it was the reflection from the far window of a cottage on the hillside, or a car door being opened, or a discarded glass bottle among the ferns. If it was none of these things, it could only be a true sign, a burst of energy, giving him a signal. *A way to the gate!* The thought formed half-acknowledged in his mind. It meant nothing, yet everything, as if he'd remembered a line from a poem learned long ago. *Abandon the earth, take back the stars! Your kingdom awaits!*

Whose voice was it that sang in his brain? When had he learned these words? They kindled excitement within him, yet there was a cost. Fear flapped there, too, in darkness. He could almost smell its carrion breath, the stink of its wet feathers. Fear and ecstasy. It must be a flashback to some forgotten drug experience. He smiled, comforted.

The train began to slow down. There was a squeal of brakes, and a tunnel of trees engulfed the carriages, hiding the land beyond. Without thinking, the traveller was on his feet, pulling down the old canvas bag from the overhead storage area, which contained all the artefacts of his life. The station, hardly more than a siding, came into view as he moved towards the door, nodding once at the girl-child, ignoring the reprimanding stare of her mother.

This was the place.

*

The station was small, the air warm and ripe against his skin. He was the only person to get off the train here. The moment his feet touched the concrete of the platform, he scanned the sky for omens, but high trees eclipsed his view, their branches flounced with autumn's yellowing leaves.

As he surrendered his ticket, he received a sour up-and-down glance from a gaunt, inbred-looking individual skulking in the inspector's booth beside the station gateway. The traveller did not bother to smile or speak. As he sauntered out into the empty street beyond, adjusting his backpack for comfort, a familiar sense of unreality stole across his senses. These are cardboard buildings, cardboard props for a second-rate drama. It was not really a town, more a village, and a forgotten one at that. The sense of history was faint, although he was aware that people had lived in this place for many centuries. It had never witnessed any events of importance, he was sure, being no more than a receptacle for a few mundane souls who sped from womb to grave with less purpose than animals, or perhaps, he thought charitably, the *same* purpose as animals. The place looked empty, but he knew that, had he walked in the other direction, he would have come across the heart of it: the lone, understocked supermarket, the row of pubs, a small cinema showing films considerably out of date. This conviction was not the result of some psychometric skill, but merely of a familiarity with towns of this type. You had to look hard for the romance in this country. Abroad, little towns seemed to possess a bustling other-life, like insects below the grass. There were often mysteries to uncover, mysteries that could be cherished, like gems unexpectedly discovered in a rock that had seemed uniformly grey. Here, the social structure demanded a different kind of behaviour – upright, polite, mannered – but that usually meant the mysteries, when they were coaxed from hiding, were all the more delightful and perverse. He sniffed the air. Something had called to him from the train.

A flash of light beckoned from down the deserted street, like a hand extended from behind the buildings, gesturing 'Come, come.' He sensed it as a gift from the future, a trail to follow.

Walking towards the signal, with the sun hanging high in the sky, the traveller was a solitary figure in an uncluttered scene. He felt as if this was the ending of something, not the beginning. He could walk away out of existence. Yet his boots made a solid, satisfactory sound against the road and his flesh felt real and comfortable about his bones. He was a good performer.

The road led out of the town straight into the landscape of hills and heath. The traveller felt his spirits lift, and tested the air for exciting perfumes. There might be a solitary stone manor squatting in the furze, where deranged family members feuded with sanity. There might be a cottage where a love-sick desertee mulled over the painful intricacies of his or her past. There might be a farm, with buxom daughters and leery sons, where a traveller might weave a little mischief for a while. The countryside seemed the proper setting for such scenarios. If he walked, he was sure to stumble across the thing he had come here to find. The richness and variety of the human race enchanted him; he was not repelled by weaknesses or failings and was tolerant of most behaviours, even the least endearing. Difficult people interested him far more than those whose conversations and ideas inspired the spirit, or whose physical beauty constricted breath in the throat. He sought out the unusual, observing behaviours with cool, yet committed interest. He loved them all.

He had been travelling for many years, and had lost count of the exact figure. He had visited many countries to which it was easy to gain access, and several where it wasn't. He wore a wide-brimmed hat that shadowed his eyes, shutting out the history of the world, if not his own history, to the casual observer. Sometimes he would play the role of enigmatic stranger, dark and impenetrable; at other times, he would be the world's fool, the travelling jester, and at these times, he might play an instrument or tell stories. Some countries reacted more favourably to this persona than others. In England, he observed the code of reticence and became the withdrawn one, the stranger on a train. Few people sat next to him on his travels, but those that did he generally liked to communicate with. Now, at least for a while, he wanted to feel the bones of the planet beneath his feet.

Something had gone awry in Cresterfield. He had begun dreaming of the closed gateway again, and the dreams had urged him to act. It was like trying to find his way through a cluttered room in the dark, where objects were hard and sharp, positioned to bruise his uncertain limbs. What was this obsession with gateways? He still could not understand it, and his waking mind shrank from examining the image. All he could do was obey the instinct when it seized him, use the old magic as a battering ram to force the gate, to blow it apart. He was aware that the gate was not a physical object, but a psychic portal within himself. What lay beyond he did not know, and sometimes he feared it might be death or madness. Still, to ignore the compulsion when it came was unthinkable, worse than ignoring the most intense sexual need. He had to spend himself in ritual, direct energy towards the obstruction in his mind. So far, satisfaction had eluded him. His performances quieted the urge, sometimes for months at a time, but never sated it. Desperation had driven him to greater excesses in Cresterfield, and he had left incriminating evidence behind him. This was not the first time it had happened, but this country was small, and it was more difficult to pass unnoticed. He'd wondered, at first, whether he would be pursued, and was alert for it, but he was adept at covering his tracks, and had sensed no invisible eyes upon him, or other, less familiar, organs of sight. Here, in this timeless wilderness, he would vanish into the landscape. He would walk the moors and see what the future exposed to him, or exposed him to. There was always the hope that this time someone or something would happen to him that might change his life, liberate him, reveal to him the answers to the puzzles of his existence.

It was a moist country, rich with the fecund smells of earth. Hills swelled towards the horizon, punctuated by the moving pale dots that were sheep. The sky was a high, bleached blue, and once out of the town, a waspish wind scoured the land. The traveller walked in an appreciative daze. He saw some people with dogs striding through the heather; he heard the pixie call of excited children. The polished hides of parked cars burned in the distance, winking glares where they caught the sun. These things did not call to him. He was aware of the timeless ambience of this land. Perhaps the things he saw and heard were simply ghosts, or echoes, of high summer that would fade into the approaching cold. When his steps faltered, he had come to a crossroads. The light, the flash in the sky he'd seen from the train, had been his guide, both physically and mentally. He knew it would continue to be. Something was waiting to be discovered.

Chapter One

Friday, 16th October: Little Moor

Lily Winter stood at the top of the hill, looking down across the grounds of the deserted manor-house in the valley below. She often paused here in her walks, for she liked to stare at the choked garden, with its still, stagnant lake, and at the dark, forbidding towers of the house itself. She had always been nervous of exploring the place in person, even though she and her twin brother, Owen, had a fascination for abandoned old houses. Long Eden. Its name alone conjured stories. Lily had concocted many languid romances in her mind as she'd sat upon the hill, gazing down. Long Eden had been empty since before her birth. The people who'd once lived there, with their imagined laughter, tragedies, riches and fantastical parties, had all left the area, no doubt to avoid death duties and expense. Lily sometimes wondered what the true story was.

A chill breeze, smelling of smoke, of autumn, moulded her long skirt around her goose-pimpled legs. She felt cold, but enjoyed the experience of it, the promise of another season, something new, yet familiar.

The distant, mournful blare of a train's horn broke Lily's reverie, brought her back into the afternoon. October. The month of brown and red and yellow; the smoke month. Today was the sixteenth day. She would count the others, each with its own unique flavour, until the end.

Two red setters bounded over the crest of the hill and gambolled, barking, towards her, their owner following.

'Amber! Lester!' Lily called and hunkered down, extending her arms. The animals threw themselves against her, ecstatic with pleasure at this unexpected meeting.

'Dogs! Dogs!' A middle-aged woman came striding behind her charges. She was dressed in yellow jodhpurs and polished black riding boots, a thick, quilted jacket hanging open to reveal a startling white jumper, which covered a bosom resplendent with gold chains.

Lily stood up, her hands upon the dogs' heads, their tails beating against her bare legs. 'Hello, Mrs Eager. How are you today?'

The woman smiled up at her. Lily was considerably taller than herself. 'Fine. But, you must be freezing.' She pantomimed a shiver. 'No coat or tights! What are you thinking of, child?'

'It's all right. I don't feel the cold.'

'Ah, youth!' sighed the woman.

Lily didn't like being called a child. She was a woman, nearly twenty years old. Barbara Eager was a pleasant sort, but a relative newcomer to Little Moor. She had brought her values with her, ways that had settled uneasily over the community, although she was not disliked. She and her husband ran the big hotel, The White House, which was popular with walking tourists in summer, and used at weekends by the locals as a pub. During the week, everyone tended to favour The Black Dog, which was run by a surly, one-eyed tyrant and his mean-spirited wife, both of whom were over-familiar or acid with their clientele according to their moods. Owen had told Lily he had once walked past The Black Dog in the small hours of the morning and had heard the landlord and his wife having sex; her wild moans had drifted from the open window. Lily was unsure whether this could be true. Owen was prone to fantasizing. Mr and Mrs Eager, on the other hand, would have a comfortable, mannered relationship. She would utter no moan of passion or otherwise, but perhaps a polite cough. Lily couldn't help smiling at this thought.

Barbara was oblivious, as she was of most things subtle in Little Moor. She smiled back. 'Well, it's a lovely day, and the smells are divine! What are you up to, Lily?' There was a note in her voice, which she could never contain, that revealed her slight disapproval of the fact that neither Lily nor Owen worked for a living. She often tried to interrogate them about where their income came from, which Lily and Owen both side-stepped with dexterity. There was no secret, but it amused them to frustrate the woman. Their mother had left them with an adequate income. Once a month, Owen and Lily drove into the nearest town, Patterham, and withdrew the interest on the account, which was more than enough for their needs. Owen had buried some of it in the walled garden to their house. Just in case.

'I'm just walking,' Lily said. 'Thinking.' Sometimes, she offered to do jobs for Barbara, to make the woman feel better, but today was not one of her most altruistic days.

'You must do a lot of thinking,' Barbara said, somewhat sharply.

Lily shrugged, and then said abruptly, 'I'm going to write a book.'

'Oh, how splendid!' Barbara's face bloomed with delighted relief. 'You know, you ought to come to my little writing circle some time. Get some feedback. It'd be good for you.'

'Thanks,' Lily said. 'I might.' She had no intention of ever doing so. Barbara's group comprised several middle-aged women and men, all well-heeled, who had retired to the moors from affluent occupations. Lily suspected that most of them were entirely talentless. The thought of writing something had only just come to her. She had no idea whether she'd be able to do it or not. It might be a boring thing to do, in the event.

'So, what are you writing about?' Barbara asked, and then grinned roguishly. 'Or haven't you reached the stage where you want to talk about it yet?'

'Well, I have a few ideas . . .' Lily screwed up her face. 'It's quite difficult.'

'Oh, I know!' Barbara's hand shot out to grab Lily's arm in a moment of artistic understanding. 'You know me and my little scribblings . . . It's such agony some-times, like trying to dig your way out of a buried cave with your bare hands!'

'Is it?' Lily didn't fancy getting involved in anything that sounded so painful.

'Oh yes! Sometimes the muse sits on my shoulder, but most often not. I have a devil of a job tempting her back!' She laughed with inappropriate loudness.

'Mmm, well, I don't think I've even met my muse yet.'

'Oh, don't worry, you will!'

Barbara summoned her dogs, who had lost interest in Lily and were now investigating cow-pats a few feet away. 'Are you walking back down the hill, dear?'

'If you like.' Lily put her hands into her skirt pockets and strolled along beside the woman. She noticed Bar-bara casting condemning glances at her down-at-heel work-boots, which were in fact a pair of Owen's, and also at her chest: because of the cold, it was obvious she was not wearing a bra. Lily could almost feel Barbara's itching desire to take her in hand, dress her up, give her a purpose in life. She had yet to meet the Eager daughter, Audrey, who was away at university studying law. Lily knew she'd dislike her intensely. Audrey had never come to Little Moor during the holidays, as she always went

4

abroad, travelling with friends. Barbara was always talking about this paragon of intelligence, wit and beauty,
and didn't seem to take offence that her daughter hadn't
even bothered to come and see The White House. Her
parents had lived there for nearly a year now.

'We're having a barbecue for Hallowe'en,' Barbara
said. 'Few fireworks and sausages. Sort of combination
with Guy Fawkes' Night. Will you and Owen come?'

'Hallowe'en's on Saturday this year,' Lily answered.
'We always come to The White House on Saturdays.'

Barbara smiled uneasily. 'So young to be such creatures of habit,' she said. 'But I'd planned for the "do" to
be on the Friday night, in any case.'

They'd reached the bottom of hill and Barbara
was clambering over the stile. Woods bustled darkly
away to their right, while the black stones of Long Eden
to the left were now hidden from view. Lily paused and
looked backwards before following Barbara into the
lane.

'What is it, dear?' Barbara asked. Lily looked as if
she'd heard something.

Lily turned round and shrugged. 'Nothing. It's just
the pull of the day, I think.'

Barbara laughed. 'My, how poetic! The pull of the
day! What do you mean by it?'

They had begun to walk along the lane that led back
to the village. 'I don't know, really. Some moments are
just significant, aren't they?' Lily had only just realized
she'd experienced such a moment, and wasn't quite sure
when it had happened. Only the taste of it lingered in
her heart.

'The sooner you start writing, the better!' Barbara
said. 'I hope you're not going to show us all up!'

Lily smiled. 'Not much chance of that, Mrs Eager.'

*

Low Mede was an old house rooted on the outskirts of Little Moor. It was three-storeyed, yet somehow appeared low slung and rambling, and was built of warm red brick. This was the home of the Cranton family, like the Eagers, relative newcomers to the village. The house possessed an air of tranquillity, a mellow ambience suited to the autumn season. Within it, however, tensions stretched and reverberated like wires.

Louis Cranton was out in the garden, staring down at the fading plants in a flower-bed, worrying about his daughter, Verity. They had not had a row exactly, but in his eyes it had been an argument: without raised voices, without bitter words, an exchange of chilled silence. The subject had been a familiar one. Everything had been said countless times before. Verity had done nothing with herself since she'd left college, which seemed such a waste to Louis, and he could not help, on occasion, telling her so. He did not begrudge the money he'd invested in her future, but felt pained she herself seemed to care so little about it. Her degree in Modern Studies had been a first; she could have pursued many avenues to success. But, whenever he broached the subject, Verity quietly, chillingly, reminded him she was happy to care for him and her brother, Daniel. She did not trust her father to look after the pair of them.

Although he found it uncomfortable to think about, Louis suspected something more than filial duty kept Verity in Little Moor. The village was a sanctuary, a time capsule, in which she could conceal herself. Why, and from what? She was an articulate and attractive girl. When she chose to, she could make friends easily, but the only people she spent time with, other than her family, were older women in the village. She seemed happy, but Louis was uneasy. Perhaps he was projecting his own desires on to the girl. The accident that had

6

killed his wife, Janine, had also left him disabled. He could no longer court the world's wonders, flit from country to country, sampling life's most potent liquors. He'd had no formal education, and was a self-made man, so successfully self-made that the forced early retirement had not posed a financial threat to him. He wanted the best for his children. Verity, he felt, was brilliant, capable of achieving the very best, while Daniel, he had to admit, did not share his sister's fine intellect.

He should worry more about Daniel, surely, with his disappointingly mediocre grades at school and his youthful, lazy disposition. Also, Daniel had an over-active imagination. As a child, he'd always chatted to invisible 'friends', and been able to 'see' what people in other rooms, even houses, were doing. Janine had been more worried about it than Louis, because she'd been the one to confirm Daniel's 'predictions' by talking with the people concerned. As he'd grown older, this tendency had abated, but he'd always been rather a solitary child. Now he seemed withdrawn from normal teenagers, preferring the company of an unsavoury band of local acquaintances, all of whom looked as if they practised the Black Mass with their families on a regular basis, or had slithered out of some H.P. Lovecraft story about incestuous hill-billies.

Louis had tried to get his son to bring friends home from school for the weekend – healthy, ordinary lads – but Daniel resisted this in an unrelentingly passive manner. Louis deplored Daniel's choice in reading matter, the most tacky of popular occult novels – surely an unhealthy interest for a growing boy – and was positively unnerved by the posters which adorned the walls of Daniel's rooms: demons, devils, peculiar animals. Perhaps it was just a phase. Louis himself had never experienced such a phase, but life had been very different back in the Fifties. He wished Daniel could get a girlfriend. He was seventeen years old now, and a goodlooking lad, if a little too slender. He didn't do himself any favours by dressing so scruffily when he was at home, but perhaps the sort of girls Daniel might prefer would like that. At least, while he was still at the private grammar school Louis had sent him to, Daniel couldn't grow his hair to an unacceptable length. The school was strict about things like that.

Louis surveyed the garden and leaned down painfully, putting his weight on his stick, to pluck a thin weed from the flower-bed at his feet. Verity's last words to him as he'd limped in anger from the drawing-room had been, 'And you spend too much time bending and stretching out there. Hire a gardener. It's time you faced your limitations.' He knew she was right. There was more pain than pleasure involved in caring for his private domain. Still, he had a peevish urge to defy her. Sometimes, she was too much the fount of all knowledge – perhaps a legacy of her university education – which he found irritating and humiliating. Sometimes, he wept alone at night, with only a bottle of whisky for company, the lights burning low in his study. He wept for Janine, his lost light, and for his ruined body. Sometimes he thought, I'd do anything, anything, to be fit again. But there was never any angel or devil listening, who could manifest before him and name a price.

The Crantons had lived in Low Mede since the spring of the year before, moving in in the wake of an army of interior decorators, who had restored the six-bedroomed building to its original splendour: wood stripped of a century of paint, dried flowers gushing from ornate vases, glossy floors spread with sumptuous Persian rugs. Louis had been out of hospital four months then, and had been able to walk small distances, aided by two sticks. Now he

8

only needed one stick, but a stroll anywhere further than down to one of the two village pubs both exhausted and was torture to him. Age conspired with his injured bones and muscles to prevent a full recovery.

At least he could look forward to one of his little pleasures this evening: the writers' circle held upstairs at The White House, in Barbara Eager's living-room. Now that he had the time, Louis wrote reams of poetry – bad poetry, he knew – but because there was so little he could do physically, it no longer seemed like a waste of time. Poetry, no matter how clumsy, had been his one solace during the dreadful grieving time following Janine's death and his own slow recuperation. The countryside around Little Moor inspired him; he wrote mawkishly of the seasons, the land, lost youth and love, time's passing. Once a month, he enjoyed the indulgence of reading his work aloud to a receptive audience; their criticism was gentle, and in return, he held his tongue concerning their own efforts. Barbara Eager had collected what she considered to be the group's best work and had published it herself. It was sold in the local post office and also on the front counter at the tiny part-time library near The Black Dog. Most copies had been bought by the writers themselves to give to friends and relatives back in the real world, part of the lives they had left behind. Verity had never seen her father's poetry; Louis could not have stood it if she had. She would only recognize its badness, and consequently praise him in a patronizing manner.

A noise from the house advised him of the arrival of his patroness. On Fridays, Barbara Eager drove in her Land Rover to Ellbrook, a small town seven miles west that boasted a large supermarket on its outskirts. Without actually saying so, she made it plain she didn't think Louis got out enough, and had briskly offered to take him with her on her excursions. He sat in the café attached to the shop, while she marched round behind a shopping trolley, and later, after they had drunk coffee together, she would drive them home the 'picturesque' way. This took them beneath the canopy of an ancient forest, known locally as Herman's Wood, through which the road cut east. The forest spread right to the edge of Little Moor. When the weather was fine, Barbara would say, 'How about getting back to nature, then?' and would wrench the steering wheel around, so that the Land Rover bounced off the lane and up one of the off-road tracks. After a short, bone-jolting ride, she would stop the vehicle with a screech of the hand-brake. Then she would help Louis down from the passenger seat and take his arm, leading him a short way into the trees. They would talk about poetry and writers, and complain about television programmes they'd both seen. Then Barbara Eager would look at her watch, make a groaning sound and hurry Louis back to the Land Rover. She had to be back at The White House to help her husband, Barney, open up for the evening. Once a week, Louis went to the Eagers' for dinner. Barney would play him marching band CDs on his hi-fi system and break open exquisite brandies. Louis liked the Eagers. He was grateful for the way in which they enhanced his diminished life.

Barbara Eager breezed into Low Mede without knocking on the door or ringing the bell. The front door was always ajar in warm weather until evening. She called out a bright greeting, which invoked Verity from the dining-room. Barbara couldn't repress the slight shudder that always accompanied a first sighting of the girl. She was somehow sinister, with her lean, rigid stance and expressionless face. Barbara had never seen her wearing dark clothes – most of her dresses were long and of a discreet floral print – but Verity still managed to give the impression that she dressed in black. Barbara knew she had little time for her, yet always attempted to be friendly with the girl for Louis's sake. Secretly, Barbara felt Verity to be a cold, selfish creature, someone who needed a good talking to, bringing down a peg. How different she was to Audrey, with her busy life, her ambitions and skills.

'He's in the garden,' Verity told her, without returning a greeting. 'I'll call him for you.'

'Thank you,' Barbara said shortly. She sensed the atmosphere immediately. There had been a disagreement. When Verity and Louis were on good terms, Verity would say hello to Barbara, and then direct her to wherever Louis was in the house. On bad days Barbara was kept waiting in the dark, highly polished hallway, while Verity behaved like a chatelaine, jealously keeping the keys of the house, and seemingly the keys to the lives of those who lived there.

Barbara's heart contracted when Louis came out of the lounge. He looked fragile. She wanted to rush forward and hug him, but of course that would be entirely inappropriate, and Verity was lurking behind him in the doorway, her eyes like flints. Barbara experienced a spasm of anger that Verity could do this to Louis. The girl did not seem to appreciate (or simply did not care) how delicate he was, how the storms of her moods buffeted his waning strengths.

'Louis, you're having dinner with us tonight!' Barbara announced impulsively. 'Come back to The White House with me after we've been to Ellbrook.'

Louis visibly brightened. 'Oh, that's very . . .'

'Dad, you should come home first for your massage,' Verity interrupted. She addressed Barbara. 'I give him aromatherapy on Friday evenings. He needs it before going down to the pub.'

Barbara acknowledged a slight censure in Verity's tone. She wanted to say, 'Well, give me the oils, and I'll do it.' She'd done a short course on therapeutic massage at her women's group before she'd moved to Little Moor, and certainly felt she had the expertise. But because of how she felt about Louis, she couldn't bring herself to suggest it. In the event, Louis himself intervened.

'I'll have it tomorrow, Vez. It won't make that much difference.'

'Suit yourself,' Verity answered, 'but don't complain to me about aches and pains.'

Louis directed a crooked smile at Barbara, which Verity could not see. He rolled his eyes. It was tragic, what life had done to him. Barbara could see a ghost of his former self in his smile. He was still a very handsome man, with his stooped, lean form and thick, greying hair. She wanted to cure all of Louis's aches, but their friendship was polite and restrained. She could barely voice her sympathy for him.

'Have you got your list?' Verity said.

Louis nodded. 'Yes.'

'Well, don't forget to bring the shopping home with you tonight.'

'I won't.'

She speaks to him as if she's his wife, Barbara thought with distaste, or his mother. 'I'll give him a lift back tonight,' she said, and realized she was taking part in Verity's game. You didn't let children walk the streets alone at night. They had to be escorted.

After her father had left the house, Verity Cranton stood alone in the hallway, closed her eyes and allowed herself a few moments to soak up the atmosphere she adored. Her hand reached out to touch the glossy sphere on top of the newel post at the bottom of the stairs. She could hear the grandmother clock ticking precisely in the dining-room, the hum of the fridge-freezer coming from the kitchen. Everything was perfectly still. It was blissful when Daniel and her father were both out, a time when she could walk the rooms of the house to experience the satisfaction of everything being in its place, the perfect symmetry of the furniture and paintings and ornaments, that drew her eyes sensuously like a well-composed picture. In this house, Verity felt completely at home, which was more than an appreciation of her possessions being around her, the spaciousness of the building, the expensive decor. The house seemed to hug her closely. She needed nothing more than the simple life in Little Moor provided for her. If she dreamed of romance, she was cynical and experienced enough to realize that dreams were often preferable to reality. She liked her own company, and on the occasions she needed outside stimuli, the gentle friendship of the few women she'd become acquainted with was more than adequate to satisfy her.

The cross words she'd had with her father a short time before had left an unpleasant resonance behind them. Verity walked slowly into the drawing-room, with the intention of cleansing the atmosphere there. Like Daniel, she was a very sensitive person, although she chose to hide and repress her more psychic aspects, and had always done so. She suspected that Louis wanted to get rid of her, that he didn't particularly like her as a person, and resented her presence. She had never been close to either of her parents, and the loss of her mother had made barely an impact on her life. She remembered when the news had come to her, in the final year of her studies at university, the phone call from her maternal grandmother at her digs. Verity was very similar to her grandmother – they had always understood one another, even when Verity had been a prim and undemonstrative child.

'Vez, I have something very unpleasant to tell you,' her grandmother had said. 'I'm afraid there's been an accident. Janine is dead.'

'Oh,' Verity had answered. She could think of nothing else to say. No tide of emotion had crashed over her head, no horrified incredulity, panic or grief. In fact, she recalled a premonition earlier in the day which she'd impatiently ignored.

There had been a brief silence and then her grandmother had asked, 'Are you upset?'

The question, under the circumstances, should have seemed bizarre, but despite the distance and the impersonality of the instrument in her hand, Verity knew instinctively that on the other end of the line a remote soul was completely in tune with her own. Neither of them felt upset.

'I'm shocked,' Verity had eventually responded in an even voice.

'Yes. Your father is badly hurt. Perhaps you should come home.'

Netty, the girl Verity shared a house with, reacted far more strongly when the news was broken to her. She wanted to hug Verity and weep with her. She ran to the off-licence to fetch a nepenthe of cheap vodka. Verity was glad that her icy stillness was interpreted as horrified numbness. She drank the vodka, wondering how this event would affect her life. Surely, she wouldn't be expected to give up her studies at this crucial stage?

After the funeral, which Louis was too ill to attend, everyone went back to Janine's parents' house. There, Verity had begun to weep. Her grandfather had hurried to console her, but she had shaken him off impatiently. She didn't need his sentimental words.

'Don't you understand?' she'd cried. 'I'm crying because I cannot grieve! All these people, look at them, they all feel more for her than I ever did!' She instantly became aware of the monstrousness of her words. Her grandfather had withdrawn as if scalded, and there was a weary recognition in his eyes. He had lived with a woman like Verity for many years. Janine had been his darling, his true daughter. Verity could tell he was sad that Janine had spawned a frozen monster like her mother. Yet Verity could not regret her outburst. It was the simple truth.

That was the only time Verity had ever considered her passionlessness might be abnormal, or even disabling in some way. She had known a similar outburst would not happen again. Scant weeks after this event, her life had become catastrophic, as if she'd incurred a psychic backlash for her behaviour. It had ended in one man committing suicide and another man's wife going insane. Louis knew nothing about this, and if Daniel had intuited it, he never mentioned it. In Little Moor, Verity could shut the door on the past. She believed she had thrown away the key.

The argument with Louis had been about the usual topic: how she should get away and immerse herself in a suitable career, meet people, find a boyfriend. Verity never shouted back at Louis, no matter how frustrated he became, how loud his voice. He, after all, was ignorant of her reasons for choosing the life she lived. She was prepared to hang on doggedly until the house became hers; she would not let him push her out. Anyway, he needed her, no matter how he liked to deny it. Although he annoyed her at times, and she considered him a weak, emotional person, she did not dislike him. Often, she felt

15

surprisingly protective towards him, in the same way that she looked after her belongings, kept them clean and in the correct place. As well as massaging what she hoped was energy into his damaged body, she bought his clothes for him to keep him spry, and had arranged for a local hairdresser to come to the house regularly to keep him well-groomed. Similarly, because she was not a good cook, she had hired someone to prepare their meals, to make jam and pickled onions for them, bake pies using fruit from the small orchard at the bottom of the garden. The rest of the housekeeping duties she kept jealously to herself. The house was large, but she devoted herself to its care. When Louis had shown an interest in the garden – a hitherto unknown interest – she had grudgingly ordered a lawn-mower he could sit down in, and various tools adapted to his needs. He no longer went shooting, which had been his favourite recreation in the past, so she supposed the gardening was therapeutic for him.

Verity now also kept the accounts, presenting neatly written cheques to Louis for him to sign. The attic had been converted into two rooms and a bathroom for Daniel, where he could live comfortably in an infuriating slobbishness that Verity could ignore. The door to the attic stairs was kept shut. Daniel would come in through the front door, rampage up the stairs and disappear into his lair. The only annoyance was the thump of the raucous music he liked to listen to, but even that was slight; the rooms had been soundproofed. Once a month, the cook's two grand-daughters came and cleaned up there. Sometimes, Daniel would be around, and the sound of high-pitched flirty giggling would come down the attic stairs. Verity was forever slamming the door shut as she passed it, although she sensed Daniel abhorred the giggling as much as she did.

Verity extended her honed senses into the drawing-room, imagining she was pushing back a gritty, grey cloud. Presently, all residue of the argument had been expunged. She breathed deeply in satisfaction, felt better. A sound from the kitchen advised her Mrs Roan had come to begin dinner. It was always eaten early on a Friday, because it was Louis's night at The White House. Now, Verity would eat alone. She doubted Daniel would put in an appearance, and would not appreciate it if he did. She herself favoured late meals, eaten in dim light with expensive cutlery and accompanied by acid wines. She felt more concerned about the correct placement of tableware than she ever did for other people. She and Mrs Roan had a mutual respect for one another. Mrs Roan was pleased a young person in 'this day and age' had an appreciation of a well-kept house, while Verity admired Mrs Roan's polite distance and tidy way of working. Verity was altogether approved of by the village women. Even those she visited could not claim to know her, but she could keep up an even stream of conversation and was knowledgeable about the subjects that interested them. The only thing she was not given to was gossip, but that was generally kept for more intimate friends anyway.

As she turned to leave the room, someone called, 'Verity!' The voice was urgent, as if warning her of something. Alarmed, Verity wheeled round, for the voice had sounded as if it was in the room behind her. There was, as she should have known, nothing there.

'What?' she demanded irritably. For years, she had shut out this kind of silliness, messages from nowhere. It annoyed her. But there was no response to her enquiry. As she passed from the drawing-room into the hall, she felt the day change. Involuntarily, she shivered, then repressed the feeling with a firm thought. The only

17

prospect for the future was the preparation of dinner, the consuming of dinner, and all the other regular routines she had created for herself. She would let nothing else in.

Chapter Two

Same day: Little Moor (continued)

Lily Winter knew that her brother was going to be out all night again. He always told her he'd be back late, not to wait up, but invariably when he went out at tea-time on a Friday, he would not return until morning. Sometimes he'd be asleep in the kitchen when Lily went down for her breakfast. Sometimes he'd be in the parlour on the floor. But she knew he never came in and went to bed. What he got up to on his mysterious nights out she did not enquire. Not that she wasn't curious – she was – but they had a mutual respect for one another. Owen needed his private times. They shared so much, knew each other so well, yet he had a need to escape their relationship sometimes. Lily did not begrudge this.

Now Owen sat at the kitchen table, one foot up among the milk bottles, dirty plates and old papers, lacing his boots. He possessed a startling pale beauty, which only became apparent upon long acquaintance. People generally thought there was something strange, or even unpleasant, about Owen when they first met him. Like Lily, he was very tall, but whereas Lily dyed her fair hair red, Owen's was a white-blond mane, invariably unwashed, and generally held back in a pony-tail at his neck. On the occasions he allowed Lily to brush it or wash it for him, she told him he looked like an angel. 'You only need wings,' she'd say.

Lily was listlessly transferring dishes from the table to the sink. She cleaned the house properly once a week, on Fridays, while Owen was out, and she took pleasure in relaxing in tidy surroundings, playing CDs, drinking a bottle of wine all by herself, dancing alone in the firelight of the parlour. She never wanted anyone else to share these evenings with her; it would spoil them.

'Barbara Eager invited me to her writing group today,' she said.

Owen made a disparaging sound. 'What ever for?' His voice, accompanied by his satyr's smile, was not the debased drawl that might be expected, but clipped and cultured.

'I thought I might write something.'

'You don't need her kind for that!'

Lily smiled to herself. Owen always supported her whims, however impractical they seemed. If she wanted to write, then she would and could, as far as he was concerned.

'I don't know what to write about,' she said.

Owen went across to the sink and hugged her. He kissed the top of her head. 'Just do it,' he said. 'Will you let me read it?'

'Of course I will – when I think of something.' She paused. 'O, is it a normal day today?'

Owen grinned. 'Well, it was until now. What's happened?'

She shrugged. 'I don't know. I feel excited. It's hard to explain, but it's how I used to feel when I was a kid, on my way to a party or something. Haven't you felt anything?'

Owen pulled a face and was silent for a moment. 'No, I don't think so.' He ruffled his sister's hair. 'It must be a female thing. Anyway, I'm off now. Don't wait up.'

Lily watched him walk down the lane from the kitchen window. She saw him turn into the drive of Low Mede, which was just visible if she leaned forward. Owen had struck up a friendship with Daniel Cranton. Lily couldn't

20

work out why. She knew all three of Owen's other regular friends, who were locals, and Daniel didn't seem to conform to their type. He was an outsider, less rough, less mature, but more educated. Unlike the other three, Luke, Bobby and Ray, Daniel was never brought into the cottage. Lily wondered if her brother had a special purpose in mind for the Cranton boy, and hoped he knew what he was doing. Little Moor was their home, but they still had to be careful. She remembered her mother, Helen, saying to her, 'You are my little jewels. You are precious and you are different.' Perhaps mothers said things like that to their children all the time, but Lily had always felt there was some secret message in the words. Helen Winter had repeated the message often, in many different ways. 'Look at the snow. It is as strange and wonderful as you are. You cannot see all the stars in the sky, but they are there. Just imagine them. Then you can see. *You* can do that. Look, look at Orion. That is the stargate, and it is a secret.' Lily wished she had kept a record of all the messages, because surely together they would have told a whole story. Like who their father was, for example, and why Helen had been so secretive about her past. Lily had accepted that she and Owen were different, and not just in obvious ways. It scared her that he had started seeing Daniel Cranton so much, but she couldn't identify why exactly. Luke, Bobby and Ray were no great intellects and they were native to the area; from them she felt no threat. But the other ... Tomorrow she must go to one of their secret places and think of an answer to it all. Sometimes, that worked.

Verity was in the middle of her early dinner when the doorbell rang. Three long, importunate rings. She set down her knife and fork and waited for the sound of Daniel's heavy feet thundering down the stairs. It did not come. The doorbell rang again, a long, insulting intrusion. Annoyed, Verity put down her napkin and went into the hall. The muffled thump of music drifted down from upstairs. Why on earth Daniel didn't listen out for his friends when he was expecting them, Verity couldn't tell. Perhaps he did it on purpose to aggravate her. She went to the door, her face a mask of disapproval. Owen Winter was lounging against one of the wooden pillars of the porch. Of all Daniel's horrible friends, he had to be the worst. Verity hated the way he looked at her, the way he dressed, his idle way of moving. She thought his face was odd, so much so, you had to stare at it, an experience wholly without delight in her opinion. There was something unwholesome about Owen Winter. If Verity had had any concern for her brother at all, she might have done something to dissolve the friendship. 'He's upstairs,' she said and turned away from the open door. It grieved her to have the creature in the house, treading upon her floors, touching her stair-rail, but it would grieve her more to wait on him and fetch Daniel herself.

Without speaking, Owen Winter loped towards the stairs. Verity went back into the dining-room and sat down, but felt unable to recommence her meal until Daniel and his friend had left the house. She waited tensely, every sense alert. What a joyous day it would be when her brother finally left home. He was like a persistent stain that no amount of scrubbing could remove. She was aware that the comforts Louis's affluence provided would inevitably delay this day of release. Daniel was lazy. She would have to remind her father about his education. Perhaps a little pressure needed to be applied. Daniel's choice of friends appalled her: local roughnecks lacking any points of merit. She knew Owen Winter sometimes drove them all to towns where they'd go to nightclubs which catered for their antisocial tastes. Perhaps Daniel took drugs. She would do nothing to prevent that. It could surely only speed his departure from home. If it wasn't for the fact he had his own rooms in the house, Verity would have had to take action about him. Fortunately, he could be ignored most of the time.

She heard Daniel and Owen trooping down the stairs, laughing coarsely in that particularly grating way uncouth young males seemed to adopt. Daniel was a slender, graceful boy. Why he had to sound like a herd of wildebeest whenever he slouched around the house she could not explain. 'Get out,' she murmured under her breath, clutching a fork. 'Just get out.'

Owen hadn't brought the car, which meant he'd decided they wouldn't be clubbing it tonight. This signalled that one of the group's more esoteric pursuits was presaged. Daniel always felt nervous about this, even though he was fascinated by the unseen and the whiff of forbidden knowledge. There was no pattern to Owen's behaviour, but some Fridays he insisted they all went to the High Place, a hill deep within Herman's Wood, where a natural circle was formed at the summit, hemmed by ancient trees. Here, Owen enacted his own arcane rituals, in which the others were expected to participate. It was a necessary part of being a member of the group, but something which Daniel didn't really enjoy. He felt that Owen was partly mad, but as this madness was never threatening, it could be overlooked. Still, the forays into the woods to the High Place sometimes frightened Daniel.

Perhaps this was because of his own hidden talents, which he never spoke about to anyone, not even Owen. While the others, excepting perhaps Owen, were happy to smoke dope and drink beer, then do whatever Owen directed in intoxicated cheeriness, Daniel was attuned to the energies they invoked, the watching presence of the trees. Often he saw shadowy shapes lurking at the edge of the circle, attracted by what the group were doing. They were not malign, but they had the potential to be mischievous. Daniel eventually found it was better to smoke as much dope and drink as much beer as he could before anything started. Then he could do whatever Owen asked without feeling scared or weird: the chanting, the strange, shuffling dancing, the rituals of snarling words and significant pantomimes of malevolence. The other three didn't seem to question what Owen did, or asked them to do, but neither did they seem particularly committed to it. This was Owen's obsession; they simply went along with it to enjoy the benefits of Owen's friendship. He had money, he had his own house, he had a car, he had charisma.

Like Lily Winter, Daniel was unsure why Owen was interested in him. They had struck up a friendship only a couple of weeks after the Crantons had moved to Little Moor. Daniel had been walking past the Winters' cottage one afternoon and Owen had been working on his car in the driveway. As Daniel had come down the lane, Owen had straightened up from the car, wiping his hands on a rag, watching Daniel intently. Daniel had been sure Owen had recognized something in him, and this made him feel ashamed. He'd always been chastised by his parents for his peculiarities and dreaded anyone else becoming aware of them now. Owen, however, had just said, 'Hi, you've moved in down there, haven't you?' Their friendship had come easily after that, which had surprised Daniel. Why he couldn't tell Owen about his odd premonitions and feelings, he didn't know. Surely Owen would be deeply interested? Yet Daniel feared scorn or punishment and kept silent, repressing the unbidden feelings as much as he could. In private, he could indulge himself and dream strange, new realities, but he had learned at an early age that this indulgence was not to be shared.

The first time Owen had taken him to the High Place, he'd been horrified, and had barely kept control of himself, anxious that no one should notice how much the proceedings affected him. Since then, he had mastered getting drunk and how to act. It came as second nature now. He was aware of how different he was from the others, and also of how his background and slightly younger age sometimes grated against their own. Occasionally, this manifested as verbal baiting, but he had discovered how to combat that, and to give as good as he got. When he stood up for himself, Owen seemed pleased. Then he would say something really cruel. Daniel found it harder to answer Owen back than any of the others.

Owen had set off in the direction of Herman's Wood, his hands in his pockets, his long stride lazily devouring the lane. 'Where are the others?' Daniel asked, hurrying to keep up.

'Meeting us there,' Owen replied shortly. He seemed to be in a distant mood.

They walked in silence, until they came to the place where a path, almost hidden by undergrowth, led into the trees. It was almost dark and the woods, on the right of the lane, looked oppressive and dangerous. Owen led the way into the moist shadows, his hands still in his pockets. Daniel hit out at trailing thorns that snagged his clothing. He wanted this part to be over. It was like a trial, a test, the journey through the woods to the sanctuary of the High Place.

The deciduous trees gave way to pines, and the ground

was spongy with fallen needles underfoot. When they approached the High Place, Daniel could see two lights burning up among the trees. The High Place was crowned by a ring of ancient oaks, and there was a hollow in the middle, where the group built fires. A solitary figure, a sentinel, was silhouetted against the light of one of the lamps. Daniel recognized the aggressive stance of Ray Perks, his least favourite of the group. He felt that Bobby and Luke actually liked him most of the time, while Ray just played at it to keep Owen happy. In another situation, Ray would be the one to jump on Daniel in a dark street, knock him senseless, take his money, his watch, kick him in resentment for his comfortable life. Ray came from the most shunned of the village families. Apart from Ray, his three sisters and his mother, the rest of the family seemed ancient and senile, including the father. If you walked past their run-down cottage, one of the ancients would invariably shout obscenities at you from the garden, or a window of the house. Bobby and Luke came from farming families, and were boisterous and crude, but mostly well-meaning.

Owen and Daniel climbed the hill. Ray said, 'All right?' as Owen passed him.

'Yeah.' Owen walked directly down to the hollow, where Luke and Bobby were already building a fire. Daniel followed, uncomfortably aware of Ray slouching behind him. Owen took a can of beer from one of the four-packs lying near the fire. 'Have one, Daniel,' he said, gesturing. Daniel helped himself. He would need to drink at least three of these before he felt part of the group again.

For about ten minutes the youths drank beer, while Owen rolled a joint. They bantered awkwardly with one another, casting sidelong glances at their mentor. Owen lit up, and exhaled a perfect plume of silvery smoke

26

which rose up to the treetops. His head was cast back, his eyes alight with some weird inner quirk; he seemed elemental, threatening. 'He's not one of us,' Daniel thought, but what Owen might actually be, he could not guess. The youths had formed a circle, which Owen dominated through his pallor and his presence. He passed the joint languidly to Ray, who noisily inhaled. The sparking end of the joint illumined his face and his generous and satyr-like features were cast in red shadow. Daniel was sitting next to him. The group had fallen silent, as if Owen had willed it. Daniel's heart was beating fast. He didn't want to be there, yet lacked the will to leave. He knew that Owen would pick on him tonight; he'd been spared too many times these last few weeks. Ray handed him the joint, and he took careful, measured inhalations. The dope helped; it altered his reality, made the ridiculous seem sane and required. He could feel Bobby's impatience, waiting for the joint to be passed on, yet was reluctant to hand it over. He wanted it all, needed its temporary gift of tranquillity. Eventually, unspoken pressure from the others was too heavy to ignore and Daniel relinquished the joint. Owen was already rolling another, his pale hair falling forward over his face, hiding his expression, but Daniel knew he was smiling. The thought of that smile made Daniel angry, fuelled a spark of passion, some creature-thing, deep inside him.

Having lit the second joint, Owen rose to his feet and began to walk around the others. His circling seemed to create a boundary that separated them all from the world beyond the hilltop, round and round. He began to hum softly beneath his breath a monotonous note. Daniel's head started to spin, slowly. The effects of the drug helped him sense the circle of presence Owen was creating; he could feel it rotating. Something seemed to uncurl and stretch within his body; he wondered if it was the same for the others. Owen's pace increased and his throat opened to a deep resonant tone. Familiar with this ritual, the rest of the group were all sitting upright, eyes fixed ahead, focusing on a point in the midst of their circle. The air was spinning round them, faster and faster, until all that existed was the small space they occupied. The smell of the forest, the earth itself, seemed to intensify within the circle, hot, humid, fecund. Daniel could feel his throat pulsing with the beat of blood, then his breast, his stomach, his loins. His arms felt hot; his fingers tingled. It was like fainting without losing consciousness.

Suddenly, Owen uttered a screech and jumped into the centre of the circle to land on all fours, head thrown back, mouth gaping, eyes starting, throat corded. Then he shook his head like an animal, his pale hair threshing around his shoulders. He reared up a little to rest his hands on his thighs, his knees cracking. His head turned as he inspected each member of his group. None of them had any doubt that he judged them, found them wanting, but they were all he had. He had begun to hum beneath his breath again, a tuneless melody. Then he fixed his eyes on Daniel, and nodded once. It was a summons.

Daniel felt the ground beneath him grow hot. It seemed to be steaming, but that might have been the smoke in his eyes. Owen was a crouched, predatory thing in the centre of the circle, his long hands quivering as they hung over his knees, his pale, attenuated face livid along the cheek-bones. He did not speak, but Daniel could almost hear Owen's voice whispering in his head. 'Come forward, come to me. Do as I tell you.' Daniel crawled towards the centre of the circle. Were the others relieved they had not been chosen?

'Your sacrifice,' Owen said aloud, and he resumed his place between Luke and Ray at the circle's edge.

Sacrifice. Sacrifice to the earth. She takes from us. We give.

Daniel unzipped his trousers. He knelt in the dirt beside the smouldering, crackling fire, and scrabbled in the peaty soil with his fingers. His will was not his own; he had no control over this. As he dug into the body of the earth, the hunger came, and the sense of being removed from his own mind. The other youths had started to chant, slap their hands against the ground. Daniel dug in time to their rhythm. By the time their voices had risen to a howl, he was stabbing the earth, stabbing it, letting her take him.

Out on the moors, the traveller sleeps among the rocks, upon the sheep-cropped wilderness meadows. He breathes deeply, his cheek against the earth. And as he sleeps and breathes, he feels. It is like a voice calling his name, this deep resonance that beats through the bones, the flesh, the blood of the moors, the body of the earth. In the morning, he will remember, and he will follow the call. Now, he sleeps and dreams, male and hard against the earth.

Chapter Three

Saturday, 17th October: High Crag House, Cornwall

Enniel Prussoe sat at his desk, staring at the printout of the message which recently had been displayed on his monitor screen, encrypted information from his electronic mail address. Dim afternoon light streamed in through the stained glass behind him, covering him in muted colours. His high brow was furrowed, his long, slender fingers tapped his lips. Long, dark red hair was contained neatly at his neck in a black towelling band. His clothes were casual but expensive; he looked like someone who should be working for a record company or an up-market advertising agency. His skin was pale, almost translucent, yet his eyes were very dark. He appeared to be a man of thirty, yet was far, far older than that. When he walked the streets of the country's cities, very few would have been able to tell that Enniel was not completely human. He was Grigori, a son of angels.

Enniel was very tall, as were most of his kind, but for one or two stunted throwbacks that emerged from time to time. His differences from humanity were not glaring; he did not drink blood, sleep by day, change into something hideous at the full of the moon or kill people unnecessarily. Neither did he possess wings and fly. Enniel knew that his forebears, contrary to popular, or biblical, belief, had never physically flown across the world with messages from heaven. Sometimes, they had worn the wings of vultures upon their shoulders, and in shamanic trance had coursed the astral planes like birds.

But the journeys had always been psychic rather than actual. Over the centuries, through the writings and oral traditions of ignorant peoples, the myths had changed and history had mutated into symbols. The history of the Grigori was wrapped in mummifying layers of symbols. Irritating human scholars insisted on trying to unwrap the layers, but the Grigori confounded their efforts. Whenever the academics and archaeologists got too close, the authorities of the Eastern countries in which they were working would mysteriously revoke their permits or war would commence. Iraq, which, as Enniel knew, was the cradle of civilization, where the Grigori had been created and the secrets of prehistory still lay concealed in buried cities, had been successfully closed to Western study for years. Sacred sites were being destroyed all the time, their damning knowledge broken up and fragmented. Gone were the meticulously kept records and chronicles of the Anannage, the first angels who had appeared in this world and changed the course of human history. The inventory of the cultivation programmes of the Garden in Eden: gone. The details of the diaspora, when the rebel Anannage, with their human consorts and hybrid children, had fled to all corners of the earth: gone. All that survived were the legends of the fallen angels, who had bred with human women and spawned races of monsters and giants. Of these, the Anakim had been the most fearsome – the outcast demon face of the giants – and nowadays the term was used to indicate the most unpredictable and troublesome Grigori individuals.

Living among humans, the descendants of the ancient rebel angel families had shrunk from calling themselves Anannage, the Mesopotamian term for their forebears, and adopted Grigori, from the Greek. They knew the pure bloodstrain had been diluted and polluted with

31

human genetic material. Nevertheless, some Grigori still yearned to reclaim their original status.

Accounts of Grigori history found in many corners of the world, with their myriad terms and permutations, were confusing. What remained of the truth still lay in darkness in the most inaccessible places, in the chambers beneath the Sphinx, in the tombs of kings, hidden beneath tons of sand, in deep, lightless caves in the high mountains of Zagros. The Grigori left it there, let it sleep, confident of their control of human affairs. The ancient paintings of the bird-shamans, with their ceremonial wings and the details of their rituals, would forever remain buried beneath desert sands.

The main difference between Enniel and humanity was his knowledge, for he and his people remembered far more than humanity did. Prehistory was not a mystery to Enniel. He knew the answers to the puzzles of the Pyramids, the secrets of the stars, the historical information concealed within all the ancient myths. In his mind lay all the wonders of the true magic, the oldest magic. Using it was no more unusual to Enniel than turning on a TV was for most humans. And he hardly aged. This was perhaps an inconvenience at times, for the Grigori had always liked to walk unseen among the little people of the world, the unawakened, the ignorant. Still, over the centuries, they had learned to shape their flesh to a degree and could disguise their longevity. Deaths could be faked, new relatives produced at will. There were also other tools that Enniel's people had at their disposal to shroud their existence.

Enniel was a member of the Parzupheim, the worldwide governing body of the Grigori families, which, as well as controlling the affairs of its own kind, held significant interests in human commerce. Grigori money fuelled many corporations. Juntas rose and fell on the strength of Grigori wealth. Perhaps because of their long lives, Enniel's people had a passion for making money, gambling with it and being creative with it. They liked to inject affluence into certain floundering societies, or cause financial famine in others. Theirs was the world of wheels within wheels, the laundering of money, arms dealing and drug-trafficking.

Enniel's working day consisted mainly of talking on the phone and using computer information networks, making data fly around the world, changing the future. The Grigori had taken well to the advance of human technology. In this respect, they regarded the little people as their workers, the ones who could get their hands dirty inventing and building. Grigori merely took advantage of the finished products. Their own evolution was geared more towards spiritual matters.

Enniel likened his occupation to the fluttering of the hypothetical butterfly's wings, which in Chaos Theory could cause a hurricane halfway around the world.

Today, however, the instantaneous dance of data had caused Enniel only consternation. The message was emphatic, spoken straight from the inner chambers of the Parzupheim: *Track down the Anakim, contain him. It is time for us to intervene*. Enniel did not want this responsibility. He sensed the unpredictable nature of his prey, and knew that his capture would have unwelcome and incalculable consequences.

Drawing in his breath, Enniel screwed up the printout, transferred it to an ashtray and set fire to it with the onyx lighter that stood next to his monitor. He watched the flames devour the paper into a curl of diminished blackness, then stood up and paced around his study. The room was large, opulent, filled with the curios of dead nations, which were unspeakably valuable. Enniel picked up a statuette of an ancient Sumerian demon, its detail worn away until only a suggestion of its features remained. Enniel weighed it in his hands, considered hurling it against the high stone fireplace. If only other evils from the past could be so easily destroyed.

The end of the millennium approached, and, as all high-ranking Grigori had suspected and feared, momentous and inevitable changes were preparing to occur. Planets and stars slid towards their inexorable positions in the heavens, influencing the political climate on the earth, and the lives of those who lived there. And as with the butterfly of the Chaos Theory, sometimes it was something small and fluttering that initiated the greater changes. The beating of tiny wings, growing and growing, like a shadow play upon the world, until there were mighty pinions sweeping hurricanes of transformation from pole to pole. Far better, then, if one was to stem the changes, to press a thumb against the helpless butterfly and squash it flat. Or else, the pretty insect could be netted and transferred to a sealed jar, where the beat of its wings could have little effect. The jar could be opened occasionally when the winds of change needed to be invoked, but anything other than that was unthinkable.

Enniel replaced the statuette upon its table. No, the insect must be netted, the power of its wings analysed and channelled.

The Parzupheim intended to do just that. They believed they were acting in the best interests of all the creatures upon the earth. Whilst they might play with humanity, they also felt they should be responsible for the little people and endeavour to protect them whenever possible. In any case, a world without toys would be a terribly dull place.

Enniel knew that one of his wards, the artist Aninka Prussoe, was currently waiting to see him. He could feel her presence in the front hall of the house, her tension, her nervousness. Enniel had summoned her to the house to interview her about recent events in Cresterfield, where she lived. Aninka had no idea what she had become mixed up in, poor child. Neither did Enniel have any intention of enlightening her too fully. She would not understand the implications, and might prove obstructive to his aims. The problem with so many of the young, Enniel thought, was that they foolishly considered the past should be abandoned and forgotten. They wanted the fast, colourful world of humanity, its trivialities and surface gloss. They were glamorized by it all. Aninka, courted by the artistic world because of her talents (a gift of her heritage, though she chose to ignore it), was perhaps one of the worst examples. Maturity would bring common sense, Enniel knew. She could not maintain her heretical beliefs for centuries, when her inhuman condition would force her to seek the asylum of her own kind, but in the meantime she insisted on playing the role of the rebel child, transforming herself into a beacon for the spirits of corruption. Enniel was annoyed by this, for now was too delicate a time for maverick Grigori to be charging about the world. They would be gathered up and used by the powers that instigated change, the powers of time. For this reason, Enniel would coax Aninka's story from her and then use her as a lure to capture his prey.

As he sauntered back to his desk to call a member of his staff on the intercom so that Aninka could be brought to his study, Enniel's eyes were drawn to a tapestry hanging upon the wall, half-hidden in the shadows cast by the long curtains beside the coloured window. The tapestry had been designed by a famous Pre-Raphaelite painter in the early part of the century, but its existence was not proclaimed in any catalogue of the artist's work. It depicted one of the ringleaders of the original Anannage rebellion standing in a field of corn, dressed in a robe of white and gold: Shemyaza, the beautiful seducer, whose lust had caused the downfall of his race. Enniel thought he detected a smugness hovering around the ascetic yet sensual features.

Thought you could be rid of my influence? Fool! You are wrong to think I would leave you in peace. Why should you prosper while I suffer?

Shemyaza had been punished severely for his actions, and in the myths of the Grigori, he suffered eternal torment, his soul held in limbo, neither in this world nor the next. Still, his spirit prevailed in the hearts of those considered Anakim and their followers, trouble-makers, fired by the frustrated bitterness of Shemyaza's hatred.

Enniel was a powerful man, and he had powerful allies, but still he feared the task he had been given. He knew powers existed that were greater than the combined might of his people, and in the forthcoming chase, the prey might well turn and devour the hunters.

Aninka Prussoe knew she was being kept waiting on purpose. The hall of the old house was dark and silent, but for the ticking of the grandfather clock under the stairs. A wash of green and ruby light fell down the stairs on to the black and white tiled floor from the stained-glass windows above the first landing. It was like a museum, or a mausoleum. The grim, reclining angelic effigy of grey stone against the wall did nothing to dispel the gloomy atmosphere. Once, she could have wandered into one of the parlours, or the library, to amuse herself until her guardian, Enniel, had the time and politeness to see her. Now she felt like a visitor, and the hall kept her at bay. Only once Enniel had accepted her presence could she feel comfortable roaming the house.

Aninka stood up and paced across the hall, her high heels staccato and echoing against the tiles. She peeled off her long black kid gloves and slapped them against the palm of one hand. She was nervous. Last night, at her cousin Noah's in the North, she had somehow managed to fire herself up again. She'd convinced herself she must speak honestly to her guardian about her part in the atrocity which had taken place in Cresterfield. Now, entombed by the silence of his oppressive house, she wondered whether she had been right. Wouldn't he scorn her for her involvement, chastise her for her stupidity? She was not the guilty party, but she was afraid she'd be sent from this place feeling as if she was. She had so rarely returned to the house since she'd left it as a teenager to attend university in the city. The release had been euphoric. Not until she'd escaped had she realized how oppressed she'd been within its walls. Enniel had not rebuked her for her absences from family celebrations, but, alone in her room in the city, she'd sensed the condensed activity going on back home, the space where her soul should be in the collective gathering. In some ways, she knew she could never really be absent. In her dreams they summoned her, and she went there, denied of choice. It was easy to believe she'd adopted the life beyond the family, free of all it implied. In truth, her 'real life' could only ever be a sham, something she could play at until time decreed she must seek the sanctuary of the enclosing walls once more. Enniel let her play; he indulged her – and her cousins, most of whom had fled to immerse themselves in the hustle of mundane life. They were all still bound to him, and knew it. *Perhaps I should have sent an occasional letter,* she thought.

Someone came through the curtains that obscured a corridor ahead of her – soft-footed, politely distant and utterly correct, her guardian's apprentice. They called him a *bouteiller*, more commonly known as a butler. 'Austin,' she said. 'I've been here nearly twenty minutes!'

37

The *bouteiller* bowed. He was a tall man, apparently of early middle age, severely handsome, his steel-grey hair held in a knot at the nape of his neck. Aninka was only an inch or so shorter than he. 'Apologies, Miss Aninka. Mr Enniel has been on the phone.'

'Is that any reason to leave me sitting here in the hall like a stranger?'

'With respect, Miss Aninka, that was your choice. This house is your home; you were free to wait where you liked.'

Aninka could not respond. The old devil knew only too well how she felt. 'Well, take me to him, then. Let's not drop the formalities.'

Austin led the way into the corridor. Beyond the curtain, no natural light shone. Peacock lamps illumined the hallway only dimly, their ancient coloured glass too thick and rheumy to provide much brilliance. Here the floor was carpeted, and the smell of cedar wood was strong. How long was it since she'd last visited: three years, four? Childhood memories came back with startling clarity. The feel of the ancient plush against small, bare feet. She knew the feel and the character of each goblin carving on the wall panels. Every one of them had experienced her childish, exploring hands. She had named them, too: Aster, Colly, Sarry-bun.

The corridor ended at a T-junction where a woman in black was seated in a high-backed chair before an imposing double doorway. Beside her was a table, highly polished, which supported a florid bowl of carnations of an almost unnatural deep red. Aninka repressed a shudder. 'Good morning, Aunt,' she said. The woman neither responded, nor even acknowledged Aninka's presence. Her face was white, her eyes dark and staring. She did not look mad, merely contemplative. She had the ability to make anyone feel like a ghost.

Austin knocked politely on the double doors and then

slid them apart. Aninka drew in her breath and marched through the aperture. The doors whispered shut behind her.

Enniel had positioned himself against the window of stained glass. This was the famous peacock window; the tail was fully seventeen feet across. The body of the bird changed into a serpent; it had a serpent's head. Enniel was relaxed. He could have been Aninka's age.

'Good of you to see me, Enniel,' Aninka said. 'You must be busy.' She wanted to be sarcastic, but failed.

'Not as busy as you, presumably,' he answered silkily, 'seeing as you so rarely have the time to visit me.'

It could easily become an argument. Aninka refused to be drawn in. 'Well, after Noah called you, I knew I'd have to see you. I feel it's urgent we talk.'

Enniel gestured towards a bulky leather sofa at the side of the room. Beside it, a tray of tea things waited on a spindly table. All was prepared. 'Please, sit down.'

Aninka perched herself precariously on the edge. She wanted to appear at ease, but it was difficult. Echoes of previous visits marred the atmosphere. Ghosts of her own raised voice could be heard in the dark tapestries upon the panelled walls. She found her hands were clutching each other in her lap. Enniel slid down beside her and set about pouring her a cup of tea, Assam, his preferred brew.

'So, there has been a spot of . . . unpleasantness,' he began. She was relieved he did not intend an overture to their interview of questions about her life, her friends, her career. Normally, he wanted to put all that under minute inspection.

'Thank you for getting me out of a mess,' she said.

Enniel pulled a wry face. 'It wasn't that difficult. The right words in the right ear, accompanied by suitable inducements, were enough to ensure the case was neatly wrapped up as nothing other than the mass suicide of a lunatic cult. Grigori influence, as you well know, can accomplish anything. There was no danger of you being implicated, even if witnesses had seen you coming and going from the house in Brontë Close.'

Aninka shook her head. 'I was ... perhaps unwise in my choice of friends.' She referred to Othman rather than his human victims.

'Do not chastise yourself, my dear. What's done is done. Nobody blames you.' He handed her the tea in a large ancient cup decorated with delicate enamel paintings of dragons. The cup wobbled unevenly upon its saucer. She took it.

'I want to tell you how it happened; then you can judge for yourself. I've been living in Cresterfield for a couple of years, as you know ...'

He interrupted. 'Of course, you had your exhibition there recently. I read about it in the paper. Did it go well?'

'Yes ... It attracted many members of the family.' She risked a smile. 'My best customers, of course.' She paused. 'But there was one ... I had not met him before. He said he'd been travelling abroad.'

Even now, several weeks after the event, her heart had begun to race as she started to recount her story. She had told everything to her cousin Noah before, of course, but still, it made her feel cold. She could not speak without shaking. This, more than what she had witnessed and experienced, unnerved her. Normally, she always felt strong, nothing could ruffle her feathers. What naivety!

Aninka's Story: Cresterfield, July
The gallery had been one of those austere, over-lit places, not to her taste at all. As usual the opening night had attracted the art

élite of the town, a breed Aninka despised. She smiled at them pleasantly, nodded at their conversation while thinking of more interesting things. Noah and two other cousins, Tearah and Rachel, had come to offer support; she'd been seeing a lot of them recently. There had been plans to move on to a Thai restaurant later – just the four of them. They were confident they could sneak away without having to take Leonora Ramwithe, the gallery proprietor, and her excruciating husband, with them. Then he *had* arrived. His height alerted Aninka to the possibility he might be Grigori immediately, and she had whispered to Rachel, 'Who's that? Ours, by any chance?'

Rachel had not known him either.

He had not come over to them directly, but had wandered around, wineglass in hand, to inspect Aninka's paintings. She winced as he paused at the piece she considered the weakest. He was certainly her type: rather forbidding in appearance, dressed in tight black leather trousers and a loose dark shirt. His dusty-looking fair hair hung unbound down his back. 'Go and speak to him,' she said to Rachel.

Her cousin, a willowy, frail-looking girl, gave her a quizzical glance. 'Am I to be your procuress tonight?' she teased. 'What about our private meal?'

'I am curious. I was not suggesting we break bread together,' Aninka answered.

Rachel shook her head. 'He is clearly one of us. He'll come over himself shortly.'

But what if he didn't? Aninka noticed Leonora glide over to the new arrival in her bloated cloud of chiffon. The gallery owner gestured widely as she spoke about the paintings. A proprietorial paw touched the newcomer's shoulder. Aninka could tell he would soon be gathered up and sucked into Leonora's clique for the rest of the night. But then the moment had to come. Leonora looked in her direction. He had asked her about the artist. Presently, a billowing descent, newcomer in tow.

'This is Aninka Prussoe,' said Leonora, as if the artist was a fitting of the gallery, fixed to the wall.

He had smiled. 'A pretty name. Are you foreign?'

'Yes, very.' He had taken her hand, kissed it. The gesture was corny, if not vile. Still, she felt elated. His beauty, at close hand, was even more stunning.

'Your work is interesting,' he said. 'A Pre-Raphaelite revival? Should sell a lot as prints.'

Am I supposed to care that you disapprove? she thought, instinctively bridling. 'I paint what I like. This is what I like. Modern art does little for me.'

'Aninka is very successful,' Leonora added, needlessly. It was clear the newcomer had dismissed the woman from his attention.

'And you are?' Tearah demanded. She was more imperious than either of her female cousins, and more heavily built. A Grigori Amazon with chestnut hair, which she wore cropped, for some reason.

He'd bowed to her. 'Othman. Peverel Othman.'

Inevitably, he'd accompanied them to the restaurant. The cousins had been guarded, unable to decide whether Othman was Grigori or not. At times he seemed to drop hints, yet, when a carefully probing question was delivered, gave the unexpected answer. Rachel and Aninka decamped to the ladies' room. Here, they discussed Othman. They could reach no clear conclusion. He appeared to be Grigori, having the same dress sense and appearance, yet he might simply be a tall outsider who was drawn to the Look. Many people were. It had been quite in vogue for nearly two decades now. Othman had told them he'd been travelling, and had spoken of the places he'd visited: India, Norway, France. There seemed no pattern. He asked Aninka a lot of questions about her work, especially the subject matter. 'You clearly emulate Waterhouse and his ilk, yet you have painted mythologies they rarely touched.'

'I am not a plagiarist,' Aninka answered. 'Babylonian mythology interests me a great deal. I feel there is much to be learned from it about the current world.' That was a big enough hint, surely. He did not seem to recognize it as such.

'It's all very biblical, though. Are you a religious woman?'

'It's pre-biblical, actually,' Aninka answered. 'The stories of those times are very colourful. It has nothing to do with Judaeo-Christian religion.'

Still he did not respond. He could not be Grigori, then, surely, unless he was playing with them.

At the end of the meal, he asked if he could call her. She gave him her phone number. 'Are you staying here long?'

'Depends on what I find to interest me,' he'd answered.

He did not call her for over two weeks, by which time, she'd given up on him.

Enniel interrupted Aninka's discourse at this point. He went to his desk and pressed one of the buttons on a tape recorder. Aninka hadn't realized he'd been taping their conversation. 'This is only the beginning,' she said. 'There's so much more.'

'I know that,' Enniel replied, 'but I don't want to tire you. I want you to recall everything in detail, and there's no rush.'

Aninka rubbed her forehead. A headache was starting. 'Do you never think about what a burden our heritage is to us?'

Enniel laughed. 'A common complaint of the young! My dear, if you insist on spending so much time among humans, you will start thinking like them.'

Aninka felt a hot surge of irritation pass through her. 'I'm claustrophobic among family. To be honest, most of the time I want to forget what I am.'

'And it seems you have been unusually successful,' Enniel remarked lightly. 'Otherwise you wouldn't have found yourself in that unsavoury situation.'

Chapter Four

Same day: Little Moor

On Saturday morning, the traveller rose from his bed of ferns and heather. He looked around himself, hunting for signs. There it was: the flash of light. He moved without stiffness towards it; a star in the sky, the reflection of light on glass. Mid-morning, he found a cluster of houses nestling in the cupped hands of a valley. The road that led to it was hewn into the land itself, its high banks thick with seeding grasses. There was a deep, loamy smell, as if some elemental creature was breathing hard beneath the soil. He came to a crossroads where a black and white sign pointed towards the houses and said 'Little Moor'. Little more than what? wondered the traveller, smiling to himself. The other roads, it would seem, led to nowhere.

Verity Cranton was roused from peaceful sleep by the insistent ringing of the doorbell. For a moment, she was disoriented and couldn't remember what day it was. She glanced at her bedside clock; eight-thirty. Early for someone to come calling. Strange. Louis was generally out of bed by eight every morning, so she lay waiting for him to answer the door. Some quality of the ringing had awakened a memory within her. The urgency of it. She thought of heralds, news, bad news. The ringing came again. Where *was* her father? Reluctantly, Verity got out of bed. She shrugged herself into her dressing-gown as she walked across the landing. Whoever was at the door now had their finger pressed continuously on the bell.

'All right, all right,' Verity muttered beneath her breath. What could be so urgent? She wondered, briefly, whether something could have happened to Daniel, and then ran down the stairs, filled with a brutal optimism.

A whey-faced man in a grey suit stood in the porch. 'Miss Cranton?' he said.

Verity pulled the collar of her dressing-gown together. The air was chilly, the garden beyond the door still and empty. There was a strange, static quality to the morning. The moment before she answered the question seemed abnormally long. 'Yes. What do you want?'

She was waiting for it. *Is Daniel Cranton your brother?* She was almost smiling.

The man was clutching a briefcase. 'I am Oswald Grise.' He proffered her a business card, which revealed he was a solicitor. 'I have come to collect you. You *were* notified.'

'No, I wasn't. I have no idea what you're talking about. You'd better explain.'

The man frowned in slight impatience. 'Miss Cranton, I think you're aware of why I'm here. You did sign the contract. And you were notified of the date.' He looked at his watch. 'We have two hours' drive ahead of us. Perhaps I could come in and wait while you get ready to leave.' He made to step over the threshold, but Verity would not let him pass.

'There is obviously some of kind of mistake. I really don't know what you're talking about. What contract? What date?' She had begun to feel uneasy, even threatened, to the point where she wished Louis would make an appearance.

'The marriage,' said the man. '*Your* marriage.'

Verity uttered a shocked laugh. 'You have the wrong person, I'm afraid! I'm not getting married. You've come to the wrong house.'

'I've come to the right house. Please don't delay any longer, Miss Cranton. We're cutting it fine as it is.'

'This is a joke,' Verity said. 'Just who am I supposed to be marrying?'

Grise looked at her in disbelief. Verity realized he thought she was lying, covering up. This was absurd.

'You are due to marry Mr Ambleton at twelve noon today. Mr Anthony Ambleton. *Surely* you remember.'

Verity's vision went momentarily black. She could not draw breath. For a terrifying few seconds, she wondered whether she really had signed some kind of contract, and subsequently erased the memory of it from her mind. Was that possible? Then, bewilderment and fear were replaced by anger. 'Go away!' she hissed. 'Get off my property!' She made to close the door in Grise's face, but he stepped forward quickly and prevented it.

'Now, Miss Cranton, please don't make any fuss. You've had the money, you signed the contract. Now you are required to fulfil your part of the agreement. Should you refuse, you will find yourself in trouble.'

'I don't care!' Verity cried. 'If you don't leave now, I'm calling the police. Ambleton's mad! I never signed a contract, never! I haven't seen him for over a year. This is ridiculous!'

'Mr Ambleton is absolutely sure you agreed to marry him, Miss Cranton.'

'I signed nothing! Get out of here!'

'Vez?'

Verity turned in relief. Louis had come down the stairs. Strangely, he was dressed in a dark suit and tie. 'Dad! Tell this man to go. Get rid of him.'

Louis smiled, that crooked, wry smile. 'Come on now, Vez. Run upstairs and get dressed. We don't want to be late, do we?'

Verity froze. 'Dad?'

Louis limped forward and smiled at Grise. 'I'll have her ready in a moment or two.'

'No you bloody won't!' Verity snapped. 'This is crazy! I'm not marrying that creep! You can't make me!' He wants to be rid of me, she thought. He's in on this. He wants to get rid of me.

'You will marry him,' Louis answered in an even tone. 'You have no choice. It's all arranged. It'll all work out. You'll see.'

'No!'

In horror, Verity tried to pull away as her father took hold of her arm, but his grip was surprisingly strong. Grise stepped into the house, taking her other arm in a firm grasp.

'Don't play up, Vez,' Louis said. 'You're going to be a bride. He's waited for this. He went through so much. Now he's much better and you'll be happy with him, Vez. For ever.'

Together, the men frogmarched her back towards the stairs.

Verity kicked and struggled, but could not escape. She began to scream.

The doorbell woke her up.

For a few moments, Verity could only gasp and splutter on the bed. She was drenched in sweat, her heart racing. She wanted to cry. A nightmare. Thank God, a nightmare! Perhaps it had all happened in an instant in her dreaming mind. Someone really was ringing the doorbell, and it had conjured the ghastly images in her head. One thing she was sure of, she would not answer the door this time. However, it seemed Louis wasn't going to either, and it was doubtful Daniel could be raised from his senseless slumber. Easier to raise the dead. Verity lay still, listening to the insistent rings. Oh, for God's sake!

Impatiently, she got out of bed and put on her dressing-gown, firmly quelling any trepidation in her mind. Purposefully, she went down to the front door and flung it wide. A young man was slouched in the porch. He looked unwashed, his long, lank hair hanging over his eyes, hiding his face. He looked as if he could be some unsavoury friend of Daniel's who'd been sleeping rough for a year.

'Verity,' he said. 'Oh, Verity.'

'Who the hell are you?'

He brushed back his hair, so she could see his face. He was pale, filthy, his eyes clouded and rheumy. Her flesh chilled. 'It's me, Pete. I've come such a long way.'

This is a dream, Verity thought, another dream.

'I love you, Vez,' said the man. 'Let me in. Let me show you how much I love you.'

'You don't exist,' Verity said.

Before she could shut the door, the man held out his dirty arms to her. 'Look,' he said.

She caught a glimpse of the wounds on his inner forearms, long, vertical, gaping wounds from wrist to elbow. They were drained of blood now, after all this time. Verity slammed the door shut. 'Wake up,' she told herself. 'Wake up.'

The doorbell rang again. 'Vez, let me in! I love you.' His voice was muffled.

'*Wake up, you stupid bitch! Wake up!*'

He started to hammer on the door. 'I won't leave you. I'll stay here! I love you!'

'You're dead!' Verity screamed. 'Go away! You're dead!'

'And you are the Guardian of the Dead,' said a soft voice at her shoulder.

She jerked awake.

When the doorbell rang again, she cried out and put her pillow over her ears. 'No! No!' Would this nightmare ever end? She would not get out of bed this time, no. She would will herself into another dream or true reality. After a few moments, she calmed herself. The doorbell was still ringing intermittently. Then it fell silent. She thought she heard voices outside. Verity held her breath, her whole body tense. Something tapped her window. She yelped and pulled the duvet over her head. 'Go away! Leave me alone! Go away!'

'Ve-ri-tee!' The voice came from outside, then something else hit her window. She realized it was a handful of stones, or at least sounded as if it was.

'Vez! Wake up! I'm locked out!'

Daniel! She lunged upwards and knelt on the bed to look out of the window. Daniel and Owen Winter stood in the drive, looking up at her.

Verity opened the window. This felt real, now. Yes. It was safe, wasn't it?

'What the bloody hell are you playing at, Daniel?' she demanded, conscious of the odious Winter boy's eyes greedily inspecting her thin nightdress.

'I've lost my key,' Daniel said in a placatory tone. 'Let us in.'

'Hang on.' Verity was just about to go downstairs, when a tremor of fear shivered through her. No. Nothing would induce her to open that door again. She found her handbag at the bottom of the bed and delved in it to find her key. 'Let yourself in!' she said, as she threw it out of the window.

Lily Winter woke up and knew that her brother Owen had not come home yet. The house felt empty around her, and cold. This was not just a metaphysical coldness, but because Owen always got up earlier than she did and lit the stove in the kitchen, so that there would be hot water ready for her when she got out of bed.

'Damn!' Lily rolled over and glanced at her clock. Nine-thirty. She had woken up half an hour earlier than usual. Three cats were positioned around her bed, which signified they had not been fed. 'All right,' Lily said. 'Don't look at me like that!'

She got out of bed and put on her dressing-gown. After going to the toilet and throwing cold water on her face, she padded barefoot downstairs, grimacing at the stove as she ventured into the kitchen. She hated having to light the thing. The cats had begun to mew and rub around her legs in anticipation. Lily pushed her un-brushed hair back behind her ears and opened up a tin of cat food. All the cats' bowls were dirty. Lily forked new food on to the dried remains of last night's meal and covered the reeking gobs of meat with a sprinkling of cat biscuits. The cats' ravenous passion gave voice to new frenzy as Lily began to put the bowls down on the floor. Presently, their cries were silenced, and Lily was able to pick her way through the crouching furry throng to put the kettle on. Then, she picked up the mail lying on the doormat beside the back door – all of it looked boring – and sat down at the kitchen table to open it. Before the kettle had boiled, the back door opened and Owen walked in. She felt annoyed with him. This was the first time he hadn't been in the house on a Saturday morning when she had woken up. She did not approve of this new development in his habits. She did her part of the domestic chores; he should do his.

'Good morning to you!' Lily said. 'You neglect your duties, sibling. Where is my lit stove?'

Owen grinned at her and shrugged off his coat. 'You are a lazy bitch,' he said good-naturedly.

'I know, but that's not the point. I do the cleaning

and cook most of the meals. You see to the stove, feed the cats and do my breakfast on Saturdays. I spent hours tidying up last night! And most of the mess was yours! Is it too much to expect the stove to be lit this morning? No! You're so selfish sometimes!'

'For God's sake, Lil, it's not that serious! Don't be so carpy!' Owen sat down at the table to take off his boots.

Lily felt a pang of affection as she looked at his bony shoulders. He seemed vulnerable somehow. 'Where have you been till now?' Normally, she didn't question him about his activities.

'Just out,' he replied. His face was grubby, as if he'd been sleeping on dirt.

Lily shook her head. 'You'll be caught!' she said malevolently.

Owen raised his brows. 'Doing what?'

'Whatever it is you're up to.'

'I doubt it,' Owen said. 'Come and sit down. I'll do the stove and make breakfast.'

'Peace offering.'

'It won't happen again,' Owen said. 'I lost track of time.'

Lily held out for a few moments, standing rigidly against the sink, then went to sit down. Owen smiled at her.

'Have you been with that Cranton boy all night?' Lily ventured.

Owen's smile clouded. Lily cóuld tell she'd crossed a forbidden boundary, but refused to go back. 'Well?'

'What is that to you?'

She pulled a sour face. 'Dunno. He seems like an odd choice of friend. He's just a kid.'

'He's bright,' Owen said. 'Young for his age, I'll admit, but interesting company.'

'I can't see Ray and the others liking him much.'

'Well, they do.' Owen stood up and went to the stove.

'O?'

'Mmm?'

Lily had to voice an uncomfortable suspicion. 'That boy's too young, much too young. You should be careful.'

Owen directed a quizzical glance at her. 'What *are* you implying, sister dear.'

Lily shrugged awkwardly. 'I think you know. Cranton's a good-looking lad, but his family are outsiders, O. They're different. You know what I mean.'

'Not exactly, no. If you are trying to find out whether I'm fucking Daniel, the answer is no. Thanks a lot, Lil.'

'I'm sorry,' Lily said. 'I just had to . . .'

'That's OK, forget it. Why don't you go and get dressed. It's cold in here. I'll have this lit by the time you come down.'

Lily stood up. She went to where her brother was crouched by the stove, and leaned down to hug him, kissing the top of his head. 'I love you,' she said. 'I worry about you.'

Owen patted her arm. 'I like it when you're jealous,' he said. 'Makes me feel wanted.'

Lily laughed and went back upstairs. She took off her dressing-gown and nightdress and sat on her bed for a few moments. Her suspicions concerning Daniel Cranton weren't totally allayed. She didn't want to feel possessive of Owen, yet resented outsiders taking up his time. She and Owen hadn't shared closeness for several months now. Was it possible they could drift apart completely, to become separate entities? She hated to think of that. 'Owen,' she murmured, staring at the window. Her eyes were full of tears. He was her world.

Her quiet utterance of his name was an invocation.

She heard him coming up the stairs. He came into her room and said, sorrowfully, 'Lily. Don't!'

She showed him her tear-streaked face, turning just her head to look at him. 'What?'

'Don't get upset.' He sat down beside her and stroked her naked shoulder. 'You are beautiful.' He parted her hair and kissed her neck.

'But am I enough?'

Owen smiled. 'Don't be stupid.'

'We don't share so often, not like we used to. I'm scared we're drifting apart.'

'Do you want to share now?'

'Do you?'

'I always do, but I wait on you, my love. It's your temple we worship in, after all.'

In response, Lily pulled away from him and lay down on her narrow bed. The impulse, when it came, was always hot and sudden. 'Now,' she said. He was her only lover.

Barbara and Barney Eager sat up in bed together, sipping tea and sharing the Saturday newspaper. Barbara loved Saturdays; they had a certain feel, an air of excitement, they were like a holiday. She, of course, no longer had any days off work, but the cheerful atmosphere conjured by the weekend drinkers affected her benignly. Barney, unaware he was being watched, frowned at the paper, his lower lip stuck out. Barbara couldn't help thinking of Louis Cranton's attenuated and ravaged handsomeness, the tiredness in his dark eyes. She lived in fear of witnessing a rapid physical decline in her friend; other times she dreamed of his miraculous recovery, a return to vigour. Last night, he'd made a jovial remark about the winter cold being bad for his bones. Barbara had winced; a wing of terror brushed her face. Perhaps she didn't do enough for him. His children were no help. Daniel was affable enough, but a sponger, whereas Verity seemed a cold, calculating creature. At first, Barbara had attempted to befriend the girl, but her efforts had been rebuffed. She felt Verity looked down on her, yet she seemed content to sit gossiping with the locals when it suited her. Strange girl.

Barney appeared to have no suspicions concerning his wife's feelings for Louis Cranton. Probably because he saw Louis as less than a man. Barbara eyed him covertly. Had he ever been handsome? It was hard to recall now. When she'd met him, he'd certainly been dashing in his uniform. They had spent the first two years of their married life stationed abroad in Cyprus. Barbara had hoped for a glamorous life with him. She'd always done her duty. Barney, however, had few expectations from life, and lacked any poetry of soul. Barbara could never really talk to him. She realized she was sitting in bed with a stranger, someone who had never wanted to know her fully, someone she knew only superficially. What would he think of his wife's inner life, if it should be revealed to him? Shock, ridicule, perhaps even concern, would manifest.

In her dreams, Barbara was strong and powerful. She did not see herself as a slim, limpid beauty, but a statuesque Valkyrie, who stalked a wild fantasy landscape, making things happen and having Experiences. Barbara's imagination was fecund. She did not read the most lurid of her fantasies aloud to the other members of her writing group. Now, she wondered: did Barney have unspoken desires, secret thoughts? It seemed unlikely. But perhaps he dreamed of a wild and dangerous military career, of himself as a hero. Barbara hoped he did. Barney was no hero in reality. He had never had a classic bone structure, and his face now seemed to be falling downwards off his skull, as if some vital inner framework had been removed. His body had become soft and toneless.

Barbara herself fought the advance of age, even though she sometimes felt she was holding the enemy at bay with diminishing troops. She had been the one to initiate the twice-weekly work-out sessions in the musty village hall, previously home only to sporadic flower shows and drab social events. She tried to pamper her body, but, mulishly, like a sulky child, it failed to respond with the alacrity and enthusiasm she hoped to instil. This was not a condition she pondered often, because it filled her with a weary sadness. The most cruel thing about life, she thought, was not the fact that you aged and decayed, but that you appreciated youth and vitality only when it was too late. *That* was cruel. It was as if you possessed in ignorance some unbelievable supernatural power, which you were only told about as the gift was taken away. *I could have done this, and this* . . . Dreams. She was fifty-two now, and her life seemed to have ended here in Little Moor. The things she did today, she would probably do every day until she was too infirm to carry on managing The White House. Don't be ungrateful, she scolded herself. You have money, you have health, you have friends. She could also indulge her obsessions and articulate her dreams via her writing circle. With these more positive thoughts in mind, Barbara got out of bed. *Who knows, something unexpected and thrilling might always be around the corner* . . . Barney glanced up at her, smiling absent-mindedly. Outside, the day was becoming unseasonably warm.

When Verity Cranton went into the kitchen to turn down the central heating, someone else's black cat was sitting on the outer window-sill, looking in. It made

Verity jump as she caught sight of its silhouette, because it was the most enormous cat she'd ever seen. Her intention was to shoo it away, but when she opened the back door, the cat jumped down off the sill and ran into the house. Verity shrank back against the door. Was it a domestic cat? She'd never seen one that size. Its coat was long, and its tail was as bushy as a fox's. The animal brushed against her legs as it passed her. The sensation, though brief, was pleasant. Verity watched, with mixed feelings, as the cat went directly to the ethnic mat in front of the range, stuck a back leg in the air, and began washing itself, very much at home. Verity had never owned pets. She suspected that, as with people, there was a cost for caring about them. Also, she sensed kindred spirits in the most aloof examples of the feline species she had encountered, and the comparisons made her uncomfortable. 'You can't come in here,' she said aloud, feeling embarrassed when the animal ignored her. She couldn't help feeling it had understood her words completely. She approached it, but felt wary of touching it, nervous it might strike out. When she came too close it stopped washing and stared at her with enormous orange eyes. There certainly seemed to be a warning in the eyes. It was only a cat. She could fetch a mop or a broom and drive it away. The cat blinked at her and then rolled on to its back in invitation. Cautiously, Verity extended a hand and touched the long black fur on its belly. What appeared to be smooth and groomed turned out to be a mat of feline dreadlocks. The cat wriggled, encouraging her caress. Then it grabbed her hand firmly with its forepaws, curling its body round so it could kick with its back legs. Verity froze. She knew if she tried to pull away now, it would bite, scratch. Stupid of her to touch it, stupid. The cat stared at her for a few moments, and then its grip slackened, allowing her to remove her hand.

It seemed to be saying, I could have hurt you badly, but I didn't. Verity touched its wide head and it pushed against her hand, beginning to purr.

The houses of Little Moor surrounded a small post office and general shop, as if, the traveller thought, they had been drawn against their will to this lone node of communication with the world. Nearby, a white building protected the rise of a hill, and there was a sign to proclaim it a boarding-house and inn. Shiny cars were parked outside, beneath an ancient monkey-puzzle tree.

As a preliminary investigation, the traveller went into the post office, which was also a small off-licence, to purchase a bottle of beer. The interior of the shop was stuffed with merchandise of the most unlikely variety. A mature female in powder and cardigan held court behind the old glass-topped counter, and there was a squinting crone sitting on a stool next to a bead curtain that obviously led to the living quarters. The silence which followed his entrance suggested these two had recently been involved in dispute; it was more than the cautious silence reserved for strangers. The postmistress looked at him hard, ready to purse her mouth into disapproval, so he took off his hat and smiled. She visibly smoothed herself.

'Shut the door!' said the crone. 'Open doors let the air in.'

'Mother!' said the postmistress, in tolerant embarrassment as the traveller shut the door more firmly. 'What can I do for you, sir?'

The traveller voiced his requirements in his most velvety tone, eyeing the dusty collection of bottles on the shelf behind the counter. The postmistress asked him whether he'd prefer one of the bottles she kept in the cellar. They had no fridge.

57

'Won't keep you a moment,' said the postmistress, dodging through the bead curtain, with an owlish backward glance that he guessed was meant to be sultry.

A stillness descended into the shop and the traveller could hear the low buzz of a motorbike far away. 'Don't get paid for this!' said the old woman unexpectedly. The traveller smiled at her enquiringly. 'I count the post,' continued the woman, 'count it all, every one. No pay for it.'

'Oh.' The stillness became rather stiff. Did it really take this long to fetch a bottle from the cellar, he wondered? Perhaps the postmistress was applying a further layer of powder to her nose for his benefit. He felt the burning scrutiny of the crone, heard her rustle like dry leaves or ancient cloth upon her seat.

'Smell the past,' she said. 'Smell it.'

'I beg your pardon?' He turned to glance at her.

'Coming back,' she answered.

He could smell her age, and another half-familiar smell, like long-shuttered attics opened to the sun.

'Here she comes,' said the old woman. The traveller thought she meant her daughter, but the door opened behind him and another customer came in. 'Hello dear!' said the old woman, in a tone of some affection.

It was a girl, maybe eighteen years old. She carried a large wicker basket which was hung over one arm and pressed tightly against her body. She was very tall and wore a long dress in a faded floral print and scuffed men's work-boots. Her arms were bare and, he could see, rather scratched, as if she'd been playing with a boisterous kitten.

'Hi, Mrs Manden,' she said, and put her basket on the counter. She gave the traveller only the shortest of inspections. Here she comes, indeed! he was thinking. This was the lure, the gem in the heart of the rock, he was sure of it. After years of practice he could sniff out items of interest very quickly. Her long, abundant hair was the most beautiful shade of dark red, probably dyed, but enchanting none the less. Her face, admittedly, was plain, but her eyes were wide and contained the hidden shred of 'otherness' he had trained himself to spot.

The postmistress breezed through the curtain, clutching the bottle the traveller had ordered, her mouth pasted with a fresh layer of thick red lipstick. She smiled airily at the girl. 'Hello, Lily love,' she said, and then redirected her attention to the traveller. 'Staying in Lil'Moor, are you?' she enquired brightly, as he counted out his change.

He couldn't help smiling at the unintentional pun and was tempted to answer, 'Well, I will if she's amenable,' but opted for, 'It's a lovely spot. I hope to stay here, yes.'

'We get a lot of tourists,' said the postmistress. 'Where are you staying? At The White House?'

'I haven't decided yet.'

'There's no decision to it,' said the girl, quite coldly. 'It's the only place for tourists around here.'

'In that case, my mind is made up,' said the traveller, putting the bottle into one of the pockets of his long coat.

'Want me to open that for you?' asked the postmistress.

He shook his head. 'No thank you.'

'You're not one of those people who use their teeth, are you?' The postmistress touched her throat provocatively.

The traveller put on his hat. 'I always carry a bottle opener with me,' he said. 'Good day to you.'

Outside, he waited for the girl, Lily, to emerge. Of course, she spent considerable time chatting to the postmistress and her mother. He sat down on a convenient

59

boulder and opened up the bottle, swigging idly as he waited. He never wasted an opportunity. He knew, through past encounters, that it was best to act on impulse, or else he would regret at leisure. It was his duty, while roaming the world, to cram as much experience into his life as possible. He wanted to taste every fruit there was on offer, even if it was sour. More than anything, he liked to experience the effect he had on other people.

Eventually, the bell above the post-office door made a muffled 'ting!' and the Lily maid walked out into the sunlight. She paused for a moment and squinted up at the sky. Her basket was laden with tins and she had bought a couple of oranges that had the wizened appearance typical of small-store produce kept long on the shelf. When she realized she was being observed, she assumed an almost guilty expression, as if she had been seen doing something shameful. She nodded curtly, hesitated with a half-open mouth, as if about to speak, and then began to walk away up the road. Once she looked back. Satisfied, the traveller stood up, threw the empty bottle into a waste bin outside the shop and headed for The White House.

He would take a room there for a night at least. The interior of the place was all polished dark wood and horse brasses, with a token grandfather clock ticking in the hallway. There was an old noticeboard hung on the wall, which had once advertised church activities, it seemed, but all it displayed now were a few bright leaflets for tourists, explaining where sites of historical interest and stately homes could be found. The traveller could not remember having seen a church nearby. It was necessary to ring a counter bell for service; clearly The White House was not crammed with business at the moment. A man, ex-military in type, came through from a room at the back. The traveller assessed him swiftly: retired, wife somewhere else in the building, hearty group of local friends, perhaps the father of a difficult child who had grown into a difficult adult. He did not fall prey to the traveller's charms at all, however well directed they were, and maintained a stiff, unwelcoming mien as his new guest signed the register. The traveller's appearance was perhaps not typical of the usual White House clientele, and it was likely he'd only been permitted to stay there because trade was slack. The proprietor would undoubtedly prefer to fill his inn with family holiday-makers and respectable moor-walkers. The traveller's attire and long hair probably suggested untold dissipations to this conventional creature, who would also scorn all males who had not enjoyed army life at some time. Enchanting delusion! The traveller envisaged many interesting encounters would be had with the landlord; his name was Mr Eager.

'Dinner at six-thirty!' he said. The traveller imagined a peremptory gong would be rung at that time, and woe betide the listless guest who ignored its summons.

His room was comfortable, if a little too flouncy. Mrs Eager would also be flouncy, of course, for the decor was her signature. The traveller would strike up a friendship with her, to the disgust of her husband. He wondered whether the Lily maid ever came to The White House. His first impression of her suggested she was not the type to drink out in pubs. Once he'd made the acquaintance of Mrs Eager, he might be able to find out.

Daniel Cranton came into the kitchen, where Verity was preparing a tray of coffee and sandwiches for Louis. This morning had been the first time Owen had asked to come back into the house with him after a night at the High Place. He was unsure of Owen's motives for that –

aware that Owen always had motives for everything he did. They had shared some toast in the kitchen, burned because Daniel cooked for himself very rarely.

'You and the Winter lout left a mess on the table,' Verity said. 'If you must invite that hooligan into the house, at least clear up after him.'

Daniel, who was patient with his sister, ignored the remark. 'Whose is that cat?'

Verity peered at the animal on the rug as if she'd just noticed it. 'Oh, I don't know. It just came in.'

Daniel gave Verity a penetrating look, from which she turned away.

'It's bloody enormous!' he said.

Verity did not feel that such an obvious remark deserved a response.

'Are you going to keep it?' Daniel asked. There was a scoffing incredulity in his voice.

'I might . . .' She paused. 'Of course, it could get under Dad's feet, trip him up.'

Daniel went over to the rug and, with some difficulty, picked up the cat. 'Very black!' he said. 'And very big!'

Verity was pleased that the animal struggled to get away from him. Once back on the rug, it shook itself like a dog and then sat down to wash itself thoroughly.

'Not very friendly, is it?' Daniel said.

'Cats are not toys or babies,' Verity answered, shouldering Daniel out of the way as she wiped down the table. 'Are you in for lunch?'

'Yeah, I suppose so.'

Verity pursed her lips. She wished she could sweep her brother out of the house, tidy up in his wake, remove his presence from the atmosphere. Having him around made the place feel dirty.

'Not off with your *friends* today?'

'Later. Maybe.' Privately, Daniel hoped not. Owen

never saw his friends on Saturday evenings, but sometimes they got together in the afternoon. Daniel felt wrung out after the previous night's activities. Most of it was a blur in his memory, which he didn't want to probe. Owen picked on him the least to perform the sacrifices, yet when he did, it seemed to bleed some vital part from Daniel's body and soul. The others seemed less affected by it, even appeared to enjoy it. Daniel had passed the point where he could tell himself to drop Owen Winter's friendship. He'd tried it in the past, but Owen only had to appear again and Daniel would be powerless. Mostly, they all had a good time. Daniel preferred going out to nightclubs and visiting pubs in Cresterfield or Patterham to the High Place meetings. On a good night like that, he could convince himself his friendship with Owen and the others was normal. At other times, in the dark, in the woods, he knew he had become part of something too compelling to cast away, something to which he had donated a part of himself that would never be returned, and could not be yanked back. He sensed that he and the others were inextricably linked, moving towards something huge and dangerous, always moving. Blind.

'You look terrible,' Verity remarked, breaking his reverie. 'What were you doing all night?'

She had begun to cut a loaf of bread into thick slices. The sight of the bright, sawing blade made Daniel feel nauseous. He had to look away, yet the rhythmic flash continued to register in the corner of his sight.

'Why so interested?' She normally did not ask Daniel about what he did. He knew she did not care one way or the other, yet an instinct advised him this was something to pity her for, because it was a minor symptom of some larger dysfunction.

'I don't think you should spend so much time with Winter. He's *unwholesome*.'

Daniel knew Verity's comments were inspired by a desire on her part never to lay eyes on Owen if at all possible, and did not signify any concern for himself. Yet he did not feel he could defend Owen, because half of him agreed with Verity's words. 'Who else is there to hang around with in this place?'

'You won't have to stay here much longer,' Verity said quickly, so quickly it made Daniel suspicious immediately. 'You could go to college next year. It would do you good.'

'Not as much as you think it would do you,' he couldn't help saying.

'You can't want to stay here! It's bad enough travelling to school every day, surely!'

Daniel hadn't really thought about it. He lived very much for the moment. 'I dunno . . .' he said, lapsing into the tone that usually silenced Verity and kindled her annoyance.

Predictably, she made an exasperated sound and stalked to the fridge, pausing only to smile down at the monstrous cat. 'Just 'cause Dad nags you, don't nag me,' Daniel said. He thought he would tweak a nerve with that remark.

'At least I've seen the world outside,' Verity answered smoothly.

Daniel was disappointed, having hoped for a bitter retort. Still, Verity's suggestion was something he'd have to think about eventually. If he went away, would the link between himself and the others be broken? Would he be free or drawn back against his will? Would Owen come after him? He shuddered at the thought, suddenly presented with the image in his mind of a moonlit night, himself in a small room alone, and a figure outside below, looking up at his window, forming a wordless summoning. To dispel the thought, he jumped up quickly. The cat hissed in alarm.

'What is it?' Verity asked. She looked, absurdly, frightened. For a few moments the pair of them shared a single terror; a look passed between them.

Daniel shook his head. 'Nothing.' But he wondered, What's her fear? Is she part of it? He recognized the brief affinity, and that unnerved him more than anything.

Chapter Five

Same day: Little Moor (continued)

'I met somebody very odd today.' Lily Winter was unloading her post-office produce on to the kitchen table. Owen, at ease in the now cosy house, had his feet up on the table. They were bare, the nails like dirty claws. He was carving a piece of wood with a sharp penknife.

'Where?' he asked.

'In the post office. A stranger. He looked at me in a weird way.'

'He?'

'Yes. He.' She frowned, wondering whether she should tell her brother about the strange effect the meeting had had on her. She had walked away from the post office keenly aware of the stranger's scrutiny. He was interested in her, she was sure. This was flattering, but worrying, too. As she'd walked back up the lane, she'd found herself thinking about what it would be like to touch him. She had never experienced such feelings for a man other than with Owen. Surely it wasn't normal to feel that way after such a short acquaintance? He was staying at The White House. For how long? 'I had the absurd feeling he recognized me,' she said aloud.

Owen glanced up at her sharply. 'Old flame of Mum's?' They knew so little of their mother's past, and nothing about their own father. Always, the unspoken fascination, even a hope, hung between them.

She shrugged. 'Is that possible?'

'You should know that it is.'

'But why would he come here? The women at the post office didn't know him.'

Owen grinned. 'That is *not* a definite sign!'

'Isn't it?'

Lily was sure the villagers knew more about their mother than they'd ever let on to Owen and herself. She suspected this must be because of scandal. Without a doubt, their mother had not been married when they'd been born. Helen Winter had never ignored her children's questions when she'd been alive, but had fielded their curiosity with skill. Instead of refusing to speak about their father, she would make up outrageous stories: he was an explorer, a famous scientist, an artist, an opera singer. As children, Owen and Lily had loved the stories, and sometimes had believed them for a short while. Until the next time. Lily could remember Owen saying to her, 'One day she'll tell the truth. She'll have to, because she'll run out of untruths.' Then they had come to Little Moor. Then Helen had died. Why here? Their mother had told them about an aunt who'd left her a house. Had Helen deliberately come back here to die?

Sometimes, the older women in the village spoke to Lily about her mother, but never about an aunt. Lily had asked about this unknown female, but the answers had been vague. The woman had either been very boring or a creature of mystery. She'd searched for evidence of the aunt in the cottage, or evidence of her own mother's childhood. Nothing. It would be too wonderful if the stranger had some connection with their mother. Yet hadn't she lied to Owen? Why had she said the stranger recognized her? Wasn't that just what she *wanted* him to do? It was all too odd. She felt that something fast and wild was coming into their lives. Routine would break up. Daniel Cranton had been the beginning of it, but this, this was something bigger. She was convinced of it.

Half of her was terrified, half of her welcomed it with open arms. 'He was too young to have known Mum,' she said at last.

Owen grunted in reply.

'Are we going for a drink tonight?' Lily asked. It was a ritual question.

At six-thirty, the traveller presented himself downstairs just as Mr Eager was about to bang the anticipated gong with a little felt-covered hammer. He nodded cheerily to the landlord who, surprisingly, went quite red about the neck and face. The traveller wore new black jeans and an open-necked black shirt, which revealed the white hollow of his throat, the place where it looked as if someone had gouged a hole in the soft, bloodless flesh with a knuckle. His long hair was tied firmly back at the neck and he had willed himself into a pleasing state of suave, groomed, aristocratic vagueness. He defied the landlord to call his appearance disreputable; he would be faintly patronizing with the man tonight, as a lesson.

At dinner, the landlord's wife made an appearance. An inbred-looking teenage girl waited on the table, but a tall, bosomy creature with dyed copper hair appeared from the kitchen during the soup to welcome the new guest. Only four other diners were present; two of them appeared to be train-spotters sadly off-course, looking for a line, while the others were a young couple, perhaps honeymooners, who whispered a lot. The traveller found the food to be good, which surprised him. He complimented Mrs Eager on it. 'Do you mind if I join you for a moment?' she enquired, as he sat waiting for his main course.

'Not at all.' He gestured languidly at the chair opposite his own.

'As you can imagine, we get few visitors this time of year, although strangely we have quite a few regulars who come for Christmas.'

The traveller inhaled deeply and silently. The woman smelled of heavy, Oriental scent, which, to him, failed to conceal the clinging aroma of flesh past its prime. 'It must be an entirely appropriate place to spend the winter holiday,' he said.

Mrs Eager smiled. 'Actually, we rarely get snow.'

He grinned. 'Well, stomachs should be satisfied, if not aesthetic requirements.'

'How long will you be staying with us, Mr . . .?'

The traveller held out his hand, which Mrs Eager took without hesitation. Her handshake was firm and dry. 'Othman,' he said. 'Peverel Othman.' He sensed immediately the woman's spirit of yearning, her unfulfilled dreams.

'What an unusual name!'

He shrugged. 'I'm exploring this part of the country. How long I stay here depends on what I find to interest me.' The words were carefully delivered, his gaze direct.

Barbara Eager's posture momentarily froze. He could tell she was wondering whether she was right to interpret that remark as slightly flirtatious. Still, he admired the fact she did not colour up; most women of her type would have done.

'Well, Mr Othman, if you're excited by wild landscapes and small communities, then we can expect to accommodate you for some time.' She stood up. 'Here is your meal. I wish you *bon appétit*.'

'Thank you, Mrs Eager.' He thought he'd offended her.

'Barbara,' she said.

He realized he hadn't.

*

After dinner, Peverel Othman took a pint of beer out into The White House garden, and sat against a wall where a late-blooming climbing rose exuded its scent behind him. Gradually, as the evening thickened, other guests drifted outside to sit at the wooden picnic tables, and locals also began to arrive. Car doors slammed; a few children made an appearance. Then there was a glimmer of white, and the Lily maid herself walked into the garden, dressed in pale cotton and wrapped in a fringed, woollen shawl. She sat down alone at one of the tables, and self-consciously fiddled with her hair, kicking the bench with her feet.

Delightful! thought the traveller, how unbelievably opportune! He had not imagined the girl would come this close to him so soon, although he knew the seeds of interest he'd planted must have taken root. He wondered whether he should approach her right away. No, perhaps a minute or two of observation first .·. . He watched her, savouring the moments before contact was made. She seemed so fey, so fragile, almost awkward. Once or twice she nodded and smiled at people she knew, but no one made a move to join her. A moth fluttered above her head, and briefly landed on her hair. Othman shivered with anticipation.

Presently, a tall young man came out of The White House, carrying two full glasses. He sat down beside the girl and placed a drink in front of her. They did not speak, but simply sat there, side by side, looking into the dusk. The traveller suppressed a frisson of annoyance, even though he'd known it was unlikely the girl would be alone. Her partner was hardly more than a boy, pallid and scrawny, his hair unkempt and the starved curve of his jaw like a blade. He wore old, frayed jeans and a huge, shapeless jumper full of holes. He and the exquisite girl lifted their glasses in unison, drank, did not speak.

The traveller had finished his beer. He stood up, cradling the empty glass, and walked towards the lit garden door of the pub as if to purchase another. Just as he was within reasonable speaking distance of the Lily maid and her companion, the girl began to say something. He could not hear the words, but the boy nodded distractedly.

'Hello there,' said the traveller, and they both turned their heads in his direction. He smiled and gestured towards the pub with his glass. 'We meet again!'

At this point, if there was no sign of welcome, he could carry on walking without loss of dignity. The girl frowned at him, and then smiled wanly. She leaned towards her companion and began murmuring in his ear, dismissing the traveller from her attention.

Othman walked past without pausing and went into the bar. He did not feel annoyed, only mystified. He employed a careful choreography when intruding into people's lives and yet, on this occasion, it appeared his first movements, which were often the most devastating, had somehow failed to arouse. He was puzzled by this, and checked his appearance in the mirror behind the bar. Barbara Eager, on duty at the pumps, was oblivious of his mood and happily chatted into the air around his body as she filled his glass.

He had obviously made a mistake. Some people were immune to his allure because of an innate lack of imagination. It was pointless to bother with individuals like that; too much work. He'd simply made an error of judgement. He looked around the bar. Perhaps someone else? What he saw did not inspire him. Barbara Eager, with her frustrated desires, was not enough to sustain him. Tomorrow, then, he would be moving on. A pity. His pique was destined to last no more than a few minutes.

'Don't you?' Barbara Eager said.

The traveller shook himself into the present. 'I beg your pardon?'

'I said how much I love this time of year, the smells, the feelings, don't you?' She waved dangerous, lacquered claws in the air.

The traveller nodded. 'Yes,' he said. Barbara Eager, he was sure, considered herself to be an amateur poet, and probably ran a small writing circle in the village. She would have been easy prey, if he'd been interested. 'Could I ask you something?'

She puffed up with pleasure. 'Of course!'

'The young couple out there, a girl with red hair and a shawl, the pale boy: do you know them?'

The question was obviously not the one Mrs Eager had anticipated. Her face had fallen a little. 'Oh, you mean the Winter twins?'

'Twins? I don't think so.' Even as he said it, he realized he was wrong. Of course they were twins.

'Well, they're the only people who fit that description,' said Mrs Eager. 'Why?'

'I met the girl – Lily? – earlier today.'

'Mmm.' Mrs Eager leaned conspiratorially over the bar. 'They . . .'

He wouldn't let her say what she wanted to say. 'What are they drinking?'

Barbara Eager straightened up abruptly. Later she might wonder, with her poet's mind, why his softly spoken words had made her feel as if she'd been slapped across the face. 'They usually drink cider,' she said. 'Are you buying for them?'

He nodded. Barbara worked the pump with a pursed mouth. 'What's that scent you're wearing?' he asked her, smiling.

*

Lily and Owen watched the traveller go back into the pub. 'Was that him?' Owen asked. 'The one you met today?'

Lily nodded. 'Yes.' She waited for Owen's verdict, as her brother stared at the glowing door to The White House, where the traveller seemed to have left a dark impression on the light.

'Interesting,' Owen said at last.

Lily felt relieved. 'I thought that, too.'

Owen turned back to the table, took a drink. 'He'll come out again in a minute, come and speak to you again.'

Lily twirled her glass in a cider puddle on the table. 'Yes, I know. Do you mind?'

Owen grinned. 'Of course not. But we must stick together, disguise ourselves. We have to suss him out.'

'Do you think he's – well – *significant*?' Lily asked.

'I can't tell yet, but there's something about him,' Owen answered. 'Probably just because he's a new face, and the way he looks.'

'We can pretend to be anything we like,' Lily said. 'He doesn't know us.'

Peverel Othman wasn't normally so obvious in his manoeuvres as to approach his prey so directly and so quickly, but he realized there was little point in trying to deny how deeply Lily Winter had aroused his interest. Her resistance called for dramatic measures. Carrying the drinks on a metal tray, Peverel Othman went back out into the garden. He would not have been surprised if the twins had already left, but they were still sitting together at the table. Lily was leaning down to fuss over a mongrel dog with a madly wagging tail that had come to sniff around her ankles.

'Mind if I join you?' he asked, sitting down. The twins

looked at him with some surprise and the dog slunk away. He put the drinks down in front of them. 'I hope you don't mind. I feel like a bit of company and I'm afraid you' – he wagged a finger at the girl – 'are the only person I've met around here.'

She laughed without reserve, a reaction he hadn't expected. 'Hardly met!' she said. Perhaps she felt safer with her brother there. The evening light suited her. How could he have thought her plain?

Othman shrugged and grinned sheepishly. 'I know, but everyone else in this place is . . .' He pulled a face.

'We call it a pre-graveyard,' Lily said, nodding. 'I know what you mean.'

'You're Lily Winter, right?' So far, he hadn't looked at the boy.

She didn't seem too pleased he'd found that much out about her, perhaps because there were other things to discover, which she feared he'd also picked up. 'And you are . . .?' she asked, a little coldly.

He told her.

'Are you foreign?' she asked. 'No, of course not. Are you a gypsy, then, or something? What an unusual name.'

He shrugged again, offering no further explanation.

'This is my brother, Owen,' she said, gesturing to her companion. 'Or did you know that, too?'

Othman shook his head. 'No. Pleased to meet you.'

He met the boy's eyes for the first time, expecting territorial surliness, and found, to his relief, he was merely looking at Lily's eyes again. Uncanny: a mixture of caution, amusement, and a certain cynical awareness of his purpose. He realized, half with displeasure, that these two somehow *knew* him. Was this a disadvantage or not? The boy was more presentable than he'd first thought as well. How fortunate to find these creatures here; their acquaintance might provide more experience than he could have hoped for.

'He *lurked* outside the post office for me,' Lily said to her brother, flapping a hand at Othman. She did not deceive him. She and Owen had undoubtedly discussed the matter already.

Owen smiled.

'I do not deny it,' said Othman. 'As a contrast to the hags in there, you were like a goddess!'

The twins exchanged a secret glance, but it did not altogether exclude him. They were willing to play, he felt. He experienced a delirious moment of weakness, as if the performance was not his, but theirs. It was a strange and unfamiliar sensation, but not unpleasant.

'Are you on holiday?' Lily asked him, drinking from the glass he had given her, but keeping it low over the table. Her eyes smiled at him over its rim.

'A travelling holiday,' he said. The twins both made noises of interest, so he began to relate some stories about his experiences, a few of which were fabrications and distinctly less interesting than the truth.

'So, are you lost now?' asked the boy. 'This is nowhere. How did you end up here?'

'I never know how I end up anywhere. I just keep moving. It's the best way, I find. Sometimes, I discover wonderful things. I don't look for them, I just make myself receptive. How did you end up here?'

'We live here,' Lily said.

'You don't seem typical of the natives.'

She made a careless gesture. 'Well . . .'

'Our mother was an outsider. We inherited the house,' Owen said.

It was perhaps rather an odd way to put it, but at least it implied that they lived alone and might have spacious accommodation. The traveller had the distinct impression that Owen was thinking the words: 'Wasn't that what you wanted to know?', but was aware he might be projecting his own desires on to these people, reading more into their behaviour than was actually there.

'So, what is there to see around here?' he asked, taking a drink.

'Nothing!' the twins said, in unison. They laughed.

'There is always something,' Othman said, 'anywhere. Always something.'

'Don't count on it,' Lily said. 'What sort of thing are you looking for?'

He shrugged. 'Just places of interest.'

'Monuments, ruins, that sort of thing?'

'Yes, that sort of thing. I like history.'

'Oh, there's plenty of that here,' Lily said. 'History. No present, though, and certainly no future. Nothing changes.'

'Sounds idyllic.'

'Depends on what you like, I suppose,' she said. 'Living here gets very boring.'

'If you don't like it, why stay?' he asked. 'Couldn't you sell your house?'

'We could,' Owen said, 'but if we went to a bigger town, we'd have to work. Our income is enough for Lil'Moor. We don't want to work for anyone.'

'I can't say I blame you,' Othman said. It was a sentiment he shared.

'You're staying here, then?' Lily asked.

'For the time being. I acted on your recommendation.'

'It was hardly that!' she said. 'What do you think of the Eagers?'

'I don't think Mister likes me. She seems all right.'

Lily nodded. 'They've only been here a year or so. Now, they think they own the place!'

'They do a lot,' Owen said, which implied criticism rather than praise.

'She once wanted to start up some kind of church business,' Lily said. 'Must have got the idea from some sad women's novel about country life. Fêtes and things, I ask you! It was absurd. Lil'Moor doesn't even have a vicar of its own. A man comes out from Patterham now and again, that's all. Hardly anyone ever goes to church any more. It's so old-fashioned!'

'I didn't see a church,' Othman said.

'Oh, it's a way out of the village,' Lily told him. 'Almost as if Lil'Moor was bigger at one time, and has just shrunk away from it. You'd like it; it's very old.'

'We could show it to you,' Owen said. Lily looked at him sharply and then smiled.

'Yes, we could. Do you want us to?'

'It's very kind of you.'

'It's just something to do!' she said, and stood up. 'Well, come on, then.'

'What? Now?' Othman was taken aback.

'Better by moonlight,' Lily said. 'Come on.'

There was no moon, but the clear sky lent a ghostly radiance to the land. As they walked together in the middle of the road, Othman again experienced a feeling of being overwhelmed. Lily appeared to have undergone a dramatic personality change. Gone was the reticent, innocent reserve of their encounter in the post office. She chattered the entire time they walked, mainly about other people in the village.

'They don't think much of us,' she said.

'Why drink in the pub, then?' he asked.

'Because they hide the fact they don't think much of us,' Owen said. 'But we still *know*. They might think they don't want us around, but they'd be disappointed if we weren't. We're part of this place.'

'I don't care what they think,' Lily said.

'You must get lonely sometimes,' Othman said. The thought of them living alone together in isolation suddenly made him feel uneasy.

'Oh no,' Lily said. 'Never.'

'We have a car,' Owen said. 'We drive to places, don't we, Lily?'

'We drive to places,' she said. Othman was beginning to wonder if they were not rather simple in the head.

The church was really quite unremarkable, and not as old as the twins had suggested. Its most significant feature was that it had been built in such a bleak spot. It was surrounded by gravestones that were kept in check by a dilapidated fence. Several tired-looking yew trees provided the traditional vigilance for the dead. It was a place where lone spectres might walk, but there were none in evidence tonight. The most peculiar thing about it was that it appeared to have no name, but Othman supposed the large wooden board bearing the dedication and proclaiming service times and suchlike had rotted away.

'It's locked up,' Lily said. She was wearing her shawl low on her arms, and Othman could see her skin was pimpled with cold.

The three of them stood against the fence, looking at the graveyard. It seemed they had made rather a pointless journey.

'Let's show him the ringstone,' Owen said to his sister.

'That's a good idea.'

It seemed rather staged. The traveller was unsure of what to expect, but wondered whether he was about to be on the receiving end of a joke.

They went through a lich-gate that seemed unnecessarily imposing, or part of an older structure. A straight gravel path ran up to the church doors, and appeared to circle the building. Othman was bemused to see there was a TV aerial sticking out from the church roof.

'It's round the back,' Lily said, running into the shadow of the church.

'We used to come here a lot with our mother years ago,' Owen said. 'While she sat inside the place, dreaming, we played out here in the graveyard.' He looked around himself. 'I haven't been here for a long time. It looks smaller now, and even more decrepit.'

'It seems an odd place for a woman to come and dream,' Othman observed.

Owen shrugged. 'Well, she was an odd woman, I suppose.'

The ringstone was nothing more than a listing gravestone, its engraving long weathered into nonsense. 'This is it,' Lily said. She was leaning on the stone, her white hands gripping it at the top.

'And what is it, exactly?' asked the traveller.

Lily and her brother started laughing. Othman felt decidedly uncomfortable. 'We must join hands around it,' Lily said.

'How pagan,' Othman observed, unimpressed.

'Oh, probably,' Lily agreed, 'but it's a custom.' She held out her hands and wiggled the fingers. 'Join hands.'

Reluctantly, Othman complied. Lily's fingers were warm and dry; Owen's icy cold. 'Do we have to make a wish, or something?' Othman asked. He felt absurdly awkward.

'No, we circle,' Lily replied. She pulled on his arm.

I can't believe I'm doing this, Othman thought, stumbling round the stone. I have no control over these people. They are wild. 'Whose grave is this?' he asked.

'Don't know,' Lily said. 'It's not important.'

He suspected that circling the ringstone was a custom traditional only to the Winter twins, and strongly hoped no stray dog-walkers from the village would come along to observe this ridiculous ritual. 'That's enough,' he said, after a few minutes, pulling away from their hands. They did not object.

'Tomorrow, we could take you somewhere else,' Owen said.

They escorted him back to The White House and cheerily waved goodbye, promising further entertainment the following day. Othman was not sure of his feelings about Owen and Lily Winter. In some ways, they annoyed him, and Lily was not at all like he had imagined her to be. She should have been a shy virgin whom he could have initiated into the ways of the flesh, the uncharted regions of pleasure. He suspected now she was not a virgin at all. How disappointing. There would be no scholar's bedroom, with bookcases full of slim volumes. There would be no delicate water-colours on the wall, painted by her own untutored hand. The scratches on her arms, which he'd fondly thought she might have incurred playing with a favourite cat in some secluded, scented garden, had probably happened while she'd been fixing her car, or something equally mundane. Still, she and her brother were unusual people, even if not in the direction he'd hoped.

When Othman went back into The White House, Barbara Eager was still hovering around the bar cleaning glasses; it was not as late as he'd thought. She offered to make him some meat sandwiches, which he gladly accepted, and he sat down in the guests' lounge to read a local paper while she made them up. Mr Eager sauntered in, pushing out his belly, and attempted to be sociable. He asked Othman whether he played golf.

'I'm afraid not.'

'Hrrm, hrrrh.' The landlord was either clearing his

throat or playing for time. 'Sitting with the Winters, were you?' he said eventually. 'Rum pair, rum pair.' Mr Eager shook his head in perplexity. Othman made no comment. 'Bit of square-bashing wouldn't harm the lad . . .'

'They seem very young to live alone,' Othman said.

'Tch, yes!' said Mr Eager. 'The mother died five years ago, but they keep the old place up. They're looked out for around here.' He glanced at the traveller in a knowing, and slightly threatening, manner.

Barbara Eager had come into the room, carrying a tray. She had obviously overheard her husband's remarks. 'Helen Winter was a very private person, I believe,' she said, offering the traveller a plate of sandwiches. 'She came here when the twins were about twelve. Had a little money, I think. She always kept herself to herself, and never mentioned what had happened to her husband, but she was a good woman. The twins have run a little wild perhaps, since she died, but grief can do funny things to people, can't it? You spent the evening with Lily and Owen?'

The traveller nodded. 'Yes, they're very quaint, but I enjoyed their company.'

'We look out for them here in Lil'Moor,' Barbara Eager said. 'We have a close community.' Her concern explained why she'd seemed a little frosty with him earlier on, but it was certainly at odds with the way the twins thought they were regarded in the village. Poor waifs. They lived in a fantasy world. How would his intrusion affect it? He hoped to find out very soon.

Lily is dreaming. She is flying across the landscape, which is rendered black and white by the round, heavy moon. She can see her shadow rippling over the dewy

81

fields, and smell the scents of the earth rising up to surround her in natural perfume. With her arms spread out like wings, she circles Herman's Wood and dips low into a valley, skimming the twitching ears of slumbering sheep. Then she is up, describing the curve of the hills in her flight, soaring towards the dark obelisks of Long Eden's silent towers. The estate is spread out below her in moonlight, and it seems the gardens are not quite so overgrown as they appear to be in daylight. The seeding lawns have been cut short, the rhododendrons trained back from the winding pathways. The gravel on the sweeping driveway looks freshly raked, and there are no weeds.

She is flying high across the sinister yew walks, until her shadow is flung over the limpid waters of the lake. It seems to her that the surface of the water is glowing. She imagines herself as a great swan coming in to land lightly upon the lake and swoops downwards. She can see the island, its tangled trees now neat and pruned. A lawn leads from the water's edge to a clearing in the middle of the island. Here, she can see the pale, glistening columns of a Grecian-looking temple. Such follies are common in the grounds of stately homes, she thinks. As she circles lazily around the temple, a tall, male figure walks down its shallow front steps. There is something vaguely familiar about him. Once on the lawn, the man looks up at her and holds out one arm in a gesture of summoning. Lily is drawn to him instantly, and realizes with some alarm that it is the stranger she met in the post office that morning. He is naked to the waist, his long, pale hair loose around his shoulders, spilling down on to his chest. She has never seen such a beautiful man before. He reaches up towards her and the air lets go of her. Weightlessly, she falls down into his waiting arms. His limbs seem abnormally long, as if he stretched them out to pluck her from the sky. The man utters no sound, but, like a giant serpent, entwines his body with hers. The embrace is so complete, so overwhelming, that Lily feels as if she might lose consciousness and slip from this dream into another. She does not want that: this is a dream in which she wants to remain.

The scent of the stranger is overpowering, redolent of ripened corn and ozone. Lily feels drunk on it. A thought floats into her mind like a drifting feather: *I have come home. At last . . .*

Without speaking, the stranger draws her away from his chest and drapes her across his extended arms, admiring her as if she were an expensive garment. He holds her sensitively and with ease. Feeling both insubstantial and paralysed with wonder, Lily stares up into his eyes. Within their shadowy depths spins a vortex of timeless stars. Lily is beginning to feel that same vortex spinning within her belly, her womb, the core of her female power. The maelstrom of sensation is spreading throughout her whole body, encompassing her completely, until time itself seems to be shifting and contracting around her.

Still gazing down upon her, the stranger starts to move towards the lake, holding her carefully, reverently, as if she were some precious, fragile thing. At the water's edge, he gently sets her down. When her feet touch the ground, Lily becomes acutely aware that the world around her is far removed in time from the world that she knows. The air smells different, somehow fresher, clear of industrial taint. And the stars fill the sky above her, their light unfiltered by the artificial radiance of street-lamps. They are so bright, they make her think of fierce angels, holding swords of flame to illumine the halls of heaven. Holding court in their midst, the moon is enormous and fiery white, a queen among angels.

Awed, Lily looks down at the lake. The water's surface is like polished glass in the moonlight, a mirror for her reflection. She, too, has moved in time. Around her pale legs hangs a long, pleated skirt of turquoise-dyed linen. Her breasts are bare and her hair, squarely cut, is waxed into coils with silver beads attached to the end of each lock. It is a style she associates with Ancient Egyptian women although some instinct tells her that her appearance and apparel are not, in fact, Egyptian. Some other culture, then, even more ancient, forgotten even in myth.

As she gazes at her reflection, details seem to form around her, becoming more definite, changing her appearance further. Now she sees that her face is partly covered by a veil of penny-sized silver disks. As this awareness comes to her, she is suddenly conscious of the veil's weight upon her head, and hears the silvery tinkle of the disks as she moves. Her eyes, visible above the veil, are heavily made-up, and there is a blue crescent moon marked upon her forehead. Her gaze is slipping downwards. Even as she looks, an image forms on her belly. Through the sheerness of her skirt, a huge and startling eye stares out, completely covering her lower abdomen. She puts her hands against the skin to trace its outline and can feel that the flesh is slightly raised. Not a painting, then, but a tattoo.

Lily raises her eyes to the sky to gaze at the moon. She feels incredibly powerful. Is this exotic, unknown woman the person she really is inside? Distant memories tug at her mind. Has she experienced this dream before? A quiet hiss behind her makes her turn round.

The stranger has also transformed, but in him the changes are far more dramatic. In his place stands a magnificent beast with the body of a lion and the necks and heads of seven horned serpents, with crowns upon their horns. Within the face of each serpent, Lily recognizes seven different personae staring out at her: a prophet, a hermit, a poet, a satyr, a scholar, a hunter and a warrior. A voice, which she senses is her own, whispers in her mind: *Behold the seven kings of the earth, the seven sages of old* . . .

Without fear, Lily approaches the beast and touches its warm flank, feeling its muscles shudder beneath her hand. She grasps the long, shaggy hair on its shoulders and, with natural ease, swings herself up on its back. The beast gives a great leap and rises high into the air. Lily's exhilaration is complete. Light is streaming from her hair in sparks. The force of the night stars crashes through the tattooed eye on her belly and pours throughout her whole body. She feels herself growing hot with an ignition of lust.

The beast circles the island and then shoots off towards Herman's Wood, throwing an enormous shivering shadow over the hilltops. Lily grips the beast with her thighs, urging him onwards. Looking down, she sees a clearing in the trees and recognizes it as the High Place in the centre of the woods. Then, without warning, the beast begins to plummet towards the ground. Sure that they are about to crash right through the earth, Lily throws her arms up across her face and utters an alarmed cry. She feels the wind of their flight tugging her from the beast's back. She is losing her grip! Down, down . . .

The impact, when it came, was simply the shock of awakening.

Lily opened her eyes, gasping, to find that her body was threshing around wildly upon her bed. The feeling of flight was still very much with her, as well as the power of the beast's acceleration towards the earth. With awakening came stillness. Her panicked body subsided into relaxation.

Lily sat up, exhausted and shocked. She had never dreamed anything like that before; it had been so vivid. Quickly, she inspected her belly, expecting to find it still tattooed, but, of course, the skin was bare.

Chapter Six

Sunday, 18th October: High Crag House, Cornwall
After breakfast Aninka took a short walk around the grounds of the house, finding all the places where she'd loved to play as a child. Enniel had sent word he could not recommence their interview until after lunch. Feeling on edge and depressed, Aninka was drawn to the shadowed hollow, hidden by ancient hollies, where her cousin Noah had first made love to her, accepting the gift of her virginity with fumbling ardour. Aninka stooped to scramble in among the prickly, dusty branches. She sat down upon the ground, in hiding. Stiff dead leaves pricked her skin through the fabric of her jeans. It would have been appropriate for tears to come, but her eyes were dry. Worse, a fantasy came of an alternative life where there had been no horror in Cresterfield, and she had brought Peverel Othman down here to the house to meet her family. She would have shown him this place, and they would have laughed together beneath the holly, their eyes meeting mid-laughter, and their expression changing to that of desire.

Aninka made an impatient noise to dispel this sad dream and virtually threw herself away from the holly patch. Such fantasies were dangerous. She had to keep in her mind the reason why she was here.

As she walked back to the house, she saw Enniel's tall figure standing at the french windows in the main drawing-room. He thought she was a liability, Aninka was sure. Damn him! Gritting her teeth, she raised her arm in a cheery wave. After the briefest pause, Enniel responded in kind.

He's doing nothing at the moment, Aninka thought. We could be getting this horrible confession business over with, but no, he makes me wait!

She presented herself at Enniel's study ten minutes late on purpose. This time she noticed the tape recorder as soon as she entered the room. Who else would be listening to her confessions in the future, apart from her guardian? It was not a comforting thought.

Enniel made a show of turning his computer off, despite the fact that Aninka could not see the monitor screen from where she was sitting on the leather couch.

'I expect you're waiting for the juicy bits!' she said in an attempt at crudeness, as Enniel came to sit beside her.

He pulled a wry expression: 'It depends on your definition of "juice".'

Aninka rolled her eyes. 'What do you want: gore, sex, mutilation, murder? I have a selection.'

Enniel sighed patiently. 'My dear, just begin where we left off, the tape's already running.'

Aninka's Story: Cresterfield, July

Aninka and Peverel Othman's first arranged meeting took place in a small, rather dingy pub on the outskirts of the city. She could not imagine why he'd chosen such a venue. Eccentricity, presumably. He'd called her the evening before and, at first, she had pretended not to remember who he was. She did not want him to know how, since she'd met him, her heart had been leaping involuntarily every time the phone had rung. A hint of laughter in his voice suggested he was perfectly aware of this, however. At Aninka's request, her cousin Noah had made some discreet enquiries about Peverel Othman among local family members, but no one had heard of him. Still, he perplexed her, for he did not seem to be merely human. She recognized the contradictions within herself: since leaving home, she'd worked hard to be utterly absorbed into human culture, yet now found herself hoping this potential lover might be something more than just a man.

When she had entered the pub, he was already waiting there for her, folded into a corner too small for him, his limbs sprawling gracefully, hugged by leather. She spotted him the instant she walked through the door, even though the room was crowded with noisy young people – none of whom was Aninka's type. So as not to appear too eager, she bought herself a drink at the bar before pushing through the jostling, over-perfumed bodies to reach Othman's corner. His hair was tied back, accentuating the chiselled lines of his jaw and cheek-bones. Hunger flexed in Aninka's belly at the sight of him. He greeted her with a half-smile, cynical and amused. This annoyed her, for she feared she had given him the upper hand.

Sitting opposite Othman, Aninka drank gin and tonic under the yellow lights, dressed in black silk among the frowzy girls with ragged perms, and boys with shaved necks. Again, Othman questioned her gently about herself; nothing too intrusive. She sought to repay the interrogation, but he evaded answering her questions in any depth. This did not surprise her, somehow. 'So what do you do with yourself?' she asked.

He shrugged. 'This and that. Some things above board, others not. I'm interested in art and antiquities.'

'Hence the travelling.'

'Yeah.'

'Are you a dealer?'

He smiled. 'When I need to be.'

His opaque answers began to irritate her. She decided to talk about herself instead. He seemed eager to pay attention. She spoke of her inspirations, the stories of Inanna, Ereshkigal, and – daringly – the earlier myths of Anu, Enlil, Ninkharsag. He did not bite by adding comments of his own, a response which she thought a Grigori would be unable to resist. Perhaps he did not recognize her words as bait.

In a pause in the conversation she said, 'I thought you weren't going to call me. It's been some time since we met.' She hoped to draw him out a little, at least, with that.

'Ah, well, I've made friends,' he told her.

Was that why he'd delayed in contacting her? A pang of jealousy slithered through her. She imagined the other women who must populate his life, all adoring him, because he looked so fine. She felt herself withdraw from the occasion. She would not be second-best. 'Good for you,' she said, churlishly.

'I'd like you to meet them,' he said, undeterred.

'Why?' Did he want to impress them with his famous, or semi-famous, acquaintance?

'I think you'd find each other interesting.'

'I'm very picky about my friends,' Aninka said. 'I have to be.' The comment hung between them. He did not question her about it.

'So am I.'

'Is this why we're here?' Aninka asked. 'Are you expecting someone else?'

He shook his head. 'No. We're here because it's honest. I feel like being honest tonight.'

'What's honest about it?'

He gestured languidly at the room, although he did not take his eyes, of a most penetrating blue, from her own. 'The lack of trimmings, the lack of pretence. Would you prefer to be sipping Spritzer in some wine bar?'

'Yes, actually. Sorry to disappoint.' She was wondering: Why am I here? Their exchanges had become stilted, maybe even hostile. Perhaps she should make an effort.

'So what are your friends like, then? Why would I find them interesting?'

'They are artists, of a kind,' he answered. 'Of the dark arts.'

'What?' She injected a little distaste into her voice.

'Magic,' he said. 'Surely, you're interested in that? All those paintings?'

'I'm not sure I believe in it,' she answered stiffly, lying. 'It's an excuse for perversion, I think.'

'Not an excuse, but often an expression,' Othman said.

'Just what do you think I am?' She cringed at the cliché.

'I didn't want to imply anything,' he said. 'I think we've set off on the wrong path. Let me explain. These people, they are into reconstructing the ancient rites of Sumeria. It's very impressive. In fact, when I first attended one of their rituals, it reminded me of your paintings: the colours, the costumes. It's all very innocent, actually.'

'Oh, I see.' Inside, she was smiling. Whatever these people did, it could only be a poor and indistinct reflection of everything she already knew. Othman suddenly seemed pathetic. He had called her only once he'd found something he thought was bizarre enough to impress her. He liked to appear interesting and mysterious, she could tell. Still, he was beautiful. She wanted to touch him. Once she'd achieved that, she could dismiss him.

'Would you like to meet them, then?' he asked.

Aninka detected a faint note of urgency in his voice. 'They don't mind outsiders knowing about them?'

'You won't be an outsider,' he said. 'You'll be with me.'

'You work quickly, to build such trust in only two weeks,' Aninka said.

He smiled.

Later, he escorted her to her car. She asked him if he'd like to come home with her. This was perhaps a risk, for she knew hardly anything about him, but he declined anyhow. 'Thanks for the drink,' she said and kissed his cheek, hoping he'd take it further. He didn't.

'I'll call you,' he said, and watched her drive away.

The next day, at her drawing board, she tried not to think about him. Probably he wouldn't call her now for another couple of weeks, if at all. He was interested in her, she felt, but it might not be carnal. What, then? She drew attenuated figures, wreathed in flowing hair, wearing his face. She drew a naked man, cupping his genitals in his hands, offering them like a sacrifice. That was perhaps her own magic.

He called in the late afternoon. Was she free that night? 'My friends are meeting later. Would you like to come?'

So quickly? *'Are you sure it's all right?'* she asked.

He was quite sure.

She met him at a lay-by on a dual carriageway at the edge of a residential area, where the houses were pricey. Here, he made her wait. Watching the drizzle obscure her windscreen, she smoked three cigarettes, wondering if she was doing the right thing. What was she walking into? Othman didn't know anything about her. She could handle herself in any situation, but the family disapproved of overt displays of difference. She hoped she would not have to compromise her decision never to behave in any manner other than completely human.

A sleek, black car drew up behind her at the lay-by. He has money, she thought. Othman got out of it and loped towards her. She watched him in the rear-view mirror, her heart pounding. He came up to her door and she pressed a button to lower the window. 'Shall I follow you?' she asked.

He shook his head. 'No. Mind if I ride with you?'

'Get in.'

She gripped the steering wheel, fraught with nerves as he curled himself into the passenger seat. The front of his hair was wet from the drizzle outside. 'I haven't brought anything with me,' she said, as she started the car. 'Was I supposed to? Wine or something?'

'No. Take the second turning off the next roundabout.'

Othman directed her on to a new estate, built in the Victorian style, and even named Victoria Heights. Sharp-edged Gothic anachronisms loured beyond tarmacked driveways, where large silver, black or white cars were parked. Swags of lace and dried flowers were evident in nearly every bay window.

'Your friends meet here?' Aninka asked. She had expected a shabby communal building hired out for the evening, or else leased on a low rent.

'Yes. Like it?'

She gave him an arch glance. 'Hardly the venue I anticipated. It's so suburban. What must the neighbours think?'

'You should know it's the ideal place, the only place,' Othman answered. There seemed to be a message behind his words. 'Turn right here.'

Aninka swung the car on to a road named Brontë Close. All the houses were detached; five or six-bedroomed, by the look of them. The street-lights were all imitation gas-lamps. In the approaching dusk, it was quite effective, but she wouldn't have wanted to live there.

'It's like a conservation area,' Othman said. 'They're not allowed to have visible satellite dishes, unsightly gardens or unworthy vehicles parked out front.'

'Well, we can all play at it,' Aninka remarked.

Othman did not comment. 'Here, pull over.'

The house was called Grey Gables, although it was made of very red brick. Pointed eaves and tall chimneys combined to provide aesthetic effect. The drive sloped downwards to the road. Three cars were parked there: two BMWs and the latest Audi.

Aninka followed Othman up to the porticoed front door. She had dressed in a very businesslike fashion: a long-skirted suit of dull, black silk that hugged her figure. Her make-up was precise and severe, and she'd wound her long black hair up into a chignon. She felt like a PR person, or a cosmetics executive. Was this costume her armour? She wasn't sure what to expect.

The door was opened by a woman of early middle age, wearing a plum-coloured crushed-velvet caftan, embroidered in bright emerald and gold. Her bosom was adorned with a tangle of coloured beads and pendants, which immediately attracted the eye. Yet when Aninka's gaze was drawn to her face, the woman appeared plain: no make-up, and her hair was a mousy colour, straight and parted in the middle, wispily brushing her shoulders.

The woman's face lit up when she saw who was standing at her threshold. 'Pev, how lovely you could come!'

Othman stepped forward to embrace the woman, Aninka hovering behind. She could hear the buzz of voices emanating from somewhere in the house.

Othman disentangled himself from the woman's clutch and gestured at his companion. 'Wendy, this is Aninka. Aninka Prussoe, the artist.'

Aninka took hold of the proffered hand. Her palm felt cold against the woman's warm, dry fingers.

'Pleased to meet you. I'm Wendy Marks. It's good of you to come. Pev has told us so much about you.'

'My pleasure,' Aninka murmured, wondering exactly what this slight acquaintance of hers had told these people.

Wendy stepped back and waved them in. 'Come in, come in.' She led her guests into a vast drawing-room, decorated in Morris wallpaper, which was virtually covered by an array of Rossetti and De Morgan prints in ornate frames. Aninka couldn't resist a quick inspection to see whether any of her own work was present. It wasn't. The people standing and sitting around the room could have stepped from the paintings. Hair rippled abundantly across the shoulders of the women, who swanned about in billowing gowns, anachronistically romantic rather than correct in historical detail. Similarly, the men were all wearing embroidered waistcoats, loose shirts and high boots. Aninka immediately felt incredibly visible in her tailored clothes. Also, apart from Othman, she was the tallest person in the room.

'Would you like something to drink?' Wendy Marks asked her. 'Mineral water, fruit juice, or something a little stronger?'

Aninka opted for caution. 'A mineral water will be fine.'

'Now, you must let me introduce you to everyone . . .'

The group numbered ten people. Three of the women had evidently changed their names to some degree to reflect their esoteric interests, whereas the men had retained their original names. Apart from Wendy Marks and her jovial, skinny husband, Ivan, who owned Grey Gables, there was another married couple, Una and Ernie Brock. To Aninka, they did not seem the type of people to be interested in exotic rites, both being round and small, and looking rather like children dressed up in colourful clothes. Serafina (no surname) was the youngest of the group, a fey, white-faced creature, with thin, dyed black hair which hung nearly to her waist, who strove never to smile and wore mainly black. It was immediately obvious to Aninka that the girl fancied Othman desperately, from the way she became more sepulchral in his presence in an attempt to appear interesting. No doubt he would find that attractive, as it mirrored some of his own affectations. Serafina barely acknowledged Aninka, other than through a brief glance, probably to establish her age and appearance with regard to competing for Othman. Three single men were present: Farrell Sharpe, Nick Emmett and Martin Fortney. All three looked like teachers or computer programmers, although Nick had a certain appeal, Aninka thought. Despite the beard and short hair, a look she loathed, his eyes were compelling. She deduced he was a womanizer, and emitted conflicting signals while being introduced to him, which she hoped would confuse him. A slightly overweight thirty-something female with bright-red hair and violently applied make-up was introduced as Misty Kennedy. Misty? Aninka thought. Hardly. A large amount of Kennedy bosom was displayed, which was thrust mercilessly beneath Othman's nose, as Misty breathed greetings in a quasi-mystical manner. The final group member was Enid Morningstar, a starved-looking, earnest New-Ager, who had not yet hit thirty, but who would doubtlessly never recover once she had. She asked Aninka for her birth sign. Aninka replied, 'The feathered serpent,' to which the woman responded, 'Er . . . I've not heard of that. Is it from a new system?'

Not wishing to explain, Aninka nodded. 'I read about it in a book.'

'Oh, you must tell me about it.'

Aninka shrugged. 'Sorry. I borrowed it from a friend, ages ago. Can't remember the title.'

'Oh . . .' Enid's face fell. She would no doubt be scouring her mail-order catalogues at the first opportunity.

Dinner was served at nine.

The party moved into the dining-room, where an enormous table, covered in black crushed velvet and adorned with silver cutlery awaited the feasters. Othman and Aninka were seated on either side of Wendy Marks at the head of the table. Misty Kennedy pushed herself in beside Othman, earning malevolent stares from Serafina, who found herself between two of the wispy beards. Nick Emmett sat next to Aninka.

As Wendy dived back and forth from table to hostess trolley, serving exquisitely prepared dishes to her guests, Aninka wondered how this tame and convivial gathering could turn into something which had pricked the interest of Peverel Othman. It all seemed so middle-class and ordinary, despite the clothes and the prevailing interest in astrology. Aninka liked the people for their very ordinariness; they were friendly, and articulate enough to be pleasant dinner companions. Nick Emmett had heard of her work, and claimed to have recently bought a birthday card for a friend bearing one of her paintings. '"Inanna Removing Her Jewelled Collar at the Gate",' he said.

Aninka was impressed he'd remembered the title and told him to visit her exhibition in town, where the original was displayed.

'Perhaps you could show it to me yourself, and we could have lunch afterwards,' he offered.

Aninka pulled a sly, yet smiling face, to show him she had his measure. 'Perhaps. I'm very busy,' she said.

Wendy, possibly having noticed Nick was manoeuvring for a seduction, distracted Aninka's attention. She told her how she was a picture-framer and restorer, and that her husband, Ivan, had a successful antiques business, with a small gallery attached to his shop. Clearly Wendy's tastes were very much in accord with Aninka's. She felt it necessary to apologize for not having any of Aninka's work.

Misty Kennedy appeared to have been deep in breathy

96

conversation with Othman, but was obviously the sort of woman who kept a separate antenna tuned to every conversation in the room. 'I help out, you know,' she interrupted. 'Buying stock, especially paintings. Perhaps we could put one of yours in the gallery, dear.'

Aninka noticed that Wendy had flushed a little. 'Misty helps Ivan out,' she said quietly, and then to Misty, 'I'm sure Aninka doesn't need to try and sell her work in little shops like ours.'

'I'd love to give you a print, Wendy,' Aninka said, feeling suddenly defensive for the woman. 'Not for the shop, for yourself. Perhaps you'd like to come and choose one. I have plenty at my flat in town.'

Wendy looked slightly surprised at the offer. 'That's very kind of you. I'm sure I don't deserve it.'

Aninka shook her head. 'Please. I'd like to.'

Wendy smiled tightly and, for the briefest of moments, touched Aninka's hand. 'Thank you.'

After the pavlova had been cleared away and coffee had been consumed, Wendy said, 'I hope you'd like to attend a small ritual we'll enact shortly. It isn't a working rite, rather a theatrical ceremony.'

Aninka glanced around the room. 'Here? Of course, I mean, I'd love to . . .'

Wendy laughed. 'Oh, I know how we must appear to you! Our excursions into the occult are gentle and therapeutic. We have an interest in ancient cultures – as do you, of course. I like to try and re-create a feeling for the past, when life was . . .' She shrugged. '. . . I can't say less violent or more artistic, because I'm sure that's simply a glamorized view, but at least when people perhaps had more integrity, and an appreciation of life, death and the world around them. Does that make sense to you?'

'Very much so,' Aninka said. 'If your "therapeutic rituals" celebrate those things, then you must be on the right track.'

Wendy smiled in what might have been relief. Aninka realized that the woman didn't want to appear shallow or stupid.

'We have a temple in the garage,' she said.

Ivan Marks had converted the two-car garage into a replica of a Sumerian temple, the details of which he and Wendy had gleaned from books on archaeology and children's encyclopaedias of the ancient world. Although many of the details were modern embellishments, Aninka was impressed by what she saw. The breeze-blocked walls were hidden by columns and hangings. Huge bowls of incense burned in the shadows. Lights flickered in chalices of wax. Behind an altar at the back of the garage, the wall had been plaster-boarded, and someone had painted, quite effectively, simplistic versions of ancient Sumerian bas-reliefs, representing some of the mythical epics: scenes from the stories of Gilgamesh and the Flood. Around the edge, zoomorphic god-forms were depicted bestowing gifts upon the smaller figures of men and women.

The atmosphere was altogether conducive to meditation and the working of magic. There were no unpleasant reverberations lingering in the air, which confirmed Wendy's claims about the gentle nature of their work. Prior to the ritual, the celebrants all disappeared into the guest-rooms of the house and emerged in full costume: fringed robes, sashes and stylized wigs. Enid, it appeared, was the official seamstress of the group, and had an eye for detail. No one suggested Aninka or Othman should get changed. They were directed to a wooden bench at the back of the temple and requested to sit quietly while the ritual was performed.

In the event, very little magic took place, as the group re-enacted the biblical story of Nebuchadnezzar and his vizier/ prophet, Daniel. Aninka realized she was spectating at a mystical play rather than a ritual. Ivan Marks, who'd written the script, had expanded upon the story, and later admitted to Aninka that he'd made the embellishments up, rather than researched them from old documents. Othman smiled once or twice at Aninka, but made no whispered remarks. In fact, he'd seemed quite distant all evening.

Later, the group went back into the house and the wine was opened. Although they had not fasted to work, Aninka noticed they had not touched alcohol until their ceremony was completed.

The evening ended pleasantly. Aninka gave Wendy Marks her number and told her to call soon. Nick Emmett was diverted with a vague promise. Serafina glowered as Aninka preceded Othman from the house to the car. Aninka was surprised he'd maintained such a laid-back presence, apparently content to sit back and watch the group hover around her instead. As they belted up in the car, with Wendy and Ivan standing on the threshold of the house to wave goodbye, Aninka wondered again what Othman's interest was in these people. They were nice — no other word for it — but she couldn't see how they could possibly fascinate someone like Peverel Othman, unless he was something other than he appeared.

As they drove off down Brontë Close, Aninka asked, 'How did you meet them?'

Othman lit a cigarette, the first he'd had all night. 'Through the Goth wench.'

'Serafina.' Aninka noticed her own voice was sharp.

'Yeah. Met her at a club.'

'I can't help wondering how she *got involved with them. They're all very much of a type, but for her.'*

'Then you must ask her,' Othman said.

'They don't seem your type either,' Aninka added, ignoring his last remark.

'How do you know what my type is?' he enquired.

'Just a hunch.'

Othman snickered to himself. 'They're like a private ant colony,' he said. 'I love to watch them, study their group dynamics.'

'How altruistic of you!'

'Well, at least I'm not tempted to show off!'

'Aren't you?'

'No. That business about the feathered serpent! What are you on?'

Aninka slammed on the brakes. They had almost reached the dual carriageway once more. 'What the hell do you mean?'

Othman gazed straight ahead. 'Keep driving, my dear, we're almost there.'

'You're an insulting, posturing dickhead. Get out of my car.'

Othman actually looked taken aback. 'Oh, have we stopped playing now?'

'We never started. Get out!' Aninka drummed her fingernails against the steering wheel, glaring through the windscreen. Some part of her wondered whether Othman would do something terrible now. Attack her.

'I'm sorry,' he said. 'I didn't mean to upset you.'

She risked a glance at him. 'I don't know what it is we're doing, seeing each other. It's weird. You're just so snide.'

'I'm too old,' he answered. 'I forget . . . sometimes. Aninka, I know you. You know me. You're right. I am Grigori.'

Aninka rolled her eyes. She felt both relieved and alarmed. 'Why on earth didn't you say? What has all this stupid charade been for?'

Othman smiled engagingly, putting his head on one side. 'I get bored easily. I wanted to keep you guessing.'

Aninka's car glided away from the kerb. The affair began that night.

Aninka could say no more than this to Enniel. The details of her love-making with Peverel Othman were private. Enniel made no comment when she abruptly ceased her narrative, other than to say, 'Shall we pause for the day now?'

Aninka nodded. 'Yes. All right.' She was sitting on the sofa, while Enniel was a distant presence behind his desk. It had been another gloomy day; night had crept down unnoticeably through a misty fusk.

Aninka stood up to stretch her legs. Enniel's office felt cold. 'I should have realized all was not right,' she said. 'I had suspicions, but I ignored them.'

'He was a good lover, of course,' Enniel remarked.

When Aninka looked at him, he was staring at her without embarrassment. She turned away, shrugged, became aware that she was hugging herself. 'Yes. I suppose I fell in love with him. He was infuriating sometimes, with his capricious ways, and his secretiveness, but I always felt there was some great sadness inside him.' She laughed coldly. 'Why is it a female always believes she can heal the soul of a grieving male? He was hiding tragedy within. I could smell it, and I wanted to draw it out.'

It pained her to remember their first kiss, in the dark of her living-room. He'd grabbed her the moment the door was closed. No one had ever kissed her like that; tenderness and force in equal measure. They had made love upon the floor. His beauty had been like a scorching flame, and his gentleness had made her cry with pleasure and a wistful melancholy. The memory was too sweet, and therefore agonizing to recall. She knew she would never experience any of that again, and it was hard to carry on living, knowing that. Even now, the act of recollection brought tears to her eyes.

'This is so difficult,' she said to Enniel.

He poured her a large brandy and brought it over to her without words, offering her his silk handkerchief along with the glass. 'It is important you tell me everything,' he said. 'You don't know how important.'

Aninka blinked at him, sipping the fiery liquor. 'He must be punished.'

Enniel touched her face. 'Rest assured; that will happen, and is doubtless happening already. He will be punishing himself.'

Aninka shook her head fiercely. 'I don't think so! Othman is a beast, an Anakim, without compassion!'

'He may be these things,' Enniel said gently, and then

drew in his breath, as if he'd been about to say more, but had changed his mind.

'Yes?' Aninka prompted. 'What else?'

Enniel shook his head and smiled. 'It is you who has the information, my dear. I am merely a sympathetic ear.'

He doesn't realize I've grown up, Aninka thought. He believes I can't tell he's lying to me.

Chapter Seven

Same day: Little Moor

Verity had been in a furious temper when she'd gone to bed on Saturday night. It had been altogether a strange day. First the dreams, then the arrival of the cat, then the conversation with Daniel. Verity was used to routine and none of these things happened regularly. She had deliberately buried all thoughts of her past, and they rarely disinterred themselves to worry her. Why she should suddenly start dreaming of people she had long discarded, she could not imagine. Nothing had happened to invoke them. She felt very peculiar all day, somehow liquid in her joints and floating in her mind. The dreams had obviously disrupted her sleep more than she'd realized. Neither Louis nor Daniel seemed to notice anything different about her.

The black cat lay contentedly before the range in the kitchen all day, interrupting his rest only to eat the sliced chicken Verity put before him and drink a dish of milk. She knew in her heart he was going to stay, even though he had evidently been cared for recently. She wondered what she should call him; he was so big and so black. The name 'Satan' sprang to mind, for it seemed apt, but Verity shrank from calling the word out loud anywhere in the house. She felt spooked enough as it was. Instead, she decided to call him Raven; that was a black enough name without being too sinister. Louis had seemed pleased about the cat. Verity knew her father thought that caring for the animal would be good for her, but his misguided sentimentality did not gall her enough to throw the creature out.

While they ate their dinner that evening – Daniel secreted upstairs in his lair – Louis had said to her, 'It's good to have a pet. We need some life about the place.'

Verity shrugged and daintily spooned soup into her mouth. She wished her father would drop the subject. It was nothing to do with him.

'What was that racket this morning?' Louis asked. 'It woke me.'

'Daniel,' Verity answered. 'He'd lost his key.'

'Ah . . .'

'And how was your evening at The White House?' It was an act of charity, Verity felt, to ask Louis about his activities.

'Very nice,' Louis answered, and then paused significantly. Verity sensed an unwelcome remark was imminent.

'We should have the Eagers over for dinner some time,' Louis said. 'I'm always eating there.'

Verity grimaced, wondering whether she could stomach a whole evening of Barbara Eager's forced jollity. 'As you like,' she said. It was as if Louis had been asking her permission.

'We could have a bit of a dinner party,' Louis said. 'Invite a couple of Daniel's friends. The Winters, perhaps.'

This unexpected suggestion jolted Verity out of her complacency. 'The Winters? Are you serious? I doubt they know how to use knives and forks.'

Louis frowned. 'Don't be a snob, Vez. Lily Winter seems a pleasant girl.'

'She might be, but Owen Winter is a filthy slob. I don't know how you can contemplate having him in the house.'

'Barbara seems to think they're both OK.'

'Oh well, that's settled then!' Verity snapped. 'No doubt Mrs Eager thinks they're quaint, like an arrangement of dried flowers or rusty old farm machinery used as ornaments. Yes, I can just see Owen Winter as a rustic ornament in The White House!'

'I wish you wouldn't be so snappy all the time,' Louis said. 'The Winters might be a bit scruffy, but they have no parents, so they're bound to run a bit wild. It wouldn't do any harm to be friendly.'

By this, Verity gathered Barbara Eager must have said something about the Winters the previous night. Do-gooding busybody. 'Oh, honestly, Dad! Owen Winter is a bad influence on Daniel. You shouldn't encourage him. They were out all night on Friday, God knows what they get up to. Aren't you concerned about what Daniel might be doing?'

For a moment father and daughter looked at one another intensely. Then Louis seemed to gather himself together. 'I don't believe *you* care, madam!' He struggled awkwardly to his feet. 'I'll arrange something for next week. It's about time we started socializing more.'

So Verity had gone to bed in a foul mood, her temper alleviated only by the attentions of the cat, who trotted up the stairs at her side, his long tail brushing her legs. Things are getting out of control, she thought, and then banished the idea. No. No. Bad to let things get out of control. Let Louis have his little dinner party. It was bound to be a disaster. The thought of facing Owen Winter's satyr smile by candlelight was chilling. Still, she could be as rude to him as she liked. She didn't care what the Eagers thought, or Winter's mousy sister. Perhaps the Winters wouldn't accept an invitation to Low Mede.

She lay in bed fantasizing about a hundred witty retorts across the dinner table. The cat jumped on to the bed and began washing himself. She could feel his comforting weight against her legs, his soft, private purr.

In the morning, she'd woken to the distant chime of church bells from a neighbouring village. She heard Raven chirruping, the soft thump of his feet as he ran across the floor. Her window was open a crack. It admitted the unmistakable smells of autumn. Sunlight fell dreamily into the room. Everything seemed to be in soft focus. Verity was aware that she had awoken in good spirits. She sat up in bed, smiling down at the cat, who was rolling around on the floor. Then, her face creased into a slight frown of disapproval. Raven appeared to be fighting with her underwear, biting the fabric, whilst mewing and purring to himself. There was something distinctly lascivious about his behaviour, and Verity was a little disgusted by his evident enjoyment of the smells her body had left upon the cloth. She clapped her hands and said, 'Hey!' The cat lay back and stared at her through slitted eyes, his back legs still idly kicking, entangled in the straps of her bra.

Eva Manden, Little Moor's postmistress, was worried about her mother. The old lady hadn't been right since they'd closed the shop on Saturday afternoon. Eva had woken in the early hours of Sunday morning, alerted by an unfamiliar sound. She had found her mother wandering up and down the landing in moonlight, feeling along the walls with her crinkled hands.

'What is it, Mother?' she'd demanded. 'Do you want the toilet?'

'Out of my way!' cried the old woman in an uncharacteristically strong voice. 'I'm looking for a way out.'

'Go back to bed,' Eva soothed, moving to take hold of the woman in her arms.

Unexpectedly, her mother lashed out at her. 'Get your

hands off me, girl! I need to get out. It's time. It's nearly time!'

'Time for what?' Eva's heart sank. Her mother's voice sounded so young.

In the moonlight, the old woman's eyes were glinting with an icy fire. Youth still lived there, and power. 'Something I doubt you'll be happy about. Something I deserve. They've come back, Evie. Like it or not, they've come back!'

Eva had pressed herself against the wall. Her lungs ached as if the air had been punched from her body. It couldn't be. No. That was all over, over and done with. She only had to wait for her mother to die now. There could be no return.

The old woman looked at her daughter with clever, glittering eyes. 'You can't stop it. I know what you think, but there's nothing you can do to stop it.'

Eva attempted to claw reality back. 'Mother, you're dreaming. Come with me. Come back to bed. I could make you a nice hot drink.'

For a few moments, the old woman stared up at the high window above the stairs. She drew in her breath slowly, tasting the air. 'Can smell it,' she said. 'The smell of a man, of more than a man.' Then her shoulders had slumped. Whatever brief energy had enlivened her had fled. 'Bed, yes.' Her voice had shrunk back to a whine. 'And a nice cup of Ovaltine.'

Relieved, Eva led her mother back to her own room. Perhaps it had been an isolated episode. It had to be.

At lunchtime, the traveller had a visitor. He had been hanging around The White House in the hope that Lily and Owen would turn up and was therefore surprised, and even a little disappointed, when Owen arrived alone. The boy was wearing the same tatty jumper he'd worn the previous evening and a pair of very scuffed leather trousers, perhaps influenced by Othman's own attire. He had also apparently brushed his hair. His flawless skin looked shockingly clean against the oily wool of his jumper.

'Lily's busy,' he said. 'I've got the car outside. I'll show you around.'

The Winter car was a big, rounded vehicle upholstered in leather, with walnut interior trim. It smelled of age. Owen drove with the habitual terrifying confidence of the young.

'Lily's making a meal,' he said, as the car bowled along one of the lanes leading from Little Moor. 'A meal for you. For tonight.' He grinned at Othman.

'That's nice. Where are you taking me?'

'Just for a walk through the woods. They're very ancient. That's the sort of thing you want, isn't it?'

'Drive on!' Othman poked his hand out of the car window, letting his fingers run through the whipping grass of the steep hedgerows.

'You could cut yourself,' said Owen, 'lose a finger. Are you afraid of blood?'

Owen parked the car in a passing-place, where a five-barred gate gave access to a field. The woods began just to the left of the gate. Owen and Othman walked down the lane a short way, until Owen led the way into the woods. He knew he was taking Othman to the High Place, even though he was trying to tell himself he wasn't. The High Place was special to Owen; it had always drawn him. It was as if a quiet, insistent voice spoke to his inner mind, telling him what he should do there. The images came to him vividly, the circling, the chanting, the sexual communion with the earth. He had sensed he was taking part in something that had occurred in that spot for many centuries, and hoped Peverel Othman would pick up on something there, perhaps confirm Owen's suspicions, and hopes, about the place.

Owen and Lily had discussed Peverel Othman in great detail after they'd left him on Saturday night. Both decided he must be an occultist, because there was something around him which reeked of magic. 'He is very handsome,' Lily had said, which had surprised Owen. Lily had never commented on men other than himself before. Although he'd experienced a distinct thrill of jealousy at her words, he'd recognized a thread of excitement as well. It had been Lily's decision that Owen should spend some time alone with the stranger. She'd seemed a little jumpy that morning, and had spoken vaguely of disturbing dreams. Owen was secretly relieved she hadn't seemed too eager to see Othman again immediately.

Owen led the way along a narrow track, brushing bracken aside. The path widened as they drew near to the High Place, and Othman increased his pace to walk beside Owen. 'The Eagers told me a little about you and Lily,' he said.

Owen rolled his eyes. 'I can imagine.'

'No, it was quite complimentary actually. I'm sorry about your mother.'

Owen shrugged. 'She was ill for a while. We've always had to look after ourselves a lot.' They had reached the foot of the hill. Here, Othman paused, forcing Owen to turn and look at him. Othman was standing with his hands on his hips, his head thrown back. 'This is interesting,' he said.

Owen's heart jumped in his chest. Othman did seem to have picked up on the atmosphere. He beckoned for Othman to follow him up the hill. 'Wait till you see it properly,' he said.

They emerged through the bracken and walked down to the centre of the hollow. Othman turned round a few times, nodding to himself. He was smiling widely. 'Is this a place you and Lily visit often, too?'

Owen wrinkled his nose, his hands deep in his trouser pockets. 'Not really. That is, Lily doesn't come here. It's one of my places.' He paused, physically restraining himself from saying any more. He had an urge to tell Othman about Daniel, how he had sensed something unusual and powerful about the boy, how he brought him to this place in the hope of making something happen. The only problem was he didn't know exactly *what* he was hoping would happen. Although he suspected Othman might be able to advise him on these activities, he still shrank from betraying too much.

'I see,' Othman said. His voice was amused.

Owen felt himself blush and had to turn away, afraid Othman had helped himself to information from his mind. Daniel sometimes did that without realizing it, betraying himself with an idle remark on something Owen knew he hadn't spoken aloud, although Daniel always denied his talent when Owen mentioned it.

'There are many places like this,' Othman said. 'Ancient sites throughout the world, where residues of power remain.'

'You feel that, then?' Owen asked quickly.

Othman nodded. 'Of course. This was probably a pagan site a long time ago.' He grinned. 'Perhaps still is!'

Owen laughed uneasily. An image had come into his mind of performing his rites with Othman present. It was almost as if the thought had been planted there.

Othman moved closer to him. 'You feel an affinity with this place, don't you?'

Owen took a step away. 'I suppose so.'

'Well, let's absorb its presence together, then. Close your eyes.'

Owen laughed again. 'OK, if you want to.'

Othman shut his own eyes, but after a moment, opened them once more. By his side, Owen was standing with his head thrown back, his eyes peacefully closed, his lips slightly parted. Othman realized the boy was really quite beautiful. He looked like a dying saint, or someone inviting a kiss. He reached out and took Owen's hand in his own. There was resistance at first, then a returning pressure. Othman ignored any presence that might reside in the land and instead tasted the flow of energy that emanated from the boy's body. He sensed untapped strengths, and something that had a flavour of familiarity about it. Before Othman could investigate this further, Owen pulled away.

My dalliance with these waifs might be short, Othman thought, but not without refreshment.

'Well,' Owen said. 'Did you feel anything?'

'I felt only you,' Othman replied.

Owen smiled uneasily. Perhaps he'd been wrong about the man. 'Oh well, let's go. I'll take you across the hills.'

Othman noticed that Owen kept his distance as they continued their walk through the woods. Not wishing to discomfort the boy, Othman kept up a stream of idle conversation, and by the time they left the cover of the trees and emerged into a field, Owen seemed more at ease. Othman knew he would have to tread carefully with this one.

At the brow of a hill, Owen paused. The fields swept down towards what appeared to be the grounds of a stately home. When Othman first caught sight of it, he experienced a sudden shock throughout his body. It was accompanied by a feeling of desperate longing. The sensations crashed over him like a numbingly cold wave. He gasped for breath, gripped by an unexpected vertigo.

Owen glanced at him. 'Are you all right? You look weird.'

Othman shook his head. 'It's nothing. I'm out of condition, a bit winded.' It was hard to maintain control of these feelings. He felt like weeping. Something must have happened at the house below, some trauma which had left psychic residue behind, which he had picked up on. Still, he was not usually affected so badly by such things. He felt that if he tried hard enough, he would be able to recall exactly what had transpired in this place, almost as if he'd lived it himself. That too was strange. He felt very uncomfortable, as if unwelcome memories were about to surface in his mind. A star had guided him here. Was this place connected with what lay waiting for him? For now, he must walk away, until he'd had time to think. Later, a visit to the house would be necessary, but not yet.

Owen followed him as he walked back down the hill. He looked puzzled. 'Are you sure you're all right?'

'Yes. Just ignore me. I'm fine.' Othman forced a smile. 'Who lives in that place back there?'

Owen laughed. 'No one! Didn't you notice the state the gardens were in? The house is all boarded up. Everyone left a long time ago.'

'Have you ever had a look around it?'

Owen shook his head, pulling a sour face. 'No! Lily and I have never liked it. It's called Long Eden. Crawling with ghosts.'

Othman was inclined to agree.

They went back to the car and Owen drove them out on to the moors. Here, they tramped around, climbing rocks and looking into caves. Othman felt his spirits become restored. Owen was pleasant enough company, although he sensed the boy's reticence and reserve. That only spoke of secrets to be uncovered. By the time Owen suggested they go back to the cottage to eat, Othman felt completely buoyant once more.

On the drive back to Little Moor, Othman wondered what the Winter house might be like. It could be large and look haunted, with ivy over the eaves, or small and cottagey, hugged by climbing roses. He dismissed the possibility of it being nothing more than a grey semi-detached house, bought by the mother from a district council. The reality, however, was none of these options.

It was a detached house, though not large, situated on a winding lane, where family homes were widely spaced. It was surrounded by tall evergreens and had rather a raddled appearance. Owen parked the car in a muddy drive at the side of the house, and when Othman got out, he could see a distorted wire chicken-run behind the house, where a few ragged birds were scampering up and down. There was a kennel and a chain, but no dog, and a bare clematis was growing against one of the walls. The back door was painted in an unsightly flaking turquoise colour.

Owen scraped mud from the soles of his boots on a piece of metal by the door and Othman did likewise. Then they went inside.

The back door led straight to the kitchen, which was steamy with the smells of cooking food. Pots bubbled on an old gas stove. Othman looked around himself with interest. The walls were of bare brick, except for one that had been inexpertly whitewashed; splashes of white marked the brown tiled floor. Bunches of herbs hung from one of the roof beams, but were so dusty that it did not look as if they were used for anything. Three crates of apples under the table gave off an over-ripe smell, one of them occupied by an elderly cat, asleep among the fruit. A group of new kitchen units against one of the walls were the sole concession to modernity but, white as they were among so much dark and earth, they looked absurd and out of place. Their Formica surfaces were already scored by cutting knives, and the scratches had been stained brown by tea. At one time, someone had begun to turn this dilapidated house into a home, but the job had never been finished, and there was no sign of recent work. Strange. The twins' mother must have lived here for several years.

'Hope you don't mind the mess,' Owen said, and went to open a door, calling, 'Lily!' into the space beyond.

Othman stood in the middle of the kitchen, bombarded by the images before him. He sat down on a wooden chair by the table, and Owen said, 'No, don't sit there. Go into the parlour.' He gestured to show the way.

The parlour was surprisingly comfortable; a woman had made her mark here. Perhaps the mother had begun renovations in this room. The walls were covered in framed embroidered samplers and a large, welcoming fire was burning in the huge stone hearth. Again, the walls were of bare brick, but in this room, it was simply rustic, a decorative effect. A beautiful old Persian rug covered most of the floor, but around its edges the boards gleamed with honey-coloured varnish. Othman threw himself into a well-padded chair and Owen offered him some wine. 'Home made,' he said. 'But you'll like it.'

Othman was not prepared to disagree, although he had a refined palate which objected to brutality. Owen poured out a glass of pale liquid from what appeared to be a crystal decanter. 'We make it from apples,' he said. Othman was pleased to find the wine tasted of fairly well-bred sherry.

Then Lily came into the room. She looked enchanting, wearing a simple, long black dress, her hair held back with a silky scarf. She had painted her lips with a smudge of pale lipstick and her lashes were spiky with mascara. Othman's heart warmed. He wished she had been with them for the afternoon.

'Did you have a good time?' she asked, sitting down on the arm of Othman's chair. He burned with the proximity of her body. She smelled of soap and floral scent.

'Yes, it was very interesting,' he said.

'Where did you take him, Owen?' she asked.

Owen sat down on the rug at their feet. 'Just for a walk around,' he said.

Othman detected that Owen didn't want his sister to know exactly where they'd been, and wondered if he should pretend he didn't realize this and tell her. Owen's reaction might be interesting. Lily, however, jumped up from her seat before Othman could make a decision.

'The food's ready now,' she said. 'We'll eat in here, shall we?'

The meal was wholesome, if rather sloppy. Lily and Owen kept up an inane chatter the whole time, plates balanced on their knees. When everyone had finished eating, Lily piled up the plates in the hearth, and refilled the wineglasses. Her cheeks had become slightly flushed. She curled up on the floor by Othman's feet and, twirling her glass in her hands, said, 'When are you leaving Little Moor?'

He smiled down at her. 'Soon,' he said.

'Where do you live?'

He shrugged. 'Actually, I don't really have a home base at present. I prefer travelling around.'

Owen was lying on his stomach in front of them, his

chin in his hands. 'But how do you pay for that? Do you work?'

Othman paused. He did not appreciate the interrogation. 'Sometimes.'

Lily uttered a squeal. 'You're rich, aren't you!' She seemed pleased with her deduction.

Othman shrugged again. 'I've inherited money, yes, but that's no excuse for being lazy.'

'Oh,' Lily said, having digested this information. 'Do you have . . . a girlfriend, or a wife?'

Othman leaned back in his chair and blinked at the ceiling. 'No.' He frowned. 'There was someone, a long time ago, but . . .' He was unsure of what had made him say that.

'Oh,' Lily's voice was soft. 'Did . . . did something happen to her?'

Othman glanced down at her. 'We just split up. These things happen.'

Lily giggled nervously and blushed. 'Oh yes, of course.' A silence came into the room.

'There's no one,' Othman said, and sat up straight again, with a sigh. He held out his empty glass to Owen. The boy gave him a studied, calculating look that went on for a few seconds too long before he got up and refilled the glass.

Lily extended a cautious hand and traced a pattern on one of Othman's boots. 'You are a very strange man,' she said.

'How strange?' he asked.

'Well, we don't like people much, but you are different. We like you, don't we, Owen?'

Owen was silent as he handed Othman a filled glass. He looked as if he wanted to have a discussion about this with his sister before committing himself.

'O!' Lily snapped in a warning voice.

'You seem all right,' Owen said grudgingly, sitting down on the floor again.

'I'm flattered,' Othman replied in an acid tone. Owen flicked a wary glance at him.

'Do you like us?' Lily asked him shyly. She did not look up at him, but Othman could see her colour had deepened around the face. Her little ears had gone scarlet. He reached out and put a hand on her shoulder.

'I think you know the answer to that,' he said.

Owen jumped up and helped himself to more wine. Othman could almost smell the boy's anxiety. He, more than innocent Lily, sensed the potential simmering in the room. Othman observed Owen's taut back. His reserve must be broken down.

'I think you two have many secrets,' Othman said. 'I want you to know you can trust me. I am intrigued by unusual people. I suppose I'm quite unusual myself. Like calls to like, as they say.'

'You think we're like you?' Lily said. She sounded surprised.

Othman reached out to stroke her hair. 'Absolutely.'

'We do have secrets,' Lily admitted, then paused, looking across at her brother. Owen appeared hypnotized by Othman's hand caressing his sister's hair.

'Owen and I are very close,' Lily said in a slow, earnest voice. 'We always have been.'

Aha, Othman thought. I should have realized. He got out of his chair and sat down on the rug next to Lily. There was a quivering desire emanating from her, unformed and unchannelled. 'You mustn't worry about it,' he said. 'It's perfectly natural.'

Owen sat down again opposite them. His eyes looked wild, but not altogether with anger. Othman saw, with some satisfaction, that Owen was actually quite drunk, a fact he was attempting to conceal. 'It is clear to me that you are made for each other,' Othman said, with a smile. He looked directly into Owen's eyes. 'Please don't be afraid of me. I have no intention of abusing you.' Still maintaining eye contact with Owen, he gently pulled Lily against his side and held out his other arm to Owen. 'Come to me. Let us embrace as friends. There is nothing to fear.'

Owen did not move.

'Please, O!' Lily pleaded.

Reluctantly, Owen came to Othman's other side, but his body was stiff and unyielding as Othman put his free arm around it.

'Don't you know that the love of siblings is sacred in some places in the world?' Othman said.

Lily giggled nervously, a sound which tailed off into silence.

'Look at me, Lily.' Othman willed her face to turn up to him. He could see she was anxious, uncertain, but recognized within her eyes a hunger for him. 'I can teach you,' Othman said.

'Can you?' Lily's voice was husky.

Othman became aware of Owen's mounting unease on his other side. The boy would have to be attended to first. He nodded at Lily, smiling. 'Oh, yes. I can teach both of you.' He paused. 'Owen, look at me.'

Owen's eyes, when he turned his face, were guarded. He had no hunger, particularly, but a certain curiosity. Othman could see ideas and desires swimming unseen beneath the surface of Owen's conscious mind. These would have to be brought out.

Gently, he spoke to the twins, his voice instilling a sense of languor. He conjured images with words, took them on a journey through their minds to a place where the sun shone on the sandy reaches of an infinite beach and waves burned silver against the shore. In this place, anything was possible.

He could feel both of them relaxing against him. The words he spoke gradually changed, until they made no sense at all, just a string of sounds that were compelling and hypnotic.

Owen's head lolled against Othman's shoulder. Sensing the moment had come, Othman gently withdrew his arms from the twins. He steadied Lily with one hand, leaving her kneeling beside him, her head bowed. Then he turned to Owen.

The boy's eyes were almost closed. Othman took him in his arms, felt the brief jerk of alarm. 'Do not fear,' he murmured, and covered Owen's lips with his own. Owen's taste was faintly familiar, and a name was whispered through Othman's brain: *Taziel* . . . For the most fleeting of moments, a screaming face rose before his mind's eye. Othman banished it firmly, and the face flew shrieking into a void. This was no time for harsh memories. Othman sensed that, had he wanted to, he could have had Owen now, but it was not the time. The kiss was enough: deep, pervading, the first offering of the greatest passion.

Othman's jaw was aching when he released Owen and turned to his sister. Lily was, surprisingly, a little more resistant. She clutched his arms painfully, her lips unyielding beneath his own. This was because she desired him more, Othman thought, and was afraid of the strength of it. Still, she relented, as he'd known she would; she became heavy and fluid against him. He moved his hands over her body, squeezed her breasts. His own desire screamed for release, yet he curbed it, beat it down. Not yet.

Drawing away from the girl, he reached out for Owen and pulled the two of them together, guiding their faces into a kiss. 'Love one another,' he said. 'From such things comes strength.'

Lily uttered a soft moan, drawing her brother back into her arms. They fell on to the rug, apparently now oblivious of Othman's presence. He sat up, leaned against the chair, wiping his mouth. His mind was buzzing; he felt slightly faint. The twins were joined through him. He was part of their love-making. In their hearts, they did not embrace each other, but him. Sitting there beside them, he could feel through his own fingers the explorations they made of each other's body. They made love without finesse, untutored and inexperienced. Othman finished the wine, watching, while they struggled together on the rug before the fire. This was the first step.

The night was clear, and the call of the moon lured Barbara Eager into the forest. She'd parked the Land Rover at the side of the road, and had let the dogs out of the back for their run. Despite the luminous sky, the arms of the trees looked forbidding and enclosed. The scents of the woodland, and the fields beyond, were overwhelming, as if the landscape was being squeezed of its essence by the night. Barbara could feel a story-poem brewing within her, which was perhaps why she had unconsciously chosen to bring the dogs to Herman's Wood, instead of taking them for a quick run through the village. It had been an odd night at The White House – a strange, excited, almost hostile atmosphere had seemed to smoke at the edges of the lounge bar. Voices had been sharp, the oldster regulars almost carping in their demands for their usual drinks. They'd been like a flock of chickens with a fox prowling round the edge of their run. The chicken wire was too flimsy to keep the threat at bay so they moved restlessly back and forth in the dry dirt, afraid yet expectant. Was there pleasure to be found in the jaws of the fox? That would make a good first line, she thought, and repeated it over and over in her head so as not to forget it.

The dogs had run off among the trees; she could hear them snuffling about, although their dark red coats were invisible in the gloom. 'Amber, Lester!' she called, as she ventured on to one of the well-worn, fern-brushed pathways. The wood always unnerved Barbara whenever she ventured among its trees alone, yet it was a feeling she quite enjoyed. It brought back a flavour of youth. She heard one of the dogs bark – it sounded like Amber. Moonlight came down sparingly on to the track before her. The shadows of the ferns were monstrous, almost prehistoric. She wondered how long this wood had been there, how much human experience the sentinel trees had absorbed. This was a poet's place, she decided.

The walk took her around the right edge of the wood, where the spreading fields were never far from sight. She passed a place where a lone folly reared dark from the grass, a massive stone arch, sheep huddled beneath its shadow. All this land, of course, belonged to the Murkasters, a shadowy, aristocratic family who had lived in the manor-house, Long Eden, and who had abandoned their seat nearly twenty years ago. Barbara was interested in local history, but had never managed to find that much out about the Murkasters. At least nothing too fascinating. There were few family scandals on record. All she had found out was that the Murkasters had locked up the house, sold most of its interior effects and left the area. Why? She began to imagine what private scandals might have precipitated the move. Skeletons in the closet? Mad relatives locked in attics, who had escaped and run amok on a murder spree? She smiled to herself. Although, from an imaginative point of view, the ideas were attractive, they were untenable. Any spectacular events would have been recorded in the press, and Barbara had already scoured the microfiches of local papers, held in the library at Patterham.

The baroque towers of Long Eden could now be seen through a thin fringe of trees as the path nudged the right boundary of the wood. Most of the house itself was obscured by the gardens. Barbara was facing the left side of the building and was on a level with its grounds. From the hill where she'd met Lily on Friday morning, the front of the house looked smaller. Perhaps that was something to do with perspective.

Barbara had to climb over a makeshift horse jump of fallen boughs that local riders must have erected. She wished she could get inside Long Eden and soak up the atmosphere. Who held the keys to the place now? Surely there must be a local caretaker?

The dogs had disappeared up the path, although she could still hear their barked exchanges and the sound of cracking twigs. The track now snaked upwards and to the left, veering away from the fields and the view of Long Eden. It led through a widely spaced grove of aspens, which in daylight remained in perpetual green shadow, despite the wide gaps between the trees. Barbara especially disliked this area. If anything, it seemed less sinister at night because you could see less of it. She crested the hill and descended it, turning left at the bottom on to a wider valley track, where pines grew on the opposite rise. She imagined galloping horses coming along the path at full tilt. Ghost horses? To dispel a sudden, greater unease, she whistled for the dogs, but shrank from calling their names in the immensity of the wood.

The path wound to the right, and gently downwards, leading her inexorably into the heart of the forest.

Perhaps she had come too far. It was easy to feel safe in Little Moor, distant as it was from city crime and city dementia, but it was perhaps foolish to be out here alone, with her dogs gambolling away from her. All it needed was for one lunatic to be on the prowl, and Barbara Eager might be no more. Oh, for the innocence or the true safety of a childhood in the Forties, when women did not have to think about such things. She knew that if she followed this path, it would take her past the High Place, and then directly to the edge of the wood where her vehicle was parked, but it was quite a long walk. Still, she balked at retracing her steps through the aspens. Again, she whistled to the dogs, but the demons of the night had got into them. They wanted none of her discipline. The High Place loomed into view through the trees; its mound looked man-made, rising up above all the other, gentler slopes. Amber and Lester came bounding out of the bracken to leap around their mistress's legs for a few moments. Barbara grabbed hold of their collars and uttered a few low, chastising words. She wished she had brought their leads with them, so she could have kept them by her side as she completed their exercise. Straightening up, she began to drag them along the path. They thought it was a game, wriggling and struggling against her hold, tails wagging furiously. Then Barbara noticed the light.

It was a pulsing, yellow-white glow illuminating the thick trunks of the trees on the summit of the High Place. Someone was up there. Barbara experienced a horrifying chill. It could be youths, yobbos. Something worse, perhaps. A lone madman searching the night, waiting for a solitary female to cross his path. Don't be ridiculous! she told herself firmly and made to scurry past, hoping she wouldn't be noticed by whoever, or whatever, occupied the High Place. As she drew nearer, she thought she could hear women's voices, soft singing, or chanting. Could it be local witches on the hill? Barbara was afraid of such things, even though her romantic soul championed the idea of female sorcery. Perhaps she should go back before she was noticed. The dogs seemed to be intrigued by whatever was happening above them. They had begun to whine and strain more forcefully against Barbara's hold, twisting her fingers in their collars. Finally, she could not hold them, and in breaking away from her, they pushed her into the bracken, leaped over her like deer, and raced up through the undergrowth, giving tongue like hounds. Barbara heard screaming, undeniably female and human in origin. Her dogs had never attacked anybody before. They were generally far too soppy.

Oblivious of any previous reticence, she charged up the hill, her palms smarting from breaking her fall. She saw a number of slight figures, dressed in floating white, bobbing back and forth among the trees, Amber and Lester in playful pursuit, barking hysterically. Girls, they were only girls! Impotently, Barbara called out the dogs' names, but of course they ignored her. She emerged from the bracken. Candles in covered glass bowls were arranged about the central hollow. It certainly seemed as if she had disturbed some kind of pagan ceremony.

The female figures were all flitting about, uttering strange low cries. They did not seem to see Barbara and soon she found herself in the midst of them, in a tangle of wafting veils. Who were these girls? They did not seem to be Little Moor residents. Barbara attempted to speak to them, but they all ignored her and their high-pitched wailing drowned out her voice. She wanted them all to stop gadding about so that she could regain control of her animals. The dogs did not seem to be inflicting harm. They thought the chasing was a game, but it was clear the girls were terrified. Eventually, Barbara managed to grab hold of a girl's arm. 'Stop running about!' she said. 'It's just encouraging them.' For a moment, she looked into the shocked, elfin face of a beautiful young woman, whose head and shoulders were wreathed in a floating mist of fair hair. She seemed horrified to discover an outsider was present, but did not speak.

Barbara began to apologize and explain about the dogs, when a hideous transformation made her push the girl away in disgust and horror. The woman was not young at all, but an ancient female, clad in floating muslin, one drooping dug exposed, where the cloth fell away. The toothless mouth was open in surprise, the bagged eyes staring. Barbara's hands flew to her mouth. With an abysmal howl, the woman ran away, down the slope, between the trees. The other women, at first still running about like chickens, suddenly condensed into a tight group and followed the first woman down the hill. They must have gathered up their candlelights as they fled, because Barbara found herself in relative darkness. Thankfully, Amber and Lester had elected to stay with her on the High Place rather than follow the fleeing females. Crones, Barbara thought. They were crones. There was no sign of them now. All was silent. Not even the sound of a single twig breaking. Frightened, Barbara hauled the dogs off the hill and virtually ran all the way back to the Land Rover, terrified the crones would suddenly manifest in front of her on the path, and exact a revenge for the disruption of their ritual. Had they been real? Barbara had never seen a ghost and didn't know whether she believed in them or not. Yet the woman she'd grabbed hold of had felt real enough. The illusion, though, of youth: that had been weird. Was it just because she'd expected to see younger people?

When she got back to The White House, flushed and breathless, she headed straight to the bar and poured herself a large brandy. Only once she'd finished it and poured herself another did she notice that someone was sitting in the corner of the room. Barbara uttered a shocked cry and backed against the Optics, causing glasses on the shelf behind her to shake dangerously.

'Barbara, it's me.' The voice was amused. Peverel Othman.

'Oh, you gave me a turn!' Barbara said. 'What are you doing here?' She'd thought, at first, he'd been sitting in darkness, but one of the low-wattage lamps was burning behind him.

'Barney said it was all right for me to sit here and read the paper. I prefer the atmosphere in here to that of the residents' lounge. I hope you don't mind.'

Barbara came out from behind the bar. 'No, no. I'm just a bit jumpy. I've seen the strangest thing in the woods tonight.'

Othman laughed. 'Oh really! Are you going to tell me about it, or is it too disgusting?'

Barbara also laughed, though less freely. 'Come into the back,' she said. 'I'll make us a coffee and tell you about it.'

'Thanks.'

Once she had installed Othman at her kitchen table and put the kettle on, Barbara became conscious of his presence on a physical level. She'd been fired up by her experience in the woods, and had needed company. Now she was aware she was alone with a man who, on two occasions, had made suggestive remarks to her. How would he interpret her invitation now? She had ambivalent feelings about it. As she made cheese sandwiches, precisely cutting the bread, Barbara babbled about what she'd seen at the High Place. Othman listened without commenting, his eyes watching her steadily. She flicked the occasional glance at him. God, he was unbelievably attractive. Just the look in his eyes made her feel slightly faint. She didn't normally go for the long-haired look. She liked a man to be neat and trim, exact in his mannerisms, military types. Othman was lounging and lazy, the precise opposite. 'What do you think?' she asked, shoving a plate of sandwiches in front of her guest and sitting down opposite him.

Othman was smiling widely, his eyes sleepy. 'Sounds like you surprised the local coven!' he said, and bit into the sandwich.

'I've not been aware of one before,' Barbara said, 'and I often walk through those woods at night.'

Othman shrugged. 'Perhaps it was the right time for you to see it. Perhaps they're recruiting!'

'I'm not sure how to take that remark!' Barbara said. 'I've already told you they were hags. Do I qualify, then?'

Othman shook his head. 'No offence meant. You know you're a very attractive woman.'

Barbara felt a panic begin. She wanted to take this further, yet was nervous of doing so. She laughed. 'You certainly know how to flatter, Mr Othman!' She jumped up and forcefully depressed the plunger of the cafetière. Suddenly the action seemed too erotic for words. She looked at Othman and he was smirking at her. She wanted to say something cool and sophisticated like 'Are you making a pass at me?' but shrank from doing so, in case he wasn't. What would a handsome creature like Peverel Othman see in her? He could have his pick of any nubile young things. Was he interested in older women for their freak value? Or was he simply playing with her feelings, imagining her (rightly perhaps) to be a frustrated, middle-aged wife, who could do with a bit of excitement?

'I've seen the place you're talking about,' he said. His tone had changed. The flirtation had gone. 'It's a very old site, and possesses echoes of . . . shall we say earth power? Sometimes that can make you see things which normally would be invisible. Perhaps that was what you saw tonight. An echo, a memory, ideas made into pictures. Perhaps even just a stray dream.' He was aware that his own presence in Little Moor might conjure such things.

'Really!' Barbara said. 'Are you interested in things like that? I must admit I am. Interested, but scared!' She laughed.

'Oh, there's nothing to be scared of,' Othman said, sipping his steaming hot coffee. 'It's a matter of interpretation. Someone else might have seen fairies dancing on the hill tonight. You saw young girls who turned out to be crones. Perhaps that's an interesting message from your own subconscious.'

Barbara disliked the implications in that. She laughed falsely. 'It's more likely to have been some New Age types who got chased off by my dogs. I just wasn't expecting it.' Othman made no comment.

'So, how did your day go with the Winters?' Barbara asked, partly to change the subject, mostly out of curiosity.

'Very enjoyable.'

'They seem to have taken a shine to you.'

'They are interesting people.'

'Oh, yes, absolutely.' Barbara sat down again. She felt safer now, talking about someone else. 'I feel sorry for them, actually. Can't help feeling they're wasting their lives, rather, stuck here in the village.'

'They seem to think they're outsiders, regarded as a bit peculiar.'

Barbara frowned and shook her head vigorously. 'Oh no! At least, I don't think of them that way. As a matter of fact, I find them very interesting, too. Lily is a creative girl. I intend to encourage her.'

Othman laughed, a reaction with which Barbara was not altogether comfortable. Did he think she was a busybody?

Later Othman lay in his bed, musing over the evening's events. He'd been gentle with the Winter twins, remaining only a spectator of their love-making, even though his body had ached to plunder and possess. He'd left the house before they'd finished, letting himself out quietly. Lily had seen him go, but had said nothing; her eyes glazed as she travelled the haunting plane of physical ecstasy. Tomorrow, he might call on them again.

Barbara Eager, Othman knew, was a ripe fruit for plucking. Still, he did not intend to gather the harvest himself. That would be too easy. He'd have to sniff around, see what was cooking in the slow-burning fires of village life. In the meantime, he'd prime her, wake up her senses a little. He'd met so few people yet. The Winters were into the things that interested him, and could clearly be encouraged. Then there was the old house, Long Eden, abandoned by its owners, with a secret story to tell. Something was certainly going on in the village, which must be why he'd been drawn to it. Old women cavorting in the woods? He thought of the crone he'd met in the post office, her strange remarks. He felt he was working out a riddle and the answer was just hovering on the edge of his perception. Tomorrow he'd apply himself to its solution.

Chapter Eight

Monday, 19th October: Little Moor

Lily awoke feeling uneasy, a headache already needling her temples. She was alone in the bed. Owen must have crept out earlier without disturbing her. This perhaps indicated he, too, must be feeling strange about the previous night's events. They had never actually slept together all night before. After Othman had gone, they'd clumsily made their way upstairs, still kissing, still caressing, to fall upon the bed in Lily's room. She had never, in her life, wanted Owen so badly as last night. It seemed nothing could satisfy her.

Now even the simple recollection of what she and Owen had revealed to Othman made Lily's face go red. She felt sure something more than sex had occurred. She and Owen had been influenced in some way. Why had she felt the compulsion to make veiled remarks about her relationship with Owen to Othman? She'd never spoken of it to anyone before, and had believed she never would. In her dream on Saturday night, Othman had transformed into a beast. Perhaps there was an important message there for her. The man was dangerous, she thought. He was an Opener, a type of person Lily's mother had once warned her about, who could charm people's secrets from them and then use the information against them. Last night, the knowledge that Othman was watching her with Owen had only enhanced her desire. She remembered how she'd thought about Othman on her walk back from the post office on Saturday, and how, in her dream, she'd fallen into his open arms from the sky. *What would it be like to touch him intimately?* Half in dread, half in anticipation, Lily had a feeling she was soon going to find out.

When she went downstairs, she discovered Owen had gone out. The kitchen had a desolate air. In the parlour, she found their clothes lying around, amid the empty wineglasses. How could she ever face Othman again? What if he *told* someone about what had happened?

Listlessly, Lily tidied the house in a desultory manner. Then she sat down at the lace-covered table beneath the parlour window, with an empty writing-pad before her. When she'd talked to Barbara Eager about writing something, she hadn't been that serious. Now she felt compelled to write about what was happening to her. She would turn it all into a fairy-story. She began to write: *There was once a girl, who lived below the mountains* . . .

She paused, tapped her lips with her biro, wrote: *She had been asleep for a thousand thousand years* . . . Oh, that had been done before too many times. The enchanted sleeper. Yet, strangely, that was how she felt. She *had* been asleep, and her dreams had kept a peculiar reality at bay. Now she could feel it creeping up on her. She would give it the face of a monster.

Peverel Othman rose early and took a stroll down to the post office to buy a newspaper. Monday morning: the village felt deserted. The day was overcast, yet warm; the air smelled of autumn. Othman liked the seasons of spring and autumn, with their sense of change, of birth and death, more than florid summer or the black clutch of winter. Excitement came with these turning times, and the possibility for wonders. The human spirit, deep in its sanitized nest of mundane life, stirred and twitched, roused instinctively by the vibrations in the air of potential and power. Othman himself felt powerful that day.

131

His body felt liquid about his bones. His bones felt like tempered steel.

Again, when he entered the post office, there was a sense of a conversation being hushed. The woman behind the counter stood very still, her eyes fixed on the crone, who was hunched on her stool. It seemed his entrance had brought tension with it. Othman sauntered over to the counter to inspect the paltry array of papers. 'Dull morning,' he remarked.

The postmistress made an effort. 'Perhaps it'll brighten up later.' She beamed rather wolfishly at Othman.

Othman picked up a paper. 'I'll take this.'

'Thirty pence, please.'

While this exchange was taking place, Othman was aware of a furtive, rustling movement emanating from the stool of the crone. He glanced to find her standing, stooped and swaying, just behind him.

'Mother,' began the postmistress.

Leaning forward, the old woman extended a bony paw to Othman's arm, pinching the material of his shirt between thumb and forefinger. Her neck craned out like an old buzzard's. Othman noticed the fine, papery nostrils twitch. She was smelling him.

'Mother!' the postmistress hurried out from behind her counter and took hold of the old woman's shoulders, in an attempt to drag her away from Othman. He could see the crone's eyes were alight with a weird excitement.

'She has her *days*,' said the daughter. 'I'm sorry about this.'

'It's quite all right.' Othman tucked his paper beneath his arm. Before he could leave the shop, the old woman struggled free of her daughter's hold.

'I want it back!' she cried. 'Give it back to me!'

Othman thought she meant the paper. He raised his

132

brows at the postmistress and waved the paper aloft, as if to defend himself from the advancing, tottering crone.

The postmistress shook her head. 'Please, I don't mean to sound rude, but could you leave now? She has turns, you see. I do apologize.'

Othman found himself pressed up against the door, and felt behind his back for the handle. This was absurd. The old hag was looking at him as if she was about to attack and devour him. He could easily strike out and floor her, but knew that would perhaps not be looked upon as kindly by the daughter. What a lunatic! The old bag should be locked up! He could even smell the crone now: a sweet sickly odour combined with the aroma of piss. She opened her mouth to display an uneven array of peg-like teeth, then made a lunge for him. Othman opened the door and stepped through backwards. The crone fell on to her hands and knees before him, and began to crawl towards him, drool hanging from her gaping lips. 'You must give it to me: the sweet, sweet liquor,' she croaked. 'Give me back what is mine, the thighs, the dainty feet.'

The postmistress had hurried out after her mother. Othman did not wait around to see how she would cope with the demented hag. Without another glance, he headed back towards The White House. What a strange episode! In the midst of a private, amused thought about the vagaries of human dotage, a realization came to him. He stopped walking. Was it possible? Was it? He glanced back, noticed the postmistress still dragging her clawing, mewling mother back into the shop. *Give it back to me ...* What had she recognized in him? Othman narrowed his eyes, and sniffed the air. Had he missed something about Little Moor, something vital? Perhaps it was his imagination, but he thought now he could detect a subnote to the perfume of autumn, a smell of blood and cedar. Someone had been here before him. Grigori. One of his own kind.

Eva Manden managed to wrestle her mother back into the shop. Why was it the old woman seemed to have such strength when it was necessary to curb her behaviour? 'Let me go, you bitch!' cried the crone, and struck her daughter across the face.

Eva backed away, leaned against the closed door. 'Get on your chair, you witch!'

'Let me after him, girl! You can't stop me!'

'I bloody well can!' Eva said in a low voice. 'If you come near me, I'll kick you! Get on the chair!'

Mumbling, the old woman crab-walked back to her stool, muttering muted obscenities.

Eva rubbed her cheek-bone, which was still smarting from the blow. She pushed back her hair. Perhaps she should close the shop for the day.

'You can't stop it,' said the crone in a mocking tone. 'I know how much you want to keep me like this, want to see me die, but you can't! They're back.'

Taking a deep breath, and glancing quickly to check her mother really had sat down again and wasn't waiting to make a break for it, Eva went back behind the counter. She felt shaken and ashamed. 'You're being stupid, Mum. That young man's just a tourist, a guest at The White House. You made a right fool of yourself. Now he'll think you're senile.' Which you are, Eva amended silently.

The old woman champed her meagre teeth together. 'Oh, he knows,' she said. 'He knows all right. And he'll be back for me now. Soon.'

'Rubbish!' Eva tidied the papers on the counter. Her mother laughed, a particularly evil sound. 'Be quiet!'

Eva snapped, thinking, Don't let her rattle you. She'll get worse.

Eva noticed a stream of liquid had begun to run across the wooden floor. The old woman was grinning malevolently. I feel tired, Eva thought, too tired to cope with this. Her mother hadn't deliberately wet herself for months. When she did, it was always a petty act of spite. Eva knew the old woman was not incontinent. Now she'd have to close the shop and take her mother into the back so she could be changed and cleaned. The task repulsed her, yet a mindless, uncontrollable sense of duty made her keep on doing it. Without uttering a word of censure, she led the old woman through the bead curtain into the house beyond. Silently, she fetched clean clothes, and ran warm water into a bowl for washing. The old woman said nothing, merely wriggled around on the kitchen chair, making odd noises to herself. Eva applied herself to the task of cleaning her mother's body and changing her clothes. It was pointless to complain, and she wouldn't give the old woman the satisfaction of seeing she was annoyed, or even upset.

'I want to go to the centre,' wheedled the old woman as Eva eased her into a clean skirt.

Damn her, Eva thought. Her mother could read her mood, sense how edgy Eva was. Today was a good day for asking favours, especially if the favour involved getting the old woman out of her hair for a few hours.

'It's too late,' Eva said, 'everyone will be there by now.' She knew her argument was a sham. Even though it made her uneasy letting her mother get together with all the other oldsters in the village, she just needed some respite today.

'No it's not. Ring Perks. She'll send someone to fetch me.' There was no hint of age in the old woman's voice now. She sounded strong and cold.

Eva paused, wanting to refuse badly, but knowing that soon she would relent. She eyed the old telephone sitting on the shelf beneath the window. The respite would be short-lived. Whenever her mother went to the centre, she came back unmanageable and weird.

'Ring her,' said the crone. 'You selfish little cow. I know you want to get rid of me, but you'd cut off your nose to spite your face and make me sit here all day.'

Eva filled the mop bucket with water and added detergent. 'I have to clean up your mess first,' she said.

'Ring *now*,' said the old woman.

Eva glanced at her mother. There was steel in the ancient eyes now, and something more. Eva suppressed a shiver, put down her rubber gloves. She picked up the phone.

Verity had had a pleasing day. Daniel had gone to school, her father had been closeted away in his study, no doubt composing bad poetry for his muse, Barbara Eager, and she'd had the whole house to herself. Cleaning had been a pleasure. Raven had accompanied her from room to room. He had not demanded affection or even come too close to her, simply flopping down on the floor near each doorway and remaining there until she'd finished tidying the room. She felt his presence in her life had stemmed the bad dreams from the past, because there had been no recurrence of the nightmares of Saturday morning. It was odd how safe she felt with the cat in her room. And yet, before Saturday, she had never felt unsafe. Peculiar. Now Verity was steeling herself for her brother's arrival home from school. Mrs Roan was already preparing dinner and, her tasks accomplished for the day, Verity wandered into the kitchen, with the intention of sharing a cup of tea with the woman. Raven came at her heels. Mrs Roan looked up from her potato peeling at the kitchen table, and smiled at Verity.

'Hello, Mrs Roan. Would you like a cup of tea?'

'Yes please, Miss Cranton.'

Verity liked the formal relationship she had with the woman, the hint of gentility. She performed this ritual of the tea every day.

'Oh, what a big cat!' Mrs Roan remarked as Raven followed Verity to the sink.

'Yes, isn't he?' Raven had not met the cook yet; he'd been asleep on Verity's bed the previous day while the woman had performed her work.

'I didn't know you had a cat, Miss Cranton.'

'Well, I've only just got him,' Verity answered.

'Was he expensive?'

Verity was very reluctant to admit that Raven was a stray. Mrs Roan might know his true owners, even though she hadn't yet appeared to recognize him as belonging to someone else. 'Yes, he was,' she lied.

'What breed is he, then?'

'Oh – er – Sumerian,' Verity answered airily. 'It's a new, long-haired breed, part Oriental, like the Somali, I suppose.'

'Somali?' Mrs Roan looked doubtful. 'Don't know what that is, but you've a handsome devil there, no mistake.'

'Mmm. I suppose my father hasn't told you yet, but he's invited a few people over to dinner on Wednesday.'

'Oh, that'll be nice.' Mrs Roan's eyes lit up at the prospect of preparing a spread. To her, cookery was an art.

'Well, I shall have a think about the menu, and let you know tomorrow.'

'Can I ask who you're inviting?'

Verity hesitated, and then, realizing village gossip

would do the rounds soon enough, so as to render a lie embarrassing, said, 'The Eagers from The White House and the Winter twins.'

'The Winter twins?' There was surprise in Mrs Roan's voice, Verity noticed, but also something else. It was a kind of awe.

'Yes, that's right. My brother's friendly with the boy.'

Mrs Roan laughed. 'It'll be a lark for them – going out to dinner.' Verity could tell from the woman's tone that she approved of the arrangement. Odd.

'Actually, I don't know the Winters that well.'

'Lily is a fine girl, and Owen, well he's a bit of a lad, I know, but a rascal rather than a bad 'un.'

'Oh, is that what he is?' This last remark was delivered *sotto voce* as Verity poured the tea. 'Perhaps you could pick me up some cat food tomorrow, Mrs Roan. I've been feeding Raven on chicken and tinned tuna.'

Mrs Roan laughed again, apparently in a frolicking good humour. 'Oh, you mustn't do that. He'll get a taste for it. They say a cat is a man who's forgotten his shape, and a taste of the good life might jog his memory.'

'Oh, do they say that? I've never heard it.' Verity glanced down at Raven, who was eyeing the milk jug speculatively.

Daniel Cranton was worried. He had not seen Owen, or any of the others, since Owen had left Low Mede on Saturday morning. Although Daniel knew Owen always went to The White House on Saturday nights with his sister, and Bobby and the others excluded him from their activities when Owen was absent, Owen normally called on Sundays. He liked to drive out on to the moors, where he and his friends would drink cider out of plastic bottles. Generally, not all of the group could make the Sunday excursions because of shadowy family obligations, which they'd rather not own up about. Quite often, Owen would end up driving out with Daniel alone, which Daniel much preferred. Although Sundays were strictly kept for drinking and idle chatter, Owen's conversation was always more interesting when the others weren't around. Yesterday Owen hadn't called. Because of the way he'd felt after Friday night, Daniel was at first relieved, but by five o'clock he was wondering if he'd done something to offend Owen. It was unlike him not to maintain the routine. At half past five, Daniel had telephoned the cottage, and Lily had answered him. She'd sounded surprised he'd called, but then Daniel had only ever rung the cottage twice before, and on both occasions Owen had answered. There was a frost in Lily's tone as she curtly informed Daniel that Owen was out. Daniel had wanted to know where he'd gone, and with whom; his words were stammered and his face went red as he spoke. 'Someone we met last night,' Lily had answered, 'a guest at The White House.'

Daniel felt partially reassured because Owen hadn't gone out with the others without inviting him, but who was this newcomer? Owen didn't take up with people, or even show an interest in them, unless there was something to be gained from the experience.

'You'd better call him tomorrow evening,' Lily said, and put down the phone.

Daniel had stared at the receiver for a moment. He'd felt excluded and weirdly excited. Departures from routine in Little Moor were big events.

When he got home from school on Monday, Louis called to him from his study. 'Daniel, have you got a minute?'

Daniel slouched in the doorway. 'What is it?'

Louis suppressed the desire to say, 'Stand up straight, boy!' and forced a smile. 'I was wondering whether you'd pop over to the cottage and ask the Winters if they could come to dinner Wednesday night.'

Daniel could not prevent a ferocious blush coming to his face. 'Lily and Owen? Why?'

'Well, I'm inviting the Eagers over, and I thought it would be nice if all our friends could get together.' If Louis had hoped the invitation would please Daniel, it seemed he was to be disappointed. The boy looked mortified. So, the olive branch extended from one generation to another was not to be appreciated. No doubt Daniel thought his father would embarrass him in front of the twins. Or perhaps he balked at exposing them to Verity. 'What's up, Daniel? Not ashamed of your old dad, are you?' The jocularity, Louis knew, sounded strained. He felt it sounded as if he was pleading.

'No, no,' Daniel said hastily. 'I'm just surprised, that's all.'

Louis turned round slowly in his chair, wincing as a limb shrieked in pain. 'Look, lad. We've been here in Little Moor long enough.' He paused. 'Shut the door and come in, will you?'

Frowning a little, Daniel did so. He was worried about what his father might come out with, but held his tongue.

'It's like this. Verity's shut away in this old place, or else gossiping with the old women in the village. All I ever do is go to The White House and see the Eagers. You, of all us, have made more friends around here. I just want to open the house up a bit. Inviting our friends round is just a start. We haven't had any formal visitors here since we moved in.'

'What does Vez think about this?' Daniel wondered, in fact, whether his father had yet informed her about the arrangements.

'Well, you know Vez!' Louis laughed loudly. 'She's

not that keen on Owen, we both know that, but I hope she'll get on with the sister. Barbara thinks Lily's a lovely girl. Vez could do with a friend more her own age.'

Daniel could not imagine Lily Winter and his sister becoming friends. He himself knew little of Lily, but she seemed to be an insular person, who shared Verity's unsociable habits. There were no girlfriends that he knew of, and the only social life she had was with her brother. Lily made no move to speak to Owen's friends. Bobby and the others rarely visited the cottage and stayed more than a few minutes. Daniel himself had never set foot inside the place. 'Lily's a bit of a loner as well,' he said.

'Well, I know she gets on all right with Barbara,' Louis said. 'Anyway, we can only ask her and Owen if they want to come. What do you think?'

Daniel could not voice his thoughts. He imagined a horrible scenario around the dining-table: Owen sarcastic and awkward; Lily silent and staring at her plate; Verity a glowering presence at the head of the table; Barbara and Louis talking too brightly and loudly; Barney looking completely out of place. And himself? Daniel would sit there squirming, desperate for the dreadful meal to be over. He knew, without a doubt, that Owen would accept the invitation. Then he remembered he hadn't seen Owen the day before. At least now he had an excuse to visit the cottage and find out whether Owen was annoyed with him or not. 'Well, to be honest, Dad, I don't know how everyone will mix. It might be a bit . . . I dunno, weird. But I'll ask Lily and Owen if you want me to.'

'Good lad!' Louis smiled sadly to himself for a moment and then said, 'You are happy here, Daniel, aren't you?'

'Yeah. Course. It's a bit quiet, but, well, Owen takes

us out to clubs and stuff. It's not too far from the towns here, is it?' He realized, the moment he saw his father's smile, that this proposed dinner party was very important to Louis. It was easy to forget that for Louis, it must sometimes seem as if his life had ended in the crash. Daniel felt a sentimental wave of affection for his father sweep over him. Louis was a good parent; he never put restrictions on Daniel's behaviour, virtually let him have his own flat in the house, gave him money without question. In comparison with the parents of some of his friends at school, Louis was a saint.

As if he'd been reading Daniel's mind, Louis said, 'You know you can always have friends from school to stay for the weekend, don't you?'

'Yeah, I know.' Daniel shrugged. 'I don't think they'd be into it much, though.'

'Oh well, never mind.'

'I'll just get changed,' Daniel said, 'then I'll go over to the cottage. OK?'

'Fine, fine. Tell them to come over about seven-thirty.'

'Will do.'

Daniel actually felt very nervous of visiting the cottage. It was unknown territory to him, and he knew that his arrival there would be an invasion, if only in Lily's eyes. He was perplexed with himself as to why he was so desperate to see Owen now, and to discover if something had happened to their friendship without him knowing it.

There was music coming from the cottage as he approached it. The parlour windows were open. He could even hear Lily's voice singing. The back door was also open. Daniel knocked on it. This elicited no response, so he half ventured over the threshold and called out,

'Hello?' He could see the kitchen was a mess, plates and cups everywhere.

Owen appeared from a door at the back of the kitchen. 'Daniel!' His surprise provided Daniel with the image of Owen totally without artifice. It was as if he'd been caught without his mask on, a mask he'd worn all the time in Daniel's company before.

'Hi . . . Sorry to barge in. I've got a message for you.'

'No, it's OK, come in.'

The volume of the music went down in the other room, and Lily's voice came: 'O, who is it?'

'Daniel,' Owen answered.

Daniel stepped into the kitchen, and Lily put her head around the parlour door. The look she directed at him was almost malevolent. Her face was flushed, even slightly damp, her hair in disarray. Perhaps she'd been dancing. 'Oh. Hello,' she said, and then shut the door again. The music came on once more.

Owen was dressed in black jeans, with a white shirt that hung open. 'Coffee?' he enquired.

'Yeah, thanks.'

'Sit down. You look as if you're about to be tortured to death!' The sarcasm was back, the mask securely in place. 'So what's this mysterious message?'

Daniel sighed. 'Well, Dad's got this idea to get me and my friends together with him and the Eagers. He's invited you and Lily to dinner on Wednesday night.' Daniel rolled his eyes to indicate the preposterousness of parental behaviour. He didn't want to show how much he wanted Owen to accept the idea.

'Really! And what does your lovely sister think of this?'

'Who cares!' Daniel said, more harshly than he'd intended. 'There'll be free booze and food. We can eat with them and go up to my rooms after, if you like.'

Owen shrugged and pulled a face. 'Yeah, OK, sounds all right. I'll ask Lily.'

'Do you think she'll come?'

Owen smiled. 'Yeah. She's not as scary as you think she is.'

'I don't think she's scary.' Daniel felt the familiar unwelcome heat rise to his face.

'Well, *you* ask her, then!'

'No! I . . .'

'Go on!' Owen opened the parlour door and shouted his sister's name over the music. She came to stand in the doorway, arms folded. Daniel thought she looked angry, somehow wild, and not at all approachable.

'Daniel wants to ask you something,' Owen said.

Lily directed a hot glance at Daniel. 'What? What do you want to ask me?'

Daniel could barely speak. 'Um . . . to come to dinner at ours on Wednesday night.'

Lily burst out laughing. 'My God! Are you serious?'

Daniel nodded, face aflame. He could tell Owen was enjoying his humiliation. 'It's my dad's idea,' he added, thinking how pathetic that sounded once the words were out.

'Oh, *Daddy's* idea!' Lily said. Then she seemed to sober up and sauntered into the room. 'We're not high society, Daniel Cranton. What's brought this on? Does your father want to inspect us, or something, decide whether Owen's a *suitable* chum for his little boy?'

'No,' Daniel said. Her remarks annoyed him enough to fight back a little. 'He's just being friendly. He's like that. The Eagers are coming, too.'

Lily rolled her eyes and laughed again, though less abrasively. 'Jesus, what a gathering!'

'There you are, Lil,' Owen said. 'You can talk to Babs baby about your writing.'

'I've written one paragraph,' Lily said. 'There's nothing to talk about yet.' She smiled at Daniel. 'Will it be posh food and everything?'

Daniel nodded. 'Yeah, I expect so. Wine and stuff.'

'Oooh!' Lily grinned at Owen. 'What do you think?'

He pantomimed an extravagant bow. 'I would be happy to escort you, my lady.'

'OK,' said Lily, 'we'll come.'

Daniel had not imagined it would be so easy. Perhaps he had misjudged Lily after all. She was prickly, yes, but nowhere near as bad as Verity.

Lily sat down beside Daniel at the table. For a few moments, she stared at him intently, which Daniel could not interpret. 'You're very good-looking,' she said after a while.

Daniel felt as if the foundations of the cottage had cracked beneath his chair. Totally unable to cope with this remark, he blushed even more furiously and mumbled something incoherent.

'Don't be embarrassed,' Lily said. 'That was a compliment.' There was something feverish about the girl, a suppressed sense of excitement. Daniel did not flatter himself that he, or his invitation, was responsible for her mood.

'Er . . . thank you.'

'That's why I get jealous when Owen disappears with you on Friday nights.'

'Lil, shut up,' Owen said.

Daniel wondered whether he could leave the cottage immediately without causing offence. No matter what he'd said to Owen, Lily *was* scary. He'd just never imagined what kind of scary it would be.

'Just a joke,' Lily said. She grinned. 'Thanks for the invitation, anyway. I'm looking forward to intruding on O's private territory.'

'Ignore her,' Owen said. 'She's just winding you up.'

Lily jumped up and pushed her brother affectionately in the chest. 'Get lost!' She danced, literally, back into the parlour.

Owen shook his head and grinned ruefully. 'Don't mind her, Daniel. That was Lily actually being nice to you.'

'It's OK.' Daniel accepted the mug Owen handed to him. It was sticky on the outside, and had clearly not seen washing-up liquid for a considerable time. 'I called you yesterday.'

'Oh, did you?' Owen seemed bland, which Daniel took as suspicious.

'Yeah, Lily said you were out. I had a *boring* day.'

'Sorry to deprive you of my company.' Owen paused, as if considering something. 'I've met this weird guy. Interesting person, but what he's doing here in Little Moor, God only knows. We went out yesterday. I showed him some of the sights; the woods and stuff.'

'Oh. Right. How long's he staying?'

Owen shrugged. 'Don't know. Perhaps you should meet him.'

Daniel dreaded a newcomer being invited to the Friday night ceremonies at the High Place. He saw himself, debased. The dread must have shown in his face.

'There's nothing to worry about, Daniel.' Owen extended a hand, his fingers brushing Daniel's jaw.

Daniel flinched. Owen had never touched him before.

Monday evenings were quiet at The White House. While Barney carefully polished glasses behind the bar – had he always done that so much? Barbara wondered – Barbara asked Peverel Othman if he'd like to accompany her on a walk over the hills. She had to exercise the dogs.

Othman had been considering going round to the Winters' cottage again, but, in the light of certain ideas and thoughts he was incubating, decided to wait a while. A walk with Barbara, however, might prove fruitful.

Barbara, remembering the previous evening with Othman in the kitchen at the hotel, felt as nervous and fluttery as a teenager to be out alone with him. Would he make a pass at her? As they strolled down Green Lane towards the stile that marked the public footpath across the hills, she chattered on in a girlish fashion, but Othman only nodded and smiled at her; he seemed preoccupied. Courteously, he helped her over the stile, and a ragged banner of crows lifted from the copse in the middle of the field beyond. The sky was bloody in the West. Dark came on them swiftly.

'How long have you lived here in Little Moor?' Othman asked, interrupting a description Barbara was giving of some of her innovations in the village.

'Oh – er – not that long, a year or so. Why?' Barbara had noticed the rather pointed end of the question.

'I'm interested in local history. Wondered how much you knew about the place.'

'Oh, I'm very interested in it, too!' Barbara revved herself up for the discussion. 'I'm sure there's a wealth of history associated with Little Moor. Not least to do with that rather sinister-looking pile over there.' She pointed to the right, where the baroque turrets of Long Eden ranked silent and watchful against the sky. 'That's where the local gentry used to live, but, for some reason, they closed up the house and left the village about twenty years ago.' She laughed. 'Dark secrets, no doubt.'

'Tell me about it.'

'There's little to tell, really. The villagers either don't know, or won't divulge, much about the family. They had a fabulous name: the Murkasters. A suitable title for dark and deadly deeds! When I first came here, I wanted to know all about them, of course. I was looking for inspiration for my work. The impression I got was that people resented them for moving away – felt abandoned, I suppose. The Murkasters must have donated a lot to the community at one time. There's a hall in the village, used as an old people's centre, that they built. And there's the local library. Admittedly it's tiny, but it has a back room stuffed full of quite rare books that I believe came from the Murkasters. There are also some almshouses, which again the family had built. It's all a bit shadowy, but I think there's some kind of trust, which allows for older people in the village to live in the almshouses for free. I hope the fund doesn't run out. That would certainly put the lid on it for the Murkasters as far as the people here are concerned!'

'The Murkasters seem to have been altruists, then. I wonder why they moved away?'

'Well, it's fun to think of mysterious reasons, but I suspect it was a case of the younger members of the family wanting a little more life than could be offered by Little Moor. I expect they have property all over the place, or something.'

'Were they titled?'

'I don't think so. There might have been an "honourable" somewhere along the line.'

Othman had stopped walking, standing to stare at Long Eden. 'Can we go over and have a look?'

'Isn't it a bit too dark, now?' Barbara felt nervous of venturing beneath the night-shadow of the house. Also, she was not certain whether there was a caretaker around or not. There might be dogs patrolling. She hated the thought of being run off the place as a trespasser. 'We could take a walk up tomorrow afternoon, if you like.'

She could see Othman smiling at her through the darkness.

'Barbara! I believe you're scared!' He took her arm, an electrifying sensation. 'Come along, I won't let anything hurt you.'

Barbara allowed him to lead her in the direction of the house. It was ridiculous. He must be at least twenty-five years her junior, yet she felt so much younger than him. She realized this situation might have its benefits. 'I'm not scared. It's just that we might be trespassing. I can't believe they haven't got any security around the place. Won't it look suspicious creeping up on the place by night?'

'The place looks deserted!' Othman argued. 'Come on. Be adventurous.'

Barbara relented. 'Well, all right. Just for a little while.' She called to the dogs, who appeared happy to follow them.

They had to climb through a dilapidated fence that marked the boundary of Long Eden's grounds. There had once been a wall, but much of it had crumbled, to be replaced by the makeshift wooden panels. That indicated a decline in fortune, perhaps. The Murkasters might not have been able to keep the place up, which had prompted them to move away. But in that case, why hadn't they sold the property?

To Barbara, it was like entering an enchanted garden. Moonlight illumined the overgrown terraces, the weed-thick lake, with its ivy-bound summer-house, the strangled follies, where carved faces peered through the foliage. 'It's beautiful,' she murmured. Beyond the jungled garden, the house was black and massive.

'Seems rather a waste, doesn't it?' Othman said.

Amber and Lester were racing off across the ruined lawns. One of them barked, and the sound echoed, far.

'It makes me feel sad,' Barbara said. They found their way on to a gravel pathway obscured by brambles. 'But it's so romantic, too.' She let the remark hang. Othman had made no move towards her, offered no sign of interest. Perhaps she was being too forward, but the remark could be interpreted as innocent, or simply artistic, if she should receive a rebuke of some kind.

'It's *very* romantic,' Othman replied, but he did not look at her, and he had released her arm.

The main lawn felt endless as they stood in its centre, knee-high in dying grasses, staring up at the frontage of Long Eden. Barbara felt particularly sensitive, as if she was hearing, or feeling, echoes of things that had happened here in the garden. She thought of croquet, parties, women in white dresses, laughter, and strangely, music from the Twenties playing on an old gramophone. 'Why did they go?' she murmured, thinking aloud.

'The windows are all boarded up,' Othman said. 'That's why there's no reflection from them. That's why it's so dark and eerie.'

'Well, they'd have to secure the place, wouldn't they? I'd love to look inside!' She laughed. 'But by day, I think. This place must be overrun with ghosts! Out here, I like them, but I think I'd be frightened of them inside the house.'

'Barbara, would you mind if I just . . . soaked up the atmosphere for a moment or two?' Othman asked. 'I'd like to sit quietly here. It won't take long.'

He sat down in the long grass, and assumed a meditative posture. Barbara was surprised, but then told herself she shouldn't be surprised by anything Othman did. She hardly knew him. Obviously, he was a bit of a New Age type person, but then she had dabbled a little with alternative therapies and suchlike herself.

'Of course!' she said and sat down cross-legged in front

of him. 'Carry on. I'll just sit here a while, too. I hope the dogs aren't getting into mischief!'

Othman smiled at her, then closed his eyes. Barbara studied his face in repose. He really was astoundingly beautiful. She admired his high cheek-bones, his long precise jaw, the brush-stroke sweep of his brows, his dusty fair hair escaping in curving tendrils from his pony-tail. It made her ache to look at him. He was beyond her, she knew. If anything *could* happen between them, it would be brief. Then he would move on, to affect other people, elsewhere, in the same way. At that moment, Barbara decided she wanted a piece of Peverel Othman, however small, and however short a time she could hold on to it. Her looks hadn't deserted her completely, and she had the benefit of experience. Moreover working in The White House had toned up her ability to flirt. Never before had she considered being unfaithful to Barney, but this was too unique an opportunity to miss.

Othman was aware of Barbara's scrutiny and could catch the stream of her thoughts, pouring like a mist from her aura. He was flattered she appreciated his difference, and how special it was. He didn't blame her for wanting a piece of it. They all felt that way. Still, he must put that to the back of his mind, and open up to whatever resonances remained here in this place.

At first, there was nothing but the buzz and hum of distant, human echoes. He rose above himself, and scanned the landscape. If anything, it was too regular. Cloaked, perhaps. He sensed a smothered pulse of energy coming from the High Place in the woods, but the house itself seemed wrapped in velvet. It was aware of him, and knew he was aware of it, but he was unsure whether there was a sense of recognition or not. 'I am looking for my people,' he offered it, in simple geometric forms. 'Have they been here?'

There was a sense of quickening, of condensed alertness, almost of wariness. It was possible for buildings to acquire a certain limited sentience from generations of human occupants, but he was looking for the singular *genius loci*, its guardian spirit, which would signal the presence, past or present, of his kin. Houses, to his people, were not just shelters, but protectors, too. If this place had been closed up, it was possible a guardian form had been created there, who was enjoined to silence, to keep the secrets. He would have to win its confidence before it would reveal anything to him. The spirit of a place would have only limited intelligence. Perhaps he would have to give it a sign.

'Barbara,' he said, and opened his eyes. She was still staring at him.

'Yes?' She was waiting to hear what he'd picked up, waiting for ghost stories. He looked ethereal in the moonlight, his skin so pellucid it seemed it glowed with light from within. He made no move towards her, yet it seemed they were touching. The contact of eyes was more physical than she could ever have believed possible. Barbara's vision blurred as her eyes filled with water, yet she refused to blink and break the contact. Othman was shining now, brilliant through her tears. Her body tingled with energy. She could not breathe; did not want to. Holding the stare for as long as she could, Barbara eventually had to give in, throw back her head, suck in breath. As her head cracked back, sound was squeezed from her chest. For a moment, she felt dizzy and blind, then a sudden, unexpected and powerful orgasm pulsed up through her belly. It was like being electrocuted, as if a conducting metal rod had been plunged through the top of her head, down her spine, into the earth. She juddered uncontrollably around this conductor, weak and helpless in its pulsing waves. Then, as abruptly as it had come, the sensation fled. She fell backwards on to the grass, feeling sick and faint. The sky spun overhead, the moon circling crazily above her. Pain filled her head. Othman leaned over her, put his cool fingers against her temples, and the pain diminished, as if it was being sucked back into a black hole deep within her. She heard the echoes of lamenting cries inside her mind.

'I'm sorry,' Othman said. 'I hope you weren't hurt.'

Barbara had begun to cry, and was powerless to stop herself. 'What happened? What happened?'

'The atmosphere here, it's very powerful. I didn't mean to do that.' He helped Barbara sit up. 'Come on. We should go now.'

Barbara pulled a handkerchief from her jacket pocket, wiped her eyes and blew her nose. She managed a shaky laugh. 'I don't know why I'm crying. That was ... unbelievable. How did it happen?' She didn't know whether Othman was aware of how his stare had actually affected her. Maybe he thought she'd just got a headache from it.

'Just echoes,' he answered. 'You must be quite psychic.'

'Oh, I don't know about that.' Barbara tried to inject some normality back into her voice. 'Where are the dogs? Amber! Lester!' She heard barking from some distance away.

'They're back in the field,' Othman said. He offered his arm, which Barbara took, and they began to walk back towards the garden boundary.

Barbara still felt dazed. She was wondering whether she'd just been unfaithful to Barney or not. Nothing like that had ever happened to her before. Her underwear felt uncomfortably wet. How long had it been since she'd felt pleasure like that? God, did this man realize what he'd done to her? She risked a sneaky glance. Othman was tall and silent at her side. She hadn't really thought about how tall he was before. In fact, it seemed he was taller now than he had been. She must be going mad. This was all too bizarre.

'Did you pick up much about the place?' Barbara asked.

Othman shrugged. 'A little.' He patted her hand where it was hooked through his elbow. 'Thanks for helping me.'

'I feel I should be thanking you,' she ventured, boldly.

Othman smiled at her. He knew she was waiting for him to say something about what had happened, was looking for some sign that he returned her interest. He couldn't be bothered to deal with that now. All he was concerned about was that the house had witnessed what he'd done, watched his transformation and the transfer of power. In return, he had caught a glimpse of the guardian, an immense bird-like creature, essentially Grigori in origin.

When Grigori felt the need to emplace guardians, they generally employed two: one physical, one spiritual. Othman had picked up no sense of a physical guardian, but he'd seen the shadow of a spiritual presence. These psychically conjured creatures were always bird-like, reflecting the ancient myths of the simurgh, the anzu bird and the roc. The simurgh was an ancient Persian king of the birds, a giver of prophecies to mankind, and reputedly possessed of the knowledge of all the ages. The roc, another Persian mythical creature, was the fabulous bird of the sun, of enormous size and strength, and the anzu bird-demon of the Sumerians was remembered for stealing the Tablets of Destiny from the god Ellil. All of these mythical birds had their roots in symbols of death and transformation, as well as of flight into the realms of heaven. Thousands of years ago, the early shamans had entered a state known as the death trance and, like the enormous birds of their folk tales, had soared along the Milky Way, the river of the stars.

Because of their ancient affinity with bird shamanism, the Grigori often worked with bird-like symbols: the peacock, the vulture and more mythical avian creatures. Often the guardians drawn from these symbols were aggressive, but then they had to be, in order to defend effectively whatever property or site they had been created to protect.

Othman had certainly not been offered an invitation to enter the house, but the manifestation of the guardian could be interpreted as an acknowledgement. Othman felt highly excited, but the pleasure of this sensation was to prolong the moment before he allowed himself release. As for Barbara, he knew he'd awoken something within her, of which she was not yet fully aware. He would enjoy watching her discover this thing.

Chapter Nine

Tuesday, 20th October: High Crag House, Cornwall

High Crag seemed so empty. Aninka wondered how many people were living there. It was so different from how she remembered it, a place of bustle and activity. She'd been an insider, then, of course. Perhaps its inner workings were concealed from her now, and children played in rooms away from earshot, and women-folk laughed together, sampling the gin bottle in the afternoons.

Enniel had been out all day Monday, which had given Aninka time alone. This was a welcome break, during which she could gather her thoughts. Although she was eager to finish telling the depressing tale of her last couple of months in Cresterfield, she was also dreading reaching its climax. It was not the kind of experience a person wanted to live through twice. Since coming to Cornwall, she had started dreaming about some of her old friends. The dream was recurring and always began the same way, with herself getting out of her car outside Wendy Marks's house on a summer evening. Above her the sky was a deep, livid purple, and the air thick with sweet, floral scent. She paused for a moment before walking up the driveway and, every time, she experienced the most poignant stab of joy, melancholy, serenity and sadness: an impossible *mélange* of feeling. Then, she'd gone into the house, and they were all there in the drawing-room, waiting for her, dressed in their ceremonial robes. They seemed friendly, pleased to see her, yet she'd sensed an undercurrent of wistful disappointment, as if they suspected she could have warned them of what would happen. She tried to explain to them, but they couldn't understand her words. She was speaking in a tongue they could not possibly know; it had not been used for thousands of years.

On Tuesday, Enniel returned, and sent a dependant to look for Aninka after lunch.

'How much do you want to know?' Aninka asked him, settling on to the sofa in Enniel's office. 'All the little details, or just the main events?'

Enniel turned on the tape recorder. 'Everything. Everything you can remember.'

'What are you going to do with those tapes?' Aninka said. 'Who's going to listen to them?'

Enniel inspected her gravely. 'You need not fear about your private business being made public within the family. Any information you give us will be treated with the utmost discretion.'

'Something's going on,' Aninka said. 'Isn't it?'

Enniel steepled his fingers against his lips, smiled. 'Please, I'd like you to begin. Omit no detail.'

Aninka's Story: Cresterfield, July–September

After the initial meetings with Othman and his group of friends, it now seemed to Aninka as if a year's worth of living had been crammed into a mere couple of months. After the night when Peverel Othman had introduced her to the Markses and their friends, Aninka had begun to see him on a regular basis, at least two nights a week, often as many as four. Still, despite this frequent interaction, she spent the entire time aching with longing to see him, touch him. Minutes spent apart were an eternity. She squandered hours gazing out of the window in her studio, blindly staring at the cityscape below, thinking only of him. In a box in her desk drawer, she kept the strands of pale hair her lover had left in her hairbrush one morning. Sometimes, she would open the drawer, take out the box and remove its lid to smell the contents, breathing deeply to conjure a ghost of his presence in the room. She dared not tell him about this, for she guessed he wouldn't appreciate her hanging on to bits of him, in which a shred of influence and power might remain. He was a mystery to her. She loved him.

Othman never invited Aninka to where he was living. Repeated questioning elicited the vague information that he was staying in a boarding-house on the outskirts of the city. Eventually he gave her a phone number where he could be contacted, but on the occasions she tried to reach him, the phone was always answered by a machine with a robotic voice. Othman was maddeningly opaque about what he did when he wasn't in Aninka's company. Occasionally, Aninka became overwhelmed with jealousy and paranoia: there must be another woman, perhaps several. He might even be living with someone, or married. Once she asked him coolly about this. She didn't want to make a scene, but explained she needed to know. 'There is no one else,' he answered simply, his expression slightly surprised, as if he couldn't imagine why she'd suspect such a thing. 'I live alone.'

'Who was your last lover?' she asked, pushing and prodding to scrape out the information she hungered to examine.

He looked her directly in the eye. 'A Grigori,' he answered. 'It was abroad, in Europe.'

'What was her name?'

Othman smiled. 'His name, my Ninka, not her.'

That made Aninka feel better. She was more inclined to be jealous of her own sex. But Othman wouldn't tell her the name.

'He was a musician. You might have heard of him. So I'm not going to tell you.'

How could he want to keep such secrets from her? 'I want to know all about you. Is that so bad?'

He shook his head. 'No, I don't suppose so, but I'm not curious like that myself, so it's hard to empathize.' He kissed her. 'I live for the moment, Ninka. This is what is real.' He learned quickly how he could silence her questions with sex.

As a lover, he was accomplished and skilled, yet often Aninka was made uneasy by the suspicion that he was somehow removed from their love-making, content to bring her pleasure and observe her response, rather than satisfy himself. A couple of times, when he stayed the night, Aninka woke up to find him sitting in the darkness on the other side of the room. He said he found it hard to sleep. Sometimes she dreamed of him watching her as she slept, dreaming of him. Often she asked him, 'What do you want from me?' And he would smile, touch her face tenderly, and say, 'Just this.' Although she could not persuade him to confirm it, she gathered he was a lot older than herself, but certainly not as old as her guardian, Enniel, and other elders of her immediate family.

Often she would lie awake to watch him sleeping beside her. She hungered to prise his secrets from him, exorcize the sadness she felt he concealed. What was his tragedy? Why wouldn't he confide in her? Was it to do with the past lover in Europe? When she dared to ask him about his past, suggesting there might be things he'd like to share with her, he would only smile, and perhaps stroke a long finger across her jaw. 'Ah, my Ninka, you think there's more to me than there is.' She did not believe that for a minute.

On the only other occasion she mentioned his past affair, Othman had almost lost his temper. The quick flash of anger in his eyes had shocked her. 'Don't ask me about it!' he'd shouted. 'It's none of your business, and I want to forget it. Can't you get that into your head?'

'I think you were hurt – badly – and that hurts me!' Aninka responded. 'Don't shout at me because I care about you. Doesn't it occur to you I ask you these questions because I'm concerned, not because I'm just curious?'

He extinguished his anger immediately, and took her in his arms. 'Forgive me. There's no need to be concerned. It's over. I just don't want to talk about it.' He kissed her. 'Perhaps, one day, but not yet.'

She allowed herself to be mollified by that.

Othman liked to go to night-clubs and pubs devoted to loud music, where members of alternative subcultures gathered. No smart boys or girls with perms in these establishments, but the reek of patchouli oil and bursts of brightly coloured hair. Aninka was happy to dress for the part and accompany Othman to these places. She felt they must appear predatory and sensual, secretive creatures of the night. Othman talked to many people; they were drawn to him. Aninka preferred to distance herself from these conversations, a silent presence in the background. She took pleasure, however, in watching the girls feast their eyes upon Othman. It amused her that many of the boys did the same, boys who would sigh and crumple beneath Othman's touch, should he deign to reach out for them, after which they'd swear vehemently to themselves they weren't 'queer', as they would term it.

Sometimes, they'd see Serafina among the crowds in the dark rooms they visited, but she never acknowledged them. Othman told Aninka he'd instructed Serafina to keep their friendship secret. That had been a glaring clue, perhaps, which Aninka had dismissed without examining.

One night, they had been sitting in a hot, noisy bar, with the usual group of adoring people hanging on to Othman's every word. One girl, with a typical mop of dyed black hair and heavy eye make-up, had become emboldened by alcohol. She said to Othman, 'You look like an angel, a fallen angel.'

Aninka, uncharacteristically, responded. 'But that is exactly what he is, my dear.'

The girl seemed surprised Aninka had spoken and laughed uneasily, while Othman flicked a wry, slightly warning glance in Aninka's direction.

'He's got Nefilim blood in him,' Aninka continued doggedly. These people would have heard of the term Nefilim, if not of Grigori, because the old myths of the fallen angels — tragic, *beautiful and doomed — had become popular in the Gothic subculture, as attractive to the darkly inspired young as the legends of vampires.* 'Look at him. His height, his beauty. You should see his dick.'

Othman bridled at that. She saw a frown form on his face, and took satisfaction from it. 'Are you drunk?' he enquired in an icy voice.

Aninka took a sip of her gin and tonic. She wasn't sure why she was feeling so aggressive. All eyes were now upon her. She had the stage. 'He's a throwback,' she said. 'Many people are. If the angels mated with women to create the Nefilim, it's got to be in all our genes.'

'If you believe in the Bible,' one girl said with scorn. 'Personally, I think it's all bullshit. I don't believe in the Christian god, therefore I don't believe in all that angel rubbish.'

Aninka directed a basilisk stare at her. She felt an urge to gather power within herself, forge it into a spear of light and hit the brat between the eyes with it. 'Really?' she said and laughed. 'My dear, you should know that those legends are not found only in the Bible, but in many other texts, from several different cultures. In fact, the Bible barely touches upon them. It would be wise of you, I think, to know what you're talking about before you open your mouth.'

The girl with black hair, who'd first spoken, was grinning. Aninka perceived a mutual dislike for the sceptic. 'That's true,' she said, nodding to Aninka. 'I've read some books on it all.' She smiled smugly at her antagonist. 'It's very likely that a race existed thousands of years ago, who were more advanced than humanity. Some of them broke the law of their people by giving humans secret knowledge and having affairs with human women. That's where the legends of the Nefilim come from: they were half-breeds, monstrous . . .' She glanced at Othman. 'Well, monstrous only in the sense that they were very tall and strong. Giants.' She put her head on one side to study Othman, who looked like thunder incarnate. 'I think you're right,' she said to

Aninka. 'He is a throwback. It's obvious.' She laughed delight-edly, clearly glad of the opportunity to stare at Othman without being obvious. 'You're a Nefilim, Pev.'

'If you believe that,' said the sceptic, 'you might as well believe that the gods were spacemen.'

'What do you believe?' the black-haired girl asked Othman.

He shrugged. 'If you want to think I'm a member of a superior race, I'm not going to argue with you!'

Everyone laughed. Othman had cut the subject dead. When conversation started up again, the matter under discussion was trivial. Aninka knew Othman had thrown out a psychic screen. He was right to. She chastised herself for contravening one of her own rules. How could she allude to the subject of the Fallen Ones, when it was something she wanted to deny in herself?

Later, back in the flat, as Othman took a shower in her bathroom, Aninka sat in her darkened living-room and thought about the conversation. The children of the Fallen Ones, the rebel Anannage, that is what we are, she thought. They don't realize it, and we forget, but that is what we are. Grigori? We deceive ourselves that we are lofty scientists and scholars, but changing our name to Grigori changed nothing. We are still Nefilim, the sons and daughters of seducers and warmongers.

The weight of history pressed down upon her, bringing with it a depression. Aninka didn't want to be different, nor to have to hide what she was. It meant nothing to her, she thought. It was irrelevant, now, in this modern world. Yet her family, and all the other families like them, held on to the past, wrapping themselves in secrecy. If we could just forget, Aninka thought, then it wouldn't matter. We could just be.

Othman came into the room, naked and gleaming, drying the long rags of his hair with a towel. She spoke her thoughts to him, seeking sympathy. He only laughed.

'Don't lie to yourself. You want to be different. You say you love humans, yet you look down upon them. Those women tonight, they would have said to each other later, "Who does she think she

is?'', and if you'd heard them, you'd have answered, ''More than you, kids.'' Get real, Aninka. You are Grigori, and you love it.' He came up behind the sofa and put his wet hands on her shoulders. 'There is no shame in it. We are what we are.'

Aninka pulled away from him, annoyed. 'We are not that different from them any more. We have lost most of what made us superior, if that's what you want to call it. We're just hanging on to a memory of something that has passed. Genetically, we are half-human anyway.' She got up and marched to the window, blinked furiously at the glittering nightscape outside.

Othman obviously didn't want to argue with her, but sat down on the sofa to watch a movie. Aninka wanted to hit him. Part of what she loved about him was the fact that he seemed so different to other Grigori she had met, less obsessed with his heritage. She wanted him to agree with her and scorn the others. They had the potential to bring their race closer to reality. They could have children together and give them ordinary names like Sharon and John, never tell them about their racial history. Aninka liked the thought of that: Grigori growing up without ever being aware that they were unlike the other children with whom they played and learned. In her euphoria at this idea, she was sure the differences between the Grigori and humanity were now so minute that her children would never suspect there was anything unusual about themselves. Thinking these things, looking down at her lover illumined by the flickering light of the TV screen, she realized she felt more for him than for any other man she had met. Children? What was she thinking of? Othman had never even told her he loved her, never mind suggested their relationship might involve commitment.

He looked up at her, as if guessing what was on her mind. 'Aninka, face it, you cannot be like them. Your longevity alone sets you apart. Even if you had human friends you trusted enough to confide in, and who could accept your difference, you would still have to watch them age and die. As they withered, they would see you remaining young, and whatever affinity you'd managed to *create would be destroyed. It comes out, in the end, in all of us. Even our children. They have to be aware of what they are because, otherwise, they'd be regarded as freaks. We have to protect ourselves, and part of that involves never being able to become that close to humans. I can see you find that hard to accept, but you won't do yourself any favours by denying it.'*

'It's not fair!' Aninka said. She felt swamped by sadness.

Othman sighed. 'I can't understand what the problem is. If someone could wave a magic wand and make you human, you wouldn't like it. You're far too vain. A wrinkle, to you, would be a major catastrophe. There will come times in the future when you'll have to fake it, for convenience's sake, but you'll find yourself backing out of situations, changing your life and your environment, to avoid it. Believe me, I know.' He held out an arm. 'Now, stop fretting and come over here. Let's watch the film.'

She hesitated, then went to him. He pulled her close, kissed her hair. 'Aninka, if you weren't Grigori, I wouldn't be here with you like this. We couldn't talk. Be thankful for what you have.'

Othman's opinion of the Markses and their friends seemed scathing. He commented on their naivety and laughed about it. Aninka wondered why he wanted to spend time with them. Every Friday, he went to attend their rituals, and now Aninka went with him. He never appeared to want to get involved in their magical work, but seemed eager to spectate. Perhaps, Aninka thought with disappointment, it was a nostalgia for his heritage that lured him to the converted garage on Victoria Heights once a week. Aninka recognized a similar contradiction within herself. Despite her avowed rejection of Grigori culture, she was sometimes tempted to nudge the group along and even enlighten them a little. They were groping around in darkness, guessing how to recreate the past, and sometimes going wide of the mark in authenticity. Ivan wrote most of the rituals himself, using ancient material as a base, but adding a lot of his own ideas. Aninka possessed knowledge that could help them, but refrained from imparting it. She mustn't fall into that trap. Wendy asked her a few times if she'd like to become actively involved, but Aninka refused. 'I'm happy just to get artistic inspiration from it,' she said.

Wendy Marks had phoned Aninka on the Monday morning after Othman had taken her to Victoria Heights for the first time. After a few minutes' conversation concerning the prints they had talked about, Aninka invited Wendy over to the flat. They had started the afternoon drinking coffee and discussing art, but later Aninka had cracked open a wine box and they'd got drunk together. It marked the beginning of a proper friendship. After a couple of weeks, Aninka was visiting Grey Gables regularly by herself, and often met up with Wendy in the city for lunch. Aninka quickly learned that Wendy's husband, Ivan, was having an affair with Misty Kennedy. At least, Wendy suspected that he was. She said there had been confrontations in the past, but all her accusations had been denied. Now she just felt peevish, jealous and paranoid mentioning it. Aninka sympathized with Wendy. She thought her new friend to be a far superior creature to the blowsy Misty, but was also secretly grateful her marriage was in shreds, because it meant Wendy had a lot of free time, of which Aninka could take advantage.

Enid Morningstar had been round at Wendy's one afternoon, when Aninka called over with a bottle of wine and a need to get drunk in female company. At first, she'd been annoyed to find Enid sitting in the kitchen. Aninka had begun to confide in Wendy about Peverel Othman, revealing only that she couldn't work out his feelings for her and that she was falling heavily in love with him, but this was more than she wanted to discuss in front of Enid. However, Enid was round to rake through the debris of a particularly messy divorce, and after several bottles of wine, Aninka found that she had warmed to the woman. This was what she loved: women drinking together, talking about men. Her experiences and her feelings were not that different from Wendy's and Enid's. They didn't think she was odd or inhuman, *therefore she couldn't be. She liked the affinity she felt for these women. It made her feel comfortable inside to know that she had proper friends, and that they were human. One day, she dared to think, she might know them and trust them well enough to reveal the truth about herself. She felt sure they would assuage her fears, tell her the past didn't matter and that she was just the same as they were.*

When Ivan came home – late, after seeing Misty no doubt – Aninka and Enid got a cab together back to the city. While the dark streets flashed past, Enid offered to make Aninka some clothes. Aninka, who dressed expensively, politely demurred, which surprisingly elicited a hot response. 'I can create things for you that are just as well made as what you're wearing, but for at least half the price. You're so tall, you must have to pay a fortune to get things that fit you.' Enid shut her mouth with a snap. 'Oh, I'm sorry. That was a bit personal. You're like a model, Aninka. I envy you.'

Money didn't matter to Aninka, but obviously it did to Enid, who was divorced and poor, so Aninka relented. Consequently, design and fitting sessions were arranged, and Enid became a regular figure in Aninka's life. Enid lived quite nearby, though in a distinctly less salubrious area. Aninka was delighted with the clothes Enid designed for her, and was careful to pay the exact asking price so as not to offend her new friend. However, she did buy Enid an expensive bottle of perfume after the woman had admired the scent in Aninka's flat. This was accepted with grace. On the nights when Aninka didn't see Othman, she started going out to pubs and cinemas with Enid.

During this time, Aninka saw hardly anything of her cousins. Looking back, she could see that Othman had influenced her in this matter more than she'd realized. At the beginning of their relationship, she'd wanted to introduce him properly to Noah and the others, but Othman made it clear he wasn't keen on the idea. Perhaps other Grigori would have been suspicious of him, and would have seen things in him to which Aninka's obsessive love blinded her. Noah kept calling for the first couple of weeks, but Aninka only sporadically answered the messages he left on her answering machine, and then told him she was very busy working on new commissions. He must have sensed her disinterest in his gossip, because eventually his calls stopped. Aninka worried about it sometimes, then Othman would imprint himself across her mind, and she'd forget about it. Tearah and Rachel called round a couple of times, perhaps at Noah's request. Aninka found she didn't want them to know about her affair with Othman. She made up a story about a human lover she'd taken on, and added a few lascivious jokes about him, which she knew her cousins would appreciate.

'Call us when you get bored,' Rachel said as she and Tearah left the flat after the second visit.

Aninka assured them that she would. She hadn't seen either of them since.

Chapter Ten

Same day: Little Moor

On Tuesday morning, Peverel Othman woke up weeping. He lay in bed, with yellow sunlight slicing between the partly drawn curtains of his room, trying to remember what he had dreamed. The sense of loss and grief in his heart was familiar – he woke with that often – but there was something different this time: a sense of urgency, of approach, of revelation. There were things to be done. This time, he must do everything correctly.

After a light breakfast at The White House, Othman went directly to the post office, where he found Eva Manden alone in the shop. He selected a paper from the neat pile on the front counter, and then asked Eva where her mother was.

'I must apologize for the way she behaved yesterday!' Eva blurted. 'She's very old and has these funny turns sometimes.'

'It doesn't matter,' Othman said. 'I hope it isn't on account of me that you've banned her from the shop!'

'Oh no!' Eva shook her head. 'She's not banned! She's at the day centre . . .' The slightest frown creased her brow, which she quickly erased.

'Oh? You're lucky to have such facilities in so small a place.'

'Yes . . . That'll be thirty pence. Is there anything else?'

Her reluctance to talk about her mother did not escape Othman. 'No. Thanks. Bye.'

Outside, he stood still for a moment and opened

himself up to any passing information in the air. Presently, he began to walk slowly down the road, away from The White House.

Mariam Alderly was having a bad day with the old ones. They seemed spooked, restless. For fifteen years, Mariam had been the official care-person for the elderly at the Murkaster day centre in Little Moor. Now she wondered how long it would be until she joined the others, mumbling in the plastic chairs before the stage. She was sixty-two, widowed, and paid by the Murkaster trust a small amount that now complemented her pension. Cora Perks had phoned her yesterday, asking a few covert questions. Each woman had sensed the anxiety behind the other's words, but they'd confessed nothing. The call from Eva Manden had been equally strained. The postmistress had kept her mother away deliberately from the centre for months, claiming, obliquely, that it affected Emilia badly, made her difficult to cope with. Therefore Mariam had been surprised to receive the call informing her Emilia Manden would be attending again; surprised and disappointed. Emilia was the ringleader in any trouble-making behaviour. Things had been running quite smoothly since she'd been confined to the post office during the day. Emilia's arrival at the centre, late yesterday morning, had seemed to kindle a new tide of rebellion in Mariam's charges. Emilia was an old minx, that was certain, and more alert and cunning than the rest of them put together. Something was afoot, and Mariam felt jumpy because of it. For a start there had been a lot of whispering yesterday, conversations which were silenced whenever Mariam approached. She could feel the keen gaze of the ancient eyes, and a hint of scorn behind the silence, the atmosphere of suppressed excitement. She was intruding into something. Was it a petty war, sparked by gossip? That was possible. When they weren't ganging up against her, the old people spent their time sniping at one another, bound by the ancient tie, but hating each other for it. They had also started a spontaneous chant half an hour before David Perks came with the Murkaster trust minibus to take them all home. It had been a terrible racket, and Mariam had feared complaints from the smart new bungalows down the lane.

At one time, Mariam had been able to handle the old ones without difficulty. Now, it was becoming more taxing; perhaps she herself was getting too old for the job. The Murkaster trust was administered by a firm of solicitors in Patterham. Mariam wondered whether they'd be prepared to fund another helper at the centre. She could only suggest it. This thought lightened her mood a little and she went to prepare the morning tea.

Othman paused where a side road joined the main road through the village, and after closing his eyes and sniffing the air for a few moments, he turned to follow it: Endark Lane. Presently, he came across a large two-storeyed building, which had an imposing façade of dirty stone columns and what appeared to be a heraldic device above the door: a peacock gripping an arrow in its claws. Below this device was a stone ribbon bearing the single carved word 'Murkaster'. Othman tried the door, found it unlocked, and went into the building. After crossing a gloomy hallway, he entered a large dusty room beyond. Arched, stained-glass windows were positioned high in the walls. Dwarfed by the room, a group of elderly people sat in modern, plastic chairs near a stage at the far end. Othman noticed a middle-aged woman handing out tea. He walked towards the group, and the tea-maker became aware of his presence. She stood up straight, her face registering surprise. She seemed frozen.

'Good morning!' Othman announced.

Ancient heads all turned to stare. He walked into the middle of the circle of chairs and turned round slowly to inspect each raddled face. The mother of Eva Manden raised a hand and stabbed the air emphatically with a rigid finger. She said nothing, but her eyes were bright.

Mariam's first thought when the tall, long-haired man walked into the middle of her charges was that he was a Murkaster. Her heart almost stopped for a moment. 'Can I help you?' she enquired.

The man turned and looked at her with deep blue yet snake-like eyes. She realized then he was no Murkaster, even though there was something very familiar about him. He was too fair; all the Murkasters had had rich, auburn hair and golden eyes. And yet, despite his fairness, there was something dark about this one, dark as a wood-shadow.

Othman, as he regarded this female, was aware that she was insignificant. However, she was a relative outsider, and he hoped she wouldn't be a prohibitive presence while he examined the old ones for signs of Grigori attachment. Before he could speak, a loud cackle pealed out from the throat of Emilia Manden.

'I told you,' she cawed to her confederates. 'Didn't I tell you?'

Around her, grumbles of assent started up. Othman smiled. Dismissing the carer from his attention for the time being, he went to each of the old people in turn, making a fluttering gesture with his hands, which he concealed from the carer. As he did so, a fleeting bloom of light illuminated the wrinkles and eager eyes of each face. Yes, it was there, tired and worn out, but still lingering: the taint of Grigori. When he reached Emilia, he actually reached out to touch her cheek. 'Hello again!'

'Not that!' snapped the old woman, jerking away. 'We want the juice. It's been too long for that.'

Othman withdrew his hand. He laughed politely.

Mariam was becoming increasingly discomfited. 'Excuse me,' she said, in what she hoped sounded like a firm voice, 'but would you mind telling me what you're doing here?'

Her question provoked a sibilant hiss from Emilia Manden. 'Get out of here, you silly bitch!' she cried, drawing herself shakily out of her chair and tottering erect. Her grey hair hung unbound down her back; she was an image of ancient, female power. 'Get out, Mariam Alderly! We have private business!' Her voice echoed through the hall.

Mariam felt strangely dizzy. 'Emilia . . .' she began, in a soothing tone, but Othman interrupted her.

'I'm sorry to cause a fuss, but I'm staying here in the village for a while, and would like to offer my services for some voluntary work.' He turned a beaming smile on Mariam, who visibly softened under its light.

'That's very kind of you, Mr . . .?'

'Othman, Peverel Othman.'

Mariam now felt light-headed, floating rather than dizzy. She had an intense desire to accommodate the requirements of this imposing, handsome man. In her right mind, she would have wondered about him; he did not look like a volunteer. 'Right. Have you got experience of working with older people?'

'Oh yes. It's something I'm always involved in. And I like to fill my time with worthwhile work wherever I am. I'm staying at The White House. Mrs Eager told me about the day centre.'

'Oh, I see. Well, in that case, I'm sure we can do with an extra pair of hands.'

'So what can I do to help?'

Mariam wanted to sit down. She felt overwhelmingly grateful someone was here to help her. 'Well, we generally have a game of housey-housey after tea. P'raps you'd like to call the numbers for us.'

The old people all uttered eager murmurs of assent. Ignored, Emilia Manden sat down again, fixing Othman with a glinting raptor's eye. Othman made a covert signal to her. He recognized her seniority in status among these people, but it was totally inappropriate to arouse the carer's suspicions. He hoped Emilia Manden would go along with him for now.

Lily felt uneasy. Why hadn't Peverel Othman come back to see her and Owen? Was he disgusted by what had happened on Sunday night? She couldn't bear to talk to Owen about it. In fact, the thought of sharing with Owen now made her feel slightly sick. Last night, he'd gone out with the Cranton boy again. Lily still wasn't convinced Owen didn't have a thing about him. Why had she agreed to go to that wretched meal at Low Mede? At the time it had seemed like a good idea. At the time, she had actually warmed to Daniel Cranton, and had wanted to put aside her jealousies. Now she had changed her mind again. What was happening? It felt as if her life was cracking apart, and something, which had been contained, was flowing out, changing everything. She wrote in her notebook: *I was asleep for a thousand years, and he woke me up. But he did more than kiss me . . .*

Sighing, she put down her pen, stood up and went into the kitchen. Here, she put the kettle on for her fifth cup of tea of the morning, and picked up one of her cats, Titus. As the kettle groaned and bubbled in the silence of the room, she swayed around to unheard music, cradling the cat against her shoulder. Why hadn't Othman come? Should she go to The White House to look for him? No. No. Don't be stupid! Where was Owen now? Was he with Othman? Surely he wouldn't go without her? Her thoughts were too crowded; she didn't want them. If only she had someone to talk to. Lily surprised herself with that thought. Normally, Owen was the only confidant she needed, and if he was absent, her desire to talk could always wait until he returned home. She had lived here in Little Moor for the greater part of her life, yet didn't have a friend. She knew it hadn't been that way when she and her mother and brother had lived in the town further south. She could remember friends from school there, summer evenings spent playing outside together. But since moving to Little Moor, she'd struck up no new friendships, and the ones from her childhood had faded away through distance and time. She'd known girls at Patterham High, and had not been unpopular, but had never confided in any of them, or spent time with them in the evenings and at weekends. There was something about the village that repelled outsiders, and the local girls all kept a distance from Lily, in a furtive kind of way. They were polite but unapproachable.

Lily swayed on the spot, considering an idea that came to her. She could go and call on Barbara Eager. Barbara was forever hinting at visiting the cottage, and Lily knew the woman longed to take her in hand. She could go and ask about the writing circle, or tell Barbara about the Crantons' invitation. Two excuses! What more could she need? This, she told herself, had nothing to do with the desire to come across Peverel Othman.

Lily washed her face at the kitchen sink, dried herself on a tea-towel that smelled of cat food, and put on a pair of Owen's boots. Halfway to the back door, she reconsidered, and changed the boots for a pair of sandals. Then she caught sight of herself in the mirror above the sink and decided her hair could do with a brush. As she was dragging a greasy comb through the tangles, she noticed there was a large tomato-sauce stain on her dress. Uttering a muted cry of annoyance, she picked up a damp, grey rag from the draining board. After scrubbing uselessly at the stain for a few seconds, she stamped her foot and wriggled out of the dress, which she threw on the kitchen floor. Beneath it, she was naked. What to wear? What to wear? Lily darted upstairs. Perhaps she should put some knickers on. She did not possess a bra. Eventually, she found a faded lilac-coloured dress, which she thought might once have belonged to her mother, and which wasn't too wrinkled. In fact, it looked quite good. She inspected herself in the cloudy cheval-glass in her bedroom. And groaned. Then, grabbing a long cardigan with holes recently darned, she hurried out of the house before she could change her mind.

It felt strange, going to The White House during the day, but then Lily knew that all buildings possessed different personae for the dark hours and the light. As usual the small reception desk in the hall was unstaffed, with a printed notice sitting on the counter, advising potential residents to make enquiries in the bar.

Shuni Perks, a girl of Lily's age, and sister of Owen's friend, Ray, was slouched behind the bar, chewing her nails. She always made Lily shudder; there was something *basement-like* about Shuni Perks which Lily detested, a hint of damp and must and fungus. 'Is Mrs Eager about?' Lily tried to sound pleasant and friendly.

Shuni didn't look too pleased to see her, but there was

caution in her posture, rather than hostility. 'Yeah, upstairs.'

There was a pause. 'Well, I'd like to see her. Could you get her for me?'

Shuni smirked in a half-cocky, half-nervous manner and thumbed an intercom button on the wall beside the Optics. Lily heard Barbara's breathless 'Ye-ess?'

'Lily Winter's here to see you,' Shuni said. It was almost as if she expected Barbara to be embarrassed.

'Lily? Oh, right. I'll come down.'

'Hear that?' Shuni said.

Lily nodded and moved away from the bar, hands deep in her cardigan pockets. She wondered what she was doing here. She wondered why she felt so excited and tense.

Barbara breezed into the bar just as Lily was drifting back into the hallway, having been made uncomfortable by Shuni's covert scrutiny. Barbara, as ever, was impeccably dressed in a cream trouser suit with a full-length, wafting waistcoat. Her hair tumbled luxuriously, almost impudently, over her shoulders. Lily realized that Barbara was actually a very attractive woman, and must have been absolutely stunning twenty years ago. 'Lily! What a surprise! I was just doing the accounts. Horrible job! What a welcome distraction! What can I do for you?'

Confronted, Lily felt completely dumb. Perhaps Barbara's friendliness hadn't meant anything. Perhaps she was like that with all her customers. Was Lily intruding now? She felt her face grow hot. 'Er – well – my writing and – um – Low Mede – the meal . . .' She shrugged helplessly.

'Aha!' Barbara laughed delightedly, putting the palms of her hands together before her face. 'I see! You're worried about the do at the Crantons', aren't you!' She put a proprietorial arm around Lily's shoulders and dragged her towards the door marked 'Private' in the hall. 'There's no need to worry, Louis's a perfectly lovely man! It won't be formal, or anything.'

Relieved, Lily went along with Barbara's assumption. 'Well, I was a bit worried about what to wear and stuff. I've got some dresses of Mum's, but . . .'

She followed Barbara up the private stairway to the Eagers' first-floor flat. The air smelled of fruit. Incense or burning oil, she thought.

'Why don't you buy something new?' Barbara suggested, gesturing for Lily to precede her into an airy lounge. She hoped she wasn't being presumptuous, but it was common knowledge the twins had a private income. Poor things, they just didn't know how to manage their money, or themselves. Barbara itched to have a hand in their affairs, confident she could work miracles.

Lily was afraid to sit down on the pale sofa, in case she got it dirty. 'I suppose I could,' she said, 'but there isn't much time now.'

'Tell you what!' Barbara said, brightly, balancing in a girlish manner on the arm of the sofa. 'I could drive you to Patterham tomorrow morning. How about that? We could go shopping together!'

Lily hadn't expected that. 'That's nice of you, Mrs Eager . . . Thanks.'

'It'll be fun. Now, come and sit down. And please – it's Barbara.'

Timidly, Lily edged around a black-lacquered occasional table and sat on the edge of the sofa. Please don't leave marks, she told herself. Barbara went to make tea, and Lily inspected her surroundings. It was so elegant. She wished the cottage could be like this: clean and fragrant and airy. Barbara had collected all kinds of knick-knacks which stood on various display stands and shelves around the walls. There were a couple of dark old portraits of shadowy women, obviously genuine antiques.

Barbara came back, carrying a wooden tray, rag-rolled by hand in dusty-blue paint. There was an enormous teapot in fiery red china and red mugs, decorated with birds of paradise in gold, jade and purple. What lovely things, Lily thought. I wish I had lovely things. She realized she wouldn't know where to start.

Barbara sat down next to Lily and poured tea, Earl Grey. 'I hope you like this,' she beamed, handing Lily a mug. 'So, you also mentioned your writing downstairs. How are you getting on?' She was flattered that Lily had obviously come to her for advice or feedback.

'It's harder than I thought,' Lily answered, sipping the delicately flavoured tea. Owen and she drank tea like tar: almost black and with several spoons of sugar each. Barbara had not offered sugar. 'I mean, there's so much I want to say, and I can think it right through, but when I come to write down my thoughts, it sounds stupid or boring.'

Barbara smiled encouragingly. 'Everybody says that! Your writing's probably not as bad as you think.' She hoped she was right. 'You must bring something along to one of my meetings.'

Lily couldn't help frowning. 'Well, maybe . . .'

'Or if you prefer,' added Barbara intuitively, 'you could bring it round when I'm on my own, and I'll read it through, and we could talk about it.'

'That would be better,' said Lily. She wondered how she could introduce the subject of Peverel Othman without being obvious. Perhaps Barbara hadn't paid that much attention to him, or disliked him for having long hair and no tie. Lily would hate it if she mentioned him, and Barbara screwed up her nose in distaste, or murmured things about *unsuitability*. Lily was always very conscious of being unsuitable in society that considered itself polite.

Barbara touched Lily's arm. 'I'm so pleased you've come to see me.'

Lily grinned awkwardly. Perhaps it had been a mistake to come. 'I was at home on my own,' she said lamely, and then took a deep breath. 'We've got to know one of your guests . . .'

'Oh, that will be Pev!' Barbara said.

Lily winced at the intimate short-form of his name. 'Yes. Peverel Othman.'

Poor girl, thought Barbara. Here she is, struggling to make conversation, and it all comes out so stilted! She wondered how she could put Lily at her ease. 'Not the usual sort we attract round here, is he?'

Lily smiled. 'No. Not really.'

'He seems to have taken a shine to you and Owen.'

Lily wondered how much she wanted to talk about Othman with Barbara. There was no way she could, or should, confess even a little of what had happened in the cottage on Sunday night. Yet talking about him seemed the next best thing to seeing him. 'It makes a change,' she said. 'I don't get to see many people.'

Barbara's face assumed an expression of concern. 'Oh, Lily, are you lonely?' She felt that might be too direct for this retreating creature, and half expected Lily to make some excuse and leave abruptly.

'Not lonely,' Lily answered, surprisingly readily. 'But something.' She smiled tightly at Barbara. 'I must be boring you.'

Barbara shook her head vigorously. 'No, no! I am *concerned* about you, Lily. You're such an attractive, bright girl . . .' She winced at her patronizing tone. 'I'm sorry. That sounds terrible. I don't mean to be condescending, but I suppose there's no easy way to say it. I think you could do a lot more with your life.' There, it was said. Would Lily leave now, take offence?

Lily, however, was clearly not a predictable creature.

'That could be said of most people in the village,' she answered. 'This is our life. Quite small. I'm not unhappy, though. Owen and I have everything we need. I don't hanker for anything else.' She wondered whether this was true. Things seemed to have changed recently.

Barbara wanted to say that Lily could tidy herself up a bit, do something with the cottage, but felt these suggestions were too forward. She would have to get to know Lily better, nudge her along gently rather than charge in. 'Well, I'm glad you came to see me.' She risked a more personal remark. 'I don't get to see my own daughter very often.'

Lily nodded. 'Yes, I know.'

'Do you miss your mother?'

'Not now. Well, sometimes, I suppose.' She smiled, more freely this time. 'I'm always surrounded by boys – Owen and his friends.'

Barbara laughed. 'Me too, actually. To be honest, the women in Little Moor don't seem to get that friendly with people they think are outsiders, and I must admit I'm not that keen on the "newcomers", you know, the despised commuters, etc.' She giggled girlishly at this confession.

'It's funny to hear you say that,' Lily said. 'I thought you knew everyone in the village.'

'I'm acquainted with everyone, because of the pub, but I wouldn't say I *knew* them.' Barbara drained her mug. 'More tea?'

'Please.'

As Barbara poured milk into the mugs, someone knocked on the lounge door. Barbara looked up, but before she could say anything, Peverel Othman walked into the room.

Lily was astounded. This was so unexpected. And how well did he know Barbara now to come walking into her private rooms so casually?

'Oh, Pev!' Barbara exclaimed in surprise.

Lily noticed the woman had gone quite pink, but then so had she. She could feel her face burning.

'Hope I'm not intruding,' Othman said, looming over them. 'Hello, Lily.'

Lily muttered a greeting.

'Oh no, you're not intruding,' Barbara gushed. 'Sit down and have a cup of tea with us.' She went quickly to the sideboard to fetch another mug. Sitting down again, she said, 'We were just discussing an invitation we've both had.'

Othman had slid into a chair beside the sofa. 'What's this, excitement in Little Moor? A party?'

Barbara laughed. 'Not exactly. Louis Cranton, a friend of mine, is having a little do tomorrow night. Lily's brother is a friend of Louis's son, Daniel, so Lily and Owen have been invited, too.'

'Oh, that's a shame,' Othman said.

Barbara frowned. 'Why?'

'Well, I was going to take Lily and Owen out for dinner myself tomorrow night.' He smiled at Lily, leaning forward to take the mug of tea Barbara offered him. 'I was hoping I could persuade Owen to drive us into Patterham.'

Lily felt unable to speak. She couldn't help thinking about the last time she'd seen Othman. What did he think of her and Owen now? How could they possibly go out for dinner without mentioning what had happened in the cottage on Sunday night? The thought of discussing it terrified her, yet she felt crushed that she and Owen had a prior engagement. She wanted to be with

Othman, yet she didn't. The contradictory feelings confused her, because they were so alien to her simple life.

'Oh, isn't that nice of Pev, Lily,' Barbara said uncertainly, sensing the change in atmosphere. She realized, with a sinking feeling of defeat, that Lily was interested in Peverel Othman. Pretty young Lily. Barbara strove to dampen any surges of jealousy. She liked the girl, and Othman was incredibly handsome. Who could blame her for fancying him?

'Never mind. We'll just have to do it another time,' Othman said. 'Although I might be moving on shortly.'

Lily looked at him in alarm. 'Already?' she blurted.

Othman shrugged, smiling. 'Well, soon . . .'

'Look, I've just thought of something,' Barbara said. 'Why don't I ask Louis if Pev can come along tomorrow night with Barney and me?' She turned to Othman. 'Louis is a very interesting person, and I know his cook is wonderful, so you'll have a lovely evening!'

'Will Mr Cranton mind?' Lily asked. The idea appealed to her. It might be easier to be in Othman's company if other people were there, too.

'I'm sure he won't,' Barbara said. 'I'll phone him in a minute.'

'That's very kind of you, Barbara,' Othman said. He stretched out his long, black-clad legs, seemingly perfectly at home in this room, even though he was a large and intrusive presence against the muted colours. 'How's Owen?' he asked Lily.

Lily felt herself blush again, having only just recovered from the last surge of heat. 'Fine.'

'I meant to come and see you both last night, but I went for a walk with my landlady instead. We had a look round the old manor-house across the fields.' He frowned at Barbara. 'What's it called? Something Eden?'

'Long Eden,' Barbara said in a carefully neutral tone.

Lily looked at her askance. Something had happened between Barbara and Othman last night. She just knew it. Don't be jealous, she told herself. Barbara is a beautiful woman, even if she is a bit old. No wonder Pev fancies her. She suddenly felt very grubby and skinny.

'Quite an interesting place,' Othman said, apparently oblivious to the conflicting emotions he had triggered in his companions. 'I wonder why it's shut up like that.'

'It scares me,' Lily said. 'I don't like it.'

'Oh? I thought you and Owen were keen on old buildings.'

'Only some old buildings,' Lily said.

Barbara was wondering why Othman had come into the room. This was the first time he'd approached her in her private rooms. Was it because he wanted to see her, or because he'd found out Lily Winter was present? No reason had been offered for his entrance. She also felt he was trying to embarrass her by mentioning the previous evening's walk. Perhaps a measure of chastisement was in order. 'Anyway, Pev, you haven't told us why you're here. Is there something I can do for you?'

Othman, she noticed with satisfaction, did look taken aback by her question. Clearly he now thought he had a right to invade her space. She would have to push him back a little; the game would be enjoyable.

'I was hoping you'd be able to suggest something for me to do. I'm at a loose end.' He smiled widely, a captivating grin.

Barbara suddenly wished Lily wasn't there. Strange how this man could juggle her feelings simply using his expressions. She laughed. 'It's a good job I don't have *all* my guests expecting me to entertain them!'

Othman smiled thinly. He wouldn't have bothered coming up to the room, but for the covert enquiry at the bar concerning Barbara's whereabouts, which had prompted the sluggish barmaid to reveal that Lily Winter was visiting. Othman wanted to observe her, and Barbara's prickly behaviour, which could only be perceived as an obstruction, annoyed him. He thought he'd got her hooked. The truth was that after leaving the day centre he'd had no immediate plans. He needed to make more acquaintances in the village. Barbara's suggestion that he accompany her to this dinner party was fortuitous. 'Well, perhaps there's something I can do for you,' he said. 'I don't like to be idle.'

Barbara's instinctive response to this idea was to ask, 'What exactly *are* you doing here in Little Moor?', but she did not voice it. Her usual guests, walkers and tourists, were content either to ramble around the countryside or to explore by car. Othman had no transport, and seemed to possess no purpose for his visit. She wondered, for the first time, whether Peverel Othman was actually hiding from something by staying in the village. He was keen to get to know people, almost as if he'd recently moved here and intended on staying. Was that his plan? Yet he'd talked of moving on soon. Othman was a person of mystery. Perhaps she was unwise in befriending him and putting herself at risk by spending time alone in his company. These thoughts passed through her mind very quickly, enabling her to respond without a noticeable pause. 'I won't hear of that, Pev. Why don't you walk over to Long Eden again. You might see more in daylight.'

Othman said nothing for a moment, then stood up. 'Yes, that's a good idea. Thanks. And thanks for the tea. Goodbye, Lily.'

It had been that simple to get rid of him. As he left the room, Barbara wondered whether she'd offended him. He made her angry, in a strange kind of way; she wanted to provoke him. Yet the undeniable attraction to the man was still there. She poured herself another mug of tea. Lily had gone very quiet, tapping her mug against her teeth.

'He's an odd one,' Barbara said, to break the silence.

'Mmm.' Lily flicked a furtive glance at Barbara.

Barbara touched Lily lightly on the arm. 'Be careful, won't you,' she said. 'We don't know that much about him.'

'OK,' said Lily.

Peverel Othman walked down the road like a grey cloud, his hands in his pockets. He sent out calls from his throbbing mind, angry calls; he felt thwarted. Woman, corruptible nothing! Alone, he allowed his masks of smiles and pleasantries to slip. If anyone should have seen his face at that moment, they would have witnessed the truth of him; light leaked from his serpent eyes. Pure Grigori, he abandoned the need to use human methods of navigating around. The microcosm of Little Moor, its leafy lanes in russet plumage, its grey walls seamed with moss, became insubstantial to him. He let his senses guide him, the other senses. Such was the intensity of his inner concentration that he did not even notice that his body passed *through* the tall iron gates of Long Eden, rather than around them. Rage had conjured this unexpected effect. Material impediments shuddered at the passage of his flesh, mutated to a fluid substance. He could have crawled, snake-like, over the tumbled stones of the wall, but in his rage he kept a straight path, through everything, while remaining consciously ignorant of what was happening.

Such concentrated anger was an unfamiliar sensation to him. He felt it rarely, only when he sensed he was losing control, however slightly. Fury always brought with it a memory of a memory that he could not place, and the brief image in his mind of a gate closing. Again the imperative came to him, nebulous and worrying: he must open the gate. But what gate? Was it physical? Where was it? Time and again, he had called upon the darkest powers of his imagination to give him the information he needed, to blast wide the shutters in his mind. He always failed, but one day, he knew, he would hit upon the right sequence of events and perform the right actions to blow the damned gate, whatever it was, into infinity. He sensed that immeasurable power lay waiting for him to claim it, beyond the gate.

Long Eden appeared around a corner of the driveway; its massive black stones looked damp, its boarded windows impenetrable. At the sight of it, Othman's inhuman rage diminished, eclipsed by curiosity. After his visit to the old people's day centre, and all the other information he'd gathered, it seemed almost certain that a Grigori family had once lived in Long Eden. The name of the house alone was a clue. Eden had been the country where, over eight thousand years ago, the Anannage had lived. Most Grigori strongholds were named after the Anannage settlement in Eden: The High House, Cedar House, Bright House, High Crag. Othman had seen many such names on his travels. Now, it was essential he accessed whatever remained of Grigori power in Little Moor, in an attempt to satisfy a hunger for power which had hounded him through his life. Power to open. Some of the Murkasters' power, he was sure, lingered at the High Place. Why hadn't he realized immediately the significance of that name? Scholars translating the old documents had often misinterpreted the words. It was common to find it transcribed as heaven. The High Place among the crags in Eden. Home. And here was a piece of it.

Othman walked round the side of the house to a yard

at the back, where the doors of deserted stables hung open. He inspected the outbuildings, hoping he might find some way in which he could penetrate the main house. Restored to emotional equilibrium, his body could no longer insinuate itself unconsciously through solid objects. He wondered how strong the guardian of the house might be. Othman knew he was powerful, and often subjugated people and spirits weaker than himself, but his was a lazy sense of power. He balked at confronting entities that might be a match for him.

Most of the buildings were tumbledown, vandalized. Graffiti marked their inner walls, old beers cans and the other flotsam of youthful festivities littered the floors. A depressing scene. Othman was glad the house itself had been secured; mindless destruction could so easily have been its fate.

A line of one-storeyed rooms stuck out from the right of the house, enclosing that side of the yard. These must have been the sculleries, laundry-rooms and suchlike. It was amazing the locals hadn't ripped out the boards that covered the windows. Othman wondered whether he could use that route, or whether others had tried it before and failed. He could see that the boards were heavily marked, as if by a penknife. He refused to think of claws. Experimentally, he banged his fist against one of the boards; it felt utterly solid, as if it was about two inches thick. Whoever had secured the place had taken great pains to make sure it remained that way. He could see no sign of nails; the joins, if they existed, were seamless.

Wandering back into the centre of the yard, Othman threw back his head to take in the massive vista of Long Eden. The blind eyes of its windows seemed to regard him, as if they could see by an extra sense, or could smell his presence. 'Let me in,' he said, under his breath. 'You know you want to.' The house remained impassive. He had the curious feeling that there were people hiding within it, listening with suspended breath, waiting for him to leave. He sensed fear. Was it possible there really *were* people left inside? Knowing his people as he did, that was not as incredible as it sounded. He would have to find out exactly why they'd left the village, abandoned their family seat. His enquiries could begin with the old ones in the community. He would give them what they wanted, for a price. He felt nothing would be gained from lingering in this spot just now. Other visits were long overdue; a return to the Winters' cottage, for example. He had been acutely aware of Lily's confusion earlier. It was perhaps time to tweak a few nerves.

A ragged shape suddenly launched itself upon him from the shadows as he walked beneath the stable arch. Othman cried out in surprise, thinking of feathers and claws. He was not prepared to engage in combat with the guardian, preferring less violent and more subtle methods of persuasion. But no shadowy, winged entity hovered behind him. Another surge of annoyance crested through him. It was only Emilia Manden.

'Thought I'd find you here.' Her voice was cracked, a hideous parody of a seductive tone.

'What do you want?' Othman asked coldly. The woman was supposed to dance to his tune, and he was in no mood for music at the moment.

Emilia laughed in an imitation of girlish glee. 'Oh, come now, Peverel Othman. You know exactly what I want. I've waited long enough for it.'

'Not from me, you haven't.' He made to walk past her, but the crone grabbed his arm. There was still strength in her grip, but then it was common for the cosmetic effects of quickening to be the first to disappear.

'You're all one and the same,' Emilia said. 'You've

done this to me. Now put it right.' She indicated her shrunken body. Her loathing for it was clear in her eyes, those strangely bright, youthful eyes. Othman loathed it, too. He did not want to touch it.

'I have other things to attend to – first,' Othman said, and smiled, lightly patting the old woman's fingers where they dug into his arm. 'You can wait. As you said, you've waited a long time already.'

Emilia shook her head. 'Oh no. There is the pact, and you are all party to it. I've kept my side – my silence. I've been patient. Now, you must give me my reward, the fruit of healing and of life.' She paused, put her head on one side. 'I know what you people are like. You need followers, people to do this for you and that for you. You're lazy. Give me life and I'll work for you. You know I'll have no choice.' Her voice became provocative. In the half light beneath the arch, it was easy to believe she was a lot younger than she appeared. 'You have come for the house, haven't you, but you can't get in. Maybe I can help you.'

'You know a way in?' Othman's voice was sharp. He realized he'd made a mistake, let her see his eagerness.

Emilia took a few steps away from him. 'They lied to us, you know. Told us we'd be fine. We had no idea how quickly the dissolution would come. They didn't care. They just left. We were nothing to them. Nothing . . .'

'Why did they leave?' Othman asked. He was aware that Emilia was determined to make herself useful, and was succeeding.

'No more, not yet,' she replied. 'You know what I want. After that, we can talk.' She glanced around herself. 'But not here. You never know who might be listening.'

It was true the atmosphere around them was that of intense concentration. 'Where?' Othman asked.

'Not the woods,' Emilia said. 'They're neither safe nor free. The village is patchy, but the safest places are where the new houses are.'

'Is there anywhere near there we can have privacy?'

'We'll have to see, won't we . . .'

Emilia walked unevenly towards the drive, and Othman followed her. He felt faintly nauseous, knowing what he'd have to do. But it was perhaps expedient.

Emilia took his arm as they walked down the lane. 'I was very beautiful once,' she said. 'And I will be so again.'

Othman remained silent. He sensed unseen eyes at the cottage windows, from the shadowed gardens. People knew what was happening, he was sure.

They turned on to Endark Lane, and walked past the looming portico of the Murkasters' hall. Here, Emilia seemed to want to hurry. Cruelly, Othman hung back. 'What about here?'

Emilia did not answer, but stuck out her lower jaw and dragged him on. Othman laughed softly. 'They can't hurt you. How can they?' He paused. 'But aren't you worried that *I can*?'

Emilia did not slow her pace. 'I've got things you need. You need me. You'll not harm me.' She glanced at him. 'You are not like *them*.'

'If you say so.' He smiled to himself. He thought he must be *much worse* than the Murkasters, who had fled.

The new bungalows all stood precisely in a row on the right side of the road. They had names like 'Sunnyside', with long drives sweeping round to porticoed front doors where electric lanterns hung, festooned with wreaths of moths. There seemed to be a large number of moths about. Othman felt another memory tickle his mind, just below consciousness, but swiftly suppressed it. Strange feelings and moods were coming upon him more frequently now.

Few of the bungalows had net curtains or blinds. Othman saw huge televisions flickering, shadowy figures moving about in dim, comforting light. Sounds came from the houses, family sounds. He curled his lip in disgust. Only so much meat, he thought, nothing more.

Where the row of bungalows ended, there was a lane, leading to a small children's playing field, where a bright plastic slide glowed in the dusk, and swings moved restlessly. Othman looked back at the bungalows. Their gardens were long, but he felt he was still fairly visible from any of the kitchen windows. 'Here?' he asked. 'I'll get arrested!'

'They won't see,' Emilia said. 'They are blind to most things. Anyway, it won't take long.'

Sighing, Othman rolled back his sleeve. His skin shone palely as if lit from within. 'You must let me concentrate for a moment,' he said.

Emilia made a whickering noise. Then he heard her swallow thickly. He turned his back on her. Holding on to his exposed wrist, he summoned his inner energy from the dark abyss, the void which traversed space and time, and from where essences of power could be called into the present. In some Grigori, this ability and its products were just memories. Othman could feel it now, rushing down the tides of time towards him, crashing into his body, electrifying its fibres. If he turned to the woman now, the sight of his face would burn her. He considered doing that for a moment, then, without turning, offered her his arm. 'Take it, then.'

Surely, anyone looking from a window at the back of the bungalows would see him. Light leaked from his clothes, his eyes, irradiating the hunched form of the old woman. He felt her grab his arm, fasten her loose old mouth upon it. She desired to bite, to suck his fluids, but lacked the teeth, fortunately. He did not want to bestow such favours. Instead, she sucked with as much power as her ruined facial muscles could muster, sucked the light from him, the life, from the place where the skin was thin. There were other places, but he would not give her access to them. In the event, she drew blood, too, but not much.

Othman snatched his arm away. It burned horribly, the burn of intense cold. He could hear Emilia gagging and gasping behind him. 'That's enough,' he said. He drew the life-force back inside himself, sent it crashing like a waning tide back through the centuries. Othman shook his head to clear his sight. Already, he felt drained, and his arm had begun to throb. It made him feel sick to think of the old woman gobbling away at him. He had never been that keen on providing sustenance, only taking it interested him.

He turned and saw her wiping her mouth. There was little immediate outward change, although her mouth glowed slightly at the corners from the ether which had passed through her lips. Her replenishment would take time, but already she seemed to stand straighter, held herself with more confidence. 'Take me for a drink,' she said. 'Then we'll talk.'

Othman had no desire to take Emilia to The White House, and, besides, his visit to the Winters' was overdue. 'Not tonight,' he said. 'I have a prior arrangement.'

'Tonight,' Emilia insisted. 'We'll go to The Black Dog. Don't worry, I won't embarrass you with your lady friend at the new place.'

He presumed she meant Barbara. Othman made a show of looking at his watch, which he wore only for effect. He knew exactly what time it was. 'Well, just for a short time,' he said.

*

Where The White House was light and airy, The Black Dog was dark and suffocating. The entrance was low and ancient; the plaque above the door said 'Burchard Leonard' – no indication of his wife. Othman followed Emilia into the smoky, beery atmosphere of the bar. It was packed with locals: farm people, oldsters. The clientele consisted mainly of men, but for one or two women sitting on rickety stools against the bar. In time-honoured fashion, all went quiet when Othman and Emilia entered the room. Othman experienced the typical feeling of having entered someone's front room. It was madness to have agreed to accompany the old woman here.

Someone said, 'Evenin' 'Milia.'

Emilia acknowledged the greeting with a grunt, and shuffled up to the bar. Behind it, the tyrant of The Black Dog held sway, a fat man in a tatty shirt. One eyelid drooped over his missing eye. The other resembled the eye of a bird, direct, penetrating and soulless.

'What'll it be, missus?' he said.

'A bottle of stout,' Emilia answered, and jerked her head at Othman. 'He's buying.'

Othman ordered himself a Scotch and soda. He could not imagine how Emilia could talk to him in this place without everyone listening in, but then that might have been her intention.

'I'll be using the snug,' Emilia announced.

'Then you'll be needing the light,' said the landlord.

Emilia, carrying her bottle of stout with a glass over it, led the way to a glass-paned door at the back of the room. Here, she and Othman descended into a musty dimness. Leonard had put the lights on, but they did little to affect the overall dismal gloom of the room. Three steps led down to a small area where three battered tables stood. Leatherette benches lined two of the walls, and a few stools were tucked beneath the tables. It was very cold.

'We can talk in here,' Emilia said, sitting down on one of the benches.

Othman opted for a stool. He felt ridiculous. Whatever the old woman could tell him couldn't possibly be worth this abysmal experience. 'So talk to me,' he said. 'I can't say I'm enjoying the surroundings, and, in fact, must confess I'm eager to escape them.'

'Burch isn't one for fancy trimmings,' Emilia said conversationally, sipping her stout with puckered lips.

'Tell me about the Murkasters,' Othman said. He took out a packet of cigarettes and lit one. The smoke smelled pure and clean in the overall mousiness of the subterranean snug.

'Well, they left,' Emilia answered.

'That much is obvious. Why?'

'You think they told us much? No. I'll tell you about me, about the past.'

Othman wasn't sure how much he wanted to know of this, or whether it would be of any use to him. Still, he could shut the old biddy up if he got bored. She could have ten minutes of his time before he walked out on her.

It seemed the Murkasters had lived in Little Moor for as long as Emilia could remember. As Othman suspected, she was older than she appeared – one hundred and fifty-three years old. When she was seventeen, she'd been taken into 'service' at Long Eden, as all young people in the village were required to do for a time. Those whom the Murkasters favoured were granted privileges – longevity being one of them. Emilia described the Murkasters as the serpent people, because of their height, their slimness, and their snaky eyes. She didn't know how many individuals the family comprised, but had met about twenty of them herself. On her second visit to Long Eden, a Murkaster male had taken her virginity:

droit de seigneur had apparently been one of the Murkasters' demands upon the villagers. No Grigori virgin girl would have lowered herself to being deflowered by a human, yet every young human in Little Moor, male or female, was taken by the Grigori males.

'Their women were sacrosanct, shrouded,' Emilia told Othman. 'They were ruled by the Lady Lilieth, and she was a stern body.' Emilia sighed. 'We knew our place, but times were good then. Strangers were kept out of Little Moor in those days, but there were none of those walking-about holidays then, bringing strangers in.'

The Murkasters had brought wealth to the village, a golden age. They appeared to have been benevolent, although Emilia spoke vaguely of 'tithes' and 'taxes', which Othman interpreted as involving the commerce of flesh and life. Their behaviour seemed typical of a loner throng, shut away in the wilderness, using the local population for their entertainment, labour and for certain experiments, which had been conducted beneath the house. Othman did not think the Murkasters had hungered for power particularly; they seemed to have been stagnant, lazy. Emilia had little of interest to tell. She had not personally witnessed any of the Murkasters' scientific or alchemical work, which she called 'secret'. Youths and girls occasionally disappeared into the private areas of Long Eden, never to emerge again, but not on a regular basis. 'We knew how different they were from us – always had,' Emilia said. 'Knew they weren't quite *human*, I suppose. They looked like us well enough, but they were very tall. Like you.' She drank noisily from her glass. Othman was silent, drawing on his cigarette, swilling his whisky round his glass. He did not prompt her. 'Still, they kept us fat. Know what I mean? The village was fat, the fields were lush. They did things to the land for us. They built the church, and in there, they showed us the mysteries.'

Othman's ears pricked up. 'The church? Is that the one some way out of the village?'

Emilia nodded. 'Still there, though hardly used. They had their own people in there years back. Some say they had the bishop on their payroll. It is called the church of St Shem.'

'Shemyaza,' said Othman. The name seemed to grip his spine like a claw. To the Grigori Shemyaza was both a god and a devil, their creator and destroyer, the leader of the rebel Anannage.

Emilia nodded again. 'That's him. We had him hung over the altar, but they took that with them when they went. Left only a space behind, but there's Christ hanging there now. Those that came after put that there.'

Othman decided he'd have to try and look around the church. Normally, Shemyaza's essence was invoked only in the most secret rites of the Grigori, when his dark influence was needed to produce a specific result, but such rituals were, to his knowledge, never performed in a place frequented by human dependants. The Murkasters, then, had been slightly more daring than Othman had thought. 'What mysteries did they teach you?'

'The Ways,' Emilia said. 'How to bend all things; how to hide in the world. They taught us the language of fire, and we could speak it. On the altar burned a perpetual flame. They called it the Tree.' She sighed deeply. 'The flame died in there when they left. They killed it, because they didn't want anyone else to know about it. With the flame gone, we were lost.' She indicated her own shrunken body. 'This is what happened. Without the flame, the Ways would not work for us. We could only remember them.'

'So why *did* the Murkasters leave?' It seemed to prise this information from the woman, but she didn't know the answer.

'They made trouble for themselves.' Emilia put down her glass. 'I'm still thirsty. Talking makes my throat dry. It's not what it was, my throat.'

'Then we'd better leave,' Othman said. He drained the remains of his Scotch, stubbed out his cigarette.

'Oh, you've not heard it all yet,' Emilia said. 'Why d'you want to go when the story's not finished.'

Othman sighed. 'Just what *can* you tell me? It seems to me you know very little.'

'I know that a woman caused their troubles, the one Lord Kashday got with child.'

'Same again?' said Othman, standing up.

Emilia Manden grinned at him, held out her glass.

When he went back into the bar, everyone watched him in silence. Burchard Leonard glared at him through his single, disturbing eye. How many of these people were like Emilia? Othman wondered. He did not want to inspect them too closely, afraid of inviting the hunger he'd awoken in Emilia. If they wanted to, they could probably tear him limb from limb, devour him whole. Greed for lost youth could make them do that, he knew. He knew only too well.

His flesh shrank against his spine as he hurried back into the snug. Putting down Emilia's bottle of stout, he said, 'Well, tell me the rest. I shall be late for my appointment if I don't get out of here soon.'

'Where are you going?' Emilia's eyes were narrowed.

'None of your business.'

'The Winter cottage?'

Othman wondered whether Emilia had been watching his movements. 'Now why should I be going there?' He grinned over his glass at her.

'Because you must know about them. You must be able to smell it on them.'

'Perhaps I can. Perhaps not.'

'We all took the vow for her before she died, you know. Promised to keep the silence. They know nothing, those children. They are innocent. But we knew they'd draw you people back eventually. They are our insurance. The Lord made us promise to take care of Helen, if she returned, and we did. But she was sickening even before she came back. The only reason she returned was because she knew what was happening to her, and she feared for the kiddies. She knew they'd be safe here.'

'Their mother? Owen and Lily's mother?'

Emilia nodded. 'Course. The Murkasters tried often, you know, to take wives from our people. Little Moor would have become something great if it had worked, but it hardly ever did. When the seed of their men took in our women the children always died. Then Helen Winter carried twins to term . . .'

Othman was stunned. Owen and Lily were kin to him, however distant. No wonder he'd been attracted to them. And they didn't even know. He smiled to himself. What intriguing possibilities this information presented. They were Grigori half-breeds.

'Helen had a bad time of it, of course. There was always a strange thing going on between her and the Lord. She hated him and loved him; true passion, I suppose. But what exactly happened that night, I don't know.' She shook her head.

'What night?' Othman wished she was capable of telling a story without rambling, and without missing out important details.

'The night they had to go.' Emilia sounded annoyed he hadn't worked this out for himself. 'All we saw was the light in the sky, and the *sounds* − sounds like big wheels turning under the earth. Then, something came out of the sky, creatures. They were just glowing outlines, but so huge! And ghastly!' Emilia grimaced and smacked her lips. 'We could see them above the trees. Monsters! Lions with wings and beaks and eagle's claws! It was like a war in the sky when they came! Such lights! And they fell down upon the house.' Her eyes glowed at the memory, then her face fell. 'The next day, the Murkasters had gone. Only some of Kashday's menials were left to clear up, and the name of the solicitors' firm in Patterham who would be handling their finances from then on. The hall was built for us. They knew what would happen, of course they did, and wanted to ease their consciences a little.' She looked directly at Othman. 'Have they sent you? Or have you come to us by other means?'

Othman saw no reason to lie. 'By other means,' he said. 'The Murkasters are unknown to me.'

'But you are like them, aren't you?'

'In some ways. You know that.' He rubbed the livid bruise on his wrist in a pointed manner. 'So Lily and Owen Winter are half-breed Grigori, and they are unaware of this.'

Emilia nodded. 'That's the truth of it. It's safer that they don't know. At least, that's what Helen thought.'

'What happened to her after that night?'

Emilia shrugged. 'Gone. Disappeared like the others. But the solicitors gave me a letter from Kashday, asking that she be looked after, so I guessed she'd turn up again one day. And she did. Didn't tell us anything, though. I let her keep her secrets. Mind you, I think whatever happened that night when the monsters came did something bad to her. She was on her way to death by the time she came back here.'

'Kashday Murkaster left her well provided for, then?'

'Very much so, I would think. I know she didn't

intend to come back here originally, but she was afraid for the twins when she got sick. Wanted to keep them away from the world, so that no one would guess they were anything other than normal kids. Kashday gave her her freedom and the money to enjoy it, I suppose. No one knows what happened to him, or where he went. It must have hurt Helen to come back here, to remember. But the children were a blessing for her.'

'They have no other relatives in Little Moor?'

'No. Helen was a strange one. She was an outsider, came here originally to work as housekeeper for Farmer Lennocks. He never had a woman, see. She was a young thing, very pretty. Lennocks was scared of her and in love with her both. Why she ran from the world and hid away here in Little Moor, she never confessed, but she was fond of sashaying around the place. Caught the eye of the Murkasters, of course. They wanted her in service, but she wouldn't have it. Wasn't local, you see, didn't understand the system. Kashday would ride over to Lennocks's on his big bay and talk to her as she hung out the washing or fed the chickens. You could hear her laughter if you walked the path through the spinney nearby. She loved him coming to talk to her. She played with him, without realizing what it was she played with. The Lord would send me over with presents for her: a jewelled pin, a bowl of roses, a phial of cedar oil. Lady Lilieth would invite her to tea at Long Eden for the Lord's sake, and she had the nerve to go, by Shem she did! I remember her walking across the fields in summer, barefoot, with her hair all tangled and wild, her dress loose around her legs, singing as she went. 'Hello, Emilia Manden!' she would shout to me, and wave. She irked me, her behaviour and everything. No respect, no under-standing. But we had to play along. What the Lord wanted, we had to want as well.'

Othman's mind was filled with the picture Emilia was conjuring. Helen Winter lived more vividly than anything else she had spoken of. 'Helen,' he said.

Emilia glanced at him sharply. 'She was a sorceress of her own kind, true enough. But he had her in the end. Maybe he told her too much, I don't know. All I do know is that when Helen Winter lost her head to anger, and came storming back across the fields to Lennocks, and shut herself away in the farmhouse, and no one, but *no one* could get her out again, soon the trouble came. *She* caused it, we all think that, but, still, we had to protect her because it was what he would have wanted.'

'Strange you should remain loyal to a man who abandoned you,' Othman said.

'If we went back on our loyalty, he would *never* come back,' Emilia said.

Othman put his elbows on the table, cupped his chin in his hands. 'So, how do I get into the house?'

'There're more than bolts and boards shutting the place up, that's for sure. You'll have to convince the place to let you in.'

Othman sighed. 'Have *you* ever been inside it since it was closed up?'

Emilia shook her head. 'No. It wouldn't let *me* in, but you, you're one of them, aren't you? It might listen to you.'

Othman remembered his experience outside the house when he'd visited it with Barbara. It had not felt completely hostile, but very wary. He wondered what had become of the Murkasters. Emilia's talk of monstrous, spectral beasts suggested Kerubim to him, which reeked of intervention from the Parzupheim. The Kerubim were the Grigori's angelic army, and, true to the cliché, they were creatures that took no prisoners. It seemed unlikely that many of Kashday's people would have survived such an attack, and even if they had, the survivors would not have escaped the subsequent round-up by the Parzupheim. If they still lived, they'd be under Parzupheim control now. The Murkasters must have seriously transgressed in some way, but clearly Emilia had no knowledge of that. The truth might just reside in the hidden memories of the Winters, though. Helen still lived in them.

He stood up. 'Finish your drink, Emilia. I'll walk you home.'

'No need,' said the old woman. 'I'm quite safe to find my own way back. You get to the cottage. I'm thinking you'll be more eager to get there now.'

Othman paused. 'Thank you for what you've told me, Emilia. You've been most helpful.'

She shrugged. 'There's a cost, Peverel Othman. You know that. A debt to be paid.'

'I shall, of course, do what I can, but I am only one man. You must protect me from the greed of your friends.'

Emilia cackled. 'Think I want to share you? No. Don't worry. I'll brush your tracks. Give me back my life and power, and there's nothing I won't do for you.'

Othman smiled. He felt a faint stirring of respect for the woman. 'Then I shall look upon you as my right-hand woman.'

'Left hand,' said Emilia, lifting her glass. 'Let's get that right.'

Chapter Eleven

Same day: Little Moor (continued)

When she'd got back from The White House, Lily had told Owen about Peverel Othman's behaviour with Barbara. Owen had reacted strongly. 'Seems like he's playing with all of us!' It was the first time he'd alluded, however thinly, to what had transpired in the parlour with Othman looking on.

'I wonder what he wants,' Lily said. She told Owen how Othman had been planning to take them out to dinner.

'So he could come back here afterwards?' Owen snapped. 'We must be careful, Lil. I don't want a repeat of that.'

Lily felt ashamed, as if she was personally responsible for what had happened.

Lily and Owen were sitting watching television in the parlour when Othman arrived. Both seemed flummoxed to see him as it was now after nine. 'I would have come earlier,' he said, 'but I took a lady out for a drink.'

'Barbara?' Lily demanded, looking sad she'd been unable to prevent the word bursting from her.

Othman laughed. 'Emilia Manden, actually.'

Lily frowned. 'Why?'

'Oh, I'm very interested in local history, and Emilia is a mine of information.' He sat down in a chair before the fire. Owen was studying him carefully, as if unsure of what to say or do.

'Little Moor seems to be a source of fascination for you,' he said. 'I can't think why.'

Othman gestured with open hands. 'The world is a fascinating place, and I travel within it. I come to places like this to unearth their secrets. There are always plenty.'

'I'll make some tea,' said Lily, getting up.

Othman waited for her to go into the kitchen. 'Owen, I think you can help me.'

'Oh?' Owen would not sit down. 'How?'

'I'd like to see inside the church you took me to the other night.'

'It's locked.'

'Then perhaps we can break in.'

Owen grinned in a tight, guarded way. 'All right. But why?'

Othman leaned forward on his seat. 'I'm finding out *interesting* things about Little Moor. Things that I think will interest you, too.'

He noticed that Owen looked wary immediately. Clearly he had his own secrets. 'Such as?'

Othman shrugged. 'It can wait. Do you know anything about the family that used to live in the manor-house, Long Eden?'

Owen pulled a face. 'No. They've gone. Have you unearthed some scandals about them, or something?' He didn't seem that interested.

'There's more to them than you think.' He decided, for now, to keep the information about the Winters' connection with Long Eden a secret. He wanted to observe the twins for a while longer before he told them about it.

'So what's in it for you?' Owen asked, sarcastically. 'Other than an academic interest, of course.'

'You seem to have a poor view of me,' Othman said.

Owen used his eyebrows. 'I can't help it. I wonder what we got into with you, the other night. You were playing with us. I'm not too pleased about that. It's upset Lily.'

'I don't want to upset anyone, least of all Lily.'

'What are you, some kind of sick pervert?'

Othman had not expected such a hostile reaction from Owen. He felt he was losing ground with the boy. At that moment, Lily came back in, carrying a tray. She obviously sensed the atmosphere, but chose to ignore it. Owen still stood belligerently next to Othman's chair. Othman wished he could put him at his ease. He'd seemed fine when Othman had arrived.

'So what are these Crantons like, then?' he asked Lily.

'You'd better ask Owen,' she replied, pouring tea and avoiding Othman's eyes. 'I hardly know them. Owen's very friendly with Daniel Cranton.'

'They're all right,' Owen said mulishly.

Othman was alert to the nuances in tone, and mentally filed a note about it. 'Can we go to the church tonight, Owen?'

'Church?' Lily was frowning.

'I want to get inside it,' Othman said to her. 'Your brother says that it will mean breaking in.'

Lily shrugged. 'Yes. I expect so. But there's nothing of interest in there. It's virtually bare. The pews and everything are all fairly modern, and there are clean spaces on the walls where things must have been hung up in the past. It's not a very inspiring church.'

Othman remembered Emilia's words about how the Murkasters had taken everything away with them when they'd left the village. Some things, however, they might not have thought to take with them in their hurry. Thoughts, feelings, the recordings of experience that might still linger in the stones of the church. 'Well, let's just say I have a *talent* for sensing things that aren't there. It doesn't matter to me if the walls are bare.'

'You'd better take torches,' Lily said. 'And before you ask, no, I don't want to come.' She grinned, and then, as a troublesome thought obviously crossed her mind, the grin slowly fell from her face. 'Will you be coming back afterwards, Pev?' It was the first time she'd used the short form of his name.

He shook his head. 'No, not tonight.' He detected the wave of relief that flooded through Owen's body.

Outside, the night had succumbed to a faint misty drizzle. Owen wore a huge old parka coat with the hood up. By the time they'd walked halfway to the church, Othman's hair was soaked.

'I hope all this is worth it!' Owen said. They had reached the lich-gate.

Othman shone his torch around. 'There's no sign of the name of the church anywhere. St Shem's, isn't it?'

Owen pulled a thoughtful face. 'Yeah, I think so. I suppose this place is a bit weird. No name, its innards removed, so to speak. Did that happen at the same time those Murkaster characters took themselves off?'

'I think so, yes.'

Owen grinned. 'This is getting interesting after all. What have you uncovered? Dark doings?'

'We can but hope,' Othman said dryly, pushing open the lich-gate. He thought it puzzling that Lily and Owen hadn't pieced things together for themselves. They were curious people, yet they'd never thought to turn their curiosity towards Long Eden, the church and the vanished Murkasters. Either their mother or their father must have had something to do with that.

Othman and Owen walked up the slight slope to the church. It stood squat and huddled in the rain, as if its shoulders were hunched against the weather. Othman prowled around the outside of the building, looking for a way in. Owen stood a short distance off, shining the torch obligingly in the directions Othman indicated. They found a cracked window on the north side of the building, which appeared to belong to a sort of kitchen area. When they shone the torch through the glass, they saw a stainless-steel sink and a drainer. Bars covered the window, but it was clear they weren't that secure. 'If we could get a few of the bars out as carefully as we can,' Othman said, 'we might be able to make it look as if no one's been in there afterwards. Put them back.'

'OK.' Owen tugged at one of the bars and a stream of powdered stone fell down the wall. 'I hope there's nothing guarding this place – from the inside!' He laughed.

Othman, for once, was not inclined to share the laughter. The thought had occurred to him, too, and he had far more idea than Owen what such a guardian could be like. Tension seemed to condense around them as they worked on the bars. Othman attempted conversation to lighten the atmosphere. 'So, do people actually still use this place as a church?'

'Yeah, but not that often. There's a vicar comes out now and again, but I've never been here then, so they could be conducting the Black Mass up here for all I know!'

'So when have you been here?'

'Oh, our mother brought us up a couple of times when we were kids. She liked to sit in the church and think. We used to play outside, mostly.'

Othman had a very clear image of Helen Winter in his head. Sitting in a ray of sunlight on the bare pews, wearing a light, summery dress, her legs bare, a posy of wild flowers clutched in her lap, her eyes raised dreamily to the place where once Shemyaza had hung. 'The ring stone,' Othman said. 'What is its significance?'

Owen glanced at him, looked slightly embarrassed.

'Oh, that. We just used to lark around when we were kids, that's all. Games, you know.'

Othman gave him a wry smile. 'So what was all that performance the other night in aid of?'

'You wanted entertainment, you got it. Are you complaining?'

Othman laughed quietly, but said nothing. He pulled another bar free. 'Can you get your skinny arse through here now?'

'Uh-oh. You go first, Mr Othman!' Owen shone the torch through the hole.

Othman knocked out some of the loose glass and squeezed his way in. 'Hand me the torch. Are you coming in, lily-boy, or what?'

Owen dropped on to the tiled floor beside him. They were in a small room, which was empty but for the sink and drainer. It was clear that cupboards had once adorned the walls, but they had been removed. A door led into a short corridor, and from there into the main body of the church. Othman thought the design was unusual. It did not speak traditional church to him at all. Still the atmosphere seemed fairly dead. He cautiously extended his senses as he swept the beam of his torch around the cavernous inner space. Nothing. Just a few faint echoes that meant very little. Owen stood beside him. 'You see. There's nothing much here.'

'Mmm.' Othman walked up to the altar, which was covered with a mildewed white draping. The whole place smelled musty and damp. A bowl of dead flowers stood on the floor. He shone the torch upon the brass crucifix behind the altar, straining to feel something, anything. Very faintly, an image came: the hanged man, hanging from one foot, bound for eternity. Othman closed his eyes, willing the image to become clearer. According to the legends, Shemyaza's physical body had been destroyed by his people, after his transgressions with humanity had been discovered, while the body of his soul, his immortality, had been cast into the constellation of Orion, where it still hung to this day. Now the effigy of the rebel leader burned in Othman's mind's eye. It pressed upon him urgently, like a silent, insistent reminder of something he had forgotten. Othman shuddered and opened his eyes, sucking in his breath. Perhaps his imagination was playing tricks on him, making him sense what he wanted to sense, see what he expected to see. Emilia had spoken of a perpetual flame that had once burned here, in this building. But where? Again, he swept the torch beam around the vaulted room, catching Owen in the light, his pale hair stark, his face hollow. Son of Shemyaza, Othman thought, and smiled. Could he tell Owen now? No, not yet. Then as the torch beam raked across the corbels overhead, Othman caught sight of a significant carving. He swept the beam backwards, spotlighting the stone figure of an angel, bound and hanging upside-down. It was the Fallen One. Looking up at the image of Shemyaza captured in stone made Othman feel as if he had been punched in the stomach. He lowered the beam, still conscious of the figure hanging unseen above him.

'Here, hold this.' He handed Owen the torch. 'Can you just sit quietly while I do a little work?'

Owen shrugged. 'If you want. What kind of work?'

Othman tapped his head. 'Using this.' He took off his jacket. He felt the strongest reluctance to face the image of Shemyaza again, but knew he must suffer it, for the sake of acquiring knowledge.

Owen sighed and sat down on the front pew. He watched, with rising disquiet, as Othman began unbuttoning his shirt. 'What are you doing?'

'Stripping off. What does it look like?'

Owen laughed nervously. 'Why? It's freezing! Are you crazy?'

'A little cold never hurt anyone, and no, I'm not crazy. I just need to use my skin, that's all.'

'Weird.' Owen stood up and walked to the back of the church, apparently examining the empty walls.

Othman ignored him. Once naked, he sat down upon his clothes and assumed a meditative posture. Was there anything left of 'Saint Shem' in this place? He had to find out.

In the first image, it was summertime and the church door was open, admitting the light. Shadowy people sat upon the floor. There were no pews. The walls were adorned with pictures of serpents and peacocks. The bronze effigy of Shemyaza was exquisite, almost life-size. He hung there, naked but for his bonds, his hair trailing down like a sheaf of corn or feathers. Peacock feathers and corn-ears were plaited into his hair. One eye was open, staring into eternity, the other closed. He neither smiled nor frowned. In his mind, Othman made obeisance to this image. He both honoured and feared it. In his life, he had inflicted pain upon many people without feeling the slightest twinge of compassion, yet contemplation of Shemyaza's martyrdom kindled panic in Othman's heart. Perhaps it was the same for all his people.

The second image was more specific. A group of people were dismantling the church, or more accurately the temple, in a hurry. The effigy of Shemyaza was taken down and wrapped in linen, bound with cords. The paintings were removed and stacked in enormous crates. The silverware, the cups of gold were similarly packed away. Outside, it seemed a war was taking place in the sky. Unnatural beams of light crashed through the high windows of the building, as if seeking out prey, which Othman recognized as the presence of Kerubim. People cringed and scuttled away from the light. They were all human. The Grigori were elsewhere. Othman directed his inner sight around the room. The perpetual flame burned within the altar, yet he could see it was only a tiny discharge of something far more powerful. The true flame had never resided here in the church. This place had been constructed mainly for the benefit of the villagers. What had the Murkasters done to provoke the wrath of the Parzupheim? As far as Othman could tell, their activities had been fairly harmless and commonplace, although they seemed to have involved more of the local community than was normally thought wise, and had certainly flirted with revealing some of their secrets. Was that it? But in that case, why the apparent full-force attack upon the Murkasters? It was bizarre. For his own reasons, Othman objected to those who sought to govern the movements of others of his kind. His movements, after all, would always be considered suspect. His heart went out to the Murkasters. He felt he knew exactly what had happened to them, and it was not a flight into exile.

He was about to draw himself back to full consciousness, when a final image blazed across his mind. The gate! As he stared at it, it flickered before him, transforming into a myriad representations of portals – stone, wooden, trellises of light – some gigantic, some tiny, mere mouseholes. Then, as quickly as it had come, the image disappeared.

Shuddering, Othman pulled his mind back into the present, and sat blinking upon the cold stone. Owen must have heard him sigh. Othman heard his feet upon the flagstones behind him.

'Well?' said Owen.

Othman shook his head. He felt stiff, ancient. 'Help me up.'

Reluctantly, Owen offered his hand. 'Are you all right?'

'Yes, yes.' Othman slumped down on to the front pew. 'Hand me my things, would you?' His soaking hair had stuck to his back and shoulders.

'What did you find out?'

Othman glanced at Owen. The questions were inconvenient. 'Not much. I don't think the Murkasters used this building very often. It was built for the villagers. And it was just a church.'

'Oh.' Owen looked disappointed.

Othman began to dress himself.

'Are you psychic?' Owen asked him.

'That's one word for it, I suppose.'

Owen sat down beside him. 'I have a friend who's like that. Daniel Cranton. You'll meet him tomorrow.'

'Oh, really?' Othman's interest perked up.

'Yeah, well, Daniel doesn't know it, and certainly can't use it, but it's just a feeling I have. I get feelings like that . . . and other things . . .'

Othman patted his shoulder. 'Well, we're all psychic to a degree.'

'How much do you know about that kind of stuff?'

'Enough.' He shivered. A listening presence seemed to have crept up on them. It was similar to the feeling he'd picked up at the house: cautious, wary. 'I think we should go now.'

Owen glanced around himself nervously. 'Yeah. I think so, too.'

Outside, Othman looked back at the church for a few moments. A wind had come up and the rain was coming down harder.

'Let's get back,' Owen said. 'You'll catch your death out in this. Come and have a coffee or something.'

Othman gave him an arch glance. 'Didn't think I'd be welcome.'

Owen shrugged. 'Forget it. I was just ... confused about what happened the other night.'

'Want to talk about it?'

'No, yeah, maybe.'

They walked back down to the lich-gate. 'One thing I must tell you,' Othman said. 'You and Lily are special people, Owen. Different to everyone else around here. That is one of the reasons why you are lovers. It has nothing to do with incest, and you mustn't feel bad about it.' He could tell Owen was extremely uncomfortable listening to these frank words, but Othman felt there was no point in skirting the issue.

'We don't feel bad about it,' Owen said mulishly. 'We do what we like, and I don't give a fuck what anyone else thinks. Neither does Lily.'

'Of course you don't. And you shouldn't. I don't have a *sordid* interest in your affairs, Owen. I find you both very attractive, and have become fond of you quickly. I also appreciate your difference, and would like to help you.'

'We don't need any help. We're fine.'

Othman sighed. Had he chosen the wrong way to deal with this? 'What about this Cranton boy? Lily resents him, doesn't she?'

'She's just jealous. Daniel's an outsider, and we've never become friendly with outsiders before.' He glanced at Othman. 'Except for you.'

'I'm not as much of an outsider as you think,' he said. 'What do you propose to use this Daniel for?'

'Nothing!' Owen said, too loudly. He felt he'd said far too much already, and was now regretting it. He certainly didn't want to talk to Othman about what happened at the High Place. That, more than anything he did with Lily, made him feel guilty. He knew that something about the High Place and its properties was forbidden.

'Oh come on, Owen!' Othman said harshly. 'Stop treating me like a fool. I know you want me to think you're more stupid than you are, but you can't hide the truth from me. If you want to keep secrets, learn to control your thoughts and your feelings. They glare out of you like TV advertisements half the time! I asked you a reasonable question, and I expect a reasonable answer. What do you propose to use Daniel Cranton for?'

'I don't know,' Owen said. He stopped walking, forcing Othman to halt as well.

Rain ran down Othman's face, down his drenched hair. He waited patiently, allowing Owen to wrestle with the difficult decision of confiding in him or not. 'You can trust me,' he said.

Owen stared at him. 'You know that place in the woods I took you to,' he began.

'The High Place?'

Owen nodded. 'Well, Daniel can . . . when Daniel's there, something *happens*. It's like an electric current or something, but you can absorb it.'

'You will have to show this to me.'

Owen sighed. That, he supposed, was inevitable. 'I don't think Daniel will go for that. Most of the time he won't even admit to me that he has psychic talents. Also, he doesn't know you.'

'Then you must convince him.'

'Mmm.' Owen began walking again.

'Do what you feel,' Othman said. 'Exactly what you feel. There are no judges upon this earth, other than human judges, and their judgements are worthless.' He laughed. 'You are trying to live by their rules, aren't you, and it doesn't work. Always, you are driven to break them. Then you feel bad about it. Like when we were all together the other night.'

Owen looked at him. 'Don't get the wrong idea. I've no problem about what happened, just what you might be getting out of it.'

'Well, now I hope you realize I'm concerned about you, and wouldn't do anything to hurt you or Lily. That's all the problems cleared up?'

'Yes.'

'So there's no reason why you shouldn't follow your instincts concerning Daniel Cranton, then?'

Owen was silent. A realization came to him concerning what Othman was actually suggesting. Eventually Owen said, 'You *want* me to, don't you?'

They had arrived back at the cottage. At the gate, Othman leaned forward and kissed Owen briefly on the lips. 'Soon, I will be showing you unimaginable wonders,' he said. 'Just be patient and trust me. I won't come in. The White House is only up the road. Just think about what I've said, and I'll see you tomorrow night.'

Owen watched him go. What *is* that man? he wondered. Is he dangerous or useful?

Lily rapped her knuckles against the parlour window-pane. She'd obviously been watching out for them. Owen raised a hand, went inside. Lily came flying into the kitchen. 'He kissed you! I saw!'

Owen took her in his arms, hugged her tight. 'I love you,' he said.

Lily was laughing. He realized she was excited. The remark about the kiss had not been made in censure, but desire.

Chapter Twelve

Wednesday, 21st October: High Crag House, Cornwall

Enniel knew that Aninka would be divulging the end of her story during their next interview. As she made herself comfortable, as usual, on the sofa in his office, Aninka noticed a covered trolley beside the drinks cabinet. She recognized the outlines of plates heaped with food; more comforts than usual were to be provided, then. Enniel had no doubt guessed this last session would be the most traumatic for her. Already, her mouth felt dry at the prospect.

'You will speak plainly, won't you,' Enniel said gently, placing a globe of brandy into her hands. Normally, he reserved the administering of liquor until the end of the session.

Aninka nodded. 'Yes. I've already made up my mind about that.' She glanced at him. 'It will not be easy, but I'll do it.'

Enniel smiled tightly and sat down behind his desk, creating the distance between them Aninka always needed to begin resuming her story. 'Shall we start?' His fingers hovered over the tape recorder.

'Not yet.' Aninka took a drink. 'Enniel, I need to know why all this is so important to you. I get the feeling I was involved in something much bigger than I realized. I wonder how you're going to use the information I'm giving you.'

Enniel withdrew his hand from the tape recorder. His expression was quizzical. 'I don't really know until I've heard the whole story. I have only suspicions, at present. I'm sorry, my dear, but I can't say more than that. Not yet. Now, can we begin?'

Aninka's Story: Cresterfield, October

The last Friday night Aninka spent with Othman began like any other. Aninka drove over to Grey Gables early, after Othman had called her to tell her he'd be late and would see her at the Markses' later on. She parked her car at the bottom of the drive. The smell of baking muffins wafted from Wendy's kitchen window, a scent which mingled pleasingly with the fruity, smoky late-summer aromas that filled the air. Aninka hadn't seen Wendy since the previous weekend as she'd had to go to Birmingham to organize a new exhibition of her work. Aninka had only been away for three days, but the enforced separation from Othman had been almost unendurable. She'd returned to the flat in the early hours of Friday morning, and had almost wept to find him there waiting for her. She'd wanted to devour him with love, and consequently had had very little sleep.

As she walked up the sloping driveway to Wendy's house, Aninka remembered thinking how contented she was. Perhaps that had been tempting fate.

Ivan let Aninka in, greeting her with a brief hug and kiss. No one else had arrived yet.

Wendy was busy preparing an ornate salad in the kitchen. 'Mmm, garlic!' Aninka said as she took off her soft wool jacket and slung it over a high stool.

Wendy seemed effervescent, bustling around in an almost manic manner. 'Wait till you taste it!'

'Oh, a new recipe?'

'Variation on an old favourite. Pev has given me some ingredients to try.'

Othman had not struck Aninka as being interested in cookery before. She couldn't help smiling. 'Really! This is a side of the man I've never seen!'

Wendy picked up a little crock bowl full of what looked like raw incense: herbs, small twigs, chopped root. 'Here it is. I think it has an unpronounceable name, can't remember it.'

Aninka took the bowl and sniffed. It was sweet, like a flowery perfume, but also acrid when it hit the back of her throat. She pulled a face. 'I'm not sure I want to eat this!'

'Oh, don't worry. It tastes divine. Ivan and I have had some already.' Wendy giggled in an uncharacteristic manner. Aninka felt slightly unnerved: Wendy didn't seem herself. 'I told Pev last week about . . . well, he came round one evening to see Ivan, and arrived before Ivan got home from work. I don't know quite how it happened, but I ended up telling him about . . .' She lowered her voice, her eyes flicking briefly to the kitchen door. '. . . Misty.'

It was news to Aninka that Othman had visited the Markses without her. Still, should she be surprised? She knew so little about his movements when he wasn't with her, and she only spent a few nights a week with him. No doubt, hearing about the domestic problems of the Markses would have amused him; more ant behaviour to observe. 'Was he a sympathetic listener?' Her voice, she noticed, was sharp. Wendy appeared to be oblivious of Aninka's tone.

'Oh, very. Our discussion was quite frank. He told me I needed a tonic, and Ivan, too. Our lives have become . . . very routine. This herbal mixture has been very beneficial. I feel wonderful!'

Aninka picked up the crock bowl again, and stirred its contents with her finger. A suspicion came to her. Grigori rituals sometimes involved the use of haoma, a concoction of hallucinogenic herbs which could be eaten or smoked to induce ecstasy. Haoma was a highly secret substance. Would Othman dare to give some to the Markses? Aninka herself had never taken it. Once she'd been old enough to make a choice, she'd refused to become involved in magical work with her family. Children, naturally, weren't ever given haoma.

'What's in it?' Aninka asked.

Wendy shrugged. 'Oh, just herbs and stuff. It's all harmless, and none of the ingredients is illegal. Pev assured us of that. He said we could grow them all in our garden, if we wanted to.'

'And you're going to feed it to everyone tonight?'

Wendy frowned. 'Why not? There's no harm in cheering everyone up.'

'I thought you all abstained from intoxicating substances until you'd performed your ritual.' Aninka knew she sounded accusatory, but didn't care. In her opinion, Othman was undermining the group, but perhaps he didn't know Wendy planned to use the mixture in her meal tonight.

'These are natural herbs,' Wendy said. 'It's not the same. Pev said the ancient Sumerians used to use them. It's a very old recipe.'

Aninka realized then that her suspicions concerning haoma were probably correct. What on earth was Othman playing at? Wendy was behaving differently tonight; there was an unfamiliar brittleness about her. Aninka could sense an edgy distance between herself and her friend. Had Othman said anything to cause that?

'Pev has been very helpful to us recently,' Wendy said. 'He's been having a few chats with Ivan about the rituals.'

'Has he?' Aninka interrupted sharply.

'Yes. Didn't he tell you? Well, he and Ivan have written something between them. Ivan says it's splendid. We'll have to use scripts, of course, because it's so new, and no one's seen it yet, but we're going to enact it tonight . . .'

'Let me see it,' Aninka said. She tried to keep the urgency from her voice. 'I mean, can I see it?'

Wendy frowned again. 'I don't think Ivan wants anyone to see it yet. It's to be a surprise . . .'

'Since when have you performed a ritual without everyone reading it first?' Aninka asked. 'I think we should see it, Wend.'

Wendy had paused in the act of slicing a cucumber. 'What's

the matter?' she asked. 'It sounds as if you don't trust Pev.' She smiled. 'I hope you're not jealous!'

Aninka shook her head. 'Oh, please! Of course not. I'm just surprised Pev has done this. He's mentioned nothing to me.'

'He probably just wants to surprise you, too,' Wendy said, resuming her slicing. She clearly had no suspicions. 'I don't think he's actually written any of the ritual himself, but he's lent Ivan some wonderful old books he's found.'

'What kind of books?'

'Well, I suppose they'd be archaeological. Some scholar writing about ancient rites.'

Aninka's flesh froze. 'What kind of rites? Different to what you've been doing?'

Wendy laughed. 'Oh, don't look so alarmed! They're not that different, apparently, but just a little more . . . authentic.' She paused, and directed a look of appeal at Aninka. 'Look, Ninka, you've been an enormous help to me recently. Please don't think I don't appreciate that. I value our friendship. But it's been good to see more of Pev, too. He's helped me get a new perspective on things, a man's view, I suppose. You know how worried I was about my marriage.'

'I understand that,' Aninka said, 'but why didn't you tell me about it? What did you think I'd say? I must admit I'm disappointed that you felt you had to keep Pev's visits secret from me. He is my partner, after all.' It unnerved Aninka that Peverel Othman had been paying visits to the Markses without her. Even more so that he seemed to be influencing their activities.

Wendy dropped her eyes. 'Well, there didn't seem that much to tell you! I . . . I really didn't think to mention it, and anyway, I've only seen you a couple of times since it began, and then never alone.' She sighed. 'Look, Pev has just been here to see Ivan once or twice during the past two weeks. And while you've been away, he's come for dinner every night. I think he was missing you.' She looked up at Aninka and smiled hopefully. 'We do enjoy his company, Ninka. Please don't be cross about this. Pev's so knowledgeable about the past.'

'Wendy, I don't think . . .' Aninka began, but couldn't think how to voice her suspicions without sounding as if she was being possessive about Othman. It was obvious the Markses thought highly of him, and believed he genuinely liked them and had an interest in their ceremonies. Aninka, having heard his scornful tirades against the group, knew otherwise. Or did she? To whom was Othman actually lying?

What is he up to? Aninka thought. Were his true motives for becoming associated with the group about to be revealed?

When Othman arrived, he was in a cheerful humour. As he greeted Aninka with a brief kiss to the cheek, she asked him in an undertone, 'So, you've taken on the role of director, then?'

'There's nothing wrong with a little direction, surely?' Othman responded lightly, and then avoided her eyes, moving away to greet the others, who were all waiting for his attention.

Aninka felt uneasy, but was unable to say anything more to Othman without being heard. Presumably, that was deliberate on Othman's part. She sensed he was 'off' with her. What had she done to upset him since this morning?

Wendy emerged, beaming, from the kitchen. 'Pev!' She hurried forward to embrace him, hanging on to him for just a little too long.

Aninka felt faintly sick. Were Wendy and Othman being awkward with her because something had happened between them while she'd been away? She felt as if the ground was shifting beneath her feet.

Othman handed Wendy a carrier bag, which clinked as it moved. 'A rare vintage for my lady!' he said.

Wendy cooed and batted her eyelashes – a reaction Aninka would have expected from Misty Kennedy rather than her friend. The bag contained three bottles of what appeared to be wine, which Aninka presumed were expensive. Nick Emmett apparently noticed her uneven temper. He appeared at her shoulder as everyone went to take their seats in the dining-room. 'Are you all right, Aninka? You look very frowny tonight.'

'Mm? Oh, I'm fine. Fine.' Aninka made an effort to smother her misgivings. It appeared she was the only one who could sense an unfamiliar tension in the air.

The wine was opened as Wendy brought the main course through from the kitchen. Aninka wanted to remind everyone that they usually abstained from alcohol until later, but sensed that the observation would not be appreciated tonight. Things were different.

Othman, sitting opposite Aninka, filled her glass. 'Try it,' he said.

Aninka eyed the liquid suspiciously; it was bright green in colour, like absinthe. 'You are full of unexpected delights,' she said smoothly, but did not take the glass he offered. 'First salad condiments, now expensive liquor.'

'Do try it,' Othman said again. His eyes, she thought, were utterly cold. A thread of feeling, which contained both panic and misery, wove down her spine. Pev, what is happening?

Holding his eyes with her own, Aninka sipped the wine. She felt as if he'd offered her a cup of poison, and she was demonstrating her love for him by accepting it. The drink was unexpectedly sweet, almost honeyed, with the ghost of tart herbs in its flavour. She realized its perfume was similar to that of the herb mixture Wendy had put in the salad. Haoma, Aninka thought, now sure of it. 'What is this?' she asked lightly. 'A vintage untombed from the vaults of Ur, or something?'

'Don't be ridiculous!' Othman answered with a wide grin. 'Can't you see the bottles are only three hundred years old?'

Aninka put down her glass. She felt estranged from her lover, as if she'd only just met him. This might as well be the first night he'd brought her to this house.

Wendy was heaping Aninka's plate with moussaka and salad. The red and white cabbage was speckled with the dust of Othman's mystery condiment. Aninka resolved not to touch it. She wanted, at that moment, to leave the house. Nick Emmett seemed a hot and unwelcome presence at her left side while, across from her, the ghoulish Serafina looked like a malevolent imp. For once, Serafina had managed to grab the seat next to Othman before Misty Kennedy had claimed it, and was now sitting there with a smug air of conquest. Let her have him, Aninka thought. She's welcome. Sadly, she wished this could be true. How much power people have over you when you love them. The thought was frightening.

A whoop of laughter came from down the table. Misty Kennedy had dropped a forkful of moussaka down her cleavage. Ivan, red-faced and grinning, was using his own fork to retrieve it. Aninka glanced at Wendy and was shocked by what she saw. Instead of wearing the tight expression of disapproval and defeat that Aninka would have expected, Wendy was smiling benignly at the tableau. Aninka felt totally disorientated. Was it possible she was sitting among strangers who had replaced the people she knew? She ate a small forkful of her moussaka.

'You're not eating much,' Nick said, with apparent concern. 'It's really very good, too. Are you sure you're all right?'

'Absolutely,' Aninka responded sharply. She took a drink of wine instead, forcing down the acid, sweet liquid. She felt she'd have to get drunk now to cope with the strange mood of the night, the suggestion of cold indifference from her lover, and Wendy's bizarre behaviour. He's going to get them all drunk or stoned she thought. The rite will be a travesty, or perhaps it's necessary to be intoxicated to perform it. She glanced again at Misty and Ivan flirting unashamedly down the table. She drank more wine, and ate more moussaka. Perhaps the drink had stimulated her appetite, for now she felt ravenous. But she would not touch the salad.

She realized the pressure she'd thought was Nick's thigh against her own was actually his hand. She flicked a discreet glance down at her lap, prompting Nick to squeeze her flesh, just below the groin. She stared at his fingers. There was no impulse to push him away. Encouraged, he pressed his hand against her crotch. Aninka looked him in the eye. He appeared to be very drunk. She wondered, vaguely, why she didn't feel angry or disgusted at his importunity. Nick's tongue shot out to lick his lips in a suggestive manner. Aninka felt herself grow hot and recognized the undeniable stab of lust that pushed through her belly.

By the end of the main course, the group were all laughing and talking loudly. Inhibitions were clearly lowered, if not cast away. Aninka sat in a daze, an observer, while Nick Emmett continued to caress her thigh. Wendy looked as if she was about to slip off her chair and disappear beneath the table. Serafina's black eye make-up had begun to slide down her face, and her red lipstick was smeared around her mouth, giving her a totally dissipated appearance. Once Othman's wine was finished, Ivan had produced some bottle of his own: a young, dry red. Aninka noticed that Othman continually filled Serafina's glass with wine for her. It looked as if the girl might be sick at any moment. Down the table, Misty was inserting lettuce fragments down the front of her dress, and Ivan, cheered on by the other men, was retrieving them with his mouth. Wendy watched with a passive smile as her husband came up for air and then plunged his face into Misty's bosom again. Aninka could not speak. She felt separate from the proceedings, yet tranquil.

There was no carefully produced dessert to end the meal that night. Othman got to his feet, and cried, 'Let the rite begin!' He looked feral, powerful, the very image of a Fallen One, his hair tumbling over his shoulders, his eyes wide and dark, yet shining with an inner light.

The group all cheered and followed Othman in a shambling, giggling line to the garage. Aninka and Nick came last. Before they left the dining-room, Nick virtually threw Aninka up against the wall. Her body felt liquid; she did not resist, nor did she want to. She felt his hand slide beneath the silk of her underwear, a sudden invasion of her body. His fingers rubbed her furiously for a few seconds, further igniting her desire. She realized, dimly, she must be affected by Othman's wine, yet was so intoxicated that she did not care. Someone called her name from the corridor that led to the garage, and Nick released her. They stared at one another for a couple of seconds, each aware that soon they would be slaking their lust with one another.

Nick smiled. 'Come on.' Aninka followed him to the garage.

The candles and incense were already lit, and Ivan had put a tape on the hi-fi system, which was concealed behind one of the wall hangings. The sound of rhythmic chanting pumped softly in the background. The group arranged themselves in a circle. Aninka noticed that none of them had bothered getting changed into regalia tonight. Was that an oversight because of their drunkenness? Othman stood with his back to the group, before the altar. He had stripped to the waist, his hair hanging down like a flag of dusty, pale rags, its longest locks brushing the waistband of his leather trousers. Aninka's heart turned over in her chest at the sight of him, then Nick Emmett took her hand in his own. She knew that Othman would not be with her this night, and that he would not care that another man was claiming the privilege.

After a few moments of shuffling and whispering, the group fell silent. Othman raised his arms. He began to speak in a tongue unfamiliar to the group, but which Aninka recognized as a dialect of ancient Persia. She herself was not fluent in it, because it was used only in high ceremonial rites among her people, but she had heard it occasionally at weddings and funerals. Even then, it was used only sparingly, to describe the inner secrets of love and death. Now Othman began the elemental invocations to create the inner temple. At each of the four quarters around the circle, he paused and uttered an incantation, his long fingers describing intricate gestures through the smoke of incense. In the east, he cried, 'Yazatas Vayu!' Aninka experienced a feeling of mild shock. He was uttering the hidden names, which were kept secret from the majority of humans, other than those who had miraculously held on to vestiges of the old ways, and who had their own esoteric societies. The names themselves possessed great *power. As Othman called to the angel of the wind, a ghost of a breeze lifted the hangings around the temple. In the south, he cried, 'Yazatas anam nanat!' and the air became moist with the presence of water. In the west, he called, 'Yazatas atar neryosang!' and the candles blazed more brightly. In the north, Othman called, 'Yazatas zam!' and a smell of ripe earth filled the air.*

Aninka felt as if her hair was crackling with static; her heart was beating hard. This was Grigori magic, performed here in this suburban house, among people whom she could not imagine possessed the spiritual strength to cope with it. She hoped they would be safe, and spoke a brief prayer to Anahita, a benign goddess-form: 'Protect them!'

Othman turned to face the group. His countenance looked sensuously demonic. Aninka doubted he would recognize her now if she spoke to him. Why, Pev? she asked silently. Why this? What is it you're looking for? She felt immeasurably sorrowful.

He began a whispered chant and presently the rest of the group joined in: 'Armaity, druj, marezehdika.'

Aninka would not speak the words. They would, she felt, turn her tongue black: words of hatred and falsehood. An insistent, gentle voice in her mind, perhaps even the presence of Anahita herself, urged Aninka to break away from the group and run from the house without looking back once. The voice was not strong enough. Aninka was held immobile in the web of the chanted words.

She turned to Nick to say something, utter some warning if she could, but found she could not make herself understood. She was speaking the same language as Othman. Nick laughed at her, clearly delighted. Aninka shut her mouth, tried to begin again, her lips twisting around the words. She had lost the ability to speak in English. It felt as if she'd split into two people: one was the silent Aninka, who was appalled by what was happening; the other was a woman who could speak in an ancient tongue and who welcomed the ceremony to come. This woman beat the silent

Aninka back, and soon there was only She, a creature stripped of contemporary restraints, an archetype of her people.

The other members of the group were still swaying and chanting the words. They turned to one another and began to remove each other's clothes. Othman presided over them like a flame, approving their actions. Aninka caught his eye, and dropped her jaw to hiss and snarl at him. His eyes burned back at her. She dropped to all fours, and Nick Emmett was tearing her clothes from her back. Turning round, she lashed out at him, her clawed fingers ripping his shirt. She lunged up to rend the fabric with her teeth. Nick laughed, holding on to her wrists to keep her from mauling him. There was no sense whatever that what they were doing was either irregular or debauched. The rest of the group, now whispering their chant, had gathered round Aninka and Nick in a tight circle. Their hot breath misted on the air. Aninka lay naked upon the richly coloured rugs. Nick removed the rest of his clothes. He knelt between Aninka's parted thighs and entered her slowly. No detail was spared for the onlookers, yet it did not disturb Aninka that people were watching. No part of herself was aghast or ashamed.

What followed was a surreal spectacle of heaving bodies and bizarre cries. At one point, Aninka closed her eyes, and opened them to find Ernie Brock's scarlet face behind Nick's shoulder. The weight of two men was upon her. She wrapped her legs around both of them, as if her limbs were suddenly twice their normal length. The pleasure experienced by her body was intense, unlike anything she'd felt before. It was sex without emotion, purely physical, as if the commerce of bodies was delicious food and she was starving for it.

There came a moment of stillness, when she realized she was alone within the group. Rising unsteadily to her feet, she picked a weaving path among the writhing shapes around her. Othman had Serafina spread-eagled on the altar, and was fucking her with an expressionless face, standing between her dangling legs, staring at the wall. He noticed Aninka approaching and withdrew. 'You *want her? It's good. Taste.'* The girl's skinny, white body looked like something made from icing sugar, friable and sweet. Aninka licked the concave belly, then let Othman drag her by her hair to sample more secret flavours. There was a candle of pain inside her as he pierced her body from behind. His fingers dug into her breasts like claws. She bit the girl, and the resulting scream sounded like a heavenly choir. Lifting her head, she bayed out a string of words. It was a guttural croak, like a vomiting sound. 'Dushmata, dushhakta, dush ahu!' And there was a greater foreign presence in the room with them, enveloping them all in a mist of ancient hungry lust and excitement. Othman thrust Aninka away, and, raising his arms, began to shout out the words of an invocation. 'Angra mainyu! Dushhavarshta!' Serafina's thin body wriggled and jerked upon the altar.

It's coming down, Aninka thought, the first coherent thought she'd had for what seemed like hours. She sensed something forming around them, enveloping the house. It was like a swirling black hole, a void, the gateway to the abyss.

Why, Pev? she thought again sadly, and his voice answered her, the voice she knew, from before this terrible night: *the gate. I have to go beyond the gate. Cannot stop. Have to . . . The pain, the sorrow of grief, the love, my love.*

There was more, but a sudden movement eclipsed the words from Aninka's mind.

Wendy had leapt to her feet, and was bursting out of the mêlée of struggling bodies, her body shaking with hysterical laughter. She began to extinguish all the candles in the room, her voluptuous body an amorphous white shape flitting in slow motion from quarter to quarter. Soon, everything was in darkness but for the muted glow of the incense bowls. Serafina began to howl, to sing, to chatter. She squeaked like a rodent, barked like a bitch. Aninka's head was suffused with an excruciating pain. *I have to get out!* She sensed, then, in a shining moment of clarity, exactly what was happening. Othman was about to sacrifice Serafina to *the being whose essence was beginning to envelop the temple. Was he truly so greedy for power?*

'Why, Pev, why?' Aninka's voice was a hoarse scream.

'It is the only way,' he answered, his voice like a coil of thick smoke through the dark. 'The gate is closed to me, but there are others who are stronger, who can open it for me.'

'But not this! You can't summon this!' Aninka's voice tailed off. She had no idea what Othman meant about gates. All she knew was that something terrible was about to happen. A string of words whispered through her mind, felt rather than thought. *The False One, he's coming . . . Deep within her, an instinct screamed out in a desperate voice: 'Flee, or it will suck in your soul!'*

Somehow, she found the strength to pull herself away from Othman and the binding power he was creating. She fell heavily to the floor, uttering a cry of pain as she twisted her ankle. Crawling, she hauled her body, which suddenly felt too heavy to move, towards the door of the garage, visible only as a darker rectangle in the dim light. It seemed a thousand clawing fingers sought to hold her back, snagging her hair, raking the skin of her back and buttocks. The door didn't seem to be getting any closer, and Aninka began to weep in fear and frustration. Oh Great Shem, help me! Help me! *Then the door was in front of her, and with stiff, unwieldy fingers, she managed to turn the handle and push it open. With a final burst of effort, she threw herself across the threshold. She wanted to curl up and sleep, cover her head, but knew she needed more distance between herself and what was happening behind her. With her limbs shrieking in agony, she dragged herself up the short corridor that led back to the main body of the house. She could see a light ahead, too bright. She could hear the hum of kitchen appliances. Eventually, she reached the sanctuary of the kitchen, which was filled with the comforting aromas of cooking. Here, Aninka lay down, gibbering, upon the tiled floor, curling into a foetal position in an attempt to protect herself from what she knew was coming down to the house. Her* throat was dry, and it hurt her to sob. She put her hands hard against her ears, screwed up her eyes. No sound. No light. Only darkness.

She must have awoken only a couple of hours later. Her head was astoundingly clear. For a brief moment, memories came hurtling back, but she dismissed them. With utter calm, she stood up and went naked to Wendy's bedroom, where she took a skirt and jumper from the wardrobe. Pausing only to retrieve her handbag from the dining-room, she walked out of the house barefoot, closing the front door gently behind her, and went to her car. The clock on the dashboard told her it was three a.m. Her mind blank, Aninka drove carefully home. She turned on the radio, hummed along to vacuous pop songs.

Back at her flat, she took a long shower, then dried her hair and went to bed. It was impossible to sleep. Revolting images of what had happened assailed her mind, memories she had to banish with force. She did not want to think about it. At five o'clock, she glanced at her bedside alarm. *Pev, where are you?* She chided herself for the thought even as it formed in her brain. He had revealed himself as false, yet still some part of her felt it was something from the past, something too dreadful to be articulated, which impelled him to do the things he did. She loved him. She could not help it. *There must be an explanation for why he needed to call upon the False One. She would listen without judging him, if he'd only come to her. Now!*

He'll not come here, *a cruel, cold voice whispered in her mind.* You are nothing to him. You never were. You'll never see him again.

Aninka groaned and turned away from the clock. The voice, for all its cruelty, spoke the truth. She knew it did.

Aninka didn't get out of bed until three o'clock in the afternoon. She'd heard her answerphone take a couple of calls from her agent and Noah. Had Noah somehow picked up on what had happened to her? She hadn't heard from him for weeks. Her body and mind felt numb, which allowed her to examine the previous night's events with a certain sang froid. Her people had a name for Othman's kind: Anakim. Users, berserkers, abusers. He was sick. People like the Markses and their friends were just playthings to such a man. Should she call Wendy? It was perhaps significant that no one had bothered to get in touch with Aninka herself. Did they scorn her for walking out on their ritual antics, or did they feel ashamed? Was she regarded as Othman's ally or as a traitor? Aninka stared at the phone by her bed. She repeated Othman's number in her head, but could not force herself to call him and leave a message. Yet the thought still plagued her, despite her earlier conviction she'd never see him again: would he call her soon?

At half past three, Aninka got out of bed and shrugged herself into the balm of a silk dressing-gown. She inspected her body for bruises, found a mark upon her hip. In the kitchen she took a half-empty magnum of champagne from the fridge, found it flat, but drank it anyway, from the bottle. She wandered into her work-room, still swigging, and threw a rag over the painting on the easel. It looked like him. Then, she sat on the floor by the window and spent a few cleansing minutes crying. This, she told herself passionlessly as she wept, was a purge. She had loved him, given him her heart, and he had only disgusted and disappointed her in return.

After the release of weeping, she phoned Noah back. As the line purred in her ear, she wondered whether she was going to tell him anything. This sort of thing should be reported, but she shrank from mentioning to any authorities her own involvement in the proceedings. Noah was out. His voice drawled out of the machine at the other end of the line.

'Returned your call,' Aninka said, after the tone. 'I'm in. Where are you?'

The living-room smelled stale. She opened a window, let in the city sounds. Then came a few minutes' recrimination. She should

*have realized Othman was off the rails. His behaviour had
provided a casebook of warning signals. How stupid to be
glamorized by his beauty. Stupid, stupid. Had she learned nothing
from life? Irritated with herself, she flopped down on to the sofa
and picked up the TV remote control. Blankly, she watched the
news; wars here, famine there, political bickering. Was nothing
good happening in the world, nowadays? She called Noah again,
said, 'I need to speak to you,' to the machine. She would not
contact any of her other cousins, because she didn't feel able to
cope with their outbursts, and there was no way she could speak to
anyone at the moment without saying something, something,
about last night.*

*The local news came on the TV. Aninka wasn't interested. It
was all too petty for words. Vandalism at a local church, money
for a charity, a celebrity grinning like a mask at the camera.
'Bollocks!' Aninka said aloud, and muted the sound on the TV.
She picked up a magazine, leafed through it. Articles on orgasms
and relationships. This she did not need. Perhaps there was a
film on another TV channel. She threw down the magazine and
glanced at the screen. Her body froze.*

*There was a picture on the screen of a face she knew, an out of
focus, bleached image. Serafina. Aninka grabbed the remote and
padded up the sound.*

*'If anyone has any information they think might help the police,
please call one of the following numbers . . .'*

What?

*The piece was finished. Aninka stood up, stared at the TV,
energized by a kind of bleak dread. She had to wait until the end
of the report for the main headlines to be repeated. There it was.
No surprise, really. It sickened her it was no surprise. Girl found
dead in car park, sexually assaulted. Serafina.*

*Aninka picked up the phone, dialled Wendy's number without
thinking. It was answered almost immediately. 'Wendy?' Aninka
said.*

'No, I'm sorry, Wendy's not here. Who's calling, please?'

There was something about the voice that Aninka didn't like. She put down the phone without saying anything more.

In the bedroom, she dressed quickly, pulling on black trousers, black shirt, a leather jacket, biker boots. She wound up her hair, and as she left the flat, picked up a pair of shades from on top of the microwave in the kitchen.

It was getting near rush hour and already traffic filled the streets of the city. Aninka sat fuming in a tailback. She lit a cigarette and turned on the radio, pushing buttons until she found the local station. Inane music filled the car. Aninka looked at her watch. How long till a news report? The traffic began to move. Aninka edged towards the other side of the city.

Out on the dual carriageway, she put her foot down, flying up the outside lane. Her hands were wet upon the steering wheel. She pulled on to Victoria Heights and parked her car by a row of shops. Here, she went into the newsagents and bought a paper and some cigarettes. Catching a glimpse of her reflection in the shop window, she realized she was too conspicuous in her terrorist garb. She took off the shades and the leather jacket. Only her height betrayed her now, she thought.

It took her five minutes to walk up the hill to the turning which led to Brontë Close. There was a phone box at the end of the road. Obeying her instincts, the wordless shout of alarm in her guts, Aninka went into the phone box and picked up the phone. She could see all the way down Brontë Close, and, as she feared, it was packed with police vehicles. Red and white tape fluttered in the breeze, marking an exclusion zone. Ambulances were there, TV crews. Neighbours were crowding against the tape, ghoulishly craning forward. Aninka's spine crawled. She feared recognition, pursuit.

As she walked briskly back to her car, she expected a police vehicle to draw up alongside her at any moment. 'Would you mind answering a few questions?' Her heart was hammering in her chest by the time she nervelessly operated the central locking of her car and swung into the driver's seat. Without pausing, she

233

set off smoothly, trying to appear calm. She was a woman who'd stopped to buy cigarettes and a paper, to make a phone call. That was all. Not suspicious at all. Had any of Wendy's neighbours noticed her on the occasions she'd called at Brontë Close? What about friends, relatives, who weren't connected with the magical group? Had any members spoken of knowing Aninka to anyone?

She drove round to Noah's house. His car was parked out front. Weak with relief, Aninka ran up the steps and rang the doorbell. There was no immediate response. She rang again, a long, impatient pressure on the button. Eventually, the intercom sputtered and Noah said, 'Yeah?'

'It's me,' Aninka answered. 'Let me in now, you bastard!'

She heard the locking mechanism churn and opened the door. The long, Victorian hallway was almost in darkness. 'Noah?' she called.

He came down the wide stairway, belting a bath-robe. 'What is it?'

'Were you asleep?' Aninka gabbled. 'I've been calling you all day! You might have answered the phone.'

'I've been in bed,' Noah answered. 'What's up?'

'I don't suppose you've seen the news?'

She followed him into the kitchen. He looked sleepy, sensual, dragged from a bed of lust, no doubt. 'No.' He took a carton of fresh orange juice from the fridge, swigged from it. 'Should I have?'

'I'm in trouble, Noah. That guy I met, Peverel Othman. He's Anakim. People are dead, hurt. Something terrible's happened . . .' She felt tears come, despised herself for it. 'Give me a drink, will you.'

Noah said nothing, but got her a glass of wine. 'Have you called home?'

'No! Noah, what am I going to do? I'm implicated. I was with him. Bloody hell!' She blinked back tears, wiping her face, then drank some wine, and scrabbled in her bag for a cigarette.

'You'd better tell me about it.' It was typical of Noah to be

*like this, deadpan, unconcerned. It was one of the things she liked
most about him. He never got hysterical, or over-reacted. She
followed him into his living-room, one of his living-rooms.*

*There, he dragged the story out of her with cold, probing
questions. When she'd finished, he put a full bottle of wine down
on the coffee table in front of her, and went to the phone.*

*'What are you doing?' Aninka asked, refilling her glass. She
felt better now, drained. She'd passed the story on. It didn't feel
like hers any more.*

'What do you think?'

She stood up. 'You can't! Please don't.'

*'Ninka, we have to. Fuck Othman, we need to get you out of
this mess.' He pushed his hair back behind his free ear, changed
his stance. Someone had answered. 'Hi, it's Noah. Can I speak to
Enniel?'*

*Aninka made a sound and sat down again. She didn't want to
hear this conversation, but couldn't force herself to leave the room.
Noah spoke quietly, relating the bare facts in a flat tone. 'Uh
huh, I'll tell her. Right. Bye.' He put down the phone.*

'Well?' Aninka asked.

*He shrugged. 'They'll see to it. Don't worry. You have to go
home, talk to Enniel.'*

Aninka groaned. 'Oh great!'

*'What did you expect?' Noah strolled over to her, sat down in
a chair opposite, laced his hands loosely between his knees.*

*'It wasn't my fault,' Aninka said. 'Stop staring at me like
that. Don't judge me, OK?'*

*'I wasn't,' Noah answered. 'I was just thinking this was all I
needed. I was having such a good time.'*

'Sorry to interrupt.'

*'Couldn't be helped. I don't mind, really. Do you want to stay
here for a couple of days?'*

'I'd like to. When have I got to see Enniel?'

'When you're ready. There's no rush.'

Aninka sighed miserably. 'I can't believe this is happening!'

Noah stood up, reached out to stroke her hair. 'Never mind. Perhaps you'd better keep the TV on, see what's happened. Do you mind if I go back upstairs?'

She shook her head. 'No, I'll be fine.'

Left alone, she sat staring at the TV for a while before she dared turn it on. Halfway through the second Australian soap opera, Noah came back downstairs. He was dressed, his hair wet. He helped himself to one of Aninka's two remaining cigarettes from the packet she'd left on the coffee table. Shyly, two young Goth types followed him into the room, one male, one female. He told them to go to the kitchen and they slunk out.

Noah sat and held Aninka's hand as they watched the local news report. At one point, Aninka said, 'Turn it off,' but Noah wouldn't. Everyone was dead. Everyone. The house on Brontë Close would go down in history as a place of carnage. The connection had already been made with Serafina. Some piece of evidence must have been with her body when she'd been found earlier that day. Thankfully, the method of killing wasn't re-vealed. They were just bodies. Bodies removed from a house. Aninka turned away from the footage of covered stretchers being carried into the ambulances. It was impossible to believe that Wendy, Enid and the others were extinguished from life. She found herself wondering what their faces had looked like when they'd been found. It was terrible.

'You need more than wine,' Noah said, and offered her pills. Taking these, she slept on the sofa, waking up in the middle of the night, to find Noah and his friends watching a video, a pirate copy of a recently released blockbuster. Her mouth felt sour, her head thick. Noah told the girl to make Aninka a sandwich, and the boy went with her to the kitchen. 'This is my cousin,' Noah told them, as if it mattered. Hadn't they wondered who this strange female was as she'd slept?

'He's got to be stopped,' Aninka said. 'I want to stop him.'

Noah raised an eyebrow. 'Is that your responsibility? You've reported in. What else can you do?'

*Aninka paused, wondering whether she should tell the truth.
'Noah, he touched me, he invaded every pore of me. He used me.
He killed my friends. What other reasons do I need?'*

*'There is only one reason,' Noah answered. 'Our own security.
And there are people who will see to that. The rest . . .' He
waved a hand at her dismissively. 'Unimportant. Brief lives
snuffed out. On the scale of time, they missed only a second. It's
irrelevant. You've attached too much emotional dross to it.'*

*'I can't look at people in that way,' Aninka replied. 'I can't be
so heartless.'*

*'Save your heart for your own,' Noah said, patting her knee.
'Anyway, I expect your friend, Peverel Othman, will be long gone
by now. He's old, Ninka. He knows the score. He knows our
people will come looking for him. They'll never find him. He's
probably done this kind of thing a thousand times before. All we
can do is cover up the mess, deal with people, quieten things down.
You know this. It's our legacy.'*

Aninka was shivering. She could tell Enniel more about
what Noah had said to her during the few days she'd
spent in his house, but could see little point. No doubt
Noah had already related all this to her guardian
anyway. Once she lapsed into silence, Enniel waited a
few moments for her to continue and then turned off the
tape recorder. He drew in a long breath, tapping his lips
with arched fingertips. Aninka couldn't break the silence.
She felt sick, disorientated. In her guts was a terrible
longing, a crippling sense of grief.

'Do you know the significance of the gate Othman
spoke of?' Enniel said.

Aninka jumped at the sound of his voice. It was over
now. She'd done her part, and had no desire to speak of
it further. She shook her head. 'Should I?'

Enniel screwed up his face. 'Well . . . I'm only guessing
of course, but over the centuries many misguided Grigori

237

have tried to reopen the stargate, our access to the Source, that which was lost to us a long time ago.'

Aninka frowned and shrugged. 'I don't pay much attention to legends.'

Enniel laughed dryly. 'You have made that clear to me. Still, just because something has become distant in time, you shouldn't dismiss it entirely.'

'So what is the stargate? Where is it?'

Enniel stood up and walked slowly across the room to stand staring at a tapestry next to the window. 'It's not a physical gate, my dear, but symbolically it is seen as the constellation of Orion. It is a psychic portal to which our ancestors had access. In trance, they concentrated their attention upon Orion and were able to pass through it to a place beyond space and time, the Source of the universe, a void that exists for ever in no-time, before the creation of the multiverse, all the different universes that comprise our multireality.'

Aninka shook her head. 'You're losing me, Enniel. Do I have to hear this? What has this to do with Othman?'

Enniel ignored her interruption. 'Beyond the stargate, the Anannage could commune with the very fabric of creation, what is known to the less articulate as God. It is where we acquired our knowledge, the knowledge that set us apart from the other races of the earth, made us what we are, or were.' He turned away from the tapestry. 'But the gate has been closed to us for millennia, since the Fall. Did Othman ever say anything else to you about a gate? Anything, no matter how brief or apparently trivial?'

Aninka frowned. 'I can't remember. I don't think so.' She opened her mouth, then shut it quickly.

'Yes?' Enniel enquired lightly.

'It's, well, not much, but Pev sometimes talked in his

sleep. Usually, it was gibberish, or it didn't even wake me up, but once he sounded really upset, so I tried to wake him. He cried out and almost flew at me. Then he said, "They have closed the gate for eternity. I am within it." It was a bit weird, but he calmed down very quickly, then told me he'd had a nightmare about being bound up, or something.'

Enniel nodded. 'Ah ... You did not mention this in your narrative.'

Aninka felt a surge of anger. She experienced a need to move and went to help herself to more brandy. 'There is a lot of stuff I haven't told you, because I can't remember it all at once. Do you want to know about him going with me to supermarkets or taking my clothes to the cleaners? How do I know what is important and what isn't? I've revealed to you some of the most intimate details of my life, and now you're complaining because I haven't told you enough!' She drank half a glass of brandy in one swallow. It burned the back of her throat, but she refused to cough, blinking back the tears which followed, because she didn't want Enniel to think she was crying.

Enniel came to her side, put a hand upon her shoulder. 'Ninka,' he said softly. There was concern in his voice, and sympathy. Aninka was prey to his compassion. When he gently pulled her against him, she could only cling to him and weep. 'I love him,' she said. 'I still do. Even after all that. What's wrong with me?'

Enniel stroked her back. 'Ssh. It's all right. You can't help loving him.'

Aninka raised her head. 'But he's *evil*. I hate myself for what I feel! Why can't I stop? It's so pointless and self-destructive! What has he done to me?'

Enniel led her back to the sofa and sat down beside her, cradling her against him. 'He is a very special man,

Ninka. People can't help but love him. That is part of his power that cannot be taken away or limited.'

'You know him, don't you,' Aninka said. It gave her comfort to think that.

'No,' Enniel replied. 'I don't. But I know *of* him. I have not been given sanction to disclose any further information to you, Ninka. I'm sorry about that. Stay here a while longer, and the situation may change.'

Aninka uttered a watery laugh. 'I want to hide for ever. I want to be a child again.' She drew away from Enniel. 'Thanks. I'd like to stay a while.'

Chapter Thirteen

Same day: Little Moor

Verity found, much to her own annoyance, that she was looking forward to the dinner party. Tuesday, she had given Mrs Roan a list of provisions to buy, and together they had discussed the menu over tea. After breakfast the following morning, Verity herself had driven with Mrs Roan over to the supermarket outside Patterham, where they had spent a very pleasant hour choosing the right ingredients for the meal. Verity bought bunches of flowers from the garage attached to the supermarket, and it was in a spirit of excitement that the two women drove back to Little Moor.

Raven was waiting just inside the door as they entered the house. Verity stooped to stroke his broad head. He did not particularly like being picked up, she'd found, but enjoyed a decorous caress, as long as she did not touch his body. Huge pluming tail held aloft, Raven preceded the women into the kitchen, where the initial preparations were begun.

Louis had shrewdly allowed Verity to organize everything herself, but was secretly pleased she seemed to be enjoying it. He ventured into the kitchen area at lunchtime, and, seeing his daughter's obvious excitement, decided he'd suggested this meal not one moment too soon. Clearly, this was what Verity needed. He hoped her mood would carry over into the evening, so that no one would think he lived with a miserable, sour-faced creature. How wonderful it would be if she befriended the Winter girl, for example. Louis's imagination roamed.

He thought of seeing the two young women going off on shopping expeditions, their heads bent over some mutual creative project, dressing up and filling the house with the air of perfume before they drove off together to some party or an assignation with boys in a pub. Louis sighed. If only that could happen.

Verity caught him day-dreaming. 'Stop moping around, Dad, and get out of the way. On second thoughts, peel these mushrooms.'

Smiling, Louis was happy to comply.

Lily appraised herself in the cheval-glass in her bedroom. It was six o'clock and she'd not long got back home after her visit to Patterham with Barbara. They'd stopped for coffee in a wonderful dimly lit bar, and had ended up chatting for longer than they'd intended, Lily's magical bags of purchases beneath the table. Barbara had taken her to several dress shops, where Lily had tried on a number of outfits. Barbara had hummed and ahed, while Lily twirled in front of her. 'Well?'

'Mmm. No.'

To Lily all the floating fabrics were beautiful, and she'd have been happy to buy nearly every garment she'd tried on. Barbara, however, was looking for something special. Eventually, they found it. A floor-length dress of translucent voile, tight to the bust, then flowing out in a mass of soft swathes. The colours were oceanic, dark greens, muted aquamarines. It was also very expensive, but as it went so well with Lily's red hair, and accentuated her slim figure so attractively, it had to be the one. Then leggings and a long-sleeved top had to be acquired to be worn underneath the dress, which would otherwise be rather too 'saucy', as Barbara put it. Lily would have liked to go for bright orange, but Barbara politely suggested black.

Now Lily examined herself in the mirror, intoxicated by her own reflection. She'd washed her hair, pinned some of it up, while the rest fell over her shoulders. She felt like a mermaid, or a transformed mermaid, something that belonged in the ocean, but had come to dry land to cause mischief, to break hearts. She dismissed the thought of Peverel Othman from her mind, and sat down to apply her make-up.

In his bedroom, Owen Winter made his own preparation, no less carefully. He wore the leather trousers he kept for the weekend excursions to night-clubs with his friends. He wore a loose white shirt. He felt strangely clean and scoured. There was no cheval-glass in Owen's room, but a fading, image-warping mirror above the dust-coated dressing-table. Here Owen regarded himself. He thought he looked like a ghost, but the image was pleasing.

At seven-thirty, Barbara and Barney met Peverel Othman in the hall of The White House. They were walking up to Low Mede rather than travelling in the Land Rover so that Barbara could drink, even though the air was rather chill, and there was a smell of rain in it. Othman's hair hung loose around his shoulders. Barbara thought he looked like a rock star. She wanted to touch him, and knew that she could: reach out with the fingertips and touch. It was more delicious not to do it. Barney looked at Othman askance, probably, Barbara thought, wondering what he was doing socializing with a person of Othman's type. If Audrey had brought one home as a boyfriend, Barney would have gagged.

The three of them walked through the dark. Othman was wearing a strongly scented aftershave, like nothing Barbara had ever smelled before. 'What is it?' she asked.

His smile was white and feral through the darkness. 'Something very old. It's probably gone off by now.'

Barney, if he ever wore aftershave, went for sensible smells, potions that smelled like clean male sweat, salty, but with no hint of musk.

Low Mede looked welcoming, huddled amid its garland of old trees. Amber lights shone from the windows; the chimneys reared reassuringly against the sky. Barbara turned her heel on the gravel of the drive, causing a few moments' activity, as she hopped around to retrieve her shoe, holding on to Othman's hard arm for support. She could smell the perfume of his own body beneath that of the aftershave, a scent of corn and ozone. It was unbearable. She made a promise to herself that she would have him, eventually. She could not stand it if she didn't.

As they stood in the porch, having rung the ornate, cast-iron bell, Lily and Owen came wafting up the drive behind them. Barbara fought to suppress the heat of jealousy that rose in her breast. Lily was wearing the beautiful dress, which floated around her body like water weed. Over it, she wore a fringed shawl. So young, so slim, so graceful. Barbara reminded herself severely that she had been the one to choose the dress, and should not be upset if it complimented the girl so well. Lily held lightly on to her brother's arm. Barbara had never seen Owen look so appealing either. It was as if the potential of the twins had been coaxed out, or unleashed, she wasn't sure which.

'Hi!' Lily said, raising an arm in greeting.

'You look lovely!' Barbara enthused.

Lily smiled at Barney and Othman, drinking in the approving inspection. She seemed feverish, over-excited, as if on her way to the opening night of a play, or a magical ball.

'Evening, Mrs Eager,' Owen drawled. 'Thanks for taking Lily out today.'

'A pleasure,' Barbara said. 'And please, call me Barbara.'

The door to Low Mede opened, and Verity Cranton stood at the threshold. Barbara felt herself tense up, but Verity seemed quite relaxed. She smiled and said, 'Hello. Come in.'

The hall of Low Mede was bathed in low light, and the air was thick with the scent of flowers, underscored by the smell of wood polish. A huge display of fresh blooms erupted over the hall table. The floor boards gleamed dully around the edge of the Persian rug that covered most of the floor.

Verity led the way into the lounge. She was wearing a long, black dress, her hair pinned up in a chignon. Barbara thought she looked about thirty-five, but a very attractive thirty-five. What would Othman think of her? Would he be attracted by Verity's precise aloofness?

'This is Peverel Othman,' Barbara said to Verity, and then, 'and this is my husband, Barney.'

Verity submitted the men to a brief inspection, inclining her head to each.

'And this is my sister, Lily,' said Owen. 'I don't think you've met.'

'No,' said Verity, not looking at Owen. 'Hello.'

Lily shrugged awkwardly. 'Hi.'

Verity glided over to a sideboard. 'What would everyone like to drink?'

Barbara was surprised by Verity's demeanour. She seemed the perfect hostess. As the drinks orders were taken, Louis came into the room, leaning on his stick. His face betrayed his pain, but only slightly. Louis brought with him a more congenial atmosphere. He greeted Barney with loud joviality, joked with the

245

Winter twins, complimented Lily on her outfit. Lily went red in a pretty fashion, and bashfully accepted the praise. Everyone was directed to seats, while Verity drifted among them, dispensing drinks from a silver tray.

Daniel Cranton hovered outside the room, listening to the laughter and conversation coming through the door. He felt awkward about joining the party, embarrassed about seeing Owen in this unfamiliar setting. It all seemed so false to him, a travesty. What was Owen thinking now, having to sit among all that chit-chat, that silly, shallow socializing? There would be sarcastic comments to follow, Daniel was sure. He braced himself and went into the room.

Owen looked completely at home, sprawled on the sofa next to his sister. He glanced at Daniel as he came through the door, flashing a heart-stopping smile.

'Daniel! You might have changed!' Verity scolded, and then as the atmosphere congealed around her harsh tone, softened it with a mocking laugh.

Daniel was dressed in ripped jeans and an old, faded black T-shirt. Louis couldn't help wincing inside, conscious of the fact that the Winters had at least made an effort. Typical of Daniel, he supposed. 'Drink, son?' he said.

Daniel nodded sulkily, immediately aware he had made a mistake in his choice of clothes – a choice over which he had deliberated for at least an hour. He'd been convinced Owen would turn up looking extremely scruffy and had dressed down in an attempt to defuse the situation. Yet here was Owen looking groomed and splendid, his sister as elegant and appealing as a slender supermodel beside him.

Presently, Verity disappeared discreetly from the room, only to put her head around the door a few minutes later to announce that dinner was ready. Louis offered Lily his arm in a gallant fashion and they led the way across the hall. Louis caught a glimpse of himself in the long mirror beside the front door. So long since a beautiful woman had held his arm. He liked the picture, and experienced the first, faint stirrings of desire, after a long desert of arid feeling.

Behind him, Barbara froze upon her husband's arm. Was this pretty little waif going to captivate every man Barbara was interested in? She had noticed Louis's glance into the mirror, and read its significance only too keenly.

'You ladies are outnumbered tonight,' Louis said as they all sat down. He had suggested the Winter twins sit either side of him near the top of the table. 'But it seems we gentlemen must consider ourselves fortunate to be in the company of such lovely creatures as yourselves!'

Verity smiled thinly from the other end of the table, wondering how much her father had had to drink before the guests arrived.

'Barbara tells me you write,' Louis said to Lily as they began the soup.

She coloured again. 'Well, a little.' She wished Barbara wouldn't tell people that.

'I hope you'll come to our meetings soon,' he continued.

'I don't think I'm ready for that yet,' Lily answered, and then, because she thought that might have sounded rude, 'I need to practise a bit first.'

'Lily's being very coy about her writing,' Barbara said, stranded further down the table. She was sitting next to Barney, with Daniel Cranton opposite. Peverel Othman was being very quiet and reserved, concentrating on his soup, and not looking at anyone.

Lily couldn't help feeling that Barbara's remark was a little barbed. Had she done something to offend the woman?

'Then she must be the same as Dad,' Verity said, daintily sipping her soup. She'd sensed that Barbara was jealous of Lily Winter, and decided to play a card of her own. This dinner might be even more interesting than she'd hoped. Othman was looking at her. 'My father refuses to show me any of his work.'

Othman smiled. Verity felt her spine stiffen. His glance made her feel more conscious of herself, her elegant gown, the long sweep of her neck. All in all, she felt very attractive tonight. The diners seemed like toys lined up, ready for her to begin play.

Louis had begun to laugh. 'Aren't they cruel to us!' he said to Lily.

To Daniel, the meal seemed to be progressing in the excruciating manner he'd dreaded. The sharp comments, the subtle interplay between the diners, grated on his nerves. Also, the stranger he was sitting next to unnerved him. What was he doing here? First, Daniel had heard that Owen had befriended the man, then this interloper had invaded Low Mede. From his appearance, Daniel guessed he might be interested in Owen's secret activities in the woods. Had Owen taken him to the High Place already? Had he told him about Daniel?

Barbara had begun to talk. She was aware that her voice was a trifle too loud, and her accent more cultivated than usual. Inside, she was a maelstrom of conflicting feelings, dominated by a bright green stripe of pure jealousy. She couldn't help it. Verity and Lily looked so lovely in the candlelight, which played on their creamy, young skins, and highlighted their rich, red hair. Verity looked like Audrey Hepburn in her prime; Lily like Kate Moss at her most gamine. While Barbara felt her age, conscious of her wide hips, her less than creamy breast which was partially exposed by the low top of her trouser suit. Apart from Barney, and Daniel, who didn't count, because he was hardly more than a child, she was in the company of extremely attractive men. Normally, in these conditions, she would be sparkling. But tonight, the sparkle seemed gaudy, obvious and tarnished. Not fresh. Not fresh at all. 'Pev's very interested in our local history,' Barbara said. 'He's been poking around our old ruins.' Why, at that moment, did she have to catch Verity Cranton's eye?

Verity smiled in a long, slow fashion, fascinated by the flush of red that crept up Barbara's bosom to her neck. 'Is that so?' she said to Othman, in a sultry, pointed manner.

'I've been delving around the old manor-house, Long Eden,' Othman said, pushing his empty soup plate away a little. 'The place seems shrouded in mystery.'

'Really? In what way?' Verity had never been interested in Little Moor's history, and was only dimly aware Long Eden existed. Now, because this puzzling man – puzzling simply because he was here in this company – was interested in the house, she suddenly became interested herself.

'The Murkasters, the family who lived there, simply upped and left some years ago,' Othman explained. 'No reason given. The house is empty and boarded up, yet it hasn't been sold. It seems odd, wouldn't you say? No one seems to know much about the Murkasters, or rather, if you ask any of the locals about them, they get extremely cagey. Personally, I find that *very* fascinating.'

'You like mysteries, then?' Verity enquired.

'Very much so. I have a nose for them. I'm wondering whether some scandal happened at Long Eden. You never know, the bastard heirs to the place might actually still be living here in Little Moor, but unaware of what they are.'

Verity laughed. 'That's quite a conclusion to jump to

in so short a time! You obviously like scandals as much as you like mysteries.'

'Often the two go hand in hand,' Othman said. He smiled at Owen.

Lily was staring at her plate. How dare he! He must be alluding to herself and Owen.

'But don't you think there might be a danger in probing other people's secrets?' Owen said with utter *sang froid*. He took a sip of wine. 'Especially if there are scandals involved. You never know who you might upset, and what they might be capable of.'

'I assure you, I'm always aware of what people are capable of,' Othman answered coolly, 'perhaps more so than they are themselves.'

Daniel was by this time convinced Othman knew all about what went on at the High Place. He felt the man was tormenting him personally with his hidden knowledge.

Verity stood up. 'If you'll excuse me, I'll just see to the next course.' She began to gather up the soup plates.

'I'll help,' Owen offered, jumping to his feet and collecting plates before Verity could protest.

He followed her into the darkened kitchen. Verity hurriedly slammed down her cargo on the table and ran to turn on the light.

'It's getting a bit heated in there,' Owen said.

'Just put those by the sink,' Verity answered, refusing to comment on his remark. It was hard for her to equate this slim, beautiful young man with the scruffy yob she usually encountered. The transformation confused her, yet she sensed Owen was completely in control of how he appeared to people. That unnerved her. It made her think he was, therefore, not to be controlled by her.

'Is there anything I can do?' Owen asked her.

Verity fussed over a hostess trolley, where the main

course was being kept warm. 'Not really. Everything's here.'

'You look different, tonight,' Owen said. 'I approve.'

'I am indifferent to your opinions,' Verity answered coldly. 'Excuse me.' She began to wheel the trolley from the room.

'Why do you hate me?'

Verity did not want to get drawn into this conversation. What was Winter playing at? And she knew he was *playing*. 'I have no feelings about you one way or the other,' she said. 'You're Daniel's friend, and he's my little brother. If you think I'm going to be nice to you just because you've had a bath tonight, forget it. I'm the person who has to put up with your slobby behaviour the rest of the time when you're hanging around here.' She realized she'd said too much. That was what Winter wanted. She should simply have walked out of the room. Still, it was difficult to make a dignified exit while pushing a hostess trolley.

'It's harder to be hostile than friendly,' Owen said, 'but then, that's your choice.' He gestured with his arm for her to lead the way back to the dining-room.

Verity felt nettled. The Winter lout had scored a point.

Back in the dining-room, the conversation still revolved around the vanished Murkasters. Everyone, apart from Daniel, was conjecturing what their secret scandal might be. It seemed that in the short time it had taken Owen and Verity to go to the kitchen and back, the wine had affected everyone's spirits. Even Lily looked animated. 'It was a murder,' she was saying, caressing her empty glass. 'It *has* to be.' She turned to Daniel. 'What do *you* think, Daniel?'

Daniel looked miserable at having been addressed. Owen went to stand behind his chair, and put his hands on Daniel's shoulders. 'Daniel undoubtedly knows the truth, but will keep silent.'

'Really?' Lily said. 'How does he know the truth?'

'Because he's psychic,' Owen said. 'Very psychic.'

'No I'm not!' Daniel spluttered. He wished Owen would move his hands. It was impossible to think while they lay upon his body.

Peverel Othman turned in his seat and put a hand on Daniel's arm. 'Then you must tell us what you know,' he said.

Daniel felt as if he was held in an electric field. Othman's touch somehow confirmed and intensified the presence of Owen. These men knew him. His soul felt naked. He could not speak; he knew that if he did, he would speak in tongues. He didn't want to talk about his abilities. Then Othman withdrew his hand and Owen moved away.

Daniel said, 'They were driven out. They can't come back.' As usual, he didn't know where the words came from. It was if another consciousness, who knew everything, was using his mouth. He did know, however, that what he'd said was utterly true.

'You see,' said Owen, swinging back into his place.

'Daniel!' said Louis in surprise.

Daniel rubbed his eyes with one hand. His vision was blurred. More words spilled from his reluctant lips. 'It was the evil of a woman and the weakness of a man.'

'What do you mean, evil?' Othman demanded. 'Weakness?'

Daniel looked at him and saw the man had gone very pale. What Daniel said had disturbed him somehow. 'It has always been this way, since the beginning, and it will always be their downfall. Even now he searches for her.'

Listening to these words, Othman wanted to lash out

and strike Daniel, silence him. His words fell as prophecies, but to Othman they sounded like accusations.

Louis broke the tense atmosphere. He laughed and addressed the other diners. 'Dan's always been a bit sensitive to atmospheres, you know. We thought he was most peculiar as a child!'

'Tell more,' said Barbara, in a quiet voice, her eyes round.

Daniel shrugged, furious with his father for his last remark. 'I can't.' He reached for his wine, nervously gulped it, conscious of Othman's eyes upon him.

Verity was moving round the table, filling people's plates. 'Oh come on, Daniel, you were always spouting weird stuff off when you were a kid. Tell them some more, for God's sake!' She laughed, although in her heart there was a thread of unease. As long as everyone's attention was focused on her brother, no one would guess she herself possessed a similar talent. She smiled at Daniel, conveying that he should play everyone along just to shut them up. He should lie, if necessary. She knew Daniel would be entirely aware of what she thought.

Verity's unexpected support made Daniel feel better. 'Vez, you know *nothing* about me!' he answered, laughing. He realized that somehow he had become a part of the evening, and was included in the gathering. What he said would be listened to by the others.

'Oh, scary!' Verity said.

Daniel handed her a plate. Where was the habitual harsh retort? Verity was not herself tonight either. When they looked at one another, a charge of communication passed between them, similar to what had happened in the kitchen the other morning. Strange. Was he developing some kind of friendship with his sister?

'I think we should begin investigating along the

obvious channels,' said Barbara. 'You know, look in the library archives or something. There must be records concerning the sale of Long Eden's effects.'

'That's true,' said Lily. 'We could begin there.' Caught up in the excitement of the evening, she had forgotten her misgivings about Long Eden.

Owen rolled his eyes. 'You'll be starting a society about it next,' he said. He stabbed with his fingers in the air to punctuate an imaginary plaque. 'Friends of Long Eden.'

'You've got no imagination,' Lily answered. She grinned at Barbara. 'There could be a book on the secret story of the Murkasters. *We* could write it!'

'Oh please!' Barney said, red of face. 'Barbara's got too many interests as it is! I'll end up running the pub on my own!'

'*Hotel*, if you don't mind,' Barbara said icily, and then to Lily, 'I think that's a great idea!' As the alcohol warmed her blood, her jealous feelings were dissipating. Lily was innocent and naive. She really had no idea how she affected the men.

'Perhaps we could have a seance with Daniel, too,' Othman suggested.

'Er, no!' Daniel answered quickly.

'Certainly not!' Verity exclaimed, rather too loudly, and then in a softer tone. 'Certainly not in this house, anyway.'

'Certainly not *anywhere*,' Daniel added. He looked Othman in the eye. 'I'm not into that. Really.'

Othman was studying him carefully, which made Daniel feel uncomfortable. 'That's OK. I understand. Still, I'd like to talk to you some time, if that's all right.'

Daniel looked desperately at Owen in appeal. Owen appeared slightly disapproving.

'I'm very possessive of Daniel,' he said. 'I don't want anyone else dabbling around with his talents.'

'Aha,' said Lily. 'So *this* is what you two get up to. I did wonder!'

'Daniel, is that true?' Verity asked sharply. Surely he wouldn't be so stupid?

Daniel glanced at her. 'Not really, no.' He looked back at Owen. 'Stop it. Please.'

Owen blinked, shook his head. A signal. 'It's OK, Daniel.' He turned to Louis, who had been silently observing the conversation. 'Do you believe in any of this stuff?'

Louis held Owen's eyes for a moment. He wondered whether he'd been interpreting the subtext to the recent exchanges correctly. 'As a matter of fact, no,' he said stiffly, pouring himself some more wine. 'But whatever other people want to believe is up to them. I'm a sceptic, but I have an open mind. Silly not to, really.'

'Absolutely!' Othman agreed. 'It's the only possible way to think.'

'Then you don't mind Daniel being involved?' Owen persisted.

The boy was too bright, Louis thought wearily. 'I . . . I don't know,' he answered. 'It's all a bit beyond me. Something I've never thought about. Daniel's always had a bit of an over-active imagination. I wouldn't want him to get hurt . . .'

'This is mad,' said Daniel, unaware of how much he was enjoying the attention.

'I agree,' said Verity. 'Daniel, you mustn't mess around in things like that. It can be dangerous. Dad, tell him!'

'Oh, don't worry,' Lily said. 'They're just winding us up.' She pulled a face at her brother. 'Aren't you, O?'

Owen put his head on one side, smiled in a charming manner. 'Of course, sibling.'

255

'I find it all very interesting,' Barbara said, realizing, too late, that Lily had effectively closed the subject.

After the meal was finished, everyone moved back into the lounge, where Louis put on a compilation CD of Sixties rock music. The younger people found they had little to complain about, as much of it was fashionable again now. Lily asked to hear a Jefferson Airplane track, 'White Rabbit', and when it came on, slowly danced alone on the rug in front of the fire.

'I'd join you,' Louis said, then indicated his legs, 'but alas . . .'

'No matter,' said Lily. She put down her glass on the mantelpiece and took Louis in her arms. 'We can just sway.'

Delighted laughter escaped Louis's surprised lips. 'Oh, oh . . . Er, yes.'

Verity and Daniel exchanged an embarrassed glance.

'Dance?' said Othman to Verity.

'O K.' It was preferable to join in rather than witness her father lurching about on his own with the Winter girl. She stood up and proceeded to dance several feet apart from Othman. Discreetly, she observed he was a good mover and put more effort into her own performance.

Not to be left out, Barbara hauled Barney to his feet, who shuffled awkwardly to the unfamiliar music. She waved her arms about a lot.

Owen went to sit next to Daniel on the sofa. 'A home disco,' he said. 'How quaint.'

'Don't ask me to dance,' Daniel answered. 'Just don't.'

'It's amazing how different people can be when you put them in an unfamiliar situation,' Owen said. 'Your sister, Lily, your dad, even old Barney bopping away there.'

Daniel sighed and leaned his head back against the

sofa, his knees drawn up to his chest. 'What a night.' He glanced at Owen. 'What were you playing at in there? All this psychic stuff.'

'It's true, isn't it?' Owen replied.

Daniel felt uncomfortable. 'It's not something I'd want to cultivate. Sometimes I just say things or experience peculiar feelings, but nothing more than that. I don't think I'm really psychic.'

'You are, Daniel,' Owen insisted. 'It's one of the things I like about you.'

'Why are we talking about this now?'

'Well, things are just happening now, aren't they? Haven't you noticed?' He didn't wait for an answer. 'I'm making decisions about things. Important decisions. Things are getting clearer now.'

'What are you on about?'

'We'll talk about it later,' Owen said. 'I think an escape to your lair is in order soon. I have a ready rolled spliff in my pocket that's itching to be smoked.'

Daniel laughed. 'Sounds appealing.'

'But first I'll have to walk Lily home.'

Daniel paused before answering. Lily was still throwing herself around to the music. 'She doesn't look ready to go yet.'

'So. We can wait.'

Alcohol and music, an intoxicating combination. Lily said she wanted to dance all night, which reminded her of a song from the old musical *My Fair Lady*. She asked Louis if he had the sound-track. When he said he had, and found the CD, Lily and Barbara sang along to the words, joined by Barney and Louis.

Verity and Othman sat down. Verity too was enjoying herself immensely. She hadn't danced for years. 'To-night's turned out very differently to how I expected,' she said.

'Better, I hope?' Othman said.

She nodded. 'Much. The Winters aren't quite what I thought they were.'

'They certainly aren't!' Othman agreed.

'Oh? And were you aware of what I thought of them? What's that Owen's been saying about me?'

'Nothing,' Othman said. 'It was just a bit obvious.'

'Oh dear!' She glanced at Owen, who was still talking to Daniel on the sofa. 'Still, I do wonder if he's quite the right sort of friend for Daniel. There's something very sinister about Owen Winter.'

'You're too protective.'

'No I'm not,' Verity protested. 'I'm not protective at all!'

'Perhaps we could go for a drink one evening,' Othman said.

Verity smiled at him. 'Perhaps.'

'You and I, and Owen and Lily. We could drive out somewhere.'

'Oh. Yes. Perhaps.' That wasn't quite what Verity would have preferred.

The party broke up about one o'clock, when it became obvious Lily was rather the worse for wear. One moment she was prancing around with Barbara on the hearth rug, the next she had flopped down next to Owen on the sofa with the slurred announcement, 'I need my bed. I'm going home.' She tried to stand up and fell back down again.

'I'll take you,' Owen said.

''S'only across the road,' Lily said, flapping a hand at him.

'I'll take you. Shut up.' Owen hoisted her to her feet and retrieved her shawl, which was draped over a chair.

The others seemed to take this as a cue, and began to say their goodbyes. Daniel went with Lily and Owen to the door. 'We didn't get to have our smoke. Oh well, never mind.'

'Are you kidding?' Owen said. 'I'll be back in a bit. Just let me lay this drunken floozie out on her bed.'

'It's late,' Daniel said. 'I have to be up in the morning.'

'So skive off for a day. I doubt your dad and Verity will be up early by the look of them.'

'Bed!' yelled Lily. 'O, I feel funny.'

'Wait up,' said Owen to Daniel, as he began to drag Lily down the drive.

'Back door,' Daniel answered in a low voice. 'Lock it after you.' The Eagers stumbled past him, cheerily repeating farewells, Othman following more sober in their wake. Verity came to stand beside Daniel on the doorstep, hugging her bare arms against the night chill.

'See you soon,' Othman said, following the Eagers down the drive.

'Bye!' Louis yelled from behind his children.

'Dad, you're drunk!' Verity said. 'Get back inside. I'll make us all a coffee.'

Louis grabbed his daughter, ignored her protests and kissed her cheek. 'Thank you for giving us a wonderful evening!'

'Oh, *Dad*!' Verity said, but she was smiling.

Daniel and Verity left Louis in the lounge and went out to the kitchen, Verity to make coffee. She wasn't sure why Daniel trailed her. 'Daniel, those trousers!' she said, shaking her head as she put the kettle on. 'You really are the limit sometimes. I can see your backside through the holes!'

'How was I to know everyone was dressing up?' Daniel said. He went to the window and looked out. He seemed nervous.

'Are you all right?' Verity asked sharply. She was still quietly discomfited by the earlier talk of psychic matters.

Daniel looked round. 'Yes.'

'You looked out there like there was . . . something out there,' Verity said.

Daniel laughed. 'Don't get spooked. Owen *was* winding everyone up earlier. I'm not that psychic, really.'

'That's a relief.' Verity spooned coffee into the cafetière. 'Ghosts scare me.'

'Me too.' Daniel continued to stare out of the window.

Raven meowed unexpectedly. Verity jumped. The cat had been asleep on one of the kitchen chairs. She hadn't noticed him. 'Oh, do you want some milk?' Her voice sounded too loud. Raven chirruped obligingly.

'Vez . . .'

'What?'

'What do you think of Owen?'

Verity went to the fridge. 'Daniel, you *know* what I think of Owen. Why is my opinion important all of a sudden?'

'I just thought you seemed to get on better tonight.'

Verity sighed. The drink had made her feel charitable. 'Well, I suppose he was on his best behaviour. His sister seems pleasant enough, though a bit dizzy.' She bent to pour milk into Raven's dish, and as she stood up, caught sight of a looming, pale shape beyond the kitchen window. She uttered a stifled scream. Daniel hurried to open the back door, and Owen Winter came into the kitchen.

'Jesus!' Verity said. 'You scared the hell out of me!' Owen appeared surprised to see her there.

'Oh, sorry.'

'What are you doing back here?'

'We're going upstairs,' Daniel said. He looked agonized.

'Oh, I see. Sneaking your friends in after bedtime. Daniel, what about school in the morning?'

'Thanks, Vez.'

'Well, you've got to get up.' Verity felt uncomfortable beneath Owen's silent scrutiny. What could she do? Order him out?

'We'll be quiet,' Owen said. 'I just want to borrow some CDs. Won't be long.'

'You should have done that earlier.' The kettle clicked off. Verity poured water into the cafetière, placed it on the waiting tray. She was not going to offer Winter coffee, or let him feel too at home. 'Well, just don't be too long.'

While she sat with her father in the lounge, sipping the coffee and listening to him ramble on about when he used to dance the night away as a young man, Verity heard the front door slam. Good riddance, she thought, comforted.

Outside the lounge door, Daniel tiptoed back up the stairs to his private rooms, where Owen was lounging on the bed, smoking the joint. He closed the door, and Owen said, 'Lock it. We don't want frosty-knickers sneaking in here.'

'She won't; she never comes up here,' Daniel said, but he locked the door. 'She'll think you've gone now.' He would have to wait until he was sure Verity was asleep before he attempted to smuggle Owen out. Exactly how long would Owen stay? Daniel was glad to have him there, but worried about what Verity would think if she found out.

'They treat you like a kid,' Owen said. 'Here.' He offered the joint.

Daniel took it and sat down on the bed. 'I know. They always will until I move out.'

Owen lay back and closed his eyes. 'Can I stay here tonight?'

'You only live across the road!'

'Oh, do I? I forgot.'

'You just want to cause trouble for me, don't you?'

'Is that what you think?' Owen opened his eyes.

Daniel passed the joint back. He was aware of the shift in the atmosphere, and his heart began to race. Was this what he thought it was? If so, what did he do about it? Ever since he'd first met Owen he'd been waiting for something to happen. The things they had done together at the High Place with the others had been just a preamble. Inevitably, it all led to this. Daniel and Owen alone at night, after an evening's drinking, and Owen saying he wanted to stay. That's what Daniel had been waiting for. The request: can I stay? It had had to come from Owen. So many times the opportunity had been there, but the question had never come.

'I don't know what I think,' Daniel said carefully. 'Why do you want to stay here?'

Owen might answer he was too tired, or too drunk, to stagger home. He might make some other facetious reply. He took a long drag off the joint. 'This might come as an unwelcome shock, but I want to stay because I want to sleep with you.' He exhaled slowly, waiting.

Daniel said nothing, looking at his hands clasped tightly in his lap.

'Tell me to get out, then,' Owen said.

Daniel shrugged. 'I just feel like my brain's melted.' He shook his head. 'God!' The silence stretched out, moment upon tense moment. Owen took another draw off the joint and stared at the ceiling. Soon, Daniel felt, he would get up and walk out. What then?

Daniel uttered a strangled cry and threw himself against Owen's side. Owen coughed. 'Ouch!' But he put his arm round Daniel's body, loosely.

Daniel felt it would be better if he kept his eyes shut

tight, so he wouldn't have to think about what he was doing, the implications of it, or whether he wanted it or not. If he just kept his eyes shut tight . . .

Owen rolled him on to his back. Daniel could hear him laughing. He felt Owen's lips brush his own. 'I take it this means yes,' Owen said.

To Othman, it was like a fine brandy, a perfect Armagnac, rolled around the tongue. Such fiery, yet delicate flavours! The garden of Low Mede was ancient, timeless. Hanging there, a ragged shadow some inches above the ground, hidden among the old-fashioned shrubs, the ecstatic bouquets of flowers rooted in the earth, Othman enjoyed vicariously the pleasures of the flesh. Hadn't he primed Owen for this? Yes. Owen, innocent sibling, unaware of his latent abilities. The Cranton boy, too, a power-house, a receiver and transmitter, long unused. It should have been dragged out of him and used while he was still suckling the breast.

A dim light shone in the attic room, but no shadows moved across it. Othman could tell that Daniel thought Owen was skilled and experienced. Othman knew Owen was not. Lily was his only lover, his only testing ground. Owen was scared and exhilarated, aware of the fragile nature of Daniel's offering of love. They were incapable of sex, as such, but were learning the communion, the special language of fingers, sensitive against flesh. They kissed, and were afraid to stop, because then they might have to do something else. Othman floated in the waves of their timid passion. It was like a drug to him. They were oblivious of his presence lapping up the etheric cream seeping from their souls. The only acceptable sustenance. Blood, flesh: what were these? Coarse, brutish victuals, the things that dogs ate. With his more refined palate, Peverel Othman could only imbibe a more subtle sustenance.

Chapter Fourteen

Thursday, 22nd October: Little Moor

While Owen Winter timidly made love to her brother in the attic room, Verity Cranton lay in her single bed, dreaming. She dreamed she was lying in her bed with the curtains open, and moonlight was falling into the room, across the floor in bars and coins of white radiance. She felt warm and cosy, utterly secure, and could hear the heating system humming, the slow tick of the clock downstairs in the hall. She was thinking about the evening, the dinner party's success, and how, for once, she had genuinely enjoyed other people's company. It had been so long since she had socialized like that. Not since she'd fled the flat, and Netty's tears, Netty's hurt, accusing eyes. She wondered how she'd been seduced into it now. Her resolutions had been strong. She had designed a new life for herself, a new persona. The severe creature she had become scorned the company of others, the taking of alcohol in excess. It could lead to unpleasant things.

In her dream, Verity turned on her side in the bed, one hand beneath her cheek. She did not feel at all sleepy. Where was Raven? He had taken to sleeping across her feet, but she could not feel the pressure of his body now. She leaned over the side of the bed to see whether the cat was asleep on the rug. There was his great black shape curled up. She called his name softly, patted the duvet. 'Raven, come on. Here . . .'

She saw the large head lift, his eyes open, enormous and colourless, but glowing. She held out her hand, a ghostly shape in the darkness. Best not to think of disembodied hands. They might belong to a disembodied voice. 'Raven . . . Raven . . .'

Slowly the cat began to stretch out his paws. His mouth opened wide in a yawn. He began to move towards her. How enormous his shadow looked, flowing across the rug. He was a magnificent animal. His shadow, rather than his body, seemed to spill on to her bed, and she reached out to stroke his silken fur. She could feel the powerful muscles beneath the skin. How deceptive was a cat's skin! It seemed delicate, easily torn, yet she knew it could withstand greater heat or more intense cold than any human integument. It was tougher, too, harder to break. Raven began to purr. He was so heavy. Verity closed her eyes and grabbed hold of the cat, pulling him towards her. In bed, he allowed her to hug him. It was strange how he'd tolerate greater intimacy with her in the privacy of her bedroom. Downstairs, every part of his body was off-limits but for his broad head.

His paws kneaded her shoulders, and his purr hummed close to her face. The weight of the cat was like the weight of man, Verity thought, and unconsciously her legs opened a little beneath the duvet. The paw on her right shoulder was clawing at her night-dress. She reached up to stop him scratching her skin, put her hand over the paw and stroked it. How long his diminutive toes felt. It could almost have been a furred hand lying there. She traced her finger along Raven's foreleg. How thick it was. As thick as the arm of a woman, or a young man. For a moment, her breath stilled. This was a dream, after all. She did not open her eyes, but ran her hand up the furred limb, encountered an elbow, biceps, a shoulder, the hollow of a throat. All sleekly furred. Her hand ran down over the back, describing muscles beneath the skin. She cupped a firm, pelted buttock, felt the upper part of a thigh. The beast-man – not Raven, surely not Raven – was still purring.

She felt the clawed hand, with its long agile fingers, gently stroke her shoulder just inside her night-dress. Still she did not open her eyes. She was afraid of what she might see, even though the touch and presence of the creature excited her. She felt no sense of threat, only a heavy desire hanging in the air. She reached up to clasp the hand that was moving inside her night-dress. She felt the bony knuckles through the fur, the naked palm with its raised pads. He raised her arms above her head. Verity moaned, opened her legs wider. The duvet was between them. She wanted to kick it off, feel all that fur against her body. The creature's breath was warm upon her throat. She felt a rough tongue licking the top part of her right breast. She felt the brief, playful nip of sharp teeth. Her back arched. He let go of her arms and she felt the weight of him lift from her body. She opened her eyes, afraid of losing him.

There was a black silhouette kneeling over her. She could see the moonlight shining on his fur, but could make out no details of the face, other than the sulphur glow of his eyes. Were there lips to kiss, or simply the wedge-shaped muzzle of a cat? He had a long mane, like a lion. Verity threw back the duvet covers, and ran her fingers over the mattress beside her. The beast-man was very still, watching her, perhaps considering. Come to me, dream creature, Verity thought. In dreams, a thought must be as loud as a shout. She began to pull off her night-dress, and a timorous hand was offered to help her. Her body shone pale as ashes in the owl light, white to his depthless black. She leaned on one elbow, reached out to stroke his belly, found beneath it the naked, wet penis, erect, nothing like the organ of a man, yet as large and hard. At her touch, the creature uttered a soft growl and pounced forward. Verity clasped him to her, wriggling beneath him, wondering whether she should guide the dream-cock into her waiting body, her aching body. But the beast-man had other ideas. He turned her on to her belly and bit the back of her neck. *Like a cat, of course, like a cat!* Verity raised her hips. He found her instantly, entering her with one swift thrust. Then he remained still, growling around her flesh where it was gripped in his teeth. His claws had found her breasts. She could feel the needling caress. For what seemed like long minutes they were locked together in stillness, then he began to move, rapid, tiny thrusts, hardly a movement at all. Verity moaned in pleasure and luxury. She had never felt anything like this: the unusual organ that felt so different inside her, the odd flicking movements. An orgasm was already beginning to rise within her. She tried to hold it at bay, wanting to enjoy this experience for as long as possible. Just before the wave of feeling crested, the creature stopped moving. She could feel the contractions of his penis inside her as he ejaculated his alien seed into her. Then he tore himself out of her. She had forgotten. The organ of a male cat was barbed. The pain seared right through her, in time to the spasms of a powerful climax. She howled, the cry of a female cat in heat, her hips bucking upon the bed. But he had already left her, flowed off the bed like a liquid shadow, back into the world of dreams.

Lily, in her drunken sleep, dreams of the house of her ancestors. She knows she is in the garden, and its fabulous terraces are set out before her, disappearing down and down into a mist. The air smells strongly of perfumes she has never smelled before. The world feels different. It is not her world, its contours are unfamiliar, yet she knows, at the same time, it is the earth. She is standing on a gravel path with a rockery behind her, where small-leafed climbing plants spill over the stones. Below her lies the next terrace of the garden, beds of plants set out in a geometric pattern. When she turns, she sees behind her a screen of cedars rearing against the sky, their branches spreading out to obscure the high building behind them. Yet the sun dapples its walls; she can see the glow of hot stone. It is a hot country. Turning slowly, she looks down upon the garden. Small figures are working there among the neat crops, paddling in the irrigation streams, panniers tied to their bent backs. Other, taller figures, stand by, as if supervising. They are strangers. She does not know them. Someone comes towards her along the path, appearing between a hedge of evergreens. She presumes it is a man, although she can't be sure. This person is very tall, and has long hair which flows loose around his shoulders and chest. His skull and his face are long, like those of ancient Egyptians, yet his features are sensual and beautiful. He is wearing a long robe, belted at the waist, and sandals on his feet. Lily realizes she is in the past; this is history. The person speaks to her, and she apprehends that what she thought was a man is a woman.

'My lady, all is ready for your inspection.' The woman bows slightly.

Lily does not have to look up to this person. She too is very tall. What is she supposed to say? Even as she thinks this, her body replies, 'Very good, I shall be along shortly.'

Lily knows then that this is not her body, she is merely lodging in it, and the consciousness that owns it has now become aware of her presence. She feels the body tense, the intake of breath, very shallow. Then the whispered thought, *Who are you?*

I am Lily, she answers. *Who are you?*

The true owner of this body! What do you want?

Nothing. I am dreaming. I'm not really here.

Lily senses laughter. This strange, tall woman seems to take it in her stride, finding an alien presence in her mind and flesh. 'Do you want to see the garden, child?' she says aloud.

Yes, please.

The woman will not give her name, although Lily senses she could look for it in this borrowed mind if she tried hard enough. However, it seems rude to do that when her hostess is being so kind. They walk down the terraces, between the dark hedges, into the areas of light, and back into shadow. Water spills over the terraces, and great wooden wheels turn in dark pools, which are come upon unexpectedly. As the woman with whom Lily travels passes the workers, they bow from the waist. She acknowledges them warmly.

Are you a queen? Lily has to ask.

'No, my dear, not a queen. I suppose you could say I am a gardener.'

They walk down the steps of the hanging gardens, and the light of the raw sun reflects brilliantly off the water as it tumbles down the tiers of cultivation. Ahead is a series of domed buildings, constructed of obsidian glass. 'These are the greenhouses,' explains Lily's hostess. 'We have created a new strain of corn here. It is very important. We did not think the seeds would sprout, but now they have.'

They turn down a narrow path, tall evergreen bushes to either side. The entrance to one of the greenhouses is straight ahead. The path is wet as if it has been recently hosed. Then there is a man blocking the pathway. He is standing with his back to them, very tall, a flag of thick golden hair spread out over his shoulders, trailing down his spine. At first, Lily thinks he has wings: six of them, iridescent as crystal, glowing with peacock colours. Then the image shifts, and he is simply a tall man. The woman says abruptly, 'What are you doing here?' Her voice is sharp, almost hostile, but there is a secret tone behind it. Lily can feel her surprise, the sensations of both disapproval and pleasure. Momentarily, the woman has forgotten about her parasitic traveller. The man turns, and Lily knows him, although his skin is paler, almost translucent, the blue veins faintly visible below the surface. His eyes are bluer, too, an unnatural peacock blue.

Pev . . .

'Shemyaza,' says the woman. 'If they catch you here, you are dead.'

'My lady Ninlil.' The one she called Shemyaza sweeps a mocking bow. 'Then you must refrain from betraying me.'

'What *are* you doing here?'

Shemyaza shrugs and saunters into the greenhouse. 'Working.' Ninlil follows him. A strange light envelops them, sunlight through the obsidian. Lily can see the circular ranks of plants growing thickly within. It is like a maze. One of the small people – a human man, Lily now realizes – is adjusting some irrigation taps just inside the doorway. Ninlil makes an abrupt gesture and the human bows and leaves the building quickly.

'Shem, you are confined to the High House until this matter has been dealt with,' Ninlil says. Lily can feel her despair. She wants to help this man, but knows he is stubborn and proud.

'Their rules, not mine.'

'Then why don't you get out?' Ninlil snaps. 'Get out of here, go down the the lower plains, anywhere! You flaunt your transgressions in their faces and they will punish you. Don't you realize that?' She pauses. 'The woman isn't worth it.'

Shemyaza wheels around at that. He looks furious. Lily feels Ninlil wince inside, although she doesn't show it. 'Don't presume to judge affairs of which you are ignorant!' he says. His voice is low, reasonable, although his eyes are shouting and wild.

'Ishtahar is using you, Shem. Why can't you see that?' Ninlil holds out her hands in appeal, as if to show she is concealing nothing. 'She wants your knowledge and the power to hold council.'

'She deserves it.'

'No!' Ninlil wrings her hands together. 'Her people can't cope with it, they are far too primitive. You will cause catastrophe if you give her what she wants!'

'Don't you think I haven't heard all this before?' Shemyaza plucks a leaf from what appears to be the prototype of a tomato plant. 'I refuse to hide or bend to the will of anyone I consider ignorant. I shall explain my position to the Parzupheim as and when required. My opinions are valid. Humans aren't animals, Ninlil, and we have been treating them as such for far too long.'

'That is your loins speaking!' Ninlil announces. 'Humanity will never be Anannage. You are deceiving yourself if you think otherwise.'

He nods. 'True, but we can mingle, Ninlil. We can become one. Humanity must gain, and Anannage might lose a little, but it is the only *proper* way. We are Watchers, aren't we? We have chosen to come to this place and reveal ourselves to them, therefore we should assimilate ourselves with their culture.'

Lily feels Ninlil's defeat as her own. 'My word will not be enough to save you, Shemyaza. If you persist in this, they will banish you, despite your beauty, despite your wisdom, despite your inordinate capacity to love. The High Lord values you, but not enough.'

He laughs. 'Banish me? Never! The Lord loves me. I can talk him round.'

'Your folly has blinded you to reality, Shem.' Ninlil reaches out to touch his bare arm. His skin is smooth and warm. 'Go back to the High House. Please!'

'No, I am completing my tasks here as normal.' Shemyaza clasps Ninlil's hand. 'Don't worry. Everything will be resolved.'

Lily feels Ninlil's thoughts. *No, you are wrong, you are so wrong.*

Lily woke up in darkness, struggling to keep the flavour, the smells and textures of her dream vivid in her memory. Dry-mouthed, still half-drunk, she scrambled from her bed and hurried to her dressing-table where her notepad lay. Fumbling, she turned on a lamp standing dustily among the empty perfume bottles and dried jars of face cream. In a scrawling, barely legible hand, she scribbled down all she could remember. 'Shemyaza,' she said aloud, the name clear and resonant in her head. Where had she heard that name before?

Naked, she ran out on to the landing and hurried, without knocking, into Owen's room. She felt she had to tell him about the dream. It was important. It was only after she had excitedly begun to speak that she realized the room was empty. She hardly needed to turn on the light to confirm that Owen's bed had not been slept in. For a moment, she felt numb, and sat down on his bed. She could remember him bringing her home. Where had he gone? What time was it? She picked up Owen's alarm clock. Two-thirty. 'Owen, you bastard!' she said aloud. 'Where are you?' Probably he'd gone sneaking off with Othman to investigate the church again, or something.

Sighing, Lily got to her feet. She felt ill, nauseous and

light-headed. Had she made a fool of herself at the Crantons'? She could remember dancing with Louis, but nothing too horrendous. Her throat was dry. She needed a drink.

After going to her room for her dressing-gown, Lily went downstairs. The house had that horrible desolate feeling it always had when Owen stayed out all night. Lily found half an inch of cloudy orange squash at the bottom of a bottle in the back of the pantry. This she diluted in a murky glass and drank down in one gulping swallow. The squash felt sticky and too sweet on her tongue, feeding her thirst rather than quenching it. She drank water from the tap, taking up handfuls and splashing it into her mouth, almost choking when someone knocked at the kitchen door. For a moment Lily stood frozen, stooped, water dripping from her chin, the ends of her hair. Then she straightened up, wiped her mouth, went to the door and said, 'Who is it?' Could Owen have forgotten his key? It seemed unlikely. He'd never locked himself out before.

'Lily, it's me. Can I come in?'

'Pev?' Lily opened the door. Othman stood at the threshold, a dark shadow among a host of shadows. Lily brushed back her hair. 'What do you want? It's the middle of the night. Where's Owen?' She wondered then, with dread, if anything could have happened to her brother.

Othman came into the kitchen, filling it with his presence. 'Owen's fine. He's still at the Crantons'.'

'Oh.' Lily frowned, but decided not to pursue any thoughts on the matter. She was wondering just how much Othman looked like the man in her dream. Perhaps the differences were greater than she thought, but then Othman looked thin, even rather unhealthy, and his hair was dull in comparison to the mane of Shemyaza. His

273

eyes did not burn in the same way. Perhaps she had dreamed of an idealized version of the man.

'I saw your light on, wondered if you'd like some company.'

'Bit late to be out walking, isn't it?' Lily had unconsciously hugged herself, as if protecting her body.

Othman shrugged. 'I needed to clear my head.'

'I'll make us a drink.'

Othman laughed. 'Oh Lily, do you always fly to the kettle whenever you're unnerved?'

She grinned uncertainly. 'Don't you want a coffee or anything?'

Othman came towards her, put his hands upon her shoulders. Lily felt her legs go weak, suddenly conscious of last night's make-up smeared under her eyes. He might not be the radiant being of her dream, but Peverel Othman was still the most beautiful man she had ever met.

'I knew you were alone,' Othman said. 'It doesn't happen very often, so I thought I should make good use of the opportunity.'

'I have just dreamed about you, or someone who looked like you,' Lily said, uncurling her arms from their position of defence and tentatively placing her hands flat against Othman's chest.

'Good,' said Othman. He leaned forward to kiss her, and Lily was alarmed by the sense of repressed hunger in every taut fibre of his body. He must have been desperate to get her alone, she thought, for this hunger to be waiting here. She allowed him to open her dressing-gown, run his hands over her body. Such long, cool hands.

Outside, in the lane, Emilia Manden watched with interest what was happening in the cottage. She was able to observe everything clearly, surfing a tide of Othman's energy in her body. Already, she felt better, stronger and more alert. Earlier that day, she'd noticed her hair had begun to grow dark at the roots again, pushing out the grey, and, even more miraculously, there were painful lumps in her gums where new teeth were shifting against the flesh.

So, Othman was taking his pleasure with Helen's daughter, was he? That made sense. He would impregnate her, of course, continue the process the Lord had started. Soon, Othman would want Emilia as well, once she had filled out again, regained her beauty. She felt no envy towards Lily. Lily was merely fulfilling her natural function.

Emilia sat down on the fence opposite the cottage, swinging her legs in the night air. She watched Othman and Lily disappear from the kitchen, undoubtedly up into Lily's bedroom. Presently the unmistakable sounds of a woman's pleasure came through the open bedroom window, drifted out into the lane. Oh, he was seeing to her well, he was, but they'd all had the knack for that. More than men, the Grigori, all of them. Emilia had sometimes overheard Owen making love to Lily on the rare occasions one of her nocturnal prowls round the village had coincided with the twins' desire to be close. Lily hadn't made noises like that then, though! Quite reserved in comparison. Emilia giggled to herself. The village had become like a dried-up old stick since the Murkasters had left. All the passion gone, all the lust. Even the fields had suffered for it. Times would change now. This one would bring it all back. She was sure of it.

Chapter Fifteen

Same day: Little Moor (continued)

Barbara woke up with rather a headache, and, for some reason, a feeling of guilt. Barney had already got up, and she could hear the sounds of the drayman unloading his barrels outside. At first, the previous evening's events were rather a blur in her mind. She remembered the food, the dancing, even her twinges of jealousy over Lily and Verity. Then the painful recollection flooded through her: dancing with Louis to an old song, swaying in front of the fire, and Louis putting his cheek against hers, saying, 'Oh, Barbara, if only this body of mine hadn't betrayed me.'

She had pressed herself more firmly against him. 'Don't be ridiculous, Lou. You're still a very attractive man.'

Louis had looked at her then, almost warily. 'Tonight, I feel like I'm coming awake after a long sleep, coming out of a coma.'

'I'm glad,' Barbara said, and then, with drunken bravado, she risked a provocative remark. 'I've been waiting here for you.'

'Have you?' Louis squeezed her, the ends of his fingers touching the side of her breast.

At that moment, Barbara had noticed Barney watching them. He had been standing with cigar in hand, whisky glass raised, his eyes like stones. Barbara had felt the heat rush through her, had to laugh in a high, braying manner in order to defuse the moment. She'd grinned at Barney, but he'd only pulled a sour face and turned away.

The subject hadn't been mentioned on the way home, but then that was typical of Barney. He'd nurse his painful suspicions in silence, curled around them. He'd never accuse, shout or get violent. Othman had left them at the end of Low Mede's drive, talking about going for a walk to sober up. Barney hadn't even said good night. Walking down the lane to The White House, Barbara had kept up a cheerful chatter, conscious of her voice being slurred. The atmosphere of the early morning seemed heavy, drowsy, dripping with floating bags of emotions that were ready to burst. Barbara had commented on the night, the feeling of it. Barney had grunted in response. He had no imagination at all. Barbara forcefully prevented the hot spasm of irritation that shot through her from escaping her lips in harsh words.

In bed, Barney had wanted to have sex, which again, Barbara supposed, was typical. He obviously needed to reassert his rights, exercise his ownership of her. Still, Barbara made no objection: the night seemed conducive to carnal urges. While Barney heaved and grunted on top of her, she fantasized happily: first about Othman (although it was very difficult to imagine Barney's large, hairy body being Othman's), and then about Louis. Poor Louis, so damaged. Barbara thought he probably hadn't had a woman since his wife had died. She wanted to smother him in love, make him feel good about himself. The evening had started so badly, what with all those silly thoughts she'd had about the girls, but by the end of it, she'd felt empowered, attractive again. No young girl could do for Louis what she could. She imagined he would be a sensitive lover; they could talk about poetry in bed, languorous in the afterglow of love.

Perhaps if Barney had whispered some endearment to her, she would have felt guilty about her secret desires, but he simply rolled off her without a word, leaving her unsatisfied. Barbara didn't care. She stared out of the window at the sky and began to make plans.

Othman left the Winters' cottage early in the morning. Lily guessed he didn't want to risk running into Owen, although she did not mention it. In the kitchen, Othman kissed her tenderly, stroked her face. 'I'll see you soon.' Lily wondered whether difficulties with Owen were presaged. Othman certainly seemed eager to pursue an affair with her, and she had the feeling Owen was not to be included in it as she'd first thought.

She washed the dishes in a dream, replaying all the events of the previous night in her imagination. She'd asked Othman questions about himself, from which he managed to slip away by asking her about her mother and what their lives had been like before she had brought her children to Little Moor. He seemed very interested in Helen Winter, reminding Lily of how Owen had suggested Othman might be *an old friend* of their mother's. A cold dart had gone through her, prompting her to blurt, 'Are you my father?', which seemed absurd now. It was obvious he was far too young. He'd laughed at her question, ruffled her hair, leaning over her in the bed. 'No, Lily, I'm not, though even if I was, I'd still be here with you like this, for my people have no taboo about such things.'

'Who *are* your people, Pev?' Lily asked.

'A very old family,' he answered. 'Far older than you can imagine. I can trace my lineage back before Adam.'

Lily laughed at him. She did not believe that was the exact truth. 'Why are you interested in us?'

He'd stroked her bare arm. 'Because you're special, my lovely. Soon, I will be able to tell you more, and then you'll understand completely. But not yet.'

When he made love to her, Lily experienced

fragmented visions, flashbacks, she thought, to her dream of Shemyaza. She told him about this. 'Who is Shemyaza? Have you ever heard such a name?'

'He's dead,' Othman said abruptly. 'He lived a long time ago.'

'But you know who he is . . . He *is* a real person?'

Othman shrugged, reaching out to her bedside table for a cigarette. 'Yes, I suppose so, in a sense. He lives on only in legend.'

'But I've never heard of him. Why would I dream of him? And there was so much detail, Pev! It was like I was really there. I could feel it, smell it. Could I really invent this person? He wasn't human, and neither was the woman who carried me. They were something else. *Anannage*. You see, I remember the name. I feel like I know it.'

'You must have heard of . . . *him* before,' Othman said.

Lily noticed he was oddly reluctant to say the name.

'The old church here in Little Moor is dedicated to him,' he continued, 'to St Shem.'

'Of course!' said Lily, although she doubted she would have made the connection herself. 'But why would I dream of a saint, and why make him look like you? And if he was a saint, then he would have been human, so why . . .'

'The imagination is a strange country,' Othman interrupted. 'The so-called St Shem was never really a saint. The dedication of the church must just have been a cover-up in case any strangers wandered through the village. Your mother must have told you stories about him when you were a child, which you've remembered through your dream.'

'But there was a story behind the dream, I just know it. It was like I simply stepped in and witnessed a small part of it. I didn't understand it, and I want to know more.'

'Perhaps you'll dream yourself back into that forgotten country,' Othman said, and covered any further questions she might utter with a kiss.

Later, Lily said to him, 'You've changed my life.'

'I know,' he answered and smiled, leaning back beside her, his long, beautiful body warm against her flesh, his hair tangled with hers.

Who was he and where had he come from? How had he insinuated himself into their lives in this way, turned everything upside-down? He had brought magic with him, Lily felt. He made things happen. What would she feel if he left her now? Could she survive, go back to how she was before? The last thoughts cast a cloud over her mood. She did not want to think about it.

When Owen came in, Lily realized she hadn't been thinking about him at all, or even wondered why he'd stayed out all night. He seemed in a bad mood as he slammed around the kitchen, scraping a breakfast together for himself. Lily felt tense, sure that Peverel Othman's presence was imprinted all over her body. Surely Owen could *smell* that Othman had been here?

Owen sat down. 'Lil, we have to talk.'

Lily froze. *He knew!* She laughed nervously. 'What about?'

'Just sit down, will you.'

She did so, waiting for the attack. He was stirring cereal round in his bowl, staring at the table. Lily was frightened. She'd never seen Owen like this, so serious.

Owen sighed, looked up at her. His eyes were dark. 'I stayed at the Crantons' last night.'

Lily said nothing, tried to swallow without gulping.

Owen rolled his eyes. 'Well, where's the outburst? At least make me feel better by shouting at me.'

Lily frowned. 'What? What do you mean?'

Owen stood up, gripped the back of his chair. 'Why is it you've been sniping at me with remarks about Daniel for the past few days, but now you've conveniently forgotten about it?'

Lily stared at him. He was talking about jealousy. Soon, the accusation would come. 'I realized I was being stupid, and too possessive.' Answer *that*, she thought triumphantly.

'Oh right, so that means you don't mind that I slept with Daniel last night.'

Lily found an irrepressible laugh bubbling out of her mouth. She put her hands over it to stop it.

Owen looked furious. 'What's so funny?'

Lily shook her head. Two days ago, she'd have been crucified by the thought of Owen touching anyone else. Now, all she felt was relief, a shift of blame. 'You won't believe this, but I thought you were going to tell me off!'

'What for?' Owen asked, in a cold voice.

Lily grinned. She couldn't stop herself. 'Well, while you were at Low Mede, Pev came here. While you were in bed with Daniel, I was in bed with Pev. Isn't that a coincidence!' She leaped up and busied herself at the sink, so she wouldn't have to look Owen in the eye. She couldn't stop laughing.

Owen came up behind her, grabbed her shoulder, pushed her round. Before she could protest, he slapped her face. The twins stared at each other in shock. Nothing like this had happened before, never had they raised a hand against one another in anger.

Lily hit Owen back. 'You bastard, how dare you!' The blow was stronger than his, sent him crashing into the table. 'You *dare* to get angry with me over Pev, O. I've always known you've been itching to get your hands on Cranton. How *dare* you get jealous now!'

Owen straightened up, rubbing his face. Lily's blow had been a closed fist, not an open palm. 'Perhaps that's true,' he said quietly. 'But I never did anything about it before – because of you. How weird that's all changed now, since Peverel Othman arrived on the scene. How convenient that I was over at Low Mede so he could come sniffing round you. It was his idea, you know, for me to be with Daniel.'

Lily digested this information. It did not displease her as much as Owen might think. Othman had wanted her alone. He had wanted her. 'So what are we going to do now?'

Owen paused for a moment. 'We don't fight. We mustn't separate. Not now.'

Lily pushed her hair off her face. 'You think something's going on, don't you.'

Owen nodded. 'Yes, but I haven't worked out what, yet. Othman told me things about us – he thinks, or *knows*, there's something different about us. He wants us, Lil. Don't flatter yourself he's in love with you, or anything. He wants more than that – from both of us. So don't go falling for him. It could be dangerous.'

Lily drew in her breath. 'And are you in love with Daniel Cranton?' she enquired archly.

'Daniel is a need, not particularly an obsession,' Owen answered obliquely. He rubbed the back of his neck, rolled his head around. 'We have to find out what Othman knows about us. Until we do, we're vulnerable.'

'He asks about Mum a lot.' Lily frowned. 'I still wonder whether he knew her. He looks only a few years older than us, but I get the feeling he's a lot older than that.'

'We'll play along for a while. It's all we can do.' Owen went back to his breakfast, and Lily sat down opposite him again, her elbows on the table.

'Is this thing with Daniel going to be regular?'

'I don't know. What about you and Othman?'

Lily looked away. 'I want him, O. I won't deny it. He makes me feel . . .' She wriggled her shoulders. 'I don't know. He fascinates me. Do you mind?'

'Well, as you rightly pointed out, I'm hardly in the position to.' Owen sighed deeply, and put down his spoon, reached for his sister's hands. 'Lily, we must stick together. Let's be frank with one another. Our sharing was never that regular, was it. I suppose something like this was bound to happen. We were isolated. Now we're not. But it doesn't change the way I feel about you. You're still my goddess.'

Lily smiled uncertainly. She wished she could share Owen's belief that their relationship would not be changed by all that had happened, and all that would happen, soon.

Barbara breezed into The White House, barely able to contain her excitement. She had been to the small local library, and, after a rather difficult episode persuading the librarian to let her look at the auction details of Long Eden, had spent the afternoon leafing through the old invoices and papers. Although she'd unearthed no juicy scandals – a personal letter inadvertently bundled up with the receipts would have been nice – she had discovered that the Murkasters had sold off the least valuable of their effects, and that a dozen or so paintings from the house had been bought by a local man. It had been twenty years ago, but she hoped desperately that Mr G. Thormund still lived in Larkington, a village nearby. Now, if her investigations proved fruitful, she had a means through which to impress Peverel Othman.

She went straight to her sitting-room and dragged out the telephone directory from beneath a pile of magazines behind one of the chairs. Thormund, G. She found it almost too easily, and the address matched what she'd written in her notebook: Leaning Willows, Larkington. Barbara wrote down the number and went to fetch herself a gin and tonic. Then she sat down on the sofa, phone in hand, and tapped in the number. She almost held her breath as the calling tone purred out, a connection from Barbara to the past. She felt it strongly. Then, just as she'd taken a mouthful of gin, the phone was answered. 'Larkington 572.' The voice was male, plummy, elderly. Barbara gulped down the gin.

'Good afternoon. Am I speaking to a Mr G. Thormund?'

'Godfrey Thormund, yes. What can I do for you?'

Barbara fell into her element. 'I am Barbara Eager, the proprietor of The White House hotel in Little Moor. I'm involved in a writing project about the manor-house, Long Eden, which as you must know is situated in the village. I understand you bought a number of old paintings from the auction at Long Eden some years ago, and was wondering if you still owned them.'

'Yes,' came the rather cautious reply.

'I don't want to inconvenience you at all, Mr Thormund, but I'd be extremely grateful if you'd allow me to view the paintings some time.'

'Writing project, you say,' said Godfrey Thormund. Barbara sensed mulishness.

'Yes. I run a writers' group here in the village, and we're aiming to produce our second book soon. Long Eden's boarded up now, and the gardens have gone wild. I'm hoping to find some representation of the house when it was lived in. Looking for inspiration, I suppose! But, of course, I'd like to see *any* painting that once hung in the old place.'

284

'Had a few meals at The White House,' said Godfrey Thormund. 'With my daughter.'

'Lovely! Perhaps we've met already, then.'

'Next Tuesday morning,' said Thormund abruptly.

'I beg your pardon?' Barbara had heard him, but hadn't expected co-operation so soon.

'Tuesday morning. Ten-thirty?'

'Oh, yes, that would be wonderful. Thank you *so* much. Would it be all right if I brought a colleague with me?'

'Just one? I don't want crowds.'

'Just one, Mr Thormund. I can't tell you how much I appreciate this.'

After she'd put down the phone, Barbara had to sit for a few moments, quickly finishing the gin. How opportune! Not only had she secured a viewing of the paintings, but their owner had been most specific about wanting no more than two people to call. It was only once her heart had slowed down she realized she hadn't asked for directions to Leaning Willows. Still, that simply meant more time would have to be spent looking for the place. She didn't mind about that.

Chapter Sixteen

Same day: Little Moor (continued)

Owen left the cottage at lunchtime, and afterwards Lily was unable to settle. She'd phoned Barbara Eager, only to be told the woman was out. Lily wondered whether she'd have confessed to Barbara that she'd slept with Peverel Othman, realizing it was perhaps lucky Barbara hadn't been available. Lily wanted to talk to someone, but instinct advised her Barbara wouldn't be too pleased if she heard Lily's news. She lay on the sagging sofa in the darkened parlour, drinking home-made wine straight from the bottle. Her body still tingled at the memory of Othman's touch. She couldn't resist sifting through the memory of their love-making, reliving it in her mind. It made her feel hot and alive between her legs: she wanted more. Should she go and look for him now? No, she must be cool about this, not too pushy. She thought about her mother, how she'd brought the twins to the village, the idyllic life they'd lived together here. All Lily's early memories of Little Moor were of summertime. Then came the shadowy time when Helen had become ill. Lily had found it all so painful, she'd refused to think about it since. Now, perhaps, she needed to examine her memory.

Many of the local women had come to the cottage back then, while Helen lay pale and thin in her bed upstairs. Lily and Owen had been fifteen, very wrapped up in one another, which Lily now realized their mother had encouraged. She must have known she was going to die. There had been whispered injunctions from the bed of sickness that Lily and Owen must stick together. They would be well provided for, whatever happened. Lily had fallen into a kind of numbness: going to school, getting out of the cottage whenever she could at evenings and weekends. During this period, she and Owen had shared for the first time.

They had walked to the High Place in Herman's Wood, a place particularly loved by Owen, but which Lily secretly found rather scary. She remembered it had been a Thursday evening, high summer, the night warm and scented. At the High Place, Owen had said, 'She *is* dying, Lil.' Lily hadn't wanted to talk about it, but Owen had been insistent. 'We have to think about what we're going to do. I don't think we're old enough to live alone.'

Lily had been horrified. They had no living relatives that they knew of. Where would they go? In fear and misery, she had begun to cry. 'She mustn't die! She mustn't! How can she do this to us?'

Owen had comforted her, as he always did: a hug, a kiss upon her wet cheek. It had been Lily who'd become aware of the first stirrings of desire. As Owen cupped her face with his long fingers, she'd looked up at his face, and realized he was beautiful. 'I don't want anyone else,' she said. 'It has to be me and you. For ever. We don't have anyone else.'

Owen had stared back at her, his eyes steady. Lily thought about how her brother's body had become estranged from her as they'd grown older. The shared baths had ended some years ago. They never slept together in the same bed now. Helen, in some subtle way, had drawn a line between them, but perhaps the carefully worded advice from the sick-bed indicated she had reeled this invisible barrier back into herself. Lily and Owen had been growing up during this time of less physical intimacy. He was nearly a man now, and she was certainly a woman. A calm, definite thought came to Lily as she lay there in her brother's arms. Owen, she knew, was hers. Acquaintances at school whispered and giggled about sex and boyfriends, but it was, in the main part, a fantasy for them. She could have what those girls craved at any time. It seemed a natural progression. There were no boys as beautiful or as intelligent as Owen, no others who understood her as he did.

'We must share everything,' she said to him. 'Do you understand?'

She ran her hand down his chest, his stomach, and found by the waiting hardness in his groin that he did understand.

Their love-making had been a ritual, an act of worship to gods unnamed, which they repeated as often as they felt was necessary to strengthen their bond. It had been that way since then. Until now. Othman was different. He kindled a wilder passion. With Owen, it had seemed necessary, a function performed to maintain a certain closeness. With Othman she had found simple pleasure, and she wanted more of it.

The villagers had looked after Lily and Owen after Helen died. Lily supposed she and her brother must have legal guardians somewhere, because surely no one under eighteen could have owned property or lived alone? Things had been taken care of. That meant people *knew*. It was time Lily was told exactly what that was. She remembered Eva Manden's old mother saying something to her not long after Helen had died. 'We'll all look out for you kids now, don't you worry. It's what your mother wanted. You're special, my girl.'

At the time, Lily had thought the old woman was just trying to be kind. Now she wondered.

A little tipsy, Lily went down to the post office to find

out. She was disappointed to find Eva's mother wasn't in her usual place on the stool by the bead curtain. 'Hello, Lily love,' said Eva as usual.

'Hi,' Lily answered. 'Is your mother about?'

Eva had frowned a little. 'No, dear. Why?'

'I wanted to talk to her. About my mother.'

Eva had known this would have to happen some day. Poor kid. Didn't she deserve to know? Eva was unsure. Personally, she thought that if Helen Winter had wanted the twins to find out who their father was, she'd have told them. 'What do you want to know?' Eva said.

'Everything,' Lily answered. 'Why did she come back here?'

Eva knew that the only reason Helen had returned to Little Moor was to hide the twins in safety, among people who understood what they were. 'Er ... well, apart from the cottage being left to her, perhaps your mum liked the quiet life, and Little Moor certainly has that, doesn't it!'

'There's more to it than that!' Lily said. 'I know there is.'

Eva drew in her breath, looking uncomfortable. By now, she could tell that Lily had been drinking. She came out from behind the counter. 'Well, perhaps your mum had private reasons for coming back, Lily, but if so, I don't know them.'

'Your mother does,' Lily accused. 'She was always talking to Mum.'

Eva nodded. 'Yes, I know, but if your mum told her anything, she's kept it close.' Eva didn't like lying to Lily. She knew that promises had been made to Helen Winter during her last illness. After the funeral, Emilia had dealt with the solicitors in Patterham on Helen's behalf, securing the twins' financial future. Emilia must have known by then, of course, what was happening to her body. Still, as energy waned, she had directed what was left of it towards the children, even if it had been from a distance. Emilia had never wanted a close relationship with them, but then she wasn't even that close to her own daughter. She had created a cloak of concealment around the twins, guarding them from suspicious eyes. Still, Eva did not want to divulge any of this to Lily. Although she couldn't admit it consciously, deep down Eva was afraid that her mother would *know* if she told the truth, and she was sensibly wary of upsetting Emilia. 'You look a bit peaky, dear. Why don't you sit down? I'll fetch you a cold drink.'

Lily flopped on to Emilia's stool by the bead curtain, her limbs splayed awkwardly. 'Yes, yes. I will.' She looked dazed.

No wonder! Eva thought as she went down to the cellar. She felt sorry for Lily, not least because she had picked up on the gossip muttered in the post office concerning Owen's friendship with the Cranton boy. That was seen as dangerous. The Crantons were outsiders. Bobby, Ray and Luke were natives, through and through. They were Owen's guardians, but even they had been unable to prevent the Cranton boy from being drawn into Owen's circle. And the weekend excursions to night-clubs, another unwise activity, were commented upon. Owen should be content to stay here in the village. He had friends here, who looked out for him. The Lord knows what could happen out there in the world. One day, Owen's difference might be noticed. One day, his heritage would have to manifest itself. That was one reason why it was so important for Owen and Lily to live as husband and wife. Neither of them should have lovers from outside, for in the moments of intimacy was the danger of revelation. Even Eva knew that, and she, for the most part, tried to ignore that aspect of Little Moor's history.

Eva returned to the shop with a glass of home-made ginger beer, which Lily drank without pausing.

'Now what's really worrying you?' Eva asked gently, thinking of Owen.

Lily sighed and wiped her mouth with the back of a hand. 'It might sound stupid, but I keep thinking there's a secret – about Owen and me, about our mother. I think people in Little Moor know what it is.'

Eva put a hand on Lily's shoulder. She'd managed to compose some convincing answers while pouring out the ginger beer. 'There's no secret, dear. Your mother was well thought of around here, and we all look out for you now. That's all there is to it.'

'Where does the money come from? Mum never worked for a living. Was she rich?'

Eva paused. 'I don't know, dear. I suppose so.'

'Do you know who my father is? Was it his money? He must have abandoned her, of course, but my aunt must have known who he was.'

Eva's instinct was to flinch away from the demand for truth in Lily's hot eyes. 'I think your father is dead,' she said carefully. 'I'm sure he didn't abandon your mother, or you and Owen. I expect he did leave her some money, don't you?'

'But why did she never speak about him?'

'Some things are best carried to the grave, Lily. If she'd wanted you to know about him, she would have told you.'

'But it's our right to know!' Lily exclaimed. 'It's not fair. It feels like a conspiracy now!' She eyed Eva fiercely. 'What about our aunt? I know nothing about her, either. It's like she never existed.'

Eva couldn't bear to look Lily in the eye and keep on

lying, but neither did she want to invite a barrage of awkward questions if she admitted the truth about the fictional aunt. She felt torn. How much simpler it would be to tell the poor girl everything, yet how difficult, too. 'Lily, I don't know anything about your family . . .'

Lily nodded. 'It was your mother who was always around when Mum was ill. Mum had dozens of friends in the village. They must have known about her. I really want to speak to your mother, Miss Manden.'

Let it go out of my hands, then, Eva thought. Emilia and her cronies were the ringleaders behind the secrecy. It was nothing to do with Eva, who'd never been involved with the Murkasters. Emilia had kept her away from all that, which Eva had correctly interpreted as jealousy. Emilia had not wanted to share her intimacy with the Murkasters with her young, attractive daughter. 'I'll tell her,' Eva said.

Lily sighed. 'Thanks. I'm sorry to bother you, but I'm feeling a bit bothered myself at the moment.'

So am I, thought Eva. She knew something was afoot in the village, but Emilia kept her in the dark. Perhaps Lily coming here asking questions was just a single component of what was buzzing beneath the surface of life at present.

As Lily left the post office, she missed Peverel Othman escorting Emilia Manden back from the day centre. If she'd seen them, she might not have recognized Emilia, who was looking so spry and vivacious.

Emilia knew that her daughter Eva was choosing to overlook the obvious changes in her, and was experiencing a kind of selective blindness, which suited Emilia fine. Eva was rebellious. She never had understood the special relationship Emilia had enjoyed with the Grigori. Been jealous, no doubt.

Emilia felt Othman was taunting the old ones in the village by turning up at the day centre as and when it suited him. A few of the more alert ones had realized Othman must have given Emilia some essence; she could feel their jealousy. All he was prepared to give the rest of them, it seemed, was his presence. Perhaps that in itself was a promise. Emilia wanted more than simple promises.

'You'll come in?' Emilia said as she and Othman approached the back door to the building. The garden was in shade, and it was cold on the porch. There was a strong scent of ripe apples in the air.

'I don't think . . .'

'Maybe I phrased that wrong,' Emilia said in a firm voice. 'You *are* coming in. I'm ready for more.'

'Well, maybe I'm not.'

'Is that so? Be careful, Othman, I can have a pack of famished hounds down on your back while you lie asleep at night. I can tell your little Winter friends a few things about you.'

'How brave you are, to threaten me,' Othman said.

'No. If you harmed me, everyone would know, because they saw you walking home with me. Harm me, and you'd have to leave here immediately, and you don't want that, do you?'

With a resigned sigh, Othman followed Emilia into the dark house. Emilia was a hunched shadow in the kitchen. 'You find me repulsive, don't you,' she said. 'Don't worry, I won't inflict this rotting flesh on you. Give me some light, and you can go. Come on, give me your wrist.'

Othman directed a penetrating stare at her. His eyes seemed to burn. 'Think you know it all, don't you,' he said. 'Come here.'

Emilia paused a moment, then complied. He'd let her have it one way or another, she didn't care which.

With cold, insensitive hands, Othman roughly pushed the old woman over the table, belly first. An irrepressible thrill ignited Emilia's flesh. He wouldn't, surely? A twenty-year-old memory twitched in her belly as Othman fastidiously removed her voluminous underwear. 'Sweet Emilia,' he said, and she braced herself for the delicious thrust.

Perversely, and obviously so as not to let her have it all her own way, he sodomized her to transfer the energy. Emilia was numb to any pain this caused. All she could feel was the raw spilling of his power, rapidly travelling through her veins and arteries, her bones. She could almost feel her hair and nails thrusting out with new growth as he pushed inside her. She could feel her flesh filling out. It took him some time to finish. Whether this was deliberate or not, Emilia couldn't tell. She did not stand up immediately once he withdrew, allowing him some time to rearrange his appearance. She'd nearly been burned before, looking at them too early. Othman was a tool to her; she felt completely passionless about it.

'Happy now?' he asked.

She stood up, straightened her dress. Her vague reflection in the window seemed taller than she remembered. 'Very,' she answered.

'Then I hope you'll be satisfied for a while. I can't keep doing this, you must realize that. What I've just given you should be enough for now.'

At that point, she turned, and was delighted by the subtle shift in Othman's expression. That, more than his words, told her he spoke the truth. He was surprised by his own magic. 'That's fine by me.' She smiled. 'But when you're tired of that sweet, innocent girl, and fancy something with a bit of bite, you know where to find me. And you know you'll need that eventually.'

Othman smiled thinly, but did not answer. He went out of the door without another word.

Emilia leaned against the table, her heart still pounding. She felt something trickle down her leg, and did not look for a moment, believing it must be his seed. When she did look, she saw blood. Her womanhood had come back to her, so quickly. Furtively, Emilia went upstairs.

Barbara was full of her news when she managed to waylay Othman on the stairs of The White House. He could barely understand her babble, he felt so exhausted. Emilia Manden was like a sponge. It had been his own hurt pride which had prompted the method by which he'd given her energy, but in retrospect, it had been a stupid choice. He'd given too much of himself.

'Are you all right?' Barbara asked. 'You look ill.'

'Bit of a hangover, I think,' he answered. 'Not used to drinking that much.'

'Oh dear! Perhaps you'd better have a lie down before dinner.'

'Yes,' Othman replied weakly.

He went directly to his room and lay sprawled on the bed, his head throbbing with pain in time to his heartbeat. All he'd acquired from covertly supping from Owen and Daniel's love-making had been taken away again. Some of it he'd given to Lily, with the intention of gently awakening her latent qualities. The rest had been sucked out of him by Emilia. It was a pity Owen was so suspicious of him, otherwise he could simply have asked the boy outright to help him replenish his strength. Soon, he would have to cultivate Owen's trust, but tonight he felt too tired. Sleep was in order, nothing else.

As he drifted between sleep and wakefulness, he thought about the dream Lily had related to him. He did not want to think about it, but forced himself to confront the issue. It was a mystery to him why she should dream of Shemyaza so vividly, but he did not like it. Perhaps racial memories were beginning to surface in her mind since one of her own kind had come into her life, but if so, she must not realize it yet. As she'd spoken, with such innocent enthusiasm, about all that she'd seen, Othman had wanted to take her hands and explain her dream to her. He knew that in her mind she had visited the Garden in Eden. Ninlil, remembered as a goddess, had been one of its main administrators. It was clear that Lily's dream had eavesdropped on a crucial time in Anannage history. Why? Why had her sleeping psyche been drawn to that particular scene? Did it reflect exactly what had happened? Had that conversation between Ninlil and Shemyaza really taken place all that time ago? Shemyaza had broken the laws of his people, and had been punished for it. Othman was not blind to the parallels that could be drawn with his own life. Before he died, Shemyaza had influenced many others, ultimately causing the rebellion among the Anannage which had divided and scattered its people. Unlike Othman, however, Shemyaza had been influenced by love – or so it was remembered. The human maiden Ishtahar, conniving priestess or bewitched devotee, had seduced Shemyaza's knowledge from him, and in return he had passed Anannage secrets to her. She, and others like her, had subsequently borne the children of her rebel Anannage lover. Over the centuries, the descendants of those children had become a hidden race among humanity. Grigori.

'And I am one of them,' Othman said aloud to the empty room, imagining Lily's face before him.

One day, he might tell Lily everything, but not yet. Once he was sure about what power remained in Little

Moor, and what he could do with it, he would think about enlightening the Winter twins concerning their origins. He wasn't sure how they'd take it. Disbelief at first, of course, but Lily, with her romantic tendencies, would eventually accept it. Owen? Difficult to predict his reaction. Perhaps, if Lily continued to dream of the Garden and her ancestors, it might help with convincing Owen. Othman wondered again whether there was a message for himself in Lily's dream. All his life the legend of Shemyaza and Ishtahar had been a story he'd shrunk from reading or discussing, even during his education as a child. Something about the myth made him feel uneasy, the *idea* of the hanged man was sickening to him. Shemyaza had been punished for loving a human woman and for divulging secrets to her. Othman thought, uncomfortably, of Emilia. Perhaps caution was called for in dealing with her. Othman never dismissed omens or portents out of hand.

Now he felt a familiar contraction start up in his belly. The compulsion to act was building up inside him again, to find the gate, to open it. Fragmented images of invocation and summoning, the offering of human flesh, raced before his mind's eye like wisps of smoke or cloud. In this hypnagogic state, his mind began to string information together and encountered the thought that the gate he yearned to breach might be the stargate Orion, the famous gate of Grigori myth, where the dreaded Shemyaza hung, his soul-face burned beyond recognition, his etheric body twisted and deformed. But as soon as the thought was encountered, Othman's conscious mind blocked it, as if turning him away from the scene of a hideous accident where bodies lay dismembered and howls of lamentation filled the air.

*

297

Barbara worried when Othman missed dinner, and brought a tray up to his room. Othman sought to allay her fears; the mention of calling a doctor unnerved him. 'I'll be fine tomorrow,' he told her.

The night was calm, its atmosphere unrippled by any thought or desire. Owen and Lily slept in their separate beds, having their separate dreams. Verity Cranton slumbered, with Raven curled innocently over her feet. Daniel lit a candle before he went to bed and stared at its shivering flame. He'd felt tired all day, which had helped to back up his story of feeling ill and missing school. Earlier, he had yearned for Owen to be there beside him, regretting the reticence of their embraces, wishing he'd had the confidence to ask for more, to take more. Now he felt at peace, sensually drowsy and comfortable in his bed and in his skin. Barbara and Barney Eager slept side by side, not touching. Barbara did not dream of forbidden lovers. She dreamed of summertime, and vast meadows.

The only person who slept uneasily was Eva Manden. She was still in shock. After shutting up the shop at five-thirty, she had gone back into the house. The sight that had greeted her in the kitchen was one she would never forget. At first, she'd thought a stranger had invaded the house, for a slim, elegant female figure stood at the sink, her back to the door, apparently engaged in peeling some potatoes. She was wearing a floral printed summer dress, her legs and feet bare. For one dreadful, heart-stopping moment, Eva had thought it was Helen Winter, but that was ridiculous for Helen was dead, and this woman's hair was dark, not pale.

'Excuse me?' Eva began, and the woman turned. Even then realization hadn't hit her, not even when the stranger had said, 'Evie dear, go and sit down. I'll get dinner ready.' The woman's dark chestnut hair fell over her shoulders in abundant shining waves. She wore no

298

make-up on her fine-boned face other than very red lipstick, which accentuated her generous mouth.

'Who . . .?' Eva began, but the words died in her throat.

'Evie, can't you see? I'm feeling so much better.' The woman held out her hands, one of which still clutched a potato peeler.

'Mother,' said Eva, feeling her way into one of the kitchen chairs, her eyes bulging. She dared not look away from the vision at the sink.

'That's right, dear. What is the matter with you? You look like you've seen a ghost!' Emilia laughed and turned back to her peeling.

'What's happened?' Eva asked in a hoarse voice.

'I would have thought you could work that out for yourself, dear. Would you like chops or a pie?'

'Who's done this?' Eva demanded. 'Who? Are *they* back? Are they?'

Emilia looked over her shoulder, swung her hair. 'Calm down, dear. You sound hysterical. I must say you pay very little attention to what goes on around here, but that doesn't really surprise me. The Murkasters haven't returned, no, but a relation of theirs has. Peverel Othman.'

The name meant little to Eva, who had deliberately been excluded from village gossip concerning the travel-ler, at the insistence of her mother. All still obeyed the words of Emilia Manden. At one time she had held the whip for the Murkasters in Little Moor.

Eva had begun to shake. 'This is an abomination,' she said. 'I know what you really look like. This isn't real!'

Emilia merely laughed. Then her face set into a harder expression and she came towards the table, leaned upon it on stiff arms. Eva cowered back in her chair. 'My dear,' said Emilia. 'Take a good look. *This* is what I'm really like, what I've always been like. I'm just lucky because I've found a way around the injustice, the fucking unbelievable injustice, of nature. You think the decaying body was me? You think the sagging tits, the slab shanks, the dried-up old cunt, was me? No. *This* is me. And it's the same for every god-damned ancient bint in the world, whatever nature's done to them. Just remember that.'

Mother and daughter stared at one another in silence. Eva was speechless. She felt she could sense her own blood drying in her veins, her own flesh desiccating. This woman before her looked at least twenty years her junior. Emilia reached out with the potato peeler, gently touched the end of her daughter's nose with it, smiled sweetly. 'Chops, I think,' she said. 'I just fancy some *red* meat.'

Chapter Seventeen

Friday, 23rd October: High Crag House, Cornwall
The day had closed in upon itself, shrouds of dark cloud surrounded High Crag House. After their talk had ended in his office, Enniel had escorted Aninka to one of the smaller dining-rooms for dinner. They dined alone. Soft candlelight bloomed above the polished table and caught the inner spark in the lead crystal goblets set before each plate. A fire burned in the hearth behind Aninka's chair. She felt drained and drowsy. The meal had been consumed, punctuated only by small talk. Enniel had poured rich, red wine into Aninka's goblet whenever she'd drunk more than half of it. She felt warm towards her guardian now. He had surprised her with his tenderness and sympathy. He offered her a cigarette and lit it for her. She watched him carefully as she leaned forward to the flame he offered her. He was a supremely handsome example of his kind. Only now could she see him as a man and not just a surrogate parent. She thought that if he asked to sleep with her tonight, she would comply. However, she also knew that any such suggestion would have to come from her. Perhaps it would be healing for her if she attempted a seduction, and imprinted another man's hands over the memory of Othman's touch.

'Is Noah right?' she asked, exhaling a plume of smoke.

Enniel leaned back in his chair, his eyes cautious. He clearly hadn't expected Aninka to raise the subject of her torment again tonight. 'About what, exactly?'

Aninka rested her chin on one hand. 'That you'll just

cover things up, cement over the cracks and forget about what happened in Cresterfield.'

Enniel shook his head. 'No, all efforts will be made to track Othman down. Noah is only right in that usually Anakim are long gone by the time their delinquencies are made public. And they are difficult to pursue, because, as your cousin correctly pointed out, they are generally mature and experienced individuals. That does not mean, however, that we *won't* catch him.'

'What will happen to him if you do?'

Enniel smiled. 'That depends on whether he's alive or not. If he is, we shall attempt rehabilitation. If that fails, and the success rate is not high, he will be incarcerated until this lifespan has run its course. It is not in our codes to kill our own kind, Aninka. Once, in the distant past, we were forced to, when the High Lord of the Anannage turned brother against brother in a futile attempt to annihilate the Nefilim half-breeds, but it won't happen again.'

Aninka sighed. 'Great Shem, not more of that old hogwash! I'm sick of people living in the past. It's over, and has been over for thousands of years. It has no bearing on the present.'

Enniel refused to rise to her bait. 'You are young,' he answered. 'As you grow older, all "that old hogwash", as you refer to it, will mean more to you. We are still living it, Aninka, because it is a story that never ended. We are responsible for the way that the world works now: its science, its religions, even its wars. We were exiled from the Source, the One, the place of our origin. The gate closed for us. But some foolish Grigori recklessly attempt to claw it open again. Now do you see why what you experienced in Cresterfield is important to us?'

Aninka frowned. 'I'm not sure exactly what happened there. I knew Othman was attempting to call something . . . *horrible* up, but why? I can't understand why Serafina and the others had to die. I thought at the time it was just an excuse for an orgy, but then . . .' She shook her head, grimacing. 'I realize now Pev's intention was always more than just sex.'

Enniel regarded her steadily for a few moments. In his heart he was considering just how much he should tell Aninka. He could see her pain permeating the colours of her aura, dampening its glow. 'Well, I think we can assume that Othman has undoubtedly tried that trick many times before.'

'What trick?'

'The conjuration. I think his motive is a lust for power. Perhaps he senses, subliminally, that accessing the stargate would help him. The gate is sealed and he calls up demonic presences to do his work for him, in an attempt to open the gate once more. But force of that kind will never succeed. Othman failed in Cresterfield, as he has undoubtedly failed before. I believe that he will continue to assault the gate in this way, and that his methods will never be successful. It's possible that his actions are for the most part unconscious. If not, he probably would have worked out for himself by now that his techniques are wrong. He offered Serafina's life-force and the power of her sexual energy to a demon, which was clearly accepted as delicious sustenance. Presumably, in payment for this feast the demon was supposed to act as a psychic battering ram against the stargate. Unfortunately, it appears that the entity not only failed or refused to carry out this task, but devoured the life-force of every other human who was unlucky enough to be there! Of course, I can only guess at whether that was Othman's intention or not, but I'm pretty sure it was.'

Aninka narrowed her eyes at Enniel. 'You know a lot about his attempts at this kind of thing, don't you?'

Enniel shrugged. 'Let's just say we've found evidence of this type of activity before, and events suggested the same person was behind it. But we had not connected it with Peverel Othman before you gave us your information. Now that we know exactly what's going on, we must put a stop to it.'

Aninka stubbed out the cigarette angrily. 'I want to help,' she said. 'I want to find him.'

'You feel humiliated and extremely hurt,' Enniel said smoothly. 'That's understandable. Grief squeezes your soul. You want revenge, not just for what Othman did to the little people, but for what he's done to you. Think very hard, my dear, before embarking upon some heroic course. Your anger means nothing to a man like Peverel Othman.'

'I don't care,' Aninka said. 'I can't just go back to my life and forget about this.'

'Indeed not. I have found an apartment for you in London.'

'That's not what I mean!'

Enniel shook his head, gently smiling at her. 'Aninka, I have been forced to donate a sizeable amount of priceless family relics to the museum in Cresterfield, as part of the deal for getting you out of this mess. They will probably end up in private collections in South America, without ever being appreciated by the public eye over here. I'm not blaming you, but your inexperience allowed you to get involved with Othman. Do you really think you're capable of bringing him down?'

'He would never have targeted a mature Grigori,' Aninka said. 'I don't even blame myself for getting involved. And I don't know whether I'm capable or not of dealing with Othman. I just want to try.'

'You are very precious to me, my dear. I would hate for you to be hurt.'

She looked at her guardian. He was still smiling. 'You knew I'd say these things, didn't you?'

'Of course. It's quite natural, and you are a creature of spirit. Proud, I should say.' He leaned towards her across the table, reaching for her hand that lay there. 'This renegade, who has offended you so badly, is not unknown to us, but then you guessed that.'

Aninka ran her thumb along Enniel's palm. 'So what else can you tell me about him?' She dared to hope a bottle of wine had loosened her guardian's tongue.

'Well, as I said, his activities have come to our attention before, but nothing quite so unpleasant as the Cresterfield incident. Peverel Othman, just one of many aliases, of course, was first noticed about two years ago when he lived in Europe. He came to England about twelve months ago, leaving a devastation of wrecked lives behind him. Once here, he started dabbling. He covers his tracks well, but usually he targets the most influential people: politicians, celebrities. The motive appears to be money. He earns his living by corruption. Until recently, we had not connected his operations with the evidence that had been found relating to demonic sacrifice. I suspect he's gone for small fry often in the past to consummate his unsavoury urges, but masked his behaviour with his more overt and relatively less destructive games with the rich and famous. His operations are generally more subtle than this – he has, for example, never been connected with murder before. Not directly. In fact, he has been a shadowy presence, hovering on the edge of our perceptions for quite some time. We have kept an eye on him, but also kept our distance. Maybe he has gone completely berserk now. I cannot say.'

Aninka was stunned. 'Haven't you called him to you, spoken to him? You just let him get on with whatever he was doing?'

'Othman has been interviewed by members of the Parzupheim in the past, but it was a long time ago. He was warned not to threaten our security. He never did.' Enniel leaned back again, releasing her hand. 'It is not our function to worry about humanity, Aninka. They are a nuisance we have to live with and co-operate with, to a large degree. You are upset because your human friends have been killed, but that really is no concern of ours. Yes, we must now try and entrap Peverel Othman, but for our own safety. He could be capable of anything. Just don't mistake our motives.'

Aninka smiled, too weary to be angry about the way Enniel spoke about her dead friends. He could never understand her feelings. 'You talk like him, you know. In your position, he would say the same, I'm sure.'

Enniel pulled a wry face, shrugged. 'Oh dear. I'm not sure what that says about me! We're investigating his movements in Europe now.'

'You'll find his ex-lover over there.'

Enniel raised one eyebrow. 'You are interested in that, of course.'

Aninka ducked her head. 'Well, yes. I'd like to meet him.'

'What's left of him.'

'Who is it?' Aninka demanded. 'You know who it is, don't you, or how else would you know what condition he's in?'

Enniel gestured with one hand. 'Conjecture, my dear. I'm simply looking at the state of *you* now and taking a wild guess.'

'There's plenty left of me!' Aninka said, and smiled. When she spoke, the suggestion in her voice was plain. 'Would you like to find out how much?'

Enniel considered this offer. 'Very much so. I'm surprised, Ninka. I thought you disliked me.'

'Well, I've grown up,' she replied. 'I've caught up with you, somewhat. When I was a child, you were nothing more to me than the voice of authority. Now I can see you're an attractive man. Have you had the others, Noah, Tearah and Rachel?'

Enniel rolled his eyes. 'Don't make me sound greedy. Do you really need to know?'

Aninka stood up. 'No. Can we go upstairs now?'

Enniel took her to his grand bedroom, with its crimson and violet tapestries, its stained-glass windows, hidden by thick blue velvet drapes. The bed was enormous, like the bed of a king, decorated with carved peacocks. Here, Enniel performed one of his functions as head of the family. He was bound to submit to whomever wanted him, the giver of seed and of life and warmth. Aninka's parents had given her to him to raise because he was respected and would ensure a suitable future for her. She had not seen them since she was a baby, and could not remember them. This was not unusual among the Grigori. Now, as she lay naked on Enniel's bed, she thought about them. No doubt they would have expected this to happen several years before. It had been Aninka who resisted. She had not asked and Enniel would never have offered. It was not part of his duty to do that.

He stood at the foot of the bed and undressed himself slowly, let down his dark red hair, casting off the image of efficient businessman and becoming pure Grigori. He flexed his long body, shook out his hair, the soft lighting affectionately caressing his perfect limbs. It was the only foreplay Aninka needed. She held out her arms to him. 'Come to me.'

Chapter Eighteen

Same day: Little Moor

Barbara was quite surprised at lunchtime on Friday when Peverel Othman asked her if he could attend her writers' meeting that evening.

'But of course,' she said. 'Are you intending to contribute?'

'I'd have no other reason for attending, would I?' He smiled roguishly to imply that Barbara's company might be reason enough.

Barbara herself wondered exactly what his motives might be. She had met Mariam Alderly in the store earlier that morning, and had been forced to smother her surprise when Mariam had laid a hand on her arm and announced, 'I must thank you for sending Pev to us, Barbara. He's a godsend!' She had patted the canvas bag hanging over her arm. 'I can get out and about a bit during the day now. It's a great weight off me, I can tell you!'

'Er . . . yes. *What* exactly is Pev doing for you, Mari?'

'The voluntary work, as you suggested, of course!' Mariam laughed, an unfamiliar twinkle in her eye. 'The old ones love him! And he's the only person I've met who can keep the old witch Emilia Manden under control!' She leaned closer, casting a furtive glance to left and right. 'Mind you, Emilia hasn't shown up today! I'm hoping he's persuaded her not to come any more. I know he takes her out for walks, and suchlike, so perhaps she's contented with that now.'

Barbara was stunned by this information. *Voluntary*

work? Walks with local old women? 'Well, one thing I do know, Mari, our Mr Othman is a continual box of surprises! I had no idea he . . . he'd take me up on the suggestion.' She had, in fact, never mentioned the old people's day centre to him.

'Well, thanks anyway,' said Mariam, almost skipping to the door. 'Toodle-oo.'

Now Barbara was confronted with the decision as to whether she should face Peverel Othman out or not over the matter. They were in the bar, Othman in the process of devouring a hearty lunch. Barbara sat down opposite him. 'Aren't you back a bit early? I thought the old people's centre was open until three-thirty.'

If he was unsettled by her remark, he hid it well. He didn't even pause in his chewing, dab his mouth with a timely napkin, or take a drink of his beer. Instead, he laughed, swallowed. 'Oh Barbara, you've caught me out!'

Barbara put her head on one side. 'Apparently, I suggested you should get involved in voluntary work. Forgive me, but the memory of that suggestion escapes me!'

Othman shrugged, forked up another helping of shepherd's pie. 'OK, I exaggerated, well *lied*, I suppose, but I couldn't see the old biddy who runs the place letting a perfect stranger in without at least some respectable recommendation. Your name works wonders in Little Moor, Barbara. It's like a free pass.'

'Pev,' Barbara began in a stern tone, 'I find it hard to believe you really want to work with old people. What are you up to?'

'You shouldn't make assumptions about me. You hardly know me.'

'Quite.'

He put down his fork, rested his chin in his hands. 'Very well. If you must know, I want to get to know the old people in order to expedite my enquiries concerning the Murkasters.'

'This has become quite an obsession,' Barbara remarked dryly. 'So much so, I can't help thinking that researching the Murkasters is your sole reason for being here in the village.'

He grinned. 'OK, Ms Holmes, you worked it out.' He leaned forward. 'But don't advertise it, all right?'

'What is your interest in them, or is that a secret, too?'

'I'm a writer,' Othman said, 'and I like to grub around in mysteries. This book could be a big one, but I'm cautious about treading on the wrong toes, especially the wrong *powerful* toes.'

Barbara shook her head. 'And there you were the other night, inciting us all at Louis's to start doing your research for you!'

Othman pulled a mock frown. 'No, I didn't. As I recall, you and Lily ran off with the bit between your teeth without any coercion from me!' He laughed. 'But don't go thinking you can gazump me by sending a manuscript off to a publisher before I get mine in. Anyway, I'm contracted.'

'I wouldn't dream of it!' Barbara said. She felt rather dizzy. The reasons for Othman's secrecy and slightly sinister behaviour seemed obvious now. 'So what are you going to bring to the meeting tonight, some of your manuscript?'

He shook his head. 'No. And I would prefer it if you didn't mention what I'm working on to anyone, not even the Winters. I'll find something to bring, don't worry.'

'You can tell us about getting published,' Barbara said. 'I presume you've had books out before?'

'A couple,' Othman said casually, applying himself to his lunch once more.

*

By Friday afternoon, Lily was starting to panic because Othman hadn't called on her again. Owen picked up on her restlessness, and probably divined its cause, but made no comment other than a sarcastic, 'Are you premenstrual, or something?' Lily went for a walk to escape her brother's observation, leaving him delving in the fractious innards of the car, with Ray Perks looking on. Owen had been seeing less of his friends recently, Lily thought as she passed them. Bobby had phoned twice since the weekend and she suspected Owen hadn't bothered returning the calls.

Her feet led her unconsciously to the post office, and it was only when her hand was actually on the door that she realized what she was doing.

'Lily!' Eva Manden exclaimed, as if in horror, as Lily walked into the shop.

'Hi,' Lily said, eyeing the empty stool by the curtain. 'Your mother not here again?'

'No,' Eva said. 'She's not. I did tell her you'd called, Lily, but . . .'

'Evie, who is it?' called a husky, female voice from beyond the curtain.

Eva said nothing, looking at Lily in mute appeal. Then she whispered. 'Please, just go!'

Lily took a single step backwards, surprised by Eva's expression and words, but before she could leave the shop, another woman came through the bead curtain. 'Lily Winter,' she said, one hand on the door-frame, another lifting a cigarette to her lush mouth. Lily had never seen such a beautiful woman.

'Hello,' she said, and frowned. 'Do I know you?' She couldn't remember having met the woman before, and surely she wouldn't forget such a stunning sight?

The woman sashayed into the dingy shop, lighting up its dusty corners with her presence. 'I knew your mother,' she said. 'In fact, this is her dress. She gave it to me.' She indicated the loose, faded red folds that fell flatteringly around her slender body. Lily did not recognize it, but then her mother had always had a wardrobe stuffed full of clothes, most of which she never wore. The woman held out a hand, flashed a wide smile. Tentatively, Lily took the offered hand, shook it. The woman's grip was strong and dry. 'I'm Emma,' she said. 'Emma Manden.'

'Oh,' said Lily, 'a relation?' She glanced at Eva, whose expression was that of stone, blank and hard.

'That's right,' said Emma. 'I understand you've been asking about your mother?'

Lily nodded. 'Yes. I wanted to talk to Mrs Manden. She knew her very well.'

'Unfortunately, Mrs Manden isn't very well,' said Emma. 'In fact, she's had to go away.'

'Oh, I'm sorry.' Lily glanced once again at Eva, who still appeared to be frozen.

'That's why I'm here,' said Emma, 'to help. Anyway, I knew your mother very well, too, so perhaps we could go for a walk and have a chat about her.' She looked at Eva. 'You don't need me this afternoon, do you?'

'Do what you like,' answered Eva in a flat voice. She turned away and busied herself straightening some magazines on the shelf behind the counter.

Emma put an elegant hand on Lily's shoulder. 'Well, would you like to walk with me?'

Lily shrugged. 'Well, er, yes. I suppose so.'

They went out of the shop. Lily was privately thinking that Emma Manden looked too young to have known her mother that well, but then, as she'd already come to suspect with Peverel Othman, appearances might be deceptive.

'Will Mrs Manden be all right?' she asked, as they walked down the lane. She let Emma choose the route.

'Oh, I doubt it,' Emma replied, wrinkling her nose. 'But then, she's very old. Poor old Eva will be devastated, of course, but it can't be helped. Personally, I think Emilia's better off dead. It must be dreadful to get so old and frail, don't you think?'

Lily liked Emma's forthright attitude. She seemed an easy person to be with, as if Lily had known her for years. 'Oh yes. The thought of it scares me. If I think about it, that is.'

Emma linked her arm through Lily's. 'Well, I doubt you think about it very often, and why should you!'

Lily was slightly disturbed, and slightly thrilled, when this unusual female leaned over and kissed her cheek. 'Er . . . thanks.'

'Anyway, such a lovely thing as yourself, I doubt you'll ever get old. The very thought is an abomination!' Emma laughed in a free, ringing manner, the sheer essence of laughter.

'Have we met before?' Lily asked.

'Oh yes,' Emma answered, 'but I looked different then.'

'Much younger, I suppose?'

'Well, age can make a change to appearance, can't it!'

Emma was leading them out of the village. 'Where are we going?' she asked. She sensed Emma had a definite destination in mind.

'Oh, just walking. Do you mind? Let's allow our feet to guide us.'

Your feet, thought Lily, but she didn't object.

'Isn't it warm for October,' Lily said, to break a silence.

'Yes. I expect it's very cold everywhere else in the country. Little Moor is enchanted by heat, a heat that pervades everything, even flesh!' Emma pinched Lily's arm.

'That's weird!' Lily said, giggling. She was beginning to think Emma Manden was rather an odd woman.

'Weird, yes,' agreed Emma. 'Ask me about your mother.'

'Well, actually, it's my father I'm rather more interested in.' Lily felt no awkwardness about confessing this to Emma.

Emma laughed. 'Ah, I see! Well, I don't blame you!'

Lily's heart leaped in her chest. 'You knew him?'

'Oh, *very* well!' Emma smiled at Lily. 'I expect you're going to ask me what he was like.'

'Well, I would like to know. Mum never told us anything. I want to know why it's such a big secret.'

'It's only a secret to those who don't know,' Emma said, rather enigmatically. 'Scandal, you know, in a small community like this, breeds all manner of intrigue.'

'Scandal,' said Lily, deadpan.

Emma stopped walking. Lily noticed they had come to the overgrown gateway of Long Eden. Emma was staring down at the wilderness of the driveway. She made a move in that direction. 'You don't want to go in there, do you?' Lily asked.

'Yes,' said Emma. 'I do. What's the matter?'

'I don't like it,' Lily answered, disengaging her arm from Emma's. 'It spooks me.'

'Nothing to be afraid of,' Emma said. 'Not for *you*, Lily Winter, especially not for you.'

'What do you mean?' Lily asked, but Emma was already squeezing between the rusting, sagging bars of the gates like an eel. Lily paused for a moment, then reluctantly followed. By the time she'd wrenched her body through the gate, Emma was some yards up the drive. Lily had to run to catch up. Emma glanced behind herself, noticed Lily's pursuit, and also began to run. She did not slow down until the shadow of Long Eden fell over her, where she glowed within it. Lily came gasping to a halt before her, beyond the fingers of shade.

'Well, here we are!' Emma said, her hands on her hips, her head thrown back as if to bask in the shadow of the house. 'I've always loved this place. It's such a shame it's not cared for any more. But then, perhaps it is.'

Lily was gasping for breath. Was she that unfit? Emma wasn't breathing even slightly heavily. The enormous towers of the house seemed to loom over Lily with oppressive intent. She'd never liked it here, not even when she and Owen, as children, had been obsessed with grubbing around old ruins. She wanted to tell Emma how much she hated it, but, for some stupid reason, didn't want to say anything like that when the house could *hear* her. 'I wouldn't want to live here,' Lily said. 'It's too big.' Even though she stood beyond the shadow, she had to shiver. 'When are you going to tell me about my father?'

'Lily, come here.' Emma held out her arms, extended them from the shade. Light danced upon the golden hairs on her skin.

'No,' said Lily. 'I don't want to.'

'Come under the wing,' said Emma. 'Don't be afraid. This is your *home*, Lily.'

'No, it's not,' Lily said, backing away. She wanted to get away from Emma now. The woman was mad, could even be dangerous.

'But it *is* your home,' Emma continued in a gentle, coaxing voice. 'This is your father's house, the High Lord Kashday. This is his seat, his place of power. You are the daughter of this house.' The soft chanting tone of Emma's voice, more than the actual words she spoke, raised the hair on Lily's head. She dared not take her eyes away from Emma's, afraid of looking at the black stones behind her, rearing so high.

'My father?' she said.

Emma nodded. 'That is correct, my dear. Helen, your mother, was seduced by the lord of this house. You. Your brother. The progeny.'

Lily shook her head, even laughed a little, nervously. 'That's impossible!'

'Why? Surely you should know that *nothing* is impossible?' Emma folded her arms. 'I was here when your mother first came to Little Moor. I knew her well. She left here twenty years ago, and came back when you were in your early teens.'

'My aunt –' Lily began.

Emma shook her head. 'There was no aunt, Lily, no relative of flesh and blood. You belong to this village and its people. If anything, the women of Little Moor are *all* your aunts. It is we who have cared for you since Helen died.'

Lily frowned. 'I don't understand. This is all too much . . .'

Emma sighed. 'Ah, your father was fine, my Lily, a fine man. You would have loved him, and he would have loved you. Such a pity.'

'Is it really true?' Lily asked in a weak voice. She felt numb, somehow immune to the words. Surely she should feel shocked or excited, bursting with questions. Strangely, there were none.

Emma nodded. 'Quite true. It's the secret they've been keeping from you, all this time. I just had to tell you. It's only right.'

Still smiling, she came out of the shadows, into the sunlight. 'Don't be afraid, Lily. There's no need. Your mother, I know, wanted this to remain secret, but things are happening now, and I think it's vital you become aware of your heritage. Soon, you will understand what I mean. Be careful of strangers.'

Lily shuddered. How much did this woman know about her? Perhaps it was a lie, this thing about her father. Perhaps Emma was playing with her. Yet there were the listening shadows of the house thrown out over the unseasonably warm day, grabbing sunlight and, somehow, in a totally invisible, indescribable way, backing up Emma's words. That house. Lily risked a glance at it. He had walked through those battened doors. He had stood there, once, gazing at this spot where one day his daughter would stand. Lily could almost see him, a tall, insubstantial shadow in the arch of the porch, standing beneath the coat of arms, devoid of mottoes, proclaiming only 'Murkaster'.

'You see,' murmured Emma. 'You must come home. Soon, if not today.'

Lily could no longer deny the urge to escape, which had been building within her since Emma had revealed her knowledge. Emma's vivid presence filled Lily's head. It was impossible to think about what she'd heard while she was with Emma. 'I have to go,' she said, taking a few steps back, dragging her eyes away from the house towards Emma's bland, beautiful face. Emma had taken a packet of cigarettes and a slim, ladies' lighter from her skirt pocket and was lighting up. The sun flashed on the chased silver casing of the lighter. The air, momentarily, smelled of petrol.

'Of course you do,' she said. 'I quite understand. This must be . . . a shock to you. You must go away and think about what I've told you.' She paused, exhaled smoke in a silvery plume, smoke which had touched the inside of her body. 'Perhaps you should not mention any of this to Owen, just yet.'

'Why not?' In fact, Lily hadn't yet considered telling her brother. But she might tell Peverel Othman.

'Tell no one,' Emma said firmly. 'You are being welcomed into the ways of women, Lily, *certain* ways. I must ask you to trust me.'

Hadn't Othman asked that of her, too? Lily shrugged. 'All right.' She had no intention of keeping to it.

'I mean what I say, my dear,' Emma continued, her eyes fixed unblinkingly upon Lily's. 'Especially, you must not speak to any of your new friends. If you *want* Peverel Othman – and I know you do – you must keep silent for now. This knowledge is your tool of control over him. He must not realize you know.'

Lily looked away, felt herself blush. 'I *don't* want him,' she said.

Emma came towards her on light feet, touched her hair. 'Lily, my dear, don't lie to me. He has spoken to certain people here in Little Moor. He knows about you. Othman is more than he seems, a very powerful, dangerous man. You don't realize how close you are to being burned, which is why you must trust me. I know how to handle his type, how to wield the whip to keep the jaws at bay. This is a simple truth.' She smiled. 'I know you are wondering how I have the right to say these things to you, but all I can tell you is that I am aware of your mother's history, and your own, and really do know what's best for you. It is no coincidence I have come back here now, just as your world is beginning to change. And it *is* changing, isn't it? I've come back here *especially* to help you. As a test, I will say this: he will not come to you tonight, nor tomorrow. The next night he may well come to you, but not before.' She stepped back into the shadow. 'Now go. We shall talk again soon. I look forward to it.'

Lily stared at her for a few moments, and then turned,

ran without stopping all the way back down the drive. At the gates, she looked back as she squeezed herself through the bars, but there was no sign of Emma Manden. The shadows seemed to have swallowed her.

Chapter Nineteen

Same day: Cresterfield and Little Moor

Daniel Cranton was both embarrassed and delighted to find that Owen had come in the old car to meet him from school. They had not seen each other since very early Thursday morning, when Owen had sneaked out of the house; it felt like an eternity to Daniel.

As he walked down the school driveway with a group of friends, one of them said, 'My God, who's that?'

Owen had parked the car just beyond the gates, and was leaning against the bonnet, dressed in his city evening clothes of leather and black linen, wearing a pair of shades, his hair a yellow-white mane around his head and shoulders. He was smoking what appeared to be a cigarette, but Daniel knew Owen well enough to suspect it might be more than that. Daniel kept silent during the interminable stroll to the gates, while his friends, who suddenly seemed absurdly young and naive, conjectured about which girl might be the one for whom this outlandish interloper was waiting. In the manner of young males finding themselves in the presence of a superior specimen of their kind, who was clearly a member of a different youth culture to their own, they began to make insulting remarks, which grew ever louder as they approached the car. Daniel cringed inwardly. In a way, he wanted to run, so that no one would know that Owen was waiting there for him. Another, braver part of him, welcomed the moment of surprise when this fact became obvious.

'Fucking weirdo!' one of the boys said loudly, the

proud owner of a haircut seen only in places where alternative culture never ventured.

Owen raised his shades. To make matters worse, he was wearing smudged eye-liner, obviously already dressed for this evening's entertainment. 'Fancy a lift, boy?' he drawled in a fake American accent.

This invoked a babble of outraged and confused braying from Daniel's companions.

'Give it a rest, O,' Daniel said, and walked round to get in the passenger side of the car, before anyone could say anything else.

Owen got in, grinning, and started the engine.

'Thanks,' Daniel said. 'Remember I have to come back here on Monday and explain myself.'

'Only a few more months,' Owen said airily. 'You could leave now, if you wanted to.'

Daniel declined to respond. And live with you after my father and sister go berserk? he thought. He couldn't bear to look at his school friends, who had all stopped to gawp at Daniel sitting in the car. He could feel his face was bright red. They must know, he thought, they must all know. Oh God!

'What a bunch of pussies!' Owen said, grimacing at the schoolboys. 'Prematurely middle-aged. From school to Daddy's curse of terminal adulthood in a single step, no doubt.' He swung the car around, dangerously close to where the group stood. Daniel stared at his hands, mortified.

'We don't all have the benefit of a private income,' he said sourly. 'Not everyone has the freedom you have, me included.'

'True. Can't say it bothers me particularly.' Owen pushed a tape into the cassette deck, thus precluding further conversation. He drove recklessly through Patterham town centre, narrowly missing pedestrians. Daniel could tell Owen was in a dangerous mood. What this signified in respect of himself, he couldn't guess. Owen had never picked him up before, so what had happened on Wednesday night must have changed things. However, there was no sign that Owen had been desperate to see Daniel. Perhaps a talk was presaged, a request to forget their brief, fumbling intimacy. That might be best, Daniel thought. He wasn't sure he could cope with anything else, even though he yearned for it.

Owen gave no explanation as to why he'd driven over to Patterham, although Daniel noticed some bags from music shops on the back seat, indicating Owen had been treating himself. Perhaps it was a coincidence he'd been about to go home at school closing time. Daniel took off his tie, loosened his shirt collar. He didn't like Owen seeing him in uniform. It made him feel young and conventional.

They drove without speaking until the countryside spread out to either side and the road climbed towards the hilltops. Then Owen said, 'We'll call in at yours so you can get changed.'

'Where are we going?'

'Cresterfield. I thought we'd go to Marlene's tonight.'

Daniel frowned. 'It's a bit early, isn't it?' The club didn't open until ten.

'We can eat in town. I'll treat you.'

'What about the others, Ray and everyone?'

Owen didn't answer for a moment. 'They're busy tonight.'

Daniel had never known Ray and the others to be 'busy', unless Owen was involved. Surely this was a good sign rather than a bad one. Owen clearly wanted to be alone with him. Daniel felt a little encouraged, though more nervous. How could they possibly speak about what had happened? It seemed like a vaguely prurient dream now.

Little Moor appeared empty as they drove up the lane. Owen turned the car on to Low Mede's drive. Daniel noticed him glance quickly at his own cottage before he swung the vehicle beneath a convenient screen of willow branches that drooped across the gravel. Did Lily know that Owen was here? How much did Lily know?

'Be quick,' Owen said. He leaned back in his seat and lit a cigarette.

'Aren't you coming in?'

'No. Go on, then!'

In the attic room Daniel dressed carefully, outlined his eyes in black, messed up the hair he was not allowed to dye or grow. The house was quiet around him; not even Verity was at home. Perhaps she'd gone out with Louis. Daniel left a note on the kitchen table, paused to stroke Raven's head, plucking up the courage to go back outside. He felt that by donning his other-life attire, he was making some kind of obvious invitation, which Owen would scorn. Presently he heard the car horn being sounded, forcing him to leave the sanctuary of the house.

Owen made no comment as Daniel got back into the car, pulling on a leather jacket adorned with careful paintings of band logos. They left Little Moor the way they'd come in, without passing the cottage.

An hour's drive later, they reached the city. Nothing had been said, as loud music had filled the interior of the car the entire time. Owen parked up in a multi-storey and they went to an American restaurant nearby that served Creole food. Daniel felt out of place. He'd never eaten out with Owen before, and their clothes invoked curious glances from the staff of the restaurant. Even the fact that the early hour meant the place was nearly empty didn't make Daniel feel any easier. Owen ate sparingly, drinking ice-cold bottles of imported Mexican beer. It didn't feel natural for them to be sitting there like a boy and girl out on a date. It felt weird. What was Owen playing at? He didn't seem to care, sitting there, swigging beer, gazing around the place. Was this supposed to be a treat for Daniel? If so, it didn't feel like one. Not one word was uttered about Wednesday night, not about the meal or the events after it. Owen talked about music, the CDs he'd bought, which bands he planned to go and see live in the near future. Was he nervous? He didn't seem so. The conversation was normal, how he'd be with Ray and the others on the nights when they didn't visit the High Place, but now it seemed strained, false.

When Daniel had finished eating – he'd been surprisingly hungry, which was a blessing considering there was nothing else to do but eat as he listened to Owen – Owen paid for the meal with a credit card. Daniel had never seen Owen use one before. Everything was strange now, different.

'We'll go to The Angus,' said Owen. This was a pub where the local alternative types met up before going out clubbing. At seven o'clock, it, too, was nearly empty, but the music was blaring. Owen put some money in the juke box, then a couple of girls he was acquainted with came in and joined them. Owen introduced them to Daniel, even though he must have met them before. Cressida and Letiel, assumed names, he presumed. They all used assumed names. Both were tall and skinny, dressed in lacy black rags, with much fishnet-clad thigh and bare cleavage exposed. Cressida had thigh-length scarlet plaits, Letiel an astounding mane of green hair extensions. Both were talkative and flirty. Daniel had a feeling Owen had arranged for the girls to meet them there and his heart sank. Girls were always forcing their telephone numbers on Owen, but as far as Daniel knew, he'd never made use of them before. They were enthusing about some band they'd been to see the night before, and Owen joined in with their conversation, apparently fascinated. Daniel sat at the bar, frozen with misery and confusion, ignored by the others, who were standing up around him. Owen was drinking too much. How would he drive home? That he might not intend to was unbearable to think about. Daniel decided he might as well get drunk, too. He asked Owen to buy him a Jack Daniels, which he thought to be a sophisticated drink. Owen gave him a ten-pound note from his jacket without even looking at him.

'Do you want a drink?' Daniel asked the girls.

They asked for vodkas, sensing affluence, and downed their half-pints of cider quickly.

Alcohol made the time pass quickly. A number of Letiel and Cressida's friends arrived in groups of two or three, and by the time they were due to move on to Marlene's, Owen and Daniel were in a crowd of about twenty people. Letiel had made an effort to talk to Daniel, and had been telling him about her college course in fashion. When asked what he did, he waspishly told the truth, expecting mockery. Letiel only said, 'I wish I'd bothered to stay on at school, now. You can't wait to get out, can you? It's the environment, I think. Stultifying. Still, I wasted a couple of years. It's so much harder now. I wish I had your guts.'

Daniel didn't think it was necessary to have guts to obey the injunctions of his father and his sister. He was surprised by Letiel's reaction, but perhaps she was just being kind. As they left the pub, she linked her arm through Daniel's to walk up the road. He felt slightly drunk, at the stage when it still feels good. Perhaps a Coke was in order once they reached Marlene's. He didn't want to be ill.

Letiel offered to buy him a drink, and laughed when he told her what he wanted, although not spitefully. 'You're very down to earth, Daniel,' she said. 'It's obvious you've got great self-control!' She had seen him gulping down the Jack Daniels in The Angus, seemingly with the sole intention of becoming unconscious as quickly as possible. Owen had moved away, chatting animatedly with a few of the people they'd come in with. Daniel felt ignored. Sod him then, he thought. If Owen wanted to play games, he could get on with it.

'Have you got a girlfriend?' Letiel asked.

Daniel caught a glimpse of himself in the mirror behind the bar. 'No,' he said. 'I'm gay.' It had been surprisingly easy to say.

'Boyfriend, then?' Letiel continued quickly.

Daniel thought it was significant she hadn't asked if he was with Owen. 'No, there was someone, but . . .' He smiled fiercely, the dressing over the pain. 'He wasn't sure what he was into. It was a bit . . . difficult.'

'Poor you.'

'It's OK now.'

Letiel put a hand on his arm, smiled at him. He could feel her empathy. She, too, had been let down by men. How odd to find this affinity. He hadn't thought of that.

'He wasn't bored with you,' Daniel said. He didn't know why he said it; the words just came out.

Letiel looked at him. 'Pardon?'

Daniel shrugged, about to dismiss what he'd said, but there was more. 'He was just a shallow, stupid fucker who fancied everything that moved. Also, he took money from you. You didn't lose the twenty, like you thought, like he said. He took it.'

'Who?' Letiel's voice was almost inaudible.

'Con . . . Connor? Was it Connor?'

Letiel nodded. Then she narrowed her eyes. 'Who told you?'

'No one,' Daniel said. 'Apparently, I'm psychic.'

Later in the evening Daniel found himself sitting with Letiel and a couple of her friends in the shadows at the edge of the dance floor. Thick beams of coloured light roved across the gyrating bodies bewitched by the rhythm of the music. Daniel couldn't remember how he'd moved there from the bar, even though he'd stopped drinking. Letiel dragged him up to dance a couple of times, though his heart wasn't in it tonight. He saw Owen dancing with Cressida. She shook her head, so that her long red plaits whipped through the air. She grinned in pleasure as she twisted her slim, agile body around to the music. Owen was caught in a spotlight of red rays, his hair looked pink. He seemed to be dancing alone, Cressida a mere elemental shadow around him. How beautiful he looked. Painfully, Daniel decided he needed another drink; anything to numb the agony which was growing inside him like an infection. He didn't want to ask Owen for money again, and managed to scrape together enough change from his pockets to buy another Jack Daniels. When he returned to his seat, Cressida came sidling up to him. He could smell her perfume and her sweat. She shuddered like a race-horse who'd just won a race. She was, he realized, stunning to look at. This did not help his mood.

'Letty told me,' she shouted in Daniel's ear, which under the circumstances might as well have been a whisper.

Daniel raised his hands to indicate he couldn't hear her properly over the din of the music.

Cressida screwed up her face, made a vexed gesture, and then dragged him to the ladies' toilets, where the pound and thud of the music was muted. The small room, with its inadequate couple of cubicles and cracked mirror, was infested with hot, perfumed bodies, both male and female, who were squeezing around the mirror to adjust their war-paint, and shrieking gossip at one another. Apart from a cursory glance as Daniel and Cressida pushed themselves through the noisy gathering, nobody paid them any attention. Cressida squashed Daniel up against the back wall.

'You have to help me,' she hissed in an undertone.

'How?' Daniel dreaded some awful confidence concerning Owen was about to be revealed.

'Letty told me about you being psychic. It was incredible what you said to her.' Cressida had raised her voice a little.

'It doesn't happen very often,' said Daniel. 'It's not a party trick.' He could sense he was being off-hand and short with the girl, but it didn't seem to deter her.

'There's something I need to know.' A few people left the room, and briefly a fist of music punched through the door.

Daniel sighed impatiently. 'I don't think I can help you.' The few people left around the mirror were now suspiciously quiet, listening.

'It's about a friend of mine,' Cressida persisted. 'Serafina. Perhaps you read about it?'

Daniel shrugged, said nothing.

'She was *murdered*,' Cressida said. 'It was in the papers a few weeks ago, on the news, everything. They found her body in a car park at night. You *must* have heard about it!'

There was no emotional crescendo behind her words. She looked, Daniel thought, sick rather than ghoulishly fascinated. He rarely took any notice of the news, although a dim memory of the TV coverage surfaced in his mind, a picture of a white-faced girl, an image retained because it belonged to his own subculture. 'What do you want me to do about it?'

'Can't you *look into it*?' Cressida said. 'Can't you help find out what happened to her?'

Daniel held up his hands, backed towards the door. 'No, no.' He found he was laughing. 'You're crazy.'

'But you're *psychic*!' Cressida insisted. 'You could help, couldn't you?' She pulled a silver bangle from her left wrist. 'Here, this was hers. She gave it to me. I always wear it now.'

Daniel looked at the offered object as if it was a poisonous insect. He didn't want to touch it. 'I'm not psychic in that way,' he said. 'I'm sorry . . .'

Cressida, who was not wholly sober, grabbed Daniel's arm and forced the bangle over his hand. 'Take it! Please!'

The silver burned his skin, cold even though Cressida had just taken it from her own wrist. With a wordless cry of disgust, he pulled it from his arm and threw it on to the floor. Everyone had gone very still. Bile rose in Daniel's throat. He pushed a horde of insistent images and sensations from his mind, a sweet, sickly smell, powdery dark shadows, moving shapes, an ache behind the eyes.

Daniel is in the hallway of a house and everything is tilting before his eyes, as if he's watching a badly filmed video. He is the camera, and can only see in the direction in which his tunnel vision is pointed. Daniel looks around himself; he has never had a waking vision as clear as this. There are paintings on the wall, huge Pre-Raphaelite prints, but he cannot pause to look at them. Something is drawing him onwards. Stumbling, Daniel progresses down a corridor. He knows he is getting closer to the thing he's been brought here to see. A vibration is building up – within himself and within the walls of the house. The light is strange; no colour at all.

He comes upon a dark room. There is a sweet, sickly smell and a sense of dark shapes writhing around in a warm fog. Daniel's eyes hurt so much, it feels as if all his tears have evaporated, the ducts withered, and no matter how much he tries to blink, he can't make the bathing fluid flow. His eyeballs are searing. Fear grips his body and his mind. His senses are aware of something too hideous to be borne. Unable to prevent himself, he looks up and sees it: a swirling, lightless void churning above the heads of everyone present. From this black hole emanates the most inexpressible evil and hunger. Daniel cannot bear to look at it for long, and forces his camera vision downwards. Before him he sees the white body of a girl, naked upon some kind of table. A huge black figure leans over her – a man, who is familiar yet a stranger. As Daniel watches, he can see the etheric body of the girl rising up out of her flesh. Her soul is being drawn up into the void. In the moment before she is engulfed, she seems to become aware of Daniel as another astral form. For one terrible moment, she looks at him. She cannot speak, but her eyes are crying, 'Help me!' He can do nothing. She is drawn up, devoured. An unearthly roar pervades the room and Daniel's mind. He knows that the void is consuming everyone around him. He cannot see for the smoke, cannot hear for the screaming. Terror is a real presence around him. From his own throat comes a long, desperate wail.

Daniel realized he was kneeling on the floor of the ladies' room, in a night-club in Cresterfield, his arms clutching his stomach. Cressida and some of the others were leaning over him, their arms a hesitant feathery protection

330

around his shoulders. 'Are you all right?' 'Do you want anything?'

'She wanted him to do it,' Daniel said, searching for Cressida's eyes in the throng. He could not recognize faces at that point, only eyes. He found her exotic make-up, her cat's eyes, staring wildly at him.

'*What?*'

'It's true. It was part of it, the power, the . . . I don't know, can't interpret. She knew him. She loved him. He was a god, a man . . . no. I don't know.' He felt very weak, reality settled around him, everything becoming normal once more. He wanted Owen. He needed to tell him about this.

'You saw them?' Cressida murmured, coaxing.

He nodded, then shook his head. Part of the strangeness of what had happened was that there were no words in any human language to describe what he'd felt, seen, smelled and heard. It was impossible to articulate, for it was beyond this reality, beyond life. An *other*ness. 'There is something else,' he said to Cressida. 'Something else in this world. Here all the time. Here now.' He had begun to shiver.

'I don't understand,' Cressida answered. 'What *something*?'

'I can't tell you. No words. They don't exist.'

Cressida helped him to his feet. 'I'm sorry, Daniel. I'm a complete cow! I'm really sorry.' She hugged him to her, to her salty-musk animal scent of races won.

Everyone stared at the silver bangle on the floor, but no one would pick it up. Daniel said, 'I have a name. Shem . . . Shem-yah-zah.'

'Who? The murderer?'

Daniel shuddered violently. He thought he was going to vomit, but the feeling passed abruptly. 'A name. That's all.'

'It could be a place, or anything,' someone suggested.

A girl said, 'Are you going to tell someone about this? You know, the police, or something?'

'No!' Daniel said. 'I couldn't go through that.'

'You could send an anonymous note, or make a phone call.' This came from a boy who looked at least three years younger than Daniel, his face plastered in black and white make-up.

'Do what you like, but keep me out of it.' Daniel began to move towards the door. It seemed miles away.

'Do you want a drink?' Cressida asked him, as the hot, clawing atmosphere of the club embraced them again.

He nodded. 'Yes. Something strong.'

Cressida took him back to Letiel, and excuses were offered concerning faintness, being too hot, a 'bug'.

'What happened?' Letiel asked him with knowing eyes. She was not to be deluded.

'Nothing. I just felt weird.'

Cressida came back with Owen. Daniel wasn't sure whether he was pleased to see him or not. Owen handed Daniel a glass. 'Drink that and get your jacket. We're going.' Even though he didn't raise his voice that much, Daniel could hear him perfectly despite the music.

'You can't drive!' Daniel yelled, his own voice diminutive beneath the din.

'I'm fine. Come on.'

Cressida and Letiel accompanied them to the door. 'See you soon?' Letiel asked Daniel.

He nodded. 'Yes, I expect so.' He gripped her arm briefly.

'Call me,' she said. 'Owen has the number.'

'Of course he has.'

She chose to ignore the caustic innuendo. 'I mean it. *Call* me.'

Daniel smiled weakly. He saw Cressida reach up and

put her arms around Owen's neck, her face raised for a kiss. Owen stooped a little, offered her his cheek, then patted her face. 'Bye, Cress. See you soon.'

Outside in the city, it was autumn-cold, as if the unnatural warmth that smothered Little Moor's nights didn't extend beyond the village itself. Daniel felt drunk, although Owen appeared to have sobered up very quickly. He strode ahead, perhaps angry. Daniel couldn't speak to him. The images he'd received from the silver bracelet still echoed round his head, which otherwise felt empty and dark; receding echoes of sight and sound.

The drive back to Little Moor was completed in utter silence, not even a tape to break the night. Owen stared straight ahead, lost in his own thoughts. Daniel was thinking, It is over, it never started. It is over. The whole evening had seemed a travesty of enjoyment. All that meaningless waffle in the night-club, the sordid incident with Cressida. What's happening to me? thought Daniel. The ability to *know* things seemed preposterous, somehow false and staged. It had been as if someone else had put the words into his mouth, someone who really possessed the ability, who stood hidden nearby, transmitting messages as Daniel gabbled out his fragments of information. He wanted to talk to Owen about it, but feared ridicule. Yet wasn't it Owen who'd suggested Daniel was psychic? Perhaps it was some freak psychological aberration playing itself out now, his desire for Owen made tangible by the appearance of being what Owen wanted. The silence was too hard to break. Daniel dared not violate it.

Owen pulled up in the lane outside Low Mede. Daniel opened the car door. The engine purred to itself, Owen stared ahead. Daniel wanted to cry, 'What have I done? Tell me!' He knew that if he let Owen go now without saying anything, the chance, however slim and fragile it was, would be lost for ever. He looked at the house.

There was a dim light burning behind the curtains of his father's study, but otherwise the house was in darkness. Verity would probably be in the lounge watching TV without the light on. Normally, on a Friday night, Owen would come back to Low Mede to scrounge sandwiches, drink coffee, lounge in the attic room, smoking joints. Was this ritual forbidden now?

'Are you coming in?' Daniel asked.

Owen glanced at him. 'You mean you want me to?'

Daniel shrugged. 'It's not that late.'

Owen sighed. 'I don't know, Daniel.'

'Oh, suit yourself!' Daniel was filled with a brief wave of anger. 'Suddenly we're not friends. OK, if that's the way you want it.'

He got out of the car and slammed the door. As he walked, not too quickly, up the drive, he heard Owen pull the car on to the gravel. The headlights went off as Daniel put his key in the door.

'Daniel.'

He said nothing but let Owen follow him into the house. Immediately they both assumed their habitual Friday night behaviour of sneaking as quietly as possible to the kitchen, in order to avoid confrontation with any other members of the household.

Daniel went directly to fill the kettle. Owen gently shut the door, standing just inside the room. He lit a cigarette.

'Did Cressida tell you what happened?' Daniel asked.

Owen ventured forward and sat on the edge of the table, his back to Daniel. 'A bit.'

'You seem really interested!'

Owen rubbed his face with one hand. 'I am, Daniel. I just can't think at the moment.'

'You didn't have to pick me up this afternoon. We didn't have to go to Cresterfield. Don't punish me, O.'

Owen looked over his shoulder. 'I'm not. To be honest, I don't know why I came to the school. I shouldn't have. I don't even know if it was my idea.'

'What do you mean?'

Owen shook his head. 'Nothing.' He stood up again, stubbed out his cigarette, hardly smoked, in a saucer on the dresser. 'Look, it's senseless me being here.' Daniel saw him take a deep breath before he turned round. 'The truth is, I *can't* be friends any more, Daniel. It just won't work. I've wrecked it, not you. When I picked you up today, I wanted to say things, but it was obvious I couldn't. It's unfair on you. I'm sorry if you had a bad time tonight.'

'So this is it, then, is it? You walk out of here and we never speak again?' Daniel managed to laugh. 'I can't believe you! You're so fucking selfish!'

'OK, you want the truth, then have it. I'd rather not speak to you again than have to watch you go off with someone like Letty or Cress. I can't do it, Daniel. It's in me to want you, and it's obvious you feel differently. If I hadn't been there tonight, you would have got together with Letty. Every time I looked at you she was all over you. Whenever our eyes met, you looked as if you were scared of what I might think. I was in your way. I took you out to dinner to talk about this, but I could tell you were dreading I'd say something. So I didn't. The look on your face when I picked you up from school said it all. It was horror, Daniel. I embarrassed you, didn't I? You think that makes me feel good? You think that makes me want to sit here and make small talk with you?' Owen pulled a sour face and swiped the air with his hand. 'You see? You see?'

Daniel digested this outburst, unable, for a moment, to say anything in response. The kettle grunted and whined in the silence of the room. Owen sat down on the table again and put his face in his hands. Daniel wanted to go to him, hold him, but it wasn't that easy. There was a barrier to be breached. 'O, Wednesday night . . .' he began.

Owen groaned and interrupted. 'Please, don't. It's too grotesque!' He hugged himself defensively.

Daniel went up beside him, put his hand on Owen's arm. He wanted to offer reassurance, encouragement, but a maelstrom of images silenced his words. Heavy breathing, but of terror, not desire. Owen's taut body, his hammering heart, his hunger to plunder and invade held back. As well as this, a pitiful ache of longing, of feelings impossible to articulate, a sense of history, of timelessness, a silver reed of connection stretching back and back into the black, diamond-studded night of eternity and magic, the earth, the power, a circle. Then, the sister. She: hanging there in the spangled sky, a flame of whiteness; the goddess. He: her acolyte. The only one. Owen was virgin, but for her. A severed umbilical cord, waving free, emanated from her belly. But she was not distressed by this. It was Owen who was drifting alone.

Daniel withdrew his hand, flexed his fingers. They felt frozen. 'O, I had no idea,' he said.

Owen looked at him. There were tears on his face, his eyes were red.

'About Lily,' Daniel said.

'You know about that?' Owen asked.

He nodded. 'Yes. It is inside you and speaks to me. There was no need to pretend the other night. You should have told me. It wouldn't have mattered. I wasn't there to be impressed. It was my first time, too, remember.' He took Owen's hands in his own, pulled them away from Owen's face. 'I don't want Letty, or anyone like her. I feel the same as you do. You're so stupid, O.

You've deafed me out all evening. I wondered what I'd done.'

Owen managed a shaky laugh. 'So I get a second chance?'

'You haven't used up the first one yet.'

As they kissed, the kettle clicked off. With Owen sitting on the table, they were the same height. Owen wrapped his legs around Daniel's thighs, pulled him closer. Daniel heard a door open somewhere else in the house, far away. It was Owen who broke the kiss, but he didn't push Daniel away. 'Verity might come in.'

The thought slightly excited Daniel. 'So what?'

'So she certainly won't be pleased for us. Come on, things are difficult enough with her as it is.'

Daniel pulled Owen close against him, put his face against Owen's throat. 'I don't care.' He pressed his tongue against Owen's skin, tasted salt.

Owen murmured in pleasure, wrapped his arms tightly around Daniel, as Daniel gently sucked the skin.

The door opened and Verity walked into the room. Owen and Daniel both looked at her, frozen. She did not appear to notice they were embracing or, if she did, paid no attention. 'Is Raven in here?'

Daniel thought she looked drunk. Her eyes were slightly unfocused, her normally perfectly arranged hair ragged round her shoulders. She had the appearance of a woman who'd just come from a lover's embrace.

'I don't know,' he said. He could feel Owen panicking to push him away, but refused to allow it. Verity's unconcern was fascinating, if bizarre.

'Raven! Raven!' Verity inspected all the chairs pushed under the kitchen table, even the one beside Daniel and Owen. 'Ah, here you are!'

She dragged the cat off the chair. He seemed to spill over her arms like an enormous fur coat. Daniel felt slightly unnerved that the animal had remained hidden and overheard his conversation with Owen, then chided himself for such a ridiculous thought.

'I'm going to bed now,' Verity said. 'Can you remember to lock up, Daniel, when Owen goes?'

'Owen's not leaving,' Daniel said. 'He's staying with me tonight.'

'Right. I'll do the bolts, then.'

'Are you OK, Vez?'

She looked puzzled, a little disorientated, as she swayed towards the door, carrying the enormous cat. 'Hmm? Oh, yes, fine.'

'Where's Dad?'

'Oh, he came in some time ago. Probably in bed.' She stared at the handle on the door, as if wondering how she could open it with her arms full of cat. Owen disentangled himself from Daniel and went to open it for her. 'Thanks,' she said. 'Good night.'

Owen stared at Daniel in mute shock as Verity left the room. Daniel shrugged.

'What is she *on*?' Owen asked.

Daniel laughed, shook his head. 'Fuck knows. I think she's been drinking.'

'I can't believe that just happened. It *did* happen, didn't it?'

Daniel nodded, grinned. 'I wonder what she's been up to tonight? You don't suppose she's had a man in or something?' He laughed. 'Your friend, Peverel Othman, was chatting quite cosily with her the other night. Do you think he might have been round?'

Owen's face fell, and Daniel perceived immediately he'd touched a sensitive spot. It was because of Lily. Of course. 'I'm sorry, O. I didn't mean to . . .'

'It's OK. Forget it. Othman seems to get in everywhere, like smoke or a bad smell. It's possible he was here. I wouldn't put it past him.' He smiled warily. 'I expect you know, with your intuitive senses, that he's been after Lily.'

'Sort of, yes.'

'I need to talk to you about him, but not yet.' He came back to Daniel, took his hands in his own. 'Tonight is ours. I want to forget Othman, Lily, everything. Just for a while.'

In the attic room, Owen and Daniel undressed in moonlight. There was a reverence to their disrobing that reminded Daniel of their nights at the High Place, only this was more sedate, contained. The previous Wednesday, they had clawed at one another, fully clothed, as if the clothes themselves could provide a safe distance. Here, there were no barriers. Naked, they sat down on the floor, crossed-legged, their knees touching, holding hands. It seemed natural to alter consciousness through controlled breathing, as Owen had instructed at the High Place, as if both were aware of the sacred aspect of what they were doing. Daniel felt a flurry of activity at the back of his brain, as if something was rustling there, waiting to take flight; an image or a sound. He opened his eyes and Owen was staring at him. 'Something is coming through,' Daniel said. He stood up and went to lie down on the bed, feeling a little dizzy. After a moment, Owen followed him, lay down beside him, stroked his face.

'I can see things,' Daniel said. 'It feels strange. Hurts a bit. It's like a headache or a pressure in my brain, like diving deep under water.'

'What can you see?'

Daniel stared at the ceiling. 'A garden. *The* garden. People. It's where you come from, O. A long time ago.' He could sense strongly that the scene he was seeing somehow belonged to Owen; Daniel was only a medium to channel the information.

'What else?' Owen asked.

'Wait.' Daniel closed his eyes, pressed the fingers of one hand against his frowning brow. 'Listen.' He reached out, traced the contours of Owen's body, felt him stir beneath his hand. 'Mountain ranges. There is another High Place, O, back in time. There are cedar trees, the lofty bright dwelling, the gardens, the valleys of fire below. It's very beautiful. Stroke me, O. Stroke my back.' He relaxed, surrendering to the exquisite pleasures of the caress. It was as if his eyes were still open. The colours of the landscape in bright sunlight made him want to squint. 'There's a woman. Very tall, dressed in a deep blue robe. She's talking to me.'

'What's she saying?' Owen's voice was soft, coaxing.

Daniel frowned. The woman seemed to be speaking urgently, making emphatic hand gestures, yet it was like trying to decipher the noise coming from a badly tuned radio. 'I don't understand you,' he said. 'Talk slowly.' He felt there was something she wanted desperately to tell him, something that related to Owen. 'Give me your name,' Daniel said, and a single word came with clarity.

Ninlil. That was her name, he was sure of it.

'What's she saying?' Owen prompted. 'Talk to me, Daniel. Tell me.'

With his eyes closed, Daniel reached up to silence Owen's questions with his fingertips. Since she had given him her name, the woman's voice was coming to him more clearly now. She had so much information to impart and there wasn't much time. He nodded. 'Yes. Yes. I will tell him.' He took hold of one of Owen's hands, although he did not open his eyes. 'They came to Eden, O, and created the Garden there. The tall people, who were different. They made the reservoirs and the waterways and cultivated the land. They brought people up to the High Place from below and made them work for them.'

The information started to degrade, flashing at Daniel in a series of abrupt and garbled ideas. He spoke quickly to keep up, relaying as much as he could, knowing that some of it was streaking past his consciousness. 'The tree of knowledge – the serpent of Eden – feathered serpent – winged man – sword of light. I see him. And her: the daughter of earth. Ishtahar – priestess – Eye Priestess – the sacred gate. He's her lover. Fire. Pain. Knowledge, they gave humankind the knowledge – made things happen – created changes . . . The dawn of civilization, it's started . . .' Daniel suddenly gagged, as if gasping for breath.

'Who were they?' Owen murmured. 'These people. Who *were* they?'

Daniel twitched, shivered. 'Many names: Anannage, Watchers, Nefilim, Grigori, Elohim, angels. They were known as many things.'

'Bible stuff . . .'

'Genesis, but not Bible stuff.' Daniel sighed. 'History that became legends.' He rubbed his face and opened his eyes. 'Where is this coming from? What does it mean?'

Owen rested his cheek against the pillow. His eyes were dark shadows. 'I don't know, Daniel. You're talking about the Garden of Eden, I think.'

'Am I? It was the Garden *in* Eden. Eden was a country. I know that.' He exhaled slowly. 'Fading now. Getting smaller. I can see this room, and I can see the garden, too, but it's fading.'

'What about the woman – Ninlil?'

'She's gone. She had to go.'

Owen was silent for a moment, still stroking Daniel's

back. The skin was pimpled with cold. 'This is for us, Daniel. It's important, isn't it?'

Daniel moved closer to him. 'I think so. I don't know. I can't work out what's happening. It's very strange.'

'Let's get into bed. You're cold.'

They huddled beneath the duvet. The sheet felt icy beneath them. Daniel shivered in Owen's arms. 'It's getting stronger every day, O, these feelings I get, these pictures I see. It scares me.'

'Ssh.' Owen kissed his forehead. 'Forget it for now.'

'I say things without thinking, and they mean something. The girls tonight. The bracelet.' He shuddered. 'It was vile.'

'It's over now.'

'No, it's not. Make it go.' He hugged Owen tightly, wanting desperately for the contact of warm skin to obliterate the crowding, threatening images that seemed eager to break through into his mind. He didn't want to think about Cressida's dead friend. It was nothing to do with him. His inner landscape was the garden, the history that he felt was connected with Owen. Distant pictures. The kindly Ninlil, gentle words. They could work it out together in the dark, the pictures of love. This was what his gift was for, not something to be snatched from his mind by hungry, pawing hands, imprinting disgusting thoughts and images in his head. He murmured a soft sound of encouragement as Owen's timorous hands crept over his body. He knew Owen was afraid of this familiar yet so alien territory. He could tell that Owen thought it was like putting his hand to a mirror and finding that his fingers could slide through the glass into another world, touch the image that lay there, the image of himself. It was disorientating for him, but desire kindled courage. Owen kissed Daniel's chest, ran his tongue over the lean stomach.

Lying with his eyes open, Daniel could see stars flashing against the dark of his room. He sensed that by being passive, he would become a channel, and more information would come to him. His arms were flung out straight to either side, in the position of crucifixion. His cock was engorged, pointing towards his belly. This was some archetypal stance. Daniel did not understand it, but he felt its power. When Owen buried his face between Daniel's legs and took the boy's cock in his mouth, the garden unfolded around Daniel once more, called back by the rising energy within him. He felt delirious, drunk, euphoric, beyond action, a vessel. As Owen pleasured him, it seemed he left his body, flying back in time.

Daniel is soaring above the garden like a bird, or a spirit without the encumbrance of flesh. Then lightning crashes over the mountains, and the sky becomes dark. Daniel senses panic, but, as an observer, experiences no fear. An image of a tumbling brazier spins before his mind's eye; he sees the coals scatter, feels a brief, agonizing tug of grief and loss. He has entered the reality of the past.

They are going to the valley of fire, all of them, where the hot blood of the earth bubbles up from perpetual wounds in the stone. Daniel is among them, his hands bound. He is their prisoner: tall warriors, whose images shimmer before Daniel's eyes. Sometimes they look like the pictures of angels he saw as a child in an illustrated Bible. Then they are simply soldiers again, stern and tall and alien to the eye, with their long faces and serpent eyes. He knows them: they are Anannage. A gust of smoke blows across his eyes; he smells sulphur, tastes metal. The warriors pause at a lip of rock, and look down.

The body is hanging from a gibbet in the valley, swinging from one foot; Daniel sees it twist in the hot

343

wings of the wind. He thinks, That is my master down there, and feels again a terrible sense of sorrow. Beside him, he hears a woman's wailing cry, and turns his head, empowered by a sense of rage and vengefulness. Her fault! She is much smaller than the warriors who are restraining her; her skin is darker. Her breasts are bare and across her belly is tattooed the image of a giant eye. *So, she has achieved the position she craved, become his Eye Priestess!* Her hair hangs in black, dusty rags around her shoulders; her eyes, red from weeping or the unforgiving air, roll wildly in her head. Her lips are torn and bleeding. Even in her agony and disarray, she is a creature of great beauty. Sensuality oozes from her straining limbs. Daniel realizes she is trying to escape her captors and throw herself from the rock into the valley below. She looks as though she might succeed, but another Anannage, who appears older than the others and who wears a pale-coloured robe, gestures at the warriors, and they begin to drag her away. She screams from her raw throat, 'Shemyaza, Shemyaza!' That name. Below, the body is turning, blackened by fire, the eyes livid in the seared face. What will happen to *her* now? Will she remain an oracle, or will she be claimed by another of the Elders?

Ninlil appears at Daniel's side. He is relieved to see her there. Her voice is clear, sorrowful. 'Listen, child. Although they hang and burn his body, his spirit will be flung into the starry firmament of Orion. Once again, the power to travel through the gate will be his, but this time, it will be a prison, not the doorway to the stars, the Source. One day, he will be released, and there will be an accounting. On that day, his descendants will come into their own, but for many thousands of years, his name will be reviled by humankind, and this deed will be a hatred upon women, and the stigma of an original sin. Yet there is recompense. From this moment forward,

Ishtahar the seductress will be revered as the greatest goddess. All other goddesses will spring from her name, her memory.' Ninlil steps past Daniel and speaks in a resonant voice that echoes from the rocks, 'Shemyaza, we vanquish your power. You no longer have the means to return to the One through the dimensions of the stars. At the gate, Orion, you will for ever remain.' She steps back, her head hanging upon her breast. Daniel knows it has been hard and painful for her to deliver those words, an onerous duty.

The scene is beginning to fade from his mind. He can feel bonds around his body, restricting all movement. The bonds are beginning to move, and he realizes with horror that he has been held in the grip of a giant serpent. A silver bracelet spins upon the air, around and around. He is flying through space, a void.

Daniel snapped back to reality. Owen was leaning over him. As the sensations of the vision faded, Daniel became aware of his physical body. The attentions of Owen's lips and tongue seemed to have taken him to another plane, an altered state of consciousness. It was impossible to achieve orgasm; he could only rise higher and higher within his own mind, travel unimagined landscapes, penetrate the deepest temples of the psyche. Now he felt capable of anything, able to secure the most hidden knowledge. Owen seemed to be waiting for instructions. He knelt between Daniel's legs, his head bowed, moonlight kindling white fire in his hair. Daniel felt a moment's sorrow, knowing Owen could not share the visions, but only help create them in Daniel's mind. They had to go further, reach for something, break through a barrier of consciousness.

Daniel held out his arms, summoning Owen into his embrace. Owen's skin felt cool, while Daniel's was burning hot. He realized then that what they were doing, and must do, was more than simply sex on a physical level and transcended the gratification of the flesh. Their intimacy created a cauldron of power, sexual energy set apart from the base instincts of reproduction or carnal release. It was holy.

They kissed and Daniel wrapped his limbs around Owen's body, aware of himself as being like the encircling serpent. He felt Owen slippery and hard against him. There was no barrier, no resistance. Surely it should not be this easy? Owen slid into Daniel's body like a fish. Was this magic, too?

Colours are erupting before Daniel's inner eye, fluid globules of vivid green and blue and red. He is flying, beating his wings through space and time, so huge he fills the entire universe. Galaxies flash past him, peppering his wings with sparkling dust. He is wheeling around, somersaulting in the void, delirious with ecstasy. Daniel feels a surge within his body, a small feeling which is getting larger and wilder like an approaching hurricane. He senses that many millennia are rushing past him. He is pulled through centuries of time. And then the constellation of Orion is before him and he is zooming in upon it, sucked forward, unable to break his flight.

Daniel cried out, tried to shut his inner eye, and all was flame; scarlet, blue, gold. He knew he should be terrified, but the only feeling he experienced was that of power, and a recognition of rage. Owen's fingernails were digging deep into his shoulders, it seemed the whole world was violent, bucking motion and burning lust.

The eye of the storm: a single, clear image comes to him: the soul of Shemyaza hanging among the stars, within the starry pentacle of Orion. He looks like the transparent outline of a man, his hair surrounding him as if he is floating in water, his body bound by an enormous serpent. Daniel's perspective shifts, and around Shemyaza he sees Orion as a mighty portal hanging in the heavens. It is as if Shemyaza's soul were frozen there in space, unable to move. Daniel senses that beyond this imprisoned astral body, beyond the blocked gate, exists a great void, a place as wonderful as it is terrifying. This place is God. But Shemyaza acts as a barrier. No one can reach through the gate to the Source.

As a thunderous orgasm built up within his body, Daniel reached out to the image of the hanged man. His hands curled around the coils of the great cosmic serpent that bound Shemyaza and he was tugging at it, ripping it free, releasing its prisoner. The serpent burst into a thousand spinning points of light, a thousand stars, and Daniel shuddered to the release of climax. He cried the name, 'Shemyaza!' but it blew away from his mouth.

Owen groaned and shuddered, collapsing on to Daniel's body. Lying dazed, Daniel was surrounded by a smell of ozone, the primal scent of male potency that had been bound up for ten millennia. The smell was so thick upon the air, it made Daniel want to retch. He could feel Owen's heart racing against his body, felt his skin slick with sweat. The echo of Daniel's cry seemed to be flying round the house below, and somewhere, somewhere, it touched a thing that recognized it, that claimed ownership.

'Daniel,' said Owen, 'Daniel.' He sounded afraid, perhaps aghast at himself.

Daniel put his arms around him. 'It's all right,' he said, but in his heart, he knew it wasn't. He shouldn't have said the name. If he hadn't, it wouldn't have been heard, but it was too late now.

Owen slept in Daniel's arms, but until the light came through the window, Daniel lay awake, tense and listening, waiting for the breathing at the door, for a shadow to pour across the floor, rear up before him, black.

Chapter Twenty

Same day: Little Moor (continued)

Apart from Barbara and Peverel Othman, only Louis and two others turned up for the writers' meeting at The White House – a married couple, Ellie and Ted Richards, who were prematurely middle-aged and not exactly the most dynamic contributors to the group. Barbara was disappointed; she'd wanted to show Othman off to everyone. Also, the rather enclosed circle had electric possibilities that might prove troublesome. She hardly dared look at Louis when he came in. His aftershave tantalized her nose as he walked slowly past her into the living-room, after a formal 'Hello'. Barbara was burning a scented oil on the hearth called Jasmine Nights, perhaps a provocative choice.

To make things worse, Peverel Othman didn't want to participate in the way Barbara had hoped.

'I hadn't intended to lecture anyone tonight,' he said. 'To be honest, my writing career is hardly glamorous. I have two self-published novels, that's all. I don't really feel qualified to advise anyone.'

'What kind of novels do you write?' Ellie Richards asked.

'Horror,' Othman said, fixing Ellie with a voluptuous feral grin. 'And sex.'

Barbara noticed the woman's colour rise. Louis caught Barbara's eye, smiled in what she supposed was sympathy. She smiled back.

'The horror genre fascinates me,' Louis began, and much to Barbara's intense gratitude, he started a discussion on the subject which seemed to keep everyone happy. Othman made caustic, but amusing, remarks. Ellie tittered and blushed. Ted asked embarrassingly inane questions. But at least it kept things going. After an hour or so, Barbara went to fetch the refreshments Mrs Moon had prepared earlier. She hoped Louis or Othman would follow her into the kitchen, but neither of them did. For a few moments, she stared out of the kitchen window over the garden of the pub. People were still sitting out there; the warm weather hadn't let up. What do I want? she asked herself, sucking on a pickled onion she'd absentmindedly taken from one of the dishes on her hostess trolley.

When Barbara wheeled her refreshments back into the lounge, the conversation had taken a turn. They were discussing alternative methods of healing, which had obviously arisen from talk of the supernatural. Had Louis instigated that?

'The mind is capable of anything,' Othman was saying. 'Thought can accomplish miracles.' He gestured towards Louis. 'I take it you haven't tried it for yourself?' Barbara was aghast that Othman could make such a bald, insensitive remark, but Louis didn't seem upset by it.

'Well, I've had aromatherapy,' he said, 'but what else can you suggest? My debilities are the result of severe physical injury. Can the power of the mind do anything about that?'

'Of course,' Othman replied coolly. 'It just depends on which mind you use to accomplish it.'

'Someone else's?' Louis said. There was a sharpness beneath the polite tone.

Othman shrugged. 'I would recommend a visit to a competent healer, yes.'

'Do you know any?' Ellie Richards asked, her brow creased earnestly. Clearly she was embarrassed by the discussion of Louis's condition.

'They are found easily enough,' Othman said, accepting a glass of wine from Barbara. 'Buy any New Age magazine and you'll come across hundreds of adverts.'

'No personal recommendation, then?' Barbara asked. She stood behind Louis's chair, protectively.

Othman paused. 'Alas, no.'

By ten o'clock, it was obvious to everyone that Louis was very weary and ready to go home. Perhaps the talk of healers had exhausted him. The Richardses said their goodbyes and left. Barbara offered to drive Louis back to Low Mede.

'Allow me,' Othman said. 'You have to clear up, Barbara. Lend me your truck.'

Barbara laughed in surprise. 'You're not insured!'

'Oh, and the lanes of Little Moor are crawling with police, are they? Don't worry. I've driven Land Rovers before.' He drew her aside a little way as Louis was putting his coat on. 'Barbara, I think I can do something for Louis,' he said in a low voice.

'What?' Barbara's heart seemed to contract in her chest.

Othman held up his hands. 'I have many accomplishments. Healing is one of them.'

'Pev!' She inserted a warning into her voice.

'Ssh! It's true, really. I learned it in the Far East a few years ago. I didn't want to say anything earlier, because I don't like talking about it much.'

'Mmm. From what I can gather, there's quite a lot you don't like talking about!'

'Please let me do this, Barbara. I know you'd do anything to help Louis; so let me do this.'

Barbara sighed. 'You are a walking miracle, Peverel Othman. Is there nothing you can't do?'

'Hardly. I've lived hundreds upon hundreds of lives,

and I remember every one of them, so I've learned just about every possible skill a person can.'

Barbara shook her head, smiled. 'I think you're probably a disgusting rogue, Pev. You could be a liar and a con-man, but if you're telling the truth about this, take the truck with my blessing!'

'Keys?' said Othman.

'How long're you planning on staying around?' Louis asked, as Peverel Othman drove him back to Low Mede. The night was oppressively warm and the lichened trunks of trees along the lane glowed with a phosphorescent sickness as the headlights of the Land Rover splashed over them.

'I don't know.' Othman replied. 'I have no plans, no demands from the outside world.'

'You seem to have made a lot of friends here very quickly.'

Othman wondered whether he detected suspicion in Louis's voice. 'I always do,' he answered glibly. 'Comes from travelling a lot, I suppose.'

They came to a halt outside Low Mede. 'Well, here we are!' Louis said. He opened the door and slowly lowered himself from the passenger seat.

Othman could tell the man was in considerable pain. His aura was full of it. 'Louis,' he said, 'what would you say if I told you I could heal your body?'

Louis looked back into the vehicle. His face was ashen in the moonlight. 'What would I say? I think I'd want to know how you could do that.'

'Would you like to talk about it?'

Louis laughed, a little uneasily. 'Are you serious?'

'Very. By tomorrow morning, you could be free from pain. Your legs could be strong and agile. That's a promise.'

Louis leaned against the door-frame of the vehicle. 'And the price? I assume there is one.'

Othman smiled. 'Don't worry, I'm not trying to con you. I don't charge. It costs me nothing to do it, so why should I demand payment? I earn more than enough money by other means.'

'Then what is your motive?'

Othman shrugged. 'I don't like to see people in pain. It's unnecessary.'

'What would happen if I agreed to let you try?'

'I'd come into your house and heal you. It would take a few hours, that's all.'

'But what do you do? What do you use?'

Othman deliberated, pulled a quizzical face. 'A sort of mental energy, I suppose.'

Louis regarded him warily. 'Some talent.'

'Yes, it is. Well?'

Louis considered for a moment, then said, 'You'd better come in.'

Othman shook his head. 'Not yet. I'll just take Barbara's truck back to the pub. Then I'll return. Go into your most private room and wait for me there. Don't drink or eat anything. OK?'

Louis hesitated, and then said, 'All right. Anything's worth a try, I suppose.'

He sounded sceptical, but Othman scented the hope in his words, that dreary, desperate hope. He smiled. 'I won't be long.'

Louis let himself in and went to find Verity. She was curled on the sofa in the lounge, watching TV, drinking expensive red wine from a cut-crystal glass. 'Hi, how was the meeting?' she asked perfunctorily.

'Fine. Is Daniel in?'

Verity shook her head. 'No, he left a note. Gone to

353

some night-club with Owen Winter. They'll be back late, I expect.'

'Right . . .'

'Are you going to bed?' Verity looked at Louis intently, as if she perceived something was troubling him.

'Er, no. I'm having a visitor in a short while.'

'Oh? Who?'

'Chap from the pub, the one who came here on Wednesday with Barney and Barbara.'

Verity frowned. 'Peverel Othman? What does he want?'

Louis smiled, a little sheepishly. He didn't want to lie to Verity, but neither did he want to confess the truth. 'We started a conversation at the meeting, which we want to finish. Have a drink. Talk the night away.'

Verity grimaced. 'An odd choice of companion for you.' Without further remarks, she turned back to watching her film.

Louis said nothing, but retreated from the room. He left the front door ajar. Would Othman ring the bell? Louis went slowly to his study. His limbs were shaking, and not just from pain. Was it possible Othman could really help him? He dared not believe it could be true.

In the study Louis turned on the desk lamp, which threw a comforting yellow glow around the wood-panelled room. The fire, which had been lit in the early evening, was still faintly glowing. The room was hot, yet Louis felt too lethargic to take the few steps to the long windows and struggle with the stiff latches to let in some air. He sat down in the enormous leather armchair on the left side of the fireplace, where he could watch the door. His eyes were drawn continually to the glass-fronted case where he kept his guns. They gleamed there as a painful reminder of healthier days, when his body had been fit and active. Often, when he cleaned them, he thought about secreting them away, wrapping them in cloth in a trunk in the attic, but he still liked to handle them and also appreciated the way they looked, hanging there on the wall. Ornamental menace. None were loaded, of course, and ammunition was kept in a locked desk drawer, but . . . Louis shivered. Why should he think about that?

Minutes ticked by. Perhaps Othman would not return. Louis did not feel completely at ease with the man; there was something very odd and almost sinister about him. But at the same time, Othman possessed a quality which made people want to spend time in his company. Perhaps it was simple charisma.

At half past ten, fifteen minutes after Louis had entered the study, Othman came into the room. Louis had not heard him enter the house. Perhaps he'd been dozing. Othman was a tall, dark shape against the light from the hall. He closed the door, turned the heavy key in the lock. Louis experienced a tremor of unease. He was at this man's mercy now. 'Is that necessary?' he said.

Othman padded across the room. 'I don't want us to be disturbed. It could ruin the process.' He'd already sniffed the air to see whether the son was present, and had been relieved to find he wasn't. Daniel might be a problem in this situation because he could pick up vibrations from what was happening. Othman hadn't checked over the past day or so to see how Owen was progressing with the boy, but he considered it better to have Daniel out of the way at the moment.

Othman stood before Louis, his hands on his hips. 'Before we begin, there are some things I would like to tell you.'

Louis nodded. 'Yes?'

'You have a part to play in this as much as I do. Some of what I need you to do might unnerve you, even disgust you. Therefore, I have to ask for your complete trust in me.'

Louis looked wary. 'I don't like the sound of this. Perhaps we should just forget it.'

Othman smiled. 'I understand your feelings. Therefore I'm prepared to give you a taste of what's to come. Look on it as a trial demonstration, a test drive. Why should you believe me? You hardly know me. I understand that.'

Louis shrugged. 'That seems fair enough.' He still felt slightly threatened.

Othman walked round behind Louis's chair. 'Now, I must ask you not to look at me while we do this. It's very important, because you could get hurt. The energy I use in the healing is very strong. You will realize this for yourself shortly.'

Louis had gone rigid. What would Othman do? Would a knife come and slit his throat as he sat there, helpless? What?

Othman picked up these loud, panicked thoughts as he took off his jacket and rolled up one of his shirt sleeves. 'You must try to relax,' he said. 'It will make things easier. Please don't be afraid.'

Louis laughed. 'I'd feel better if I knew what you were going to do.'

'In simple terms, I'm going to feed you with healing energy. In a moment, I shall ask you to close your eyes. Soon, you will feel a kind of heat on your face. This will only be my arm, but you must not open your eyes and look at it. It could blind you. When you feel my flesh against your mouth, suck. It's as simple as that.'

Louis turned round in the chair, tried to look at the man behind him. 'Oh no, I'm not doing that! Are you mad? Get out!' He wondered, if he shouted loud enough, whether Verity would hear him. Would she be able to get through the locked door in time? He eyed the gun case desperately.

Othman put a long-fingered hand on Louis's shoulder. 'Please, don't get angry. I know this must sound very peculiar.'

'Peculiar? Sounds like something out of a horror film! You want me to suck your blood? What do you think I am?'

'You're disabled,' Othman answered simply. 'And desperate. You want vitality. You want strength and agility. Youth. You want Barbara Eager.'

Louis spluttered a protest, but Othman interrupted him.

'I don't care about that. I'm not claiming to be a vampire, Louis, and I'm not offering you blood. Do as I suggest and you will feel the effect for yourself immediately. It is just a test. If you really want to stay as you are, tell me to leave once more and I will. But I won't offer you this again, and you'll live the rest of your life tormenting yourself with the thought that I might have been telling the truth.'

Othman let these words hang in the silence. He could feel Louis battling with himself, the primitive, instinctive side, deeply buried, against the rational, intellectual conscious mind, which shouted to him that this was preposterous.

After a while, Louis sighed. 'All right. Do it.' He wished he could have a drink first, get used to the idea, but he was afraid Othman might take such a suggestion as an excuse.

'Relax,' said Othman. 'Just close your eyes.'

Louis sat tense in the chair, unable to obey the first instruction. His eyes were shut tight, his brow creased, his mouth a little open.

Behind the chair, Othman drew himself up to his full

height, threw back his head and composed himself to summon the energy. It came eagerly, as if desperate to be taken. Othman's flesh became hot. He raised his arm to his own mouth, and bit the skin of his wrist, sucked a little. A small amount of blood rose to the tiny wound, but the light came pouring out. Quickly, Othman put his hand over the wound, and reached round to the front of the chair. He removed his hand and put his arm against Louis's lips. Louis jumped at the contact. At first, he closed his mouth tightly.

'Take it,' Othman urged. 'It won't take a moment.'

Louis was shaking. He opened his mouth again, tentatively sucked the flesh held against it. The skin was warm, fragrant. Something like liquid fire filled Louis's mouth.

After five seconds, Othman took his arm away. The flesh tingled only slightly. Louis was no voracious monster like Emilia Manden. A slight glow still played around Louis's lips, which were shuddering. Othman knew the ichor would have tasted wonderful, literally divine.

'There now,' he said. 'It's done.' He walked around to face Louis again, adjusting the cuff of his shirt. Louis opened his eyes, blinked rapidly. 'Well?' Othman enquired.

Louis wasn't sure what he felt. The heat had come and he'd sucked at it, as instructed. He'd felt something white-hot flow into his mouth, something that was neither liquid nor solid, yet something that was more than air. The flavour of it lingered on his tongue like a fine liqueur, burned his throat in the same way. Abruptly, he lurched out of the chair, stood upright, swaying. His legs tingled, but the pain had diminished.

'I don't believe it!' he said.

'Oh, but you must,' Othman said. 'It's no illusion.'

'What are you?' Louis asked. 'Just what the hell are you?'

Othman smiled. 'An angel of deliverance. Do you want to continue the process?'

Othman's ichor had filled Louis with a wild euphoria as well as silencing the pain in his damaged limbs. He felt like laughing hysterically. This man could not be human, but at that point, Louis did not care. 'Yes!' he said. 'Yes.'

Othman sat down in the chair Louis had vacated. 'Good. Are you willing to do whatever I ask?'

Louis nodded, his eyes wild. 'Anything!'

Othman reflected, as he undid the belt to his leather trousers, that it was so easy to manipulate them once they'd had the first taste. If he told Louis now that slitting his own throat would grant him immortality, he'd believe it and do it. Too easy, really. 'Kneel before me,' he said.

Louis complied like a child, trusting. His face looked manic, almost imbecilic, his hair sticking up in all directions. Othman had to smile. He peeled back his trousers, revealed the smooth, pale flesh, the ripe fruit within. 'Drink to your fill, Louis Cranton,' he said. 'Take as much as you like. The well is depthless.'

Louis looked slightly confused. 'You want me to . . .?' He could not speak the words.

'Make yourself comfortable and close your eyes. Remember, you must not look once the energy comes.'

Louis shuffled forward on his knees. He did not think about what he was doing, concentrating only on the fizzing sense of power that coursed through his body. He wanted more. He didn't care how he got it.

At midnight, Verity turned off the TV. She was bored by it, and looked forward only to going to bed with Raven.

359

She hadn't experienced any more unusual dreams or visions since Wednesday night, but tonight she felt spicy, wild. Tonight might be the night. When she went into the hall, she noticed the front door stood open. Had Daniel come back? As she closed it, Verity remembered her father telling her that Peverel Othman was due round. She hadn't heard anyone arrive, but perhaps Louis had left the front door open on purpose. Still, that wasn't like him. Purposefully, Verity went to the study door, knocked softly, then tried to open it. She was surprised to find it locked. Louis never locked himself in there. 'Dad?' she called, knocking again. She pressed her ear against the door, but could hear nothing.

'Dad? Are you all right?' She slapped her open palms repeatedly against the wood. At first there was only silence. Panic gripped Verity's heart. Was her father lying unconscious in there? She called again and heard, with relief, a slight movement beyond the door.

The lock turned, although the door did not open. What had Louis been up to in there?

Verity opened the door and stepped into the study. The room was in darkness but for the dim light of the desk lamp, which hardly illuminated anything. A stifling heat hit her in the face, bringing beads of sweat to her upper lip with unnatural speed, followed by a fierce chill, which raised the hair on the back of her neck. At first, she thought the room was empty, but in that case, how had the key been turned in the door? Then she saw a pair of glowing eyes in the chair by the hearth. At first, she thought it must be Raven crouched on the back of the chair, but then she realized that someone was sitting there. Someone with glowing eyes. Alarmed, Verity reached for the main light switch, turned it on.

'Don't!' The voice, as loud as a thunder crack, shattered the bulbs in the chandelier and the desk lamp, but not before Verity saw. The sight was so shocking, she could hardly draw breath. Her father was sprawled on the floor before the chair, his face buried in the groin of Peverel Othman. It looked as if they had been like that for a long time. However the door had been unlocked, it hadn't been by the agency of a human hand.

Verity wanted to scream, or run out of the room, but could neither make a sound nor move. The shattering of the light bulbs seemed to have transfixed her. Now she stood immobile in the darkness. In her mind, she called, 'Raven!' but she knew the cat could not hear her. Something huge and black had engulfed her, chained her to this bestial room, while shutting out the world beyond. Time itself seemed to have stopped.

Gradually, as Verity's eyes readjusted to the dim light, the outline of the chair by the hearth exposed itself before her. Othman raised a hand, weakly.

'Come here,' he said.

Verity tried to resist the command but, in jerking movements, her limbs carried her towards the fire. She found herself looking down into the gaunt, handsome face of the stranger. He looked very tired. Louis never even raised his head. Something like luminous paint covered her father's face, shining dully. She dared not look too long. It was too vile to contemplate.

'Verity,' said Othman. 'Kiss me.'

Verity thought she might be sick; acid bubbled in her throat. She wanted to scream 'No!', or attack the man before her, but her body ignored her feelings, and obeyed Othman's words. Leaning down, Verity put her lips against his. It was a chaste kiss. She felt him sigh. 'Thank you. Please, sit here with us. Let me stroke your hair. You have beautiful hair.'

Verity kneeled down beside the chair. Her mind was slowly becoming occluded by a numbing lethargy. She felt the long fingers in her hair, the gentle caress. She pressed her face against the old leather of the chair, her eyes closed.

'You mustn't judge me, Verity,' Othman said. 'I'm healing your father.'

Verity could only listen, unable to speak. How could healing be so dark? She felt only evil around her, nothing healthy at all. It was bleak and cold and cruel. Heartless. This, she reflected miserably, was almost a reflection of herself.

Othman continued to stroke her hair. Occasionally, he made a small sound, which might have been distress or pleasure. No sound came from Louis. He barely moved.

After what seemed to be several hours of being trapped in a nightmare, Verity was partly jerked from her trance by the sound of a car in the driveway outside. Othman uttered a brief hiss and reared upright in the chair like a snake. Louis collapsed on to the floor, where he made feeble, crawling movements. Verity tensed. She heard Owen Winter call her brother's name, heard them come into the house. Would they find them here like this? 'Daniel!' she said, but realized the sound was only in her head. Her throat was closed. Gently, Othman pushed her away.

'Get up,' he said. 'You can go to your room.'

Verity's limbs felt like stone, the blood stilled in the veins. Without looking backwards, she lurched uncertainly to the door and went out into the hall.

For a few minutes, she simply stood there, mindless. Then she thought of Raven, and a few tears spilled from her eyes. 'My cat,' she murmured. 'I want my cat.'

He would be in the kitchen.

Seeing Owen and Daniel embracing made no impact on Verity's mind. How could it, after what she'd just seen? In some ways, she was glad that they were there, for despite their closeness, which normally she'd find distasteful, they were clean and pure. She felt she could see their souls shining out of them, clear light. Their love for one another surrounded them like a glowing shield. She could not tell them what she'd seen, what had happened. In their purity, they could not possibly understand the words, an alien language of darkness. She couldn't tell them to go to the study, although some part of her thought she should. Othman still had a grip on her tongue.

Once Raven was in her arms, she felt better. Owen opened the door for her and she was able to escape.

Verity went directly to her room, and put Raven down on the bed. The cat was purring, his tail moving slowly against the duvet as he watched her undress. She wanted to cry, but it seemed impossible. Naked, she slid beneath the quilt and Raven walked up the bed to purr in her ear.

'Horrible,' she murmured, '*bad* thing. Oh Raven, what's happening?' The tears came then and she pulled the cat against her.

'Don't worry,' he said. 'I'll look after you.'

Was the voice in her brain or her ears? She couldn't tell.

'The tall one can't hurt you,' Raven said. 'You're protected. You don't have to be afraid.' Then he began to lick her damp, salty cheeks with his rough tongue.

'Will you be a man again?' Verity whispered.

'Sometimes,' the cat replied, 'but not tonight.'

Downstairs, Louis lay unconscious in his study before the dead hearth. Fluids within his body flowed and ebbed upon a strange, alien tide. Fibres twisted and mutated; grew. He did not dream.

Othman was sitting on the stairs, trembling, his hands

dangling between his knees. His wrist ached now. Will it never end? he thought. He sensed Owen and Daniel's communion two storeys above him, and instinctively fed upon it. Owen was running ahead. He would have to be brought back under control.

Othman pressed the heels of his hands against his eyes. His flesh was burning. He smelled charred meat. No! He threw back his head, sucked in a lungful of breath, attempted to rise to his feet. Instead, he collapsed against the banister. It was with him again, the torment. He heard her terrible screams, the grief of it, the unbearable grief. Then the stones came down, to bury and conceal, to crush and kill, to seal the pact of the curse, *their* justice. A memory of it had been evoked in this house. Something, someone. Weakly, Othman pulled himself up against the banister. He had to get out.

It came as a whisper, as a shout. It came like a silver dart down the stairways, snaking as a trail of vapour into the hallway. It hit him between the shoulder-blades. A name. Shemyaza. The name he dreaded. He had to take it, absorb it. The impact made him nauseous.

They have awoken the spirit of the church, Othman thought. I am with them. The oldest memory, still to be recalled, stirred deep within him, forbidden and intangible, yet real and terrible. A desire to flee the house overcame him.

Outside, he vomited into the antirrhinums, a substance that tasted of smoke.

Chapter Twenty-one

Saturday, 24th October: Little Moor

Daniel woke up alone. It was full daylight, and a glance at the clock told him he'd slept till midday. Owen must have crept out earlier. Daniel lay back, first to savour the lustful memories of the night, then, less readily, to contemplate the dark images that had assailed his mind, holding sleep at bay. The name: Shemyaza. It stuck in his brain like a mantra. First in the club, then later in bed; too much of a coincidence.

He got out of bed and pulled on some jeans and a T-shirt. Again, the day was unnaturally warm for the time of year. He opened the window and an airless blast came into the room. He could see Verity out in the garden, picking the last of the summer flowers that remained and putting them into a basket. Raven was winding in and out of her legs, his huge tail held aloft. An idyllic sight, Daniel thought.

When he went into the kitchen, he was surprised to find Owen there, reading the paper and eating toast. 'Verity made me breakfast,' Owen explained.

'How was she?' Daniel still couldn't believe the apparent dramatic change in his sister's character.

'Fine. A little vague. She didn't mention anything.'

Daniel shook his head. 'Most bizarre. Have you seen Dad?'

'No.'

After breakfast, Daniel took Owen into his father's study. 'Research time,' he said.

Owen grimaced as they entered the dark, high-ceilinged room. 'Smells funny in here,' he said. 'What is it?'

Daniel sniffed. 'I don't know.' He shivered. 'I've never liked this room.'

Owen watched him go over to the floor-to-ceiling bookcases on either side of the fireplace. 'What are you looking for?'

Daniel browsed through the titles. 'Here. This section. Dad bought a lot of books up at random when we moved in, because his collection left too many spaces on the shelves. We picked up some stuff at an auction, loads of dictionaries and encyclopaedias. Here . . .'

He handed Owen a fat plain-covered volume that felt sticky to the touch, even though it was bound in cloth. '*Dictionary of World Mythology*,' Owen read. 'Volume ten? Wow. Got the rest?'

'Most of them. I think the only ones that are missing are the index volumes, if we're lucky.'

Owen wandered over to Louis's desk and sat down. He leafed through the book. 'The text is tiny. This was certainly a labour of love!'

'Look up Shemyaza,' Daniel said, then spelled the name out.

'I've heard that name before,' Owen said, and told Daniel about his visit to the old church with Peverel Othman. 'That place is dedicated to a St Shem. Pev said that was Shemyaza, I'm sure he did.'

Daniel's eyes were round. He hurried over to the desk. 'Really! This is weird. Look it up, O, quickly.'

Owen pored through the text. He frowned. 'Oh.'

'What does it say?'

'"See Semjaza."' Owen marked the text with a finger. 'Here we are. He was the leader of a band of fallen angels, known as the Grigori.'

Daniel interrupted him. 'Yes, yes! I said that, too. Remember? The name of the people who built the Garden in Eden. I'm sure that was one of the names!'

Owen smiled. 'Calm down. Let me finish.' He peered at the page. 'Originally, Shemyaza was a powerful seraph, who fell after being seduced by the wicked maiden, Ishtahar. He was punished for this and his soul now hangs between heaven and earth, head down, in the constellation of Orion.'

'Why would a church be dedicated to a fallen angel?' Daniel asked. 'That seems a bit . . . strange.'

'Dark doings in Little Moor,' Owen said with a grin. 'No wonder there's not much of a religious community! The Murkasters built that church.'

'And they were driven out!' Daniel said excitedly. 'O, I must be picking stuff up about this.' He frowned. 'But where do you fit in?'

'Excuse me?'

'The Garden in Eden, the one I saw last night. It was connected with you. I saw Shemyaza, Semjaza, whatever he's called, in the garden. He *was* hanging upside-down. In a valley of fire. Everyone was there, and a woman was screaming, trying to get to him! Look up Grigori, O.'

'Well, get me the book, then.'

After a brief search, Daniel located the book. He had already found the entry by the time he'd reached the desk. 'The Grigori were the tenth order of the bene ha-Elohim – the sons of God – known also as the Watchers, sent to earth to teach humanity, but they were seduced by the daughters of Cain, and spawned monsters upon them. It says also that the Grigori were giants, very tall. There are some names. Semjaza again, Kasdaye, Penemue, Azazel – oh, a load of them.' He frowned. 'What connection does the name Shemyaza have with the murder of a girl in Cresterfield and a church in Little Moor and . . .' He grimaced. '. . . you?'

'There might be no connection between the murder and the rest of it.' Owen said. 'You might have just been picking up stuff in Marlene's that concerned us, not Cressida.'

'But the bangle she gave me . . . the images. I saw everything.'

Owen shrugged. 'True. Are you prepared to get involved in a big psychic quest to unveil a murderer, then? If it's connected with this stuff, it might involve some shady characters. Evil angels? Isn't that black magic, or something? I'm not into that. Magic should be natural, earth-orientated stuff.' He paused significantly. 'Like the magic we do.'

Daniel nodded. 'Perhaps that's another connection. Your magic at the High Place, O. So close to the church. What did Peverel Othman say about Shemyaza? Why did he want to look round the church the other night?'

Owen paused for a moment, wondering whether he should tell Daniel. 'Well, he's looking into something, I think. Could be why he seemed keen to work with you. Remember? He did want to talk to you about your *powers*.'

'So perhaps he should.'

Owen shook his head. 'No, there's more to Peverel than meets the eye. I don't trust him.'

'Change of heart?'

'He's too interested in Lily and me.'

'Well, there's another connection, then. You are associated with my visions of the Garden, Othman's interested in Shemyaza, and also interested in you.'

'This is too weird. What are you trying to prove?'

Daniel shook his head. 'I don't know.' He put the book down. 'There is something else I want to look up.

Ninlil.' He went back to the bookcase, selected another volume, pored through it. 'I'm not sure if this helps.'

'What does it say?' Owen asked.

'Ninlil is the name of a Sumerian goddess, sister/wife of Enlil.' He risked a smile at Owen. 'Well, perhaps there is *some* connection.'

Owen's face remained impassive. 'What else does it say?'

'She's also referred to as Ninkharsag, Lady of Kharsag, the Serpent Lady.' He looked up at Owen. 'Kharsag was a settlement of the Anannage, the sons of Anu, also known as the Shining Ones, Sumerian deities. They equate with the angels of biblical legends.'

Owen shrugged. 'Seems like you got your mythologies mixed up in your visions: a Sumerian goddess wandering around the Garden of Eden?'

'Different mythologies might have different names for the same things,' Daniel said. 'We have to go to the High Place tonight. I want to do some more work on this. I want to know how all this connects to you.'

Owen wriggled his shoulders. 'I'm not sure I want to know. It makes me feel strange. Why go to the High Place anyway? Can't we do it here?'

'Come on, O. We have to find out. How long have you been conducting rituals in the woods? It's a place of power. I just *feel* it's the right place to go.'

Louis woke up feeling extremely hung over. For a while, he couldn't remember the events of the previous night, and it wasn't until he tried to sit up in bed, bracing himself for the inevitable pain, that the memory came back. There was no pain. Louis sat on the edge of his bed, his head spinning. He felt weak, sick, but there was no pain. What had Othman done to him? He couldn't bear to think about his own part in the proceedings. And

Verity, hadn't Verity been there, too? How could he ever face her again? Tentatively, Louis got to his feet. He flexed his limbs experimentally. They felt fine. What would Barbara think? He could never tell her, of course, what had happened. How could he explain it to her? He thought about phoning her, then changed his mind. He needed a day to think, to hide.

Owen didn't go back to the cottage all day. Daniel did not comment upon this, but he guessed there was a rift between Lily and her brother. There was no mention of having to go to The White House with Lily that evening, as Owen normally would. Verity wandered in and out of the house in a daze, while Louis kept to his room. Daniel supposed his father was having a bad day, but why his sister seemed so peculiar, he could not guess. While he and Owen were in the study, she came into the room a couple of times, first to open all the windows, then, ten minutes later, to close them again. On a third occasion, she came into the room and sprayed air freshener. On none of these occasions did she acknowledge or even appear to notice that the room was occupied.

'Has she gone mad?' Owen wondered.

Daniel wasn't sure. Perhaps he should talk to her – sometime.

As the sun sank, they went to the High Place. On the lane to the woods, autumn truly held sway, sickly, ripe smells fermented by the day's sun. The colours were riotous, unnaturally brilliant. Owen led the way on to the path. Once inside the shadow of the trees, he turned and embraced Daniel, the first physical contact they'd made all day. A polite distance had been maintained. Daniel stood very still in Owen's arms, listening to the rubbing creak of the forest. He could hear a rustling at ground level as if the vegetation was crackling in the heat. 'Are you afraid?' Daniel asked.

'No. Nothing's changed here.'

It seemed odd to be going to the High Place without Ray and the others. Daniel wondered how Owen had kept them at bay. He half expected them to be there waiting in the hollow, resentful and sneering. It would no longer bother him now. Daniel went to stand in the middle of the piny circle. 'Can you hear it?' He closed his eyes.

'What?'

'Something like a heartbeat.' Daniel felt very alert. This was the place where their seed had mingled in the earth. He squatted down, put his palms against the ground. It seemed hot, but that might simply be the effect of sun having fallen there all day.

Gradually, the night descended, hung in the arms of the trees, squeezed the fragrant juices from the brazen leaves. A wind started up, set the branches whispering. Daniel sat in the centre of the circle, trying to concentrate. His mind was assailed with too many images: memories. Perhaps he was trying too hard. Owen was a pale shape on the edge of his awareness. 'What do you see, Daniel?'

'Nothing.' Daniel opened his eyes. He'd been so sure this had been the place to come. 'Perhaps we have to be together.'

Owen smiled. Clearly he had no objection to that. 'I want you,' he said. 'I want to be part of you. It's like we can become greater than the sum of our parts, when we are together.'

'We can,' Daniel agreed. He looked around himself and exhaled slowly. 'Well, here we are. Maybe we should have done this a long time ago.'

Owen knelt behind him, and pulled Daniel's T-shirt

down past his shoulders, leaning forward to lick and nibble the flesh. Daniel felt a stab of light ignite within his mind. He fell back heavily against Owen, whose hands slithered down over his belly, crept beneath the waistband of his jeans. Awaken the serpent, Daniel thought. He pulled away from Owen's arms and stood up, extending his own arms towards the sky. Then he began to undress himself. When he was ready, he turned to Owen. 'Now,' he said, pointing a rigid finger at his lover.

Beneath Daniel's steady scrutiny, Owen took off his clothes. He could sense Daniel's power; it seemed almost female, dark and barely controlled. The High Place had affected him, directed his energy.

Daniel came to Owen who was still sitting on the ground. 'Don't get up,' Daniel said. Despite his obvious male attributes, he looked like a young girl, like Lily, ghost hair blowing around his shoulders. When he speared himself on Owen's lap, it felt like entering a woman.

Daniel was hungry for the visions, eager to soar the astral highways of his mind. At first, it seemed as if great wings lifted him up, but then something took hold of his etheric body, pushed him back into himself, and it was purely physical, only fragments of images flickering across his brain.

Halfway down the hill, Peverel Othman lay down among the browning bracken, extending his senses towards the boys on the summit. He shivered, his eyes open wide. So many emanations poured off the High Place, both recent and more distant. He caught fleeting impressions of Owen's group of friends, their shadowy shapes as they stabbed the earth. Then, further back. Something else. A quivering sensation of power, of flame. Othman sucked the impression into his brain, savoured it. Daniel must not pick this up. Not yet. It was simple to exude a blocking stream, which, invisibly, wrapped as a caul around Daniel's senses. He was so young, untrained. He could not fight it. Under Othman's influence, he abandoned the spiritual aspects of what he was doing and gave himself up to lust.

As the night pressed down, and the beast sounds of unfettered ecstasy filled the air above the High Place, Peverel Othman slunk away through the undergrowth. Soon, he thought. Soon.

As Emma Manden had predicted, Peverel Othman did not come to visit Lily on Friday night. Lily didn't see her brother all day, either. She sensed the growing estrangement between herself and Owen, but her thoughts were full of Othman. It was him she wanted now. In the evening, after getting home from her visit to Long Eden with Emma, Lily set about creating her usual Friday night mood, complete with favourite CDs and wine. Tonight, the mood would not come. She thought about what Emma had said. It was odd that she didn't feel more shocked about it. Was this because she didn't really believe she was the daughter of the Murkasters? There could be no other explanation, surely, for this complacent acceptance. Long Eden. Did she feel differently about the place now? She thought of its silent turrets, its great shadow on the drive. No, she felt no warmer towards the place. Still, she was curious about her father. Kashday. An unusual, foreign-sounding name. She had never even seen a picture of him.

At three o'clock in the morning, still awake, and hardly drunk, Lily felt very much alone. Owen's absence seemed more profound. She knew, in her heart, he was with Daniel Cranton. She had lost him. A brief spurt of jealousy went through her, but left no trace of its passing.

It was pushed out by a tide of panic that Othman would never come to her again, never touch her. Had he used her just for that single night? The thought was unbearable. Yet Emma had said he would come back, but not tonight.

Lily fell asleep on the sofa, a CD of ambient music set on repeat, to take her through to morning. She dreamed of the gardens again, but neither Ninlil or Shemyaza appeared to her. Then she was underground, walking along a subterranean corridor, the walls lined with paintings of birds and men with wings. The dreams were fragmented, offering little information. She woke up with a headache, feeling as if she hadn't slept at all.

Owen made no appearance all day Saturday. Neither did Othman. Lily toyed with the idea of phoning Low Mede, and even on one occasion picked up the telephone, then changed her mind. It was a strange day. Too hot. Like summer, but more fetid somehow, more condensed. She drank a bottle of strawberry wine in the afternoon, lying out on the browning lawn behind the cottage, her head in the shadow of a sundial. She wondered if Owen had left her for good. Was that possible?

Seven o'clock came and went. Then eight. No Owen. It was the first time Lily and her brother hadn't visited The White House on a Saturday evening for years. At a quarter past eight, Lily found she had put on her sandals, dragged a brush through her hair and was out of the door, walking towards the pub on her own. Old people, as if drawn from their cottages and bungalows by the heat, stood along the hedgerows, gossiping together. They all nodded at Lily as she passed. She nodded back, distracted. My aunts, she thought. It was absurd.

The garden at The White House was thronged with villagers. It seemed everyone was out that night. Lily took a half-pint of cider out to one of the tables, close to the garden wall, where ivy ticked against the wood. She sat alone. Only a week before, she had sat in this garden with Owen, and the stranger had come to them. It seemed months ago. Since then she had lost her brother and gained a lover. Perhaps that was an exaggeration. She sipped her cider. Barbara Eager came out, dressed in a sleeveless tunic and leggings, high-heeled sandals on her feet. She wafted from table to table, placing her manicured hands upon the shoulders of her customers, pausing to share a joke, a quick exchange of pleasantries. Lily hunched in the shadows beneath the ivy. She hoped she wouldn't be noticed, but was weirdly relieved when Barbara spotted her and ambled over to her table.

'Lily! Here alone?'

Lily pasted a smile across her face. She could feel her real face frowning and miserable beneath it. 'Yes. It's such a lovely night. Didn't want to stay in.'

'Where's your brother?'

Lily shrugged. 'Oh, he had something to do tonight.' She paused, then took a plunge. 'Is Pev around?'

Barbara's hesitation in replying was almost imperceptible. 'I haven't seen him since dinner. Why?'

Lily forced a smile. 'Just wondered. Looking for a drinking partner, I suppose.' She dreaded Barbara would offer her own company.

'You must know everyone here, Lily, surely!' Barbara said. 'You could sit with any of them!' There was a certain stiffness to her tone. Lily realized she had offended the woman.

'He said he might be here.'

'Well, he isn't.'

As Barbara walked away, she admonished herself for being so waspish. Jealousy was such a pointless, wasteful emotion. She hadn't spoken to Othman since the previous night, when he'd dropped off her truck keys. He'd waved

375

at her across the bar at lunchtime, and smiled from the dining-room at dinner, but she sensed he'd been avoiding her. She was desperate to ask him what had happened with Louis. Was the prognosis good? She had telephoned Low Mede at least half a dozen times during the day, only to get Louis's answering machine. Before dinner, she'd considered taking a walk down the lane to make sure Louis was all right, but a minor calamity in the kitchens had prevented her leaving The White House. She would have to pop round tomorrow.

Lily watched Barbara walk back into the pub. She resented the way the woman had been with her. Perhaps Othman had hinted at having spent the night with Lily. She realized she didn't know him at all, didn't know whether he was the sort of man to do a thing like that. Despite Barbara's remark that everyone in the garden knew Lily, not one of them came to join her, although she was conscious of their discreet scrutiny. Probably, everyone was wondering where Owen was. No doubt they'd all been making speculations concerning Daniel Cranton. A hot flush washed up Lily's neck. She didn't want to think about it. For a moment, she put her head down upon her arms, which rested on the splintery table top. She needed to talk to someone. Perhaps she should call on Emma Manden.

The sound of something being placed on the table, prompted her to raise her head quickly. She saw Peverel Othman standing across from her, smiling, his tall shape filling her eyes. He looked radiant and wicked. There appeared to be twigs in his hair.

'You're the green man from the forest,' Lily said. Her heart had grown wings. She had never been so pleased to see someone in her life.

Othman gestured at the pint glass he had placed

before her. 'A drink for my lady,' he said, and sat down on the bench opposite her.

'Thank you.' Lily pushed her own empty half-pint glass away, and dragged the full one towards her, took a sip. She wanted to demand why he hadn't been to see her, but managed to curb her tongue. She must be cool about this, and not risk frightening him off.

'Drinking alone, my Lily? So sad.' He grinned at her.

She felt he knew where Owen was, and was savouring the knowledge, something she didn't have. 'My brother has a new lover,' she said. 'But then I expect you know that. In fact, Owen seems to think it was your idea.'

Othman laughed. 'Hardly! We spoke about his feelings, and I simply advised him to follow his heart. That isn't the same as giving someone an idea, is it?'

She shook her head. 'I suppose not.' She wanted to say something about how Owen had never behaved like this before Othman had turned up in the village, then remembered her suspicions concerning Daniel had been quite long-standing. Perhaps Owen was wrong to blame Othman for making things happen.

'Would you like to walk with me tonight, Lily Winter?'

'I might.' She smiled, drank some more of her cider. 'Where?'

'A walk in the woods,' Othman answered, his eyes full of dangerous promises.

Lily felt a tremor of desire course through her. 'That would be . . . appropriate. If you are a green man, that is.'

'Oh, I am, and much more than that.' He laughed.

Owen and Daniel had been long gone by the time Peverel Othman led Lily by the hand beneath the canopy of the trees in Herman's Wood. Othman sensed they had returned to Low Mede but he couldn't be sure. Their passage had left a vapour between the trees. Lily couldn't perceive it. Not yet. He squeezed her hand.

'Why here?' Lily asked. She felt uneasy, not least because the woods had always been Owen's territory. She dreaded coming across him and his friends now.

'Forests are romantic,' Othman answered smoothly. He paused, and turned to take Lily in his arms. His face looked very dark.

Lily shuddered. She laughed nervously. 'The cottage is empty. We could go there . . .'

Othman said nothing. He pushed her gently against the wide trunk of an ancient oak, began to kiss her. She could feel the demanding hungry presence of his erection as his hips moved tantalizingly against hers. He must want her so much. This thought both surprised and delighted her. She felt slightly smug about Barbara Eager. If only the woman could see her now. She dared to run her fingers over the taut leather of Othman's trousers, expecting him to cast her passionately to the forest floor. He stepped back. 'Not yet.' Holding her hand, he led her further into the trees. He seemed to know where he was going.

Lily was not altogether pleased when she realized they were heading for the High Place. Did Othman know that was where she and Owen had first shared together? She felt it would be like him to want to make love to her there, but how could she really tell? Most of her thoughts about this man were romantic fancies. She tripped on the tangled bracken as he dragged her relentlessly up the slope.

'There's a path somewhere,' she said. He ignored her.

When they reached the summit, he let go of her hand and walked down to the hollow, where he stood with his hands on his hips, his head thrown back. He seemed to be sniffing the air. Lily went towards him, but halted a couple of feet away. She wasn't sure he wanted her close to him now.

'What do you feel, Lily?' he asked.

She shrugged. 'I don't know . . .' What kind of answer did he expect? She wasn't sure what he meant by the question.

'This is a very ancient site,' he said conversationally. 'It has been used in fertility rituals for many hundreds of years, perhaps thousands. Do you know what people used to believe about it?'

Lily shook her head. She had unconsciously begun to hug herself.

'Sit down,' Othman said.

Warily, Lily obeyed him. She was worried about incurring his disapproval.

'Men came here to worship the Goddess, the archetype of female power. They shed their seed here for her. Women had their own rites. They would come here to dance in the light of the moon and to invoke the man of the forest. They believed it would make them fertile, but not only that. The power here could give them beauty, youth, vitality, the ability to ensnare the hearts of men.'

Lily shuddered, glanced around herself nervously. She didn't like this talk; it conjured ghosts in her head. 'Owen and I used to come here,' she said.

'Of course,' Othman answered shortly, as if her remark was too obvious to have been uttered. 'The sacred flame is asleep in the earth here. Sometimes they have made it twitch in its drugged sleep. Sometimes . . .' He hunkered down in front of Lily. 'Shall we wake it up now?'

Lily's teeth had begun to chatter, even though the air was warm. 'If you like.' She wished he'd just come to her, hold her, caress her, possess her. He was behaving oddly. She didn't like it.

'Take off your dress, Lily.' His voice was quiet. He reached out and stroked her shoulder, kindling a hot thread of desire within her. He watched impassively as she unbuttoned her linen dress and drew it over her head. Beneath it, she wore only an old pair of knickers. Briefly, she wished she'd put on something a bit more alluring, sure there were holes in the fabric, greyed by too much washing. Othman took one of her hands in his own, pressed it to her left breast. With the other hand, he squeezed her right nipple. She laughed a little, but his face was serious. 'I want you to do something for me,' he said.

'What?'

'Nothing appeals to me more than the sight of a woman pleasuring herself. Will you do that for me?'

Lily was confused and embarrassed by the request. She didn't think she could do that in front of Othman. 'Well, I . . .'

'Just forget I'm here,' he said, and leaned forward to kiss her, pressing her own hand firmly against her breast. 'You can ask anything of me as well.'

'I'll feel a bit . . . strange,' Lily protested weakly.

Othman pushed her backwards so she lay on the rough pine needles. He removed her underwear, ran his hands across her flat stomach, playfully pulled at her pubic hair. 'We'll start together,' he murmured, lying down beside her. He kissed her deeply, filling her mouth with his swollen tongue. He massaged her breasts, scraped his fingernails across her belly, pushed his fingers inside her. Owen had never excited her the way this man did. It was like he made her drunk on sex, where anything was possible. As he worked dextrously at arousing her, his free hand guided her own fingers down between her legs. It no longer seemed embarrassing. Soon he was kneeling upright between her spread thighs, not touching her at all. She felt like a writhing mass of exposed nerves. As she continued the process he had begun, she was aware of him casting earth upon her. Fragments of leaves and twigs fell into her open mouth. She could see his hand moving above her. The ground beneath her body felt hot and wet like mud. Sharp things dug into her spine and buttocks. She pressed herself against them. Then Othman was pulling her hands away from herself, dragging her body up into a sitting position. She felt delirious. Now, he would take her. Waiting for it was the most exquisite pleasure.

Something moved between her open legs. Something alive.

Lily uttered a squeak, thinking of insects. Othman said, 'Relax, give yourself up to it.'

An invasive pressure, like a rough finger, touched her body. A moment of panic combined with her heightened sensuality. 'What is this?'

'You have invoked the man of the forest,' Othman said in a soothing voice. 'Relax. I am with you.' He still held her hands, her arms stretched out before her.

Lily sat quivering, her spine aching, as the spirit of the forest took on woody, loamy, mossy flesh and rose within her. It was a phallus of earth, rising up from the floor of the hollow, as thick as the organ of a stallion. The sensation was unlike anything she could ever have imagined: not exactly painful, but strange. She felt tears running down her face as the alien thing expanded within her, as if sucking up her own juices. Then it began to move, retracting back into the earth, thrusting up into her once more. It scratched her with twigs and bark, pressed painfully against her cervix. Now, as the hurt increased, her excitement mounted. She wanted the pain, wanted to be torn apart by the enormity of the alien thing that thrust into her. She pulled her hands away from Othman's grip, grasped her own breasts, added her own movements to that of the forest lover. Othman was irrelevant. When the orgasm came, she screamed loudly, the cry of a mating vixen. With her release, she felt the phallus crumble within her, reduced to fragments of leaf and mould. She howled again, filled with a sense of power and rage. If she stood up now, her head would look over the tree-tops. She was Goddess; pure female.

When Othman pushed her back on to the earth, she fought him with nails and teeth. He thrust up inside her, grinding sharp fragments into the tender flesh. She gripped his body with her thighs, snarling, clawing at his back, lunging up to bite his face. When the next orgasm crested within her, it was as if a saline tide washed all the particles of earth out of her, cleansing and healing. She could concentrate on the pure aspect of pleasure without any interference of pain, however intoxicating.

The next orgasm was calmer, leading her inside her own head. Here, she walked a long corridor, that seemed to be deep underground. She could pause to look at the wall paintings. They were of people performing rituals, dressed in cloaks of feathers. The corridor faded into dimness. She was losing it. Then, another spasm of release brought it back into sharp focus. There was a dark circular chamber, its perimeter hidden in shadow. All, in fact, was dark, but for a tiny blue glow in the centre of the room. Lily approached it. A ring of stones surrounded the light. Lily knelt beside them, leaned forward and blew upon the flame. It flickered slightly. She blew again. Her breath seemed to blow something away, an invisible obstruction that blocked the flame. It rose as a straight, blue luminance, casting azure light around the chamber. Lily saw humped, motionless forms clad in rags positioned around the ring of stones. Seven of them. She stood up. The chamber was fading now, and there was no further spasm of orgasm to rekindle the vision. She came to herself, panting upon the floor of the hollow in the High Place, Othman heavy and motionless upon her. She managed to push him off to get her breath. He lay on his back, looking at her. His expression was unreadable. Lily didn't care. He had given her something, or had he merely been a tool for her to use? She walked around the hollow, needing to move, to expel energy. Neither she nor Othman said a word. Presently, she retrieved her clothes and dressed herself. When she began to walk down the hill, Othman jumped up and said, 'Do you want me to walk you back?'

She glanced behind her briefly, shook her head, raised a hand in farewell. She needed to be alone now. The forest did not frighten her. She was part of it.

Once the girl had gone, Othman lay back down upon the earth. He could sense the flame beneath him, far below. There would be a temple, of course, an underground vault. But where was the entrance? He didn't think it was here on the High Place. There were only two viable options, he supposed. The church of St Shem, or Long Eden itself. Probably both. Now could be the time to gain entrance to Long Eden. Now the guardian of the house might let him inside.

When Lily got back to the cottage, she saw there was a light on. The thought that Owen might be home somehow reassured her. That surprised her. She felt very tired now, and sore. It was odd what sex could make you do, she thought. It did not seem odd to her what sex had appeared to make the forest floor do: that seemed only natural. She was a Murkaster, and they had been more than ordinary people. The idea of this did not seem strange now. She had acknowledged her connection with the vanished Murkasters and accepted it. Perhaps she would tell Owen about it.

She opened the front door and went into the kitchen, calling Owen's name. There was no reply. Perhaps he was in the parlour.

Lily uttered a shocked cry when she found Emma Manden lying on her sofa, drinking some of her strawberry wine. 'I hope you don't mind me letting myself in,' Emma said. 'But I wanted to wait for you. Was it good?'

Lily felt herself blush; Emma's remark brought reality crashing back in.

'I told you he would come for you tonight, didn't I?' Emma said before Lily could answer her. 'Are you all right?'

'Yes.' Lily sat down shakily on the sofa beside Emma.

Emma lightly touched her arm. 'Oh, don't worry. We've all had fun up at the High Place. I know what happened to you tonight. Unfortunately, I was never strong enough to wake the flame, but then I'm not Grigori, and you are. Well, partly.'

'What is Grigori?' Lily took the bottle of wine and swigged from it.

'The Murkasters were Grigori,' Emma said. 'They were not entirely human, which makes you the same, doesn't it?'

'If I'm not human, what am I?' Lily laughed a little. She didn't feel at all human at the moment.

'Just something else. The Grigori are an ancient race, who have existed among humanity for many thousands of years, hidden, yet not hidden. They are powerful people, and possess abilities and senses humans don't have. Perhaps you have felt the pressure of that deep in your heart, Lily. I know you must have felt different to everyone else you know.'

Lily nodded wearily. 'Well, yes, I suppose so. Mum

told us we were, anyway.' She giggled nervously. 'But *inhuman*? That's a little hard to take!'

'Any harder to take than some of the other things that have been happening?' Emma asked gently. 'Look into your heart, Lily.'

Lily sighed deeply. 'I can't think at the moment. It's all too confusing. A week ago, I was an ordinary person with a fairly ordinary life. Now my life has become full of mysteries, and I'm not myself any more.'

Emma patted her arm, then jumped up from the sofa. 'Don't worry about it, my dear. Let me run you a bath. You look exhausted. Then we can talk.'

Lily said nothing, watched Emma walk from the room. She heard the woman go upstairs. Of course, she would know this house. After a moment, Lily got to her feet. She felt stiff now, as if she'd been exercising furiously. It was an effort to get upstairs.

Emma came out of the bathroom, and took Lily's arm. 'Don't worry, you'll be fine.'

'I feel . . .' Lily's knees gave way, but Emma broke her crumpled fall.

'Come on, into the bedroom. Let's get those dirty clothes off.'

Meekly, Lily allowed the woman to take control. It reminded her of when her mother was alive, of a time when she'd come into the cottage after falling off her bike and badly grazing her legs. The disorientation. The shock. It was the same. Also, the raw soreness, although it wasn't her knees that pained her now.

When the bath was ready, Emma helped Lily limp into the bathroom. The steam rising from the water was scented with herbs. Fragments of leaves floated in the bath. 'Healing herbs,' Emma explained. 'Just get in, dear. Come on.'

The water was exactly the right temperature. Entering

it was like falling into a pair of comforting arms, relaxing against a soft body. 'Mmmm,' Lily murmured. She wanted to sink beneath the water, but Emma held her around the shoulders, gently flicking the water over her breasts and neck. She rubbed Lily's arms and legs, stroking away the forest dirt. 'There, that's better, isn't it? Shall we wash your hair?'

Emma found shampoo on a shelf next to the sink. She used the toothbrush glass – murky and unwashed – to wet Lily's hair. Lily gave herself up to the enjoyment of having her head massaged. 'It's like when Mum was alive,' she said in a slurred voice.

'Well, didn't I tell you I was a relation of sorts?' Emma said with a bright laugh. 'We all need looking after sometimes.'

When Lily got out of the bath, Emma wrapped her in a towel, and led her back to the bedroom. Lily had begun to shiver. 'Is it getting cold?'

'No. Lie on the bed, dear. I've brought something with me to make you feel better.' She held a small, glass pot in her hands, and was unscrewing the lid. 'Do you know, my mother had to do this for me once upon a time. I was very young, younger than you are now. This is a special ointment. I'll let you keep it, and you can use it for a couple of days. Take off the towel, Lily, and open your legs a little. This won't take a moment.'

The ointment stung at first, but soon eclipsed the soreness with a soothing numbness. Emma sat on the edge of the bed. 'Now I'll get you something to drink.'

'Wine,' said Lily, flapping one hand against the bed.

'No,' Emma said firmly. 'Wine won't do you any good at all. Get into bed. I shan't be long.'

Left alone, Lily began to cry. She didn't know why, because she didn't feel sad. Everything just seemed so strange. Grigori: what were they? She thought of Ninlil and Shemyaza in the garden. They hadn't seemed entirely human either.

Emma came back carrying a tray of tea things. 'I don't know, my girl. You need some lessons in housekeeping, you and that brother of yours. The place is a tip!' Her words were harsh, but she was still smiling.

'Owen isn't here any more,' Lily said. 'He . . .' She couldn't go on.

'Oh, he'll be back!' Emma said. She took her cigarettes and lighter from a pocket on her skirt. 'You've no need to worry about Owen.'

'What am I going to do?' Lily said. 'So much is happening . . .'

Emma lit a cigarette, exhaled. 'My dear, we have to work together. Basically, the situation is this. The Murkasters, being Grigori, gave certain benefits to the people of Little Moor. One of these things was an extended life-span. But when they left, the benefits went with them. The flame beneath the High Place has the power to rejuvenate but once the Grigori dampened it, none of us knew how to activate it again. The Murkasters were very selfish to leave in the way they did! But now, another Grigori has come. The man you know as Peverel Othman. What he's doing here, I'm not entirely sure, but we have to use the situation to help ourselves. He seeks to control us, but we must equally control him. If he leaves us, I shall lose everything I've regained.'

Lily felt very sleepy now. It was difficult to concentrate on Emma's words. 'Did you know Othman was coming here? Is that why you returned to Little Moor?'

Emma laughed. 'Allow me to let you in on a little secret, Lily. I never left the village!'

Lily frowned. 'But I've never met you before. Where were you hiding? Why were you hiding?'

'You've met me a thousand times. And I wasn't hiding.

Well, let's put it this way. I *was* hidden, but it was beyond my control. My body betrayed me, and I was trapped within it. You knew me as Emilia Manden, Eva's mother.'

Lily put one hand over her mouth to stifle a laugh. 'No! I don't believe it.'

'You must,' Emma said. She did not seem mad, yet her claim was outrageous. 'I know this must sound very unlikely to you, but it is the truth. That is the power of the Grigori. I smelled Othman out as soon as he got here, and I forced him to give me back what was mine.' She indicated her svelte body. 'This.'

'How did he do that?'

Emma laughed. 'Oh come, Lily dear, how do they do anything? It's all sex, the great source of power, the fount of magic.'

Lily was faced with the image of Othman making love to Emma, then realized he must have actually made love to *Emilia*. The thought was disgusting. She was so old! 'Did he really do that?'

'Oh yes. Believe it, dear. He will have his way with many people in Little Moor. You mustn't make the mistake of getting possessive about him. That path leads only to the town of hurt. The Grigori use us, but we must also use them.'

'How do they use us? Just for sex?'

Emma shook her head. 'That's only part of it. They like experimenting, and we make good subjects for their experiments. They claim to have helped evolve the human race, and who knows, it might be true. They told me they want only to help us become more like them. Of course, this might be a lie. They might just be evil, cold-hearted and curious, eager to twist and deform our bodies and our minds for their own pleasure and entertainment.'

'That's horrible!'

'Well, I could make your hair curl with stories about Long Eden when I was a girl!' She flicked ash on the carpet. 'Anyway, one of their pet projects was creating hybrids. They've always done it. You and Owen are the product of such an experiment. Othman knows that. If I were him, I'd want to reclaim Long Eden, get inside the house. Perhaps he will continue the experiments. Who can tell? We must make him want to stay, Lily. At least until you and Owen can claim the power that is yours.'

'You think we could make old people young?'

Emma laughed again, patted Lily's hand. 'That remains to be seen. I don't know how much the Grigori traits lie within you. Othman will bring them out if they're there. He's already started, hasn't he?'

Chapter Twenty-two

Same day: Abyss Recording Studios, Vienna

Taziel Levantine lay asleep at one o'clock in the afternoon. It was a grey anvil of a day; nothing worth getting up for. Taziel's clothes lay strewn around the floor of the darkened room, limp ghosts of his long body fashioned in fabric. He was dreaming. The dreams were not of his work, bled from the near-dry well of his creativity, nor of the last person he had spoken to, on the phone, before falling asleep – his woman. He dreamed of the simurgh, a bird-creature evoked from the myths of his race, which flapped carrion-scented feathers, wet with death, in his face and screamed incomprehensible prophecies. Behind the fierce claws, smoke billowed and curled. Through it, Taziel's sleeping mind could see the image of a man, hanging upside-down, twisting in the hot wind. It was a familiar haunting. Taziel twitched and grimaced in his sleep, but there was no one there to see or comfort him. He had locked the guest-room door against everyone: concerned friends, anxious engineers, disgruntled fellow musicians who saw the second hand on the clock marking off money and more money. Taziel did not want to work; it seemed a travesty. He knew he was being humoured, dragged out of the rigid pit of isolation he had clawed for himself in the remnants of his existence. His wounds were healed; he had no excuses about licking them in private. They were only scars now.

Three years ago, a man had come into his life and systematically destroyed it: Peverel Othman. He had brought with him the promise of magics unimaginable, but there had been a cost. After a sleek seduction, Othman had taken over the management of Taziel's band, all of whom were Grigori. As Taziel's work had soared to new levels of creativity, and the band's fortunes waxed strong, Othman had dabbled in the politics of the music business. He had engineered a rivalry between Taziel's band and another – for publicity, Othman claimed – but the mounting tide of jealousy and deceit had ended in tragedy. Taziel had hit out in fury, and there'd been a casualty of his rage. Taziel had escaped imprisonment only because of Grigori connections. He felt little remorse now for the crippling injury he had inflicted against the frontman of the rival band, but his heart was still broken by Othman's betrayal. When the storm broke, Othman had fled and Taziel had not seen him since. Sick with despair, Taziel had hidden himself away and some kind fluke of fate had kept the healing presence of Adele beside him. He had vowed never to work again, but his music made money, and others were not content to let him vanish without trace.

'Come back,' they had wheedled. 'Write music again, record, be happy. See light.' In the end, it had been easier to comply; their therapies were harder to bear than work. Also, his record company, Grigori-owned, owned him. They had used all manner of threats to smoke him out; he still feared prison, being incarcerated with the lowest aspects of humanity. A huge marketing machine stood ticking over, waiting to rev up, churn out hypocrisies. The company people expected Taziel to exorcize the demons of his fall and supposed resurrection in the music, and relished the lucrative thought of his fans being able to analyse his tortured soul via his lyrics. But no faces burned in Taziel's memory, and his heart was a blank slate. Adele kept him calm; she had stayed by him during the flaying times, while others had fled.

He knew that some of her friends considered her a saint, others a madwoman. It did not matter what they thought. He never abused her. They existed in a bubble of excision; everything painful she cut out of his reality before it might reach him.

Adele could not control his dreams.

'*Angra Mainyu*!' spat the simurgh, and Taziel turned over in the bed, his limbs bound in tangled sheets. The bird engulfed him in its thundering wings, thrust its beak against his head as if to break open the skull, implant a thought there. *The Hanged One is waiting for you! He is hungry for you, Taziel!* Then came wakefulness, and the insistent knocking was not against his own skull, but in the world of the flesh. He heard the door handle rattling, the sound of his name being called, 'Taz! Taz!'

'All right.' Disorientated, Taziel sat on the edge of the bed for a few moments, watching the world sway around him. He felt as if he was drawing something back into himself, something which had been roaming.

'Taz, it's the phone!'

He pulled on a long, black T-shirt and went to open the door. Outside, his closest friend and guitarist, Rafe, took a step backwards, as if he hadn't expected the door to open at all.

'Who's on the phone?' Taziel asked. He had deliberately avoided looking in the mirror on the way out, but guessed from the reflection in Rafe's expression he did not look particularly lovely. He was unshaven and, because Grigori were not particularly hairy, the patchy growth looked almost mangy. His long, fair hair was a mat of tangles.

'Enniel Prussoe.' Rafe shook his head. 'Are you OK?'

Taziel nodded dismissively, repeating the name of the caller a few times, then, 'What does *he* want?'

'Wouldn't say.'

There were no phones in the guest-rooms at the studio. They were designed to be places of rest and nothing more; business should not cross their thresholds. Taziel slouched his way to an empty meeting-room on the next floor. Rafe hovered in the doorway as Taziel seated himself in an executive swivel chair at the head of an enormous table laid with neat notepads instead of place-mats. The overcast afternoon light was softened by mar-bled paper blinds which occluded the floor-to-ceiling windows. Rafe watched as Taziel picked up the phone and the call was put through to him. After only a few seconds, Taziel swung his chair around, so that Rafe could not see his face. But Rafe heard him say 'No!' several times. The small word echoed in the immense silence of the room. Each 'No' was delivered in a different tone: first wonderment, even pleasant surprise, then fear, then adamant refusal. Rafe shifted his position uneasily. He thought Taziel Levantine was fragile and yearned to intervene.

Taziel put down the phone, but did not turn to face the door. He said, 'They're making me go to England.'

Rafe took these words as an invitation into the room. 'Why? The album's not finished yet.'

Taziel turned round then. His face looked stricken. Rafe had not seen that expression for some time, and had hoped never to see it again. 'What's happened?' He was thinking of a law suit, some unexpected legal reven-ant. Sometimes, money was not enough to satisfy the wounded, the victims. It was possible someone, some-where had reanimated the scandal.

Taziel shook his head to signify he could not explain, then made an effort to appear normal. It nearly suc-ceeded and would probably have convinced anyone other than Rafe, or Adele. 'You'll have to carry on without me as best you can. Prussoe tells me I shouldn't be away long.'

'I can come with you.'

'No. Not necessary. It's family business, that's all.' Taziel stood up. 'I'd better throw some things into a bag. Call Adele for me, will you?'

'What do I tell her?'

Taziel flashed a feral smile at his friend. 'Invent something.'

'It's nothing to do with . . .?' Rafe let the question hang, afraid of invoking bitter ghosts.

Taziel drew in his breath. 'It was never over, Rafe. And it has to be.'

Rafe watched him walk back up the corridor towards the stairs. The faint suggestion of a spring in Taziel's step made Rafe very much afraid.

Chapter Twenty-three

Aninka was told that the car would come to pick her up at seven-thirty. She spent the day mooching around the house, avoiding relatives, trying to recapture childhood memories in some rooms, trying to shun them in others. Out in the real world, among ordinary people, it was easy to forget who and what she really was. Here, she could be nothing but Grigori. It seemed unfair she had to have this heritage thrust upon her.

During the day she rang Noah, but could only reach his answering machine. She felt abandoned, chastised. What was Peverel Othman doing now? Where was he? Such questions were like hooks in her heart. She didn't want him to be Anakim, evil. She wanted him back.

Walking through a misty rain in the afternoon, lost in the tangled realms of the garden, she considered that it could have been an accident that people had died in Cresterfield. Enniel had told her that the herbal mixture Othman had given to Wendy and the others had undoubtedly contributed to their deaths. No trace of poison had been found in the bodies, however. Aninka now knew that Othman had invoked a demon which had taken their souls, but Enniel had suggested that if the Markses and their friends had not taken the haoma, they might have been able to resist the demon's power long enough to flee the garage and escape it. Cause of death had been given, officially, as heart failure brought on by group hysteria. Had Othman wanted to kill Aninka as well? She couldn't bear the thought of that, not when she had the memory of his warmth and his beauty to lay alongside it. But then, she argued, Othman had eaten the haoma-laced meal, too. Of course, Grigori had more robust constitutions than humans. Perhaps she was immune to its will-weakening effects, and Othman had known that. Yes, that must be the explanation. She wondered whether he'd tried to contact her at home since she'd left the flat. Was he aghast at what he'd done, terrified of the consequences? No. His history suggested he knew what he'd been doing. And the girl, Serafina. She had not died of poisoning or heart failure.

Now Aninka stood before the long windows in one of the drawing-rooms, chain-smoking. Rain lashed the glass, salt rain from the sea. The room was warm, enclosed. A fire burned in the enormous grate. Clocks ticked. As the darkness came, her reflection bloomed in the window, became a mirror image. She looked bewildered, hanging there like a ghost on the outside.

'Gone cold, hasn't it?' One of her guardian's servants had come into the room: Leonie, a small woman, who favoured tight clothing and elaborate hairstyles. She was biting into an apple, a women's magazine held open in one hand. Aninka had never liked this woman. She was human, a dependant, and riddled with all the resentments that that often entailed.

'It is the time of year,' Aninka answered, coldly, stubbing out a cigarette. The ashtray, an ancient hoof of some gazelle-like creature, was overflowing on to the polished mahogany of the table top.

Leonie threw herself down in a chair, one leg over the arm. She was, Aninka knew, over three hundred years old. A daughter of Methuselah, his heritage. She would not even begin to fear mortality for at least another seven centuries. She looked like a young woman of twenty-five, but there was something about her that spoke of age, a mixing of cultures past and present. Other humans were fascinated by Grigori dependants, perhaps drawn to their otherness. Leonie had been married once: a life outside. Enniel had indulged her, perhaps hadn't even noticed she'd been missing until the time she presented herself beneath the coat of arms at the threshold, suitcases at her feet, an impending divorce in the hands of the family solicitors.

'So you're off again tonight,' Leonie said, licking her fingers to flick through the magazine.

Aninka deplored such habits. 'Yes. A short visit.' She made to leave the room, conversation with Leonie being the last thing she desired at the moment.

'Enniel's arranged for you to be travelling with the famous Taz, then.'

Aninka paused. She didn't want to appear ignorant. What knowledge could Leonie have sequestered that she did not have? 'I wasn't aware my travelling arrangements were made public.'

'Hardly that! I only heard Enniel make the arrangements five minutes ago, on the phone in his office.'

'Well, I hardly expected to travel alone. Please, excuse me.'

'Aren't you curious?' Leonie asked.

Aninka glanced at her contemptuously. 'I have no doubt my guardian will inform me of all arrangements in due course.'

'But Taz, Taziel Levantine, was once a lover of the Anakim, Peverel Othman. Not only that, he's very well known. I wonder whether Lahash will bring him with him this evening . . .'

Aninka suppressed a surge of impatient interest, a desire to snap out questions which would be irritatingly side-stepped. She tapped the back of a sofa which was to hand, then turned to Leonie. She affected a nonchalant tone. 'Since you are obviously a fount of knowledge on the subject, please enlighten me. Exactly *what* have you overheard this afternoon?'

Leonie sat up, rubbing her hands gleefully. If she was aware of Aninka's frosty approach, she chose to ignore it. 'There was a scandal concerning Levantine,' she said. 'Tears, accusations, corruption, maiming . . .' She described an arc in the air with one arm, talons curled. 'Peverel Othman is a great seducer. But, of course, you know that.' She giggled. 'Oh sorry, I don't want to sound bitchy.'

Aninka leaned on the back of the sofa, slitted her eyes. 'Go on . . .' She was far from happy that the woman seemed to know all about the reasons behind her visit to the house.

'This isn't something I overheard today, you understand. This is something I read in the file that Enniel left out on his desk the other day. Still, I'm sure you'll keep a confidence about that! Taziel Levantine is a prodigy – Grigori, naturally – who has made a name for himself in the music business. Not so much over here, but in Europe, I understand. Have you heard of him?'

Aninka frowned. 'I don't think so. Is he in a band?'

'Was,' Leonie said. 'They called it depression when he had to retire temporarily. Sucked dry, more like! They were called Azliel X.'

'That sounds familiar.' Aninka strolled around to the front of the sofa and sat down, her arms spread along the back. 'So, what happened?'

'Peverel Othman managed Azliel X for a couple of years. Made their name for them, I suppose.'

'In Europe?' Aninka was thinking of how Enniel had known all this and had pretended ignorance. Now she was hearing it from the mouth of a menial. Enniel would receive a strongly worded rebuke for this.

Leonie nodded. 'They gigged over here, but it never came to much. Bad timing, I suppose. Othman and Levantine were Grigori, so you have to suppose they could have done whatever they'd wanted, but preferred to keep things low key. Levantine always had recourse to family money. Don't they always! Anyway, another band set themselves up as rivals, Atziluth. All human, they drew on a lot of cabbalistic stuff for inspiration. Playing at it, of course. They believed Levantine was into the same thing. Little did they know. The music press had great fun playing the two bands off against each other. Then, for some reason known only to himself, Othman decided to start working with Atziluth as well. It's claimed that Levantine thought he was divulging knowledge, shall we call it *hidden* knowledge, to the songwriter of the other band. Things must have got messy. Enniel's dossier didn't give too much detail. Only that Levantine blinded Atziluth's singer and suffered a breakdown. Levantine spent some time in hospital, after what was reported as a suicide attempt, although questions were asked about that. There was speculation that Othman had tried to kill Levantine.'

'So why is Enniel calling this person in now?' She thought she knew. Another wronged lover seeking revenge. It was likely this Levantine had got wind of what had happened and had approached Enniel himself.

'Well, it's all very interesting!' Leonie declared gleefully. 'While Levantine was being kept in an institution, he believed he still had psychic contact with Othman. Apparently, the Parzupheim wanted to use Levantine to keep tabs on the Anakim, and I believe he must have done, at first. Then he decided he was "healed", whatever that means, and the contact was lost. It's clear from the file that the Parzupheim were sceptical about this claim, but they respected Levantine's desire to put the whole distressing episode behind him. Now it appears Levantine has been more or less forced to become involved again. I gather he's not pleased about it.'

Aninka shook her head. 'None of this makes much sense to me. The Parzupheim are aware of what Othman gets up to, but they simply move him on when he gets too audacious, otherwise letting him have free rein. He's a special case, obviously!'

'I agree, it's strange. Perhaps Taz Levantine will be able to enlighten you.'

Aninka raised a sardonic eyebrow. She wondered how Levantine would view her, given her recent closeness to Othman.

'We'll have to see. Who is Lahash?'

'A carnifex, they say. An executioner.'

Aninka nodded slowly. 'So. They will kill him, this time.'

'Oh, I don't know about that. Perhaps just clip his wings?'

'What did you overhear just now, then?'

'Only Enniel telling someone that Levantine had been *persuaded* to get involved. He's pretty sure they can track Othman down now. You were mentioned.'

'Oh?'

'It seems they want to use you and Levantine to draw Othman out. We can only presume Lahash will do the rest. Perhaps he's there to keep an eye on you both.'

'If Enniel has fears I'll fall into Peverel Othman's arms once I see him again, he's mistaken,' Aninka said. Her heart had begun to beat a little faster. She realized she wanted to see Othman again desperately, and hoped it was only to tell him what she thought of him. Anything else was, of course, unthinkable.

'This is something big,' Leonie said. 'They're playing it down. I thought you should know.'

'Thank you,' Aninka said stiffly. She left the room.

Upstairs, in the bedroom that had been allotted to her, she packed the few belongings she had brought with her. Mundane objects like hairbrushes and lipsticks seemed absurd, removed from her existence. She made up her face, poured herself a glass of whisky from the bottle she had hidden in her suitcase. Then she sat on the bed to drink it. She felt nervous, filled with anticipation and dread. The rain beat down, bringing with it an early darkness. The room felt warm but damp. This house is like a honeycomb, Aninka thought. Each room a separate cell containing an entity, a thought, a possibility. She did not know how many of the family, servants, friends and dependants were in residence at the time. Everyone kept to their own timetable, interacting only as it suited them. No one had shown any interest in Aninka. She had dined alone with Enniel nearly every evening since the first day.

After drinking two glasses of whisky, Aninka fell into a shallow sleep, drifting on the edge of dreams, believing herself to be fully awake. A knock on her door brought her back to complete awareness. She called out unclearly, 'Yes?'

A woman who looked like a secretary and probably was came into the room. Aninka had never seen her before. 'Enniel has sent me to bring you down.'

Aninka stood up unsteadily, quickly arranged her hair in the mirror of the dressing-table, slipped her feet into her shoes. 'OK, I'm ready.'

The woman smiled sweetly, as a dental receptionist might do to a child about to undergo painful experiences.

Three Grigori were present in Enniel's study. Enniel sat behind his desk, looking relaxed. A black-haired man in a neat, dark suit stood in front of him, while a dishevelled individual with long unkempt hair was slumped on the sofa. Aninka made her own assumptions: the dapper one was the carnifex, the scruffy one Levantine. The carnifex was tall, even for a Grigori.

'Ah, my dear, come in.' Enniel summoned her from the desk. 'Your transport has arrived.'

Aninka stalked forward, shoulders back. 'I wasn't told I'd be travelling in company.'

'Do sit down,' Enniel said. 'Let me introduce you.'

Aninka sat on a high-backed chair against the wall, so that everyone would have to turn round to look at her. She noticed Taziel Levantine appraising her with cold, speculative eyes. The carnifex, Lahash, appeared faintly amused, as if she and Levantine were children he had to govern for a while.

Enniel indicated the dark-suited man. 'This is Lahash, your driver. He is a very capable person and has received instructions as to how to proceed once Othman is located. Please do not interfere at that time.'

Aninka objected to Enniel's tone. 'I only want to see the bastard brought in,' she said. She was craving a cigarette badly, but she could not bring herself to traverse the space between her chair and Enniel's desk, where a tempting wooden box full of king sizes lay. Her hands were clenched rigidly in her lap. The cigarettes burned white like candle flames.

As if sensing her need, Enniel gestured to Lahash, who came swiftly, but languidly, towards the desk. Enniel made a further signal, and Lahash picked up the cigarette box, sauntered over to Aninka and offered it to her. She managed to unclasp her frozen fingers and help herself to a cigarette. Lahash lit it for her with a petrol lighter he took from his jacket. He could not be much more than a servant, then, to obey Enniel's request in that manner. 'Thank you,' she said, and crossed her legs. The cigarette gave her confidence, its smoke was a protective screen between herself and the others in the room.

'This,' Enniel gestured towards the sofa, 'is Taziel Levantine. Like you, he has had past connections with Peverel Othman. Unlike you, he still maintains a certain link. However, we are confident that between you, it will be possible to locate our Anakim friend. I hope you have no objection, my dear, to working with Taziel in this way?'

Aninka shrugged, took a lungful of smoke. 'Whatever's needed . . .'

She noticed that Levantine rolled his eyes. In fact, she felt she would not be able to work with him at all.

Levantine stood up. 'I just want to get this over with. When do we start?'

Enniel rose, more slowly and with greater grace. 'Well, first we need to establish contact, however tenuously. Perhaps we should move to the family meditation-room. The atmosphere there is more conducive to what we need to do.'

Aninka had not been in this room for many years. They called it a meditation-room, but really it was a temple. Even before Enniel opened its doors, she could smell the pervasive incense smoke that was soaked into its walls and curtains. The room was large, to accommodate up to fifty people who might need the space to move around. Some rituals incorporated dancing and drama. The walls were painted with depictions of the Garden in Eden, rituals being conducted there by individuals wearing feathered cloaks.

Someone had prepared the room. It was already lit with tall candles, and a burner exuded a coiling steam of silvery smoke. Everyone removed their shoes at the threshold. The windows in this room were all of stained glass. Some bore representations of the peacock angels, others stylized depictions of the Shining Ones and the Fallen Ones, Azazel and Shemyaza. The largest window, which was circular, represented seven sages standing around a blue flame, their arms raised. The colours of this window were crimson, dark blue and purple, with hints of gold. Aninka had always loved it and, as a child, had spent more time staring at it than concentrating on family rituals.

The floor of the room was of dark wood, buffed to a satiny sheen. A huge golden circle was inlaid into it, marked with sigils and names of power.

Taziel Levantine went directly to the circle and sat down, cross-legged. He seemed intractable and sulky. Lahash, more urbane, waited for Enniel to precede him into the room.

Aninka was last to join the circle. She felt slightly uneasy.

Once everyone was seated, Enniel closed his eyes and threw back his head. 'We call upon thee, O Shining Ones, in the names of Ninlil and Enlil, our forebears, and the High Lord Anu. Bestow upon our sister, Aninka, and our brother, Taziel, the fruit of knowledge. Give to them the inner sight, to look upon the one named Peverel Othman.'

He bowed his head. Aninka automatically attuned to the invocation, and assumed Levantine must have done the same. She heard him exhale slowly through his nose beside her. Opening her eyes, she saw his head was slumped on to his chest.

'Hear us, O Lord of the Grigori,' Enniel said. 'We call upon thy spirit, Shemyaza, to aid us in our search for Peverel Othman. Reveal yourself to Aninka and Taziel, guide their sight. Give them a sign of the whereabouts of Peverel Othman.'

Aninka wondered why Enniel had called upon

Shemyaza in this instance. There were other figures, surely, who were more suited to the purpose of hunting?

Enniel's voice was low and soothing, as he led them into a visualization. Aninka found it easy to see once more her old home in Cresterfield, but from above. Enniel told her she could see the direction Othman had taken in his flight. It would be revealed as a trail of dirty light. Aninka immediately saw about a dozen trails in her mind's eye. Which one? She felt it was her imagination at work rather than any attempt at clear sight. Beside her, Taziel Levantine suddenly said, 'South-east.'

'Is he in London?' Enniel asked.

'No, further north. Huge area. Can't tell.' Levantine gasped and suddenly jumped to his feet. 'That's all. The trail's too cold.'

Aninka felt mildly irritated by his behaviour. She was sure he was merely seeking attention.

'Well, that's a start,' Enniel said mildly. 'I suggest you head for London, then try again.'

'There's no point!' Levantine said. 'Why should I contaminate myself by even thinking about that shit, just so you can watch from afar. You won't stop him. You know you won't. You're just using us.'

Aninka was aghast at this outburst, and also slightly impressed, much to her chagrin. She herself would never have dared to speak to Enniel in that way.

Enniel ignored the eruption. He rose to his feet, smiling. 'Well, I think you have time for dinner before you begin travelling. I'll have my secretary book you into a suitable hotel in the city. It won't matter how late it is when you arrive there.'

Lahash rose silently to his feet. Levantine was standing moodily, arms folded, with his back to everyone else.

'Did you pick anything up, Aninka?' Enniel asked.

She shook her head. 'No.' She wasn't sure how she felt about that.

At dinner, Levantine picked moodily at his food, crushingly silent, while Lahash and Enniel attempted to conduct a civilized conversation. Aninka felt dazed, hungry but sick, and barely able to concentrate on the small talk. She was conscious of the occasional covert glances cast in her direction by Taziel, his hostility. It seemed hard to believe that this was the ex-lover who'd caused Pev pain, the legacy of which she'd felt she'd had to suffer. He was like a spoiled child, sulky and rude. Since talking to Leonie, she had imagined someone very different, confident and charismatic, a match for Othman's own splendour. In reality Taziel Levantine was a mess. Perhaps she was lucky not to be in the same condition.

After the main course, Levantine suddenly announced, 'So are you going to tell us exactly what Othman is, Enniel?'

Enniel laid down his fork, paused to wipe his mouth with the corner of a napkin. He laughed politely. 'I think you know that already, Taziel. He is a troublemaker.'

Taziel rolled his eyes. 'Yeah? Is that all? Then why haven't you done anything about him before?'

'The only thing you need to know is that we are doing something about it now.' He smiled at Lahash and Aninka. 'Would you like dessert, or shall we go on straight to the brandy?'

Taziel pushed his plate away, spilling food on to the pristine table-cloth. 'Oh, for fuck's sake! I'm sick of this!'

Aninka froze. Taziel's aggressive behaviour was the last thing she wanted to witness at the moment. 'You are disgusting!' she said. 'At least behave like an adult, even if you do have the mentality of a child!'

Taziel's dark eyes whipped towards her own, his face creased into a sneer. 'Oh, *excuse me*! Keep your mouth shut, lady. If you had any sense, you'd realize we're being duped.'

'Duped?' Enniel enquired delicately. 'In what way?'

Taziel leaned forward over the table. 'What was all that Shemyaza shit in the temple? Why call on him? What's the connection?'

Aninka was surprised by Enniel's subsequent silence. It was obvious that he was lost for an answer.

Eventually, he cleared his throat and said, 'It's documented that the image of Shemyaza cropped up frequently in your delirium during your hospitalization, Taz. Clearly, you have made your own connection, and it seems only logical to utilize it now.'

Even to Aninka, who knew little of Taziel's history, that felt like too convenient an answer.

Taziel shook his head. 'It's not just that, I know it. The Shemyaza frequency is dangerous, unstable. No sensible Grigori – and Enniel I just *know* you are too sensible for words – would call upon it. Not unless it had specific bearing on the work in hand.'

Enniel raised his hands. 'All right, all right. We're driven to desperate means.'

Taziel shook his head again. 'Too glib. You can't use an archetype who's bound up in stasis as a hunter, Enniel, even if the constellation he's held in *is* Orion.'

Aninka realized that for all Taziel's dissipated appearance, his mind was sharp. She waited to see how Enniel would respond.

Her guardian leaned back in his chair, apparently totally at ease. 'All right, I'll be straight with you. From information that my ward, Aninka, has given me, it transpires that Peverel Othman has been using ritualistic means to "open the gate". It is well known that the stargate Orion would be, should it ever be unsealed, a great source of power. It is clear to me that Othman is calling upon the archetypal form of Shemyaza to aid him, perhaps even without being aware of it.'

Aninka frowned. 'He never mentioned Shemyaza's name, though.' She wondered why Enniel had not mentioned this aspect to her before.

Enniel shrugged. 'Perhaps Othman is acting instinctively.'

Taziel's eyes were like glittering flint. 'It's dangerous, Enniel. Shemyaza represents all that's dark in our culture. You want us to expose ourselves to that frequency?' He laughed coldly. 'Get real!'

'You will be protected,' Enniel answered smoothly. 'There is no risk.' He indicated Lahash, who had remained silent throughout the exchanges. 'You can put your lives into Lahash's hands without fear. He knows what to expect.'

'I wish I did!' Aninka said. 'This is a new aspect, Enniel. Why didn't you tell me about it?'

'Because it is only conjecture, my dear. I didn't want to alarm you, nor put dangerous ideas into your head. I thought it best to keep Shemyaza in his place, as it were, in bondage.'

'Which is why you called upon him in the temple, of course!' Taziel sneered. He stood up. 'You people are full of shit! I need some air!' He barged out of the room, pushing chairs from his path, leaving the door open in his wake.

'Phew!' Aninka said.

Enniel was watching the door. 'Be careful with that one, won't you Lahash,' he said.

Lahash inclined his head. 'My thoughts entirely,' he answered.

Chapter Twenty-four

Monday, 26th October: Little Moor

Owen stayed out all night again. On Monday morning,
Lily rose early, feeling surprisingly refreshed, and did not
mind that the house was empty. Emma had left, although
she had obviously cleaned up the kitchen. Sunlight
streamed into the room, promising another day of Indian
summer. Lily opened the back door, then fed the cats.
She prepared herself a bowl of cereal and went out into
the garden to eat it. There was no hint of strangeness in
the air, no alien scents, no hurrying breeze. All was
tranquil, if still unnaturally hot. Lily felt comfortable in
her body; all residue of soreness had gone. The happen-
ings on the High Place might never have been, but for
her memory. If she had dreamed of Peverel Othman
while she'd slept, she could not remember it. Neither had
she dreamed of the garden again. Today, if Owen
deigned to return to her, she would tell him some of
what she knew. The sky above her was the blue of
honesty.

In her mind she laid out the facts, as if they were
coloured cards: her father, the Grigori, Emma/Emilia,
Peverel Othman. Should she discard any of these as
being harbingers of lies? Emma, for all her eccentricities,
was convincing, and she was the first card. If she really
was an ancient crone made youthful once more, then
surely the rest must be truth as well. All that had
happened at the High Place, and Lily's oddly vivid
dreams, seemed only to confirm Emma's fantastic claims.
Lily felt that in order to move forward from this glittering

point in time, she only had to decide whether something exciting and wonderful was happening, or something terrifying and potentially destructive. Yet, how could she make this decision without living what must come with all its dreadful, fearful and exciting possibilities?

A cat jumped on to her lap, just as Owen came sauntering down the lane towards her. She could see his bright hair above the hedgerows. Lily rested her head against the back of the ancient deck-chair, watched him and waited. She wondered whether she would see signs of Daniel Cranton on him. The thought was like something growing through her gums, slightly painful but irresistible to probing.

Owen spotted her as he turned on to the short driveway. Lily sensed his desire to pause, consider, even though he did not physically appear to hesitate. She could see the wariness in his eyes. He expected confrontation.

'Daniel gone to school?' she asked politely as he came into the garden.

'Don't start.'

Lily laughed. 'Start what?' She arranged the cat over her shoulder and stood up. 'I presume you've been at Low Mede this weekend?'

'And you've been here all alone?'

Coldness, barriers. This was not conducive to the sharing of secrets.

Lily went into the cottage, and Owen followed. She turned to look at him, and realized she hardly recognized him now. If she touched him, his skin would feel different. How much of him had Daniel touched? She felt a brief, proprietorial anger. 'I have things to tell you,' she said.

Owen's face was expressionless. 'I'm not sure I want to hear them.'

'You will. Sit down.'

Owen paused before doing so. 'Well? What is it now? Another confession? This is pointless, Lil. I'm not trying to get one over on you all the time. If you've been with Othman, I think you're mad, and playing a dangerous game, but don't imagine I've been at Low Mede just because of that.'

Lily decided a lie was necessary. 'I'm not interested in why you've been at Low Mede. I don't care. Do what you like.' She paused for effect. 'I want to talk to you about our father.'

Owen pulled a quizzical face. 'I hope you're not going to say it's Othman.'

Lily shook her head. 'No, but I know who our father is. In fact, while you've been amusing yourself elsewhere, I've discovered a lot of things about who and what we are.'

Owen's expression was unhelpful. 'Who from, Othman?'

'No. Someone else. Someone who knew our mother well.' Before Owen could speak, voice the question, she reached over the table and laid a hand across his arm. 'O, we are *Murkasters*.'

She expected Owen to laugh and he did. 'Who told you that?'

She wished now it had been someone else, someone whom Owen might respect. 'It was Emma Manden, that is, Emilia Manden. O, you won't believe what's happened!'

Owen realized he might have been wrong to leave his sister alone for the past two days. Her feverish excitement unnerved him. 'Lily, Emilia's off her head. She's lost it. You can't believe what she says.' As he spoke, he imagined he could hear a key turning in an old door, at the end of a long, dark corridor in his mind. Revelation, he felt, was unrolling like an ancient manuscript, each turn uncovering another brilliant picture.

'It's true, O. I know it is. Listen . . .' She did not tell him about visiting the High Place with Othman, but related as much as Emma had told her about herself and Helen Winter's relationship with Kashday Murkaster. Owen kept silent, regarding his sister with a blank face, almost as if he refused to be impressed or surprised. She expected a sarcastic outburst when she'd finished telling him, but when he finally assumed an expression, it was faintly worried.

'Well, say something,' Lily said.

Owen wriggled his shoulders. 'You've either been hallucinating, or conned by a mad relative of the Mandens', or it's the truth. What else can I say?' He frowned, wondering how much to tell his sister about Daniel's visions. Explaining them might be embarrassing. He shook his head. 'This is unbelievable, but I suppose it makes a crazy kind of sense, too. Daniel and I have been . . . investigating things as well, Lil. Now it's your turn to listen. We know about the Grigori.' Carefully, he explained about Daniel's visions, omitting any mention of sex.

Lily began to shake as Owen's story unfolded. She hugged herself in an attempt to stop it. *Something is happening, and it's happening to us. Messages. Dreams. Everything will change.*

When Owen mentioned the names Ninlil and Shemyaza, she interrupted him to relate her dream of the garden. 'It is the same, O,' she said. Her face was white. 'How can Daniel and I see the same things? All these names are new to us.' She rubbed her arms fiercely. 'It scares me. Did Shemyaza look like Pev to Daniel, too?'

Owen shook his head. 'He didn't say so, no . . .' He paused. 'There's more, though. Daniel had a peculiar experience in Cresterfield on Friday night. Listen to this.'

When Owen had finished speaking, Lily put her hands across her face. 'Oh my God, what does this mean?' She peered at Owen through her fingers. 'Is Peverel Othman a murderer?'

'What? How did you reach *that* conclusion?'

Lily gestured wildly. 'Well, it's possible, isn't it? Daniel took the bangle, saw a murder, and picked up the name Shemyaza. Shemyaza is a fallen angel, a *bad* Grigori, and I saw Shemyaza with Pev's face . . .' She held out her arms. 'Well? What does that say to you?'

'It's a bit far-fetched is what it says,' Owen said, but he spoke without conviction. 'It's more likely to be symbolic. If we really are Kashday Murkaster's children, and there's some truth in the Grigori legends, then all this Shemyaza stuff relates directly to us. Racial memories? Shemyaza had a bad reputation, and subconsciously you could be putting that on to Othman. It would be too much of a coincidence if he'd murdered the girl Daniel heard about in Cresterfield. Wouldn't it?'

Lily slapped the table. 'O, I don't want to believe it, of course I don't. I've been alone with Othman, made love with him . . .' She shuddered. 'But in my heart, I feel he's capable of anything.'

Owen stared into her eyes. 'And does suspecting him of murder change your feelings for him?'

Lily glanced away. 'Emma says we must use him. She thinks he can help us reclaim our heritage.'

'Use him?' Owen laughed without humour. 'Lily, have you gone insane? We should get rid of him, get him out of our lives, report him to the police, anything! Even if we are Murkasters, what good is that knowledge to us, really? Do you want to break into Long Eden and set up residence there? Do you want to prove legally that the place could be ours? What *is* it you want?'

Lily closed her eyes to damp her irritation. She felt Owen was overlooking the obvious. How could they ignore the truth of who they were? 'O, we've always known we are different. How many times have you said so? All I want is for us to know ourselves, to be aware of ourselves, and yes, I want to know our history, all of it. It's got nothing to do with the house. Anyway, don't we owe it to the people here to find our power? The Murkasters abandoned them, let them wither away.'

Owen jumped to his feet. 'Listen to yourself!' he exclaimed, throwing up his arms. 'This talk of powers, inhuman relatives, is madness. We have to look at things objectively.'

Lily looked up at him. She felt slightly afraid. 'Owen, I know it's true. I just know it. There was no aunt in this cottage before us. Mum never had relatives here. She worked for a farmer named Lennocks. Emma told me. She only came back here because of who our father was. She thought Little Moor would protect us. And it has. Don't we owe these people something for that?'

Owen shook his head vigorously, then sat down again. 'The past has nothing to do with us, Lil. Supposing these Murkasters, Grigori, whatever they were, did have extraordinary power, and supposing, however unlikely it is, we could find it within ourselves, think about the responsibility that would bring. If we could give people longevity, we'd be ... well, *enslaved* by them. They would be terrified of losing us.' Owen rubbed his eyes fiercely. 'No, this is too much to take in. It's crazy. Emilia Manden is an old crazy woman, and you're too dreamy, Lil. You shouldn't listen to her. A week ago, you'd have just laughed at all this.'

'You haven't seen her,' Lily said calmly. 'Talk to

Emma, O, look at her, then tell me I'm dreaming! Listen to what she can tell you.' She smiled weakly. 'I know you must feel the same way I do. We know, in our souls, this is the truth.' She touched the place between her breasts with a closed fist. 'We are Murkasters; we are half-Grigori. Our suspicions were never wrong, O. We *are* different.'

In the afternoon, Emma Manden made an entrance. Owen was delving inside the car's engine on the mud driveway next to the cottage, Lily reading one of her mother's old books in the deck-chair on the brown lawn, the cats asleep beneath the shade of shrubs and trees. Emma came striding down the lane, her long hair swinging. She looked as if she'd just stepped from another, more magical world, into the sweltering, decaying autumn of Little Moor. Lily would not have been surprised to see seaweed in Emma's hair, or desert sand upon her bare legs. Emma ignored the open driveway, and opened the little gate into the garden, stepping on to the lawn.

'Owen, Emma's here,' Lily said, putting down her book.

Owen reared up from the innards of the car and stared at the woman, as if from behind a veil.

Emma smiled at him widely and lazily. 'Hello again, Owen Winter. Haven't seen you for a while.'

'Let's go inside,' he said.

The kitchen was cool. Lily poured lemonade for everybody, ice-cold from the fridge, but unfortunately it had gone flat. Emma's fingernails were long and red against the smudgy sides of a glass that had been in the cupboard for years. 'You two, like this house, have been running to seed,' Emma said, and took a long swallow of the drink.

'I've told Owen everything,' Lily announced, 'and he has things to tell, too.'

'I've no doubt of it,' said Emma. She lit a cigarette. 'Well, Owen, what do you think?'

Owen was openly staring at Emma. He was searching for signs of decrepitude, lines around the mouth, a crêpiness of the skin. Emma was young. There was no doubt. 'How do I know you are Emilia?' he said.

Emma grinned widely. 'You could ask my daughter.' She laughed. 'Poor Eva. She isn't happy about this, but then, she always has been a jealous girl. Was a spiteful, secretive child, in fact. What I did to deserve such a lump, I don't know!'

'And Othman did this to you, gave you back your youth?'

Emma's tone was flat, uncompromising. 'Yes. Othman did this to me. I'm afraid I don't want to go into too much detail, because it's hardly a romantic story.'

'This is all very hard to believe,' Owen said.

Emma made a careless gesture, spraying ash into the air. 'Of course it is. Departure from the ordinary makes people uncomfortable. The fabric of reality starts to fray. I quite understand. I myself am still utterly astounded whenever I pass a mirror, but my feelings are more of relief and joy than of fear.' She paused to inhale from her cigarette. 'So, Lily has told you about me, and about your father and his family. Just for convenience's sake, suppose that all this information is true. You can argue with Lily about it later, if you like. Now, what is it you can tell me? Lily seems quite excited about it, doesn't she!'

Owen was reluctant to answer. He still wasn't sure whether he should trust this strange, charismatic female who claimed to be Emilia Manden. 'It's not much,' he said.

'Owen!' Lily scolded. 'Just tell Emma what you told me. Please! I think it's important.'

Owen shrugged. 'OK. A friend of mine is psychic, and over the past few days has been picking things up about the Grigori. I suppose he could just be taking it out of my head, some racial memory or something. Does that make sense?'

Emma pulled a face. 'Possibly. Your friend is Daniel Cranton, with whom you have an intimate relationship?'

Owen glanced at Lily in an accusing manner. 'Yes. It's not something I want to be general knowledge around the village, though.'

'I appreciate that,' Emma said, 'although I think you'd find the true residents, those who were Grigori dependants, and their families, don't care a twig about such friendships. Grigori rarely made distinctions concerning gender.'

'I think Daniel's father might.' Owen grimaced. 'Anyway, that's irrelevant to this discussion. I want to know everything you can tell me about Peverel Othman.'

Emma glanced at Lily, who cast down her eyes. 'Mmm. He is not as much of a problem as you seem to think. Not yet.'

'Tell her about the bangle, O,' Lily said. Her face had gone slightly pink.

Owen did so.

Emma listened, her eyes slitted against the smoke she exhaled. 'First, I think you should consider that Daniel might have picked up the name, as a symbol to represent murder, from you, in the same way he might have received visions of the Garden in Eden. Shemyaza is a potent symbol of the Grigori. You know that. He is supposed to be able to love and kill at the same time,

417

capable of ultimate compassion and ultimate cruelty. Ultimately, he is totally immoral! His symbolic appearance in Daniel's mind is one possibility. The other is, as Lily suggests, that Peverel Othman *did* murder this girl in Cresterfield. Othman, or Shemyaza.'

'Shemyaza,' Owen said in a monotone, 'is a mythical fallen angel, who, if he lived at all, must have died about eight thousand years ago. I can't see him hanging around night-clubs in Cresterfield picking up girls and killing them.'

Emma smiled thinly. 'I wasn't speaking literally. I think certain Grigori traits are awakening within you, to which Daniel is sensitive.' She leaned forward earnestly. 'Owen, you are not without magical experience yourself. You should know how it is possible to invoke ancient mythical forms . . .' She frowned at Owen's blank expression. 'Oh well, maybe not. But it is possible. As a matter of fact I don't think Shemyaza is a real person walking around killing people. Perhaps Othman or *another* Grigori was stalking Cresterfield! But Shemyaza's *essence* may well be behind what is happening. He was reputed to be beyond love and hate, the eternal dying king. A martyr and a seducer, the hanged man of the tarot.' She flicked ash into a saucer on the table. 'These are concepts you ought to reclaim, investigate. Perhaps it would help you understand yourselves, your people, better.'

'Where are our people?' Lily asked. 'Are the Murkasters the only Grigori?'

Emma shook her head. 'Obviously not. The Grigori have always had a hand in human affairs, of that I am sure, even though my knowledge of their activities is limited. The Grigori want to keep humanity in the dark about this, of course they do. You are half-human, and have a foot in both worlds. Maybe you can rediscover

Grigori knowledge for your mother's people, those whom the Murkasters abandoned to die. They all looked out for Helen. They deserve to be repaid.'

'It could be dangerous to delve into these things,' Owen said.

Emma exhaled a snort. 'You!' she exclaimed. 'What have you been doing in Herman's Wood all these years? You were playing with fire, the *only* fire, without realizing it. That in itself was potentially dangerous!'

Owen stared at her, unable to speak.

'What has he been doing?' Lily asked.

'Something similar to what you experienced at the High Place,' Emma said, almost dismissively, with a sidelong glance. 'Your brother thought he was acting in secret, but we, the women, we knew.' She smiled at Owen, a knowing rictus.

'What *have* you been doing up there?' Lily demanded. 'Was it with Othman?'

Owen pulled a sour face. 'No! And I don't want to discuss that now. It's irrelevant.'

Emma laughed. 'Hardly. But still, that is a private issue between you. The women of this village have used the High Place for centuries for their own rites. You were drawn to that place, Owen, because it was significant to the Grigori. Notice you never came across us on the Friday nights you went there. We were aware of your activities, and considered them essential. What you did there was a re-enactment of an ancient ceremony as old as the flame itself.'

'What *is* the flame?' Lily asked. 'I think I saw it when I was at the High Place, in a room deep beneath the ground. It was in a vision, or a kind of dream, but it felt very real. A blue flame. I breathed on it to make it grow.'

'The flame is the Source,' Emma said. 'The source of

their power. Othman wants you to reawaken it. The Murkasters dampened it before they left, perhaps to keep it in reserve for a future time when they would return here.' She smiled bleakly. 'They promised to return, of course.'

'And what if they do?' Owen asked. 'What will happen to us?'

'It is important for you to become yourselves,' Emma answered obliquely. 'That will give you protection.'

'This is all too insane,' Lily said, clawing her fingers through her hair. 'I keep thinking I'm going to wake up and find this was all a nightmare. Everything's happened so quickly. I wish we could go back in time to last Saturday.' She laughed nervously. 'We should have ignored Pev when he came to us in the garden at The White House. None of this would have happened.'

'Don't kid yourself,' Emma said sharply. 'I wouldn't have let Othman leave this place without taking what was mine. You wouldn't have been able to keep out of it for long, not once the process had started. I was waiting for this time, watching you in silence, but I knew the day would come when I could come to you and tell you both the truth.'

'Do you think we will ever meet our father?' Lily wondered. 'Do you think *he* knows what is happening?'

'I can't answer that,' Emma said. 'I've no idea where he is, or what happened to him.'

'Did he know about us?' Owen asked.

Emma nodded. 'Oh yes. That was why Helen was so well provided for. He knew about you.'

'Then why has he never come for us?' Lily said.

'He might not be able to,' Emma answered. 'Let me tell you what happened the last night the Murkasters were here.

'Several days before, there had been some kind of

dispute between Helen and Kashday. As to what it was about, we only had rumours to go on, but it seems Helen wanted to have some Grigori power for herself. Kashday was besotted with her, but he must have resisted her demands. So, Helen had left Long Eden and returned to the farm where she worked. Kashday had tried to lure her out, but she was strong-willed, wouldn't have it. She kept him dangling for three days. Then, he must have relented, because he brought her back to Long Eden with him. There were undercurrents of disapproval in the house. I know Lady Lilieth argued with Kashday about Helen.

'I was at Long Eden in the afternoon, on that last day. It was the eve of Lammas, and an important family ritual would take place that night in the temple on the island in the grounds. But it was to be no ordinary ritual. Kashday had an inkling, I think, that something was about to happen, because he sent some of his people up to the church. I was there in the garden when they came back with the effigy, wrapped in a black cloth. I went to him in the early evening, to see if I could find anything out. He was on the phone, talking quickly. I remember asking what was happening. I was afraid. He said, and I can recall this as clear as day, "Emmie, tonight is very important, but I've no idea how it will turn out yet. It may be that I'll have to go away for a while, but don't worry, I've been sorting things out. I want you to speak to all the dependants for me, reassure them." Of course, I was horrified. Kashday often went away, sometimes for a couple of years at a time, but there was a tone in his voice that day that spoke of endings. I panicked. The first thing I thought of, and I was right to do so, was that the Murkasters were running away from Little Moor, and that it would mean a death sentence for me, and my kind. I pleaded with him, begged him to take me with him. He said, "I don't need to hear this, Emmie. I have problems of my own. Rest assured you will be provided for. The Murkasters do not abandon those who have helped them."

'Of course, they did abandon us. That night, monsters came out of the sky. Lady Lilieth, your aunt, had already sent all the dependants back to the village for the night, apart from Helen, and we were instructed not to approach Long Eden. Everyone was terrified. We shut ourselves in our houses, and drew the curtains against the lights outside. We heard noises like great metal wheels turning in heaven. We thought we heard cries. Rain came, and it was red, like beads of fire, or transparent blood. I lay awake that night, praying. Praying to the names they honoured, Anu, Ninlil, and him, of course, Shemyaza. "Great Lord, Hanging One, protect us," I said. He did not listen.

'In the morning, all was quiet. We were scared to go up to Long Eden, but everyone came to me, and I had to go. It was all so silent and still. I walked up the driveway, and the rest of them waited at the gates. I was terrified of what I might find, but there was no real sign of destruction. The house was not locked, and I went inside. I went from room to room, and the house was in shadow. All was dark. The sunlight was only outside. There didn't seem to be anyone around, but then I came across a man in one of the offices. I thought he was Grigori at first, but if he was, he wasn't a Murkaster. He looked up as if he'd been expecting me, and made me sit down. A solicitor. He spoke about trusts and funds, but I wasn't interested. All I could ask was, "When will they come back?" He ignored this, and made me sign things. They knew, of course, that without them, we would lose our longevity, and the arrangements they'd made were for our care in senility and decay. Horrible! So callous.

They knew . . .' Here Emma paused and wiped her face with a single, stiff finger.

Lily reached out to touch her hand. 'Oh, Emma, that was terrible.'

Emma shook herself, as if to rid herself of any contact with Lily. 'Yes. it was. It took me twenty years to become what I was, a hideous hag, while all the time, inside me, I knew I was really like this. It was an abomination, and I will never forgive Kashday for it, but . . .' She reached out quickly to touch Owen and Lily briefly. 'I do not blame you, his children, for this. I trust you will help restore the past.'

Owen wondered whether Lily thought the same as he did: that there was an implicit threat behind Emma's words. She did not blame them at the moment, no, but how would she feel if they were unable to fulfil her expectations? 'We are descended from angels,' he said, almost tonelessly. 'We have stepped from reality into fantasy. It's weird.'

'The angels were a race called the Anannage,' Emma said firmly. 'As real as you or I. Primitive people ascribed their technology and mental abilities to magic. The Anannage were a race of flesh and blood, like us.'

'But what happened to them?' Lily said. 'Everyone used to worship them, so they must have been visible about the world. How come they disappeared?'

Emma smiled. 'Look between the lines of ancient books, my dear. The Anannage, like humanity, were not beyond political squabbling, power grabbing and lust. There is truth behind the legends of the fallen angels. Lust drove Shemyaza to betray his people and abuse his power. The experiments with humanity must have been carefully controlled, but he and his fellow conspirators ruined everything by creating the Nefilim, the giants, the original half-breeds of Anannage and human. Nowadays, they prefer to call themselves Grigori, which I believe is a Greek rendition of Anannage. Originally, they were wild, uncontrollable, and cared nothing for discreet experimentation. Also, Shemyaza and the others freed humanity from the Anannage by giving them forbidden knowledge, how to use metals to make weapons being perhaps the most significant. It caused a war. The original Anannage were dispersed into the world, went into hiding, whereas the Grigori turned themselves into legends. Most myths of gods and heroes are fantastic elaborations of Grigori history. Kashday told me this. Much of the history is lost now. The events were recorded by men such as Zoroaster, Enoch and Moses, but through their human eyes and limited experience. Why do you think the chronology of the Bible states that people like Moses lived for hundreds of years? It was because the Grigori gave them longevity. But at some point, the Grigori withdrew their overt influence. Your people no doubt know why and when. But the history of the world might have been very different if it hadn't been for the Fallen Ones, who changed everything. As to whether the great Shemyaza acted through altruism or self-interest, it's impossible to say. Still, the Grigori look upon him as a god, even to this day. Well, we have to suppose *some* Grigori do.' She frowned. 'This, of course, might be one of the reasons why the Murkasters had to leave Little Moor. We have no idea how the Grigori feel about the Anannage, the past, or how they operate in the world now.' She sighed. 'I should talk to Othman further about this, now that I have my wits about me again. It is strange, very strange, what has happened to me. I feel like I've been a split personality, with this side of me held back by the senile stubbornness of Emilia. Now Emilia is dead, thank Shem.'

Owen couldn't help feeling that some of the unpredictable moods of Emilia still remained. He felt reluctant to trust Emma completely. 'We still don't know exactly why the Murkasters left,' he said. 'You've already said they worshipped Shemyaza, who was seen as a traitor by the original Anannage. If there are other Grigori around, they might see the Murkasters as traitors, too, and by default, us. They might be a danger to us.'

'That is one reason why we have to use Othman,' Emma said quickly. 'We mustn't let him become aware of how much you know at the moment. Let him believe he holds all the cards.'

'But Othman is an unknown quantity,' Owen said, 'and possibly dangerous.'

'I wish Kashday would come back!' Lily said. 'If only we could find him!'

'I wouldn't put much hope in that,' Emma replied. 'We have each other, and there are at least fifteen other Grigori dependants remaining in Little Moor. We must persuade Othman to rejuvenate them eventually, and help you bring out your own Grigori abilities, assuming you have them. However, my instincts tell me you have, at least to a degree.' Again, she touched Lily and Owen briefly. 'The dependants will be your people, and will help you. Our main problem is that there are so many outsiders in Little Moor now. We will need to control them, or drive them away without attracting attention to ourselves. This, I feel, will be a major task.'

Owen shuddered inside. His imagination offered unsavoury images. If Emma took control, he felt he and Lily would have little power of their own. Also, the problems she spoke of would undoubtedly be harder to deal with in reality than she imagined. Emma was still partly Emilia, who lived in an earlier time. The world had changed a lot in twenty years. It was now more difficult to conceal things, and to maintain isolation, from the outside world.

'Tonight, we will visit Long Eden,' Emma said.

'What about Pev?' Lily asked. 'Do you think he'll come here again today? Shall we take him with us?'

Emma shook her head adamantly. 'Certainly not! He might come sniffing around today. Owen, you must forestall him. It will be safe, I think, to tell him about Daniel's visions. He will be intrigued, and might suppose he could use Daniel to gain entrance to the house. I feel it's important that you two achieve that first, stake your claim.' She frowned. 'Somehow, we're going to have to keep Othman away from Long Eden tonight, and the only obvious way is for one of us to keep him occupied.' She pulled a sour face. 'I suppose that will have to be me. You two must go to the house and try to get inside. Do this by psychic means if necessary.'

'How?' Lily said.

Emma seemed impatient with their lack of experience in these matters. 'Sit down outside the house, and visualize going inside. Long Eden has its own spirit of protection. I'm convinced that it will recognize you and speak to you through images. If we're lucky, you'll even find a way to enter the house physically.'

'And if we can, what should we do then?' Lily asked.

'Nothing. Just do it. You need to make your presence felt. Leave the rest to me.' Emma stood up. 'Now, I'll get off, and see whether I can track Othman down. We must act quickly.'

After Emma had left, Owen and Lily stared at one another across the table. 'Are you scared?' Lily asked.

Owen nodded. 'Shitless. Is this real, Lil?'

She smiled. 'I think so. Don't you feel that it is?'

Owen exhaled a shuddering sigh. 'I don't know. I don't know. What time is it?'

Lily had to go into the parlour to find out. 'Ten to three.'

'Come on.' Owen went to the door.

'Where are we going?' Lily followed him.

'To pick Daniel up from school.'

Lily's hand went nervously to her mouth. 'Oh . . . Do I have to come?'

'You know you do. We need him, Lil. *Come on.*'

Emma Manden walked up to The White House, only to discover that Othman was out. She presumed he must have gone to the old people's day centre, and sat down with a coffee in the lounge of the hotel to wait for him. Barbara Eager walked past a few times more than seemed necessary, and Emma smiled at her politely. Eventually, Barbara could obviously contain her curiosity no longer and made a direct approach.

'My receptionist, Shuni, tells me you've been asking for one of our guests. I'm afraid he's not in at the moment. Is there anything I can do for you?'

Emma put down her cup. 'No. I'm quite content to wait, thank you.'

She could see that Barbara was confused about where she'd come from. There was no evidence of luggage, a car, or even a coat, yet Emma was a stranger to her. 'Will you be wanting a room?'

Emma grinned. 'Oh, I doubt that!' She let the implications hang.

Barbara stiffened and withdrew. Another hopeless convert, Emma thought.

By four o'clock, Othman had still not returned. Emma was worried he might have gone straight to the Winters, and considered returning to the cottage herself. Yet it might be unwise to let Othman know she had any contact with the twins. Restless, she went out into the fading sunlight, her senses twitching. She hoped Lily and Owen would have the sense to get rid of Othman as soon as possible, should he turn up at their door. In the meantime, a discreet surveillance could not do any harm.

Emma was both surprised and relieved to find the cottage locked and empty, and the Winters' car missing from the driveway. She didn't feel that they had taken Othman with them, wherever they'd gone. Still, she suspected Othman had been there recently, hopefully after the twins had left the house. Following her instincts, Emma made her way to the gates of Long Eden. She could feel a tension in the air. He'd been there, all right.

After wriggling through the bars of the rusting gate, Emma proceeded cautiously up the drive. Her senses were alert for changes of atmosphere, for movements in the rustling shadows that lined the overgrown gravel. She was confident that things were being stirred up.

She found him in the yard behind the house. For a few moments, she hid in the shadows of the arch, wreathed in twilight. He was running his hands over the bricks of the scullery wall, touching the boarded glass of the windows. It won't let you in, Emma thought, and was pleased by it. What are you, Peverel Othman? she wondered. More than Grigori somehow . . .

In the past, she'd have been able to unearth his secrets more quickly, but now, with her body and mind sapped and impoverished by the decay they had suffered, her intuitive faculties were yet to be completely restored. It would take time. Time and power. But Othman must not know that. He must believe she was utterly renewed.

'Contemplating burglary?' Emma enquired as she sauntered across the yard.

Othman jumped round, his expression of surprise at

her appearance conjuring a laugh from Emma. 'No more than you,' he said. 'What are you doing here?'

'Looking for you,' she replied. She was close to him, and could have reached out and touched him, but restrained herself. Not yet. 'How are your investigations progressing?'

'As you can see, I've yet to penetrate the house.'

'I was hoping you'd come to see me.'

'Well, I've been busy.'

'With the Winter twins?'

Othman gave her a beady stare, perhaps wondering how much she knew. 'I have been visiting them, yes.'

'When are you going to tell them about themselves?'

'Soon. The girl's no problem, but the boy is difficult.' He paused. 'He doesn't trust me.'

'How silly of him,' said Emma, lighting a cigarette. She offered her case to Othman, who took one himself, leaning close to take the flame from her lighter.

He exhaled. 'There's another boy, too. He has strong psychic ability. He's a friend of Owen's.'

'That must be Daniel Cranton,' said Emma. 'Psychic? How odd. He seems such an ordinary boy.'

She took Othman's arm and began to lead him towards the arch. He resisted at first, then relented, clearly thinking there was little he could do at the house tonight. 'Where are you taking me?' he enquired, in a jovial voice.

'To your room in The White House.'

'Emilia, my dear, I hope you're not planning to exhaust me again!'

She stopped walking, turned to face him. 'I was thinking strictly of pleasure.'

He kissed her briefly. 'I am relieved!'

Emma smiled. 'Good. And please, call me Emma now. Poor withered Emilia is dead, thank Shem!'

Barbara was hovering in the hallway as Emma and Othman entered the hotel. She smiled tightly, her eyes homing in on the linked arms. 'Will you both be having dinner here, this evening?' she asked, unable to keep the blades from her voice.

Emma laughed and Othman politely declined. 'Would it be possible to have a few sandwiches in my room? Of course, I shall pay extra for my friend.'

'I'll see,' Barbara responded icily, and swept through a door to the kitchen.

Othman and Emma went slowly up the stairs. 'She is jealous,' Emma said, pleased.

'Probably, but not for long. I paid some attention to her crippled friend, Louis, on Friday night. She'll soon have him to enjoy and will forget all about me!'

'You are too thoughful,' said Emma. 'Although I think you underestimate the effect you have on people.'

Barbara Eager was in a foul humour. She told herself this was not because Peverel Othman was upstairs in his room with a strange woman. No, it was because of the oppressive heat, the sickly odours of fruit baking on the trees and water congealing in pools around the village. Also, she had still not been able to contact Louis. The phone continued to be answered by the machine, and when she'd called round – twice – once the place had looked empty, locked up and in shadow, and on the second occasion, an unusually vague Verity Cranton had almost stumbled from the garden, saying her father was 'unwell'. Barbara had fired a barrage of questions at Verity, wondering if the girl knew about Othman's visit on Friday night. Surely, Louis should be feeling well now, if what Othman had claimed was true? Or perhaps it was a part of the healing process that Louis should get worse before he got better. Whatever was happening, Barbara could barely contain her worry. She demanded to see Louis, which roused Verity from her torpor, prompting her to gloss over into her habitual icy, stiff reserve. 'Dad doesn't want any visitors. He'll call you when he feels better. Please don't worry. I'm looking after him.'

Rebuffed, Barbara could do nothing but leave. She would have to speak to Othman about Louis. Perhaps tomorrow as they drove to Larkington, supposing he didn't shy off from the excursion because of his visitor, or, worse, suggest she should accompany them.

In the bedroom, Emma took off her dress, and lounged on the duvet in a grey silk slip. Othman ordered wine, which presently arrived with the sandwiches, brought on a tray by Shuni Perks. Othman turned off all the lights, but for a single lamp beside the bed. The room was transformed from over-tidy formality to something far more restful. Othman poured wine for himself and Emma, and handed her a glass.

'You look like something from a Forties film,' he said, with apparent approval.

Emma tossed her hair, soft shadows caught in the hollows of her throat and collar-bones. 'I enjoyed that decade. Did you?'

Othman shrugged. 'I suppose so. Events tend to blur, don't they?' He flopped down beside her, inserted a finger between the warm strap of her slip and her flawless skin. 'You are very beautiful. I feel quite pleased with my work.'

Emma extended a taloned hand and cupped his groin. 'No more than I. Also, I am looking forward to enjoying a Grigori man again. Being buggered across a table was not exactly what I had in mind.'

Othman laughed, and lay back with his arms across his face. 'I get these whims sometimes.' He made no protest as Emma undid his trousers.

'What wonderful skin you have!' she said. 'So smooth.'

'It is the skin of a boy,' Othman said. 'Goes with having the mind of a geriatric.'

'Believe me, I know what the mind of geriatric is like,' Emma said. 'And you do not appear to have one.' She pulled his trousers off.

'Perhaps, but I think I may possibly be mad.'

Emma ignored this remark and took his cock in her mouth. He made a small sound, which was almost sad. He tasted faintly of almonds.

'Do you want more from me?' he asked. 'Is that it? Are you feeling weak again?'

Emma raised her head. 'Be quiet. We are trying to be sensual. Forget about power.' The urge to demand it was great, but she controlled herself. It was important to keep Othman's mind from straying. She knew he might be capable of picking up any psychic activity buzzing around Long Eden.

Presently, she lifted herself and straddled him, pulling aside her silk underwear to impale herself upon him. This, she did slowly, in order to savour the long, gradual invasion, as her newly revitalized body accepted the first man she'd had in over twenty years. She had made love with many Grigori men in her time, and with as many human men. The Grigori had spoiled her; humans could do little for her now. After the Murkasters had left, she'd lost interest in sex, a culling of libido caused by more than the inexorable dissolution of her flesh. Othman lay impassively beneath her, but she could feel him becoming larger and harder within her body. That was the way with them; Kashday had once split her, made her bleed. But the sensations were exquisite. She could have

432

wept for being able to experience them once more. Her mind drifted as luxurious tides coursed lazily through her skin and bones. She thought about the original woman, Ishtahar, who had seduced Shemyaza. A mother of the Grigori, how beautiful she must have been. For Shemyaza, it must have been as if the earth herself had called to him. The Grigori, as presumably some of the Anannage before them, also found humans irresistible. Race called to race in lust, in desire. It must always have been this way.

The orgasm, which was screaming to be released, beat at her control. She was about to surrender herself to it, when Othman reared up and pushed her off him. He rolled her on to her back, hung there above her, staring down without expression.

'Please,' she said. A single, polite request.

He blinked slowly. She thought he would order her out, leap up and leave the room.

'What do you want?' she purred.

He said nothing, but complied with her desires, watching her face. It was an art to him, the long careful thrusts, the sudden accelerations into teasing stabs. She wanted to pull him down on to her, hold him close, but he maintained a distance, resting on stiff arms above her body. He let her climax three times before withdrawing. Without speaking, he poured himself another glass of wine and drank it down quickly. She knew he had experienced no release.

'Are you all right?' she asked him, breathless.

He smiled. 'Fine.'

'I wanted to give you pleasure.'

'You did. I have work to do.'

A tremor of panic sizzled through her. 'Tonight? What? Surely there's nothing that can't wait until tomorrow. Relax, enjoy yourself.'

'I'm in no rush.' He lay down beside her.

She rested her head on his chest. 'Where have you come from, Pev?'

'I had a childhood in Austria, if that's what you mean,' he said. His arms were behind his head, he did not enfold her as she wished he would.

'I don't think that's exactly what I mean,' Emma said. 'But I don't suppose you'll give me honest answers.' She raised herself a little to look him in the eye. 'Don't you see? Because I believe that, you can tell me anything, truth or untruth.'

'I am a searching creature, but I don't know what I'm searching for,' Othman said. His eyes, and his mouth were smiling, so where was the un-smile Emma sensed? Where did it hide?

'Tell me more.'

'I have loved a thousand times, taken lives, spread dissension, dripped poison into eager ears. I have caused wars, and stopped them. I have created religions, and turned them into jihads. Just the ordinary life of a wandering Grigori, you see?'

Emma laughed, reached over him for the wine bottle. 'Who was the last person you loved?'

Othman grinned, but Emma was sensitive to the wariness that came into his eyes. He wasn't going to let himself be seduced by her into revealing too much. 'I experienced perfect love, but felt driven to destroy it. Strange. Just didn't feel right. Felt too good, I suppose. Perhaps I destroyed it before it destroyed me.'

'Are you mourning, then?'

Othman turned down his mouth into a quizzical expression. 'No. That would be far too inconvenient.' At last, he extended an arm to pull her against him. 'Emma, you are a bad girl. Is this how you pulled Kashday Murkaster's secrets from him? Pillow talk, they call it,

434

don't they? All the great *femme fatales* of human history were adept at it.'

Emma laughed obligingly. 'You flatter me. Kashday told me no secrets.' He hadn't needed to: she'd guessed many of them. Othman, however, was a closed vault to her intuition.

'What is this business that's so urgent, then?' she asked, in a careful voice.

Othman hesitated, before answering. 'I want to talk to the psychic.'

'Daniel Cranton?' Emma supposed that would not cause any problem. If Othman was occupied with Cranton, Owen and Lily could conduct their investigations in peace. 'But why? You're Grigori. You don't need him.'

Othman smiled lazily. 'Ever heard of using a canary to test the air in a coal mine? There's a guardian at the house, and I don't have its measure yet. Did you, by the way, ever go into any of the underground sites around here while you worked for the Murkasters?'

Emma shook her head. 'No. My duties were entirely domestic. I don't think any villagers went into the secret places – and came out again.'

'It's important I find the chamber . . .'

'What chamber?'

Othman smiled. 'Where the flame burns. You talked of that, didn't you, when we first met?'

She nodded. 'Yes. I know about the flame. I think the Murkasters killed it, or took it with them. It will take a lot to revive it.'

'Perhaps it has already revived.' Othman sat up.

Emma realized he was referring to what had happened with Lily at the High Place, but did not question him. 'Are you going now?' She reached out, stroked his arm. 'Please, wait a while. I have a lot of catching up to do.'

Her hand strayed to his groin. She felt him stir beneath her fingers.

Smiling he reached out to squeeze one of her heavy breasts through the silk of her slip. She drew her breath in slowly, savouring the contact. 'You are a temptation,' he said.

'Relax for a few hours.' She lowered herself backwards, opened her legs a little.

Othman leaned over to remove her silk knickers, which she still wore. 'Just a while, then,' he said.

Chapter Twenty-five

Same day: Little Moor (continued)

Long Eden seemed less threatening to Lily with Owen and Daniel there. The building still towered up into the night, clutching its secrets within, throwing baleful shadows on to the weedy gravel of the drive, but its looming presence seemed petulant rather than sinister. She noticed that Daniel made a point of maintaining a distance between himself and Owen as they walked up the drive. Whether this was irritating or gratifying was hard to decide. Daniel looked young and vulnerable, still wearing his school uniform, although he'd removed his tie and jacket. He'd obviously been horrified to find Lily in the car when they'd gone to pick him up. After an excruciatingly silent drive back to the cottage, Lily had made sandwiches and a pot of tea, while Owen told Daniel about Emma Manden and all that she had said. Daniel had sat pale and wide-eyed, looking as if he wasn't taking in much of what Owen was saying. Lily had been able to tell he was painfully aware of her presence and that she knew about his relationship with Owen. She'd wanted to put him at ease, whilst also revelling in his discomfort. She couldn't understand her feelings. Daniel had agreed reluctantly to accompany them to Long Eden.

'Have you ever been there before?' Lily asked him.

He'd shaken his head. 'No.'

Lily could tell he wasn't very happy about having to go there. In that, at least, they were in accord. An unexpected burst of empathy had made her say, 'The place scares me to death, but at least there'll be three of us.'

'And if we really are Murkasters, we have a right to be there,' Owen said.

'We really are Murkasters,' Lily said in flat tone. She noticed Owen had managed to avoid the subject of Peverel Othman. At some point in the future, she knew she would have to speak to Daniel about her dream, and get him to talk in depth about what had happened in Cresterfield. But not yet. She didn't want Daniel to feel too at home in her territory.

Now Long Eden loomed above them. Lily could feel it watching her. She did not feel at home.

'Do we walk right up to the front door and knock?' Owen said.

'I wouldn't like the thought of anyone answering!' Lily replied.

'Or the door might just swing open,' Daniel added, 'and there'd be no one there.'

They laughed together nervously. The possibility of that, unfortunately, seemed very likely.

Something large and winged, an angel shadow, suddenly swooped out from the eaves of the house, flying low in front of them. Lily jumped and squealed, grabbing hold of Owen's arm. 'Oh, it's an owl!' She felt stupid for her outburst.

Daniel gestured up at the house. 'Perhaps there are holes in the attic windows.'

They paused to stare up at the eaves. The night shadow of Long Eden's towers lapped just before their feet. Lily tried to imagine their mother coming to this place, tried to visualize the face of the man who had possessed her here. Somehow, Helen Winter could not easily be made a part of this landscape. She had been too slippery, too quick-silvery, to have been held by the shadows of Long Eden.

'They must have named this place after the Garden,' Daniel said. 'The Garden in Eden.'

'Of course,' said Lily, extending a toe to dip into the wavelets of shade ahead of her. Gaining access to the house seemed impossible. However, she had no doubt that they'd be able to accomplish it.

'What can you feel?' Owen asked Daniel.

Daniel took in a slow breath. 'On edge, antsy.' He shook his head. 'I feel too small. Trying to penetrate the walls of this place is like trying to imagine breaking a mountain with a pin.'

'Let's go into the garden,' Lily said. She walked towards the lawn of seeding grasses. 'It must have been so beautiful once.'

If Helen Winter had a place anywhere in Long Eden, it would have to be in the garden. Lily spied the pale remains of a summer-house against a stand of yews some yards away. It was mangled by frenzied, overgrown climbing roses. Lily thought she could smell the perfume of the flowers. Even now, a few voluptuous blooms still clung to the rambling stems. She could imagine her mother pausing in the doorway of the summer-house to smell the flowers, looking back over her shoulder to the one who followed her. In there, perhaps, Kashday Murkaster had made love to Helen, with the drowsy scents of a summer night all around them, the call of a nightjar, the slow drip of falling rose petals resounding against the breathing earth.

Lily felt drawn towards the summer-house. Reality slipped away and she was walking in a summer garden with the warm night inhaling and exhaling around her. The lawn was neatly shorn and the roses climbing the walls of the summer-house rambled over trellises. Lily heard laughter, the murmur of voices. She looked back, and the lights of Long Eden spilled out over the lawns. Faintly, she could hear music, the scratch of old gramophone records being played beyond the open french windows. This was a place of opulence and contentedness.

Lily paused at the door to the summer-house. She saw a flash of pale fabric and there was her mother coming towards her. Lily gasped, murmured 'Mum!' but Helen could not see or hear her. She was smoking a cigarette, her red lips almost black in the moonlight, her arching brows disdainful of secrets. A man came up behind her, a tall silhouette. His red hair fell forward as he leaned to put his hands on Helen's shoulders. 'Feel it!' Helen said in a husky voice. 'Feel the night, Kash. It's calling to me.'

My father! Lily thought. He was like Peverel Othman, she could see that, but whereas danger lurked in the shadows of Othman, this one gave off only light. How could she doubt Emma's words about the Grigori now, seeing him there, an angel incarnate?

'I want to help you,' Helen said, taking a fierce draw off her cigarette. 'Give me the chance! You know you want to.'

'My beloved, I can't. You know that.' Kashday's voice was low, musical. It contained both humour and weariness. Lily realized this must be a demand that Helen had made many times before.

Helen glanced round at him. 'I can't understand why you're being so craven. It's something you want as well. Make me the Oracle! Give me the Eye! Take me into the flame next week! Let me open the Gate for you!'

'There are too many risks,' Kashday replied. 'I cannot be Shemyaza, and you are not Ishtahar.'

'Pah!' Helen spat. 'We are their equals!'

Kashday sighed. 'I rue the day I ever told you the old

440

stories. We are not their equals, Helen. Nowhere near. If I'd guessed you'd be like this, I'd have kept silent.'

'Be like this?' Helen was scornful. 'What do you mean by that? You have within your power the ability to get back all the things that were taken from your people so long ago. I am giving you the opportunity, and what do you do? Throw it back in my face! You are a coward, Kash!'

'The Gate was closed to us for very good reasons!' Kashday appeared to be losing patience. 'When the time is right, it will open again, but we cannot force it. You have no idea what you're asking.'

'I have courage,' Helen said. 'And that's enough!'

'No!' Kashday said. 'It is not!'

With an angry cry, Helen smacked his hands from her shoulders. She ran past Lily on to the lawn. 'I despise you! Moulder here for eternity, then! See if I care!' She ran off across the lawn, and Kashday did not follow. He watched her leave for a while, then glanced to where Lily was standing in the shadow of the nodding rose vines. Lily looked right into his eyes. She was sure he could see her. She wanted to speak, communicate with him, but her mouth wouldn't open.

'Already, she carries you,' Kashday said.

Something touched Lily's shoulder, and, for a few moments, reality became a swirling rush of colour and sound. Then she realized that Owen had come up behind her and put his arm around her. Kashday and the old summertime had gone. 'It's wistful here, isn't it?' Owen said.

Lily was shaking. 'I saw them,' she whispered. 'Our parents. Here.'

Owen peered into the dark summer-house. 'What happened?'

Lily screwed up her face, shook her head. 'It's fading

like a dream. They were arguing about something.' She reached for Owen's hand. 'Kashday saw me, O. He spoke to me. He knew about us, even before Mum did.'

Daniel tentatively approached. 'Something was happening here a moment ago. I could feel it, but I couldn't see or hear it.' The night had become still and eerie. Daniel's voice was a soft intrusion. 'Can we look round the garden?'

'Why?' Owen asked. 'Is it important?'

'I just feel like I want to.'

'OK.' They moved off together, Owen still with his arm around his sister. Lily felt both smug and uncomfortably guilty about this; strange, contradictory feelings. She felt Owen should be touching Daniel, not her, yet resented the fact it should be so. The impressions of her waking dream about her parents were slipping away from her, but she was glad it had happened. Kashday had seen her.

They wandered into the night shawl of the yews, where the moon's radiance could not penetrate other than in occasional silver coins of light. The watching stillness of the trees crept into everyone's bones. It would be so easy to become extremely frightened. Lily thought she glimpsed pointed, gnarled faces among the trees, and told the others about it. It seemed safer to laugh about it, and the sound of their laughter created an aura of protection around them. As they walked further into the tangle of yews and fading ferns, a dreamy, intoxicated mood descended slowly into their minds, dripping down like sap from the trees.

The yew walk led to wide stone steps that were covered in fallen leaves and moss. At the bottom of the steps was a lake, with a paved area where people might have sat to enjoy the view, or else climbed into boats. A narrow pathway appeared to skirt the water, but was overgrown in places and had collapsed into the water in others. The lake was surrounded by tall trees; pines on one side, oak, sycamore and beech on the other. An ornamental island, now a scrub of wild shrubs and trees, dominated the centre of the lake, speared by a single ancient poplar. Bats flirted with the water's surface, seeming to flit in and out of reality.

Lily recognized the island as the place where she had met Peverel Othman in her first dream about him, but she could see no sign of a temple through the trees. 'Now you see me, now you don't!' she said, wiggling her fingers in imitation of flickering bat wings.

For a few moments, they stood in a line, staring at the island. Lily said, 'Things have happened over there.'

'There is so much to tell,' Daniel answered, his voice faint. 'A million stories, a million pictures.'

'Can you see them?' Lily asked.

'If I let go, I feel I'd be swamped with them.' He closed his eyes and let his head drop backwards. 'Boats across the lake, breaking the line of the moon. Music and lights. Old music. Dancing. Laughter. Then there is winter, and the island is white and silent. A slow figure climbs out of a dark vessel, crawls up the bank, carrying a dim lantern.' He opened his eyes. 'It's like this place is a hundred films all showing at once.'

'We should be taping this, or writing it down,' Owen said. None of them had thought to bring a tape recorder or a notepad with them.

They sat down on the paving stones at the water's edge, which were warm beneath their hands, and scratchy with dried lichen. The lake smelled slightly fetid, but there was also an overpowering aroma of earth and fruit, so strong it seemed intoxicating. Lily said it was like taking alcohol by nose.

Daniel lay down on the warm stones. He felt he only

443

had to close his eyes for the images to come crowding in; they were so strong here. 'This is your history,' he said aloud, but he wasn't sure whether he was speaking to Lily and Owen, or to someone else.

'Tell us,' Owen said.

'There is a woman in the water,' Daniel began. He wrinkled his nose, as if perplexed. 'She's bathing, or perhaps she lives in there. Her name is . . . Mellith. She says she comes from another place. She's one of the Murkasters. She drowned in the lake. She is showing me a picture from her mind . . .

'It is the night of Lammas Eve. They walk to the temple underground. No, not through the Gate of the Cat and up to the island, but further on . . . The flame, it is waiting. She is there. Yes. So strong. She will go into the flame.' Daniel began to gasp for breath. 'Lily, Owen: your mother!'

Lily touched his arm. 'Daniel! Are you all right.'

His face was puckered up, as if in pain. 'Yes,' he hissed. 'Listen, it's all too rapid. Images. The flame! She is there, she is the Eye. No! The gate is opening, it is opening, but something's coming through! No! No!' Daniel's voice cracked. Lily and Owen were frozen, their flesh crawling, as they listened to their companion's panicked words. 'Too late! It's closing again, but they have come through! Angry! Punishing! They are like a wave of vengeance. The Murkasters are running away, and some of them are going up to the island. But the vengeance is coming after them! Forcing them into the water. They're drowning! Drowning!' Daniel's voice had become a squeal. Tears ran down his face. His breath caught in his throat and gurgled there, as if his lungs were full of liquid.

'Wake him up!' Lily cried. 'Owen, do something! He's drowning!'

444

Daniel's hand lashed out and gripped Lily's arm painfully. 'No!' His voice was strong and deep, not his own. 'It must be seen. The Grigori repeat old mistakes, in their greed and stupidity. The knowledge is not for the people of low earth. Not yet! There will be a time when the tree shall fruit once more, and all can feed from it. But not this way!'

Daniel's booming voice ebbed to a sigh. Lily and Owen exchanged a shocked glance. Who had they just heard speaking through Daniel? Not Kashday, but someone greater.

Daniel stirred upon the stones, then rubbed his nose. His voice was almost normal again. 'Now I'm walking back towards the house . . .'

'What can you see?' Owen asked softly.

'Lights in the windows,' Daniel said. He was smiling now. 'It is all lit up and there are people there.'

'Can you go in?' Lily asked.

'Of course. The doors and windows are all open. There are people on the lawn, talking, laughing. I think some of them can see me, others not.'

There was a silence as they waited for Daniel to speak again. He said nothing.

'Have you gone into the house?' Lily asked at last.

'The peacock,' Daniel said. 'It's the peacock.'

'What do you mean?' asked Owen.

'The tail of the peacock contains the eyes. It's in the walls. And down there, underneath. The blue. Peacock blue. The flame.'

Lily touched Daniel gently on the arm. 'Find the spirit of the house,' she said softly. 'As it is now, not in the past. Can you do that?'

'There are so many images,' Daniel answered, his brow creasing. 'But I'll try.'

'Tell it who we are and that we need to go inside the house,' Owen said.

445

There were a few moments' silence, and then Daniel became agitated. His head moved rapidly from side to side, and his arms flapped as if warding something away from his face.

'What is it?' Lily's voice showed her alarm.

'So big,' Daniel answered breathlessly. 'So dark. Can't speak!'

'You can't, or it can't?' Owen demanded.

'Won't let me. Pushing me out! Its beak! Its claws!' Daniel suddenly sat upright, breathing hard. He shook his head as if to clear his mind, then glanced round himself fearfully. 'It's very strong. I want to leave!' He stood up.

Owen got to his feet and put his arms round Daniel. 'Calm down. It's all right.'

'Perhaps we should go,' Lily said quickly. She was beginning to feel very uneasy. The night had assumed a threatening quality, as if something hideous was about to burst out of the trees around the lake. The thought of the walk back through the yews was not pleasant. Was there another way out of the garden?

'Scaring each other will not help,' Owen said, although he did not sound totally at ease himself. 'This is all psychological. We must be rational.'

Daniel pulled away from Owen. 'It won't let you in. It's a guardian created not to let *anyone* in.'

'What about the woman, Mellith?' Owen said. 'Can you find her again? Ask her what we must do?'

Daniel made a miserable sound. 'I don't want to. I want to get out of here.'

'Owen, let's leave it!' Lily said sharply. 'We don't know what we're getting into.'

'Lily, your friend Emma is the one who seems to think it's so important for us to get into the house! We can't give up yet.'

'But she's not here!' Lily's voice had become a wail. 'I'd feel safer if she was!'

'It's OK,' Daniel said, rubbing his arms. 'I feel a bit better now. I'll try to talk to Mellith again.'

'Are you sure?' Lily asked. 'We can always come back another time.' She glanced accusingly at Owen. 'Perhaps in daylight.'

Owen made a scornful sound, but sat down on the slabs once more. Lily and Daniel sat down as well, Daniel in the middle.

Lily laid a reassuring hand on Daniel's arm. 'Stop at any time.'

Daniel lay back and closed his eyes. He said nothing for several minutes, until Lily was beginning to think nothing would happen. Then he sighed deeply.

'He has left a key.'

'What? Who has? Where?' Owen demanded.

'Sssh!' Lily hissed. 'Let him speak.'

'You need the key to enter the house.'

'You mean it's just locked up? Is it that simple?' Owen's voice was incredulous.

'Owen!' Lily said in a low voice. 'Shut up!'

Daniel shook his head. 'The key walks. It enters the house and leaves it like smoke. It has to be petitioned.' He opened his eyes, blinked at the dark sky. 'That's all. She won't say any more.'

'It doesn't make much sense,' Lily said. 'A key that can walk around? What would it look like? Is it a real key?'

'I doubt it,' Owen answered. 'It must be symbolic. Were there no clues other than that, Daniel?'

Daniel shook his head. 'No. I'll think about it.' He sat up. 'Now, I really want to leave.'

Lily stood up and offered Daniel her hand. She sensed a shift in alliances. Owen was being awkward and unfair, she thought. Didn't he consider that what Daniel was doing for them might be dangerous for him? 'Come on. We'll go back to the cottage for supper.'

They walked quickly, approaching the lightless mass of the yews with unspoken misgivings. To break the tension, they discussed what had happened, trying to ignore the oppressive, watching shadows. We should be safe here, Lily thought. If this is our home, we should be safe. For a moment, she thought about what it would be like if suddenly the three of them should become separated. What would come for her? What would she see? The urge to hurry, to break into a run, was great. She knew she had to resist it. Later, she would ask the others if they'd felt the same. To voice such thoughts now was unthinkable. She was sure it would act as a powerful invocation of terror.

Suddenly, Daniel froze and said, 'What was that?'

'What?' Owen asked, glancing round.

Daniel looked up and moaned. 'Oh no! It's coming!'

'What is?' Lily demanded, trying to peer through the thick branches. She could see nothing. Then it came, the slow, heavy pulse of great wings. A charnel-stinking wind, hot as a predator's breath, came whistling up the yew walk.

'Run!' Daniel screamed.

Panicking, the three bumped into each other, tangled in each other's limbs, unable to move forward. Then Daniel leaped away and Lily and Owen could follow him. A terrible scream shattered the night, a screech as of huge metal teeth grinding against one another. The trees were creaking and swaying and rustling as if something gigantic were pressing down upon them. Twigs and insects spattered down on to the heads and necks of Daniel and his companions. Lily thought she felt claws snag at her hair. She was too terrified even to scream.

The end of the yew walk was in sight, a grey rectangle in the blackness ahead. Lily was afraid that once they were out on the bare stretch of the lawn, the thing pursuing them, whatever it was, could pick them off easily. Yet what else could they do but run?

They burst from the trees, and Lily squawked in dismay. Something amorphous and black squatted on the pathway ahead of them. Owen swore and yanked Daniel back. Lily, holding on to Daniel's other arm, stumbled, grazing her left knee on the mossy stone. 'What is it?' Her voice was shrill. She realized that whatever had been threatening them overhead had vanished the instant they'd come out of the trees.

Daniel laughed in relief. 'It's over,' he said, pulling away from the twins.

Lily and Owen watched as he approached the shape ahead of them. They heard him murmuring encouraging words, saw him stoop and gather something large and black in his arms. 'It's Raven, Verity's cat,' Daniel said. 'I'd know him anywhere.'

Owen exhaled in relief. 'Thank God! What the hell was that back there?' He glanced round and up, scanning the sky, but now the night was still once more.

'The guardian of the house,' Daniel said. 'It was warning us off, I think.'

Lily shuddered. 'It was disgusting!'

'A bird of prey,' Daniel told her. 'A name came to me: anzu bird.'

Lily walked up to Daniel and stroked Raven's broad head. 'Well, Raven, I think you saved us from a big, ugly bird! Thank you very much!'

Daniel laughed. 'I don't think Raven had anything to do with it! He's just out hunting, aren't you, boy?'

'But he was sitting there so still, as if he was waiting for us,' Lily said. 'I think he scared the guardian off. You look very threatening, Raven!' She smoothed the long fur on his back.

'Careful where you touch him,' Daniel said. 'He's a bit grouchy about fussing. I have scars to prove it.'

'He's very handsome,' said Lily. 'How long have you had him? I haven't seen him around.' Lily wanted to talk about mundane things like Verity's cat, rather than think about all that had just happened. It would feel safer to talk about that in the sanctuary of the cottage, with the night shut outside.

They began to walk back towards Long Eden, Owen slouching, moody and silent, behind the other two. 'Vez adopted Raven a week or so ago,' Daniel said. 'He's a stray.'

'I wonder where he's from,' Lily said. 'Perhaps he's wandered from one of the new bungalows.'

'Wherever he's come from, Vez has catnapped him.'

'He looked so scary sitting there,' Lily said. 'It really was as if he was waiting for us, in a menacing kind of way! Isn't he big!'

As they passed the house, making for the main driveway, the cat struggled from Daniel's arms and scampered off through the long grass. They could see his path as the grasses shivered in a snaking line. He went back towards the yews.

On the driveway, Lily paused and stared back at the looming towers of the house. 'Well, Long Eden, your secrets are still safe,' she said. 'At least for now.'

Clouds passed over the moon, bringing deeper darkness, as if the house was frowning. They hurried down the driveway, and didn't look back.

Verity was looking for Raven when the doorbell rang. Since Friday night, she felt safer when the cat was in the house with her at night. She knew, dimly, that something huge and incredible had happened to her life, making ineradicable changes, but her conscious mind shrank from thinking about it. She'd felt numb all weekend, and had avoided her father. Louis had seemed to avoid her, too; they'd barely glimpsed one another. Verity knew, in her heart, that her father had been healed, although she was aware he was embarrassed about showing this to her. She wondered whether she herself was responsible for bringing all the strangeness into their lives; it seemed to have begun the morning she'd had the horrible dreams, conjuring ghosts from her past. Had she opened some kind of psychic door? Verity never mulled over her own history. She wondered now whether she should have analysed it more carefully. She felt so different now; numb and sleepy, yet more alive than she'd ever been.

At first, when she heard the bell, she resolved not to answer the door. This was not because she feared finding a phantom crouching at the threshold, but merely because she expected it would be Barbara Eager, who had been pestering her all weekend. How would Louis explain himself to Barbara? Verity wondered, as the doorbell rang again. She sat in the kitchen, biting the skin around her fingernails, staring at the door that led to the hall. Eventually, the bell was silent. Whoever had pressed it so insistently had obviously given up.

Then a sharp tap upon the kitchen window made Verity swing round on her chair in alarm. She could see a pale face looking in.

Her first instinct was to let down the blinds, and she even leaped up and hurried over to grab the cords, but then the kitchen door opened and Peverel Othman walked into her house. The door had been locked, Verity was sure. She wished Raven had come home.

'Don't look so scared,' Othman said. 'It's only me.'

'What do you want?' Verity was sickened by the mere

sight of Othman, as it reminded her of what she'd seen in her father's study on Friday night. Yet his power and his beauty filled the room, bringing with it a sense of well-being and joy, as well as fascinating undercurrents of forbidden and wicked pleasures. Verity acknowledged Othman's power, and was wary of it, but she was not totally immune.

'I've come to talk to your brother.' Othman carefully closed the door and went to sit on one of the kitchen chairs. Verity remained immobile by the window.

'He's not here,' Verity answered. She realized then that Daniel had not even come in from school.

'Are you sure?' Othman asked. His mouth curled into a wry grin. He thought she was lying.

Verity sauntered over to the table. The awareness that Othman couldn't tell for himself that Daniel was out made her feel better. 'Search the house for yourself if you like,' she said. 'He's probably with Owen Winter. Now, seeing as Daniel's not here, you'd better leave.'

Othman pulled a rueful face. 'Oh Verity, I do hope you're not being prudish about what you witnessed on Friday night.'

'Prudish?' Verity's voice rose, and she felt her face flush. 'How dare you! What I object to is the way you coerced me, against my will, to be part of whatever filthy ritual you were engaged in.'

'It wasn't filthy,' Othman said. 'Only a prude would think so.'

'Get out.'

Othman stared at her with hooded eyes for a moment or two. She dared to believe she had the power to remove him from her home, even though she did not entirely want to.

'How *is* your father?' Othman enquired.

'I've no idea. I've not seen him.'

'Not a very tight-knit family, are you?' Othman stood up.

Verity realized she was too close to him, and backed away. Even as she did this, she knew it was a mistake. Othman reached out and touched her face. His fingers were neither cold nor warm. It was just a pressure.

'My dear, you are a knot of anguish. I can help you, you know.'

'Get out,' Verity repeated. She steeled herself not to pull away from his touch or drop her eyes from his gaze. 'I want nothing from you.'

'But it pains me to see you suffering. How you punish yourself! And why? What did you do that was so wrong? You wanted the best from life, and other people, lesser people, let their emotions carry them away.' He laughed. 'Oh Verity, let it go. You have built a shrine within you that calls to ghosts.'

Verity went cold. He knew about her. He knew all about her. She could not speak.

'You did exactly the right thing finishing with that puling wretch,' Othman said conversationally. 'Imagine how dreary it would have been if you'd carried on seeing him. Sick fools who kill themselves to inflict guilt are not worthy of being remembered, neither do they deserve to enjoy relationships. You did the right thing. Unfortunate, perhaps, that you did not recognize him for what he was before you stole him from your friend, Netty, but you were younger then. You would not make such a mistake now.'

'I don't want to hear this,' Verity said. 'Just go!'

'You really should accept my help,' Othman said. 'His essence is a ghoul for your vitality, and never leaves the area. He clings to you like a bad smell. You brought him home with you.' He looked past her, at the window. 'I can see him now, in fact, scratching at the pane. Would you like me to get rid of him for you? It's a very simple process.'

Verity resisted the urge to turn round, even though her skin was crawling. There's nothing there, she told herself, he's winding you up.

'Look,' said Othman.

'I don't want to.'

'Running away again? Turning your back?' Othman laughed. 'Don't be a fool, Verity. Be a woman.'

Angrily, Verity spun round, directing a fierce glance at Othman in the process. She did not expect to see anything, but did.

The face against the window was rotting, flaccid. Its filmed eyes stared in at her. She saw the mouth working upon the shape of her name. Uttering a cry of disgust, Verity put her hands against her eyes and turned away. She did not intend to turn into Othman's arms, but he'd positioned himself accurately. He felt strong and reassuring. 'Make it go!' Verity said.

'If you want me to, of course I will. Watch.'

Othman released her and went towards the door.

'Don't!' Verity cried in horror as he turned the handle.

Othman glanced back at her. 'Don't worry. Just come and watch.'

He went out into garden, where a writhing shadow crouched against the wall of the house. Verity peered nervously round the door. She saw Othman pick something up, like a bunch of tattered rags. He uttered some strange, unintelligible words and flung his burden up into the sky, where it broke up into smoky ribbons and dispersed. Othman turned to her with a smile, rubbing his hands together.

'There. All gone. Now, how about a nice strong cup of coffee?'

Verity could only stare numbly at the place in the sky where her demon had evaporated. Othman gathered her up and drew her into the kitchen with him. He kissed her cheek. 'Don't worry, Verity. We're friends now. I want to talk to you about your brother.'

Chapter Twenty-six

Same day: London

It was a Grigori hotel. Aninka heard breathing in the walls. There was nowhere to check in.

When they arrived, the night outside was wet and cold, and there was steam in the air from the Chinese restaurants that lined the narrow street. Lahash had a card which, when inserted into a brass slot beside the door, and after a certain sequence was tapped in on the keypad beneath it, gained access to the building. The door opened electronically.

Inside it was like walking into someone's hall, a private house. There were flowers, gloves on a table, carelessly tangled with a dog's lead of plaited leather and stainless steel. Letters lay in a pile on the same table; some were opened.

'Well!' said Aninka.

Lahash opened a door off the hall, looked into the room beyond. Taziel Levantine remained by the front door, now locked and sealed again, and lit a cigarette. He wore shades and looked seedy, thin like a drug addict, well-handled like a whore. So far, he had ignored Aninka almost completely. Back at High Crag House, he had got into the front passenger seat of the car beside Lahash, forcing Aninka to sit alone behind them. The back of the car was as big as a railway carriage. She had rattled around in it uncomfortably. The upholstery was of cream leather. She'd heard Taziel talking softly to Lahash, a murmur beneath some late-night music wafting from the radio. Occasionally, one of them had laughed. Was it to be like this, now? The two men as allies? She would have to change things.

'What is this place?' Aninka asked. 'It's not a hotel, is it?'

Lahash came back into the hall. 'It's late,' he said. 'Someone will be along soon.'

Aninka sat down on a chair beside the hall table and clawed through the contents of her shoulder-bag to find her cigarettes. Lahash, ever gallant, held out a light to her. She took it.

'Where are we?' She put tired cynicism into her voice.

Lahash pocketed his lighter. He himself never smoked. 'It's a boarding house. Exclusive.'

Aninka sighed, exhaled smoke. 'So where is everybody? I don't want to sit here all night. Go and find them.'

Lahash raised an eyebrow at her, but went off to investigate other areas of the building. He walked down a corridor beside the stairs. Taziel came over to the table and began looking through the letters. Aninka couldn't think of anything to say to him. She had no idea how he felt about Othman, and knew he would not tell her if she asked. Perhaps he was jealous of her, or else despised her. It really didn't matter what he felt, she thought.

She flicked ash on to the red carpet. 'This is ridiculous!'

Taziel was silent. He'd spent some time alone with Enniel before they'd left the house down south. Perhaps Enniel had scolded him, and his musician's pride couldn't take it.

Lahash appeared again, accompanied by a woman. She was Grigori, dressed in a long green caftan, her dark hair wound up on her head, tendrils of it escaping artfully in places. Her Grigori beauty was tiring. Aninka had seen too much of it recently. She yearned for human asymmetry.

457

'Good evening,' said the woman. It sounded as if she was speaking through silk. 'I hope you've had a pleasant journey. Allow me to show you to your suite.'

She preceded them up the stairs, her hips swaying a little drunkenly, Aninka thought.

On the second floor, the hostess produced a key-card from her pocket and inserted it into the door. Inside the room, soft lighting glowed ready for their entrance. Champagne in a bucket beside the sofa; Japanese cabinets, midnight drapes, a Turkish rug.

'Champagne?' Aninka tried to sound quizzical. 'This is not a honeymoon!'

The woman ignored her remark. 'Would you like something to eat? The kitchen is open twenty-four hours.'

'I would like lobster,' Aninka said. She noticed Taziel smirk.

The woman hesitated. 'Of course.'

'On a baguette, with salad.'

'For all of us,' Lahash added.

'And coffee,' Aninka said. 'Viennese, with black sugar.'

The woman inclined her head, and left the room. She appeared faintly amused.

Aninka poured herself some champagne into one of the exquisite glasses standing on a filigreed tray next to the ice bucket. The stem was a twisted serpent of indigo glass. She considered putting it into her bag before she left the place.

Lahash picked up a remote control and turned on the television. They sat and watched a late-night American media show in silence until the soft tap came at the door, signalling the arrival of their order. Aninka found she was hungry, as the aroma of rich coffee filled the room. The baguettes were accompanied by bowls of coleslaw and other assorted salads. Aninka kicked off her shoes. 'I feel quite at home,' she said.

'It's not real,' Taziel said tersely. 'None of this.'

'You might as well relax,' said Lahash.

Taziel uttered a muted snarl and scuffed across the room to open one of the bedroom doors. He disappeared inside. Aninka rolled her eyes at Lahash, who grinned wryly. 'Not a great conversationalist, is he?' Aninka said.

Lahash shrugged, then took off his jacket. Beneath it, he wore a white dress shirt and a gun in a shoulder-holster. 'Are we in a movie or something?' Aninka asked. She laughed. 'This is all too bizarre.' The gun actually made her feel nervous. She wanted to ask Lahash to hide it, but felt it would only reveal her naivety.

'No, we are not in a movie,' Lahash replied. 'It's all too real, no matter what our companion thinks.'

'What *is* going on?' Aninka hoped to draw him out.

Lahash sat down next to her on the sofa, but some distance away. 'We just have to find Peverel Othman.' He frowned. 'And soon.'

'Why? Why now?'

Lahash flicked her a glance like a serpent's tongue, black and quick and wet in an otherwise dry countenance. He knew more than he would tell her. 'He's getting into mischief, isn't he?'

Aninka stretched out on the sofa, admired the sweeping lines of her silk-clad legs, hoping Lahash would do the same. 'I'm beginning to wonder whether I did the right thing, offering to help find him. It was an impulsive decision. Maybe I should just forget about the whole thing, put it behind me.' She creased her brow. 'I'm not sure I want to see Pev again.'

'Nobody's forcing you to come,' Lahash said. 'I'm sure Enniel wouldn't mind if you backed out. Taziel, after all, is our most potent tool in this operation.'

Aninka smiled sourly. 'What I haven't mentioned is that my curiosity will be forever pricked if I don't see what happens for myself. I know I won't get any information from Enniel. No, however painful, I'll see this through.' She leaned out to refresh her glass, offered the bottle to Lahash. 'Anyway, what is this *link* Taziel has with Pev? It sounds very . . . arcane.'

'They had an association.'

'Yes, I heard about that. Ended in tears, I believe.'

'Among other things.' Lahash drained his glass. 'The bottle's finished. Shall I order more?'

Aninka caught a note in his voice, a certain speculative gleam in his eyes. 'Why not?' she said.

Lahash picked up the phone and, after a few moments, spoke into it, a private whisper. Then he turned back to Aninka. She could see from his hairline, which was auburn, that he dyed his hair black. 'Taziel's been through a hard time. He escaped with his sanity, just, but it's fragile. You must overlook his behaviour; he's damaged.'

'I heard he blinded someone, another musician. Triangle situation?'

Lahash didn't bother to lower his voice, and Aninka wondered whether Taziel could hear them. 'Yes, he blinded someone. He burned out their optic nerves.'

'Great Shem!' Aninka exclaimed, grimacing. 'How did he do that?'

'There was no weapon,' Lahash said dryly, adding, 'that was ever found.'

Aninka glanced at the closed door, behind which Taziel Levantine might be listening to them discussing his affairs. 'He must have felt very strongly.'

'We must suppose that,' Lahash said.

There was another soft knock at the door, and Lahash got up to answer it, returning with a bottle of champagne larger than the one they had just finished. 'I see you intend to make a night of this!' Aninka said. 'It must already be about half past one in the morning.' There were no clocks in the room.

'Look on this as the lull before the storm,' Lahash said, prising out the cork. It popped out and hissed sullenly, releasing a snaking steam. There was no froth, just the alchemical breath of the wine.

'Do you think something . . . unpleasant will happen?' Aninka held out her glass. She looked at Lahash's long, manicured hand – a killer's hand? – as he poured her a drink. The hairs on it were dark red and smooth, like a diminished pelt.

'I think there will be some kind of *event*,' he said, 'but don't worry, you won't be in danger. That's what I'm here for.'

Aninka laughed dryly. 'I am reassured beyond measure. What kind of *event*?'

'Obviously, most of the information I've been given is sensitive.' Lahash sat down again, sipped his drink. 'All I can tell you is that Othman is approaching a crisis. That is why the Parzupheim want him brought in.'

'I thought you might kill him.'

Lahash grinned. 'No. That would not be desirable.'

'But perhaps expedient – in the event.'

Lahash shrugged. 'I will, of course, protect you and Taziel. Don't think that Enniel looks on you as disposable.'

'This is all very sinister,' Aninka said. 'It's like a boy's game. I can't understand it, or I don't want to.'

Lahash smiled at her. 'Sometimes we forget what we are. Perhaps you should think about that. We have assimilated ourselves with human culture, but destiny occasionally pokes us to remind us of our heritage, which is inescapable. We have responsibilities, too, which we

461

took upon ourselves in the beginning, and which we cannot shirk.'

'Are you lecturing me?' Aninka asked archly.

Lahash shook his head. 'No, perhaps lecturing myself.'

'But what has Othman to do with these things you're talking about? Is it because he's Anakim, a throwback?'

'He is more than that, Ms Prussoe.'

'Do we have to be that formal? My name's Aninka. Also, I have not been given the privilege of knowing *your* second name.'

'It is Murkaster,' he told her.

Aninka opened her mouth to ask another question about Othman, but a cry from beyond Taziel's closed door silenced her. It sounded like the screech of a bird of prey.

Lahash stood up quickly.

'What was that?' Aninka asked, also rising. 'Is he all right?'

Lahash went to open the door, Aninka following. Fortunately, Taziel had not locked it. Light from the sitting-room fell over the wide bed, where Taziel lay fully clothed. He was writhing in what looked like pain. Aninka turned on the overhead light, while Lahash hurried to the bed.

'What's the matter with him?' Aninka asked, thinking of the lobster.

Lahash was leaning over Taziel. 'He's dreaming.'

'Then wake him up! It must be a nightmare.'

Taziel's face was creased in agony, and gleaming with sweat. There were marks, like scratches, on his neck and the upper part of his chest revealed by his open shirt. There was a smell in the room, salt and sear, perhaps the smell of terror.

'Wake him up!' Aninka repeated. She had become conscious of a watching presence in the room, a silence wrapped around the core of movement and energy that was Taziel Levantine. She could feel something cold and damp, and utterly beyond physical form, touching her mind.

Lahash did not touch Taziel. 'Taz,' he said. 'Taz, can you hear me?'

Aninka asked again, 'What's the matter with him?'

Lahash frowned, shook his head.

'Guardian!' Taziel wheezed. 'In the house.'

'Where?' Lahash demanded.

Taziel's body squirmed across the bed. 'Grigori stronghold. Closed up.'

'What's happening?' Aninka asked.

Lahash shrugged. 'He could have pin-pointed Othman's location, and encountered some kind of guardian, perhaps a protection Othman's conjured up. Whatever it is, it doesn't look as if it's going to let Taziel past.'

Taziel uttered a wordless sound, a plea. The temperature in the room was falling. Soon, their breath would be steaming.

Aninka moved closer to Lahash. 'Can't you stop this?'

Lahash ignored her. 'Taz, you are in control. I have surrounded you in light. You are safe. Speak!'

'Hot,' Taziel said. He had calmed down a little, although his eyes were screwed up tight. 'It's so hot.'

'What is?' Lahash sat on the edge of the bed.

'The heat is around him, it reaches up to the sky, condensing. His epiphany conjures the heat, and it is close, very close.' Taziel suddenly opened his eyes, although he did not seem to see the room or his companions. He sat up, rigid, on the bed. 'Moorland, heat. He is making heat. He has returned to Eden. In the North.'

Suddenly Taziel's back arched and he emitted a piercing howl. He began to claw at his chest and throat. 'No! No!'

Lahash grabbed Taziel's arms, pushed him back down on to the bed, where he kicked and struggled as if being attacked by an unseen assailant.

Lahash shouted out '*Aeshma vohumana, Dregvant masha, Yazatas, Daeva, Spenta mainyu!*'

Beside him, Aninka felt compelled to repeat the invocation in English, 'Through the wrath of Mazda's will, wicked magic, depart from this body. In the name of the Adorable Ones, and the spirits of fire and goodwill.'

Abruptly, Taziel's body relaxed, and he uttered a long, hissing sigh. Aninka, who'd been frozen in horror and disbelief, realized the temperature in the room had returned to normal. Taziel opened his eyes, and blinked up at Lahash. 'He is in the North,' he said. 'But we knew that, didn't we?'

Lahash nodded. 'Yes. Can you be precise?'

Taziel frowned. 'I shall have to concentrate, but not yet. The name Eden is prominent. It is a vital clue, I think.' He shook his head. 'It is clear, but unclear. I'm too subjective. Othman has been drawn towards a power source. That, too, is inevitable. What power sources are there in the North that we might not know about?'

Aninka was astounded at how quickly he appeared to regain his composure. His chest was still scored with long red weals.

'There are none – that we don't know about. But there is one that has been – shall we say *corked*?' Lahash smiled, without humour. 'It is ironic, but perhaps no coincidence I should be involved in this. There is a place called Long Eden in the North, the site of my ancestral home. My family were exiled from it twenty years ago, for transgressions. Our community service, to atone for our delinquencies, includes my employment with the Parzupheim. I am bound to them for a millennium.' His smile became grim. 'It will be there. I know it.'

Taziel reached up and took one of Lahash's hands in his own. 'I'm sorry.'

Lahash shrugged. 'It's only pertinent.' He smiled. 'Well, I have been prevented from seeing my home, and I had expected that by the time I had paid my penalty, Long Eden would be dust. In some ways, it will be good to see it again.'

'I could use a drink,' Taziel said. He lay back on the bed, still holding Lahash's hand. 'I need to talk.'

'We have plenty of champagne,' Lahash answered, and went back into the sitting-room. Aninka was left staring at Taziel. She realized, with some amusement, that there would be competition over with whom Lahash would be spending the rest of the night. Well, she had no intention of spending it alone. Pointedly, she sat down on the bed.

'Are you OK?'

She was waiting for Taziel's expression to become closed and sour, but he seemed resigned to her presence.

'Yes.' He smiled weakly, then pressed the fingers of one hand over his eyes. 'This sort of thing has been happening more often recently. I was angry at Enniel calling me in to get involved in this, but now I know it was the right thing. I'd have gone mad, otherwise. This thing has to be finished once and for all.'

'What thing?' Aninka dared to ask.

Taziel lowered his hand and gave her a knowing smile. He seemed very young now. 'You know what thing. Othman doesn't have a hold on me; he's just an unwelcome presence now and again.'

'You must have been very close for that to happen.'

He nodded. 'I thought so. But not that close, obviously, otherwise what happened wouldn't have happened.'

Lahash came back with the champagne and the glasses. He filled each one. 'A toast,' he said, distributing them to his companions. He raised his own glass. 'To our success!'

'Success!' Taziel said.

'Success,' murmured Aninka. They clinked glasses and drank. Aninka felt uneasy. Just what would their success encompass?

They drank in silence for a while, and then Lahash refilled their glasses, an action which seemed to prompt conversation once more.

'If Othman has settled somewhere else for a while,' Aninka said, 'he'll probably be making plans to re-enact his gate-opening ritual, won't he?'

Lahash nodded. 'I wouldn't be surprised.'

'Then we have to get to him soon!' Aninka cried. 'Otherwise people will be hurt!'

'Don't waste your sentiment,' Taziel said sourly. 'If he acts rashly, all to the good. We'll be able to find him easier.'

The warm feelings that Aninka had begun to extend towards Taziel evaporated. 'Not caring about what he does to people makes us just like him,' she said.

'And you don't want to be like him?' Taziel's expression was knowing. 'I bet you go hot at the crotch just thinking about being near to him again.'

Aninka refused to get angry. 'That sounds like displacement to me. Perhaps you should think about your own expectations before you criticize mine.'

Taziel flopped back on the bed, his champagne glass held upright upon his chest. 'We're infected, both of us. We are his followers, whatever our conscious minds try to tell us. Our only defence is that we should be aware of that.'

Instinctively, Aninka shivered. She wished Taziel wouldn't come out with such remarks, for they were generally unsettling.

'Taz is right,' Lahash said. 'You must be alert for his influence. As we draw nearer to him, it might become more powerful.'

Aninka laughed coldly. 'Only if he remembers us or thinks about us! I doubt he does. I believe that once he used us up, he forgot about us. *That* in my opinion is our best defence!' In her mind, she tried to silence the whispering voice that murmured, *But I want him to remember me; I want to punish him for what he did.* She glanced at Taziel and found that he was staring at her through narrowed eyes. Was it jealousy or anxiety in his expression?

'Of course,' Taziel said, 'we have to prepare ourselves for the worst.'

'The worst?' Aninka held his eyes.

'That we'll fail, be too late, or too weak. That he'll get away. That we'll not even catch sight of him. That is the worst, Aninka, isn't it?'

Chapter Twenty-seven

Tuesday, 27th October: Little Moor and Larkington

On Tuesday morning, Barbara called Low Mede again. She was now extremely worried about Louis, and had even begun to wonder whether his vile daughter had poisoned him or pushed him downstairs. She resolved to demand to speak to Louis if Verity answered the phone, and to brook no argument. If that failed, she would go round and march right into the house. Louis, however, answered the phone. Barbara was so surprised, she was lost for words for a moment, then recovered herself.

'Oh Louis! I can't tell you how relieved I am to hear your voice. I've been out of my mind with worry!'

'Wasn't feeling too well,' Louis answered, 'but I'm fine now.'

'Thank God! I take it the healing session didn't do you much good, then?'

There was a pause before he answered her question. 'Actually, it's been amazingly successful.'

There was an unfamiliar edge to Louis's voice which Barbara could not identify. 'Are you sure? You sound a bit odd.'

'Well, to be honest, I'm still rather shell-shocked . . . Barbara, I have to see you.'

'Of course. I'll come round later, if that's all right. I'm going out with Pev shortly to see some paintings.'

'Oh . . . Well, whenever you can make it.'

'This afternoon.'

Barbara put down the phone, a puzzled expression on

her face. Barney came into the room and said, 'Everything all right?'

'Yes, yes.' Barbara smiled, pushing misgivings from her mind. 'I shall be out most of the day, but I've left instructions for everybody.'

Barney gave her a withering look, which she ignored.

Barbara found Peverel Othman sitting out in the beer garden, reading a paper. He always scanned the local news; she wondered why he found it so absorbing. 'Ready?' she enquired loudly, swinging her truck keys from her fingers.

Othman glanced up, appearing, for a moment, confused. Then his expression cleared. 'Ah, the private view! I had forgotten.'

In the truck Barbara vowed not to mention Emma to Othman, then found herself saying, 'Your friend last night seemed very pleasant.'

'Yes. She's a local girl.'

Barbara pursued the topic relentlessly. 'How do you know her?'

Out of the corner of her eye, she noticed an expression of irritation cross Othman's face. He found her questions discomforting. 'The same way I know any of you.'

'Really? I've never seen her before.'

Othman smirked at her, but said nothing. Hedgerows rushed past, brushing the sides of the truck. Seeds fell in through the open windows. 'Isn't that the turning you want?' Othman said.

Barbara had nearly missed it. The old signpost was virtually hidden by brambles. She swung the truck recklessly around the tight bend, so that Othman lurched into her. 'You'll roll this thing,' he said, but didn't seem particularly concerned.

Barbara wanted to interrogate him further, let him

know how much his obliqueness annoyed her, and that it stank of deceit, but realized it could jeopardize her plans. Just *what* her plans were, she refused to examine too minutely.

Larkington was a picturesque village, nestling in a valley and bisected by a wide, shallow river. Even at this time of year, tourists milled along the narrow main street, looking into the gift-shop windows. It was a less functional place than Little Moor, being directed towards heritage theming. Barbara wondered why Little Moor had escaped this late-century grooming, which was now so popular everywhere else. After all, Long Eden and Herman's Wood were surely greater potential tourist attractions than those that other nearby villages boasted. As she drove, she looked out for Leaning Willows, hoping the house would have a name plaque displayed. They reached the other side of the village without finding it. Barbara drove for another mile or so, then backed the truck up a lane to turn round.

'Do you know where we're supposed to be going?' Othman asked.

'We'll find it,' Barbara said sharply. 'Larkington's tiny.' The trip wasn't turning out to be the convivial, carefree occasion Barbara had planned.

'Barbara, you *did* get directions?'

'Well, no,' Barbara admitted, 'but we can ask somebody if necessary.'

Othman shook his head, but he was smiling. She wished there wasn't this suggestion of barbs between them, a fence of bristles preventing easy conversation. Was it because of Emma being with him last night? Barbara wondered. She was aware of her tendency to be jealous. Now, stop it, she told herself. You have this man to yourself. Make the most of it. She affected a girlish laugh. 'Actually, I was so excited about locating the paintings, I forgot to ask Godfrey Thormund how to find him! Isn't that ridiculous?'

'It's unlikely we'll see anything revealing, even if we do track Mr Thormund down.'

'Oh? What makes you say that?' Barbara directed a sharp glance at her passenger. His use of the word 'revealing' was intriguing. What else did he know?

Othman shrugged. 'The Murkasters will have kept everything of value, won't they.'

'I get the impression you meant more than that! Come on, Pev, spill the beans. What have you found out?'

He grinned widely. 'The Murkasters weren't even human.'

Barbara laughed. 'Oh, is that all! What were they, then? Vampires?'

'No. They belonged to a race that has been around for a lot longer than humanity, and who were responsible for nudging human evolution along. You could call them scientists, I suppose. They liked to experiment with interbreeding.'

Barbara was beginning to feel uneasy. There was no laughter in Othman's words. 'You're scaring me, Pev. You sound so convincing.'

'Well, as the old saying goes, truth is often stranger than fiction. Turn left here.'

Barbara obliged and then said, 'Why here?'

'Leaning Willows will be down this lane.'

She laughed again. 'You bastard! You knew all along where it was! Have you been here already?'

'Not at all. Simple deduction. Look.' He pointed towards a group of enormous willow-trees, where a stream hurried towards the main river. 'Just a guess.'

'I can't believe what you said about the Murkasters.'

'I'm not asking you to. You asked me a question and I

471

answered it. What you do with that information is your business. Stop here.'

Barbara stopped the vehicle in front of a small gate. There was no sign of a house-name, but the garden was full of willows. 'Do you think this is it?'

Othman opened the passenger door. 'Well, there's an old guy at the window twitching his nets.'

Sighing, Barbara turned off the engine. Her day wasn't going as planned at all.

Godfrey Thormund had obviously been waiting for his visitors, for he opened the door to them before they reached the porch. He was a precise, sedate old gentleman, an example of a dying breed which Barbara held dear. The dark, polished interior of his cottage, with its slow-ticking clocks and smell of lavender reminded her of her childhood and the afternoons spent at her grandmother's house. Clematis greened the windows, and an old spaniel lay with its head on its paws before the cold hearth. The atmosphere of Leaning Willows, strangely familiar, made her feel sad. It reminded her of vanished youth and innocence. Already, she could feel a poem brewing in her mind.

Thormund cast wary glances at Othman, but was gallant to Barbara. He had a housekeeper, he said, a woman who 'came in' now and again. Coffee and biscuits were ready on a tray in the parlour. For a while, polite conversation ensued, as Thormund asked Barbara questions about The White House and related the experiences of his brother-in-law, who also owned a pub. Barbara didn't press the point about The White House actually being a hotel, for it seemed impolite. Othman sat quietly, sipping coffee, inspecting the room. Eventually, Barbara thought enough time had elapsed for the subject of their visit to be introduced.

'So, you're an art collector, then?' The walls were covered in old paintings. None of them looked like prints.

Thormund nodded. 'A hobby,' he said. 'I spend a lot of time simply sitting around and my paintings always entertain me. Better than TV.' He gestured at the walls. 'Each picture holds a memory, or has a tale to tell.'

'You must have lived here a long time, then, to have been in the area when the Long Eden auction took place.'

'My wife was alive then,' Thormund said. 'We'd not long moved here when the sale came up. I was working away a lot, civil-service job. Mary liked to go to the auctions. It was she who actually purchased the pieces from Long Eden.'

Barbara put down her cup. 'May we see them?'

Thormund nodded, and rose slowly from his chair. 'Of course. That's why you're here, isn't it? The best piece is in the dining-room. Through here.'

They ducked through the low doorway into the hall, which was flagged in cool stone. A Persian rug glowed against the grey slabs, while the panelled walls gleamed with brass ornaments.

'In here.' Thormund led the way into the dining-room, which was carpeted in red, and had the ambience of a room hardly used. Everything was polished and tidy, but the air lacked life.

The painting dominated the room. Barbara uttered a delighted gasp when she saw it. 'Oh, that's beautiful!' She hurried round the dining-table for a closer look.

The woman in the painting posed in front of a dim landscape, but behind her a representation of Long Eden was clearly discernible in the distance. 'Is she a Murkaster?' Barbara asked. The woman was dressed in a strange, Oriental fashion, with a head-dress of pendant beads. A peacock crouched at her feet, its radiant tail sweeping the ground. The colours were muted with age, but still seemed to glow and burn. The woman's face was long, her eyes slightly slanting, but to Barbara, she seemed familiar. Her hair was black, loose around her shoulders, with two plaits falling down at the front, clasped with round golden medallions.

'The painting is unnamed,' Thormund said. 'It's the best of the bunch, because all the others were a lot smaller, and mostly of horses and dogs. We thought at the time it was unusual, and probably shouldn't have been in the sale. It was the only piece of its type.'

'She's lovely,' breathed Barbara. 'Like a heroine from a myth, or a goddess.' She turned to Othman. 'A woman who was touched by a god!'

When he'd first looked at the painting, Othman had felt a charge of shock course through his flesh. The woman was the most beautiful creature he had ever seen, and some part of him *knew* her. Still, he was wary of approaching her. The long, knowing eyes seemed to trace his passage around the room.

Barbara leaned closer to look at the depiction of the house. 'Long Eden doesn't look that different,' she said. 'Although the gardens are neater. Good Lord, what's that?' She pointed to something in the gardens, a tiny figure, almost hidden among some trees.

Othman followed the line of her finger, and nearly gagged when he saw what she was pointing out. He saw the image of a man hanging upside-down by one foot from the bough of a tree. One of his eyes was open, the other closed. Shemyaza: the archetypal image. Othman's eyes flicked from the beautiful face of the woman to the distorted figure of the hanged man. He felt sick, but wasn't sure why. The image of the Hanged One seemed grotesque to him, certainly out of place in what seemed to be a portrait of the woman.

'Well, who do you think that is?' Barbara said gleefully.

'Probably one of her lovers,' Othman said. His voice was rather sour, Barbara thought.

'Yes, it is a bit odd,' Thormund said. 'Mary called him the Hanged Man. Apparently, it's an image from a tarot card. She was into that kind of thing. Always trotting off to clairvoyants and suchlike.'

'But what is it doing in this painting? Do you suppose it related to a real event?'

'Who can tell?' Thormund said. 'Mary thought it was probably symbolic, a spiritual symbol. She had the idea the Murkasters were into the occult. Bit too Dennis Wheatley for me, I'm afraid! Haven't got the same imagination.'

Barbara turned to Othman. 'Do you know, this woman looks very familiar to me. Now, who does she remind me of?'

Othman's expression was veiled. Barbara thought the painting had upset him in some way. He was not his usual, sardonic self. 'You tell me,' he said.

Barbara took a step back, narrowed her eyes at the picture. 'Lily,' she said. 'It's Lily Winter. Now I think of it, the likeness is uncanny.' She smiled at Thormund. 'Lily's a girl who lives in our village.'

'By-blow?' enquired Thormund delicately.

'I beg your pardon?' Barbara was unsure for a moment what he meant, then realization dawned. 'Oh no, I hardly think so. They only came to the village a few years ago.' She frowned. 'Still, I think their mother once lived in Little Moor. Is that possible, Pev? Do you think the Winter twins are Murkaster bastards?' She made a few calculations before Othman could answer. 'Hang on,

475

the twins would have been conceived round about the time the Murkasters left Little Moor. It *is* possible.'

'Well, the landed gentry were always renowned for being friendly with village women and servants,' Thormund said. It was clear he enjoyed a little intrigue and scandal himself.

The rest of the paintings were disappointing in comparison with the first. Barbara scanned them swiftly. Thormund told her she could come back and see his pictures again if she wanted to. Barbara thanked him warmly. 'I envy you that portrait,' she said. 'It is beautiful. There's only one thing I'd like to ask you. I hope you don't think I'm being too personal.'

'Ask away!'

'Why is it hanging in a room you clearly use only rarely? If I had that picture, I'd want to look at it all the time.'

Thormund smiled. 'Well, there's a tale to tell about that. When Mary bought it, it hung at the top of the stairs on the landing. But it spooked her. She didn't like having to walk past it every night on the way to bed. I told you she was an imaginative sort. She loved that picture, but occasionally it scared her. All she'd say was she didn't like the way the woman looked at her sometimes. So, it was moved in here. Mary said it was a daytime picture that needed light. In darkness, it brooded too much.'

Barbara smiled. 'I think I would have liked your wife! She sounds just my type.'

On the way back to Little Moor, Barbara chatted on about the picture, while Othman sat in silence beside her. Eventually Barbara commented on his mood. 'What *is* the matter with you today? You're not usually this subdued. It was as if you weren't even there at Leaning Willows. In fact, it seemed to me that the painting upset you in some way.'

476

'If it was a portrait,' Othman said in a flat voice, 'then it was a Murkaster posing for the illustration of a legend. The woman was Ishtahar.'

'Who?' Barbara took her foot off the accelerator.

'Ishtahar. A Mesopotamian woman who seduced an angel.'

'How do you know?'

'It's my field. I know, that's all.'

Barbara halted the vehicle. 'Pev, are you all right?'

He put his hand over his eyes, pressed his forefinger and thumb into the sockets. 'Yes . . . yes. I feel a bit . . . I have a headache.'

'Do you want some Paracetamol? I have some in my bag, I think.'

He shook his head. 'No. Let's find a pub. Is it too early for a drink?'

Barbara smiled as she put the Land Rover into gear. 'Not at all. It's just the right time.'

They drove for another couple of miles, up into the hills, and away from the knots of tourists. Barbara parked the Land Rover in the car park of a pub called The Green Man, which was otherwise empty. Cloud-shadowed fields sloped down behind the pub towards the river and Larkington. On the other side of the road, wilderness held sway, and the occasional dot of a walker could be seen, the red or blue of an anorak. Here, away from Little Moor, the air seemed more chilly yet cleaner.

The pub was dark inside, low-ceilinged and devoid of clientele. 'Is it open, do you suppose?' Barbara asked in a stage whisper. She called out, 'Hello?' After a few moments, a young, tired-looking woman in a drab dress and cardigan came through a door behind the bar. Behind her, from the doorway, came the thin wail of peevish children. The woman directed a scorching glance at Barbara and Othman, hardly bothering to disguise the suspicion in her eyes that here was a moneyed middle-aged housewife out with her bit of rough. The suspicion was peppered with resentment and envy disguised as scorn.

Barbara decided to abandon her welcoming expression and assumed a more reserved mien. She ordered two pints of cider, and enquired about the whereabouts of the beer garden.

Outside, she and Othman sat at a picnic table, next to an ornamental pond. It was really too cold up here to sit outside, but the pub was too quiet for conversation to be conducted freely. Barbara commented on the koi carp swimming around in the pond and then grinned at Othman, saying, 'Well, it was fairly obvious what *she* thought!' referring to the woman who'd served them.

Othman raised his brows and sipped his drink. 'Does it matter?'

Barbara laughed. 'Not at all. In fact, I was quite flattered!'

Othman ignored the remark. 'Have you seen Louis since Friday?'

Barbara shook her head. 'No. In fact, he's been avoiding me! However, I am going to see him this afternoon, come hell or high water. What did you do to him, Pev? He sounded strange on the phone this morning.'

'I performed some healing on him, as I told you I would. It can be disorientating. He probably needed a couple of days to sort his head out.'

'Will he really be completely healed? I find it hard to believe.'

'Well, you'll be able to judge for yourself later, won't you?'

There was a few moments' silence, while Barbara searched her mind for something to say to break down Othman's reserve. 'How are you feeling now?'

He shrugged. 'Better. You'll have to forgive me today; I'm not myself.'

Again, silence.

'Well, do you think we should tell Lily about the painting we saw?' Barbara chirruped.

Othman sighed through his nose. 'It's up to you.'

'Pev, you might be feeling out of sorts, but you're making this really hard work for me!'

He leaned his chin on his hands. 'I'm sorry. Perhaps I need to take my mind off my worries.'

Barbara laughed flirtatiously. 'You mean you have worries? I am surprised! Do you want to talk about them?'

He ducked his head in a boyish gesture. 'They're quite ordinary, nothing more than anyone else has. Sometimes I wonder who I am and what my purpose is. I'm drifting through life, and it doesn't feel real.'

'But you're a writer! Surely, that's a purpose!'

'It's not enough.' Othman drained his pint. 'Come on, we'd better go. You don't want to be late for Louis.'

Barbara stood her ground for a moment. 'To be honest, I'd rather be here with you.'

Othman looked down at her. When he spoke, his voice was gentler. 'You must see Louis. He deserves to see you. I think you know what I mean. But we can stop off on the way back to the village, if you like.'

Barbara stared up at him, unsure of whether she understood the implications in his words. 'Stop off?'

'You can drive the truck through the woods, can't you? We can find a private place. That is, if you want to.'

Barbara was unable to speak for a moment. She realized the path of her life had just reached a fork, the most important fork imaginable. It was as if she was given a glimpse of the future. If she declined Othman's offer, her life would continue as normal, and when she saw Louis, he would not be healed. If she chose the other path, wonders would ensue, but her life could never be the same again. And there were shadows along this path, Barbara could tell. She wanted to bound along it, wild and free, like a doe, but she could sense the unseen guns, wicked among the undergrowth, the hunters' weapons.

Barbara stood up, leaving her drink half finished. She picked up her shoulder-bag. 'Let's go, then.'

'Are you sure?' Othman's voice was a dark glitter.

'Yes. Quite.' She was prepared to accept whatever came to her.

Barbara found it difficult to concentrate on her driving as she and Othman travelled back to Little Moor. She felt both afraid and excited. No further words passed between them; in fact, Barbara felt drained of words. The sprawling shadow of Herman's Wood appeared ahead of them, to the left of the road, which sloped downwards towards the village. Barbara had to wind down the window; heat held in the valley of Little Moor seeped through the glass, making the air almost painful to breathe. 'I'm beginning to think this weather's unnatural,' Barbara said, a slight tremor of unease in her voice. 'It was certainly colder up on the moorland.'

'Valleys hold the heat.' Othman put his hand on Barbara's thigh. 'Drive in here. Find a track.'

Barbara knew all the tracks that led off the road. It was here she'd often brought Louis on the way back from their shopping expeditions. All that seemed so long ago. No talk of TV programmes and poetry now, she thought. Othman kept his hand on her leg as they bumped along the track. The air was bright with swirling red and yellow leaves, which grazed the windscreen like unearthly insects. With each jolt, Othman's fingers moved nearer to Barbara's crotch. She felt as if it might burn up from the contact. Desire like this hadn't seized her for a long time. Too long. They left the deciduous area of the wood and entered among the sombre pines. Here, Barbara pulled off the track and drove through bracken for a few yards. Othman's hand lay between her legs now; she squeezed his fingers with her thighs. They did not look at one another.

Barbara applied the brakes and the truck stopped abruptly. Othman withdrew his hand, staring through the windscreen. 'Here,' Barbara said. 'This is private enough.' She opened the driver's door, and was assailed by the smell of crushed fern. It made her feel dizzy. She jumped out of the truck and leaned against its side, breathing hard. What am I doing? she asked herself, then provided an answer: what you've been praying for.

Othman came round to her side of the truck. He put his hands against her face, pushed back her hair. His blue eyes looked faintly yellow, she thought, as if an autumn cast had come over him. He kissed her deeply, his long hands painfully squeezing her heavy breasts. When he drew back, she began unbuttoning her top. Beneath it, she wore a front-fastening bra. Othman flicked open the fastening, then stooped to nuzzle her flesh. He sucked and bit her nipples. Barbara, still leaning against the truck, threw back her head and stared up at the sky between the branches of the trees. This seemed so pagan, somehow. As if intuiting her mood, Othman lifted his head and said, 'You are like an archetypal Venus. I would like to see all of you.' He took her hand and led her away from the truck into the thick undergrowth of bracken. Ferns grew to shoulder height around them. Once the Land Rover was out of sight, Othman turned round and kissed Barbara again. Then, very precisely and slowly, he undressed her, running his hands appreciatively over her generous body. She reached out to unfasten his clothing. Once naked, they left their clothes in a mingled heap on the loamy floor, and burrowed into the bracken. He pushed her back so that the fronds curled over them, hid them.

'Pev, I have wanted this so badly,' Barbara said, wishing she didn't have to make that confession.

His hand stroked her thigh, moving up to massage her wet bush. He tore off a handful of bracken fronds and rubbed her with them, stuffing them inside her. She reached for his cock, uttered a sound of delight when she found it. After a while, she pushed his hands away, and manoeuvred herself on to hands and knees, her full buttocks pointed towards him. This was a position she especially liked, something Barney had always been reluctant to appreciate, and certainly never did now. Othman kneaded her buttocks. She was waiting for penetration, but first came his mouth, his tongue pushing inside her, his teeth pulling out fern fronds. Then, he mounted her, leaning over to bite the soft skin of her plump shoulders. For a while, he teased her with gentle pressure, before a single, swift strike that felt as if it speared her to the core. His hands reached round for her breasts, pinching the nipples hard.

Barbara felt as if her spirit was leaving her body. It was as if she was looking down on the two pale bodies, rutting like animals, the pumping buttocks, the grunts and moans.

Then Othman stopped moving and her consciousness snapped back into her physical mind. The stillness was absolute. She knew that when he moved again, it would presage the climax, and for now, she was happy to be joined to him like this, locked together. Then, she felt him begin to grow inside her, until it seemed her body must split. That was something she'd never experienced before; how could he do it? Slowly, he withdrew, before slamming back into her. Her stomach ached, somewhere deep inside. She began to cry out, then to scream in ecstasy. She was delirious as he rode her, filling her to capacity. The orgasm, when it came, was like nothing she'd ever felt before, or would do again. Her head flew back as she howled, and bucked beneath him.

When he finally withdrew from her, her head sank to rest upon her forearms. She felt disorientated, delirious. Othman gently rolled her over on to her back, stroked her face. She blinked up at the trees. 'What are you?' she murmured. Then looked at his solemn face. 'What *are* you?'

'Grigori,' he answered. 'Like the Murkasters. I am not quite human, Barbara.'

She took his hand from her face, kissed the fingertips. 'More than human.' She believed it, now.

Chapter Twenty-eight

Same day: Little Moor (continued)

Verity faced her father for the first time since Friday night at lunchtime on Tuesday. She was in the dining-room, dreamily polishing the gleaming table, when an unfamiliar tread sounded in the hall. Raven, who was sitting on the window-sill, uttered a soft, gibbering noise, and turned to face the door. Verity straightened up, the duster bunched in her hand. She was afraid it would be Othman invading her territory again. Half of her hoped it was. Then she saw her father standing there in the doorway. He said nothing at first, as if allowing her time to take in what she saw. He stood tall and straight. Even his face looked younger. Verity wondered if he expected her to comment. How could she? She was conspirator enough in his abominable act as it was. 'Do you want lunch?' she asked.

He shrugged. 'If you're making something.'

Verity could tell he didn't know what to do with his hands. They were so used to leaning on sticks or reaching out for solid surfaces. Louis apparently noticed her disapproving scrutiny because he hid his hands in his trouser pockets. Verity didn't want to walk past him. As if sensing her feelings, Raven leaped down from the window-sill and trotted out of the room, tail aloft. Louis moved aside, and Verity was able to walk past him without getting too close.

'Vez . . .' Louis began.

'Don't,' Verity snapped. 'Don't say anything. Will ham sandwiches do?' She knew that if she relented and endured a few exchanges concerning what had happened, some kind of normal life could be resumed. Everyone in the village could be told that Louis had been seeing a healer, and that the alternative therapy had worked. Most would swallow the story, she was sure. And even if they didn't, so what? Was it a punishable offence to be cured of disability? However, Verity shrank from allowing Louis that respite. She was angry at what he'd done, because he'd invited Peverel Othman into their lives. He might not be directly malevolent but corruption burgeoned wherever he trod. Verity had constructed a sterile world for herself; now it was shattered, undone. Assuming normality with her father would not help rebuild it, whereas silence and refusal to accept his condition might.

Louis followed her into the kitchen. 'I'm expecting Barbara Eager this afternoon.'

'Oh. I'll bring your lunch into the study. Go and sit down.'

'No!' Louis shouted. 'I've done enough sitting down to last a lifetime. Vez, look at me! Say something! We have to talk!'

Verity turned round, her expression icy. She wanted to screen out the image of this younger-looking, upright man, and impose upon it the crabbed familiarity of infirmity. 'I don't want to discuss it. Talk about it with your friend, Barbara. I'm sure she'll be interested.'

'We can't just ignore what's happened!' He took a few steps forward. His hair looked thicker, springing up from his head, very black.

'I will not be part of this!' Verity said.

There was a silence. Louis clawed his hands through his hair, and then walked out of the kitchen.

Raven uttered a demanding mew. Verity bent to pick the cat up. He was a comforting heaviness in her arms.

*

485

Barbara wanted to go home and change before visiting Louis, but shrank from seeing Barney. Even an unimaginative creature like him would be able to tell something had *happened* to Barbara. It would not be just the twigs in her hair, her flushed face or her green-stained clothes, but the expression in her eyes, the invisible colours radiating from her body.

Othman asked to be let out of the truck at the gates to Long Eden. He muttered something about looking round the place again. In the woods, he had seemed to have got over whatever had been nagging at his mind, but now a cloud was coming across his face again. Barbara could both see it and sense it. She wanted to soothe him, but he had drawn a barrier between them.

'Thank you,' she said as he got out of the truck.

He smiled at her. It was a weary smile, brimming with an infinite sadness that made Barbara think of news reports of starving millions, of wars and insurrections, of a single broken heart nursed alone in a dingy bedsit. 'Pev,' she said, but he shut the door.

For a moment he leaned through the open window. 'Take care, my Barbara. I will see you soon.'

Barbara watched him squeeze through the rusting bars of Long Eden's gates, knowing she would never touch him again. Her body throbbed pleasurably in memory of his presence within her. As he walked up the tangled driveway, he turned once to wave at her, before the drooping arms of the exhausted trees hid him from view. Barbara pressed the horn before driving off. She must put Peverel Othman from her mind for the moment. There were other things to think about now.

A quick glance in the rear-view mirror assured her she looked a mess, like a woman who had just stepped from a nest of passion. She could smell the forest on her, the salt-tang of sex, the musk of maleness, her own fruity, faintly bloody odour. In the driveway of Long Mede, she applied some powder to her face and attempted to brush her hair. Before she jumped down on to the gravel, she said, 'Here goes,' under her breath. As she pressed the doorbell, she was thinking, Here I am, accepting the unacceptable. This house still stood as it had always stood, the village stretched away from it, in its regular lines and wayward curves, its fields and hedgerows as they always were, yet everything had changed. A veil had been lifted, a patina of concealing dust blown away. Far from being alienated from the village by her experiences and the things Othman had said to her, Barbara felt as if she'd found a niche she had been looking for and was settling into it comfortably. That afternoon she had become the woman of her fantasies.

Louis opened the door. His appearance did not surprise her entirely. In her heart, she had always seen him this way: virile, handsome and nervy with energy.

He and Barbara looked at one another for a few moments. She saw apprehension in his face at first, which quickly softened to relief. He could *see* what she had experienced in the forest.

'Come in,' he said.

She stepped over the threshold.

Peverel Othman walked around the walls of Long Eden. Occasionally, he touched the bricks, as if searching for heat, for a message of some kind. The house tolerated his brief caresses, but remained impassive. He could feel its attention, and something new: curiosity. He was thinking hard about what he should do. Half of his mind hung back, aghast, faintly whispering that he should leave this village, abandon whatever had drawn him here. This inner self sensed danger and exposure. What would be exposed? Othman held no illusions about himself, and no guilt. He did what he did to obey an inner compunction that shielded him from remorse even as he committed acts which to some might be considered unspeakable. Now he remembered the flashes in the sky, the reflected glare, that had summoned him to Little Moor. Only fools never paid attention to omens, and normally he would be wary of any lurement, whatever its form. But here, he'd become himself too fully, insinuated himself into the lives of too many people. It was reckless.

Throughout the world, there must be hundreds of places where Grigori had lived and loved, leaving their psychic imprint on the land. Othman had passed by many of them himself, but had never felt drawn to investigate them. What made Long Eden and the village so different? Was it simply Lily and Owen, the fledgeling half-breeds? But surely, in those other places, in the most concealed corners of Eastern Europe and Asia, there were whole towns of half-breed Grigori, abandoned and ignorant of what they really were. Dimly, Othman could remember such cases; the dark villages screened by pine forests, the soaring cliffs, the corrupted rites of Christianity in ancient, crumbling churches that mirrored ceremonies only half-remembered in the genes of those who performed them. Those places had been far more mysterious and curious than Little Moor, with its open fields, its roads to civilization, tarmacked and signposted. Maybe, then, the difference was in him. A time had come, or was coming. He could feel it drawing closer, feel its predator breath on his back. So he must face it, and perhaps take strength from the power that had awakened here. He must access it fully. Perhaps then the gate of his dreams and nightmares would open and the void he sensed within himself could be filled. The house could remain impenetrable; he no longer cared. The true source lay at the High Place, and it had less consciousness than the guardian of Long Eden. If the proper offerings were made, it would not be able to resist them. It would offer itself up to Peverel Othman for a gift of blood and life essence. His only dilemma lay in choosing the sacrifice. He had considered Emma Manden, for she was strong and vibrant. But she was also too wise, too aware, and would be brave enough to fight back. Barbara and Louis were not suitable either; they were worn, despite what Othman could offer them to heal their minds and bodies. Verity was a dark miasma, trailing ghosts. She would be unpalatable. Lily and Owen he wanted to keep near him, and would not surrender them. That left, in his opinion, only one choice, which would be troublesome. Owen would object, but Othman would simply have to deal with that at the appropriate time. Daniel Cranton would be offered to the flame: the innocent, newly awoken, brimming with psychic energy, untapped and fresh. Daniel.

Othman wandered into the garden, and lay down in the seeding grass. He was tired. After a brief rest, he would go to Barbara, Louis and Verity. They would work for him now, and there'd be less resistance than from Owen the lover. Give me your son, he would say to Louis, and Louis would obey.

When Daniel got home from school, he sensed something peculiar in the atmosphere of the house as soon as he stepped over the threshold. Low Mede was silent and dark. Like an omen, the petals from Verity's flower arrangement lay all over the hall table. There was a stink of fetid water. The hot day had been occluded by thunder clouds, which had trapped the heat, making the air almost unbreathable. Daniel hadn't gone home the previous night, but had stayed with Owen at the cottage. He was glad that Lily seemed to have accepted him now.

He liked her. In the morning, Owen had driven him to school. Before he got out of the car, Daniel had said, 'I'm thinking of leaving. I can't handle these two lives.'

Owen had looked shocked. 'Leaving *where*?'

'School, of course. I can't be a schoolboy and ... whatever else I've become. This life means nothing to me now.' Daniel indicated the modern frontage of the school, the tamed creatures strolling down to its gates. 'I'm not like them any more. I've become suddenly so much older.'

'It would mean changing your life,' Owen said. 'Completely. Perhaps for ever.'

'I thought you wanted me to leave!'

Owen shook his head, perplexed. 'I do, but I know you have a certain future mapped out for you. Dropping out now would destroy that.'

'I know,' Daniel answered.

'It's up to you,' Owen told him. 'You can only do what you think best. You will have my support – and Lily's – whatever you decide.'

Daniel leaned over and kissed him, uncaring of whether anyone saw him do it. 'I'll see you later. Don't worry about picking me up, I'll get the bus.'

'Are you sure?'

'Yes. I still have some thinking to do, but first I have to steel myself for a whole day of play-acting!'

Now Daniel wished he had asked Owen to pick him up after school. His instincts told him something was wrong. The house *felt* wrong. Had something happened to his father? He went cold as he thought about how Louis had been ill all weekend. Perhaps, unconsciously, he had wished his father dead, to free himself from the life that Louis desired for him. Horrified, Daniel opened the door to his father's study. They were waiting for him there, as if they'd known he'd run to that room, as if they'd anticipated his guilty thoughts.

Peverel Othman sat in his father's big, old leather chair before the empty hearth. Behind the chair stood Louis, a man Daniel barely recognized as his father. Beside him, holding his arm, Barbara Eager, too, was a changed woman, her expression veiled and assured. Verity was sitting on the floor at Othman's feet, hugging her knees. She alone of the group looked miserable, her eyes holding a hunted expression. Daniel wanted to laugh. They all looked both sinister and ridiculous, like a horror-film family of vampires waiting for prey.

'Daniel,' Othman said, raising his head.

'What have you done to them?' Daniel demanded from the doorway, his hand still on the handle. He wasn't sure whether to run or not, although his instincts screamed danger to him.

'Done?' Othman laughed sedately. 'Look for yourself.' He rose from the chair, taller than Daniel remembered. His hair hung thick and loose around his shoulders and chest, his hands were attenuated, demonic, and his eyes, narrowed like a viper's, burned with a light that was almost invisible but which made Daniel's own eyes ache. Daniel wanted to look away. He knew that he should, but lacked the will-power. In his heart, he was aware of just how vulnerable he was, and that Othman knew that. He had dared to believe he was different, that a new, stronger self had awoken within him, but it was new-born and fragile. This man, this *creature* was more than a match for it.

Othman padded across the carpet, his posture stooped. He seemed too big to fit into the room, as if, should he straighten up, his head would brush the high ceiling, cause the light fitting to sway. Everything normal, Daniel realized, had been removed from his life. The inexplicable had come to replace it. His family were gone, the patterns of routine, the possibility of a mundane future. Was this what he had yearned for? These thoughts gave him the impetus to step back. He slammed the door in Othman's face, turned towards the front door of the house, intending to flee the place, run to Owen and Lily. He had left the front door open. Before he reached it, it crashed shut, and refused to submit to Daniel's struggles with the handle. He glanced over his shoulder. The study door remained closed. Panicking, Daniel began to run down the hall, towards the corridor that led to the kitchen, but then Peverel Othman stepped like a phantom through the closed study door, and stood before him. In his state of heightened awareness and emotion, his body recalled the most effective of its powers.

'Daniel,' he said in a soft voice. 'Don't run from me. Don't be frightened. Why are you afraid?'

Daniel would not answer. He tried to push past Othman, who grabbed hold of his shoulder with taloned fingers. Daniel cried out, beat at the hand that held him, kicked at Othman's legs. He noticed his father and sister, along with Barbara Eager, standing in the doorway to the study, watching the proceedings as if hypnotized. Then Verity cried, 'No!' and ran forward. She clawed at Othman's face and he was forced to release her brother.

'Run, Danny!' she cried, and Daniel had no avenue of escape but the stairs. As he skidded round the corner before alighting on the first floor, he saw Othman strike his sister to the ground, where she lay still. Leaning on the banister, horrified, Daniel looked into the eyes of the demon, glowing vividly now.

'Daniel!' Othman began to lope up the stairs, taking them two, three at a time. Daniel ran, scrabbled with the door to his upper-floor rooms, and slammed it shut behind him, turning the key. He did not consider that such a flimsy mechanism as a lock would not prevent Othman, a creature who could apparently walk through closed doors, gaining entrance to the room. All Daniel could think about was creating space between himself and Othman. He wondered whether he'd be able to climb out on to the roof from his room.

In his bedroom, Daniel dragged furniture across the door, his strength augmented with fear. He went to the windows, opened them wide, looked out. There was no escape, other than to jump down. But it was too far. He would be injured or killed.

Panting, Daniel backed against the wall of his room, staring at the door. All was quiet. For one, sweet, shuddering moment, he dared to wonder whether he'd just suffered some grotesque hallucination, and to believe that there was no devil outside his door. He wanted to cover his ears, believe for just a while longer, that he could not hear its breathing. He closed his eyes. Suddenly, he felt so weary. How could he fight? It was impossible.

He felt the presence of Peverel Othman before him before he raised his head and opened his eyes.

'Offer unto me what is mine,' said Othman. There was blood upon his face, but he looked beatific. His faded fair hair hung like serpents on his breast.

'What do you want?' Daniel said, his voice dull. 'What do you want with me?'

'I will not hurt you,' Othman said. 'Please don't be afraid.'

'My family,' Daniel said. 'What's happened to them? What have you done?'

Othman stepped towards him, reached out to Daniel's shivering face with one hand. The touch was exquisite, so light, yet so electric. Daniel turned his face away. 'Don't touch me!'

'Your father is healed,' Othman said softly. 'No more pain for him, no more illness. I have done this. Can't you see, my pretty boy, how good I am? I don't wish you harm, any of you. I love you all.'

'You are evil!' Daniel cried. 'Please go! Please, please go!'

'How can I leave you when you are so upset?' Othman said. 'Daniel, don't cry. It hurts me to see it. Let me kiss your tears away.'

He took Daniel's head in his hands, and Daniel knew he could have crushed it like a paper cup if he'd wanted to. Daniel felt completely powerless; there was nothing he could do. Nothing. Othman kissed his face gently, licked his tears. Then he sank down with Daniel in his arms, to sit against the side of the bed. He held Daniel in his lap, stroked his face.

Daniel looked up, and it seemed that reality was seeping away. The room was dark around him. All that existed was the demon's shining face, and there were tears in his eyes, tears that fell like tiny flames.

'I love you,' Othman said. 'You must believe it.' He hugged Daniel tightly for a moment, and Daniel could feel Othman's body trembling as if he was weeping. He knew then that Othman would kill him. Reality shifted before him, and there was a perfume in his nostrils, of flowers and dried grasses. The Garden. He saw them moving slowly, gliding phantoms at the very edges of his perception. They were tall, tall as angels. Their faces shone. And Othman was with them. He stood with a group of others on the brow of a ridge. On one side, the cultivated slope led towards shining water and the terraces of the Garden. Everyone was gesturing towards this place, discussing its features, suggesting innovations. Othman joined in with the occasional remark, but Daniel knew he was only pretending to participate, and his thoughts in reality were elsewhere. The others could not see him turning round to stare behind them all, down the spiked jumble of rocks and barren stone, the hard path that led to the lowlands and the people there, their daughters. Othman faced the Garden, but his mind looked backwards. His heart was full of a desperate yearning.

There were symbols here to interpret, Daniel thought, but he felt too tired, too weak to analyse them. The demon's face burned through the image of the Garden, and it was wet with tears.

'You are Grigori,' Daniel murmured. It was an effort to speak, but he knew he spoke the truth.

'Yes,' Othman said. 'You can truly see me.'

We could have moved to any other village, Daniel thought. It was blind chance that we chose this one. If only we'd known, on that day, that this would happen. It was waiting here for us all along. We should have known.

The touch of the demon was the essence of pleasure. He stroked Daniel's face, his throat, and his burning eyes were full of tenderness.

'If you're going to kill me, do it now,' Daniel said. 'Don't make me suffer this.' Would a demon care about suffering?

'You are cruel,' Othman said, shaking his head. 'How can you say such a thing?'

'Then let me go.' Daniel tensed, wondering if escape was still possible.

'But Daniel, you are a lover and keeper of angels. Why do you fight me? Do you fight Owen this way?'

It occurred to Daniel then that Owen knew what Othman was. They were the same. He felt sick to think that Owen hadn't warned him, perhaps even knew what was happening now. 'You are two of a kind,' Daniel said. 'I don't fight him.'

He felt Othman stiffen a little, become alert. 'You have told Owen what he is?'

'No, it was the woman, Emma. She told them everything. You know that.'

'I didn't, actually. I was hoping to reveal the truth to Lily and Owen myself.'

'Then they don't know that you are Grigori?'

Othman exhaled through his nose, and was silent for a moment before answering. 'I expect Ms Manden has told them that as well.'

'They didn't mention it to me.'

Othman looked into Daniel's eyes. It seemed the Winters were playing a few games of their own. It did not matter. He directed his attention back to Daniel. 'You must not fear me. You are right in saying Owen and I are the same. Come now, let me love you, and everything will make sense.'

He lowered his face towards Daniel, but Daniel turned away. 'No!' He managed to find the strength to roll out of Othman's arms. Othman remained where he was, looking at Daniel with a speculative eye. 'You do not understand what you're running away from.'

Daniel got up and lurched towards the door, began tearing at the obstacles he had stacked there, obeying a screaming inner urge to get out of the room. Othman leaped up and pulled him back. 'Oh no! You're not leaving me.'

Daniel struggled uselessly as Othman lifted him bodily and threw him on to the bed. Then Othman leaned down and, in a casual movement, ripped Daniel's shirt open. His face was angry now, the features seeming more prominent, his eyes a dull glow beneath hanging brows. Daniel curled up into a ball, knowing that Othman could break his limbs to destroy his defences, if necessary. There seemed to be nothing he could do to save himself.

Then came an enormous crash. Othman growled and turned towards the door. Shocked and dazed, Daniel saw it burst inwards. Shards of wood and fabric flew outwards, surrounding a leaping black shape that pounced into the room. At first, Daniel couldn't make out what the creature was or exactly how big it might be; its outline seemed blurred as if a myriad of flickering images were superimposed over one another. The creature threw itself at Othman, snarling like a monstrous cat. Othman threw up his arms to ward off the attack, but the creature lunged forward, throwing Othman back on to the bed. Daniel rolled away quickly and landed heavily on the floor. Glancing back at the bed, he could see that the animal was nothing other than Raven, Verity's cat. Raven was now clawing at Othman's upper body, his ears flat, his back legs kicking. How had a cat possessed the strength to demolish the door and its barricade? Daniel could not hope to answer such questions himself. Only escape was important now. But before Daniel could flee the room, Othman managed to tear himself free from Raven's offensive and flung the cat away from him. The animal went sailing over Daniel's head to land with a dull thump against the far wall. Daniel cringed, expecting Othman to grab hold of him again, but Raven recovered immediately. With a furious scream, he lunged towards the bed again, but by this time Othman had leaped up and soared nimbly over the debris in the doorway. Already, he was disappearing down the stairs. Raven paused for a moment and glanced at Daniel. For a split second, his image blurred again, and it seemed as if a darkly furred man was crouching there on hands and knees. Daniel gasped, scrabbled backwards. Then, with a final red-mouthed hiss, Raven jumped through the doorway and followed Othman downstairs. After a moment or two, Daniel heard a cacophony of yowling and spitting, as if a dozen or more cats were having a battle on the first-floor landing. There were sounds of things breaking, even the echo of an anguished voice from downstairs. Then, after a final feline scream, and a tremendous crash, silence. Daniel ran over to his window, looked out into the garden. He saw something like an oily black shadow slithering over the ground, covering the shrubs and fading flowers, pouring around the trees. Raven came after it, his long paws hardly seeming to touch the ground. Then Daniel saw his father coming out of the french windows of the back parlour. He looked as if he'd stepped from a photograph of a younger version of himself. In his hands he carried a gun. Verity's cries came from the house, but they were muffled as if she was being restrained.

Louis raised the gun.

The image hit Daniel like a physical slap. Louis was twenty-two, in South Africa, newly married. Verity hadn't yet been born. And there was silly Janine, with her drawling English speech, her 'darlings', her neat, pressed khaki clothes. Louis, in bright sunlight, raised a gun and fired it. In the background, the chink of ice against glass, a stuttering radio sound. The smell of gunfire. And death. Something red.

The gun went off.

Raven jumped at least ten feet into the air, somersaulted, fell heavily back to earth. There was a confusion of screaming and shouting, a blur of movement. Daniel found he had slumped against the window-sill, half kneeling. Weakly, he dragged himself to his feet. It was important to get out of the house, he knew that, yet the heat tugged at his body, clawing him down. Feebly, he crawled over the splintered furniture at the threshold to his room, and stumbled across the short landing. From downstairs, came the sound of a woman weeping inconsolably. He thought of his mother as he felt his way dizzily down the stairs.

He could see the front door, no longer closed, but standing ajar. Daniel ran towards it, the mad scramble of nightmare, when the limbs flail, the breath aches in the chest, but no ground seems to be covered. His hands were reaching, reaching for the outside. He nearly had it.

Barbara Eager appeared from the study, carrying another of Louis's old guns in her hand. She did not try to shoot Daniel, but smacked him full in the face with the butt of the weapon. He crumpled to the ground without a sound.

Barbara stood over him, peering down as if unable to identify the object at her feet.

Louis appeared from the parlour. He took the gun from her hands.

'We have to confine them both,' he said.

Barbara looked up at him. A small voice inside her wanted to ask, 'But what are we doing, Louis? *Why* are we doing this?'

Instead, she helped Louis to lift his son. Effortlessly, Louis threw the inert body over his shoulder. 'Bring the girl,' he said shortly.

Not *Verity*, not any more: just 'the girl'.

Barbara went into the study. Verity was slumped over her father's desk, holding a tissue to her nose, which was still bleeding. She was weeping. The gun cabinet hung open behind her.

'Come along,' Barbara said, in a ghost of her former voice. Verity raised her head.

'Fuck off, you old bitch!'

Barbara walked to the desk, picked up a heavy book which lay upon it, and without hesitation hit Verity over the head with it. The girl cried out and fell out of the chair to lie twitching upon the floor. Barbara peered down at her dispassionately. It looked as if Verity was still conscious, but dazed. Swiftly, Barbara grabbed hold of the girl's arms and dragged her to the door. Deep within Barbara's mind, a shocked but weak voice, was protesting, 'What are you doing? Why are you doing this?' But she ignored it. There were certain things that needed to be done now: it was part of the change in Barbara's life that had been initiated in the forest. There could be no going back.

As Barbara was dragging Verity across the hallway, Louis reappeared from the back corridor. Without saying anything, he helped Barbara carry his daughter to the cellar entrance, which stood opposite the door to the kitchen. After placing Verity's barely moving body on the top step of the cellar, Louis shut the door and locked it. He and Barbara stared at one another for a few moments, but it seemed impossible to communicate. Something was missing.

Othman came into the kitchen from the garden. He glanced at the doorway, where Barbara and Louis were held in a kind of stasis, staring expressionlessly at one another. He ran water from the tap, splashed it on to his scratched face. Then he dried himself on a tea-towel. The messiness of the past quarter hour distressed him. He disliked overt violence.

'Make us all something to eat,' he told them, and walked past them. There was blood on the hall floor. Stepping daintily over it, Othman went to close the front door, before going into the lounge, where he made himself comfortable on the sofa. While Barbara and Louis silently prepared a meal, he watched TV, flicking across the channels with the remote control. His face stung a little where the animal had clawed him. He needed to reorganize his thoughts. Things had gone well, although he would have preferred less violence. Daniel was more resistant than he'd anticipated. Still, something else nagged at his mind. He felt paranoid and uneasy. I've been too loud, he thought, and remembered the sensation of being able to walk through solid objects. He felt he must have done that many times before in dreams, but never in reality. Such overt paranormal behaviour would act like a beacon. Was it a sense of pursuit that now scratched at his mind? He walked to the window and looked out. Little Moor looked as it always had, sleepy and serene, yet somewhere, somewhere, Othman sensed imminence and approach. He had betrayed his presence and someone out there had perceived it.

Lily heard the sound of a cat-fight while she was in the kitchen stirring spaghetti round a saucepan. She went to the kitchen window and leaned over the sink, trying to see the cause of the row. Her own cats occasionally got into skirmishes with other local felines. Once a trip to the vet in Patterham had been necessary.

She could see two of her own cats, Minda and Titus, sitting upright on the front lawn, their postures that of alertness. Lily went out into the garden. The evening was oppressive, thick with impending storm. Minda and Titus ran to her as she approached them, wound around her legs, mewing loudly. 'What is it?' she said. Titus lowered himself to the ground, and growled at the hedge. Lily hunkered down, tried to peer into the shadows. She saw a flash, heard a long, sinister hiss.

'Oh, we have a visitor, do we!' She picked up a garden rake which was lying on the lawn, discarded after a half-hearted attempt at gathering leaves. With this, she poked at the interloper in the hedge. Her assault elicited a frenzy of hissing and spitting, but the animal did not move. Its furious snarls sank to a monotonous yowl, which Lily recognized as distress. Perhaps Minda or Titus had already dealt with the unwanted visitor. Lily put down the rake. The animal had stopped yowling now, and seemed to be panting. She edged forward, murmuring soothing sounds. Perhaps the cat had been run over in the lane and had crawled into the hedge seeking sanctuary. She wished Owen was home, but she had asked him to go to the supermarket to fetch some groceries. She would have to deal with this alone. What if the cat was badly injured? What could she do? Cautiously, she extended a hand, expecting the creature to lash out at her in terror, but the cat didn't move. It was a big, black, long-haired animal, similar to the one she and Owen and Daniel had seen at Long Eden. Could this be Verity's cat? She touched its head, and the cat began to purr, the ragged, desperate purr of pain. Gently, Lily stroked it. She would have to move it, even if that risked further injury. As she was contemplating how to do this, the cat tried to rise to its feet. It leaned against her arm, almost as if it sensed she was trying to help it. Lily put her hands round its body behind its front legs and gently pulled. The cat yowled in pain, but strained to come to her. It was so heavy. As it emerged from the shadow of the hedge, it seemed to grow before her eyes. She would have to try and pick it up. The cat remained passive as she hefted it into her arms. It was like trying to carry a child. There was wetness on the fur around the back legs. Blood? In the twilight, it was difficult to tell.

Staggering, and followed by Minda and Titus, Lily carried the injured cat into the cottage. Carefully, she put it down on the kitchen table, amid a jumble of unwashed plates and scattered newspapers. The cat lay on its side, its head raised, its enormous orange eyes gazing at her. Lily stroked it while she tried to locate the injury. She used a fork to part its fur, aware that her makeshift instrument was covered in tomato sauce and hardly sterile, but it seemed better than probing with clumsy fingers. There seemed to be a flesh wound on the back leg. Could be a burst abscess, she supposed, or a wire tear, perhaps even a bite. She hoped the cat would allow her to bathe the wound with salt water.

It lay quietly while she cut away some of its long fur with kitchen scissors. She could see the animal was amazingly well-muscled. Its hind leg was as sturdy as a dog's. 'You *are* good,' she murmured. She had to go upstairs to find some cotton wool, but the cat did not move while she was out of the room. As she cleaned the wound, it rested its head on the table and closed its eyes. This worried Lily for a moment, because it was not typical cat behaviour. Her cats were more likely to struggle and attack when they were hurt. This one seemed to understand her ministrations were necessary, or was it simply weak and dying? The wound did not look too bad. It was long and quite wide, although not deep. Also, there was not as much bleeding as she would have expected. She felt the cat shuddering as the salt water went into the wound, but it kept still and made no sound, other than the occasional soft gibber. It was obviously in shock. Lily decided to move the cat to the parlour, where it could lie on a blanket. She was just about to see to this, when she felt a strong compulsion to hide the cat in her mother's bedroom. She paused. This thought was absurd. Why should she think that? However, the drive was too strong to ignore. It did look like Verity's cat; surely there weren't two like this around Little Moor. Perhaps she should call Low Mede and tell Verity what had happened. Again, as she moved towards the phone, something in her mind seemed to prevent her from picking it up. No, she wouldn't call Verity. That was not a good idea.

Nonplussed, she stared at the cat for a few moments. It raised its head and stared back at her, its eyes round. 'All right,' she said, realizing, as she spoke, that the idea about the hiding-place and the decision not to call Verity had come from the cat itself. At any other time, Lily would have chided herself for her fantasies, but too much had happened recently for her to ignore this idea, however bizarre it seemed. She went back to the table, and stroked the cat's head again. It nudged her gently, purring once more. 'I wish you could talk to me,' Lily said. 'What kind of cat are you?' The cat blinked at her slowly.

Verity and Daniel hugged one another in the darkness. The light switch was outside the door, at the top of the steps. Both of them had wept, both of them were afraid. Daniel's forehead had been bleeding but the flow seemed to have congealed now. Still, he seemed feverish. Verity was worried he might have concussion or a fractured skull. Her own head ached from Barbara's blow with the book. Daniel was sleeping. He twitched in his sister's arms, dreaming. What would happen to them? Would someone come looking for them? Verity's main hope had been Raven, but she knew her father had shot at the cat in the garden. Had he survived? She dared not think that he might not have. Raven was powerful. Surely, he couldn't be killed so easily. Earlier that day Verity had called Mrs Roan and told her not to come to work for a while. She had done this to give herself time to formulate a believable story about her father and to get her own head together, but in retrospect cancelling the cook had been a stupid idea. She and Daniel needed allies now. Daniel had murmured something about how Owen Winter would find them. They had only to wait. Verity couldn't bear to argue with him, but privately she wondered how Winter could guess where they were. Louis would make up an excuse about their absence, and Owen could hardly come rampaging into the house to search for them.

Daniel had tried to explain to his sister what kind of creature Othman was. Verity supposed this was no more unlikely than all the things she'd experienced over the last week or so. At least Othman hadn't killed them outright. Did that mean he never would? What *were* his plans for the family exactly? Verity knew that Louis and Barbara had surrendered all autonomy to Othman, whereas she had been able to retain a certain amount of liberty. Othman thought he'd achieved control of her, but he'd been wrong. Now she wished she hadn't tried to help Daniel in the hallway. If she was still free, and pretending to be obedient, she might have found out what was going on and been able to fetch assistance. Because of her error, Raven had been either wounded or killed. She'd ruined everything. Too many mistakes, Verity thought. That's the story of my fucking life!

Above Verity and Daniel, in the lounge of Low Mede, Peverel Othman watched Barbara and Louis make love on the rug before the log-effect gas fire. He took some satisfaction from their relief, from Louis's almost tearful gratitude for the body he now inhabited. Othman felt he should go and visit the Winters, although for some reason, he felt compelled to stay at Low Mede. He knew he would feel vulnerable beyond its walls. He was not strong enough at the moment to control Lily and Owen. If only the oppressive heat would break in thunder and rain. He felt the weather conditions were draining him; the wounds he'd received from Verity's cat were still throbbing. He knew it was no ordinary animal, and could only assume it had some connection with the guardian of Long Eden. He could only conjecture as to why it had attacked him. Surely it should have recognized him as Grigori? Othman felt very tired. Memories tugged at his mind, which he had forcibly to repress. He must not fall apart now. They would swamp him. All of them. Whatever they were.

Chapter Twenty-nine

Same day: Patterham and Little Moor (continued)

Another hotel, this one dingy and utterly human. Aninka forced herself to like it, although in her heart she missed the opulence of the Grigori safe-house in London. They had separate rooms; nasty, functional, plastic rooms. 'What place is this?' Aninka asked, as they met in the undersized 'lounge', after dumping their baggage in their respective rooms.

'Patterham,' Lahash replied. 'We are close now to our target.'

Aninka shuddered involuntarily. She sipped from her warm gin; there was no ice available. Lahash wouldn't tell her what was going to happen, and she dared not guess. Othman was nearby, causing trouble, no doubt. Perhaps he'd found another youthful Grigori like herself to seduce and corrupt. 'Are any of your people left around here?' she asked Lahash.

He shook his head, then shrugged. 'There are not supposed to be, but I have no idea, really.' He seemed awkward in the confined space of the room, too gangly. His clothes had fitted him perfectly in London, now they seemed too small, the arms of his jacket too short. Taziel simply looked ill. He wore his shades again, but Aninka had seen the state of his eyes as he'd got out of the car: red-rimmed and blue-smudged beneath. Aninka wondered what she looked like herself. Did her face bear evidence of anxiety and exhaustion? She didn't feel exhausted. In fact, she felt quite energetic. Her heart was beating too fast continually. She likened it to the state of her body when she was about to leave home to meet someone she found very attractive; no, someone she loved. Anticipation, but with a delicious undercurrent of fear of rejection. Did her heart harbour some secret agenda? She sipped her drink again. She wanted to ask Lahash what his family had done to deserve exile, but knew she'd be invading his privacy. If he wanted to tell them, he would. That much had been established on the journey north.

Lahash finished his beer, a bottled variety poured into a glass without the benefit of prior refrigeration. 'There are some things I have to see to.' He stood up.

Aninka did not relish the thought of being left alone with Taziel Levantine, who, despite brief periods of sociability, was inclined to taciturn silence. 'Can I help?'

Lahash glanced at Taziel. 'I'd prefer it if you'd stay here.' He gave her a significant glance. OK, she was to be a baby-sitter.

She shrugged. 'Very well. Perhaps we could look around the town.' On the way to the hotel, she'd seen little to interest her, but perhaps Taziel might be more tolerable in the open air.

Lahash pulled a rueful face. 'I'm sorry, but I think it would be better if you remained here. There's a possibility Othman might frequent this town. We don't want him to see either you or Taziel here.'

'Of course.' Aninka sighed. 'I suppose we'll just have to sit here drinking warm alcohol.'

'There are worse ways to spend an afternoon.' Lahash grinned. 'I shan't be long.'

'Where are you going?'

'To meet with some people. Our reinforcements, if you like.'

'Who are they?'

'Don't ask!' Taziel interrupted. He took off his dark

glasses and rubbed his eyes wearily. 'You wouldn't want to meet them.'

'We might have to stay here a couple of days,' Lahash said smoothly. 'We can drive out somewhere for dinner later. I'll suss out a safe place.'

When he'd left the room, Aninka said, 'Exactly *who* is he meeting, Taz?'

Taziel wriggled his shoulders. It was not quite a shrug, more a gesture of discomfort. He took off his shades again to reveal the vulnerable state of his eyes. 'Kerubim,' he said. 'Grigori militia. And you don't meet them, you *conjure* them.'

Aninka grimaced. 'There is so much we don't know about our own people. Militia? I can't believe it.'

'I know *too* much,' Taziel said. 'Think yourself lucky.'

Aninka wasn't sure whether that was a sarcastic remark. 'You must have been around, then, to have amassed all this knowledge?'

'Here and there.' He carefully put down his drink, and paused, alerting Aninka to the fact a significant comment was about to be uttered. She was not disappointed. 'Most of it I learned through Peverel Othman.'

Aninka held her breath, hardly daring to speak. How could she draw him out? He glanced up at her, perhaps unsure of what her silence signified. She smiled in what she hoped would appear as sympathy. 'I know a little of what happened, but not much.'

Taziel leaned back in his chair, laced his fingers, which Aninka noticed were shaking, across his stomach. 'Othman ruined me,' he said.

'He killed my friends,' Aninka said. 'I was lucky, I suppose. Hardly damaged.'

Taziel sighed. 'I don't know why he did it to me. I wish I did. Was it because he hated me, or because he

509

didn't care one way or the other? Do you know about him, Aninka?'

Aninka frowned. 'Know what? Something other than he's a cold-blooded killer, an Anakim?'

Taziel nodded to himself. 'There is more. They won't tell me, and I can't find the knowledge I need, but there is more. That is why they're so desperate to find him now. They've been waiting. People like us, we are nothing, fodder for the beast. All this talk about Lahash protecting us is bollocks. We are disposable, Othman is not. They want him, they prize him, they fear and respect him. What is he, huh? What do you think he is?'

Aninka shrugged helplessly. 'I don't know.' She offered Taziel a cigarette, which he took. She lit her own. 'Why are we here, Taz? Do they really need us to find him? You, perhaps, but me? How am I of use to them?'

'They'll need you, don't worry. They'll send you in as bait, to talk to him. It'll be an attempt to catch him off-guard. But he's sharp. You'll have to be careful.'

'What if I refuse to do that?'

Taziel laughed. 'You won't. You know you won't.'

Aninka objected to his tone. 'What about you?'

Taziel took a long draw off the cigarette. 'I would die for him, still. But I would also like to see him dead. You know these feelings, of course, or an approximation of them.' He smiled sadly. 'I want to see him again, yet I dread it.'

'I know what you mean.'

Taziel sat upright, staring at his hands. Then he glanced at Aninka. 'I want to warn him,' he said quickly. 'You must stop me.'

'How?'

Taziel put his head in his hands. 'I'll have to get drunk, very drunk. Keep me talking. Don't leave me on my own.'

Aninka shuddered, as a memory of the night in London nudged her mind. The numbing cold, the watching presence. 'Do you think he knows we're here?' Already a seed of that feeling was around them in the chintzy hotel lounge.

Taziel shook his head. 'I can't tell. It's possible.' He rubbed his face. 'This has to be over soon. It *has* to be.'

By the time Lahash reappeared around six o'clock in the evening, both Aninka and Taziel were amiably intoxicated. Aninka went up to her room to freshen up. She splashed water on her face. There was a sense of imminence all around her. She felt excited. Soon. Soon.

Lahash knocked on her door and came into her room, barely waiting for a response. 'How has he been?'

She was drying her face on a hand-towel. 'Fine. Well, manageable. Where is he now?' She didn't want to mention Taziel's confession about alerting Othman to their presence.

'In the shower.'

'You should be with him.'

Lahash raised his brows. 'Should I?'

'I think he's unstable.' Aninka began to drag a brush through her hair. 'Are we eating out?'

'If you want to. I've found a couple of places. You're worried about Taz, aren't you?'

This one is too bright, Aninka thought. She shrugged. 'It's obvious he's distressed. You know that. Otherwise, why did you want me to stay with him this afternoon?'

'What was it he said that worried you?'

'Nothing!' Aninka answered irritably. 'It's just his general condition.' She felt she ought to tell Lahash about Taziel's fears of communicating with Othman, but shrank from doing so.

Lahash grinned in a knowing manner. 'Can you be ready in twenty minutes? Nothing too formal.'

'I'm sure I can manage.' She sat down in front of the mirror above the dressing-table. The quality of the reflection made her skin look yellow.

'I'll see to Taz.' He left the room, shutting the door quietly.

Aninka stared at herself in the mirror. I should have told him, she thought. Why didn't I tell him? The answer was obvious. She and Levantine had a common bond; she could not bring herself to break it. It was up to her to keep Taziel out of trouble, and she could only trust he'd do the same for her.

Owen looked worried as he put down the phone. 'Everything all right?' Lily asked him.

'I don't know. Daniel's not there. His dad says he's staying overnight with schoolfriends in Patterham.'

'Owen, I hope you're not jealous!' Lily teased.

'I might have upset him this morning,' Owen said. He'd already told Lily about Daniel's decision to leave school.

'Perhaps he just needs time away from us,' Lily said. 'Time to think. He's got a lot of things to ponder, not least the fact that we are not exactly what we seem.'

Owen grinned weakly. 'True. I feel no different from how I felt a couple of weeks ago, though. Do you?'

Lily shook her head. 'No. To be honest, I'm not sure how I feel.' She hadn't told Owen about the cat. It lay in the bottom of her mother's old wardrobe, among the limp, flowered dresses with their powdery aromas of summers past.

In the evening, Lily suggested a drink at The White House, to which reluctantly Owen agreed. He was still very worried about Daniel. Lily hoped that Othman would be at the pub, in the garden, where they'd first seen him.

When they arrived, the garden was empty but for a couple of tourists, who sat at a table in the light of the open door of the pub. Barbara was not around either. Lily was relieved on one count, but concerned about it on the other. Perhaps Barbara was with Othman now. Owen sat across from her, staring moodily at the lights of the pub.

'Daniel will be all right, O. Don't fret,' Lily said. She herself was fretting quite a lot, but she couldn't confide in her brother about it.

'I feel responsible,' Owen answered. 'I feel like I've done something bad to him.'

'He can make his own choices.'

Owen pulled a rueful face. 'I know, but . . .' His expression became guarded. 'Don't look now, but I think Captain Eager is on his way over to us.'

Lily resisted the urge to look round. 'Collecting glasses,' she said. A certain thrill passed through her body.

'Hrrrmph!' Barney Eager announced his intention to communicate.

'Good evening, Mr Eager,' Lily chirruped, smiling.

Barney looked very uncomfortable, miserable, in fact. 'Is everything OK?' Owen asked.

'Have you seen Barbara today?' Barney asked Lily. It was clear this question, spoken aloud, was causing him great discomfort.

'No,' Lily answered, suppressing the urge to add, 'Have you lost her?'

'She went out with your friend this morning,' Barney said.

Lily went cold. 'Pev?'

Barney nodded. 'That's the one.' Disapproval filled his voice.

'And she's not come back?' Lily demanded. 'Where's Pev now? Has he come back?'

Barney looked as if he wished he hadn't begun the conversation. 'She's probably been in and out again. It's her "do" on Friday night, you know. Busy making preparations.'

Lily stood up, glanced at Owen. 'I'm going up to his room.'

Owen reached out to grab her arm. 'No! Sit down, Lil.'

'What's going on? Where *is* he?'

'He's not in his room,' Barney said. He eyed their glasses, half full. 'Well . . . hrrrmph!' He wandered off.

Lily stood, uncertain, by the table. 'Sit down,' Owen said again. 'You heard: he's not in.'

Lily threw herself down again, took a drink. 'Do you think he's with Barbara Eager?'

'Who cares!' Owen snapped, and then paused before adding, 'Well, you obviously do.'

'Yes,' Lily admitted. 'I do. You can think what you like.'

Owen reached out to squeeze her hands, which were clasped on the table top. 'Lil, I understand. I might not like it, but I understand.'

She smiled gratefully. 'Thanks, O. We're both in a bit of a state, aren't we?'

He grinned. 'We'll survive, I'm sure.'

Lily went back into the pub to refill their glasses. She was surprised to see Barbara Eager behind the bar. 'Oh, hi!' she said. 'Um, Barney was looking for you earlier.'

Barbara's normally open, cheerful face was guarded. Lily felt a chill looking at the woman. Something had happened. 'I've been busy,' she said. 'How are you, dear?' It sounded as if nothing interested her less than Lily's welfare.

'I'm fine,' Lily said. 'Did you go out with Pev today?'

Barbara picked up a glass, already spotless, and began to polish it with a towel. 'Yes. We went to see some paintings from Long Eden.'

'Was it a long way away?' Lily persisted.

Barbara gave her a penetrating glance. 'No. Very close, in fact. Larkington.'

'Oh. What were they like?'

'Interesting,' Barbara said. 'I think you'd have liked them. Now, what are you having? Two ciders. On the house, dear.'

'Is Pev in now?' Lily asked. She knew she was battering Barbara with her questions, but refused to give up.

Barbara looked up from pouring the cider. She had a quizzical expression. 'I really don't know, Lily! Why should I?'

'Well, you've been with him all day.'

Barbara laughed. 'Dear, dear! Don't let it bother you, child. In fact, I've been at Low Mede since lunchtime.' She put the glasses on the plastic drainer in front of her. 'Enjoy your drinks.' Her attitude was smug in the extreme. Furious, Lily took the drinks back out into the garden.

'Babs is back,' she told Owen. 'She's been at Low Mede.'

Owen raised his brows. 'And didn't tell her husband. Well, well. I've a feeling she's got a bit of a thing about Daniel's dad.'

Lily giggled. It made her feel better to think Barbara had been with Louis Cranton for most of the day, rather than Peverel Othman.

Chapter Thirty

Wednesday, 28th October: Little Moor

Lily and Owen were eating breakfast when Emma knocked at the kitchen door. For whatever reason, she had decided to bring Ray Perks with her. He skulked behind her as Lily guardedly invited them in. Owen did not look pleased to see Ray, Lily noted. She wondered whether Perks knew about her brother's relationship with Daniel Cranton. Somehow, she couldn't imagine him approving of that. Owen had clearly been avoiding Ray and the others for over a week now.

Emma breezed in, as if she took Ray Perks with her on visits to the Winters regularly. 'Any tea?' she asked brightly, sitting down at the table, and taking her cigarettes from her skirt pocket.

'Sit down, Ray,' Lily said, getting up to refill the kettle. She felt slightly sorry for him, he looked so out of place.

'Hi,' Owen said without enthusiasm.

Ray brushed his hair out of his eyes in a self-conscious manner and sat down.

'I've been explaining a few things to Ray,' Emma said, lighting up. She pushed her cigarette packet towards Perks across the table, and he fumbled to help himself from it. 'You don't have to worry, Owen. Ray knows all about you now. Don't you, Ray?'

'Yeah.' Perks eyes moved furtively from side to side.

Owen stared at him coldly. He dared not guess how much Emma had told him. 'Seems we have no privacy any more.'

Emma laughed sweetly. 'Well, sometimes it helps if more than just a few people know your business. Look on it as insurance against unwelcome possibilities.'

'How comforting,' said Lily, pouring some milk into two mugs.

'I take it our friend Mr Othman hasn't called yet?' Emma said.

Lily shook her head. 'No.'

Emma exhaled smoke. 'Hmm. I couldn't locate him last night. I've a feeling he might have been at Low Mede. He's "healed" the Cranton fellow. That means Cranton will have developed a dependency.'

Owen and Lily exchanged a shocked glance. 'Daniel doesn't know about that,' Owen said.

'Perhaps not,' Emma replied. 'He will soon, though. The evidence will be apparent to all. Anyway, let's leave Pev to his dalliances for now. Our main priority is still for you two to gain access to Long Eden.'

'We need the key,' Lily said.

'Yes, I've been thinking about that,' Emma said. 'Obviously it's not an ordinary key. Perhaps it's a sequence of words or thoughts. That seems most likely to me.'

Lily leaned against the cooking range. 'And how do we guess them?'

'You can't. It would take for ever. No, you'll have to try and learn them through psychic means.' She smiled at Ray Perks. 'I've already discussed the matter with Ray. He put it quite nicely: you need the services of a "psychic hacker", and if what you say about Daniel Cranton is true, perhaps you've already found one.'

'Except Daniel isn't around,' Owen said.

'He'll probably be back tonight,' Lily said.

'Well, that should be soon enough,' Emma beamed. 'Now, Ray and I have business in Cresterfield today, but as from tomorrow, I want him to stay close to you both.

Now, now! Don't pull those faces. Trust me when I say you need the protection.'

Emma and Ray Perks stayed for only half an hour. He seemed to have fallen under Ms Manden's spell. When she told him to drink up his tea, he did so. As she left the house, she called to him and he followed her out like a puppy.

'There goes our bodyguard,' Owen said, once the door had shut. 'Who now probably thinks I'm a fucking queer.'

'Well, aren't you?' Lily enquired archly.

Owen glared at her. 'Thanks, Lil.'

She laughed and went to hug him. 'That was a joke. Do I have to pussyfoot round you now?'

He reached up to hold her arm, sighing. 'No.' There was a silence, while Lily swayed behind Owen's chair, still holding his shoulders, her cheek resting on his head. Then he said, 'Lil?'

'What?'

'I'm worried about Daniel. If what Emma suspects is true, and Othman was at Low Mede last night . . .'

'Daniel wasn't there. There's nothing to worry about.'

'If Louis was telling the truth. You know Othman was interested in talking to Daniel.'

'Owen, you're paranoid!' Lily said. 'What are you afraid of? That Pev has seduced your beloved? Daniel's staying with a friend. Stop worrying about nothing. Why don't you go and meet him from school today?'

'Yeah, I will.' He took one of Lily's hands and kissed it. 'I'll just go and look the car over.'

After Owen had gone outside, Lily took some food and water up to the invalid cat, who was still secreted in the bottom of the wardrobe in Helen's old room. He had pulled some of the faded dresses down off their hangers to make a nest, and greeted Lily with a musical meow as she opened the wardrobe door. 'And how are you today?' Lily stroked his broad head. The cat got to his feet and lumbered stiffly out on to the carpet. He seemed a lot better, even though he was limping. Lily watched in satisfaction as he devoured the food, then daintily lapped the water. She thought she should bathe his leg again, and was just standing up to fetch some salt water, when she heard the kitchen door open. Owen! she thought, and wheeled around to put the cat back in the wardrobe, but the cat backed away, his mouth wide and red in a violent snarl. He was looking at the door, with his ears flat against his head. 'In the wardrobe,' Lily whispered hoarsely. The cat seemed to understand her and leaped back in so quickly, it must have hurt his injured leg badly. Lily pushed the wardrobe door to, then went downstairs. Her heart nearly stopped when she saw Peverel Othman standing in the kitchen.

'Pev!'

He smiled at her widely. 'Lily, I've been neglecting you. I'm sorry.'

He looked terrible, his face drawn and grey, his hair lank. He leaned against the table for support.

Lily went up to him, touched his face with a nervous hand. 'Are you all right? You look ill.' She pushed back his hair and saw the livid scratch marks. 'My God, your face! What happened?' She wondered whether Barbara had done this to him.

Othman's hand flew up to his cheek. 'A cat scratch.'

'Some cat!' Lily said, then something clicked into place in her mind. Verity's cat had done this, and Othman had retaliated. Why? No wonder the cat had hissed when he'd sensed Othman had come into the cottage. 'Pev, what *is* wrong with you?'

He sat down at the table, ran his hands through his hair. 'Too many late nights.'

'With Barbara Eager, with Emma Manden?' Lily couldn't help the accusation. 'Perhaps even with Louis and Daniel Cranton? How about Verity? I doubt you've left her out.'

Othman's face had assumed a guarded expression. A smile hovered uncertainly around his mouth. 'That sounds like jealousy, Lily. I hope it isn't.'

'Then it's true?'

'Some of it. Please don't upset yourself about it. Now, how about a drink. Something strong.'

Lily folded her arms. 'Not before I get an explanation, Pev. What do you really want with us?'

Othman rubbed his face, yawned. 'OK, if that's the way you want it. You know about me, and I know about you. Me Grigori, you half-breed. I want the flame, Lily, I need its power. Look at me. Something's happening. I wasn't drawn here by coincidence.' He held out his hands to her in a gesture of appeal. 'Help me, Lily. Please.'

She wanted to remain cold and aloof, but her heart wouldn't allow it. Her feet carried her to him, even as her mind debated how to react to his plea. 'Pev.' She pulled his head against her breast, bent to kiss his hair. 'What can I do?'

'We woke the flame,' he murmured. 'We need to stoke it, call it forth. It is Grigori power, taken from the earth. Lily, something is happening to me, to my mind. I feel weak and afraid. We are kin, you and Owen and I. You must not turn away from me.'

Even as Lily held him, murmured reassurance, some icy part of her wondered whether Othman was simply acting, manipulating her feelings. Still, he looked dreadful, and his words seemed sincere enough. 'Have you seen Owen? He's outside, working on the car.'

'I noticed. I slipped past him. Wanted to talk to you first.' Othman pulled away from her a little and looked up at her face. 'Owen doesn't trust me, Lily. I don't think you do either, not completely, but I feel I can trust you.'

'Owen is probably wiser than me,' Lily said. 'So, tell me what will happen if I help you, if we both help you.'

'Give me a drink,' Othman answered. 'Then we'll talk.'

Lily fetched a bottle of wine from the pantry, which she opened and set before Othman, along with a tumbler. The wine was a bit cloudy, but Othman didn't seem to notice, or didn't care. Lily sat down opposite him, folded her arms on the table, and watched him pour a full glass, drain it in one swallow, then pour another. He gasped and sighed, throwing back his head, blinking at the ceiling.

'Well?' said Lily.

'I gather that Emma's told you about the special relationship people here in the village had with the Murkasters?'

'Yes. She wants us to reclaim our birthright, for obvious reasons.' Lily paused. 'When did she tell you this? We understood she didn't want you to know how much she'd revealed to us.'

Othman laughed uncertainly, took another drink. 'Emma doesn't have to tell me things, Lily. I can read her like a comic strip.'

Lily wasn't sure she believed that entirely. 'So, do you agree with her? Do you think we should find a way to make Long Eden ours?'

He nodded slowly, watching her carefully. 'Yes. Why not?'

'But the Murkasters were driven out. The same thing could happen to us.'

Othman considered her words. 'Long Eden is a forgotten place, Lily. I don't think you have anything to worry about. Not if you're careful.'

'Will you stay with us?'

He paused, his eyes flicking away from Lily's stare. 'For a while.'

'What are you hiding from?'

He glanced back at her. 'Nothing.'

Lily realized that this feeling of control she had over him proved to her more than his physical appearance how weak he must be at the moment. 'Have you ever killed anyone, Pev?'

His face seemed to bleach before her eyes. He looked like bone, a skull. 'Why do you ask? Is it important?'

She shrugged. 'Perhaps. Perhaps if you told me some truthful things, I might trust you more, no matter what you've done.' She leaned back in her chair. 'So, tell me . . .'

He rubbed one hand over his eyes. 'Lily, you must understand that being Grigori is not like being human. You have been brought up as human, with human values. Whatever I say to you will be judged by human morals.' He looked at her directly, as if summoning a few shreds of strength from some inner place. 'Yes, I have killed. How could I not? I am quite old, and age brings experience. If you live long enough, you will kill, too, because you will undergo every possible experience.'

'That's an easy answer. What is it like to be Grigori, Pev? If I am this thing, then tell me about it.'

He sighed. 'How can I? It's too big to describe. If you look deep inside yourself, you will find the answer. It lies there, believe me.'

'That's not enough. Tell me!'

His eyes widened as she raised her voice. He glanced towards the window, as if afraid Owen would hear her and come into the cottage. 'All right. Look upon yourself as one small part of something unimaginably huge. Grigori: one family. We are all linked, every one of us in the world. You are estranged, but you could change that if you wanted to. I don't recommend it, because, as you rightly pointed out, you might not only lose the chance to attain Long Eden, but would also suffer the penalty meted out to your father. Grigori are powerful, but they are paranoid, too. They want to remain a secret, even though they permeate human society like parasites. All true magic lies in their hands, Lily. They understand the old ways, they keep the knowledge that humans were given but have lost: the original sciences, what we call magic, the science of free energy, before the narrow perception of humanity took over. Some Grigori, like your father, want to expand upon that knowledge, and they are punished for it.' He shook his head, smiling sadly. 'We never learn our lessons. Never. We repeat the same mistakes and tread the same evolutionary cycles.'

'Then you agree that Kashday Murkaster should have been stopped.'

'No. I mean the same mistakes the Anannage, our ancestors, made, of having an unbalanced view, of fearing chaos and the more unstable spheres of the cabbala. I believe what the original Grigori did was right, but conservatives within our society espouse a more fundamentalist creed. They seek to regain what they see as respectability, perhaps to earn the approval of the Anannage once more. They believe that is the way to the ultimate understanding, the way to regain Paradise. Others, such as Kashday, take the view of the Fallen Ones, that we should find enlightenment through our own experience and experimentation.'

'Do the Anannage still exist?'

Othman shrugged. 'Who knows? If they do, they are

more efficient at keeping themselves hidden than we are! I like to think that they don't and the conservatives are wasting their time.' He leaned forward across the table. 'Lily, you can have power and I can help you get it. But first, you have to acknowledge and accept what you are, cast off the outdated, constricting values you've inherited from your mother.'

'You mean I have to become the sort of person who could kill someone?'

He stared at her for a few moments, as if deciding how to answer, then said simply, 'Yes.'

Lily stood up, went to the window. 'I don't want to,' she said. 'I'd rather just forget what I am, go back to the life I had.'

Othman came up behind her, put his hands upon her shoulders. 'And never age? One day, you would be forced to accept your inhuman condition. Neither will the villagers here let you shun your destiny. You think Emma Manden would allow it? She is strong, Lily, stronger than you. You would be wise to let me become your teacher, not her, because Emma, for all her longevity, is only human. You and I are of the same race. Let go, Lily. Come to me.'

'But I am half human,' she whispered.

'Grigori blood is stronger.'

Lily bowed her head. She could feel tears trying to escape her dry eyes. They wouldn't come. Some inner part of her had already accepted what Othman had said to her. It was like standing on the edge of a precipice and being told she could fly. Someone was now telling her to jump, to trust the information and jump. She was afraid, even though she could already feel the experience of flying.

Othman parted her hair and kissed the back of her neck. 'I need Owen, Lily. You must help me. It would be inconvenient if he opposed me, us. We must have him with us.'

Lily sighed. It was a struggle to speak. 'You are right. He doesn't trust you. I can't see how you, or I, can change that. Not immediately, anyway.'

Othman rested his chin on the top of her bowed head. 'Then we must believe a way will present itself shortly. Belief is magic, Lily. Add your will to mine.'

'All right,' said Lily.

'I will stay here now,' Othman said. 'Later I'll fetch my things from The White House.'

'Barbara won't like that!' Lily managed a weak laugh.

Othman ignored the remark, turned her round to face him. 'It's Owen we have to concern ourselves with, not Barbara. She is nothing.'

'Go to my room,' Lily said. 'He mustn't see you yet. He's worried about his boyfriend. Let him go to collect Daniel this afternoon, then he'll be happy, and in a better frame of mind to accept things.'

Othman's face became hard. Lily realized she had said something he didn't want to hear. Then he smiled. 'All right. Come to me when he's gone.'

'I will.'

Later, as she lay naked in Othman's arms, surrendering herself to his gentle love-making, Lily sensed the black shadow of the cat leaving her mother's bedroom. She moaned a little to distract Othman's attention, worried he'd sense the presence of the cat himself. She wanted to believe in Othman, wanted to become part of his world, yet a portion of her inner being made her keep silent about the cat. She would not give herself to this man completely. He had a lot more to prove to her before she'd do that.

*

Owen waited outside the school gates, chain-smoking in the car, but Daniel did not come out of the building. He waited until the caretaker came to close the gates, even though he sensed that Daniel had not been to the school that day. Anxiety mounted within him. Was there a rational explanation? Was Daniel hiding somewhere, unsure of what to do with his life? Owen had a dreadful premonition he would never see Daniel again. Something had happened. He knew it.

By the time he reached home, Owen was almost demented with worry. He stopped the car at Low Mede, went to hammer on the door, ring the bell. Barbara Eager opened the door. She did not seem surprised to see Owen. 'Hello, dear,' she said. 'What is it?'

Owen was taken aback at finding her there, opening the door to the house as if she owned it. He tried to peer round her. 'Is Daniel in?'

Barbara's face crumpled into an expression of apology. 'I'm afraid not.'

'I want to speak to his father,' Owen said. 'Or Verity.'

Barbara's face changed; it became hard. 'That's not possible. Daniel's not here, neither is Verity.'

'Who is it?' Louis's voice came from inside the house. Owen saw a male shape come into the hall behind Barbara, shadowy. It did not sound like Louis, neither did the outline look like him. But as he came towards the door, Owen realized this was Daniel's father, but changed almost beyond recognition. Othman had done this. He glanced at Barbara. Both of them were Othman's now.

'Where's Daniel?' he said, looking at the apparition of health and vigour that was Louis.

Louis put his hand on Barbara's shoulder. 'I'm sorry, Owen, but Daniel and Verity have gone to stay with my brother and his wife for a few days. I wanted some time to myself.'

'I don't believe you,' Owen said.

Louis laughed. 'But it's true.' He frowned. 'Why would I lie to you?'

'Because you've changed,' Owen said.

Barbara and Louis looked at one another and laughed. 'If we have, I can't see why that means we've become liars as well!' Barbara said.

'I want to look round his room,' Owen said. He knew it was unlikely his request would be granted, but he couldn't let these two creatures of Othman's think they'd convinced him.

'That's out of the question,' Louis said, then smiled ruefully. 'Look Owen, this is difficult, but I really think you should know that Daniel's quite upset by . . . certain things that have been going on. He wanted to get away. Surely, I don't need to say more? This is quite embarrassing.'

'I don't believe you,' Owen said again, although he could feel his determination ebbing.

Louis stepped forward and spoke in a confidential manner, an avuncular smile pasted across his face. 'Look, old chap, we all do things when we're young which are experiments with life. I think it'd be best for everyone if you just accepted that Daniel was curious about . . . well, you know. But now he's decided it's not for him.'

Owen thought that if Louis looked the way he had the last time he'd seen him, he might believe what he was saying, but this was a man who'd been charmed by Peverel Othman, who'd been *altered* by him. His resolve was battered by the shame of thinking Daniel might regret their relationship, but that was a thought implanted by Louis. Owen forced himself to remember the last time he and Daniel had been together. There had been no hint of regret. Still, it was clear that, short of barging into Low Mede, he was going to get no information here. Without another word, Owen turned away. He would have to talk to Lily, maybe even Emma. Daniel was in danger, he was sure of it, and Othman was involved.

'Bye!' called Barbara Eager as Owen retreated down the drive.

Louis closed the door, took Barbara in his arms. She pulled away. 'Lou, are we doing the right thing?'

He kissed her. 'Barbara, don't! Of course we are. We've been given another chance! Don't fight it.'

'But Daniel . . .' she said. 'And Verity. What's going to happen to them? We can't just leave them down . . . there.'

'They'll come round,' Louis said. 'Pev will talk to them. Don't worry! This is a strange, new world for us, and the kids are scared of it. Get one of the guns.'

'What?' Barbara took a step backwards. 'Why?'

Louis shook his head, smiling. 'Barbara, my dear, we have to feed the poor children. And we don't want them causing any trouble. Now, I'll make some sandwiches, you fetch the gun.' He touched her face softly. 'Everything will be fine. I know it will.'

Verity had endured a day of terror, a day during which all her phantoms had come back to torment her in the dark. Daniel had slept most of the time, but she had talked to him continually, stroking his face, his hair, glad of the contact. At times, she went cold and clammy with fear, thinking of Daniel dying in her lap. Then he would wake up, tell her he was thirsty, and she would tell him she loved him, not to leave her.

'I can't!' he said, trying to laugh.

'How do you feel?'

'Sore. Vez, what are we going to do?'

She squeezed his body. 'I don't know. Raven will come. I know he will.'

'Dad shot him,' Daniel said. 'I saw.'

'It doesn't matter,' Verity answered firmly. 'He's not just a cat, Danny, he's something more. He isn't dead. He'll come. We must believe it.'

They'd had to relieve themselves in corners of the cellar, Verity helping Daniel to stagger a distance away from where they were sitting on old sacking and a ragged car blanket. The smell of their own urine and excrement filled the stifling room, until they couldn't smell it any more.

Once Verity said to Daniel, 'Can you see anything over there?'

Some small amount of light was leaking in somewhere. They could make out dim outlines in the dark. 'See what?' Daniel asked.

Verity shuddered. 'A man.'

'No, Vez, no!' Daniel's voice sounded panicked. 'Don't say things like that. We'll scare each other to death!'

'But I know I have ghosts around me, Danny. Peverel Othman told me. I saw him get rid of one of them. He threw it up into the air like a rag.'

Daniel reached for his sister's face. 'No, Vez. He must have ... I don't know, hypnotized you. You mustn't believe what he said, or what he made you see.'

'You don't know,' Verity moaned. 'You don't know about me.' She told him then, about the married professor, who seemed as if he'd give her so much, but had proved to be a weak, puling man, who would not leave his wife, then changed his mind, then changed it back. She told Daniel about how the wife had discovered the affair, the long, useless cruelties of betrayal and indecision which had followed, the woman's breakdown and suicide attempts, the professor's decline into depression. Then there was Netty, and Netty's boyfriend. Verity hadn't wanted him as a partner, she just had wanted sex, his body. But the fool had fallen in love with her. Her coldness had invoked only deeper degrees of infatuation. She'd had to be cruel. She hadn't guessed that he, too, was so weak that her denial of his existence would send him plummeting into an abyss of despair, where death seemed the only viable option. 'Those are my ghosts, Danny,' she said, and Daniel could think of nothing to say. Now he dared not look too closely into the dark.

When the light came on, they were blinded by it and clutched each other more tightly. They heard Barbara Eager's voice, 'Oh, Louis, Louis! Look at them! Oh Louis, the smell!'

Then their father, or a man that sounded like their father used to sound when they were children. 'Put down the tray, Barbara.'

Verity squinted up the steps. She saw her father holding the gun, pointing it at them. 'Dad!' she said. 'Please, Dad!'

'Louis, you can't . . .!' Barbara's voice was cut short as Louis slammed the door. They heard the lock turn, but at least the light was left on. Verity glanced up at the naked bulb. It was old. How long would it last?

'They've left food,' Daniel said in a dull voice. 'Vez, I'm too tired to go up the steps. Will you fetch it?'

'Of course.' Verity eased herself from under Daniel's body. Now there was light, she could see the swelling on his forehead, the dried cut. His eyes looked glazed. Oh Raven, she thought as she mounted the steps. Come soon.

Barbara left Low Mede in a temper. She walked back to The White House in a daze of confusion. What was she doing? How had she become involved in all this? It was only yesterday that she and Othman had gone to visit Godfrey Thormund, only yesterday when she'd achieved her desires and enjoyed Peverel Othman in Herman's Wood, and later taken her pleasure with the rejuvenated Louis. Now she felt she was a criminal. It had shocked her to see the condition of Verity and Daniel. How could Louis do that to his own children? And yet, she'd had a part in it herself. She had been the one to inflict the wounds. What should she do now? Call the police? It would mean implicating herself, but she couldn't just leave Verity and Daniel locked in that stinking cellar, injured and hurting.

Louis had let her go. He'd only said, 'You'll be back.' He was so confident, as if he didn't believe for a minute that she'd betray him. How was she going to explain herself to Barney? Was it possible to claw back that dull, mundane, dissatisfying life with her husband? Now she yearned for it more than anything.

Yet, by the time she'd reached the hotel, her heart was longing for Louis. It was as if she hadn't seen him for a week. Mrs Moon accosted her in the hallway, wearing an expression of extreme disapproval. The staff all knew, of course, where Barbara had been spending most of her time since yesterday. They'd drawn their own conclusions.

'There's things to be seen to,' Mrs Moon said, 'for Friday.'

'Friday?' Barbara had forgotten what was planned.

'Your barbecue for All Hallows,' Mrs Moon reminded her. 'I've got to order rolls.'

'Oh, yes,' Barbara said irritably. 'Can I leave it to you, Mrs M? I'm afraid a few things have cropped up, and I'm really rather too busy to organize Friday night at the moment.'

'Charcoal,' said Mrs Moon accusingly, 'and the bonfire to be built.'

'Surely Mr Eager is the person to speak to about that?'

'He says it's your "do",' Mrs Moon persisted. She folded her arms. 'He's got things on his mind. I don't like to bother him.'

'Oh please! Speak to Shuni, and ask her to get her brothers to help!' Barbara snapped. 'Shuni knows all about it. I really can't be bothered now, Mrs Moon!'

She escaped upstairs. Fortunately, Barney was absent from the flat. Barbara poured herself a tumbler of gin, and went to sit on the sofa in the lounge. She stared at the cordless telephone for five minutes before she dialled Low Mede. Louis's voice, when he answered, was husky and seductive. She ached to hear it, and began to weep. 'Louis,' she said. 'I love you. Don't be horrible, please. Don't become someone else.'

'Barbara,' Louis answered in a gentle tone. 'I'm waiting here for you. Come when you can.'

'Your kids . . .' Barbara began. 'Louis, I feel dreadful! We've hurt them! I can't live with it! What's happening to us? You must let Daniel and Verity out, get them to a doctor!' She couldn't continue, but rested the phone against her face as she sobbed. She could hear Louis's voice, gentle, soothing.

'Everything will be all right. It'll all be over soon. Pev will take care of things.'

Barbara shuddered. 'Yes. Yes.' She sniffed. 'I have to go.' She threw the phone down as if it burned her.

The last person Owen wanted to see when he went into the cottage was Peverel Othman, yet there he was, large as life, if a little bedraggled, sitting at the kitchen table as if he'd lived there for years. 'Owen, hi!' he said.

532

Owen ignored him and slammed the door. 'Lily!'

Lily appeared from the pantry, carrying some frozen food. 'Hello, O. Where's Daniel?'

Owen turned to Othman. 'We'd better ask your friend!'

Othman raised his hands in a placating gesture. 'Whoa! What do you mean exactly?'

'Where's Daniel?' Owen demanded. 'He's missing and I know you're involved. What have you done to him?'

Othman looked surprised. 'I don't know what you're talking about! What do you mean, Daniel's missing?'

'He wasn't at school today,' Owen said. He turned to Lily. 'I've been to Low Mede. Babs Eager and Louis Cranton look like serial killers, and they tell me Daniel and Verity have gone to visit relatives. Something's going on. I don't believe a word of it.'

Othman sighed deeply. 'Great Shem,' he said in an undertone. 'I think the worst has happened.'

'Pev?' Lily walked forward, put her burden down on the table. 'What do you mean?'

'I have to come clean,' Othman said, glancing from Owen to Lily. 'I'm sorry your friend's got involved in all this, Owen. It was not my intention.'

'Involved in what?' Owen's fists were bunched. Lily was afraid he'd hit Othman.

'Sit down, both of you,' Othman said. 'I have something to explain to you.'

Lily sat down, but Owen remained standing. Othman reached for Owen's hand, but Owen snatched it away. 'Don't touch me! Just talk!'

'All right,' Othman said wearily. 'Please don't shout at me. I've had enough of shouting.' He turned to Lily. 'I have enemies, people who've been following me. I hoped it would be safe here, but . . .' He shrugged. 'I was wrong. If Daniel's gone missing, I wouldn't be surprised if he's been taken by my enemies.'

'What?' Owen cried. 'Then we must do something! Call the police.'

'No!' Othman stood up. 'Owen, you're talking shit. You don't know what we're up against. This is Grigori business, and we must deal with it our way. No police. Are you mad? What do you think will happen to you?'

Owen lowered his eyes. 'We must do something!'

Othman nodded, sat down again slowly as if in pain. 'I know. But panicking and shouting won't help. Daniel won't be harmed, if that's what you're worried about. They'll interrogate him and he'll tell them what he knows. No torture, just mind control. He's in no danger. Once they're done with him, they'll remove all memory of their existence from his mind, implant alternative memories, then let him go. I've seen it happen a hundred times. I know the routine. All we have to do is wait – and, of course, prepare our defence.'

'*Our* defence!' Owen snapped. 'We're not your allies, Othman. You can just get out of my house right now! If your enemies come here, I'll gladly tell them all I know about you!'

Othman seemed to buckle beneath Owen's verbal assault. Lily said, 'Stop it, Owen! It's not Pev's fault. Look at him, he's sick! Don't be so mean.'

'Yeah, he's sick all right!' Owen said harshly.

Othman looked up at him. 'Hate me all you like. I'm here as your protector. The people looking for me will be after you, too. They're the same ones that drove your family from Little Moor. We *are* allies, Owen, whether you like it or not.'

Owen looked at Lily. 'Is this true?'

She looked puzzled. 'I . . . I suppose so.' Othman had mentioned nothing of this to her earlier.

'Ask Emma Manden,' Othman said. 'She'll tell you.' His face creased in pain, and he clutched his side. Lily hurried over to him.

'Pev, what's the matter?'

He shook his head. 'It's nothing. Give me wine.'

'Yes, yes!' Lily ran into the pantry.

Owen looked down upon Peverel Othman.

'You don't trust me,' Othman said. 'What can I do to make you trust me?'

'Bring Daniel back,' Owen said.

'I will, I'll do everything I can. Owen, take my hand.'

Owen stared at the offered palm for a few moments, then reluctantly took it. 'Do you mean it? Will you get Daniel back? I can't wait for these bastards, whoever they are, to release him.'

Othman nodded wearily. 'Yes. Whatever you want. I just need to recuperate, get my strength back. The High Place, the flame.' His lips peeled back from his teeth as he grimaced in pain.

'What's wrong with you?' Owen asked him.

'Needles,' Othman gasped. 'In my head, in my heart, old needles, from the past, pricking me.'

'He's off his head,' Owen said to Lily as she reappeared with a fresh bottle of wine.

Lily frowned and shook her head to silence him. 'He'll be fine. He's staying with us. We'll look after him.'

Owen looked doubtful. 'I don't like having to trust him. You haven't seen what he's done to Babs and Louis.'

'I've given them nothing but strength and health,' Othman said, regaining his composure. He still held Owen's hand. 'One day, you will be able to do such things yourself, then it will not frighten you.'

'It doesn't seem to be doing you much good!' Owen

said. 'While Louis Cranton regains health and vitality, you look like hell.'

Othman shook his head. 'My condition has nothing to do with what I've done for Louis Cranton. It's the influence of my enemies. But it will pass. With your help.'

Out in the garden, Raven sat beneath an upturned wheelbarrow. His leg still pained him, and he could feel the dim desperation of Verity Cranton calling out to him from below the ground at Low Mede. His intelligence was limited in this form, but this was the form he was constrained to maintain most of the time. All he could sense were the strident feelings of the Two Legs, screaming through the air like demented ghosts. He sensed their passions, their confusion, their betrayals. And Othman. Raven sensed Othman as a ball of flame, red and black, burning inwards. He was wary of Othman, and sensed him as an intruder. Raven had been awoken for a purpose, and soon it would be fulfilled. Then might come release, or further slumber. In the presence of the dark woman of Low Mede, his bindings were loosened and he could creep forth to touch her. He was aware of her absence in his life, and knew she needed him, but other compulsions dominated his mind at present. Here, in the safety of the garden, he could gather back his strength, direct healing energy into his wound. There was work to do.

Chapter Thirty-one

Same day: Little Moor (continued)

Emma called in at the cottage again around nine-thirty in the evening. By this time, Owen and Lily had prepared a meal and they and Othman had eaten it. Now Othman lay on the sofa in the parlour watching an American film on TV. He was wearing a dressing-gown of Lily's. She and Owen had bathed him earlier. His body had looked so thin and depleted that Lily could have wept. Owen had been silent, watchful. His eyes betrayed only flickers of his thoughts, confused and conflicting.

Emma had brought Ray Perks with her again. When she saw Othman, she looked surprised, momentarily displeased, then relieved. 'I wondered what had happened to you.' She stood tall at the threshold to the parlour, appearing far stronger than Othman, who was draped over the sofa like an empty garment. Her eyes, Lily thought, held some secret knowledge, which she was relishing privately.

Othman smiled, looking past her at Ray Perks. His smile was hard. 'Who's this?' he said.

Emma came into the room, sat down on one of the chairs. 'This is Ray. He comes from an old family, and will protect Lily and Owen.'

Othman nodded. 'I can see the sense of it.'

'I'm glad.' Emma lit the inevitable cigarette. 'May we speak alone, Pev?' She glanced at Lily and Owen, noticing that they both appeared to be ill at ease in their territory.

Pev also directed his attention to the twins. Owen put

537

his arm around Lily, a convulsive, defensive gesture. 'How about if you two go out for an hour or so?' Othman suggested. 'I want to talk to Emma.'

Owen looked at Lily, who shrugged.

'All right, just an hour,' Owen said. 'Shall we go to The White House, Lil?'

'Well . . . yes . . . whatever.' Lily was surprised Owen had given in to Othman's request.

'Take Ray with you,' Emma said, 'but don't be long.'

Outside, in the road, with Lily still pulling her coat on, Ray Perks stood in front of Owen. 'Will you give it to me?' he said. His face was fierce. 'When it's time?'

Owen appeared doubtful, but said, 'Yes.'

Perks nodded and began to walk up the road, ahead of the twins. Lily caught up with Owen. 'What did he say?'

'He just reminded me of our purpose, I think,' Owen replied. He looked troubled.

Lily linked her arm through his. In silence, they strolled towards the lights of The White House, too bright against the night.

'You are in trouble,' said Emma Manden. She let the statement hang, a string of words.

Othman blinked at her. 'Tell me.'

Emma leaned back in the chair, crossed her long legs. She still wore her coat. 'Ray and I went to Cresterfield today. There was something I wanted to look into.'

Othman regarded her without expression, waiting for her to continue.

'You have been busy in Cresterfield, I think. We delved into the matter of a certain murder, a girl named Serafina. Of course, you have heard of her?'

Othman still said nothing.

'There were quite a few strange deaths in Cresterfield

around that time. It seems a group of what the media called Satanists committed mass suicide on the same night poor Serafina died. The case was closed very quickly. It was supposed the group had killed the girl before getting hysterical and suffering fatal heart attacks.' Her voice betrayed her scepticism about this story.

'There is no link between me and these people,' Othman said. His face was composed in a half-smile.

'Naturally not,' Emma agreed, 'although the case has your pawprints all over it, I'd say.'

'How did you make this absurd connection?'

Emma lifted her shoulders in a shrug. 'You did not take control of Owen and Daniel. Perhaps you should have done. You left them to their own devices, and Daniel discovered the link, although I don't think he realizes it himself. He met a friend of Serafina's in a night-club in Cresterfield, and caught the name Shemyaza when he held the dead girl's bangle. Then Lily saw the fallen angel in a dream. He wore your face. Daniel did not recognize you for what you are, and Lily has only romantic fantasies. But I know. You killed those people in Cresterfield, didn't you, before coming here. You are of Shemyaza's blood-line.'

Othman raised himself on one elbow. 'It is not your concern. It is irrelevant. Have you forgotten so much during your stint of decrepitude?'

Emma laughed. 'Not at all. I just want you to know I'm aware of your activities. Also, I wouldn't want you to try the same trick here.'

'I had no such plans.'

Emma narrowed her eyes, leaned forward, her hands like claws upon the chair arms. 'What are your plans, Peverel?'

'I shall comply with your wishes utterly. On Friday

night, I will conduct a ritual to resuscitate the perpetual flame, and the power from it will be passed on to your people. Most will be at Barbara Eager's party at The White House. I shall come there. The gates of Long Eden will be opened to us, and all will proceed as you desire.'

Emma nodded thoughtfully. 'Will you stay here?'

'I don't know. There's a possibility some of my people are looking for me. Whether Long Eden can hide me, I've yet to ascertain.' He paused, wondering whether he should confide in her about the changes he was feeling in his mind and body.

Emma seemed to guess he was withholding something from her. 'What else?' she said.

Othman thought quickly. 'There might be a problem on Friday night. It has become expedient to use Daniel Cranton in the ritual. I'm concerned about Owen's reaction, and have only two days to coerce him.'

'Where is Daniel?' Emma asked.

'His father has him,' Othman answered. 'He is safe. Daniel is vital to the success of our venture, Emma. I can't stress this too strongly. I am weak and need strength. The flame will provide it, but it will take more than the power of sex, however potent, to stoke its furnace. It needs unbound life-force. Without the flame, I can do nothing. It took nearly all of my vitality to rejuvenate you, heal Louis, and subjugate the Crantons. If I am hungry for too long, my spirit will draw back into my body what I gave to you. I know you don't want that.'

Emma was silent. She bit one of the fingernails of her left hand. 'Poor Owen,' she said at last.

'I can help him get over any emotional crisis,' Othman said, 'but first I need him close to me.'

'I understand. Well, you seem to be doing all right so

far. Two days ago, Owen would have thrown you out of the house!'

Othman lay back on the sofa, resting one forearm against his brow. Then he spoke. 'Emma, you must help me. I want you to prepare a drink for Owen when he and Lily come home.'

Emma raised one eyebrow. 'Resorting to chemical persuaders, are we?'

Othman grinned slowly. 'Herbal,' he said. 'Will you do it for me? I doubt Owen would accept it from me.' He explained the substance was in a jar in his jacket pocket, hanging behind the kitchen door. 'A teaspoonful should suffice.'

Emma shrugged. 'As you wish.' It was beginning to happen now, she thought. In two days, the old regime would be restored. Sacrifices would have to be made, but they amounted to nothing, really. Yet why did she feel so uneasy? Why was it that, in her heart, she felt a need to make alternative plans? 'Will you be strong enough by Friday?' she asked.

Othman nodded. 'Yes. I need only a brief period of recuperation.'

Emma chewed the skin around her nails, looking at him. They remained silent, until Othman raised his head and said, 'Now, Emma. Go into the kitchen and put the kettle on. They're coming back.'

Emma heard the back door open, the high sound of Lily's laughter. She, at least, seemed untroubled.

Once the twins and Ray Perks had left the kitchen, Emma made the drinks as Othman directed, sprinkling a teaspoonful of the herbal powder from his jacket pocket into Owen's coffee. A few strands of herbs spiralled round on the coffee's surface, which Emma removed with a fingernail. She sniffed the drink. It smelled faintly leafy.

Owen did not seem to notice anything unusual about the coffee. Emma watched him guardedly as he drank it. Poor boy, she thought. His will is about to be taken from him.

At Othman's discreet signal, Emma announced she was leaving. 'Be here tomorrow morning early,' Othman told her.

Emma gathered Ray Perks to her side and left.

Othman watched Owen through slitted eyes, waiting for him to manifest some physical effect from the haoma that Emma had put in his coffee. Lily was chattering brightly, but her words were nothing more than a chirruping nonsense that flapped round Othman's senses. He wanted Owen. He needed him.

Owen sat down on the hearth-rug. He felt drunk, as if he'd had more than two pints of cider. Lily's voice seemed too strident to be borne. He rested his cheek on the rug and closed his eyes, trying to summon concern about Daniel. But it seemed his head was too cloudy for his thoughts to make contact with one another. On one side of his mind was the troubling fact that Daniel was missing, on the other, his own potential concern. However much he tried to concentrate, Owen could not make the two thoughts meet. Lying on his side on the rug, he struggled to take control of his swimming mind, until he thought he felt hands upon him and had to open his eyes. Peverel Othman was kneeling beside him, Lily standing just behind, an expression of thoughtful uncertainty on her face. Owen knew then that he was in the presence of a partnership. Lily had stepped back from him, into Othman's control.

'Owen.' Othman stroked his face, rubbed his arm. 'Don't fight me. Lily hasn't. Lily knows me now. Lily trusts me.'

Owen rolled on to his back. The ceiling seemed very

far away, coruscating with flickering spots of light. His limbs felt unnaturally long, his eyes were on fire. He realized then that Othman was not stroking his face or his body, but his aura. The long pale hands hovered a couple of inches above Owen's face and arms.

'Is Daniel safe?' Owen asked, although there was no true feeling behind the question. It was just something to say.

'Yes,' Othman answered. 'He is already safe, and very soon, you and he will fulfil a special purpose.'

Owen tried to drag his burning eyes towards Othman's steady, viper gaze. 'What purpose?'

'An ending to what you have always done at the High Place, Owen. The energy of your communion with Daniel will awaken the power of the Murkasters, which will then belong to you and your sister. You must trust me.'

Owen smiled, although his eyes were dull. 'Can I give Daniel longevity?'

Othman nodded. 'Of course. Whatever you wish.' His hands descended through the nimbus of Owen's aura and touched his skin. 'Tonight, I will instruct you. It will be the first lesson of many.' He kneeled upright, and glanced at Lily. 'Prepare your brother for me. I must meditate for a short while.'

Lily's fingers were pressed against her mouth, her eyes wide. 'Prepare him?'

'Take him upstairs and bathe him. Put him to bed.'

Lily knew these words for a command, not a request.

Owen lay on his back in his bed. Around him, the yellow lamplight looked dim and cold. His mind drifted in a luxurious haze. He could not remember how he had got there, or the fact that Lily had bathed and undressed him. All that existed was a faint sense of impatience.

543

Othman came to fill the dark space at the doorway, his eyes lit by blue sparks that seemed to shine from somewhere deep within him, perhaps through centuries of time. Weakly, Owen raised his head, but could summon no feelings within him of surprise, dread or welcome. Instead, he experienced a sense of contraction, as if an unknown power within himself was coming sharply into focus, to be directed against a single objective. He had no idea what that might be.

Othman slipped into the room like a shadow. He gestured with one slender hand, a summoning. 'Rise, Owen.'

Owen sat upright, and the sheet fell away from him. He became aware of the air being chill against his skin, his breath steaming.

'Come to me,' Othman said.

Unable to resist, Owen swung his legs over the side of the bed and walked towards the shadowy shape at its end. The floor was icy cold, burning into the soles of his feet. He had to tear his toes away from the bare wood with each step.

Othman reached out with the fingers of one hand and touched Owen's cheek. 'You are so angry,' he said. His breath came as a billowing steam, creating a screen of mist between them.

'No, I'm not,' Owen replied. He frowned. It was the truth. He felt nothing.

'But you are,' Othman insisted in a soft voice. 'I can see it and smell it. You abhor me.'

Owen shook his head, perplexed. 'No . . .'

Othman also shook his head, and his hair threshed about his shoulders as if he were floating underwater. He undid the belt of his dressing-gown, and it slipped from his body. 'Look upon the agent of your displeasure.' He indicated himself. 'This flesh which has destroyed the harmony of your life. How you must detest it!'

Owen tried to take a step backwards, but found he was unable to move. 'I don't detest you ... It's ... It's ...'

'It's what?' Othman snapped. 'The fact that you feel you have no power any more, that you are a victim? The fact that Lily is no longer your faithful companion, but my lover? The fact that Daniel gave himself to me today?'

'No!' Owen pressed his fingers against his eyes. 'That's not true.'

'Yes, it is. There is nothing of yours I have not touched and possessed. Soon, I shall even possess your body as I have taken those whom you love. You have no power to resist me.'

Owen felt as if a swirling cloud of red mist was forming around him, spinning ever faster. He wanted to break it down, deny it, but its spiralling tendrils held him in their grip and he could not dispel them. 'Daniel's not in Little Moor. You said so ... Those *people* have him ...'

Othman laughed. 'I lied. Daniel has betrayed you, Owen. He laughed about you, as Lily did. Both of them prefer my attention to yours. You are weak, unskilled, a fumbling, hopeless lover. Give yourself to me now. Let me teach you.'

'No!' Owen could actually see the cone of spinning red light now. It separated Othman and himself from reality, enclosed them in a constricting space of hatred and deceit. Othman's skin and hair were glowing. He looked supremely beautiful, full of self-love. Owen felt a spurt of anger rise up within him like a fountain of hot blood. He wanted to smash that perfect face, claw away its smile, break the flawless limbs, burn away the genitals.

Othman laughed. 'Come on then, boy!' He gestured

with his hands. 'Think you can best me? Come and try!' He laughed again, the essential heart of mockery.

'You're evil!' Owen cried. He tried to lunge forward, but an invisible barrier held him back.

'Sometimes,' Othman admitted. 'I can be, but I am also the soul of love, and that is what fires you with envy. You can never be to Lily and Daniel what I am. You are like a ghost, with no substance, just a persistent whine and clumsy paws that never make contact. I despise you!'

As Othman spat out the final words, Owen experienced a feeling of shattering, as if he'd fallen through a sheet of ice. Suddenly he had hurled himself forward and, before he could gather his thoughts, he found he had grabbed Othman round the neck. He could feel Othman's laughter vibrating in his throat. The man clearly had no fear. I can kill him, Owen thought. If I believe it, I can kill him!

Othman's arms snaked around his body, and he suddenly went limp in Owen's hands. A thrill of conquest shivered through Owen's limbs. He shook Othman's neck between his hands and Othman's hair fell over his arms like a sheaf of unravelled silk. I am strong, Owen thought and bore Othman to the floor. Othman was moving feebly now, as if life was draining from him. Owen pressed harder, and then Lily's face was before his eyes. It was Lily whom he was strangling. With a yelp, Owen released Othman and jumped up. Looking down, he could see Lily naked upon the icy floor, holding out her arms to him. 'My beloved, he tricked us! Don't kill me! Love me!'

Owen was stunned. For a moment, he turned away, unsure of whether to believe what he saw at his feet. Then Lily's voice came to him, pleading. 'O, he seeks to destroy us. We must combine in love to defeat him!'

Owen looked back. It was definitely Lily lying there, rubbing at her neck with one hand, the other reaching out to him, the fingers clenching and unclenching.

'Oh Lily!' He gathered her up in his arms, buried his face against her neck. He felt her reach out for his cock, grip it in her hand. He moaned and pulled her against him.

Then the laughter came, and Owen realized it was Othman in his arms, Othman's hard fingers. painfully gripping him between the legs. With a howl, Owen pulled away, hit out at the hand that held him.

Othman let go and licked his fingers lasciviously. 'You taste sweet!' he hissed. Still the red cone of light spun around them, growing in intensity as Owen's fury rose within him.

He hurled himself against Othman once more, pushing the man's head back against the floor with a satisfying crack. His fists made contact with yielding flesh, beneath the ribs, in the stomach, between the legs. Othman had no time to retaliate. His breath came out in grunts with each strike. Owen began to weep, every blow becoming harder. The red haze around them was bloody, and blood ran across the floor. Owen felt something heavy pressing against his spine, gripping his shoulders, pushing itself into him. It was like the expression of his hatred formed into a demon which wanted to possess his mind and his flesh. He felt its limbs ease down inside his own limbs, its phallus rear up inside his cock, hard and fierce. Othman's face suddenly loomed before him, like a transparent three dimensional image. 'You only want men. You are afraid of women!'

Owen let out a furious cry of rage. 'Then let me be what you say! Isn't it what you want?' The words seemed not to be his own. He was only a channel for them. His mind was spinning, spinning, matching the rhythm of the cone of light. It was the demon who directed his flesh. He was becoming smaller and smaller, condensing down until his consciousness occupied only the furthest corner of his mind. And the demon, his beast self, plundered Othman's body, its clawed fingers ripping skin and tearing hair. A rapid succession of images flashed before Owen's eyes. He was raping Daniel, abusing Lily, then it was his own mother, Helen, beneath him, moaning in terror and pain. With this final image, the last of Owen's will surrendered and fled. His body ejaculated and was still and the red cone of light diminished, flowing into Owen's body like smoke.

Othman rolled Owen off him and stood up. His body was unmarked by bruises or scratch marks. Easier to strengthen his body against the predations of the boy than against the cat-creature at Low Mede. Tentatively, he nudged Owen with his foot. 'Mine now,' he said aloud, then laughed softly. 'All mine.'

Chapter Thirty-two

Thursday, 29th October: Little Moor

In the morning, Lily met Othman coming out of Owen's bedroom. She sensed his vitality, and half dreaded that if she went in to look upon Owen, he would be nothing more than a shrivelled husk. Othman smiled at her. 'You look like you've seen a ghost, my Lily.'

'Is he all right?' she couldn't help asking.

Othman's smile widened. 'Of course. What are you thinking of? Go and see for yourself.'

Lily went into the bedroom, with Othman following. Owen lay on his back in the bed, apparently asleep. His arms were straight by his sides above the duvet, his legs straight.

Othman touched her shoulder. 'Don't wake him,' he said. 'He will sleep for today. Tomorrow night, he will fulfil a momentous function and he must be prepared for it.'

'You're going to use him and Daniel to wake the flame completely, aren't you?' Lily said. There was bitterness in her voice. 'Aren't I good enough?'

Othman turned her round and propelled her back towards the door. 'Lily, don't be absurd! You have no idea how important you are, or how powerful. But we all have our roles to perform. You could do the job, yes, but it would be selfish to deny Owen his part.'

'I suppose so,' Lily said weakly.

Someone knocked on the kitchen door. 'Answer it,' Othman told her. 'It will be Emma.'

Reluctantly, Lily obeyed him and went downstairs to let Emma in. Ray Perks was with her. 'Leave him in the garden,' Lily said, and Emma spoke a few abrupt words over her shoulder. With a dour glance at Lily, Perks shambled over to the lawn and sat down.

Emma smiled brightly and came into the kitchen. 'What another lovely day!'

Lily pulled a sour face. To her the day felt less than lovely. A distant but nagging depression hovered menacingly in the corners of her mind.

Othman appeared at the bottom of the stairs. 'Emma, I want all the old Grigori dependants to be at The White House tomorrow evening. Can I trust you to arrange that?'

Emma nodded. 'Yes. Will you replenish any of them then?'

'I hope to. You must all wait for me there. A ritual will be enacted at the High Place to awaken the power of the flame. When this is done, I will come to you.' He smiled. 'We shall then set about rebuilding the Murkaster stronghold.'

Emma's expression had become slightly tense. 'What about outsiders? No doubt some of them will be there.'

Othman shrugged. 'They will be taken care of. Don't worry. Now, Lily, may I use the phone?'

Othman rang Barbara Eager at The White House and gave her terse instructions concerning the barbecue on Friday night. Lily could not hear Barbara's responses, but could imagine her bewilderment at Othman's tone. Still, that was not her worry now. Othman had told her that Barbara was nothing, a tool. Outside, in the garden, Raven still lay concealed. He could sense them now, gathering force, coming nearer. They had the faces of men, but the bodies of bulls. Their feet were the claws of lions, and they were winged like sphinxes. Raven could feel their inexorable march, their fiery purpose. Soon, they would be here.

The heat beat down, squeezed the air, dried the fruit rotting upon the trees. The corn fields, shorn, were bleached by the sun, and crackled beneath its glare. The sun was an eye of fire in a white sky. Ghosts walked in daylight, and there were flashes across the fields, as if hot rays of light licked fragments of broken glass. On the hills around Little Moor, vague shadowy shapes took their positions and waited. They furled their wings around them, and hid themselves from all but the most acute perceptions.

Othman waited until the afternoon before venturing over to Low Mede.

He walked into the house without ringing the doorbell, or waiting to be admitted. He found Louis in his study, drinking whisky. Othman looked for signs that might suggest Louis was weakening, such as an old photograph album open on the desk, or an evocative song being played on the hi-fi system, but Louis seemed composed, if drunk, and there was no light of sentiment in his eyes.

'Are you ready?' Othman asked him.

Louis nodded. 'For whatever it is I have to do.'

'Good. Where is Daniel?'

Louis got up from his chair. He had a tendency to pause before standing erect, a legacy of his banished pain. 'In the cellar. I thought it best to keep him and Verity there.'

When Othman came down the cellar stairs, Verity cried out and shielded her brother with her body. She recalled Othman asking her questions about Daniel only a few nights before, although she could remember the conversation only dimly now.

Othman was annoyed that Daniel had been injured. He made no remarks about it to Louis, who after all had simply been following orders, but privately deplored the boy's condition. More precious energy would have to be expended patching him up, as Daniel would be useless for his purpose in this state. Othman's nostrils flared at the stench in the cellar. Perhaps he should have come sooner. Verity cringed as he reached down to stroke her hair.

'Hush, child. Give Daniel to me.'

Verity whimpered and curled herself more tightly around Daniel. 'No! You fiend!'

Othman laughed. 'Quite.' Daniel appeared to be unconscious, his aura was weak and pale. 'Come now, Verity, don't be foolish. I've come to make Daniel better.'

Verity's face, when she raised it, was red and streaked with tears. She looked feverish. 'Like you made my father better? No! Leave us! Raven will come! Raven will help us.'

Othman straightened up, and directed a questioning glance at Louis. 'Raven?'

'Her cat,' Louis replied. 'I shot it after it attacked you.'

'Oh, of course,' Othman said, as if being reminded of some trivial event. 'He's dead, Verity. Your *cat* won't save you.'

Verity let out a wail. 'I don't believe you! He isn't dead! He's not just a cat. He has power! More power than you!'

Othman ignored her remarks and turned again to Louis. 'The beast was probably some scrap of a Murkaster creation still remaining in the vicinity. I should have been more alert for such things. Still, it's been destroyed now.' He gently touched Raven's scratch marks on his face, which had faded considerably since the previous day. Looking at Verity now, he could see

552

that she had allowed the creature to attach itself to her. There were remnants of its influence hanging around her still. It had possessed her, he could tell. Stupid girl. She'd had no idea what she'd been dealing with. He sneered at Verity. 'You welcomed an incubus into your bed, yet you shun me. You're pathetic.' He gestured at Louis. 'Bring the boy.'

Verity attempted to prevent Louis from wresting Daniel's lolling body from her arms, but Louis was strong now. He hit her in the face with his fist and she fell back on to the car blanket, where she uttered no further sound. Louis lifted Daniel in his arms. 'Where are we taking him?'

'St Shem's. Can you drive? I don't want us to be seen by any newcomers to this village, or indeed any casual observers at the Winter cottage.'

Louis nodded. 'The car's in the garage. There's a door through to it from the laundry.'

'Good.' Before they left the cellar, Othman paused to look down upon Verity. She was moving feebly upon the old blanket. 'You may release her on Saturday,' he said to Louis and then directed a lambent stare at him. 'Love her, Louis, make her well. You must love your children.'

Othman sat with Daniel on his lap in the back of the car as Louis drove his old Daimler up to St Shem's. Daniel was semi-conscious, and occasionally made a whimpering sound. Othman stroked his hair, which was spiky with blood. 'I want you to remain with Daniel until tomorrow night,' he told Louis.

Louis glanced over his shoulder. 'At the church?' He sounded surprised.

'Yes. He has to be prepared for an important ceremony which will take place on Friday night. He must be bathed and anointed.'

Louis made a disparaging sound. 'The church is virtually derelict,' he said. 'How can I bathe him there? How will I cook food?'

'Daniel will be fasting,' Othman said. 'As for the rest, you will be surprised how many facilities St Shem's has hidden away. Barbara can bring you food.'

Louis stopped the car at the lich-gate. Othman stepped out when Louis opened one of the rear doors for him. He sniffed the air and looked around to see if anyone could witness what they were doing. When he was satisfied there were no prying eyes, he signalled for Louis to lift Daniel from the back of the car. Louis followed Othman up through the forlorn graveyard. Othman stopped at the main doors.

'It's all locked up,' Louis said. 'You'll have to break in.'

Othman turned and grinned at Louis. He flexed his fingers together and cracked the knuckles. 'You think so? As it happens, I partook of a very fine meal last night which filled me with energy and strength. Watch this.' He made an abrupt, flicking gesture with his hands at the door. There was a shock, as if something had invisibly exploded, and a strange, sour taste in the air. The door to the church stood open. There was no smoke, no sign of Othman's power, other than the simple truth of the open door. 'You see?' Othman said. 'No problem.'

Louis had the wits to look disturbed. He shifted the weight of his son in his arms. 'Let's go in, then.'

Once inside, Louis began to ask awkward questions concerning why Othman had chosen this particular site, and what the ceremony tomorrow night involved. Othman was forced to seal Louis's lips with a few puissant words, to quell his curiosity. It was not desirable to explain things to Louis. Like Barbara, he was merely a tool, and, in Othman's consideration, deserved no explanation.

Othman directed Louis to lay Daniel out on the floor before the altar, while he made an inspection of the building. 'I will bring you life once more,' Othman told the brooding stones. 'Be patient.' In the vestry, he located the entrance to the underground chambers he'd expected to find, hidden beneath a threadbare carpet. After discovering the main power switch to the building, Othman descended the stone steps that led under the vestry. Fortunately, the electric lights still worked, although some of the bulbs had blown.

He emerged into a round, domed antechamber where once the ceremonial robes would have hung, and all the sacred artefacts would have been stored. Now it was empty, but for a faint lingering reek of ancient incense. Doors led off the chamber, and behind one of them, Othman located the ritual bathing area. The waters had been drained from the pool sunk into the ground, but after a brief investigation, he found the stop taps and water began to splutter out from the faucets around the rim of the pool. He would have to leave the water heating for a while, and certain items needed to be brought up to the church, such as towels, ointments, incense and candles. Lily and Emma would have to prepare the unguents and incense.

Back in the church, Louis was standing over Daniel, looking paranoid. When Othman emerged from the vestry, Louis jumped at the sound of his voice. 'There is nothing to be afraid of, I assure you.'

Louis stuck his hands in his trouser pockets. 'It's an eerie old place.'

Othman shrugged. 'If you say so. Sit down.'

Louis obeyed.

'If it will make you feel any better, I shall invoke some

protection for you. After all, we don't want anyone poking their noses in, do we?'

Louis shook his head.

Othman put his hands upon the wall and bowed his head. He visualized a glowing cloak of protection around the building, so that should anyone have the intention of approaching it, they would turn away, walk past, not even think of opening the lich-gate. As he did this, Othman was surprised himself at how powerful he felt. Over the past couple of days he'd felt drained, weak. Now it was as if some inner source was filling him with energy. He was still aware of the void deep within his mind, but he had lived with that for as long as he could remember. Was it possible that what he'd do in this place would fill that void for ever? He needed to believe it.

'Now I must go,' he said. 'Do not leave the building. I shall be as quick as I can.'

'Will you send Barbara up here?' Louis's request was hopeful.

Othman felt a twinge of sympathy. 'I shall call her from the Winters' cottage. But if she comes here, you must not be too intimate with her. I don't want any stray sexual energy thrumming around. Do you understand?'

Louis nodded.

'Good. Give me your car keys.'

Louis rummaged in his pocket and handed them over.

'I shall be back before nightfall,' Othman said.

As he drove back down to the village, he considered, for a few brief moments that he could now drive off anywhere, free himself from whatever he'd taken on by coming to this place. What is holding me here? he wondered. It was of no consequence to him, really, whether the power of the Murkaster flame was reactivated or not. He had seen many flames in his life, passed through them unscathed. Closed gateways, every one. Many times, he had attempted to call upon powers which he directed to 'open the gate', although he had no idea of what would happen, should he ever be successful. He could not think about it, only act. Trying to analyse himself, or his motives, simply caused his head to fill with white noise that prevented thought.

The car purred up to the Winters' cottage, and Othman parked it behind Owen's on the driveway. The Perks boy was still sitting on the lawn, a grudging sentinel. Othman ignored him and went into the house, where Emma and Lily were drinking tea. Emma's hand was placed over Lily's. Clearly some comforting had been going on.

'Do you have any materials with which to make incense?' Othman asked Emma. 'Something simple to purify, frankincense, sandalwood and myrrh.'

Emma smiled. 'Do you think I ever neglected my worship? I still have a few ingredients back at my daughter's house.'

'Good. Go and fetch them. Also, some animal fat, and any candles you might have.'

Emma stood up. 'This sounds urgent.'

Othman said nothing until she had left the house. Then he asked Lily, 'Has Owen stirred?'

She shook her head. 'No, he's still sleeping.' Her brow was creased into a frown that looked as if it had been there all day. 'I'm worried about him, Pev. How can he sleep this long?'

'You have nothing to worry about,' Othman said. He sat down opposite her at the table, reached for her hands. 'Poor Lily. Be at rest.' With one hand, he stroked her brow and the frown faded.

Tears came to her eyes. She took Othman's hand and kissed it. 'I love you,' she said.

Emma returned in twenty minutes with a bagful of ingredients, and Lily's kitchen became a workshop for incense-making. Othman called Barbara Eager and told her to take some food and a flask of coffee up to Louis at the church, then went into the parlour to watch TV, while Emma directed operations.

'What is this all for?' Lily whispered.

'His ritual,' Emma answered. 'He seems to want everything to be just right.'

Emma pounded some of the incense mixture into a fine powder, which she blended with animal fat. When this was done, Othman appeared from the parlour and gave her some of his haoma mix to add to the ointment. Emma had collected nearly two dozen candles of assorted colours, while Lily found a couple of boxes of plain white candles under the sink for use during power cuts. All her good candles were half-used. 'We shall need more,' Othman told Emma. 'But you'll have to get some tomorrow, now.'

The candles, incense and ointment were packed carefully into a carrier bag by Emma, along with a couple of Lily's rather scratchy towels. Before he left them, Othman kissed each woman. 'Keep a vigil over Owen tonight,' he said.

'Will you be back?' Lily asked him.

'Later. Perhaps.'

The light was fading from the land by the time Othman parked the Daimler outside St Shem's. This was the time of power; he could feel it vibrating in the air around him. The soul of the boy burned with a white luminance within the church. Soon, it would blaze like a beacon fire.

Othman dismissed Barbara Eager as soon as he entered the building. She was sitting with Louis on one of the pews, holding his hands. Othman was satisfied to note that Louis pulled his hands away from her and directed his full attention upon Othman as soon as he made an appearance.

Once Barbara had gone, they lifted Daniel and carried him down to the bathing room, Louis wincing at the shadows. Othman lit candles around the pool and extinguished the electric light. Now the room became magical, the patterns of the moving waters rippling across the walls. Othman disrobed Daniel with his own hands, his fingers lingering at the places where the skin was broken and bruised. Then he lifted the boy in his arms. Daniel moaned and moved his limbs slowly as Othman waded into the pool. He lowered Daniel tenderly into the water, which was not yet quite at the temperature of living blood. A memory surfaced in Othman's mind: the ritual bath, the eyes of a boy, trusting, the scent of earth, the sensing of the weight of mountains pressing down from above. As if this memory was the first gate to many, he became aware of a parade of images, waiting to reveal themselves to his inner eye. His first instinct was to push them back, which he did, but not before the face of Taziel Levantine, feral and screaming, reared up before him. Othman closed his eyes. Louis said, 'What is it?'

Othman shuddered. 'Nothing. A bad memory.' But now it was painful to touch Daniel's skin. He stood up and came out of the pool, dripping water across the ancient flagstones. 'You do it,' he said to Louis. 'Bathe your son.' He went to sit on the wooden bench that circled the wall of the room. He could hear Louis making small, aggrieved noises as he got his trousers wet in the pool. Othman rested his head against the cool, damp wall and closed his eyes. Suddenly, he felt weary. He remembered, then, a dream.

It came to him on a wave of scent, the cut corn, the smoke of votive pyres, the sunset red and purple across the wide sky, and the mountains in sharp relief against it. The dwellings. The high dwellings, with their great stones. His house. There was a room, over whose threshold chaos had walked. He saw a boy, his personal seer, cowering in fear and terror, and the coals were spilled from the brazier across the carpets. The boy was calling out in fear, because the elders had sent their Serafim to take his lord, his master, from this place, to another place where the earth gaped with sores and running wounds of fire. The boy would be left alone, then, with no one to protect him, perhaps sacrificed as a creature of the sinful. Othman saw the eyes of the boy, heard the voice crying, 'Master!', but it was too late, far too late, and he knew then that a curse had come from the boy's lips; he had cursed her, cursed her name, her soul, sealed it with his grief.

She.

Her veiled face, the image of an ache behind his heart and eyes. Her beauty, coming from the inside of her, covering her with a glow. Her voice. *Give it all to me. Give me knowledge for my mind is hungry. Fill the belly of my mind.* And he had done so.

Ishtahar.

Othman jerked upright, the echo of a name, whispered aloud, fleeing from his mind. Had he been sleeping?

'It is done.' Louis was standing on the edge of the pool, having draped Daniel against the side. The boy's eyes were open; he was blinking at the water.

Othman stood up, momentarily disorientated. He could sense Louis's attention and, not wishing to betray any sign of weakness, pulled himself up to his full height. From the corner of his eye, he noticed Louis cower. Satisfied, he chanted, 'Rise, Daniel.'

The boy stared up at Othman with defeated eyes. It was clear that he feared death at that moment.

'There is nothing to fear,' Othman told him. 'Nothing. I will bring you bliss.'

He could tell Daniel did not believe him, but what did that matter? There would be proof for the boy soon enough.

Othman picked up a towel, and signalled to Louis to drag Daniel from the water. Between them they wrapped the boy in the towel and led him back out into the antechamber. Here, Othman bade him lie down on the bench against the wall. Daniel said nothing, clearly believing there was no way he could change his unknown fate. Othman admired the boy's saintly composure, his innocent dignity. He knew he had made the right choice.

The antechamber was also lit by candles, which threw leaping shadows up into the dome of the ceiling. Othman had laid out the incense, lighting materials and the jar of ointment on a stone ledge which jutted out from the wall. Now he lit the incense, and the powdery, silver smoke reached out to the walls. Louis flapped a hand before his face.

Othman glared at him. 'You may go back into the church or remain here,' he said. 'The choice is yours. But you will learn more by remaining.'

'Bit smoky,' Louis muttered, but he did not leave.

Othman leaned over Daniel. It was time to induce the sacred trance and guide Daniel bodily into it. Thereafter, by careful dosing with haoma through the skin, the boy could be kept in that state until the following evening. Daniel stared up at Othman with wide, defiant eyes. Still he said nothing, clutching the towel together at his throat. Othman maintained the eye contact as he began to unbutton his shirt. He noticed Daniel's expression change subtly as he realized what would happen.

Othman saw the boy's throat move as he swallowed nervously. Yes, he thought, you know, don't you?

'Are you afraid I'll hurt you?' he murmured. 'Don't be. I shall cast fear out from you.'

Daniel made no response, but merely watched with anxious eyes as Othman finished undressing. At first, he attempted to resist when Othman reached out to pull the towel from his grasp. Then he closed his eyes and his hand dropped in submission. Othman could tell he intended to remove himself from the proceedings, powerless to avoid the inevitable, but refusing to be a collaborator. Othman smoothed Daniel's cool skin, still damp from the water. Then he took down the ointment from the ledge.

Anointed, Daniel's body gleamed in the soft, moving candlelight. He looked like a carving of polished wood, so still. Othman lifted him and placed him on the floor in the centre of the room. Louis uttered a cough, which prompted Othman's head to snap upwards. 'Silence!' Louis dropped his eyes.

Othman circled the room, uttering a virtually inaudible invocation. At various points he made complicated hand gestures. As he circled, he became aroused, transforming himself into the representation of a priapic demiurge.

Daniel lay with his eyes shut tight. He could feel the mounting power around him, familiar and yet so alien. He could hear the sound of Othman's feet padding round him on the stone floor, which sounded more like the clopping of hooves. If he surrendered himself, he would be lost, yet the urge to surrender was great. He tried to think of Owen, to conjure his lover's face before his mind's eye as a protection. He wanted to keep some part of himself intact, his consciousness, his personality. Yet when the demon touched him, with the most subtle and gentle of caresses, when the kiss came to him, which was the archetypal kiss, it was impossible to keep hold of the past. All that existed was the present moment, which stripped him of his will. The demon had anointed itself with haoma, the seducing poison. There was no pain as it invaded Daniel's body, only a sense of coldness and a rushing sound in his ears like water crashing in the distance or flames devouring dried wood. A smell of ozone and ripened corn insinuated itself beneath the cloak of the incense.

Daniel went backwards in time, saw the brazier fall, the coals scatter. He cried out, 'Master! My Lord Shemyaza!' They pulled the man away from him, the butt of a spear thrust into the small of his back. The pain was sudden and intense. He rolled over, saw them dragging his master away. He was looking at his own death, at the time when his violated body would be thrown into the pit on top of the corpse of the man he adored, and the stones would come to crush the life from him. Daniel wept, his heart full of grief and love.

Daniel's consciousness snapped back into the present. He reached for the hand of the demon who rode him, held it tight until his nails broke the skin. He had already learned that sex conjured images in his head, and this time they were unbelievably vivid. He sensed that the man who possessed him wore the aspect of a demon like a garment. Within, in ignorance, he was a being of light, and the commerce of their flesh was sacred. If Daniel concentrated on this aspect, it became more real in his mind. He felt elated. This was too much to be borne, for he knew it would be the first and last time.

Then the visions came flooding back, and time had twisted around him once more. He was being led, bound, along a stony path to the lip of a valley of fire. He had been kept in confinement for seven days, while his master had been tortured. This much his guards had told him. He had also learned that Shemyaza's confederates in crime had fled, taking their human women with them, although their freedom would undoubtedly be short-lived. The High Lord Anu was enraged, and his wrath burned cities and destroyed continents.

At the lip of fire, Daniel saw they had brought forth the woman responsible for his master's fall from grace. Ishtahar. No doubt her family had surrendered her, seeking to appease the High Lord's anger and avert his vengeance on their children. Ishtahar's hands were chained with gold before her belly, which was the cauldron of her power, the way to the stargate. Her eyes were wild.

Daniel screamed, 'Why did you do this? Why?'

And she answered. '*They* did this, not me! It is their cruel laws! I want only to be allowed to love him!'

How could he curse her? It was impossible. What the master loved, he loved.

In the valley below, the Serafim soldiers ripped Shemyaza's clothes from his body. He stood tall and unafraid, even though he must know they meant to kill him. His body was marked with the tongue of the lash, his face bruised and swollen beyond recognition. Daniel's heart contracted at the sight of his master's familiar shape, which he knew so well. *I will find you again, though it might take many lifetimes, and when I do, I will save you from harm. This I swear.*

Roughly, the Serafim threw Shemyaza to the ground and bound him in rope, which was dyed green to represent the coils of the cosmic serpent. They tied the end of the rope around one of Shemyaza's ankles, and from there looped it over the arm of a gibbet, which lay in the hot dust beside him. Daniel wanted to look away as the gibbet was raised and swung out over the wound in the earth, where acrid, searing fires and lethal fumes gushed upwards. It was too terrible a death to witness, but he also felt he owed it to his lord to suffer the sight of his execution. His own death would follow soon enough.

He and Ishtahar were forced to watch the burning, forced to smell it, hear their beloved's cries. Daniel could not tell how long it took his master to die, only that it was *too* long. Before Shemyaza's body had finished shuddering and jerking at the end of the rope, the Serafim had begun to dig a pit, in unblessed ground beside the fissure of fire, where presently the body would be cast, perhaps still possessing a faint vestige of life. Daniel knew that as soon as Shemyaza had been transferred to the pit, he himself would be thrown into it alive. Then the Serafim would fill the makeshift grave with heavy stones, and Daniel would be crushed to death as the closest minion of the Fallen One. Because of his association with the disgraced Shemyaza, no other lord or lady would speak out for him, or take him on as seer. Whatever their feelings on the matter, they would not risk incurring the wrath of the High Lord Anu, who had been offended by Shemyaza's actions. Instead, they would watch Daniel the innocent die a criminal's death. Strangely, Daniel felt no fear or dread. There was little point. His fate was inevitable, and he could only accept it. Also, what point was there in living once Shemyaza was dead? He had only to look upon Ishtahar's face to glean the answer to that.

At the last moment, when the pit was still being dug and the seconds streaming away towards the time when Daniel would be cast down to join his master in a final embrace, Ishtahar reached out for him with her chained hands. The wrists were bleeding. Her eyes called to him as she struggled against the ones who held her. He knew she wanted to take hold of him, go with him to the place where he would die. But they would not allow it. Her punishment was to live. They needed her to live, for her power was greater than that of any human woman before her. Through her desire for knowledge, she had created herself anew. Now that this new self existed in the world the Anannage would take advantage of it and use it.

The image of Ishtahar receded in Daniel's sight. He could see her lips moving, but could no longer hear her cries. He was filled with a heavy grief. She would live on, and the memory of this terrible day would continue through her children, and the children of her sisters, who had also taken Anannage lovers. Most of them had so far escaped Shemyaza's fate, but later the High Lord would attempt to hunt them down and slay their hybrid children. None of it should be happening, Daniel thought. How many times had he followed his lord to the lower plains, and crouched patiently in the dust outside Ishtahar's dwelling, wherein they had loved? Never once, during those times, had he foreseen this moment. Until the advent of Ishtahar, he had been Shemyaza's only seer, but his master had been seduced by the utterances of the woman, and had turned away from the voice he could trust. I could have warned him, Daniel thought. If I had looked into the heart of their love, I could have seen this. Too late now. Far too late . . .

Daniel was suddenly jerked back to reality. Othman was standing over him, panting. His face was a mask of terror and grief. 'Illusion!' he said. 'Why do this to me? Why torment me when I have loved you?' He put his bunched fists against his eyes, staggered backwards. 'Leave me! Go!'

Louis made an uncertain movement, unsure whether

to go to Othman or his son, or retreat from the room altogether.

Daniel sat up. He felt tranquil, visionary, full of the presence of haoma. It was then that he realized he was part of something inexorable and ordained. Slowly, he rose to his feet.

Othman winced as Daniel reached out to touch him. 'It's all right,' Daniel said. 'She is coming.'

'Who? Who?' Othman looked like a stranger, vulnerable and afraid.

Daniel shrugged and shook his head. 'Only you can speak her name. But she's coming.'

Daniel took one of Othman's tremulous hands in his own. He stroked the long, pale palm. 'Look, a single thorn in the flesh is causing you pain. Let me remove it.' Daniel placed his palm over Othman's and a light seemed to radiate from his skin.

At that moment, he knew, Othman would be forced to recognize him as holy. Then Daniel slid his hand away, leaving Othman to stare at the tiny pool of blood which had collected in the centre of his palm. It was the blood of sin.

This was the moment, then. There was a chance, like a doorway slightly ajar. Othman could reach out and open it, or shut it and walk away. He sensed that if he took Daniel in his arms now, and tomorrow night invoked something other than what he intended, the future would change. It would be so simple. Yet there was still a smell of charred flesh in his throat. Resentment wrestled with compassion. He struck Daniel's hands away. 'No!'

Daniel cringed back, sensing the change. Whatever Othman had briefly become, it had been banished. Slowly, he sank down to sit naked upon the stone floor. He would pray. It was all he could do. Pray to the truth of a god-form whose name bloomed in his mind like a beacon. *Ahura Mazda.* Pray to the light. But he knew now that the lie was coming.

Chapter Thirty-three

Friday, 30th October: Patterham and Little Moor

Aninka put on her make-up. Her heart was beating fast, erratically, within her breast. Lahash had said little, but she knew that today would see the end of it all, one way or another. Taziel had come to sit in her room – they had spent all their time together over the past couple of days. He seemed tense and weary. 'Ninka, I want to go home,' he said.

'Where's home?' she asked him.

He lay back on her bed. 'Vienna. I wish I was there now.' He rolled on to his side, stared at her. 'Will I ever go back?'

Aninka shuddered, but strove to hide the physical reaction from him. 'You won't die, Taz. Lahash will look after you.'

'Flesh may survive,' Taziel said, 'but what about the mind? I think I'd rather lose the flesh.'

Aninka stood up, went to sit next to him. She stroked his shoulder. 'Taz, shut up. Thinking like this won't do you any good. You're a tracker, that's all. Stop imagining you have more responsibility than that!'

He smiled sadly. 'You're so strong. How come you can be this calm about it? We'll see him soon, Ninka, I know we will. Aren't you afraid?'

Aninka clasped her hands together in her lap. 'I keep telling myself not to be. I remind myself of what Peverel Othman has done, what he did to my friends, what he tried to do to me. If the only fear is that when I see him again, I will remember love, then no, I am not afraid.'

She felt it would be wiser not to confess to Taziel that she was worried her rational control might slip once she faced Othman in the flesh. However, she trusted Lahash. He was like a pillar that held the sky from falling, always sensed, even if he was not physically present.

Once her make-up was perfectly applied, Aninka packed her belongings. Lahash had bought her a small figurine of a protective demon, which he'd found in an occult shop in Patterham. She looked at it fondly, handled its smooth stone, before secreting it in her bag. It had stood on the bedside table since Lahash had put it into her hands.

She carried all the bags down to the cramped hallway of the hotel, Taziel following her. He seemed disorientated, unable to make decisions or even accomplish the most basic task, such as carrying a bag. Lahash had already settled the bill and had gone to fetch the car. Aninka looked around herself. In some ways she was sad to be leaving this dingy little sanctuary, because she and the others had forged a close friendship here during their short stay. She had wondered, occasionally, whether she would end up sleeping with either Lahash or Taziel, but it hadn't happened. Now was not the time, she knew that, but even so, if something bad were to happen, she wished she could have the memory of their love to take with her to the next place. 'Stop it!' she told herself, and instructed Taziel to go out on to the street.

The day was warm, a *kind* day, which was full of summer ghosts, yet alive with the scent of the turning season, spiced by a suggestion of chill in the air. How wonderful life is, Aninka thought. How beautiful this world. She wished she didn't keep having these aching thoughts of a final kind, because it did not bode well for the future. Trust Lahash, she told herself. Buck up, Aninka. This is war, not a funeral.

The large black car came sliding up the road, and purred to a halt before Aninka and Taziel. Lahash wound down the window and smiled at them. Aninka felt a pang of remorse. She had thought him severe, unattractive. Now he seemed beautiful. 'Get in,' he said.

Aninka got in the front beside him, while Taziel got into the back seat, where he curled up to go to sleep.

'Where are we going?' Aninka asked.

'A small village near here,' Lahash answered. 'I have already dispatched the Kerubim, who are in position. Othman is there; his activities are so overt, even I can pick up the residue. It hangs above the place like a red cloud.'

Aninka shivered. 'So, what's the plan? We go right in and confront him?'

Lahash shook his head. 'That wouldn't be a good idea. No, we'll keep our distance for today, and let Taz do his stuff. Something's building up. Tonight, we move in.' He let go of the steering wheel to grip Aninka's hands briefly, which were clasped tightly in her lap. 'Don't worry. We'll be fine.'

What can I do, thought Lily, but try to continue life as normal? She was hanging the washing out at the time, her mouth stuffed with wooden pegs. The oppressive warmth raised a shimmering haze from the dried lawn around her, and, above, the sky was almost purple, as if bruised. Looking at the garden, Lily thought that it was like peering through coloured sunglasses, purple or dark pink. Her heart continued to pound much faster than usual. Not even sharing a bottle of wine with Emma could do anything to dampen her feverish excitement. Something is coming, something is happening. This was the inaudible chant that charged her blood. Lily picked up the washing basket and began to stroll back towards the cottage. Owen still lay immobile in his room. He hadn't drunk or eaten anything, but neither had he soiled the bed. It was as if he was held in suspended animation; it frightened her. She went to look in on him often, worried in case he woke up alone and afraid. He looked like a dead saint, lying there on the bed. Was it the Grigori beauty coming through in him now, this translucence, this sense of inner fire, which shone through his fine-boned face, or had Daniel coaxed this new beauty from him? Lily sponged his limbs with cool water, leaned down to kiss his genitals. 'My brother.' He did not stir.

A loud, demanding meow made Lily turn round. She expected to see one of her feline troupe bounding towards her, asking her to wait for them, but it was the enormous black cat from Low Mede. He came out from the rhododendrons, his tail aloft like a banner. 'Hello!' Lily said. 'Are you better now?' She was in the habit of talking to cats as if they themselves could speak. The cat miaowed again, leaned heavily against her legs, twining his tail between them. She could feel the muscle of it; it was almost prehensile, like a monkey's. He looked up at her, his mouth open in a silent meow, then he ran ahead a few feet, before pausing, gazing at her enquiringly, one forefoot held up. Lily moved towards him, murmuring soft words, but he ran off again, only to pause and look back at her once more. Lily put down the washing basket. She understood.

'Go on, then,' she said, and the cat ran to the garden gate, slipped under it. Lily followed and opened the gate, went out into the lane. The cat was already trotting off ahead of her. After looking back at the cottage just once, she went after it. Emma was drowsing in the parlour and Ray Perks was absent on some errand or another: no one would notice Lily was missing.

*

Long Eden seemed to be surrounded by a shimmering aura, which was clearly visible against the aching purple sky. The colours of the garden, of the house itself, seemed unnatural, as if bathed in a brilliant sunset. It was ten o'clock in the morning. Lily walked slowly up the drive. Perspective had shifted; nothing around her looked real, but everything was slightly warped, tilted, leaning, squeezed out of shape. At the edge of her vision, she caught flickers of movement as if others walked beside her, a crowd of spirits who would not make their presence completely known.

A figure stood before her on the drive, indistinct in the haze. It appeared to be a long distance away, shielding its eyes with one hand, staring down at her. Then it raised its hand in a cheerful wave before swinging round and walking towards the house. Lily knew the figure instantly. It was her mother.

Lily felt no fear. She ran forward, shouting, 'Mum!' but the woman did not turn round again and disappeared beneath the shadow of the house. When Lily hurtled up to the great front doors, Raven was sitting at the threshold, licking one of his front paws. He looked up at Lily as if to say, 'You took your time!' Then he stretched out his long body, before rearing up to scratch at the door, as if demanding entrance. Beneath his great paws, the door swung open on to darkness. Lily drew in her breath sharply, and took a step backwards. She felt a wave of cold come out of the house and wrap its chilling arms around her. Raven looked up at her, meowed peremptorily.

'Are you asking me in?' Lily said. Raven, then, was the key. They had stumbled across him, fleeing the guardian of the house, not even realizing he was there for them to use. Now she would have to deal with it alone. Owen was unconscious, Daniel was missing, only she could enter the dark of Long Eden. Still, she hesitated. 'Enter,' said Raven. Lily looked down at him. Had he really spoken? She blinked.

There was no cat on the doorstep, but a man stood before her, some monster of myth made flesh. He stood at least seven feet tall and had the head of a great cat. His skin was pelted with black fur, over which he wore a deep green robe, fringed with gold. When he spoke, his voice seemed hardly more than a whisper, yet as loud as the wind. 'Enter.' With a clawed hand, he gestured for Lily to pass him and go into the house.

Lily was transfixed. 'What *are* you?' Was this what the Grigori really looked like? Was Peverel Othman a monster beneath his flesh as well? What did that mean for herself and Owen, if they attempted to reclaim their heritage?

'I am the physical guardian of this house,' Raven replied. 'Have no fear. I am the key, as you have guessed. The spiritual guardian will not harm you in my company. It is time now, Lily Murkaster, for you to come home.'

Lahash parked the car on the edge of some woodland, and then he and Aninka half carried Taziel along a narrow lane, between high hedges. Lahash had slung a binoculars case over his shoulder. 'Where are we going?' Aninka asked. Lahash seemed to know.

He smiled at her, gestured with one hand towards a hilltop, visible on the left side of the road. 'Look! Look hard!'

The sky shimmered in a strange way, its colour a most unnatural shade of dark blue, as if it contained some red hue within it. The atmosphere was unreal; it vibrated with power, with imminence. Aninka stared at the hilltop, narrowed her eyes. A nebulous outline flickered there, like the memory of a monstrous statue which might once have stood upon the hill. Aninka had never seen Kerubim before.

'It is beautiful, and terrifying,' she said, and then glanced at Lahash. 'And you can control such a creature?'

He shrugged. 'If it obeys its instructions. I hope so. There are six of them.'

Aninka said, 'Look, Taz. Can you see it?' The suggestion of the vast shape, more than anything Enniel could tell her, brought home to Aninka exactly what she was, what her people were. So easy to forget in the humdrum world – but this?

Taziel shook his head from side to side. 'I need painkillers,' he moaned. 'Give me something. I hurt.'

'No,' Lahash answered affably. 'We don't want your mind fogged, do we?'

'Fuck you!' Taziel leaned weakly against Aninka. 'I don't want this!'

Aninka appealed to Lahash. 'Is there nothing we can do?'

'It will not be for long,' Lahash said, hardly a satisfying answer.

They followed the lane until they reached a five-barred gate on the right side, which gave access to sloping fields that rolled towards the skyline. Lahash led the way up the hills, Aninka supporting Taziel as best she could. At the top, they looked down upon a village. 'Playhouses,' said Aninka. 'So tiny.'

Lahash took out his binoculars and scanned the landscape. Then he turned to the others. 'Sit down, Taz. Rest a while.'

'The air is full of him,' Taziel answered. He collapsed on to the ground, where he lay clutching his head. Aninka squatted down beside him, stroked his back. She could feel him shuddering.

'Try and sleep,' Lahash said. 'I'll wake you in an hour or two.'

Aninka sat down and placed Taziel's head in her lap. She massaged his scalp, pressed her fingers against his closed eyes, hoping to instil some comfort. Lahash was a tall black shape beside them. He stood with folded arms, gazing down at the village.

'Where is your old home?' Aninka asked, more to make conversation and ease the tension than out of curiosity.

Lahash pointed. 'There. It hasn't changed.' His voice was hard, but Aninka felt he was trying to contain his emotions.

She looked in the direction he indicated. The house was surrounded by tall trees; in the grounds, water gleamed beneath the feverish sun. 'It's massive.'

Lahash nodded. 'I grew up there.'

'Are you very old?'

He turned to her and smiled. 'No, not very.'

'What happened?' Aninka asked him. 'Can you tell me about it?'

Lahash hunkered down in front of her. 'I don't suppose it will do any harm.' He sat down on the prickly grass.

'Well?'

'We lost everything because of a woman,' he began. He gave Aninka a rueful smile. 'My uncle, Kashday, was lord of our house. He fell in love with a human woman.'

Aninka risked a laugh. 'Sounds familiar! Such has ever been our downfall, if we are to believe all the old stories!'

Lahash nodded. 'True. Ninka, you must know about the two factions in our society.'

'Factions?' She wasn't sure.

Lahash nodded. 'They both want to find a way back to the Source, to the One, but they have different

576

methods. Many blood-lines believe we should try to emulate the ways of the Anannage, so that they will reveal themselves to us once more, and give back to us the knowledge of our ancestors. The others believe we should further our own knowledge to reopen the old stargate. My family belonged to the latter faction.'

'I see,' Aninka said cautiously. She felt she belonged to neither faction. It all sounded very paranoid to her, similar to the conspiracy theories that many humans were so fond of inventing.

Lahash sighed. 'Well, when Kashday met Helen, we had no idea what a viper he was bringing into our nest. She was bright, too intelligent to be a dependant. Pretty soon, she guessed many of our so-called secrets, what really went on in the work-rooms beneath the house, and she must have bullied other information out of Kashday. She wanted to become the Eye Priestess, the oracle. Kashday was foolish enough to believe she could be the gateway, the one who would open the closed thoroughfare to the Source.'

Aninka couldn't help expressing her surprise. 'But that's just a legend, surely! They didn't really believe they could accomplish it!'

Lahash shook his head. 'Ninka, the majority of our people are kept in ignorance. There is more truth in the old stories than you know. A perpetual flame burned in this place, but it was diminishing. We could draw sustenance from it, but we could not pass through it and use it as a gateway. Neither could we draw energies from the stars back through it to this world. Kashday persuaded the family to allow him to use Helen as Priestess for the fire festival at the corn-cutting. Lammas. It took some doing, but eventually he wore down all the arguments. Claimed he knew what he was doing. I think he did, but Helen was no Ishtahar. When she went into the flame, the gate opened, yes, but it incurred only the wrath of the elders. Something came through. The Parzupheim were alerted and sent out the Kerubim to attack us. We had no choice but to scatter. Most of us were killed, and the survivors were taken into confinement. It was terrible, a real mess.'

Aninka regarded him thoughtfully. Half of her didn't want to believe what he'd said, yet he spoke with such simple sincerity. Lahash did not seem like Enniel and other power-holding Grigori she had met, tight with secrecy and veiled insinuations. Lahash said little, but when he did speak, his words made sense.

'You are looking at me as if I'm mad,' Lahash said. 'Do you think I'm making this up?'

Aninka shook her head. 'No, of course not. But it just seems so . . . *incredible*. What happened to this woman, Helen? Was she killed?'

Lahash shrugged. 'I don't know. That is, she survived Lammas night, but having once entered the flame, I wonder how much longer she could have carried on living a normal life afterwards. Anyway, it's irrelevant. She was human, and her knowledge was limited. Kashday and Helen were hung up on the old stories, the romance of them. They must have seen themselves as Shemyaza and Ishtahar, and believed their communion possessed the same power. The instinct to re-enact such a cycle must be strong in our family's genetic blueprint. Kashday and Helen's love for one another ruined them both, ruined the family and the lives of many villagers down there, too.'

'And Peverel Othman arrives at the site of this devastation,' Aninka said quietly. 'What a coincidence!'

'It's obvious Othman has sniffed out the residue of the flame here, and is attempting to resurrect it. We left guardians, and quenched the flame as best we could, but now . . .?' Lahash looked around himself. 'You can feel it, can't you? A pressure of impending power.'

Aninka shuddered in the oppressive heat. 'That's an amazing story, Lahash.'

He smiled. 'Well, what I've told you is very condensed. There was more to it than that.'

'One day, I would like to hear it all.'

His smile widened into a pleased grin. 'Then one day, I *will* tell you, but it will take some time.'

Aninka reached out and briefly touched one of his hands. 'Let's hope we have it, then.'

He stood up. 'We will.' He lifted the binoculars to his face once more, his voice distant, as if sucked away from them, down the hill to the village and the silent, looming house of his exiled family. 'We will go to a restaurant together, and we will drink expensive wine and enjoy good food, and I shall tell you all my stories.'

'And afterwards?' Aninka asked.

He laughed. 'I'd have thought you'd had enough of Anakim to last you a lifetime.'

'You are not Anakim,' Aninka said.

Lahash turned to look at her, the binoculars held at his chest. 'Your guardian may not approve of your plans.'

'I'll tell him I want to hire you as a bodyguard.' She affected a dramatic posture. 'I've been through so much. I'm afraid of being alone now.'

Lahash shook his head, still grinning, before resuming his inspection of the surrounding countryside. She knew she had pleased him.

Lily stood in the hall of Long Eden, looking around herself in wonder and fear. *I am inside, at last. I am really inside.* The house seemed removed from reality, utterly still and silent, permeated only by a dingy light which leaked through the murky greens and golds of the stained-glass window over the stairs. There was a sweet, musty smell of age, mixed with a faint mushroom tang of dry rot. It was hard to imagine anyone having ever lived there. Raven stood patiently as Lily walked around touching the panelling on the walls, gazing up at the great metal chandeliers high overhead. Her footsteps echoed, even though she was only wearing rubber-soled pumps on her feet. She felt as if time was hanging suspended in the dusty air. What was she supposed to do? Just look around? There seemed no message for her there; no sense of welcome, or even of attention. If the house watched her, it did so covertly.

Raven said nothing, and when she addressed questions to him, he remained silent, as if he'd said all he was ever going to say to her. She did not like looking at him directly, because his appearance was too unearthly. Gazing at him would only force her to admit that the world she had inhabited since childhood was a fragile, friable thing. Monsters could walk out of the shadows at any time to alter perceptions for ever.

How could I have been so unaware of all this? Lily wondered, her fingers running over an intricate carving, sticky with old wax. It has always been part of me. Why couldn't I feel it? She peered at the carved pictures on the panelling, saw men and women with wings and fringed robes marching sideways towards a spoked globe. She touched the globe lightly. *They entered here. They entered into it* . . . She wished she knew the meaning of her thoughts.

Something moved at the back of the hall. Lily thought she saw a brief flash of muted white in the shadows. An echo of female laughter moved the air, set the chandelier swaying overhead. Now the house had flexed its bones, woken up. It would present its ghosts to her.

'Mum?' Lily moved towards the shadows, thinking she should be afraid, but feeling only curious and, in a way, impatient.

A corridor at the rear of the hall led off to the left. Lily cautiously peered around the corner, conscious of Raven still standing motionless nearby. The corridor appeared lit by a subterranean-looking, blue-green light, but there was no indication as to its source. 'Should I go down here?' Lily asked aloud.

Raven did not reply, but swiftly walked past her, his tall shape diminishing quickly down the corridor. Lily felt she would rather remain with Raven, despite the absurdity of his appearance, than be left alone. She followed him.

There was no furniture in the corridor, not even a painting on the walls. The floor beneath her feet was of bare tiles, whose colours were now indiscernible through the dust and grime that had collected over the years. Lily was a little disappointed by what she saw around herself. Everything was so bare; everything had been removed. She had hoped to walk into a shrine to the Murkasters, with the furnishings neatly covered in white sheets, simply waiting for people to come back and live there once more. Now, just by being there and breathing the dead air, Lily knew in her heart that the Murkasters never intended to come back. All they had left behind them were the phantoms of their lives. There were no physical treasures to be uncovered. *I should be dancing along these halls, in the dark, dressed in bright silks with ancient gold around my throat,* Lily thought. *They should have left something behind for me, a skin to wear, a looking-glass reflecting only history* ... The house wove a spell over her, as if melancholy dreams drifted down from the cobwebbed corners.

Ahead of her, on the left of the corridor, a door swung

silently open, spilling a wan light over the floor tiles. Raven halted in his tracks without looking round, and Lily paused. The doorway stood between them now. She thought she could hear a sound, and strained her perceptions to decipher it, but it ebbed and flowed in her mind like a badly tuned radio. *Voices, they are voices.* Once Lily had identified the sound, it became clearer. She heard low conversation, men speaking quickly.

'What does this woman mean?'

'He is out of his mind?'

'But the flame, the flame? What about the flame?'

'Can he do it?'

'No.'

'Yes. He might.'

'It could be the end of all our work.'

'Or the harvest of all our work.'

Lily hurried past. She felt that if she lingered too long, her presence would be registered, even though she knew she was only hearing a replay of something that had happened a long time ago.

The corridor opened out into a circular hall, where a mosaic pattern on the floor depicted a brace of male peacocks with their tails intertwined. A skylight in the ceiling picked out what remained of the colours of the tiles: ruby, indigo, blue and gold. Here the air smelled faintly perfumed, as if a woman had walked through it wearing Oriental scent, or once a sweet incense had been burned. Raven stood in the centre of the peacock design, his arms folded on his breast. All Lily could see of his face were the lambent embers of his burning eyes. She hesitated before him. *Where now?*

A sound came, like someone opening a window with rusty hinges, followed by a muffled crash; something falling, shattering. Then the distant laughter, and, more clearly, the low, sultry tone of a woman singing. Lily could not make out the words. Perhaps they were in a foreign language. The song called to her, invited her body to sway to its rhythm. Lily felt as if the song could carry her away, lift her bodily from the floor, so that she could float around in the air, brushing the ceiling with her fingertips. She lifted her arms high, standing on tiptoes, waiting, waiting, for someone to take her hands and lift her up.

A flickering white shape flitted past her, and abruptly the singing stopped. Lily gasped, and nearly fell, as if she really had been floating just above the ground. Someone stood just behind and to the left of Raven: a woman in a summer dress, her long hair flowing over her shoulders. She was smiling, but there was something flat and flickering about her appearance, as if she was merely a projection of an old film, playing upon the shadows.

'Mum!' Lily reached out to this apparition, but it had already disappeared. Behind the spot where Helen had appeared, a door swung open, and a white light came out, as of bright daylight. With it came a scent of gardens, strawberries and red wine. Raven took a step to the side and turned to look into the light. Taking this as encouragement, Lily cautiously moved closer to the door. Had Helen passed this way?

Inside, the room was furnished. Heavy tapestries covered the walls, depicting tall winged figures in robes, similar to those on the panelling in the main hall, but here more majestic and stylized. Lily was reminded of Egyptian wall-paintings found only in tombs. The room was dominated by a colourful painting, which hung above the great hearth, where no fire burned. Lily looked at the painting and recognized her own face, even though the woman depicted there appeared to be of ancient Middle Eastern origin, dressed in the robes of a priestess and adorned with gold. Lily was drawn by the painting

583

and stepped across the threshold. As she did so, she realized the room was not empty and that a man was sitting at an enormous desk, his head in his hands. As she entered the room, he looked up. 'Here you are,' he said. 'My tormentor, my love.' His dark red hair was tied back at the nape of his neck, but poured forward over his shoulders. He was perhaps the most beautiful man she had ever seen, other than Peverel Othman. He wore an expression of cynical resignation. He reminded her of Owen.

'Father!' she said, and suddenly there was a great flapping and chirring of wings about her head. Lily threw up her hands to protect herself and the haunted cry of a peacock echoed throughout the empty house. When she lowered her hands, the room was bare: no furniture, no painting, no phantom of Kashday. Even the carvings on the panels had become indistinct, only an arm reaching out here, the corner of a robe visible there. Lily retreated into the corridor, and saw Raven walking away from her, an unnaturally tall darkness gliding through the shadows. 'Raven, wait!' She ran to catch him up, but the cat-man neither slowed his pace nor turned around to beckon her. The corridor flashed past as Lily ran along it. How could she run so fast? It seemed as if the house was moving, while she was running on the spot.

Then, abruptly, the walls on either side of her came to a shuddering halt, and Lily realized she had stopped running. She had reached the end of the corridor.

Raven, too, had halted and now stood before a door, which was closed. Its panels were decorated by carvings of long, sweeping wings. Lily ventured forward cautiously and put her hands flat against the panels, feeling the ridges of the carvings beneath her palms. The wood felt warm and pliable, as if it was alive. She rested her cheek against it, and thought she could hear a faint, humming sound coming from beyond the door. If anything still lived in Long Eden, it was across this threshold. Lily wished another vision of her mother would appear to guide her, or that Raven would say something. But the cat-man remained silent, and no ghosts beckoned from the shadows. Summoning her courage, Lily put her hand upon the door knob and tried to turn it, but it was locked. She shook it a few times, to no avail, and then stepped back with a sigh. Glancing at Raven, she enquired, 'Can't I go in here? You're a key, aren't you? Will you open the door for me?'

Raven's eyes were a glowing amber. He said nothing, but opened his red mouth and uttered a fluting yowling sound.

'What?' Lily said. 'I don't understand. Speak!'

Raven simply repeated the note.

This was too frustrating for words. What was he trying to convey? Lily understood the language of cats only to the extent of being able to provide food, caresses or entrance to a closed room. Raven's cry had not sounded like a demand. Lily reached out and shook the door handle again, and uttered a soft sound of alarm when Raven's clawed hand shot out and gripped her wrist, pulling her away from the door. 'So what else can I do?' Lily said.

Slowly, Raven shook his head. His eyes seemed to burn into Lily's own, demanding that she recognizes the instruction he was giving. Softly, the cat-man repeated his musical cry. Lily detected a note of exasperation in it. *Are you so stupid, girl? Listen!*

Wondering whether she'd interpreted the message correctly, Lily hummed the same note. As she did so, she thought she could hear another woman's voice joining hers, singing an identical tone. Raven blinked at her in the way that cats signify approval. Encouraged, Lily drew in her breath and sang the note once more, more loudly. As before, another female voice, which seemed to echo from somewhere deep within the house, mingled with her own. The weaving duet reverberated throughout the bricks and rafters of Long Eden, until Lily's hair began to lift on her neck. She felt a great joy build up within her, and her song climaxed as a scream. Something seemed to tug away from her, a sense of release, of power. All fell to silence.

Raven turned towards the door, and Lily saw that it now stood open, revealing a long flight of steps going downwards beneath the house. The note had been the key. Lily stepped forward. 'Must I go down?'

Raven again said nothing but began to descend the stairs. Hurrying, Lily followed him. She had to feel along the walls so as not to fall, because there was no light at all. Raven soon became invisible in the darkness ahead of her. Lily's pumps slipped upon the stairs; she dreaded losing her footing and plunging down into the darkness. 'Raven!' Her voice was muffled; there was no echo.

Down, down. The stairs seemed to have no end. Lily fought a sensation of panic and claustrophobia. When she looked back, she not could see anything above her. Just as she was about to give in to her terror, turn back, and scrabble her way to the doorway, she noticed two amber lights hanging in the air ahead of her that she recognized as Raven's eyes. She heard a whispering voice murmur, 'Don't stop,' which she wasn't sure came from Raven or someone else. She went towards the eyes, noticing as she did so that the floor had levelled out. Groping, with her arms held out in front of her, she encountered Raven's body. Briefly, he put his long, furred arm around her shoulder, and then a weak light came to illuminate the short corridor in which they stood. Raven had apparently pushed open another door. Lily went towards it. Across the threshold lay an enormous room. Again, there was no visible source of light, but the whole place was illumined by a soft, yellowy radiance. Here, at last, were things that the Murkasters had left behind them in their flight.

Tentatively, Lily ventured into the room, which stretched away for as far as she could see. It was filled with tables, benches, shelves and cupboards, all of which bore strange machinery and models. Enormous books, as tall as Lily herself, lolled in a bookcase against the wall near the door. Nearby stood what appeared to be the skeleton of some extinct saurian, except that it looked more like a bird than any dinosaur Lily had seen in books or films. Some of the apparatus in the room was huge, brushing the ceiling with jointed, metal arms, supporting globes, a few of which had spikes. Lily thought this might be astronomical machinery, representing planets and stars. On the walls, reflecting the positions of the astrolabes, were great maps of the heavens, marked with red and purple lines of ink. Marvelling, Lily walked slowly to the nearest table, which was covered in metal balls that shone with many colours like oil. Some of the balls were as small as marbles, others the size of door-stops. Lily picked up a palm-sized ball; it was warm to the touch and lay heavy in her hand. What was its purpose? She became aware of faint sounds at the edge of her perception: soft, whispering voices, liquid bubbling, the clack of wood against metal and a swishing noise like a broom being brushed across the floor. She put down the ball and turned around quickly, but the sounds ceased immediately.

On another table, Lily found trays of metal instruments that looked disturbingly surgical. She picked up an object that seemed to be a strange hybrid of scalpel and pincers, and the faint noises of activity pushed against her ears once more. She smelled burning, something like charred hair. Lily dropped the instrument quickly and again the sensory impressions ceased immediately. Unnerved, Lily stood with her back to the table, looking around herself. Here she felt very uneasy; the atmosphere was tense. Also, Raven was clearly visible in the light. He stood with arms folded some feet away, terrifyingly alien, yet weirdly familiar because of his feline features. He blinked at Lily, as if to reassure her. 'You're strange!' Lily said nervously. 'I want to get used to you, but it's difficult.' Raven merely blinked again, but the brief communication helped to alleviate Lily's unease. She walked down an aisle between two rows of tables, Raven following.

'This must have been where the Murkasters worked and conducted their secret research,' Lily said. 'Did you ever work here, Raven?' She did not expect an answer. 'I don't suppose Raven's your real name, is it. If I knew your real name, would you speak to me again?'

A low, rumbling sound erupted in Raven's chest. Lily realized with some amusement that he was purring. Was that supposed to make her feel better? So loud a purr sounded distinctly threatening. 'Owen would love to see all this,' she said. 'I wish he was here.'

The aisle opened out into a circular space, ringed by work-benches. In the centre of the circle, a drain was set into the floor. Above it stood a sinister rubber-topped gurney, with leather straps dangling from its sides. Looking at it, Lily felt sick. What would she hear and smell if she should touch the ancient rubber, the cracked leather? The urge to do so was great, so Lily hurried quickly through this area, keeping her eyes ahead.

It took ten minutes to cross the laboratory. Some of the things Lily saw fascinated her and drew her attention, others repulsed her and filled her with nausea. Good feelings came from the intricate models of inexplicable mechanisms, which she handled without fear, alert for the indistinct sounds that accompanied her contact with the objects. But there were other things, such as the snaking tubes of glass and rubber, the ranks of bottles filled with ancient, murky liquids, that she would not touch.

On one table stood an array of exquisitely fashioned, tiny glass bottles, filled with luminous liquids: blue, green, pink. Lily thought they looked like perfume bottles, and picked one of them up to sniff the contents. But when she removed the cork stopper, a fierce, sour stench puffed out that made her cry out. Sweat burst from the pores of her back and shoulders. She heard a terrible scream, as of an infant in great pain. Disgusted, Lily threw the little bottle on to the floor, where it smashed, releasing a series of heart-rending whimpers. *What had happened here*? In her heart, she knew. The experiments the Murkasters had conducted on their human servants had been to do with reproduction, the creation of hybrids, and the study of these processes. She could feel their dispassion. They had not been cruel, but unable to look upon humans as anything but inferior to themselves. Sickened, Lily ran the short distance left to reach the far side of the room. She wanted to cry, filled with an enervating despair. Raven came after her, touched her shoulder with his reassuring paw-hand. Lily reached up to stroke it, grateful for his presence. 'Were they bad people?' she asked him. 'Are all Grigori like them?' Raven was not purring now.

They came to a wide doorway, which gave access to a flight of broad stone steps, leading downwards. Lily was unhappy with having to go further underground. How much further down had the Murkasters tunnelled to hide their work-rooms? However, Raven was already descending the steps, making it clear that this was the direction Lily had to go. She was not sorry to leave the laboratory behind, although she was aware she might have to cross it again to leave the house. This was not a cheering thought. She decided that instead she must direct her attention towards what lay ahead.

The walls on either side of the steps were threaded with thin veins of light, which provided weak illumination. Lily wondered where the light came from. When she touched the walls, they did not feel warm. The air smelled earthy, with a hint of stagnant pond water. Soon, Lily thought she could hear a faint echo of running water and the steps became damp beneath her feet, slippery with slime. The walls, too, were streaked with oily, fungal growths, channelled with thin streams of water. Lily was sure she must be passing deep beneath the lake in Long Eden's grounds, although she had lost her sense of direction since descending the first flight of stairs to the work-room. The atmosphere had become very oppressive, and Lily was aware of a great weight pressing down upon her. She heard a low, booming sound and couldn't dispel the image of the ceiling suddenly opening up above her, and water crashing down to drown and break her body. A seed of terror opened up within her. She wanted to turn back, run through the hideous laboratory, fly up the long flight of steps, scurry through the listening house of ghosts, find the sunlight. But she could not stop walking.

Gradually, the steps became shallower, until they levelled out into a wide tunnel. Here the walls were still plastered, although the plaster was distinctly leprous, parts of it having fallen away in chunks. Lily could see that at one time the walls had been covered in paintings similar in design to the carved panels she had seen in the house, but twenty years of neglect had taken their toll, and now little remained intact. Lights were set into the ceiling in glass globes, but they didn't look as if they were powered by electricity, being too similar to daylight, yet somehow flickering like the flames of candles. There were no longer veins of light in the walls, but that might be because they had been damaged by the damp.

The sound of water was much louder now – a muted roar – and within this sound Lily thought she could hear the echoes of cries that might have been human or the screams of birds.

Ahead of Lily, Raven ducked down beneath the lintel of an open doorway and disappeared. Lily disliked his habit of vanishing without waiting for her, but was still nervous of being alone and hurried to catch him up. She emerged into a round antechamber, which had a high, domed roof. The light was greener here. Raven had positioned himself in the centre of the room, and stood once more with folded arms, as if waiting for Lily to make her investigations of the surroundings. Around the edge of the chamber were seven columns of a soapy-looking green stone, and to the left a great closed door. Opposite the entrance, another tunnel led out of the chamber.

Lily went up to one of the columns and touched it. As she did so, the stone resonated with a musical note. Hastily, she withdrew her hand and the sound ceased abruptly. 'It's like the things in the work-room,' Lily said to the silent Raven. 'When I touch something, a sound comes.' She went to another column and put her hand against the stone. This column also emitted a note, but at a different frequency. It sounded as if it came from a musical instrument, but Lily could not think of what kind. She dared to keep her hand upon the column for a minute or so, and closed her eyes. In her mind, she saw seven shadowy figures, wearing long, fringed robes like Raven's, coming into the chamber. They were tall people, Grigori: three women and four men. Each member of the group approached a separate column and embraced it. To Lily it seemed as if they were in some way connecting with the columns and absorbing their distinct tones. She was sure that one of the group was Kashday. She opened her eyes and withdrew her hand. What was the purpose of this room? She was convinced Raven could tell her, but knew that interrogating him was pointless. For whatever reason, he was refusing to communicate with her in her own language. She eyed the cat-man speculatively. Had he always been here in Little Moor? Why had he appeared at Low Mede, and, more importantly, was Verity aware of what kind of creature he was? Somehow, Lily doubted that. Verity was ordinary, a mortal woman, whereas Lily was half-Grigori. Raven had revealed himself to her because she was different. I am becoming part of something, Lily thought. Yes, it is becoming easier now to accept what I am. I am not afraid of it. She held out her arms and threw back her head, spoke aloud to the sentinel columns. 'Show me. Show me everything.' Raven uttered a chirruping sound, which Lily took as approbation.

She walked around the chamber, touching each column to conjure its note. By keeping one hand on the column behind her, and reaching forward to the next, she could create a chord. The sounds were beautiful; she wished she could activate them all at once. What would happen then? Something she could not even imagine. When she reached the door on the left of the chamber, she saw that its central panel bore a carving of a cat-man like Raven. Perhaps it even *was* Raven. Lily tried to open the door, but Raven uttered an admonishing or warning growl. A flash of light burst before Lily's eyes.

In her mind, she saw the door fly open, and knew that the stairway behind it led up to the temple she had dreamed about, on the island in the lake. She also knew she must not go up there. It wasn't dangerous, but neither was it her destination. She stepped back from it, her fingers tingling. Raven uttered a soft, mewing sound and Lily went up to him. She felt compelled to put her arms around him and stood for a moment with her head resting just above his belly. She could hear the noises his body was making, ordinary sounds of digestion. How could such an unbelievable creature be alive and breathing, his body behaving in the same ways as her own? Surely, he could only be a phantom or a visualized thought, yet he felt so real. Raven put his hands upon her head and lifted her face to look into her eyes. What was he thinking? Lily wondered. After only a moment, he gently disengaged himself from her arms and gestured for her to follow him into the tunnel on the other side of the chamber. For a moment, Lily hesitated. Despite her earlier feelings of belonging, she felt suddenly that something hideous was waiting for her up ahead. Raven seemed to sense her misgivings and uttered soft meows of encouragement. *I am with you. I will protect you.* Reluctantly, Lily followed him.

The corridor beyond was not as well lit, and Lily stumbled as she jogged behind Raven. He appeared to be hurrying now, as if something important was waiting for their arrival. The floor began to slope upwards, the stone no longer damp beneath their feet. Raven continually increased his pace, until Lily was forced to run if she wanted to keep him in sight. The floor slanted so steeply, her legs began to ache. She cried out, 'Wait!' but Raven ignored her. Just as Lily decided she'd have to sit down and get her breath back, whether Raven waited for her or not, the tunnel opened out into another chamber. Lily stopped dead at the threshold, breathing hard, her hands braced upon her knees. Her whole body was soaked in sweat, yet she felt cold. There was a heavy pressure in the atmosphere which leadened her limbs. After a few moments, Lily raised her head, bracing herself for whatever she'd have to face. She recognized the chamber immediately.

This is it, the end of my journey. I'm here now. Something will happen.

The ceiling was high and domed, shaped like a beehive. There was little light, and although Lily could see that the walls were painted with looming figures, she could not make out the details. The rough marble floor was deeply grooved with concentric rings, each of which was at least three inches across. Lily thought a person could easily trip crossing the floor, if they didn't tread carefully. In the centre of the chamber was a wide pit, ringed with rough-hewn ornamental stones, about six inches in diameter. Interspersed at regular intervals between the stones were seven pedestals, each supporting a huddled, shapeless form, wrapped in ancient grey and brown rags. They looked like petrified mummies, all facing the centre of the pit, as if whatever had once burned there had frozen them in time. Lily could see it now, pulsing in the middle of the pit, a seed of light, a burning, icy-blue glow.

I have been here before . . .

Lily remembered the time when Peverel Othman had made love to her at the High Place, and her visualized journey beneath the ground to wake the sacred flame. She had come to this place then: the hidden sanctuary of the Murkasters' power source. Here, her father and his family had once enacted their secret rituals and the flame had burned high. Lily straightened up and stepped across the first ring on the floor. She kept her eyes fixed warily on the ragged shapes standing on the pedestals, but they appeared to be dead, or perhaps only half-crumbled statues wrapped in cloth. The figures were hideous, yet somehow fascinating. Lily felt a pull of repugnance start up in her belly as she looked at them, but was drawn to approach them. Carefully, she stepped over the grooves in the floor until she was close enough to touch the hunched figure that stood on the nearest pedestal. It emanated an acrid, powdery, dusty smell. With a trembling hand, Lily reached out and stroked the rotting cloth. Fragments of fibre came away beneath her fingers. 'They *are* mummies,' she said to herself, and shuddered, rubbing her hand on the front of her dress.

Raven had taken up a position opposite Lily, on the other side of the fire-pit. His arms were folded. 'They are guardians, like myself,' he said.

Lily looked up at him and smiled in relief. 'Ah, so now you can speak again!'

'You must wait now,' Raven said.

'For what? Will you tell me why I'm here, or what's going to happen?'

'She will come,' Raven answered shortly.

'She?' said Lily.

Raven sat down, cross-legged, outside the ring of stones surrounding the fire-pit. Lily did likewise. It seemed as if a faint thread of incense perfume was creeping into the room, gradually extinguishing the smells of rot and age. A ritual was about to begin. Lily closed her eyes and presently began to dream.

Chapter Thirty-four

Ishtahar

I am the daughter of Hebob, the farmer, who is held in esteem by the Shining Ones, the Lords who live in the High Place, beyond the lower plains. My father has spreading lands, here below the mountains. The Shining Ones came here in the time of my grandmother's mother. Before this time, it is said, we were like animals. Now we are more like them, the Tall Ones, the Anannage. They are very beautiful, but we see them rarely. Where they came from, nobody knows, but they have given us the knowledge of the mystery they call their Source, which is beyond the light of the stars. Perhaps the Anannage came down from this unfathomable place themselves, or perhaps they were once like us, smaller people who changed. The Anannage tell us that we will change, and that one day our children will spread throughout the world, like they have, taking knowledge with them.

I am the Oracle of my people, the gate to the starry firmament. Without women of my kind, the knowledge and science that the Anannage teach us cannot be practised. I am sacred.

Our temple has a tier of sloping roofs, and stands in the centre of a sea of corn, approached by four radial paths. The people of the lower plains come to it at sunset, when the swelling harvest moon hangs her belly in the sky, red as the blood of birthing. Tomorrow is the day of harvest and now I am priestess of the festival, giving sacrifice before the cutting. Here, in the temple, my sisters have helped me to feed the perpetual flame, and now it burns high, a blue blade of light. Usually, it is small, but it is never extinguished. The men sit around me in a circle as I enter the flame. They are farmers and astronomer-priests; my father is among them. At this time of year, my people need guidance on how to align the position of the harvested crops with the right constellations. It is of great importance.

My sisters fan me with sweet incense, their low, lovely voices taking me deep into the sacred trance. Through me, the Renowned Old Ones, ancestors of the Anannage, will speak. I channel their wisdom to the men, yet the meaning of the words I speak is hidden from me. I am the fount of all knowledge. My womb is the all-seeing Eye. I am the stargate, whose mind can pass without challenge through the portal of the stellar veils. Without me there can be no commerce with the ancestors, yet the men will not share their knowledge with me, or my sisters. It is forbidden.

The flame burns higher, excited by the voices of my sisters, their supple genuflexions. Their ankles are braceleted with bells, which utter sacred music. Their long hair sways like unravelled linen; their faces are veiled to prevent their breath polluting the flame. I feel the stars descend upon me, their white fire in my skin, their empyreal voices in my head, behind my eyes. It comes to me, this cold white feast of knowledge, yet I am only the taster, who must pass the plate on to the men who wait to feed. Why am I denied? I know I have the power to go further than my elders would allow. I can feel their sacred staffs pointed towards the flame, pointing towards me, and it feels like the weight of chains. Why can my spirit not fly free and move through the sacred spheres of knowledge without the commandments of men? I would bestow my power to all my sisters, and become queen of my people. The men can feel this. This is why I am denied. They fear me for they know nothing of the power of being female, generator of life and channeller of wisdom. They fear all women. Yes. It is this.

My spirit enters the gate in the constellation of Orion. The Renowned Old Ones approach me: I can sense their flaming presence, yet cannot see them with my eyes of flesh.

My lips move around sounds which have no meaning to me. The men say, 'She speaks in tongues,' and they pour sand upon the floor in precise patterns to record my words. Later, they will argue over the symbols and signs, until they are sure they know their secrets. The secrets will not be revealed to me.

Before me: this beautiful being whom I cannot understand. Neither man nor woman, there is no distinction in their kind. All I feel is the resonance of the tonal sounds they generate and their invisible hands upon my brow, igniting the fibres of my soul. And the words come, passing into the world and the ears of men.

I beseech the ancestors: 'Reveal to *me* the sacred names, for I would use them well. Give me the knowledge that men covet. Am I not worthy? Do you not look upon me with love and give me the touch of your holy hands?'

But still the words that tumble from my mouth are meaningless to me. If I try hard enough, will the forms of the words change in my head, become real? No. I have tried. I always try.

The Renowned Old Ones draw away from me, and it is time to retreat from the stargate. I feel the pull in my skin, dragging my soul back into the temple. And yet, as my spirit travels, I sense an unseen Presence: something different. It seems to me as if a voice is speaking, and, at last, the words have meaning: 'You will gather the harvest of knowledge through your own power, the power

that you have yet to discover, a power I have yet to use.'
The voice is male, and rings like a clarion across the
heavens, yet whispers as soft as the feet of a mouse
running over the grain. Now I fly across the rippling
fields of corn, and my spirit's eye can see the roofs of the
temple, ruddy in the harvest light. A perfume rises from
the corn, the smell of ozone, a salty, male scent. And on
the horizon, rising from the jagged mountains of heaven,
the dwelling-place of the Shining Ones. A yearning presence envelops me.

I rise from my trance and my sisters hold out their
hands, with their henna-red palms, to lead me from the
flame. Already the men have dismissed me from their
attention and apply themselves to debate, arguing over
the patterns in the sand. I want to spit upon their
symbols, muddle the pictograms with my hands so they
cannot read them. The Presence is still with me: I can
feel it all around. Something is coming.

Brushing aside my sisters, I am drawn out into the
immensity of the spreading fields. Here I am so small it is
a marvel. The grain sways for as far as I can see, and in
the eastern distance the mountains are dark and secret
against the sequins of the stars. It is as if the mountains
are hanging above the earth, not part of it at all. The
smell of the sky is overpowering out here. The earth god
holds sway across the fields. I walk into the corn, and it
caresses my body as I glide along the narrow path
towards the mountains.

How dare they deny me! Within the words I give to
them are the answers to the greatest questions: where we
come from and what we are. The men are too stupid to
see this, yet they are unwilling to question their gods, the
Anannage, on these mysteries. Instead, they use me,
unaware that I have the potential to be greater than
them. Fools! I throw back my head to the sky and

scream in silence, Give *me* the answers! Then, as I lower my eyes, they rest once again upon the mountains, the High Place. Women are forbidden to go there, too. I have never gazed upon one of the Anannage at close quarters. On the rare occasions they come to us, I have been shut inside the house with the other women. We looked through the slats across the windows and saw their tall shapes, but that was all. Now, as I walk this path, I defy the elders and begin to sing the forbidden tones of the Renowned Old Ones. My song is my greatest gift, and I sing it from my soul. I sing it to him whose presence is with me, and whose body is coming to me. As my song reaches its highest pitch, the tones rising through the sacred scale, a blinding light fills my mind and a powerful love fills my heart. He is coming to meet me, he is coming from the High Place, and when he arrives . . .? Oh, by all the names of all the gods, sacred and profane, I feel his soul: already it passes through mine like a veil of incense smoke, like a shower of rain at dawn. It shouts to me. May the Great Lady give me strength to bear his beauty and his power!

There. I see him upon the path, tall and pale, his robes swinging about him. He has heard my soul-song calling to him, I know this. As he draws closer, I can see that he wears a feathered cloak which hangs about him like wings. They are vulture feathers: black as night. Beneath the cloak, his robe, as I first thought, is white, belted with gold. Nearer. I can see his feathered head-dress, the plumes nodding against the night sky. He is so tall. Am I afraid? He wears the bones of a snake, wound around and around his long neck, the brittle, ivory head of the serpent gripping in its jaws the bony links of its tail. The symbol stitched in gold upon his breast is that of the Watchers. I have seen that seal before, and heard men mutter about it. They watch over us and take word of our activities back to the mountains. Usually, they hide themselves in clouds. But there are no clouds to conceal the one who comes to me now. He is a Watcher, high-ranking among his kind. Nearer. His face. I can see his face. What is it that I see? He is a serpent-man, a feathered serpent, yet how lovely to behold. His eyes are like the eyes of a viper, filled with an ancient wisdom. My knees are weak, but I must not stumble. I must walk, walk towards him. He is looking up at the sky now, towards Orion. How bright the constellations shine this night, brighter than ever before. When he speaks, his voice will be familiar, yet we have never met. The smell coming from his body is the salt smell of the sky after a storm; it is so strong now, the essence of manhood.

Here: we meet. In the mid-path between the High and the Low. He looks down at me from his great height, and it is as if he is afraid. A flame of golden light burns around his body. Does it burn with desire? I have called him, and his body heard me.

'Are you my god in heaven?' I ask him.

He holds out his hands to me and I take them in my own. 'I can be, if you want me to be,' he says, and there is a smile on his face. His hair falls from beneath the plumes on his head like a cascade of flowing white feathers. His eyes, even in the dusk, are the deepest blue.

In contrast to him, I am female power; the residue of Orion's energy hangs about my body like a veil. He recognizes this. I know it. He knows my function. Is this real? Am I still in trance? I want this man and the things that he might teach me. He enfolds me in his cloak, wings wrapped about my body. Pressed against him, I can hear his beating heart, feel the hardness in his loins.

I say to him, 'If you are my heavenly god, tell me the

hidden names, tell me what the men of the temple refuse to tell me.'

He takes my head between his long hands and looks into my face. 'You have a need,' he says, 'as I do, to experience that which is forbidden to you. If you, my lady, give me the power of the earth and all the fire within her, I will do anything you ask of me. My heaven is cold, my wings have grown tired of traversing the astral spheres and constellations, and my heart grows sick of the commandments from my brethren. The smell of the earth is ripe around you. The fruit of your body I long to taste. Seek not the stars for me, Ishtahar, oracle of Hebob. Lay open for me the depths of the earth, and the richness of her power. Please do not deny me the knowledge of this pleasure.'

There is knowledge, then, that the Anannage deny their own.

He lifts me in his arms and puts his mouth against my own. My hands steal beneath his eburneous mane. I press my wrists against the heat of his neck. His skin is smooth, like marble. He carries me into the corn and lays me down there. In the stillness of the night, I can hear the soft voices of my sisters in the temple, and the sound of it makes me aware of my flesh, my existence in the world. The air is cool now, like an urgent hand shaking the sleeper to wakefulness. The Shining One blots out the stars above me and I feel a fear rise up within my breast, like a serpent arranging itself to strike. He feels it, too. As I start away from him, he leans down and grips my hand. 'No, do not be afraid of me. For this act, you will be venerated as the highest goddess for evermore.'

I have been told the serpents are sacred. To lie with this serpent-man must be a holy act. Our love has been waiting, like a star ready to fall. It is inexorable.

I take him in my arms and he breathes in my ear the first of the forbidden words. His name: Shemyaza.

Chapter Thirty-five

Same day: Little Moor (continued)

Barbara Eager was overseeing operations at The White House. To a casual observer, it might have appeared that she was no different than she'd ever been, but Mrs Moon knew otherwise. Whispers had been circulating around the village all day, a condensation of rumours that had flown for a couple of weeks now. The Grigori were back. Like Eva Manden, Mrs Moon had a parent who had once been a Grigori dependant and, also like Eva, she welcomed their return with mixed feelings. Still, there was little anyone could do about the situation. If they'd come back, they'd come back, and that was that. The Eager woman was charmed, all right. You could see it on her like a dark glow. She was hysterical, but managed to hide it.

Peverel Othman made an appearance at six o'clock, just as a couple of Perks boys were seeing to the barbecue in the garden. A few people had already begun to arrive, mostly oldsters, although a couple of new families were present, who had brought their children with them. Mrs Moon, watching from the kitchen window at the back of the pub, shook her head at that, and pursed her lips. Fodder! she thought, but it was not her place to judge.

Othman went up to Barbara who was supervising the placement of bread rolls on a trestle table, which was covered with a glowing white cloth.

'Is everything ready?' he asked.

Barbara jumped at the sound of his voice, then turned to him with a smile. 'Yes, Pev. Everything.'

He touched her face. 'Good.'

'Is Louis coming?' Barbara asked.

'Later,' Othman replied. 'We shall all be down later.'

'What are you doing?' Barbara's eyes became momentarily alert.

Othman smiled at her gently. 'A ceremony at the High Place. Don't worry. Soon, all shall be as it was before.'

Before when? Barbara couldn't help thinking, but the thought was quickly smothered. Misgivings had been tugging at her heart all day, indistinct fears and doubts, yet her body felt exuberant and sleek, more beautiful than it had felt for years. Barbara could sense youth creeping back into her bones and flesh. Whatever she had involved herself in, it had been a voluntary act. She must accept the consequences.

All the oldsters present were watching Peverel Othman with greedy, inquisitive eyes. He acknowledged each of them with eye contact, knowing that to risk more would prove to be a waste of his energy. Just the slightest touch could set them off sucking at his soul.

Emma Manden appeared at the edge of the garden, dressed in a long, man's raincoat, her abundant hair curled Forties style around her shoulders, her lips a bruised smudge in the artificial light. Othman noticed her and thought that she looked as if she was getting ready to leave the place. Her attire spoke to him of stations and partings. She was obviously playing another role from her memory.

He summoned her: 'Emma!'

She marched over to him briskly. 'Well, everyone's here! So what happens now?'

Othman led Emma aside. 'In a few minutes, I shall leave for the High Place. I'll be back in an hour or so.'

'Can't I come with you?' Emma's eyes were defiant.

Othman hesitated, then touched Emma's arm. 'My

dear, this is a man's ritual. I'm sorry. I wish you could be present, but it is impossible.'

'I see.' Emma narrowed her eyes. He is a little afraid of me, she thought. He was not as confident as he should be, appearing too nervy and jumpy.

'It's up to you to keep everyone happy here, Emma,' Othman said. 'I'm relying on you.'

Emma shuddered involuntarily. In an hour Daniel Cranton would be dead. She chided herself for feeling uneasy about it. In the past, she'd been aware of human deaths in Long Eden. Was this one so different?

'Where is Lily?' Othman asked her.

Emma shrugged. 'I don't know. She wasn't at the cottage when I left. I think she's hiding. It's frightening her, all this.'

'She's just jealous,' Othman said, with a smile. 'She wanted to be the one to empower the flame.'

And Emma thought, how can you be so wrong? She felt no fear for Lily, and had not even bothered to search for her. Othman clearly considered her unimportant to the proceedings, intent as he was on his 'man's ritual'. There was a tiny seed of feeling within Emma whispering that Lily might spring some surprises of her own. Emma did not question this. She only thought of their brief conversations concerning the key to Long Eden, and harboured a cautious hope. She realized then that she had faith in Lily. 'Owen is ready,' she said. 'I've dressed him and put him in the kitchen.'

'Thank you,' Othman replied.

Emma watched him leave the garden of The White House, thinking, He's not as clever as he believes himself to be.

Othman prowled the lanes of Little Moor, dragging his intentions behind him like smoke. The air was like needles against his skin, invisible pricks of light. He sensed a wave about to crest, a veil about to tear. *Soon.* Like Emma, he shuddered, half in anticipation, half in dread. He could not go back on his decision.

Ray Perks was lurking on the lawn of the Winter cottage, his two cronies, Bobby and Luke, skulking behind him. Othman presumed Emma had directed them to be present. Although he had not thought of this, he saw the sense of it. They were Owen's minions and protectors, always had been. This was their hour, too, and later, if Owen was wise, he would reward them for their dumb loyalty.

Inside the cottage, Owen sat at the kitchen table, staring into space. He was dressed in loose white trousers and shirt – presumably, a hasty costume Emma or Lily had put together. Owen's hair was a shocking aureola of light around his head and shoulders. He appeared blind, or mindless. Othman did not bother to address any remarks to Owen, but simply raised him by the arm and led him into the garden. Here Othman directed Ray and the others to take Owen to the High Place. He would meet them there shortly.

For a few minutes, he sat upon the lawn in the cottage garden, composing his thoughts, condensing his strength. The sky shivered with dark colours, the stars were tiny shrieks of radiance, each proclaiming a legend, a history, a tragedy. The constellation of Orion hung like an omen high in the sky. Othman could feel them all converging on the High Place: Owen and his acolytes, Louis with his sacrificial son. Tonight the veils between the worlds were thin. He would tear them open, blast them apart, clear the astral rags that blocked his way to the gateway. When it finally opened, understanding would come to him. He felt nervous, exhilarated, as if held in the throes of a great and powerful love.

607

As he walked down the lane towards Herman's Wood, Peverel Othman's thoughts were entirely on the ritual to come. He did not notice, nor could perceive, the liquid shadow that followed him. No unearthly predators, but Emma Manden, acute and aware, covering her own back, intent on seeing with her own eyes what would happen at the High Place.

As Othman clambered up through the bracken, figures were silhouetted against the orange-purple sky at the summit of the hill. All stood motionless, as if unable to move or act until he arrived. The sky, the earth, the air, were full of a vast imminence, of the event waiting to happen. Othman felt breathless; hysteria scratched at his control. His fingers tingled, his belly churned with acid, his eyes ached. He felt like a vessel waiting to be filled, or a filled vessel waiting to be uncorked, to issue froth and foam in ferocious spurts. All eyes turned towards him as he crested the hill. Earlier in the day, he had visited the High Place to make certain preparations for the night. An unlit bonfire stood ready in the centre of the circle. This he intended to be the gateway to the flame below. Owen stood before the cone of branches and moss, his eyes downcast. Perks and his two companions were stationed around the edge of the circle, while Louis Cranton stood just outside, opposite Othman on the brow of the hill, his hands upon Daniel's shoulders, who stood before him. Daniel, dosed with haoma, did not appear tranced like Owen, but aware and serene. It was almost, Othman thought, as if he knew what fate awaited him and accepted it. That, of course, could not be possible.

While the others waited in silence, Othman lit the bonfire. It did not crackle up greedily, despite the dryness of the tinder, but snapped and fizzed in a sullen manner, a dark red glow forming at its heart. All was as it should be.

Othman raised his arms, causing Owen to lift his head languidly. There seemed no recognition in his eyes, just stupefaction.

'Tonight,' Othman said, 'we meet to reawaken the flame below. The power shall rise, and the gateway open.' He lowered his arms. 'Louis, bring forth the lamb.'

Hesitantly, Louis pushed Daniel before him into the circle. The dull ruby light of the fire did not seem to touch the boy. He was the lamb to the slaughter, pure, beautiful, burning with his own white light. Othman experienced a twinge which was almost regret; all that potential soon to be quenched, extinguished, gutted. He allowed himself to bask in the ray of pure love for Daniel which speared his being. Then he turned away to face the dark of the forest below, to invoke the elements.

In the eastern quarter, the direction of air, a wind started up as Othman chanted the invocation. It stirred the high branches of the trees, caused the bonfire to grow momentarily brighter. In the north, the direction of earth, Othman's words conjured movement from the leaf mould at his feet, and the phallus of the green wood thrust forth from the ground. In the south, for water, rain began to fall, but only on that side of the circle. In the west, as Othman conjured fire, earthlights flickered among the debris of the forest floor, and the bonfire in the centre flared up in great tongues of flame. It had begun.

Below the High Place, numb in the temple chamber, Lily opened her eyes. At first, she felt disorientated, unsure of her surroundings, still lost in the scrolls of history, reliving an ancient story of love. *Ishtahar*. She stood up. The air was warmer now, the incense perfume pervaded by the smells of corn and ozone. Across the fire-pit, Raven also got to his feet. Lily began to cry. Her heart was filled with grief, a great sense of loss. She ached for the arms of the Shining One. Shemyaza and Ishtahar's story had ended in death and tragedy. All that was left was the memory of their great love, and the peoples who had come after them. Grigori. Lily herself.

Blinking, Lily stared into the perpetual flame. What use was this knowledge to her? She knew now that her mother and Kashday Murkaster had in some way seen themselves as reflections, or avatars, of Ishtahar and Shemyaza. Helen had tried to reopen the stargate which the Renowned Old Ones had closed after Shemyaza and his brethren had committed transgressions with human women, turning away from the power of the stars and seeking the female power of the earth. Helen had failed. The flame here burned weakly, Lily understood that now. She held out her hand to it, willing it to reawaken. She felt that if the flame could fill her being it would burn away her grief.

Suddenly, without warning of any kind, the flame made a brief fizzing noise and then roared up towards the ceiling of the chamber in a buzzing blue-white column. Lily yelped in surprise, and cowered away, covering her head with her arms. Across from her, Raven uttered a panicked snarl and dropped to all fours, his ears back. The chamber was filled with a sound like electricity crackling. Lily looked up and saw the flame spattering across the ceiling. *It is awake. Did I wake it?*

Something creaked and rustled beside her. Lily shuffled backwards, her feet stumbling in the grooves on the stone floor. Around her, on their pedestals, the ancient guardians of the flame began to stir. As they stretched their desiccated forms, powder crumbled from between the cloths around their bodies. Withered limbs creaked, ruined throats strove to make sound. Lily covered her ears with her hands for she could not bear the dreadful squeaky whisperings. Something was happening above her; she could sense it. She wanted to flee the chamber, but also felt compelled to remain, even though she was afraid. Raven slunk around the circle and stationed himself behind her. She was grateful for his presence, his protection. Glancing up, she saw the domed ceiling of the chamber was laced with cracks. As the blue flame beat against it, chunks of plaster and stone began to crumble away, dropping to the floor where they exploded in clouds of dust. The flame was trying to break free into the world. I have done this, Lily thought.

The long black car pulled up on to the sloping drive of The White House. Aninka was the first to get out. The air smelled of cooking meat and smoke. Lahash helped Taziel out of the back seat. Aninka noticed Lahash was wearing black leather gloves. She shuddered, even though the air was steamy and hot.

'Stay behind me,' Lahash told her.

At sundown, Lahash had coerced Taziel into investigating the village psychically. He had winced and shuddered as his inner senses glanced off the presence of Peverel Othman. 'The place is pervaded by him,' he'd said, shivering. 'Everywhere . . . The old ones gather at The White House, they wait for their replenishment. It is there. There.'

Using his binoculars, Lahash had picked out the three-storey hotel, and had even read its name. The White House. 'There is a fire built in the garden,' he'd said, and turned to Aninka. 'Something is going to happen there.'

So The White House had drawn them. Now Aninka
could feel something gathering in the air around her. It
made her feel both nauseous and excited. Was Peverel
Othman in the garden behind the hotel?

'He might have left guardians,' Lahash said. 'Follow
me, and be careful. Do not say anything to anybody.'

We look so conspicuous, Aninka thought. Surely, the
first person we meet is going to challenge us?

Lahash led the way around the side of the building.
Aninka saw a dark crowd milling around, barely illuminated by garden spotlights. Lahash drew them all
against the hedge. It seemed no one was paying much
attention to anything that moved outside their immediate
circle.

'Taz,' Lahash whispered. 'Read these people.'

Taziel looked ready to collapse. His skin was damp.
'Dependants,' he said, almost immediately. 'Many of
them. Waiting.'

Lahash glanced at Aninka. 'Murkaster dependants.
They have been left here to rot.'

'And now Peverel Othman has found them,' Aninka
concluded.

Lahash shook his head. 'They must be destroyed.'

Aninka shuddered. 'Why? What have they done?' She
had been taught to respect dependants.

'They are Othman's potential army,' Lahash replied.
'Also, I have my instructions.' He threw back his head
and pressed one hand against his eyes. Aninka saw his
lips moving silently. She knew in her heart what he was
doing. She could feel a surge of energy, a sense of
movement and of summoning. On the hilltops around
Little Moor, the Kerubim stirred, unfolded their wings,
flexed their claws. They flowed towards The White
House, came stamping like legions, floating softly like
moths. Aninka thought of the gentle friends she had

made in Cresterfield, their hideous end. Would this have been their fate, too, if the Parzupheim had deigned to interfere in Othman's activities sooner? What about herself? Could Kerubim make distinctions once unleashed to destroy?

A woman dressed in a pale-coloured trouser-suit with a long, flowing waistcoat had noticed them. She came towards them with enquiry in her eyes. 'Can I help you? I'm the proprietor of this establishment.' Her voice reeked of exclusion. What she was really saying was 'Get out!'

'Good evening,' Lahash said, suddenly suave and urbane. 'We are looking for accommodation, actually.'

The woman subjected them to a penetrating glance. 'I see. Well, we are having a bit of a party this evening. If you'll excuse me, I'll find someone to book you in and show you to your rooms.' She smiled. 'I'm sorry, but the party is private.'

Lahash raised his hands. 'I quite understand. Before you go, could you tell me the best places to go sightseeing around here?'

Aninka was surprised by Lahash's behaviour. What was he up to? The woman seemed not at all inclined to be drawn into conversation, and no wonder, if she was a part of whatever Othman was planning. Still, despite an expression of annoyance, she began to list a few places of interest. What she could not see was what was invading her garden. Perhaps only Grigori could see them. As the woman tried to satisfy Lahash's request, to get rid of him, Aninka watched the Kerubim manifest as translucent creatures of light around them. They were enormous, hideous, beautiful. With their tongues of fire, they licked certain people in the crowd, breathed a Kerubic breath upon them. These victims fell to the ground, crumbled away, as the false life they had been given was taken from them. No chance of replenishment. No more. Younger people, apparently oblivious of what was happening, stepped over the piles of dust and rag to reach the barbecue, paper plates held in their hands, completely oblivious of what was occurring. Only a couple of the children looked anxious, glancing around themselves as if something had whispered their names in an earthy voice.

Taziel leaned against Aninka's shoulder, shielding his eyes from what was happening. Perhaps his groaning sigh alerted the landlady, perhaps she was Grigori-touched enough to sense all was not well. She glanced behind herself nervously, then back at Lahash.

'You are . . .' she began, her face creasing in anxiety. 'You are *one of them*!'

'Where is Peverel Othman?' Lahash suddenly demanded, aware his cover was blown.

'What do you want with him?' The woman's voice was suddenly harsh. Aninka saw, in her mind, a vision of a cornered she-cat, all claws and defences.

'We are colleagues of his,' Lahash answered smoothly. 'Please answer me . . . I'm sorry, I didn't catch your name.'

The woman took a step backwards. 'He's not here.'

'Then be so good as to tell me where I can find him.'

Behind the landlady, the Kerubim had begun to rear up against the sky, roaring out their triumph in voices that could not be heard by human ears. Aninka put her hands over her ears, while Taziel cried out in pain. Lahash made a gesture, and the monstrous creatures fell silent, motionless sentinels around the garden. The woman had not answered Lahash.

'If you will not tell me, I shall be forced to take the information from you by other means,' he said in an affable voice. 'Please don't be difficult.'

The woman threw back her head and flared her nostrils. When she spoke, it was with scorn. 'He's staying at a house called Low Mede further down the village. Try there. If he's not in, well . . .' She shrugged. 'He could have gone anywhere. I hardly know him.'

'You had better be telling the truth,' Lahash said with a grin. 'Otherwise, we shall be back to talk to you again. Now, where is this house you spoke of?'

Barbara watched the three strangers walk away from The White House. She knew that they meant danger to Peverel Othman. She had no choice but to go to the High Place and warn him, even though he had instructed her to wait for him at the barbecue. As she hurried down the lane, she kept visualizing an enormous hourglass in her head, the sands running quickly through its waist. For a moment, she paused, listened to the beat of her heart, the healthy sighs of her breath. The night was hot and still around her. I could go back, she thought, I could go back now and no one would be any the wiser. It will be over soon.

She even looked over her shoulder, where the ruddy light of the bonfire in her garden burned behind the hedges. Barney was there, she could go back to Barney. But Louis was waiting at the High Place, and perhaps in danger, as Peverel Othman was. Barney or Louis? After brief consideration, Barbara resumed her pace in the direction of the High Place. There was regret in her heart, but only a little.

At the High Place, the preliminary invocations had been made, the correct atmosphere induced. An essence of incense mingled with the scent of ripening fruit and pine, underscored by a hint of sweet corruption. Ray Perks and his two friends still guarded the outer limits of the circle, their hands clasped in front of them, their heads bowed. They did not look at what was happening in front of them. Louis stood to one side of the bonfire, Othman to the other. At his feet, Daniel lay naked, his eyes focused on the stars. Owen knelt between Daniel's legs, his body twitching as if being whipped by invisible flails. His fingers clawed the dirt, his lips drawn back into a snarl. Othman stared down at him from an expressionless mask. His eyes burned red with the reflection of firelight. Slowly, he raised his arms and with a final glance at Owen, threw back his head. '*Drauga! Druj! Renen! Drauga! Druj! Renen!*' The bonfire hissed and crackled, its red flames purple at their hearts. As Othman repeated the chant, Louis's lips began to move silently. Owen's back arched as if someone, or something, had grabbed hold of his hair. He cried out, a bleat of pain.

Daniel closed his eyes. If he could only shut himself away from all this, hide his being deep within his mind, he might survive. He had never heard the words Othman was chanting before, but he knew their meaning: 'Falsehood, lies, violence.' Something hideous would come, something beyond human endurance. Daniel had realized that Owen was no longer the person he knew and loved, but a stranger, Othman's cat's-paw. It would be useless to appeal to him for help. He had no will of his own any longer. As if sensing Daniel's thoughts, Owen growled like a dog and lunged forward, curling his hands around Daniel's throat. Daniel tried to struggle, to rip the constricting fingers away, but Owen was filled with unnatural strength. Daniel gasped for breath, his eyes filled with red light like a film of blood. Owen's eyes glowed like neon violet through the darkness. His engorged cock slid inside Daniel's oiled body like a blade or a tongue of flame.

Othman could feel the presence forming around him.

He had attracted the interest of the being he was trying to invoke. 'Ahriman!' he screamed in his mind. 'Come to me. Take this offering!' At his feet, Owen Winter made love to his lover, but it was a lie, a travesty of love. Around him in the air, Othman felt the imminence of the false prophet, the embodiment of falsehood, untruth and destructive love. If there were tears upon the face of the lamb, then it was only fitting. Everything was drawing to a close, a climax. When the Ahriman manifested and took the sacrifice, then the flame would be unleashed.

Daniel felt as if he was nothing more than a column of pain. He could not hate Owen for his actions, but felt a crushing disappointment that his belief in Owen had been misguided. This clawing, grunting, thrusting creature, this beast, was not the person Daniel had known, and yet, maybe he was now experiencing the truth of the Grigori, the stronger blood that drenched the humanity in Owen's veins. Only hope sustained him. Perhaps, if he kept quiet, and made no fuss, this grotesque parody of love would cease and whatever ends Othman hoped to achieve would be consummated. Then it might be possible for Daniel to escape with his life. He sensed that if he fought against what was happening now, he would be killed outright. Opening his eyes, he looked past Owen's moving silhouette and saw Othman leaning over them. To Daniel, it looked as if Othman was now over eight feet tall. His face was a leering mask, all vestige of beauty fled. That is the truth of you, Daniel thought, and gleaned a faint satisfaction from it. He was amazed at how clear his head felt. Whatever was being done to his body, his mind was free, serene. He could even scoff at Othman's demonic ritual. What did he hope to achieve? Nothing lasting could ever come of this. If it succeeded, Othman would only destroy himself.

Almost as if Othman could sense Daniel's thoughts, he uttered a guttural snarl and sprang into a stooped position. Before Daniel's eyes, his outline shimmered and was distorted. *Scoff at me now, pretty boy!* He was a demon with goat's legs, a lion's head, and a serpent was wrapped around his body, breathing fire. Daniel forced himself not to look away from the hideous spectacle. I have been drugged, he told himself. I am hallucinating. But the demon looked too real to be an hallucination. From its mouth came abomination, lies and false prophecies. '*Drauga, Druj, Renen, Aeshma, Degvant! I am the guardian of the abyss, too vile for your frail human senses to endure!*' The demon laughed, its grotesque face hanging inches above Daniel's own. Its tongue lashed out like a thick, wet worm and licked Daniel's face; its saliva stank of rotting flesh. Daniel cried out, felt his stomach tighten, then his consciousness tugged free of his body and soared up towards the treetops. Looking down, he could see the enormous demon crouched beside the fire, see himself beneath Owen, the shadowy figures of his father and the others standing nearby. Then the demon raised its arms and Owen was hurled, ejaculating, away from Daniel's body. Daniel's consciousness snapped back into his own flesh. He could feel the effects of the drug wearing off within his body and mind, yet still the image of the demon stayed clear in his eyes. Its fanged maw slavered viscous fluid, and its eyes leaked blood. It uttered a hungry, whimpering sound, reaching out with its greasy, black talons for Daniel's white flesh.

This is it, Daniel thought, quite coherently. This is my death. He wanted to close his eyes and pray, but could no longer control his body or his mind. As he stared up at the demon, its countenance shimmered. For a moment, he saw Othman looking down at him, his expression confused, then the image flickered again, to become the most beautiful face Daniel had ever seen, its facial cast indescribably sad. Then the conflicting images were banished, and the demon held sway once more, preparing to strike and feed.

In the chamber beneath the High Place, the guardians were awake, creatures of bone and tattered cloth, their faces like the skulls of reptiles or birds. As they stretched their withered spines erect, the flame changed colour to violet blue. Lily's eyes ached from looking at it, yet it was too beautiful to turn away from. The guardians did not seem to notice her presence; their concentration was centred on the flame. Lily got to her feet, felt Raven's clawed hand reach out briefly to steady her. She took a step towards the flame. As she stared into it, she could see a shape forming within it, a sinuous, female shape. Hands reached out to her: 'Come to me, my darling. Come to me.'

Lily blinked. 'Mum?'

The image shimmered and writhed within the flame, yet became more definite as Lily stared at it.

'Come to me, my daughter.' Slim, white arms extended from the flame, and there was Helen, dressed in a long, pleated skirt, her belly tattooed with an enormous eye, her breasts bared, her hair hanging down in coils.

'Lily, my daughter . . .'

Lily took a hesitant step forward. Was this image real? Behind her, Raven made a soft, encouraging sound. Reassured, Lily went towards the flame.

'Come now,' said Helen. 'This is your heritage, my child. Take it!'

Gathering all her courage in her heart, Lily reached out to take the offered hands. Around them, the guardians had begun to chant monotonous notes, which sounded like the tones that had emanated from the pillars in the antechamber. Helen was so beautiful, an icon of love and benevolence. Her hands felt real and warm in Lily's own. Her smile was just as Lily remembered it. She allowed her mother to draw her into the flame, and it did not burn her, or make her feel cold, as she'd feared. It was an energizing warmth, nothing more. Helen held Lily close and as Lily curled her arms around the slim body to return the embrace, suddenly the flame burst through the ceiling of the chamber, scattering plaster and stone. Lily felt herself melt into her mother's soul, become one with her as the flame roared upwards, tearing away earth and roots to reach the sky. And as their souls fused, combining the raw energy and light of their female power, another presence was evoked, greater than their sum, a goddess.

The flame burst through the ground, exploding the bonfire in the middle of the High Place. Flames and burning embers, stones and soil flew everywhere. Daniel saw his father tossed sideways by the force, to land in a crumpled heap on the edge of the clearing. Owen and the other youths all fell to the ground and covered their heads. The demon hanging over Daniel roared out in anger, and rearing up, wheeled round to face the flame. For a second, its eyes blazed triumph, but then, to Daniel's astonishment, it sank to its knees with a hollow, breathless moan. Daniel blinked, and the tiny action seemed to take an eternity. He saw Peverel Othman kneeling before the flame, with his arms over his eyes. The demon presence had vanished.

The flame was incredible to behold, a vivid violet blue, soaring up into the sky. Daniel scrambled on to hands and knees. Was this evil? It didn't feel like it to him. He shielded his eyes from the light, but was unable to look away. Something was rising up into the flame from below, a figure taking shape, as tall as Othman had appeared before. Slowly the rising form took on definition. Daniel realized it was the figure of a woman, wreathed in transparent peacock-blue veils, which were like smoke, or part of the flame. Her arms were held out to either side of her body, the glowing flesh tattooed from wrist to shoulder with writhing serpent forms. Upon her belly, a tattooed eye stared out. Daniel saw horror and wisdom in its gaze, grief and understanding. The eye spoke to him, called him. He looked up to the woman's face and recognized her, even though she appeared very different to the last time he had seen her, struggling and lamenting beside a pit of fire and sulphur. Ishtahar, the Master's woman: he knew her. She returned his gaze, acknowledging the contact, but only briefly. She wore her beauty like a scent, like gold, like bells; it called to all the senses.

Daniel glanced round at Owen and the others, but they were still curled up on the ground. Couldn't they feel the presence of this goddess? Didn't they want to look at her? Daniel crawled over to Owen, shook him. He *must* see her. Owen groaned, a sound of despair and terror. He had shut himself away, *refusing* to see.

The voice of the goddess, when it came, filled the world, yet it was the most gentle, soothing sound. She said one word: 'Shem.'

As that sound touched his mind, Othman saw his own body fall away from him in black flakes. He stood up. Peverel Othman lay decomposed around him, no longer flesh, no longer relevant. What was this thing? he thought, looking down at the dismal remnants. His memory was cloudy. He remembered hot, feral thoughts, bitterness, frustration, yet surely he had been asleep for millennia, and the thoughts had been dreams, nightmares of revenge that had troubled his slumber. She was before him now, but her image and her presence were difficult to perceive. Some part of him had always hoped he would find her again, but he was afraid of believing his longing had been fulfilled. Doubt and resentment had tortured his hope, beaten it down. His body ached; his soul was torn. She had murdered him, but it had been an act of love. He raised his face to her slowly. 'Ishtahar.'

She shook her head sadly, a weary smile upon her lips. Pain had hardened her, matured her, but it had softened her, too. Gone was the spark of ambition and greed. All that was left was the love of him, which she had manifested and shared with those who had invoked her for centuries. 'Shem, why are you still torturing yourself?' she asked, gesturing round the clearing. 'What have you been doing to these children?'

He felt confused at her words. What did she mean? Then, as he glanced behind himself, he remembered. The black words spilling from the mouth of his dead persona, the invocation of The Lie and the offering of life. Daniel's face looked up at him wondering, his arms around the shuddering form of Owen. They *were* beautiful. What had he been thinking of to abuse them? Hadn't his original purpose been to defend the children of humanity, to be their advocate? Why this?

Crouching in the dirt, Daniel could only stare in awe at the beings before him. He had seen Peverel Othman fall, but what had risen was something very different. He knew now who Othman was. It all made sense. His original vision in Marlene's had been literal. Othman: Shemyaza. The same. He didn't know how such a thing could be, but he knew it was the truth. Othman the Dark Priest had transformed into Shemyaza the Being of Light. And she: Ishtahar, the bound woman who had been forced to watch Shemyaza die. No wonder

Shemyaza had transgressed the code of his people for her. The power and love emanating from her was over-whelming. She was compassion and gentle comfort, passion, sex and serenity, excitement and tranquillity: all of this. The all-wise, all-seeing mother earth, the potential which dwelt within every woman. Had their love made her this, or their sacrifice?

Shemyaza sank to his knees before her as she hung in the violet light of the flame. Daniel heard him say: 'I once said to you that you would become a goddess. Didn't I tell you that? I wanted to find you again, but it was impossible.' He indicated the flakes of Peverel Othman which already were being blown away. 'There was only this, or other versions of it. I searched for something, but could not find it.'

Ishtahar made no verbal response, put both hands against her belly, where the eye stared out upon the world. Violet light spiralled there and her flesh opened. She drew forth from her womb the body of a girl, which she placed outside the flame. The girl stumbled around, disorientated, her hands out before her.

'Lily!' Daniel cried. She seemed to be blind, although her eyes were open and staring.

Ishtahar made a gesture with her hands and Lily was propelled forward to where Daniel knelt, Owen across his knees. Daniel reached out for her, pulled her down, and she curled against his side, making a strange sound of mingled weeping and laughter. Daniel looked up and the goddess was staring at him. 'Look after them.' The words rang inside his head like bells.

Then Ishtahar directed her attention back to the one who knelt before her. 'Rise, Shem. Come with me.'

Shemyaza obeyed her words. He saw her hovering in the flame before him, summoning him with an extended hand. Now, at last, they would be together again. He stepped towards the flame and it engulfed him entirely. The light burned his eyes and he closed them. Lost, familiar energy coursed through his blood and bones, but he could not reach for her. Had she abandoned him again?

He opened his eyes and raw, white sunlight made him blink. Around him, he saw the tiers and terraces of the Garden, half-hidden by a screen of cedars. Ishtahar was sitting some distance away from him, on a close-cropped lawn, in the shadow of one of the trees. She looked exactly as she had the last time he'd seen her in the flesh: a beautiful young woman, with a mischievous glint to her eyes and a humorous expression.

'What has happened?' he asked her. 'Have we gone back? Come back?' He dared to hope that all the terror of the millennia of confinement, while the black vestiges of his soul had roamed the earth, had never happened. He could begin anew, escape now with his beloved before the worst happened.

Ishtahar smiled sadly. 'I'm sorry. I have brought you here to talk. It isn't real, but I wanted us to be together in a pleasant setting.'

'Where are we?'

'In the flame, in the future. There is so much I want to say to you.'

Shemyaza went towards her, but Ishtahar held up her hand. 'No! Do not approach. That is not the reason I've brought you here.'

Shemyaza sat down upon the grass, some distance away from her. 'I am confused.' He shook his head. 'I can't think. Talk? I want none of that! I want you, to touch you. I want back what was mine.'

Ishtahar laughed. 'Ah, why did I ever think you were so different from human men? I thought that you and I were the same, but we're not.' She frowned a little.

'Listen to me. Let me tell you the things you should have realized for yourself.

'We were separated so harshly, and with such cruelty, yet I never nurtured bitterness in my heart. I remembered only love, while your fragmented spirit remembered only sundering and became twisted. Over the centuries, in the hearts and souls of women, and even men, I have become what you ordained I should be: a goddess. This I did for you. Hope never died in me, for the generations we spawned have filled me with their own hopes. I am fulfilment and the desire for fulfilment. What happened between us in the past created a destiny greater than either of us, greater than our desires. If you had escaped with your life, we would have had an *existence* on earth together, yes, but little more. Because of our sacrifice, we have given life and the seed of potential to the people of the earth. For good or for bad, this was our fate.'

Shemyaza regarded her contemplatively for a few moments. Light rippled over the skin of her bare arms as if from the reflection of water, but there was no water nearby. He did not want to think deeply or argue with her, but he could not agree with all she said. 'Ishtahar, perhaps you are right in saying that our sacrifice changed the future of the world, but you are wrong in saying that we would have had a small, meaningless life together. Our union was destined to create greater changes, to enable humanity to challenge the power of the Anannage. We were stopped, but perhaps now we have been given another chance.' He began to stand up, but Ishtahar again extended her hands to push him back.

'I cannot believe you can deceive yourself so much!' she cried. 'What is this talk of changing humanity's destiny? You wanted only to sample the mysteries of the earth through me, and turned your back on your people!

I was the one who was aware of our potential, not you! You were only interested in gratifying your desires!' She laughed gravely. 'Now you want to come to me! Can't you see that you're not ready? Coincidence has aligned so that you have been able to remember who you are, but you should thank the boy, Daniel, for that. He has always been your faithful follower, and, like you, unaware of his true self. But unlike you, he has remained unconsciously faithful to his original purpose. You, on the other hand, have done many wicked things over the years, all of which I have seen and experienced.'

Shemyaza opened his mouth to interrupt, but Ishtahar silenced him with a shout. 'No! Just listen to me! You still have many lessons to learn before what we created all that time ago can be fully reawakened, and we can be together again. Through our bonding, humanity's destiny was sealed. You can't change what has happened, but can only go forward. Now is not the right time for you to return to me, or to regain access to the Source beyond the stargate. You would only abuse that knowledge! You are Shemyaza, but at the same time you're not. Too much of Peverel Othman and the countless personae before him remain within you.'

Shemyaza raised his arms to her. 'So, what can I do? It's not my fault I became what I was. Ishtahar, you must let me come to you. Let me pass through the gate to the Source that I renounced. I am empty. I am a void. I have been alone for over ten millennia. Ishtahar, through your love, take me back to Paradise, show me my kingdom and my power!'

Ishtahar slowly shook her head, although she was still smiling. 'Our love is not enough to break the bonds that tie you to your penance. When humanity has finished partaking of the fruit from the tree of knowledge that we planted, and the seeds of that fruit engender another tree, only then can we be in the Garden again. For some, the fruits of that tree are still red with the blood of sin. Shem, you have to go on living. You have to interact with humanity by giving to them your presence, your light and your knowledge. At the end of this millennium, you will return to me, your brethren and the glory of summer in Paradise, but not yet.'

'There is nothing I wish to do on earth,' Shemyaza said. 'It has given me nothing and I am sick of it.'

'But what of your destiny?'

Shemyaza leaped to his feet. 'Destiny? What destiny? Everything I had was taken from me and I was shaped into a monster! How can you give me back the knowledge of myself and then force me back into the world?'

Ishtahar sighed. 'You make it sound as if this is easy for me. It isn't. My instinct is to take you in my arms and shelter you from everything you fear and shun. But I can't. Shem, can't you see? You are an archetype, the eternal dying king. You are the key to unlock the doors of the future. Humanity is failing, floundering around in darkness. Only you can lead them to the light. On earth, the end of the millennium approaches, which is the gateway to change. You must go back and learn to become your true self.'

As she spoke, the image of the Garden began to shimmer, take on a bluish cast. Shemyaza realized she was withdrawing from him. He wheeled around, desperately trying to reconstruct the image, but it was Ishtahar's will alone that had sustained it. He felt a sense of propulsion and found that he was standing beyond the flame once more on the High Place outside Little Moor. He screamed, 'No!'

Ishtahar had become less distinct within the flame. She gestured with her hands towards Daniel and the others. 'Shem, take these children. They are our children, and when you've learned to love them, then you can love me again.'

Shemyaza tried to lunge back into the flame, but could not penetrate it. When he spoke, his voice was ragged and weak. 'Ishtahar, you are wrong! Give me your stellar gate! Show me the way back to the One. We must remember what we were *together*.'

Again, Ishtahar shook her head. 'No, Shem. I will not. Only when you understand why will you be ready to enter the gate once more.'

Shemyaza could feel her preparing to withdraw her presence. A feeling of total desperation engulfed him, familiar and hated. The flame would not open to him, his kingdom was yet again denied to him. Ishtahar had brought him back to consciousness, only to compound the cruelties of his brethren, bind him once again for another eternity, deprived of his love, his power and his faith. She tortured him as she spoke words of love. The world's goddess now, not his. He had made her into this, and she dared to defy him. He felt his body falling forward, his head touch the earth, felt the form of his soul crumble inwards.

Taziel Levantine had his hand upon the gate of Low Mede. The house was in darkness. 'He's not here,' he said to the others. 'I don't even need to look.' A roaring sound of thunder and a mighty crack caused them all to turn round and gaze up.

'Great Shem!' Lahash exclaimed. 'The flame!'

'What is it?' Aninka cried.

The sky was speared by a blade of violet light. It looked solid, like a tube, as if it was an unearthly passage-way to the stars.

'It's the perpetual flame,' Lahash said. 'He must have

awoken it! Come on!' Already he was loping down the lane towards the woods.

Aninka and Taziel looked at one another. 'I can smell it,' Taziel said. 'I can feel its cold heat, its reawakening. The earth is vibrating. Can't you feel it?'

Aninka took his arm. 'I can feel something. Come on, we mustn't let Lahash go alone.'

Taziel resisted for a moment. 'This is it, Ninka.'

She pulled a wry face. 'I know, Taz. I know. Let's go.'

Emma Manden was still crouched among the bracken, chewing the skin around her fingernails, trying to evaluate what she'd witnessed. The man she'd known as Peverel Othman was crushed, she could see that. Whatever he'd tried to make happen certainly wasn't going to happen now. Shemyaza had thought he was alone in the Garden with Ishtahar, but their words had boomed out over the High Place like prophecies, clearly audible to all. It was obvious to Emma that the erstwhile Peverel Othman was much more than she could have imagined, and the woman in the flame had spoken of the future. The end of the millennium? That wasn't far away. Something big could happen then. Emma stood up. She'd have to get Shemyaza away from this place before what was left of him was destroyed. Ishtahar did not frighten her. She was fuelled by an instinct for survival. Shemyaza and the twins were her only recourse to longevity, and Daniel Cranton seemed to be a part of everything that had happened. Emma knew that all of these people had to be taken away from here as soon as possible, and she was the only one capable of initiating it.

Barbara Eager was fighting her way through the dark woods. It was so confusing at night, and there were so many terrifying sounds: thundering, crashes, electric crackles. Whatever Othman was doing at the High Place, she had to interrupt him. She thought she knew these woods so well, but where was the path? When she saw the tall figure ahead of her, she thought it was Othman. 'Pev!' she cried and beat her way forward, stumbling on roots and tangled fern. The figure turned and she saw its white face. Not Othman, no, but the other one: his enemy. She realized she had to stop him reaching the High Place and with a high-pitched scream, threw herself against him, her hands curled into claws. The suddenness of her attack caught the other off-guard. He stumbled backwards.

'I must kill him,' Barbara thought. Her fingers scrabbled to reach his eyes and she thrust her whole weight upon him. Then someone grabbed her hair and pulled her backwards. She came up snarling, lashing out at whoever held her. It was the woman from the hotel garden: the enemy's accomplice.

'Get out of here!' Aninka said. 'Go back!'

Barbara smacked Aninka's arm away and stepped back until all three of them were before her. 'You have to pass me first!'

'Who the hell are you?' Aninka demanded.

'Othman's creature,' Lahash said, standing up, rubbing his face.

'Who the hell are *you*?' Barbara snarled.

'We have private business with Peverel Othman,' Aninka said. 'Now get out of the way. We don't want to harm you.' She wasn't sure whether Lahash held the same view.

'Over my dead body!' Barbara screeched. She felt very powerful, and quite prepared to die to protect Peverel Othman. She knew these interlopers could sense that. They were wary of her, despite the fact they outnumbered her. Then she saw the tallest man reach towards his jacket. She sensed he hid a weapon there and without further thought plunged into the bracken. As she turned, she saw the purple light radiating from the trees above her. She was close. 'Pev!' she screamed. 'Pev! Look out!'

Aninka glanced at Lahash, sure he would shoot Barbara down in cold blood. She was wondering whether she should spoil his aim, but then realized he hadn't reached for the gun after all. He didn't have to. The next minute she was thrown sideways and the Kerubim gusted through and past them. Taziel landed heavily against her, shielding his head with his arms. Aninka pulled him close, scraping hair from her eyes. She saw them take the woman, saw the body flung up into the air as if it weighed nothing, explode in a ball of blood and bone. She cried out and hid her face, but Lahash was already pulling at her arm.

'We can't wait! Get up!'

Emma heard the sounds coming from the bottom of the hill, Barbara Eager's frantic warning. There was no time to waste. As she ran into the clearing, she saw the goddess form shoot up into the sky through the flame, and as she soared upwards, the flame began to collapse behind her. Shemyaza was a slumped form on the ground, the twins and Daniel Cranton huddled together nearby. Around the clearing were several other motionless forms, which she didn't bother to examine. They were unimportant. She could hear Lily whimpering. Daniel seemed to be the only one in possession of his senses. 'Get up!' Emma cried as she ran past him. 'Help me get them out of here!'

Before Emma could reach Shemyaza, the ground suddenly erupted around her. Seven blades of light punched up through the earth, sending up a chaotic spray of debris. Emma cringed and dodged, but kept on stumbling forward. As she reached Shemyaza and put her hands upon him, she saw the erupting flames had solidified into seven columns of white light making a circle around them all. The columns vibrated, emitting a chord of bizarre musical notes. And there were faces in the flames, faces Emma recognized: Murkasters! But there was little time to contemplate what this might mean. Already the white blades were soaring upwards towards the stars, following the ascent of the blue flame. The Murkasters were truly leaving Little Moor, for the last time, and they would never come back.

Overhead, the seven columns began to twist together, their song condensing into a throbbing choir. Emma hauled Shemyaza to his feet. He appeared mindless, and certainly didn't recognize her. 'Move!' she ordered. 'Do you want to die here?' Shemyaza blinked at her. He looked like Othman, but was also distinctly different. She could not fathom the difference exactly, but now was not the time to worry about it. Even as she continued to exhort Shemyaza to move, the air exploded around them with sound and light and movement. Thousand upon thousand of birds were rising up through the ruined earth to flutter around the circle, filling the air with a cacophony of cheeping, twittering and whirring wings. Their claws snagged in Emma's hair as she tried to drag Shemyaza towards the opposite side of the hill. There was so little time. A thunderclap of sound crashed around them as the white columns of flame broke free of the earth, trailing tails of twigs and stones. The thundering sound was almost unendurable, rolling on and on and on; deafening, roaring, ripping. Emma had to push Shemyaza ahead of her. He could barely stand, never mind walk. She saw Daniel's face peering over the brow of the hill. 'Go down!' Emma yelled, trying to make herself heard above the noise. Failing, she gestured wildly. 'The cottage! The car! Quickly!'

Aninka and Taziel stumbled after Lahash into a maelstrom of wings and light and deafening sound. Aninka was too astonished to be frightened. She'd never seen anything like this; pure chaos. Where was Othman? What the hell had he been doing up here? Lahash turned to her, pointed. 'Over there!' She could barely hear his voice, but looked in the direction he pointed. She saw the staggering form of a woman, who was helping a man escape the clearing. Her heart nearly stopped. Even though she couldn't see his face, she recognized him immediately. 'Pev!' She couldn't help shouting out the name.

'Too late for that!' Lahash said. He tried to run after their fleeing quarry, but the riot of birds swooped down to snag in his hair, peck at his body and face.

Aninka saw him lashing out with his arms. She crouched down on the edge of the circle, Taziel held against her.

'He has *become*,' Taziel whispered against her neck.

She didn't question him. Her guts felt as if they were being pulled upwards, and soon she might vomit herself inside-out. A violent wind plucked at her body, trying to toss her up into the swirling air with invisible hands. Desperately she reached out to clutch the tough stems of bracken around the circle, trying to anchor herself to the earth. Taziel cringed against her. Through slitted eyes, Aninka saw Lahash's suit jacket flapping about his body as he slipped and stumbled across the clearing. If he doesn't grab hold of something, he'll be taken, she thought, and called his name. He glanced back briefly. The Kerubim had been lured from their play with the dead woman's remains, but as soon as they approached the vortex of light, they were sucked upwards. At first, their strident song was joyful as they cavorted through the maelstrom, but then, as their spiritual fabric began to disintegrate in the wake of the flame, their song became a blood-chilling symphony of howls and shrieks. Streaks of their shining substance broke away and streamed upwards. Aninka was determined not to follow them. She had not come all this way to die like this, without even confronting the object of her pain and love. Everything in the clearing was being dragged towards the sky now: she saw twisting bodies, trees, ferns, soil, stones. Lahash, she was relieved to see, had wrapped his arms around a large tree on the left of the clearing. She hoped it would hold. 'Taz, we have to try and go backwards,' she said, even though the thought of trying to move was terrifying. Relinquishing their anchor might mean immediate death. Just as Aninka plucked up the courage to let go of one fistful of·ferns, which were beginning to come loose from the ground, everything stopped.

The silence, the stillness were abrupt, immediate and total.

Whatever energies this place had contained were now thoroughly expelled. All power had left it.

Shakily, Lahash stood up, and smoothed his hair in rather an embarrassed manner, like a cat. After a moment, he came over to Taziel and Aninka. 'Well, Taz?' he demanded. 'Where's he gone?' The unbelievable experiences of the last few minutes might never have happened.

Taziel, still shuddering against Aninka, merely moaned.

Lahash reached down and pulled Taziel upright. 'Speak! Concentrate! Where's Othman?'

Taziel's head lolled sideways. Aninka was afraid he

was dying. 'Oh, let him go!' she cried. 'This is all too much!'

Lahash ignored her. 'Taz! Pull yourself together!'

Aninka leaped up and attempted to wrest Taziel from Lahash's hold. 'Leave him alone!'

Lahash bared his teeth at her. 'Shut up! We have to keep searching! We can't let him go.' But he relinquished Taziel into her arms.

Aninka held Taziel close. His flesh felt cold. 'Who *is* Peverel Othman?' she asked in a low voice. 'Why is he so important? What the hell happened here?'

Lahash made an irritated gesture, then rubbed his face with his hands. Energy seemed to be leaking away from him. The lust to pursue was fading. 'Who is he? You wouldn't understand. Don't even ask.'

Aninka objected to his condescending tone. 'How dare you! We, more than you, appreciate what kind of creature Peverel Othman really is!'

Lahash gave her a narrow glance. 'Oh do you . . .' His voice was flat.

Taziel pulled himself away from Aninka. 'Don't fight,' he said. 'Stop shouting, for fuck's sake!'

'Are you all right?' Aninka asked. Her hands reached for him, but Taziel only gave her his hand.

'I'm fine. Things have become clear, however.' He fixed Lahash with a surprisingly steady eye. 'Peverel Othman is far more than we knew, isn't he? We were too blind, too wrapped up in the mundane world we inhabited to realize it. The clues were there all along, but we'd denied our past and shut ourselves away from the truth. Peverel Othman is an incarnation of the Watcher Shemyaza. Isn't that right, carnifex?'

'What?' Aninka said. 'What do you mean?'

Lahash studied Taziel through slitted eyes. 'Did you know that all the time?'

He shook his head. 'No. Sometimes I suspected, simply because Pev got into such crazy states about himself, and I probed his mind to try and help him. I picked up images, which I thought were ... metaphorical. They had to be. I was suspicious when Enniel called upon Shemyaza at High Crag to guide us to Othman.' He looked at Aninka. 'I should have been more persistent in questioning Enniel.' He glanced back at Lahash. 'The Parzupheim have known about Othman for a while, haven't they?'

Lahash exhaled impatiently, glanced away, then back to Taziel. 'Yes. It is something they've feared. There have always been prophecies that Shemyaza would return, and that his advent would have catastrophic consequences.'

Aninka couldn't help laughing. 'Listen to you two! Othman is Shemyaza? Are you mad? That's not possible.'

'It's true,' Taziel said. 'Tell her, Lahash. Tell her it's true.'

Lahash looked slightly uncomfortable. 'Physically, Peverel Othman has not lived for thousands of years, but his consciousness is the enduring soul of Shemyaza. At least, that is what is suspected. He has been monitored.'

'But *why*?' Aninka felt too exhausted to expand her question. There were too many questions. She could try to scoff at what she'd heard, tell herself it was nothing more than foolish beliefs dredged up from a long-dead past, yet she had just seen with her own eyes the most incredible things. Was the existence of Shemyaza in flesh any less credible?

'There will come a time,' Lahash said, 'when Shemyaza is vital to this world. But this incarnation is warped. It was thought best to contain it or kill it, to allow the soul to go free and inhabit a new host. Also, when

636

the time of reckoning comes, the Parzupheim want Shemyaza to be firmly under their control.'

Taziel shook his head. 'We'll never catch him, Lahash. We have to let him go. We'll only snare him when the time is right, and that's not now.'

'I have people to report to,' Lahash said. He glanced uncertainly across the clearing in the direction Shemyaza and his companion had taken. 'I can't just let him get away.'

Taziel said nothing, but began walking back down the hill in the direction they'd come from. 'It's all over here, now,' he said. 'Leave it, Lahash. There's nothing we can do. Believe me, *I know it!* Shemyaza has already left this place.'

Aninka followed him down, took his arm. 'Taz, this is all too weird. I can't believe it.'

'They knew what he was,' Taziel said. 'They always knew. They just didn't see fit to inform us. How did they ever think we could do anything? How? It's insane. We're lucky to be alive.'

'So he'll just go on now, killing and destroying. Taz, we can't allow that!'

'It's beyond our abilities to control,' Taziel answered. 'He's scorched us, Ninka. We are just memories of his power.'

Emma drove the old car, Daniel in the passenger seat beside her. They'd grabbed very little from the cottage and had had to restrain Lily, who'd gone crazy about leaving her cats behind. Emma had been the one to release the scrawny chickens from their run at the back of the house. They would have to survive as best they could.

The twins were in the back of the car with *him*. What should she call him now? Was he still Peverel Othman? The being of light he'd briefly become at the High Place

637

had faded now. His skin was grey and cold, but at least he was alive. She had felt the fragility of his soul as she'd carried him from the woods. He was so tall yet she'd been able to lift him in her arms like a child, or else like a man might carry a woman from danger. She'd wondered then whether he was dead. Dead from grief. But no, he was still breathing.

'We are a family now,' Daniel said.

Emma glanced at him. 'Are we? Light me a cigarette.'

She looked in the rear-view mirror, saw Lily with her arms round *him*, crying on his shoulder. Owen was sitting there staring straight ahead. Emma hoped the boy's mind hadn't been irreparably damaged. She didn't want to have to cope with anything like that. Daniel seemed to have become childlike. His voice sounded very young, although his eyes had become far too old. They'd been through too much, these kids. She took the cigarette from Daniel's outstretched hand. 'Thanks.'

'Ishtahar made us a family,' Daniel said. 'You are the housekeeper and I am the vizier.'

'Right.' Emma sucked hungrily on the cigarette. She wanted to tell Daniel to shut up. 'Get some sleep.'

'I'm not tired.' Daniel leaned back against his seat. 'Is my father dead? I hope Verity will be all right. How will she get out of the cellar?'

Emma was grateful he didn't suggest they go back to see to it themselves. 'She'll be fine. Someone will find her. Someone will come looking. The police probably.'

'I have a new father now,' Daniel said. He looked over the seat, then back at Emma. 'He is Shemyaza.'

'I know. Just relax, Daniel. You've had a very bizarre experience.'

The car glides along the twisting country lanes. There is a dim light inside. The woman driving the car concentrates on the road. The boy beside her is considering destinies. He knows that eventually Shemyaza will recognize him as his vizier and prophet, as he always has been. Daniel, around whom the lions lay down, who spoke with angels. As for Lily and Owen, their function is to help Shemyaza fulfil his own destiny. Emma has the role of defender. She will be their guardian and their weapon.

The car glides onwards into darkness. A woman's face can be seen through the windscreen, frowning hard. Draw back. A woman's face becomes the face of a lioness. Sekhmet. Goddess of War. Protectress.

Chapter Thirty-six

Tuesday, 3rd November: Little Moor
The unnatural heat had left the village, and cold had swept in in its wake. Verity had to put on her thickest coat before going out to the makeshift aviary that she and Raven had constructed the day after the night of terror. Outside, the garden looked enchanted, covered in frost. Verity whistled as she crackled her way over the lawn, leaving a green trail in the grass. Hearing her tune, Raven came bounding out of the shrubbery, jumping up around her legs like a large dog. Verity laughed, put down her basket of bird food, and squatted down to take the cat in her arms. 'I love you,' she said, burying her face in the fur of his shoulders, kissing the hard muscles beneath.

'And I you,' he replied, before uttering a feline chirrup and pulling away from her, to dance on ahead towards the aviary.

Verity had never experienced so complete a love as that which she felt for Raven. Last night, in the warmth of their bed, he had told her his true name, but it was difficult to pronounce, so she knew she would rarely use it. Sometimes, in the delirium of their love-making, she might remember it and sing it, but not in the clear, hard light of day.

He had come to her in the night of terror and darkness, smashing down the door of the cellar to reach her. She had looked up, sick from pain and fever, to see his tall body standing at the top of the stairs, wrapped in a fringed, green robe. She had never beheld such majesty and power in any living thing. 'I knew you would come,' she managed to say. He had leaped down the stairs in a single bound, his eyes full of fury and love. His rough tongue had licked her wounds, bringing a healing warmth to her body.

'Don't leave me,' she'd said to him softly as he'd carried her back to her life.

'Never,' he'd answered fiercely, and she knew he meant it.

The aftermath of the night left lingering echoes in Little Moor. There were deaths to be mourned. Nothing would ever be the same, but in some way the villagers knew they were free now. They would look to Verity for support, instinctively aware that her position in their community had changed. She was a guardian now.

On the day after the event, Lily's cats had come creeping down the lane to Low Mede, to take up stations of entreaty around the kitchen door. Since then, they had become residents.

Raven had taken Verity to Long Eden wearing his cat shape, as he never appeared before others as a man. He had taken her inside the house and showed her everything.

'If you want this, it is yours,' he told her. 'No one else will come for it.'

Verity had walked around the echoing, empty rooms, and for a while imagined herself living there, but the fantasy was short-lived. 'No,' she said. 'It will never be my home.'

On the night of the feast of Yule, Verity knew that she would gather the villagers together, and lead them to Long Eden. In the cold darkness, they would chant for the rebirth of the Sun King and burn the house down. It might take several days to burn completely, but at the end, its great stones would fall inward, hiding for ever the dark secrets of the underground chambers.

Verity also knew that soon new people would come to live at The White House. Barney Eager would not feel able to live in Little Moor after his wife had been mysteriously murdered in the woods. The new people would be young and enthusiastic. They would encourage tourists to come to the village, and no one would stop them.

Although Barbara Eager had not survived the night of terror, Louis had. What was left to Verity was a human husk, in which very little of her father remained. Still, she would care for him, wash his body, feed him, and wheel his chair out into the garden when it was fine. Raven had told her he would take a long time to die because of what Peverel Othman had done to him. Sometimes, Verity would feel pity for Louis, but mostly, she would feel nothing. Caring for him was a duty; she would not neglect it.

Verity opened the aviary and stepped inside. Raven sat down on the frosted grass and began to wash himself, content to wait outside. A myriad of brightly coloured birds lifted in a throng and blew about Verity's head like a shimmering flag of cloth. Their high songs filled her head and she held out her hands for them to land upon her. Souls. The birds were souls, released from the belly of the earth, the spirits of all who had died in the laboratories of the Murkasters and who had been released on the night of penance. Verity was their guardian now. She knew that gradually the birds would disappear as they were taken one by one to the place that had been denied them, but until that time, she would care for them herself. The birds nestled in her hair, fashioning a living head-dress of feathers and bright, beady eyes.

Perhaps, in a way, she really had become a queen of the dead, as once her dreams had prophesied.

Verity closed her eyes, enjoying the feel of the little claws tickling her scalp. She thought of Daniel, her brother. Raven had assured her he was alive, but she was worried about him. She would never forgive Louis for what he'd done. There were now photos of Daniel all over the house, put up on the walls mainly to discomfort Louis, whom Verity felt had to be reminded constantly of his part in Daniel's disappearance. She knew nearly all the details of what had happened on the night of terror, and why it had happened, because Raven had told her. She knew that Louis would have stood by and let Daniel be killed. Greed, she thought, he was so greedy, but stupid, too.

Having fed the birds, Verity let herself out of the aviary and went back towards the house. She had a busy day ahead of her: a morning meeting with the women of the village and, later, a sitting of the Little Moor council, of which she had hastily been elected secretary. As she approached the house, she heard the telephone ringing. Mrs Roan had not yet arrived, so, muttering in impatience, Verity increased her pace. She ran into the hall and threw down her basket on the hall table, lifting the phone. Raven bounded halfway up the stairs and sat looking at her intently through the banisters.

'Hello,' Verity said, in her most aloof tone.

'Vez?' The voice was weak, distant. There was a lot of interference on the line.

Verity pushed her hair back behind her ears. 'Dan? Daniel? Is that you?'

'Yes. Are you all right?'

'Yes, yes. Daniel, where *are* you?'

'It doesn't matter,' he answered. 'I'm OK.'

'But what happened . . .?'

'I can't talk. I just wanted to let you know I was still alive.'

'Dan! Daniel!'

'Take care.' The line went dead.

'He hung up,' Verity said to Raven. She felt like crying, but instead began to laugh. 'He hung up.'

Raven was a sinuous, manly form draped over the stairs, resting his head on one hand. His tail switched lazily against the carpet. 'You will hear from him again,' he said.

'Will I?' Verity wearily climbed the stairs and lay down with her head against Raven's chest. Wan sunlight came into the hall, kindling fire in the gleam of the polished wood on floor and walls. Time ticked slowly by, and Verity became aware of a sense of imminence, but there were no holy feet walking towards Little Moor.

Epilogue

The hotel was dingy, unassuming, hidden away in a run-down corner of a sooty Midlands town. They had been holed up there for three days, since the frantic drive down from Little Moor.

Emma Manden was beginning to wonder whether she'd done the right thing. Owen was imbecilic, Lily forever weeping about her cats, while Daniel seemed to want to live inside his own head – not that she could blame him. As for *the other one*, Emma was wary of approaching him. This was not the man she'd met in Little Moor. He was aloof, broken, terse and melancholic; a stranger. It was like going out into the back yard and finding an angel, fallen from heaven, flapping around in the dust with broken wings, too big and too alien to help, too beautiful to ignore and allow to die. He had shut himself away from the others, making it clear he had no desire to communicate. Emma wondered whether he was actually eating anything. Still, she knew she had to talk to him at some point. What, for example, were they going to do next? Where must they go? There had been pursuit, they all knew that, and to use any of their credit cards might prove dangerous, a means by which they could be traced. And cash was short.

She went to him in his room, and there he was, filling it with his presence, uncomfortable and confined. 'What do I call you?' she asked.

He was lying on the bed, half-dressed, apparently doing nothing. He shrugged. 'I don't care. What do you want?'

She explained, adding, 'You must help me. I need to make plans. Where can we go?'

He rubbed his face. 'There are places. London. We'll go to London. I know people there.'

'Right. Thank you. That's all I needed to know. I'll get the others organized, then.' She made to leave, then paused at the door. 'We have to carry on, you know. And you have to help me. The kids are a mess. I can't cope with it alone. After all, you are responsible.'

He frowned. 'No, I'm not. It's something I've inherited.'

Emma sighed and left the room. She felt like the keeper of a mad menagerie.

They left the town in the late afternoon, hidden among the bustle of rush-hour traffic, the darkness of the day occluded by smog and rushing lights. Daniel sat in the front with Emma as before. He seemed tired, but slightly more alert than he'd been over the past few days. Lily slept in the back, while Owen lay slumped with his head against one of the back windows, staring out at the dark. Shemyaza sat between them, apparently oblivious of their presence.

Halfway down the M1, he instructed Emma to pull off the motorway and drive into the country. She didn't question why. Perhaps they were going to make an overnight stop on their way south. She would leave that decision to him.

They came to a hill at the side of the road, perhaps an ancient earth-works of some kind. Here, Shemyaza asked Emma to stop the car. She did so, and watched as he got out. Now what? He climbed over the fence and began to walk up the hill. Emma sighed. 'Oh, for God's sake!'

Daniel, sensing her mood, lit her a cigarette. 'Don't worry,' he said. 'He's got a lot to think about.'

*

Shemyaza walked up towards the stars. At the brow of the hill, he paused, looking skywards, then sank to his knees. The air was cold around him, burrowing between the layers of his clothes, pinching his skin. He felt so numb and yet so raw. He could smell the fertile earth and the clear-water perfume of the sky. The marriage of heaven and earth. Hadn't that been what he'd always wanted? But that had been a long time ago, so long that it could hardly be important now. Ishtahar had spoken of destinies, of approaching conclusions. Shemyaza wanted none of that. He wanted to rest, seek respite with those whom he loved, live a normal life. It had been an accident that he'd become something different. Now he was faced with the end product of his illicit affair with the human woman: Lily and Owen, the hybrid twins. Without him, and his acts of lust, they would not exist. He *was* responsible for them, but he did not want to be. Neither did he want to admit that he could serve some special purpose in this chaotic, messy world, and bring about important change. He was too tired, too hurt. It was difficult to care about what happened here.

He raised his head to the sky, seeking out the constellation where some part of him had hung in exile. 'I don't want this,' he whispered, and repeated it until it became a shout. 'I don't want this!' If he sought to penetrate the psychic gate symbolized by Orion, reach the senses of the Renowned Old Ones, his words were unanswered. He could feel no hint of their presence, or any other, save his own.

The others were waiting for him. He must go back. And perhaps, one day, as he struggled towards the destiny he neither wanted nor cared about, one or more of them would betray him, and he would be hung and burned once more. Now, they were hungry for him, and wanted him to lead them. But if he couldn't give them enough, they might turn and snarl and bite. He knew enough of human nature to understand that that was not inconceivable. But he realized he did have a choice.

With a final, weary glance at the sky, Shemyaza gathered his strength and walked back down the hill to the waiting car, lit from within by a dim, yellow glow. He knew now that he would deny his destiny. No one could make him become something he did not want to be. Let the end of the millennium pass unnoticed. He would hide from it. He had not asked to be awakened.

Emma Manden watched Shemyaza come back towards the car. 'Look at him,' she thought. 'Great Shem, look at him.' And he was Great Shem. She knew that, but she had a feeling that he didn't.